THE WONDER OF

KATHLEEN E. WOODIWISS

"Live and breathe the world
Ms. Woodiwiss creates!"
Houston Chronicle

THE FLAME AND THE FLOWER
THE WOLF AND THE DOVE
SHANNA
ASHES IN THE WIND
A ROSE IN WINTER
COME LOVE A STRANGER
and
SO WORTHY MY LOVE

"Woodiwiss reigns!"
Life

"A stirring drama . . . Skillfully woven!"
Publishers Weekly

"Ingenious . . . Excellent"
Ottawa Citizen

"A publishing phenomenon!"
New York Times

Avon Books are available at special quantity discounts for bulk purchases for sales promotions, premiums, fund raising or educational use. Special books, or book excerpts, can also be created to fit specific needs.

For details write or telephone the office of the Director of Special Markets, Avon Books, Dept. FP, 105 Madison Avenue, New York, New York 10016, 212-481-5653.

KATHLEEN E. WOODIWISS

So Worthy My Love

AVON BOOKS ◈ NEW YORK

SO WORTHY MY LOVE is an original publication of Avon Books. This work is a novel. Any similarity to actual persons or events is purely coincidental.

AVON BOOKS
A division of
The Hearst Corporation
105 Madison Avenue
New York, New York 10016

To My Four-Year-Old Granddaughter,
Alexa,
Who Was The Visual Inspiration For Elise

So Worthy my Love

Prologue

*T*HE MAN WAS RELATIVELY YOUNG, perhaps five or so years past a score and ten, yet the lines of fatigue and recent deprivation were accentuated by the stubble of a beard that roughened his cheeks and chin and which seemed to age the handsome face. He was seated on a large, square-hewn block of stone that had tumbled from the jumbled ruins behind him. On a blanket spread near his feet a girl of two or more plucked listlessly at the woolen hair of a doll. She seemed to be watching and waiting.

The man tipped his head back to catch the warmth of the midday sun on his face and breathed deeply of the cool, fresh breezes that brought the brushy tang of heather to him from across the moors. His head throbbed as he reaped the rewards of his recent excesses, which a long sleepless night had done little to ease. His hands hung limply over his knees, and his chest ached with the weight of his agony.

The pounding in the back of his skull began to ease after a time, and he sighed at the release. He had come here to find some hint of a memory of brighter days when there had been three of them, and they had gamboled happily across these same slopes. The child, Elise, was not of an age to understand the permanency of their loss. She only knew this as a place where a warm, soft, and laughing person had played with her and had giggled in glee as they rolled on the sweetly smelling grass. She waited expectantly for that loving loved one to appear, but time fled and that one did not come.

Clouds gathered above their heads and hid the sun. The wind turned northerly and was suddenly cold and chilling. The man sighed again, then opened red-rimmed eyes as a light touch caressed the back of his hand. His daughter had crept close to him and now looked up at him inquiringly. Her eyes bespoke her sadness as if she too, in her own child's way, had come to understand that the memory would never again return to life and there was no further reason to stay in this place.

The man saw in the deep blue eyes, in the dark russet hair, in the delicate shape of her chin and the soft, expressive lips, a hint of the wife he had loved so completely. He swept the girl into his arms and held her close, breathing deeply to quell the sobs that threatened to wrack him. Still, he could not stop the tears welling up between his tightly closed lids. Slowly they coursed down his cheeks and fell into the soft curls.

The man coughed and held the tiny girl from him. Again their eyes met, and in that long moment was born between them a bond that nothing of this world could sever. They would ever share a touch, and it would span whatever distance separated one from the other while they remembered the one they had both loved so dearly.

Chapter 1

London became a place of unrest as tales of treason and paid recompenses began to be noised about with more frequency. Life in the city was mingled with a series of alarms as the Queen's agents sought to up-root conspirators. Wild shouts and the clatter of running feet often shattered the silence of the streets during the darkest hour of night, then would come an insistent pounding of a heavy fist upon a solidly bolted door, followed by torchlit interrogations that sometimes resulted in multiple hangings and the display of severed heads on London Bridge. The attempts on the Queen's life did not cease, but seemed to roil up from the nether realms of the earth. Mary Stuart was a prisoner of England, and Elizabeth Tudor was on the throne, and one was as much in danger of losing her life as the other.

November 7, 1585
Near the Village of Burford
Oxfordshire, England

THE TINY FLAMES of myriad squat candles frolicked in jubilant accord with the wedding guests as they stepped in lively time to the courante. The festive music of the performing minstrels filled the great

3

room of Bradbury Hall, blending with the revelrous laughter of the lords and their ladies. There was indeed much cause for celebration, for the oft-arranged betrothals and much-canceled weddings of the beauteous Arabella Stamford had finally resulted in a successful union. Just as amazing was the fact that no great disaster had yet befallen the brave swain who had so zealously sought her hand these past months. Of the six who had previously held the distinction of being the lady's betrothed, none were known to be alive, including the late Marquess of Bradbury in whose country estate the guests now celebrated. Reland Huxford, the Earl of Chadwick, had decried the possibility of a curse on one so fair and had rushed recklessly on with his courtship, heedless of the dire fates of those who had preceded him. Now triumphantly wed, he stood joined to his bride by a garland of green while all around them leather-bound tankards and silver goblets were lifted in boisterous toast to the newly espoused couple. The strong ales and heady wines did much to warm the spirits and encourage the jovial moods, and servants hastened to tap fresh casks of the dark ale and hogsheads of claret and sack lest the excitement flag and fade.

Edward Stamford was ecstatic at having finally gained a son-in-law of both wealth and title, but the giving of his daughter's hand had not been accomplished without a certain measure of pain. Reluctantly he had conceded that the wedding banquet warranted more than the usual staples, and under his baleful eye huge trenchers of suckling pig, stuffed goat, and gaudily adorned birds were set before the ravenous guests. He winced in miserly distress as the succulent meats, elaborate puddings, and tasty sweetmeats were devoured with impartial gluttony by those who had come to indulge in his rare display of largess, but if any took note of their host's lack of appetite, they kept such observations in reserve.

It was an uncommon day indeed when Edward Stamford appeared kindly disposed toward anyone. Rather, it was said of him that he was something of an opportunist who had acquired his wealth through the misfortunes or follies of others. No one could aver that these windfalls had occurred through any clever manipulations of his, but Edward was always eager to seize whatever harvest he could wrench from those who had carefully sown and nurtured. His most noteworthy, if vocally reluctant, donor was the erstwhile Lord of Bradbury Hall.

No one was cognizant of the supreme sacrifice Edward had been required to make in order to divert attention from his own involvement in the murder of the Queen's agent. By casting the blame on Seymour, he had dismally foreseen relinquishing every honor and advantage he had once aspired to gain from his daughter's union with the man. It was the very least he would lose if he were successful, he had realized, and if he failed? Well, the dangers to himself had been too enormous to even entertain. Not only had there been a threat of reprisal from her sovereign majesty, but the Marquess had for some time been touted as the finest of the Queen's champions, and tales of his prowess with a sword had been well-published. In his mildest nightmares Edward had seen himself being skewered to a wall by the nobleman's long, shining, two-edged rapier.

Cautiously he had woven his tale while Elizabeth had lent an ear to his accusations, but he had underestimated her fondness for Seymour. She had flown into a rage, incensed that a favored lord would be accused of treason and murder by one held in such low esteem. It was only when witnesses affirmed that the Marquess's gloves had been discovered beside the slain agent that Edward had gained the leverage he needed. The Queen finally had relented and, with a venging stroke, had sealed Seymour's doom by calling for his immediate execution. Dealing out swift justice to traitors, she had stripped him of his title, possessions, and estates and spitefully heaped the latter two upon his accuser. Edward's glee had been immeasurable, but fear had come quickly in its stead when Seymour vowed from his gatehouse cell at Lambeth Palace to see all those who had precipitated his fall from grace brought to justice. Though the nobleman had been scheduled to meet the headman's axe a short fortnight away, Edward had nearly crumpled beneath the onslaught of fear, wary of even closing his eyes lest he never open them again. It was the cleverness of the man which had frightened him, and he had good cause to be afraid, for it was the Marquess's plan to escape his guards when they crossed the bridge on their way to the Tower. Fate, however, decreed otherwise, and Seymour was shot and killed by a guard trying to halt his escape. Edward received the news in trembling relief and had finally deemed it safe to begin the transfer of his household from his own rather barren manor to the Marquess's wealthy estates.

Edward's swift dispatch of the Marquess was one of his most memorable exploits, but now when he displayed sympathy or opened his house or his purse to help another, there were those who were wont to believe his base intent was to reap some greater reward. It seemed precisely the case when he extended his hospitality to Elise Radborne, the daughter of a foster sister now ten and five years dead. The disappearance of Elise's father had brought about circumstances that had necessitated her flight from the family manor in London, and only too aware of the rumors of a hidden treasure, Edward had eagerly opened the east wing to her. Still, it was not in his nature to be overly generous. Since he was the only kin the girl could turn to, he had taken advantage of her plight, requiring steep rents and pressing her into service as working mistress of his newly acquired country estate of Bradbury Hall. Casually he had given the excuse that his own daughter could not be bothered by menial tasks while she attended to the preparations for her marriage to the Earl of Chadwick. Well in advance of the wedding feast, Edward had instructed his niece to restrict herself from the evening's regalement and to give her full attention to the supervision of servants as they laid out the feast. Not a drop or a crumb was to be wasted, he had sternly admonished her, and above all there was to be no sampling of the fare by the hirelings.

Though naught but ten and seven years of age, Elise Radborne was a rather resourceful young lady and not without experience in managing a large manor, for she had served as mistress of her father's house for several years past, but she was among strangers and had been placed in charge of a household staff still sympathetic to the late Marquess of Bradbury, Maxim Seymour. As loyal as the hirelings were to his memory, they were equally as critical and resentful of the new squire, for it was widely rumored among them that Edward Stamford had purloined the estates of Bradbury by conniving lies.

Elise had no way of determining what was truth and what was not. She had come to Bradbury months after the Marquess was killed in a reckless bid for freedom and had never had the occasion to become acquainted with the man. Her closest contact with him had been her discovery of his portrait in the east wing where she now resided. Previous to her arrival, the quarters had remained closed, but in the tiny cubicle where the portrait had been found, the disturbance of dust and the clean, fresh covering over the piece had given evidence of its recent placement. Curious as to why so grand a painting would be hidden away, she had made discreet inquiries, only to be told that the squire had ordered the portrait destroyed shortly after his arrival and that the servants, taking umbrage at his dictate, had spirited it away to the east wing.

Elise could hardly fault the servants for their loyalties, though she was persuaded by the evidence of the Marquess's crimes that he had not deserved such devotion. After all, he had been judged guilty of foreign intrigue, conspiring to assassinate the Queen, and of trying to conceal his duplicity by the murder of her agent. Still, when she considered how long many of the servants had been at Bradbury, some even before the event of Lord Seymour's birth, three past a score and ten years ago, Elise could understand why they would choose to reject the evidence of his guilt and remain faithful to his memory.

She was determined to remain just as sensitive to her uncle's motives in ridding the house of every reminder of the late Marquess. If the portrait represented a true likeness of the man, then one could assume that Seymour had made quite an impression on Arabella. The loss of such a magnificent suitor would have made any woman resentful of a father who had somehow been involved in his demise. If for no other purpose than to keep peace in his small family, Edward had been justified.

The challenge Elise had found herself faced with since her arrival was dealing with a staff of servants who disliked the squire. Though they kept busy and attended the duties of the house, it was done more out of respect for its previous owner. A confrontation usually ensued after a long period of continual grumbling over Edward's way of doing things. It was not their right to question the squire's orders, Elise instructed them, no matter how inane they seemed to be.

This evening was proving no exception to the rule. She had already scolded several for their unfavorable comparisons between their present master and their last, when she noticed a manservant dawdling in front of a tapped barrel. This one wore a tunic whose hood covered his head, preventing any glimpse of his features. He stood hunched over his task in such a way that his broad shoulders obstructed her view, giving rise to the suspicion that he was taking liberties with the brew, certainly an unforgivable sin in her uncle's eyes.

Bracing herself for another argument, Elise straightened her spine and smoothed her black velvet gown over the hooped farthingale, assuming her best mien as mistress of a great house. For one so young, she looked very intent and most elegant in her simple but costly garb. A white, lace-edged ruff, conservatively narrow compared to the lavish excesses of court dress, flared out from her throat and rose higher in the back, enhancing the beauty of her oval face. A bloom of rosy color brightened delicately-boned cheeks, setting off a sparkle in the jewel-blue eyes. Those sapphire orbs slanted slightly upward and were thickly fringed with silken lashes of a coal-black hue. Her brows had not been shaved as was the custom of some women, but were slashes of red-brown that swept upward across flawless, lustrous skin. Her rich auburn hair had been parted in the middle and was neatly coifed beneath a pert, black velvet attifet which formed an arc above both sides of her forehead. Two long ropes of pearls hung about her neck beneath the crisp ruff and swept downward over her bosom. A ruby-encrusted frame served as a clasp at the first full swell of her breast and held a miniature enamel painting, the profile of a woman whose image her father had often said resembled her mother.

Elise hoped she looked as imposing as the subject of the tiny portrait, for the servant would be more likely to give her the respect due her station, than if he were one of those who had witnessed her undignified masquerades as ragged urchin and Hansa youth. Pausing close behind the man, she inquired almost sweetly, "Is the wine to your liking?"

Slowly the hooded head turned until the narrow opening of the deep cowl faced her above a broad shoulder. The covering was drawn up close around the man's face, half masking it, and though his darkly translucent eyes caught the glow of nearby candles and seemed to glimmer at her from the shadows of the hood, she was forbidden a clear view of his features. He seemed much taller and somehow different from the other hirelings, lending to the suspicion that he had come from a different portion of the estate.

"Beggin' yer pardon, mistress. The ol' winemaster bid me sample the brew so's no bitter vetch'd be sourin' the tongues o' these 'ere foin folk." Though stubbled with the coarseness of a commoner's speech, his voice was deep and rich, with a full measure of warmth. He raised the flagon he held, tipping it a bit, and thoughtfully contemplated it before tapping his forefinger against its side. "Mark me word, mistress, this 'ere brew comes from the ol' stock. Has a fair ta middlin' bite, 'at it does. 'Tain't none o' 'at rot this fellow Stamford serves up."

Elise stared agog at the man, taken aback by his

unabashed affront. His audacity pricked her sense of propriety, and her voice sharpened with sarcasm. "I rather doubt *Squire* Stamford would countenance your judgment *or* your opinion, whatever it may be. Ungrateful wretch! Who are you to cast awry the good intent of one who pays your wage? For shame!"

The hireling heaved a wearisome sigh. " 'Tis a pity, it be. A rank, poor pity."

Elise settled her hands on her slender waist, and her eyes flashed with a feral gleam as she gave him a chiding retort. "Ah, now we would hear it! A complaint! Forsooth! The squire would sooner tolerate grievances from the poor beggars in the streets than from those in his own kitchen. Pray tell, good fellow, have I hindered your freedom to imbibe by my presence?"

The man raised a hand wrapped in ragged strips of cloth and scrubbed it across his mouth. "The squire'd do well ta taste his own stock. 'Tis a pity ta give 'ese foin folk 'em bitter dregs what he'd 'ave us pour."

"Are you unquestioned as a tapster, or were you just born arrogant?" Elise asked with rampant scorn.

"Arrogant?" The fellow gave a brief chortle tinged with reproof. "Well now! Ye might say I've gots me share. Been 'round ye high-blooded folk too long."

Elise caught her breath in high-flying indignation. "You have far more than your fair portion, let me assure you!"

Untouched by her criticism, the servant responded with an indolent shrug. " 'Tain't so much arr'gance as 'tis knowin' good from bad, right from wrong . . . an' sometimes it takes a wee bit o' wit 'fore ye can tell the difference 'twixt the two." Stepping close to the cask again, he began filling a second flagon. "Now when his lor'ship were 'ere . . ."

"What ho! Another loudly lamenting the loss of the

late Marquess! I have never heard the like from so many rebellious servants!" Elise complained. She noted the entry of more trenchers of food and, with an impatient wave of her hand, directed the hirelings to a trestle table some distance away, as yet unwilling to let this oafish knave escape without first setting him in his proper place. "Tell me, is there aught that man was able to teach you about good manners?"

"Aye, 'at 'ere was." The cowl muffled the deep voice as he wiped up spilled droplets with the sleeve of his tunic. "His lordship . . . the Mar'kee . . . 'Twas his very ways I followed."

"Then I'll warrant you've had a dreadfully poor tutor," Elise interrupted brusquely. " 'Tis a known fact Lord Seymour was a murderer and a traitor to the Queen. You'd do better to seek another source for your instructions."

"I've heard 'em tales meself," the servant replied, and continued with a short, scoffing laugh, "but I canna' put much store in 'em."

" 'Twas more than a tale," Elise reminded him crisply. "Or at least the Queen thought so. She stripped the man of his holdings and gave them to my uncle. Obviously she recognized the better man."

The man set the flagon down with a thump and leaned forward as if to confront her with a denial, unmindful of the cowl that fell away from his lower face. An unkempt beard of a light brown hue masked his jaw, and beneath the ragged wisps of whiskers hanging over his upper lip, his mouth was drawn back in a snarl. "Who made ye his judge, girl? Why, ye ne'er even met the man, an' ye've no ken o' the squire if ye say he's the better man."

Elise met those eyes which were now strangely piercing within the shadows of the hood. For a moment she was held frozen by the anger she saw blazing there, then she lifted her chin with an elegant air and dared counter his attack. "Are you some ancient sage that you can say whether or nay I met the man?"

Straightening to his full height, the hireling drew back slightly and folded his arms across his chest as he stared down at her with sardonic amusement. At best, the top of her head reached to the point of his bewhiskered chin, and had Elise not tilted her head back, she would have seen naught but a wide expanse of rough sacking covering his chest.

"Beggin' yer pardon, mistress." He pressed his hand to that broadness in a mocking gesture and swept her a shallow bow of apology. "I ne'er saw ye 'ere when Lor' Seymour was master, an' I was o' a mind ta think the two o' ye 'ad ne'er met."

"Actually we never did," Elise admitted, a trifle piqued at his challenging manner. The man deserved no explanation, and she wondered why she even bothered giving one. Daring to meet his taunting smile, she lent emphasis to her words. "But I would have known him just the same."

"Indeed?" He gave her an oblique stare from the depth of the cowl. "An' could ye've said 'twas him or nay had ye looked him in the eye?"

Elise's temper sparked at the servant's insolence. It was obvious he doubted her claim, and perhaps only common sense discouraged him from calling her a liar. Still, memories from a more recent time lingered in her mind, and she found it rather frustrating that she should be haunted by one she desired to forget ... the portrait of the Marquess. At first, she had laid the cause of her admiration to the mood of the painting. The Marquess's green hunting attire had added a debonair flair, while the pair of wolfhounds waiting alertly at his side had conveyed an adventuresome spirit, but in truth, it had been the handsomely aristocratic features, the darkly lashed green eyes, and the subtly taunting smile which had really attracted her and had compelled her to go back for another glimpse or two.

Elise realized the ragged servant was awaiting her reply with a tolerant stare, as if he regarded her silence as proof of a much-inflated boast. Her annoyance grew by a full measure and added to the crispness in her voice. "Obviously you smirk because you know I cannot prove my claim. The Marquess was killed attempting an escape."

"Aye, I've heard it said meself," her antagonist acknowledged. "On his way ta the Tower, he was, when he tried ta break free o' the guards an' was shot dead." The servant leaned forward again and whispered furtively as if he encountered a dire need for secrecy. "But who's ta say for sure what happened ta the Mar'kee after he tumbled from the bridge? 'Ere weren't nary a soul what ever saw him again, an' 'ere weren't no leavin's what any could find." He sighed rather sadly. "Aye, ye can reckon 'em fishes feasted well 'at night, 'ey did."

Elise shivered at the gruesome image conjured forth and, with an effort of will, dismissed what seemed to be a deliberate attempt to unsettle her. Purposefully she directed her attention to the matters at hand. " 'Tis the present feast we need attend to ..." She paused, not knowing how to address the man. "I assume your mother gave you a name."

"Aye, mistress, 'at she did. Taylor, it be. Just Taylor."

Elise swept her hand to indicate those seated at the trestle tables and instructed him on his duties. "Then, Taylor, I bid you see to the squire's guests and their cups ere he takes us both to task for dallying."

With a flourish of his own rag-covered hand Taylor

stepped into a flamboyant bow. "Yer servant, mistress."

Elise was rather astounded by his grace and could not resist a conjecture. "You copy your lord's manners well, Taylor."

A soft chuckle came from the man as he tugged the cowl closer about his face. "His lor'ship 'ad as many tutors in his youth as a toad has warts. 'Twas a game o' mine ta follow what was bein' taught."

She raised a brow in mild curiosity. "And why is it that you keep your head covered and your face hidden? I've not detected a chill in the hall."

His answer came quickly enough. "Nay, mistress, 'ere be no chill. 'Twas an accident o' birth, ye see. Why, 'ere be some what'd swoon at the merest glimpse o' me poor face. I fear 'twould be a dreadful sight for 'ese foin folks ta bear."

Elise refrained from further inquiries, having no wish to view the man's deformities. She spoke a word of dismissal and watched him until assured he was applying himself well to his task. He moved around the trestle tables, refilling a goblet here or providing a new cup there as he alternated the use of the flagons, serving the ladies and elderly from one and replenishing the goblet of the stout-armed, able-bodied men with the other. Silently Elise gave her approval, admiring his foresight in serving a milder wine to give to the less stalwart.

Scanning the hall for more laggards, Elise almost relaxed as she saw that the servants were keeping busy. She let her eyes wander from table to table, assessing what further foods were needed, and failed to notice a guest stepping near until that one pressed close against her back. The intruder slid a hand about her narrow waist and, before she could react, bent down to place a light kiss below her ear, just above the ruff.

"Elise . . . fragrant flower of the night . . ." a deep voice warmly crooned. "My soul doth yearn for your favors, sweet maid. Be kind to this poor fellow and let me taste the nectar from your lips."

Elise's temper exploded. She was not of a temperament to allow such fondling and would set this fellow back upon his heels! She came around with a hand drawn back, ready to strike this arrogant bumpkin who had so foolishly accosted her. Though her weight was slight, she had every bit of its force behind her and had every intention of landing a damaging blow to the fellow. She had visions of Reland's conceited cousin, Devlin Huxford, nuzzling her neck, for she had noticed how he had ogled her for most of the evening. Her eyes flashed with indignant rage at the thought that he should be so bold, but as she faced the man, her wrist was seized and securely held against her attempts to withdraw. She lifted a smoldering-hot gaze to the dark, swarthy face above her own and met the deep brown eyes that fairly danced with laughter.

"Quentin!" she gasped in relief. "What are you doing here?"

Smiling down at her, he brought her slender fingers in warm contact with his full and generous lips. "You look most enchanting this evening, Cousin. Certainly none the worse for having avoided the malice of the Radbornes." The corners of his mouth twitched upward teasingly. "My mother may never forgive my brothers for letting you get away."

"How can you jest so easily about your kin?" Elise asked in amazement. "They meant to do me ill, and 'twas a miracle I escaped."

"Poor Forsworth is still smarting from that blow

you smote against his head. He swears you hit him with a club, and of course Mother laid more upon him for turning his back to you." Quentin sighed in mock sympathy and slowly shook his head. "The lad will never be the same. You quite addled him, I'm sure."

"*Lord* Forsworth, or so he has dubbed himself, was addled ere I touched him," Elise derided. "Truly, I am much bemused that you came from the same stock. 'Tis evident you have risen far above your siblings in both wit and wisdom, not to mention good manners."

Pressing his hand to the rich cloth of his doublet, Quentin bent forward slightly to acknowledge her compliment. "My gratitude, fair damsel. There are certain advantages of being the eldest. As you know, Father left me the family's country estate and wealth apart from Mother's. Such comforts allow me to separate myself from the rivalries and conspiracies of my family."

Elise lifted her slim nose, denying any excusal for the faults of his kin. The widow and younger sons of Bardolf Radborne belonged to a haughty class of aristocrats who wielded their power as impartially as they would a heavy broadsword on a field of battle, hacking down with destructive blows any who stood in their way. "Uncle Bardolf was just as generous with Cassandra, and there was more than enough wealth to provide for your mother and brothers for some time to come. If her reserves are dwindling now, then her own foolishness caused the waste. She covets what my father set aside for me and claims it belongs to her sons as part of the Radborne inheritance, but a pox on her and your three brothers if they believe the lies she conjures. You know well enough that as second son, my father had to acquire his own fortune, so there is naught of ours that belongs to your family.

If not for the fact they took me prisoner and tried to force me to tell where my father had hidden the gold, I'd be inclined to think they were responsible for his abduction."

Quentin's brow furrowed in museful consideration as he folded his hands behind his back. "I agree. It seems unlikely they'd attempt to force the information from you if they already had Uncle Ramsey in their possession." He heaved a ponderous sigh. "I'm continually distressed by the games my mother and brothers play to gain riches."

"They're more than games," Elise corrected icily. "Cassandra and her brood of banal-headed dolts meant to do me harm." She paused, realizing how her aspersions might offend this member of their family and felt some chagrin at her own insensitivity. "I'm sorry, Quentin. I wound you, and I don't mean to. You're so different from the rest of your family, sometimes I forget to curb my tongue when I'm with you. I cannot understand why you ever entertained your mother's wrath and took me away from them."

An abortive laugh escaped his lips. "I fear my gallantry was shortsighted. I should have made my house secure against their trespassing. Then there'd have been no need for you to escape a second time."

"Your brothers came while you were gone, creeping into your home like thieves in the night to drag me back to London. You cannot blame yourself, Quentin."

His dark eyes probed the pools of deep blue. "I've been wondering..." His words were spoken hesitantly. "I would not ask, Elise, but I fear I must. What did my family do to you?"

Elise drew up her slender shoulders in a small, distressed shrug, not wishing to recall the cruelties of her aunt and cousins. Their abuses had extended beyond verbal insults to heavy-handed interrogations and, when that had failed, the withholding of food and simple comforts. They turned her bedchamber into a place of torment, and now that she was free, she was keenly aware that her memory of those weeks was best put behind her for the sake of her own sense of peace and well-being. "When taking actual account, Quentin, they did me no lasting harm."

Despite her charitable words, Elise realized she was still atremble over the nightmare of her imprisonment. Forcing a smile, she glanced up at her cousin. "You've not told me why you're here. I thought you had an aversion to Uncle Edward."

"I cannot deny that fact," he admitted with a chuckle, "but I would brave the vulture's nest to see the fairest gem."

"You've come too late, Quentin," Elise admonished in a lighter vein. "The nuptials have already been spoken, and Arabella is now married to yon Earl."

"My fairest Elise, I came not to see Arabella," he declared with fervor. "But you!"

"And you, Cousin, most surely tease," she accused with unfeigned skepticism. "You'd have better odds convincing me of your sincerity if you told me you came to see Uncle Edward. Arabella is a beauty no man can deny, and I'm sure many a rejected suitor came here tonight to bid her a fond adieu."

Quentin's grin was somewhat representative of a leer as he bent near her to whisper warmly, "Has no gallant troubadour ever sung sonnets praising your beauty, sweet Elise? Or were they too smitten by your perfection?" He sighed in exaggerated agony as Elise gave him a chidingly dubious stare. "Sweet maid, I do not lie! Your eyes are like gems, the most costly of sapphires. They sparkle from their fringes of black. Your brows are winged birds taking to flight, and your hair has the rich warm hue of cherrywood and a fragrance that makes me heady with delight. Your skin gleams with the soft luster of pearls...and promises to be most tasty."

Elise continued to eye him in amused disbelief, unmoved by his ardent declarations. "The wine has most surely addled your wits if you think I will believe that nonsense."

"I have not had a drop to drink!" he avowed passionately.

Disregarding his interruption, she pressed on. "I've heard many tales about you, Quentin. So many I daresay your prattle is frayed from much use. Surely many a maid has had like praises plied to her."

"Forsooth, sweet maid!" Quentin laid a hand to his breast as he feigned a mournful protest. "You do me grave injustice."

"And you, sir, beat your doublet in vain. We both know I accuse you rightly," she challenged with a teasing smile. "You're a rake worthy of the first merit. Why, 'twas only a fortnight ago I heard similar prose expressed to Arabella...and from your own lips!"

"Can you be jealous, fair Elise?" Quentin asked in hopeful glee.

Ignoring his quick riposte, she continued undisturbed. "I trust Arabella, being duly betrothed to Reland, had the good sense to ask you to leave. As your cousin, I should hope to spare you."

"Oh, sweetling," he lamented dramatically. "You ply your tongue with the skill and zeal of an ill-tempered shrew, and I am left bereft of joy."

"I doubt that." Elise spoke past the laughter in her voice. As a woman, she could readily acknowledge the dark-eyed, dark-haired Quentin Radborne had both the good looks and charm to lure innumerable feminine admirers, but she was every bit as convinced that more than a few maids had been led to a sullied doom by his cajoling words and ardent attentions. Though she enjoyed his company, she was not of a mind to let her name be linked more than it was to his.

Elise paused, hearing her name called from across the crowded hall, and glanced about until she saw her uncle beckoning impatiently to her. His sharp frown clearly betrayed his displeasure, and there was no need for her to search for a reason. To say that he was even remotely tolerant of Quentin would have been stretching the truth to the extent of farfetched. His tone sharpened with the directive, "Come, girl! An' be quick 'bout it!"

"Alas, your gatekeeper calls," Quentin remarked disparagingly.

Elise raised a querying brow at her cousin's dark humor. "My gatekeeper?"

A wry grin spread across the full lips. "If Edward could, he'd lock you up in a tower and throw away the key, just to prevent me from getting too near. He's afraid you'll either lose the treasure he has his eye on or the one called chastity."

"Then his worries are unfounded." Elise smiled and lightly tapped Quentin's doublet. "Not that you wouldn't try to claim one or the other, mind you. I'm willing neither to be divested of my purse nor added to the long list of your conquests."

Throwing back his head, Quentin gave vent to a torrent of uproarious guffaws. He could not help but admire this saucy wench for speaking her mind. She was destined to be a challenge to any man and a prize well worth the seeking.

Elise cringed inwardly, knowing how deftly his glee would enflame her uncle's temper. It was not that she was afraid of Edward, for she held in reserve the prerogative to move out of the manor if ever he became too harsh or demanding. Nevertheless there were times when she was wont to keep the peace as much as she was able, and since it was Arabella's wedding night, the occasion warranted such considerations.

Dipping into a quick curtsey, she excused herself. "'Tis my regret that I must leave your good company, dear Cousin, but as you say, my gatekeeper summons me."

Quentin nodded with a leering grin. "You may have been saved for the moment from this hoary wolf, fair damsel, but there shall come another time, I assure you."

Elise made her way through the press and joined her uncle, who cast a contemptuous sneer toward the younger man who was now making his own way through the hallful of guests. Edward bent a baleful glare upon her. "Did I not tell ye ta keep yerself ta yer duties?" he growled in low, angry tones. "I gave ye no leave ta be cavortin' with 'at Quentin fellow. Have ye no shame?"

"For what offense should I feel ashamed?" Elise rejoined softly, causing her uncle to glower in sharp displeasure. In earnest she explained, "I merely passed a word or two with my cousin in the presence of your guests. I see no fault in that."

Edward nestled his round head between his thick shoulders as he harrumphed sharply. "Aye, I saw the two o' ye laughin' an' chortlin' like ye were sharin' some vile tale."

Elise's delicate brows lifted in wonder as she observed her uncle's jeering disdain. He had a crude way of twisting his lips to display his contempt that reminded her of her own escalating exasperation with the man. The occasions were becoming more and more frequent when she found herself abhorring his manners. Of late, she had felt much relief that her own mother had been of no actual kin to Edward, but had been left as a babe in the chapel on his family's small farm. That fact alone freed her from any loyalty required by the association of blood kin, yet when she had to struggle with such contrary feelings of her own, she was beginning to feel hampered in her duties when she had to chide others for their lack of respect.

"Ye should be ashamed the way ye carry on with 'at rascal," Edward berated.

He flung a hand to indicate the man, meaning to condemn his niece further, but paused abruptly when he realized the handsome rake was now standing beside his own daughter. From all appearances, Quentin was sharing some amusing comment with the bride, for they were both laughing.

Edward puffed up like an enraged rooster and blustered, "Look at him! A body would think the man never had a care in the world the way he's makin' his rounds wit' the ladies."

"Has the Queen declared a period of mourning that we should bridle our gaiety and good humor?" Elise inquired in a guise of worry.

Somewhat befuddled by her question, Edward frowned at his niece until the realization struck that she was making light of what he had said, then his bushy brows came sharply together. "I'll thank ye, girl, ta keep a civil tongue in yer head an' stop yer foolery! Ye'd do well ta pay more attention ta yer duties so's I wouldn't have ta remind ye what they are."

His arrogance pricked Elise's pride, and though she made an effort to retain her good manners, she reminded him, "I pay rents for the east wing, Uncle, and they are more than adequate. Above that, I yield you whatever help and service I can offer. I am happy I can be of assistance, but I do not have to earn my keep, for my father left monies enough for me in my own accounts with his bankers. Nor do I have to stay here if I choose to leave. If you are uncomfortable with the arrangement, give me leave and I shall find shelter elsewhere."

A hot retort came quickly to the tip of Edward's tongue, but he was wise enough not to unleash his anger upon the girl. There was more at stake here than the rents, though those were high enough to warrant his good behavior. Yet he had little tolerance for anyone challenging his dictates, especially one from his own household or the fairer gender. His wife had meekly obeyed his will throughout their married life, taking refuge in her bedchamber when he had raged and salving her hurt feelings in bottles of port until her death. Arabella had never dared give him argument, but had submitted to his authority as if she had no desires of her own. Elise, however, had already proven herself to be of a different mold entirely.

If Edward had learned anything about his niece since her arrival at Bradbury, surely it was a realization that she had a mind and a will of her own. Her firm resolve to find her father had led her into dangers to which he would have abandoned her had he not coveted her wealth so much. He had glimpsed evidence of her strong determination when she had donned the rags of a penniless urchin, secured a ride to London on the back of a cart, and slipped beyond the invisible barrier of Fleet Street in an effort to obtain what information she could from the miscreants who had taken refuge in the lawless territory of Alsatia. When the incessant reminder of a hidden treasure finally prodded Edward to take action, he had sent a servant to find and fetch her home. Other disastrous events occurred shortly after her return, not the least of which had been a shocking confrontation with Reland. That single event had done much to convince him that Elise Radborne had a most incredible talent for brewing trouble.

Order had barely been restored to his household when she slipped away again, this time to the Stilliards, a place her father had purportedly gone to exchange some of his possessions for coffers of gold. If he had thought himself afraid of the lawless breed in Alsatia, Edward had concluded after much fretting, then he was absolutely terrified of those dreaded foreigners in the Hanseatic League. They possessed the power and wealth to influence kings and princes, and though Queen Elizabeth had proven of sterner mettle, many of her subjects had fallen prey to the Hansa. He had despaired of ever seeing his niece again and was much amazed when she came back politely escorted by one of the Hansa youth and dressed in the garb of one of the same. "Breeches on a girl!" he had railed in shock when he saw her. "'Tis not fit!"

Clearly, if he had perceived to what extent his niece would disrupt his life, Edward knew he would have haggled for steeper rents. As it was, he was convinced the twit had made the better bargain. For every coin she gave him, he was put through twice as much torment. Still, he took care now to placate her and assumed a mien of injury as he gave the excuse, "I'm only concerned for yer reputation. Quentin is not one ta bring ye honor. I can only advise ye not ta lose anythin' ta him."

"You needn't fear, Uncle," Elise promptly assured him. "I have no intention of being led astray by any man." She delivered the pointed statement, knowing full well what the elder really desired and what he was afraid Quentin would get. He was not so wise at hiding his greed as he thought he was.

Edward missed the thrust of her subtle gibe as he rushed on to criticize her position. After all, she had fled to his house in fear of her life. "Everyone knows yer father sold all an' hid the gold 'gainst yer day o' need, mainly ta keep Cassandra an' her get from sinkin' their greedy claws into his wealth when he left this world. I can tell ye for sure, girl, whilst the treasure be hidden, 'tis a fearful burden ye'll bear. Every rake'll be tryin' ta ferret ye out. An' dare I remind ye 'tis the very reason ye're here, so's I can protect ye from yer father's kin. An' there stands one o' 'em Radborne devils just awaitin' ta get his hands on what is yers."

"Quentin has wealth of his own," Elise reminded her uncle. "He has no need of mine."

"Humph! I ne'er seen a man what couldn't use a little more gold in his coffers. I tell ye, Quentin would sport his manhood with ye whilst he lifted the purse from yer side. Aye! Ye mark me words, girl. Ye keep yerself from the likes o' Quentin, an' mayhap someday ye'll get yerself a man like Reland or his cousin, Devlin."

Heaven take pity! Elise thought in abject repugnance, and muttered aloud in droll humor, "Debauchery may have its rewards after all."

"What's 'at ye say, girl?" Edward railed, taking offense at her offhandish jibe. His fists knotted as he struggled to subdue his bent toward belligerence. "Ye've lost yer wits for sure if ye think yer cousin is a better man 'an Reland!"

"Mayhap," Elise responded with a noncommittal shrug, and moved away without assuring him that his judgment of Quentin was far outstripped by her own resolve to avoid any serious involvement with her cousin. She was too concerned about her father to countenance being courted by any man, least of all by the Huxford tribe.

Chapter 2

GREED WAS FOR MANY a curse, for it greatly diminished the enjoyment of most pleasures. Not even the smallest coin could be expended without regret at its loss or without an anxious hope that its departure would bring a larger reward and somehow prove worthy of the sacrifice. Such was the case of Edward Stamford, whose satisfaction over his daughter's marriage dimmed to distressing degrees as he continued to witness the liberal glee and excesses of the revelers. His grudgingly given generosity had apparently delighted the inconsiderate masses who had come to satisfy their gluttony, but the festive strains of the musicians did little to ease his rapidly souring disposition. The laughing and cavorting guests enhanced his gnawing resentment, and he gained no greater comfort from those who were now dozing in a much-sated stupor.

"Look at 'em!" Edward muttered to himself in contempt. "They've stuffed their gullets so much on me wine an' vittles, they're wallowin' in their cups. I could've saved meself a few good coin if I'd known they'd crumple so easily."

Edward's glower ranged slowly about the room and came full around to mark the servant, Taylor, as that one paused at a nearby table. "You there! Stop dawdlin' with 'at flagon an' fill me cup!"

The fellow half turned in surprise, scrubbing the back of a hand across his mouth, but when Edward beckoned him to come, he sidled away as he mumbled, "I'll go now an' fetch ye a fresh pitcher o' ale, Squire."

"Here now! Ne'er ye mind the ale." Irate at being denied, Edward motioned the servant back. "I'll take a mug o' whate'er ye've got."

" 'Tain't fit, Squire." Taylor's voice was muffled as he tugged the cowl closer about his face. "Why, 'tis naught but the last, foul dregs o' the keg I've gots here. I'll fetch ye a good, stout ale, 'at I will, Squire," he offered, continuing his retreat. " 'Twill take me no more'n a twinklin' o' an eye." Before further protest could be made, he slid past several drunken lords and slipped out of sight.

Grinding his teeth in vexation, Edward mangled several expletives as he slammed the leather-bound tankard down upon the table. He snatched up his plumed toque and, plopping it upon his graying head, rose to his feet, ready to storm after the wayward fellow. In the next instant he was struck with a horrible fear that the full weight of the terrestrial globe had abruptly descended upon his head, for the sudden throbbing pressure within his skull nearly buckled him to his knees. He waited in cautious stillness until the first assault of pain began to ebb, then gingerly avoided any sudden movement as he scanned the hall for the impertinent servant, unwilling to let him go without a serious dressing-down.

"I'll see his foul carcass picked clean by the crows," Edward swore through snarling lips.

In his careful search for the servant, however, Edward's gaze touched upon Elise again, and the sharp spur of anger goaded him anew, for it seemed she was on the verge of creating more trouble. The young swain, Devlin Huxford, had been obvious about his interest in her during the course of the festivities and was now asserting himself in a most insistent manner by trying to pull Elise out with the other dancers. As close kin to Reland, the roué was not to be offended without expecting some dire recompense to be exacted by the Huxford clan. Yet the girl was most assuredly pressing toward that mark. One could gauge by the rigid set of her jaw that an insult was forthcoming, and it would be fortunate indeed if the young man escaped unscathed from the little minx.

The furrows between Edward's brows deepened, and he forgot the pounding in his head as he elbowed his way through the guests. He had to reach Elise before she wreaked havoc upon the evening, which he had learned by grievous experience that she was quite capable of doing.

"Do you not ken, sir? I've no knowledge of the steps," he heard his niece explain. Her statement, curt and sharp as it was, failed to gain her release from the zealous Devlin. In some exasperation Elise snatched her slender wrist free in a quick, twisting movement and fixed an aloof stare upon her persistent admirer as she straightened the white pleated cuffs of her sleeve. "And presently, sir, I have no wish to learn."

Chortling in feigned merriment, Edward crushed a padded sleeve as he laid an arm around his niece's shoulder and cajoled, "Come now, girl. Would ye have this good fellow think ye ta be a stiff-necked ol' spinster without a proper upbringin'? Why, this be young Devlin Huxford." He dropped his arm away and waited for Elise to digest this information before he added meaningfully, "Cousin ta Reland."

Elise's softening smile was sweetly apologetic, and Devlin almost preened in anticipation. He made bold to copy her uncle's manner and slipped an arm confidently about her waist. "Forgive me, Uncle," she replied, trying to delicately extricate herself from the suffocating nearness forced upon her by Devlin. "Even if he were the Queen's own son, I'd tell him to go fish in another stream." Gritting out the last words, she jabbed an elbow into the ribs of the eager swain and added rather tartly, "I'm tired of his hooks pricking me."

Edward could hardly restrain himself as the thrust of her reply pierced him. His eyes first flared with expanding rage, then darkened to a steely hardness. He glanced briefly at the reddening Devlin, who had cautiously retreated a step. The young man waited expectantly for some show of pressure that would force the maid to submit, but Edward was well-acquainted with the folly of such an act. Simply, the girl would not stand for it, and he would be left without any hope of finding the hidden treasure.

Barely controlling his ire, Edward pressed near the pertly capped head, engulfing his niece in the foul vapors of his ale-sodden breath. "Would ye bring the Huxfords down upon us, girl?" he gritted out in a rasping whisper. "Reland still stews over yer last encounter, an' ye've now set yerself 'gainst another Huxford. I'll warrant ye'll not fare well with Reland takin' up quarters in the west wing."

In a soft, questioning tone Elise reminded her kin of his earlier command. "Did you not instruct me to keep the servants busy, Uncle?" she prodded, sensing where he was most vulnerable. "Why, if not for me, the hirelings would drain your cellars dry and eat your cupboards bare. But if 'tis your wont they be left to their own gluttony, then give me leave to enjoy the dancing."

Edward blustered in some embarrassment, then, without further preamble, he seized the younger man firmly by the arm and drew him away. "Come along, Devlin," he cajoled pleasantly, "'ere be a maid right o'er here whose talents are sure ta match yer own."

Elise folded her hands demurely as she witnessed the rather confused departure of the Huxford kin. Devlin had done much to strengthen her judgment that he was a crude, inconsiderate boor who boasted mightily of his own prowess, and in this, he had surely proven himself kin to Reland Huxford.

Edward wasted no time in presenting Devlin to a young and comely widow before hastening back to his niece. It seemed prudent to find duties for her outside the hall before he had to pay dearly for her presence. "I'll have ye escort Arabella ta her chambers now. Help her ta ready herself for Reland, an' as soon as she's done, ye come down an' tell me. I'll see ta it meself that Reland is escorted up, whether he's able or nay. This feastin' needs be stopped ere I'm stripped ta me bones."

Snatching a mug of ale from a passing servant, Edward gave her no further notice, but tipped the brim to his mouth for a long draught. He had need of a full keg to salve the turmoil now roiling in his belly.

Elise felt unsure of herself in this new directive and stepped away from her uncle with some hesitancy. It was not that she was ignorant of the manner in which a bride should receive her groom, but it seemed to her that Arabella might have benefited more from the wise counsel of an older, married woman. What assurances could she give the bride when she was herself a virgin?

Elise's gaze ranged slowly about the room until it came to rest on the newly wedded couple. Arabella was as delicate as a fragile flower, tall and slender with silky brown hair and pale gray eyes that were haunted by a look of melancholy. Her temperament was pliable, much like the reed that is blown to and fro by the wind. Indeed, there were times when she appeared to have no mettle to stand firm against the dictates of others. In sharp contrast Reland was a dark-haired bear of a man whose wide, muscular chest tapered to narrow hips. Though handsome and well-tutored, he displayed a strong inclination to be both irascible and mulishly opinionated. In his boorish arrogance he enjoyed testing all whose paths he crossed and was known to guffaw in outlandish glee when his actions elicited a response of fear. In short, he was a swaggering hector until one yielded him the upper hand, then he might deign to put aside his threatening demeanor and once again act the gentleman.

Elise's mind ranged back to the time when she first encountered the Earl. She had heard of his bumptious nature and overbearing tendencies well before her arrival, but she had dismissed most of the talk as poor-spirited hearsay. She had never even so much as seen the man from afar until that day he came riding into the courtyard on the late Marquess's black Friesian stallion. The steed had come into Reland's possession by way of a betrothal gift from Edward, and even from that initial viewing of the pair together, Elise was struck with a strong aversion for the pompous attitude of the one in the saddle. She had sensed that the man reveled in the fear and awe he inspired by the sight of him riding the animal, and fulfilling her image of a crude bully, he had chortled in uproarious mirth at the servants who scurried out of his path.

Elise had paused beside the courtyard stairs to admire the beautiful, stately-gaited beast, and never considering that she might become an offense to the Earl because she did not flee in terror like the others, she had calmly stroked the cat she held. Her unruffled composure, however, had done much to squelch Reland's booming laughter and thwart his good humor. Not content to frighten lackeys, maids, and scullions, the Earl had reined the stallion about and kicked him forward in her direction. Elise recalled how shocked and alarmed she had been when she realized she was being charged at, but her moment of panic had only seemed to encourage him. Reland's laughter had risen to a deafening roar, serving to ignite her indignation. In stubborn defiance she had stood her ground, refusing to yield the man any further gratification as the monstrous horse thundered toward her. The sight of that horrendous beast advancing toward her had nearly stripped away her thin facade of bravado, but against an almost overpowering urge to flee, she had held her place and clutched the frightened, struggling cat until the brutish fellow hauled back on the reins and brought the steed to a skidding halt in front of her, then she tossed the hissing, spitting feline at the horse.

When the cat lit, it raked its claws deep into the stallion's nose as it struggled for a hold, drawing forth a terrified shriek from the steed. Like some wild, maddened beast the animal had leapt and thrashed about to dislodge his tormentor, while the equally terrified cat clung with perseverance to the steed. Not so the rider! Unprepared for this abrupt turn of events, Reland had soared through the air with limbs flailing helplessly until he crashed to earth flat on his back. His breath had left him with an audible "whoof," and he had suffered through a panic-filled moment as he fought to regain it. An enraged, bellowing curse had given loud evidence of his success, and he had sprung to his feet like a geyser of erupting fury.

Faced with this new threat, Elise recalled her decision to beat a hasty retreat into the house, but Reland had seen her move and determined otherwise.

Incensed that a mere girl could unhorse him, he had charged her back, hardly considering that her far smaller frame was actually more agile than his own rather hulkish one. Elise had both sensed and heard his ponderous approach and, when the moment was ripe, had whirled aside from his path, ducking beneath his outstretched arm. A low moan had issued through Reland's gritted teeth and increased in volume and intensity as he stumbled past.

Even before Elise had finished turning, she heard a loud splash and an even louder commotion. When she looked around, she had found Reland thrashing facedown in a nearby pond. Spewing forth a flume of water, he had gotten clumsily to his knees, then to his feet, presenting the servants with such an hilarious spectacle that their giggles and guffaws could not be contained. The wet plumes of his toque had drooped downward beneath his hooked nose, causing him to spit between gasps as he tried to expell the limp ends from his mouth. His leather-cuffed riding gloves had spilled torrents of water when he lifted his hands to rake hair and feathers from his face, while the fur-lined chamarre had dripped steady runnels all around him. His soft hide boots, the pride of his costume, had each held a jug or two of water, making his legs and feet appear swollen and misshapen as he stomped out of the pond.

Reland's ensuing bellow of rage had made the skittish stallion snort and dance away, then, as if wondering what new threat might be forthcoming, the steed had glanced about in some apprehension until he spied the cat safely ensconced on top of a stone wall a short distance away. The clear victor of the fray, the feline had licked a paw and smoothed its ruffled fur in languid repose.

Reland had slowly glared the onlookers into silence

before he faced the insolent twit who had so recklessly challenged his authority. Elise had met his glowering gaze calmly and smiled with soft, enigmatic humor, aware that he was purposefully maneuvering to entrap her in a corner of the courtyard wall as he stalked forward.

Elise retreated until she felt the stone at her back, then braced herself to give him full measure before his strength and bulk could overwhelm her. Growling a profanity, Reland seized her by the collar and, lifting her from her feet, began to shake her violently. The girl reacted, and the previous furor of the cat was diminished by the outraged vixen she became as she fought off her assailant. Scratching, biting, poking, and eye-jabbing, she was like a little wild thing until a pained yowl issued forth from the ungallant Earl.

"You little bitch!" Reland bellowed and swept a hand back to cuff her.

"Great Caesar's blood!" Edward exclaimed from the gallery. "What be ye about?" Shocked by what he was witnessing, Edward stumbled down the stairs and, with the help of servants, dragged the pair apart, but not before his niece delivered a sharp kick to Reland's shin.

"You foulsome son of a flap-eared knave!" she railed in unladylike vehemence. "What hole did you slither from?"

"Elise! Calm yerself, girl!" Edward was aghast at the insults his niece laid upon the Earl. Anxiously he explained, "This be Arabella's betrothed . . ."

"Pity Arabella!" Elise sneered. "She'll likely expire from this clumsy oaf's abuse!"

"Shush, girl, shush!" Edward wrung his hands in great distress as he tried to placate his future son-in-law. He had never been in a situation that warranted such control on his own temper. He could not turn on his niece for fear of losing a fortune. Nor could he question the Earl for fear of setting off his temper. "Please, Reland, ye must forgive the girl. She's beside herself. She's a kinswoman o' mine, barely arrived. Ye can see she has much ta learn. I beg ye, ease yer fervor, an' let us settle this in a genteel manner."

"She has maimed me steed!" Reland flung a sodden glove to indicate his mount, scattering an arc of shiny bright droplets as he once again startled the steed who threw up his head in fear. Fine trickles of blood marred the tender nose and, where the rich bridle crossed it, small droplets gleamed in the sun like tiny rubies on a strand. "He'll bear the marks 'til his death!" Almost as an afterthought Reland clutched his aching head, moaning his discomfort. "And she nearly spilled me skull upon the cobbles!"

"You need have no fear, milord," Elise snidely countered. "'Twas empty before the fall."

In a high-flying rage Reland shook his fist at her. "Ye simpleminded twit! Ye must've come from the low bogs not to know Eddy could've killed ye. Next time I'll let him trample ye in the mire!"

She responded with derisive sarcasm. "Having now met your acquaintance, my lord, *next time* I'll be more wary of what you might command of the steed."

"Reland, forgive the girl," Edward hastened to interject. "She just doesn't know . . ."

"Remember the names, girl," the Earl growled, ignoring the pleas of the elder. "Hide yerself when ye hear that Reland Huxford, Earl of Chadwick, and his big Eddy are here. I give ye fair warning."

"Eddy . . . Big Eddy . . . Eddy Reland . . . Reland Big Eddy . . ." Elise tossed her head like a child chanting a verse as she deliberately jumbled the names to convey the fact that she could disregard the man, his title, and his threat more readily than she could the stallion.

" 'Tis a fine steed you have been given. Obviously too good for you. I shall endeavor to remember him."

Reland's face darkened to a mottled red as she lifted a challenging gaze and dared him to attack her again. Edward rushed to stave off the threatening eruption, seeing the lowering brow of the man, and quickly took the younger man's elbow. "Come, my son-to-be," he chortled worriedly. "Let us seek a cup o' bitters an' rest ourselves 'fore the fire."

Edward gestured urgently for a servant to attend the dripping Earl, and when the man was led away, the squire turned a glare upon the errant Elise in dire promise of further reproof. It came when Reland was well out of earshot.

"Have ye lost yer wits?" he demanded. "Do ye want ta sour the bonds Arabella seeks with this one?" Edward thrust his hands aloft in mute supplication, then bore down upon his niece again. "Or would ye rather set me affairs awry by shamin' this good fellow in me home?"

" 'Twas *his* buffoonery that caused the fray!" Elise flared in her own defense. "He nearly ran me down with that animal!" She flung a hand toward the stallion as it was being led away by a groom. The stable boy was patting his neck affectionately, as if the animal were some long-lost friend. The steed nuzzled him in return and did not seem so threatening now. "Does it matter aught to you that Reland is an overbearing lunatic?"

"Shush!" Edward flung the command out before he threw an anxious glance over his shoulder to assure himself that the Earl had departed. "Do ye not ken, girl?" He caught her elbow and bent close to whisper, "This may be Arabella's last hope."

Elise jerked away from the cruel vise and rubbed her arm as she replied with barely restrained ire. "Better to remain a spinster than bed with the likes of *him!"*

Spinning on a heel, Elise lifted her skirts and flew up the stairs before her uncle could find his tongue. Though he called after her, she dashed along the loggia without giving acknowledgment, snatched open the door to an inner hall, and slammed the portal behind her, rattling nearby windows with the force of her passage.

Throughout the ensuing days her uncle had repeatedly demanded she give an apology to the Earl, but Elise had vowed through clenched teeth that she would move into a thorn-bound spinney before she would yield to any such request. Not sure of just what she might do, since she seemed capable of the most outrageous conduct, Edward had finally acceded and had pressed her no further.

And here she was again, Elise thought, feeling a strong repugnance for Reland. She was sure the task she had been given was tantamount to lending assistance in the sacrificial rites of a virgin being offered up to a slavering beast. In truth, she abhorred the ruffian and felt great sympathy for her cousin.

Elise quickly erased the repugnance from her face as Arabella glanced around. As if bidden by some mysterious summons, she searched the room until she found her younger cousin. Elise met her gaze and responded with a hesitant nod, recognizing an unspoken inquiry in the pale gray eyes. A fleeting frown touched the bride's smooth visage before she turned aside to speak a word to her new husband. Reland leered in heated lust as he watched her depart, and in smug triumph he glanced around at his companions, stirring a memory in Elise's mind of that same self-satisfied smirk he had worn that first day of their meeting. It was almost as if Arabella had become another possession he could use as a whip with which to lord it over others.

A few of his rowdy friends called to him in coarse repartee and, at each stroke of witty humor, chortled the louder in outrageous glee. Arabella showed only a trace of a smile as she moved with quiet dignity through the press of bantering, hooting guests and held her silence until she and Elise were climbing the stone stairs that led to the west wing.

"I am beset by folly," she murmured dismally.

Elise stared at her cousin, wondering what had finally set her awry with her state of circumstance. Arabella had always managed to maintain a reserved poise through times of conflict and turmoil, even amid her father's blustering tirades, and had actually shown a certain measure of eagerness to marry the Earl. To Elise's knowledge she had never issued a complaint against Reland before, though there were times when she displayed a discontent because of the tragedies she had suffered. She had a bent toward melancholia and long moods of depression, which even Edward tried to assuage. Much attention had been given to the grieving woman by everyone in an attempt to bring her out of doldrums, for no one could doubt she had good cause to lament.

"What troubles you, Arabella? Why do you say such a thing?" the younger cousin asked.

"Oh, Elise, try and understand. Reland is a fine and noble man . . . even a handsome man . . ."

Elise was sensitive to her cousin's uncertainty and understood only too well the troubling disquiet Reland could rouse in a young bride's breast. Indeed, if the roles were reversed and she were the one to wed the Earl, she would have vented a thousand grievances by now.

"I am beset with a cruel curse," Arabella continued

in a muted tone. She paused on a step and leaned her head listlessly against the stone wall, not caring how she crushed the jeweled attifet that adorned her meticulously dressed hair. "Heretofore every man who has vied for my hand has been torn from my side by some cruel tragedy. Where now are those who once pledged their troth to me? All fallen to some awful fate, I vow. Each plucked from my side by death or some great catastrophe. I thought it mere coincidence when the first two succumbed to some unnamed malady, then the third's life was snuffed out when thieves attacked him on the streets. 'Twas not three years ago during Eastertide the earth jerked and heaved until stones tumbled down upon our heads from a church and killed my poor William. Hardly a week betrothed, and so quickly he was taken. The fifth suitor was abducted by miscreants, and I'll warrant we'll find his bones someday. And then, the sixth..."

Delicately sweeping brows came together in querying bemusement as Elise heard the other's wistful sigh. Softly she questioned, "Was that not the Marquess of Bradbury?"

Arabella nodded slowly. "Yea... Maxim... he was the sixth."

Elise dropped a slender hand on her cousin's sleeve as she gently argued, "Surely you cannot mourn a murderous traitor."

Without answering Arabella continued her ascent and, moving down the hall, passed through her chamber doors. She crossed the anteroom and went to stand before the fireplace in the bedchamber, there pulling the veiled cap from her head and tossing it carelessly aside. "Yea, 'tis true. The Marquess's offenses were worse than the others. Accused of murder and conspiracy with Mary Stuart against the Queen, he deserved to be hunted down and slain. He could not have done more to win my hatred."

Not knowing what to reply, Elise glanced about at the spacious bedchamber and its rich appointments and wondered what had possessed the man who had once lived here within the confines of these chambers to form such unhealthy allegiances. What had turned him against the Queen...that same Queen who had fondly compared him to that other Seymour she had known in her youth? Thomas Seymour had won her affection; had Maxim Seymour deserved her hatred?

"Surely you are not cursed as you suppose, Arabella," Elise consoled. "Rather, 'twould seem you've been fortunate to escape marriage with those who were less worthy."

"How can I make you understand, dear child? You are so young, and I have grown so tired and...so old..."

"Old?" Elise repeated in amazement. "At five and twenty? Nay, you are still young, Arabella, and you have your life ahead of you. This is your wedding night...and you must prepare yourself for your husband..."

Elise saw the tears well up in the silver-gray eyes. The agony was visible in the wan smile, but there was no ease for it, nothing either of them could do.

"I must have some time alone," Arabella whispered in sudden desperation. "Delay the wedding party until I send a servant to beckon them."

"Your father asked me to attend you," Elise murmured softly. "What would you have me say to him?"

Arabella looked into the worried countenance of her cousin and hastened to reassure her. "Beg him to let me have a few moments alone so I can better prepare myself for Reland. Only a little time...just until I have calmed myself. Then you may return and assist me."

"Reland has a fair look about him." Elise offered the comment with the hope that she could bolster her cousin's spirits. "You'll no doubt be the envy of many a maid."

Arabella responded distantly, "Not as handsome as some I've known."

A small, fleeting frown chased across Elise's brow. "Do you yearn after a dead man, Arabella?"

The gray eyes stared back in mild curiosity. "A dead man? Whomever do you mean, Elise?"

"The Marquess of Bradbury, of course," the girl stated. "Does he still trouble you?"

"Oh, truly there was a man to stir a maiden's heart." Arabella touched a hanging drapery absently and caressed the velvet as if in fond recall. "Quite dashing . . . and handsome. Always a gentleman, always . . ." She snatched herself from her reverie. "But enough of this! I must be alone." Laying her hands upon her cousin's shoulders, she turned Elise about to face the door and, at her uncertain resistance, avowed, "I only seek some time to myself before my husband comes. 'Tis all I ask."

"I shall inform your father," Elise acquiesced and reluctantly made her departure. As she closed the door gently behind her, she wondered how she might approach Edward without first defeating her purpose. If she could somehow catch his eye without drawing the notice of the other men and then speak with him in private, he might prove more tractable, but if an audience of boisterous merrymakers were gathered around him, his pride would have to be dealt with more subtly.

The stairs were of stone and turned sharply with each short flight around an ornately carved newel. Her passage set the candle flames wavering in the wall sconces, and a multiplicity of shadows leapt and danced ahead of her until she was fairly dizzy with the shifting light and her ever-turning progress. Though she hurried, she concentrated carefully on the stairs lest her silken slippers miss a step and bring about a faster but infinitely more painful descent.

From below the music of tambourines, celtic harps, and lutes blended with the louder, uproarious laughter and crude, boisterous shouts of the guests, mantling the ascending approach of another on the stairs until it was too late. The man's haste was more agile than her own, and at the very last moment they both glanced up and tried to swerve, only to step in the same direction and collide. Careening off the solid, unyielding chest, Elise staggered precariously on the edge of a step. A small cry escaped her as she seemed destined to plunge headfirst down the stairs, then an arm as hard as an oaken limb came around her. For a scant moment Elise leaned in relief against the stalwart body, then long fingers encircled her slender waist, and she was lifted to a safe stance upon a higher step. She opened eyes she had not been aware she had closed and, in sudden realization, flung them wide as she recognized the rough tunic of the servant, Taylor. The hood had slipped from his head, and what she viewed was not the sort of face she had expected to see beneath the cowl. This was not some scarred and hideous beast she stared at, but a strikingly handsome man with pale-streaked tawny hair and aristocratic features half-masked by a shaggy beard.

A slight frown of concern marred the man's brow as he questioned in the same heavy tones, "Be ye well, mistress?"

Elise nodded hesitantly as she tried to sort through a moment of confusion, and then his hands left her waist and he was moving further up the stairs. Her head cleared with a snap. "Here! What are you about?

What business have you in the upper chambers?"

The man halted on a step and pivoted about with deliberate slowness, allowing the shifting light of a nearby torch to illumine his features. The green eyes seemed to bore through her, and the gaze was so bold and froward that for a brief moment Elise held her breath, frozen by those steely orbs.

"You!" she stammered, struggling against that aching, mesmerizing stare as she realized she had been duped into thinking this man was a servant. The bearded visage was etched with sterling clarity upon her consciousness, dragging forth a remembrance of a cast-off portrait in the east wing. She now knew the artist had been most adept at his trade, for Maxim Seymour, the Marquess of Bradbury, was a most magnificent man, and he was here, standing before her as a flesh and blood man. "You're . . . you're alive!"

A scowl darkened his brow for a scant second, then his mood changed with the purposefulness of a strong will. Startlingly white teeth flashed suddenly in a grin, and when he spoke, the guttural jargon was gone. In its stead was the neat, precise speech of a well-tutored gentleman.

"You have forced my hand ere I desired to reveal it, fair maid. 'Twould seem I must be well about my business or well upon my way before you raise a hue and cry."

The Marquess cast a rueful glance upward toward the top of the stairs and sighed as if disappointed in the choice he was having to make. Turning, he moved toward her and caught her arm as he stepped past her, dragging her along in a rapid descent that left her breathless.

"I'm sorry, but I cannot allow you to roam free until the proper moment is met," he apologized. "Once the news is out, you will be at liberty to go your way.... And was that not downward?"

"Stop! Please!" Elise gasped, trying to keep her footing in her haste. "I cannot ..."

Lord Seymour halted and, sweeping an arm behind her shoulders and another beneath her knees, lifted her against his chest and bore her swiftly downward as if she were but an airy froth of silks and laces. Leaving the stairs, he made his entrance into the crowded hall which had, since her departure, grown strangely subdued and was awash in deep lethargy. The servants had returned to the kitchen, awaiting the moment when the wedding party would venture to the bridal chamber, but in the main hall the guests seemed to loll in a languid, soporific stupor as if awaiting the onset of some great event. Some were vaguely aware of the proceedings, while others appeared distantly amused by the antics of this roughly dressed man.

Maxim strode to the nearest table and seated Elise unceremoniously in a large, high-backed chair that stood beside it. Bending close, he held a thin finger in front of her slender nose, and his green eyes seized hers in an unrelenting vise. "I adjure you, madam, be still. You may well be amazed by what you hear."

He whirled and, gripping the end of a long cloth that covered the bare boards of a trestle table, swept it and all its contents onto the floor where it landed with an horrendous crash.

"Ho! Good guests of Bradbury Hall," he shouted. "Now that you have supped well and sipped even better, you must needs be entertained."

The guests faced about with stupefied slowness and stared blankly, giving no hint of recognition as their eyes came to rest on this ill-garbed stranger. The hall grew silent as they appraised this new development, but their sluggish minds could not clearly grasp what was happening or even cope with the reality of it.

" 'Tis him!" an agitated fellow from nearby finally managed to choke out. " 'Tis him! Back from hell he's come!"

Confusion deepened, and a wave of halfhearted inquiries drifted through the hall. "What's that ye say? Who do ye mean?"

The one who first spoke threw up his arms in disbelief and began to chide the strangely apathetic guests. "Who, do ye ask? Great sainted mother, do ye not know this blackguard? Why, 'tis the Marquess o' Bradbury himself!"

"Lor' Se'mour?" a man slurred thickly, and slowly grinned before he slumped forward, plunging his face into a trencher of food. Startled gasps came from others who gave their full and undivided attention to the Marquess. His mildly amused smile did not waver as his gaze wandered leisurely about the room, searching for the face that belonged to his chief accuser.

"Nay! Nay! It c'naugh be!" a muddled voice argued. "The Marquess is dead! He was killed!"

A soft chuckle flowed across the room, sending shivers down Elise's spine. From the sound she could well believe that Maxim Seymour had grown horns to complete his satanic demeanor.

"So! You thought me dead, eh?" Maxim seized a sword from the wall and leapt to the top of the trestle table. "Sweet darlings and gentle men, if you think me dead, then press your breasts upon my blade and trust no ghostling lord to bring you harm. Come feel my point," he urged, then chuckled in derision when no one stepped forward to test it. His bold, accusing glare swept the room and no few felt the crawling prickle upon their napes as the full weight of his gaze fell on them. "I have not left you as some would have it . . .

at least not in *that* fashion. 'Tis perhaps true enough that I passed beyond recall." He lifted his broad shoulders in a brief, careless shrug and leisurely paced the length of the wooden plank. "And 'tis true I was sorely wounded by those laggards on the bridge who tried to halt my escape, but I fell into the stream and 'twas my fate to pass . . . as though swept by angels . . . into the hands of friends who saved me from the murky depths. So see and hear me, gentle folk! And spread the word that Maxim Taylor Seymour has come to serve vengeance on that thief who purloined his properties with a lie and gave his betrothed to another. I'm here to claim what is mine and to see justice served! Do you hear me, Edward Stamford?"

Maxim leapt across to another table and strode its length, scattering trenchers of food and tankards of ale and wine to the floor with a soft, hide boot. The stupefied guests shrank back in bewildered fright, and some stumbled and fell in their panic. Others stared about them in a daze, unable to shake the mind-confusing trance which had come upon them. Too listless and befuddled to flee, they slowly slithered into their seats or retreated further to the floor.

"Seize him! Don't let him escape!" Edward shouted from the doorway. He had left some moments ago to relieve himself and had returned to find his guests fleeing a man he had thought himself rid of. He fervently sought an end to him now. "Cut him down, do ye hear! Run him through! He's a murderer! A traitor ta the crown! The Queen will reward ye for his death!" With a wave of his hand the squire indicated those who had fallen, and stirred fear as he continued. "I ask ye now! Were these simple souls addled by heady brews . . ." He glared about him as if demanding an answer. "Or be this the work o' a hideous fiend? Has he poisoned us all?"

Terrified gasps and wailing sobs attested to willingness of the guests to believe his statement. Elise searched her mind as she tried to recall just what the Marquess had been doing at the wine cask before she interrupted him. She formed a mental image of the two flagons he had served wine from, and she stared at him in growing dread, half-afraid her uncle was right.

Several men staggered forward to seek revenge for this horrible deed which had been done to them, but Maxim Seymour rested his hands on the hilt of his sword and chuckled as he calmly awaited their stumbling advance. He seemed quite self-assured as he slowly shook his head and chided them, "Carefully consider, gentle men. 'Tis true you are much besotted with the potion I added to your cups, but 'tis not hemlock your tongues have tasted and no Socrates's doom you'll see. The most harm the brew will do is aid you in a long night's sleep, but if you test your skill against my blade, you may not fare as well. I ask you now, would you waste your life at the call of this Judas?"

"Take him!" Edward Stamford railed in mounting apprehension. "Ye mustn't let him escape!"

One of the guests plunged forward, and swords clashed as Maxim met and quickly parried the thrust. Three others rushed in to pit their skill against the Marquess, only to stumble away in defeat. The ease with which he parried the attacks dissuaded many from carrying out the bidding of their host. After all, they had come to Bradbury Hall to feast and frolic, not to do battle with a skilled swordsman.

"Haven't you brought enough sorrow to this household?" Elise cried, jumping to her feet. She was incensed that this man could hold the entire hall at bay while he worked his mischief. "Must you mar Arabella's wedding night with more pain and grief?"

The green eyes took on a steely hardness as they settled upon her. "This was my home, and this might have been my wedding night if not for the tales of this palterer. What think you that I should do, maid? Leave it to the likes of Edward Stamford without a fight?" His sardonic chuckle belied the possibility. "Watch me and see if I will!"

Edward's rising panic made him desperate. "Are there none brave enough ta take him?" he screamed. "He's a traitor! He deserves ta die!"

The bridegroom, Reland, had toasted more liberally than many of the others and was sluggish and slow as he braced his broad hands on the table and pushed himself to his feet. Immediately the guests scattered, clearing a path between the two men, for here indeed was a match worthy of the Marquess.

"Arabella is mine!" Reland thundered in a low roar, and tried to focus his blurring vision on the other. He shook his head to clear it from the thickening cobwebs and slammed a fist down upon the table. "I'll kill any man who tries to take her from me!"

Edward quickly motioned for a guest to fetch Huxford's sword and, receiving it himself, delivered the weapon to his new son-in-law. "Catch him unawares if ye can," the elder advised. "The Marquess is a shrewd one, he is."

The Earl sneered at the smaller man. "Would ye have me do yer bloodlettin', little weasel?"

A sudden sweat dappled Edward's brow, and his lips formed voiceless words for a moment as he searched for an acceptable reply. "I . . . ah . . . cannot defend . . . me daughter, Reland. Me skill with a sword is far too feeble for his lordship here." He inclined his head slightly to indicate the Marquess. "He's a wolf, Reland, an' ye know a weasel can't best a wolf. Ye're more his match. A bear set against a wolf. 'Tis the way it should be."

Placated, Reland stumbled forward a step and stood with legs braced wide apart as he gazed about him with heavily lidded eyes. The Marquess awaited him with sword in hand, and though there remained only a short distance between them, it seemed to Reland that he stared at his adversary through a long, narrow corridor. Imperceptibly everything around him grew darker until there was only a small glimmer at the far end where his enemy stood, and even that light steadily dwindled. He was very tired and weary. His limbs were too ponderous to lift. He had to rest a moment . . . only a moment . . .

Reland Huxford sank to his knees and there, with head bowed low, braced himself doggedly on stiffened arms until, like a mortally wounded bear, he sprawled forward onto the floor.

Edward was beside himself. He ran to Reland and, grasping his sword, held it aloft. "Who'll take up the challenge? Which one o' ye Huxfords'll receive the sword o' his kin?"

No one came forward, and Devlin smirked from the doorway where he leaned. "You have the sword, Squire. You carry forth the challenge."

Edward gaped at Devlin as if certain the other had lost his wits, but the jeering grin of the younger man made him drop his gaze. He stared down in horror at the weapon in his hands, realizing that no one would come to his defense. With trembling hesitancy he lifted his worried gaze to the man he had dubbed traitor, and though the taunting smile of the Marquess mocked him, he could not find the courage to lift the sword and charge his foe.

Maxim began to chuckle softly, mercilessly lashing the older man's pride. "Come now, Edward," he chided in a ridiculing tone. "Have you lost your taste for bloodletting? I am here, ready to meet your thrust."

Fear congealed in Elise's breast and ran its icy tendrils through her veins as she watched the two men. Her heart labored against the dreadful chill of the emotion, for she knew what the outcome would be if the Marquess successfully goaded her uncle into a fight. It was all too obvious that Lord Seymour meant to kill the elder.

Her mind screamed at the injustice of it, and she suddenly realized the only person who could possibly accomplish the feat of stopping Seymour was not in the room.

Whirling in desperate haste, Elise fled the hall and, lifting her heavy skirts to her knees, raced up the stairs as fast as her spinning head would allow. Arabella's chamber door stood ajar, and without pausing to knock, Elise plunged through with her cousin's name spilling from her tongue, but the sound dwindled to a whisper as a flurry of impressions assailed her.

The chambers were dark. Only a meager light shining through the doorway from the adjoining room illumined the antechamber.

The rooms were deathly quiet. Arabella was nowhere to be seen, and no sound came from the bedchamber.

The candles had been deliberately snuffed. The scent of the hot wax still lingered in the air.

Elise felt a strange foreboding as she ran into the bedchamber. There, a lone candle burned, and in the hearth the golden flames of a fire danced along a charred log, casting across the floor elongated shadows of the tall-backed chairs which stood before it. The velvet hangings of the massive bed were open, displaying the richly embroidered coverlet that was still neatly spread over the feather ticks. Nothing in the room conveyed the welcoming warmth of a bride awaiting her groom.

Stepping out onto the loggia, Elise scanned the courtyard, probing into shadows and doorways. A softly whistled tune caught her attention, and she peered through the lantern-lit gloom until she spied Quentin strolling leisurely toward the hall. She had not seen him leave, but it was apparent by his manner that he was ignorant of what was presently transpiring there. Nor would he go to Edward's aid when he entered. Her cousin was no more fond of the elder than Maxim Seymour was.

Keeping her silence, Elise slipped back into Arabella's bedchamber. If she did not find her cousin soon, Edward would have to face the challenge of the Marquess, and that one would surely have his revenge.

She felt the warmth of the fire at her back, but a sudden eerie feeling sent a shiver sinuating down her spine and compelled her to lift her gaze. There against the far wall, she saw her silhouette cast, but creeping stealthily toward her shadow from either side were a pair of other shapes, large and manly.

The chambers were not empty!

Elise leapt forward, eluding the beefy arms that reached out to seize her. A meaty *thunk* followed as the pair came together, giving evidence that the silhouettes were more than mere illusions. Where she had stood an instant before, two hefty bodies now struggled against each other, and the mumbled curses of the pair filled the silence.

"Damn ye, Fitch! Ye broke me nose! Let go!"

"She's escapin'! Catch her!"

A tall shape lunged for her, and lightfooted as a frightened hind Elise whirled away, only to crash into a pear-shaped bulk. As much surprised as she, the man teetered on one foot while he sought to wrap his thickly thewed arms about her slender form. He knocked off her cap, and in the next instant Elise found her face pressed into the folds of the brigand's roughly woven tunic. It had a wet woolen smell mingled with the strong stench of cooked fish. The encircling arms were strong and forbidding, but she fought against them in desperation, frightened of what might await her if the men took her. She lashed out, catching her hand in the pearl necklace, and distantly she was aware of the precious beads and jeweled clasp scattering across the floor, but the loss of the treasured piece did not halt her struggles as a calloused hand reached forward to muffle her outcry. It was the man who groaned in pain as her teeth sank into his fleshy palm. He snatched his hand away, but as she drew a breath to scream she quickly found a knotted cloth biting into her mouth.

The sharp heel of her slipper came down hard on the instep of the man's softly booted foot. In the very next instant she pushed with all of her strength against the protruding belly. Suddenly Elise realized she was free, and never being one to faint or yield without a good fight, she set her mind to full flight, but before her darting foot gained a step, she was smothered in the folds of a drapery torn from a window. The large cloth was promptly wound about her until she was wrapped from head to foot. Frustration and fear fused into rage, and she exploded in a fury of mindless thrashing. A thick arm closed tightly about her neck, bringing the fabric close over her face until she could not draw a full breath of air. The more she struggled, the tighter the embrace became, and when she eased her writhing, the restraint likewise eased. The message became clear. She would be taken one way or another.

"Spence, where ye be, man?" the one named Fitch called. "Let's be gone from 'ere."

The sound of hurrying footsteps approached them from behind. "I canna find the lady's cloak..."

"She'll 'ave ta make do wit' what she 'as. Let's be gone from 'ere 'fore somebody comes."

The thick cord which had held the swag in place at a window was used to bind the drapery about her, then strong arms lifted her and laid her over a broad shoulder. Gagged and trussed up like a helpless goose, Elise could only moan and wiggle in protest as she was carried out onto the loggia and whisked down the outer stairs to the courtyard. Once they came to earth, a sense of urgency seized the two. Her stout captor jogged along for a space, nearly jolting the breath from her, and then slipped through a hedge that bordered the courtyard. Of a sudden she was hurled through the air in a rather wild swoop, and she nearly strangled on the scream that erupted from her chest. It found no release beneath her gag, and she came to earth with a bounce, thankfully on a thick pile of straw. There was a moment of confused movement as a startled horse awoke and pranced nervously, making Elise aware of the fact that she had been thrown into a cart. The hushed voice of the driver soothed the animal as bundles of straw were heaped upon her, then the cart jiggled and creaked as the two men scrambled in. They stretched out on top of the straw, and their combined weight pressed her down until she could hardly breathe, much less move. The horse was urged forward, and the cart obligingly followed. The pace was slow, plodding, deliberate, and Elise's spirits plummeted as she found little hope for rescue.

The driver of the conveyance made a wide swing which brought them around to the front of the manse.

Though she had lived only a short time at Bradbury, Elise was able to discern the very moment the wooden wheels of the cart rolled onto the front lane, for her ride became immediately smoother. It was here she longed fervently to scream and alert the household to her abduction, but it was a useless wish, for the men had guaranteed her silence. Somewhere over the rattle and creak of the cart she heard the twittering chitter-chirrup of a nightingale, and she thought how strange that on this crisp winter's evening the bird should be so near.

Maxim Seymour paused and cocked his head slightly as he heard the soft chirp. His nod was more mental than noticeable. He looked into Edward's gleaming, sweating face and murmured with a sardonic smile, "You have a reprieve from the wolf, weasel. I now have what I came for, and for that you shall pay dearly."

Maxim leapt away and cast a quick glance about the hall. Hardly a score of men were capable of pursuit, but some of them would prove reluctant. Those who were loyal to Edward rallied together at his shout.

"He's escapin'! Don't let him get away! He's a traitor ta the Queen!"

Maxim tore a velvet drapery from a window and, swirling it about, flung it into the faces of those who followed, then as they struggled to disentangle themselves, he caught the edge of a long table and overturned it upon the squirming mass. He leapt to the top of another plank and, from there, sent platters of food and flagons of wine sailing down upon them. He seemed in gay spirits as he ran to the doorway and there paused to salute Edward with his sword.

" 'Tis time I bid you adieu, Squire. I trust the lot of

you will not sorrow greatly over my departure."

His arm whipped upward, and the sword sailed high to bury its point in a timber of the vaulted ceiling, there to quiver in fading throes. "Farewell, Squire," he bade with a sweeping bow. "I leave a memento to remind you that I shall return. Gird your loins against that day, or flee and hope I cannot find you."

Edward lifted his eyes and seemed entranced by the glimmer of light sent abroad by the trembling blade. Slowly the movement died, and when he glanced about him, Edward realized his foe had departed.

"After him!" he shouted, and glared about him when there was no immediate response to his command. "Would ye have the Queen think we're all cowards 'cause o' one man? She'll have our heads if we make no attempt ta stop him."

The heavy table was laboriously cast aside, and the men, incongruously bedecked with varied sauces or coyly perched carcasses of roasted blackbird, struggled against each other to get to their feet. In priggish distaste they flung aside the sticky globs and stumbled after Edward as he charged through the portal.

When they stepped outside, a rattle of hooves drew their attention to the lane in front of the manse. Beneath a canopy of winter-bare limbs that swept upward from the trees growing alongside the road, they could see the dark figure of a man on the back of the black Friesian stallion.

Edward cursed aloud as he watched the rapidly departing pair, then he turned to shout to those who stood around him, "Ta horse! Ta horse! We can't let him escape!"

Chapter 3

*T*HE SUFFOCATING CONFINEMENT of her cloth cocoon and the weight of the two men pressing the straw bundles down upon her created a hellish torment for Elise. The cord-bound drapery restricted her movements and held her arms pinned to her sides, but her mind ranged far afield, conjuring a multitude of evil deeds which might be done to her. The unknown dragged out her apprehensions until the low rumble of the wooden wheels rolling over the rutted lane seemed but a distant echo of her wildly thumping heart. Had she been the least bit prone to having fits of unbridled panic, she might have yielded to an upsurging compulsion to writhe and struggle against her bonds, but fear of what these brutish ruffians might do persuaded her to keep still and hold her peace, at least for the time being. It was little more than idiocy to provoke them while she was so vulnerable.

Her ankle and her hip were pressed down hard against the boards beneath her where the mound of straw had thinned and offered little padding. With each jolt of the cart Elise suffered a twinge of pain in both areas. It was easy to surmise that even after a short journey she would be left bruised and aching. Persistently and by slow degrees she managed to wedge a hand beneath her to cushion her hip and discovered there an opening in the fold of the drape.

Concentrating all her efforts, she wiggled her hand through and began to search the silken cord for the knot that held everything secure, then a distant drumming made her pause. She strained to listen until the sound grew more distinct, and her spirits soared as she recognized the pounding hoofbeats of a swiftly approaching steed. Someone was coming after them! Surely she would be rescued!

Her heart took up a hopeful beat, and she hardly dared to breathe as she waited for the rider to overtake them, but alas, her expectations were cruelly dashed when a sharp jolt bespoke of the cart's departure from the path. The rough conveyance jounced and lurched beneath her and, after several more heaving gyrations, finally came to a halt. The racing hooves clattered past, and a brief moment later another movement jiggled her crude bed as one of the men scrambled down, then everything grew still and quiet around them until the sounds of the night came stealing back. In the waiting hush a growing rumble arose in the distance. This time it became distinguishable as the thunderous advance of a dozen or more horses on the road. The din of the ride was liberally fused with loud shouts and questions, most of which were unintelligible to her constrained ear, but amid the windswept jargon she recognized her uncle's loud bellow.

"Ride hard, lads! We'll run that black-hearted son o' Satan ta earth an' stretch his neck for certain this time! He'll not escape us!"

Elise struggled to alert the horsemen to her presence, but the sudden thump of a foot on a straw bundle above her head warned her to be still. Warm tears of frustration coursed down her cheeks as the noise of the chase faded and silence once more regained its hold. In their haste to catch the fleeing rider, they had not even considered there was one nearby in desperate need of rescue.

Cautiously the driver took to the road again, and he plodded along for what seemed an eternity to Elise. To be sure, the monotony of their passage became well-established. Her fingers had discovered no binding knot that could be plucked free, and though she wiggled around in a continuous effort to secure the ever-evasive comfort of her crowded straw bed, the jolting of the wheels rolling over stones and into holes made the ride almost unbearable. She grew more weary and numb with each furlong they traversed, and she was certain no other rack of torture could compare to the one she had been set upon.

As the journey dragged on, doubts began to corrode her mettlesome spirit. Her mind, seeking random surcease from her distress, began to drift, and she tried to find some reasonable cause for her abduction. Why had these strangers taken her? What was their intent, and who was the lone rider on the road? The image of Maxim Seymour grew strong and tall amid the jumbled impressions that rushed at her. Surely he was the one who had passed them on the road, as affirmed by her uncle and the small band of wedding guests giving chase behind him. They would have gone after no other. But she could not even imagine what auspicious end her capture would serve such a man. Had he been of such a mind to take her prisoner, he would have surely forbade her departure from the hall. Instead, he had dismissed her with barely a glance, not caring that she was fleeing. Nay, 'twas not that traitorous renegade who wanted her. There were others who had more reason to see her taken. Cassandra and her whelps, for instance. Or the high Earl Reland bent on mischief and revenge.

The possibility that these men were working for

people bearing the same surname as her own lent Elise no amount of confidence. If she became the prisoner of her aunt and cousins again, she would be hard-pressed to continue her defiance for any length of time. Cassandra would see to that. The woman would not waste time going over ground she had already covered. She would come swiftly to the point.

Elise had overheard many whispered comments about the vindictiveness of her aunt during her childhood years, mostly from servants who had disapproved of the woman. According to gossip, the widow, Cassandra, had been in love with Ramsey Radborne even while his brother, Bardolf, was still alive. Cassandra had abhorred the beautiful, auburn-haired woman Ramsey had married, and had insisted that Deirdre was naught but a nameless wench whom he had taken pity on, much like the Stamfords who had found her as a babe. The fire flamed higher beneath the cauldron of jealousy and hatred when the young wife gave birth to a daughter, and in spiteful venom Cassandra had refused to acknowledge the girl as kin, suggesting as boldly as she dared that Elise was not a Radborne at all but the leavings of some wandering bard, just as her mother had been. Then came that sad day when Deirdre succumbed to some strange malady during the latter stages of a second pregnancy. Ramsey had grieved deeply over the loss of his wife, but much to the vexation of his sister-in-law, he had turned his attention to his young daughter.

The years had passed, and the increasingly questionable state of Cassandra's financial affairs began to concern Ramsey, for he knew the limitations of his daughter's future if he died without securing his wealth and estates for her. Cassandra's greed was such that if no precautions were taken he could easily foresee Elise being stripped of her inheritance and then being thrown upon the doubtful mercy of the world. To prevent this injustice Ramsey established accounts for her with bankers who were close friends of the family. It was further rumored that in more recent months he began to dispose of his possessions and took to traveling to and from the Stilliards on strange missions, causing rampant curiosity among the Radbornes who fretted over the removal of several large coffers from his manor during the night hours. Cassandra and her three younger sons gained this information by the torture of one of Ramsey's servants, and therefore, in their opinion, it was undeniably true.

Elise grimaced as the cart lurched around a bend, causing her heel to painfully scrape across the rough boards. She could expect no better treatment from her kin. Indeed, the Radbornes could be quite ruthless when it served their purpose. Despite all the murmured accusations and tales of vile deeds that her aunt was supposed to have done, Elise had still been amazed by the woman's unquenchable avarice. After Ramsey's kidnapping Cassandra and her sons took charge of the Radborne manor, not with the purpose of giving comfort to his daughter by any means, but to insist that he was dead, that the estates and the hidden fortune could not be inherited by a female offspring without due consent of the Queen and that everything was therefore the rightful property of the sons of Bardolf Radborne as part of their birthright. Elise refused to yield anything to her aunt, which only served to infuriate the woman, who took out her spite in harsh measures. Nor did Cassandra take it kindly when Quentin interfered and spirited Elise away to his country estate. She was even more incensed when the girl made good an escape on her own, much to the embarrassment of Forsworth.

Now here she was again, Elise thought morosely,

being swept away in a cart to some strange destination by men she had never seen before. No good would come of it, she was certain of that. So certain that she was seized with a paralyzing fear when the driver halted the small wain. She was relieved of a burdensome weight when the two men climbed down, but she could not count her blessings, for any moment she might find herself facing a greater hazard.

One of the men spoke in muted tones to the driver while the other took away the straw bundles and lifted her down. The drapery and gag were removed, and Elise was provided her first look at her abductors by way of a weak light cast from a tallow lantern. The last few months had brought a full share of scoundrels to her attention, from the meticulously well-garbed and seemingly ever-youthful Cassandra and her handsome sons to the low, base, filthy, evil-hearted thieves of Alsatia. To her surprise, these men did not appear unduly dreadful. Spence was tall, lean but strong-built, with light brown hair and kindly gray eyes, while Fitch was shorter, rounder, and somewhat pear-shaped with unruly hair and a merry twinkle in his blue eyes. Neither looked capable of doing the evil deed which they were about.

Elise recognized the driver as one who worked in the stable at Bradbury, but she promised herself that if she ever returned to that place, she would make sure that his part in this kidnapping was made known. Now she had to watch in dismay as he clucked to the nag, urging the animal back the way they had come.

Glancing about her, Elise realized she had been brought to the edge of a river. She saw no boat or waiting conveyance or mounts by which they might leave the place, and as illogical as the idea seemed, she began to wonder if she would leave the place alive. If not for the purpose of murder, then she had to believe the two men had brought her to this place for their own sordid pleasures. A cold, agonizing dread congealed within her and left her heart thudding heavily against the inner walls of her chest, but she settled the matter firmly in her mind that if there was naught else to do, she would at least give these knaves a fight worthy of her strength. She had been well-tutored at an early age and in a most unladylike fashion by a scullery maid's son on the necessity of defending oneself, and though she had not the body of a brawler, she had the temperament and determination that could equal the brawn of a much larger foe.

The men's countenances quickly changed to those of brute savages as her imagination ran rampant. A thousand disparaging titles came to her tongue, but she dared not waste the advantage of surprise. She noticed a broken branch lodged in the crotch of a nearby tree and surreptitiously stepped back until she could grasp hold of the end of it. As Fitch came near, she swung it over her head with all her might, landing a painful blow against the side of his noggin. With a loud yelp the man stumbled back into his startled companion, but Elise never paused. Catching up her velvet skirts, she made a frantic dash into the nearby copse. The pair shouted as they recovered their wits. Spence seized a lantern and the two gave chase, but the night was dark as ebon, and her black gown gave Elise the advantage. While the lantern Spence carried illuminated the two in a dim circle of light and showed them the path close at hand, its dull glow failed to reach the deeper shadows wherein Elise moved. She raced far ahead of the two who thrashed about in confused discord, her thin slippers making no sound on the damp, thick mulch of decaying leaves while the small heels secured her footing. Like a small, furtive sprite, she sprinted through the trees, now and then flinging a glance over her shoulder, and was encouraged by the slower progress of the men. Her heart thumped with the excitement of the chase, for it seemed her escape was well within her grasp.

Alas, it was not so easily gained. When she passed a narrow glade, Elise found her way barred by an impenetrable thicket. Anxiously she searched the dense growth for an opening that might allow her to slip through, only to be halted at every turn. However, after the many trials she had faced of late, Elise was not ready to accept this barrier as defeat, not when she was aware of what might await her if she did not escape.

Choosing a stealthful retreat, Elise slipped across the clearing again and entered the trees where the darkness befriended her. As the lantern-lit circle in which the men moved drew nearer, she stepped back, merging with the deeper shades of night. Though her heart threatened to give her away with its riotous thumping, she stood motionless, afraid even to breathe.

Oblivious to her proximity, the men charged forward until their progress was also halted by the brambles. Separating there, they raced in opposite directions, seeking a way around the spinney while Elise carefully left the dark void wherein she had hidden herself. Gathering her skirts, she fled back toward the spot where she had first entered the woods. Her feet fairly flew over the leaf-strewn bower, and once again she anticipated her freedom. Then suddenly her world was jolted as her slippered toe caught on a low-growing vine. A startled cry escaped her as she sprawled forward to the ground, and before the fog dissipated from her head, Fitch and Spence had regrouped and were racing back in high-kneed form.

Elise groaned in misery, but it had naught to do with the slight discomfort in her ankle. Rather, it was the inevitability of her capture which prompted her to vocally vent her disappointment.

"Unhand me!" Elise cried angrily as the two sought to lift her to her feet. Surprisingly they obeyed her command and stumbled back to await her pleasure. Beneath the light of the lantern, she plucked dead leaves and small twigs from her hair and primly brushed her velvet gown. Satisfied that she had done what she could to repair her appearance and thereby test the patience of the men, she raised a hand to Spence.

"Have a care. I'm wounded," she complained, then immediately sucked in her breath as he bumped her ankle in his eagerness to help. It had only been a small, insignificant bruise, but with such clumsy attention, she mused, it was not likely to remain so for long. "Please! My ankle!"

" 'Tis dreadful sorry I be, mistress," Spence rushed to apologize. Once again he bent to lift her up into his arms, this time using more care.

Elise was confused by his apparent show of concern, but she had no doubt that she would learn more of their game as time progressed ... if she lived that long. "I should like to know what you intend," she demanded. "Why have I been kidnapped?" Though he gave no answer, she pressed him further, anxious to gain what information she could. "Were you hired by the Radbornes? Did they promise you a purse to bring me back?"

Spence looked somewhat perplexed and slowly shook his head as he replied, "Nay, mistress. We've no ken o' the Radbornes."

Elise found no comfort in his statement. It was a simple enough matter for her aunt and cousins to make use of other names when hiring their accomplices. Of late, she had taken to tying a pouch of coins beneath her farthingale to ensure the presence of some bargaining power if circumstances warranted it. The present time seemed appropriate, but rather than letting them know she carried it on her person, she would let the pair think their reward awaited them at her uncle's house. "I can promise you a worthy purse for your trouble if you'll take me back to Bradbury Hall. I vow 'twould be more than what you can expect from the ones who've set you to this mischief. Oh, please . . . you must take me back. I'll pay you well."

"His lor'ship says we're ta take ye ta London, mistress, an' 'at's where ye'll be goin'."

"Lord Forsworth, perchance?" Elise queried and chuckled in derision. "Let me assure you, good fellow, if that be the one who's hired you, he is *not* a lord, and he's as poor as a church mouse."

"Ne'er ye worry yerself 'bout his purse, mistress. His lor'ship needs none atall wit' the pair o' us. We're as loyal as fish is ta water." Spence's flatly spoken answer made it apparent that he could not be coaxed from his mission.

Fitch ran past with a lantern as his companion carried her to the river's bank. Setting the lamp upon the ground, the portly man reached into the tall reeds growing in thick clusters along the shore and, seizing a rope, wound the cord around the length of his forearm until a boat was dragged from the grassy growth. He hastened to prepare a soft place in the prow, spreading out several fur robes, and it was upon this that Spence lowered their captive. The cockboat wallowed from side to side as the taller man stepped to the stern.

Fitch settled amidship and, placing the lantern beside him, grasped the oars. With amazingly powerful strokes, he rowed the boat from shore out into the main channel where he dropped a centerboard and stepped a stubby mast which the two of them quickly braced before hoisting a small triangular sail. The small craft took on a skipping, dancing, headless manner 'twixt the errant breezes and the strong, dark currents until Spence, lowering the rudder into the water and leaning against the tiller, brought the vessel into a steady, smooth course downstream.

The lantern was doused, and once more the night closed in about them. Elise's eyes grew accustomed to the dark, and as the boat skimmed through the water she could see the black bulk of the shore on either side. The tall shadows of the sail and the men were silhouetted against the quicksilver shine of the river, and behind them a mottled wake stretched out into darkness. As the night aged and the constant creaking of the mast lulled her senses, Elise dragged the fur robes close over her shoulder and, having some assurance that the men were on a specific mission and not intent upon rape or murder, finally yielded to sleep.

It seemed only a moment later when a dull thump disturbed Elise's slumber, and her eyelids flicked suddenly open. She stared aloft where the twigs and branches of a huge tree formed an airy canopy high above her small, floating bed. Beyond the far-reaching limbs, low clouds of a dreary gray hue scudded across the bleak sky while brisk breezes rattled the branches, tossing them to and fro. Leaves were whipped into a frenzied flight and, in jubilant freedom, pirouetted before her captive gaze, before slowly settling in a zigzagging descent and coming to rest upon her furry robes. The swirling, strengthening gusts cavorted like some mindless, invisible sprites through the woods, scudding over the river and rippling the surface with its breath. Secured by the long painter, the boat skimmed sideways over the water until it bumped against a fallen log, then as if beckoned, it drifted back to the reeds growing alongside the bank.

On another day Elise might have enjoyed the interlude, but awareness of her circumstances dispelled any leisured thoughts of pleasure. The snoring cacophony of the two men rent the peace of the morning, bringing a reminder of her captivity. She bit her lip in anguish as she tried to move, realizing the struggles of the past evening had left her unmercifully stiff and sore. She stretched carefully until her aching muscles began to loosen and she could lift herself to a sitting position. Her gaze immediately found Fitch sleeping on shore beneath the very same tree which sheltered her. The man had removed his jerkin and spread a cloak beneath him as protection against the damp chill of his leafy bed, putting the leather jerkin to use as a pillow beneath his head.

Almost lazily her eyes followed the long painter from the prow, moving upward along its taut line to a spot where it was double-looped around an overhanging branch. There it had been tied back upon itself to keep the boat some distance from shore. Except for the growing wind it might have remained where the men had planned it to stay.

Her gaze continued to trace the path of the rope from the knot, down along a loosely dangling dip, back up into the tree near the crotch of a limb where she spied Spence. He had obviously drawn the last watch and had climbed into the tree where he could keep an eye on her from above. He had wrapped the loose end of the painter several times around his ankle to further secure the boat lest he should doze, and apparently had felt safe enough to fall asleep on his perch, for his snores rivaled those of his earthbound companion.

Elise studied her choices. If she managed to climb from the boat when it bumped against the fallen log, her ankle was just sore enough to prevent her from fleeing swiftly on foot. To escape in the boat was her best choice, but even if she managed to extricate the rope from the branch, there would still be Spence to contend with.

Even as she watched, fate took a hand and set in motion a chain of events that would have astounded a casual observer. The wind had risen, and the current swung the boat outward until the painter stretched tight. The well-chafed branch could no longer stand the strain and suddenly snapped with a splintering *c-r-r-a-a-c-k*. The broken limb plummeted into the water, freeing the knot. The boat shot outward into the stronger current, and Elise seized hold of the sides as the wind filled and then took aback the loosened sail. As she was the only weight aboard and situated well forward, the craft spun in a crazy dance on its bows, catching the painter with the now-lax tiller and twining it firmly thereon before picking up a direction downstream. The rope snapped taut, and with the end of it now bound only to the foot of the dozing man, Spence received the full jolt of the thrust. Snatched sideways from his lofty perch, he sailed through the air, instantly and totally awake, but thoroughly confused. He gave voice to a bellow of fear and clutched in panic at whatever branch or twig he passed. Retaining only a handful of dry leaves, he struck the water with arms and legs akimbo and then abruptly disappeared from sight. The water was shallow, perhaps no more than half his height, and his free foot found good purchase on the bottom, but only briefly. The momentum of the boat was such that it caused him to cartwheel up from the depths like some many-limbed sea monster. His wail of distress rose to a shriek, but the sound was cut short by another plunge into the river.

The horrendous caterwauling finally snatched Fitch from the depths of noisy slumber. He could not mistake the panic in Spence's voice, and he sprang to his feet, shedding the remnants of his bed and presenting a truly astonishing sight in his baggy chausses, loosely flapping shirt, and bare feet. He stared in awe at the sight of his companion being dragged over a shallow strand while the boat drifted downriver with the stern lifted high before the morning gale. A brief vision of his lordship sternly admonishing the pair of them "that at no cost were they to let their captive escape" gave him sudden momentum. Lifting his bare feet high as he ran and pumping his arms to gain the best turn of speed, he raced along the edge of the embankment toward a downstream point from which he hoped he could intercept the flight of the wayward craft.

Elise looked back at the one in the water. Somehow Spence had managed to grasp the rope and, with much choking and spluttering, was pulling himself ever closer to the cockboat. She made her way aft to the tiller, but the painter had been twisted firmly about the rudder and, with the floundering man's weight upon it, she could budge neither. She seized an oar and, with a desperate heave, managed to lift it from the oarlock. Sliding the long, unwieldy thing out over the stern, she began to poke and harass her half-drowned captor, to such an extent that the mild-mannered Spence gave vent to loud shouts of duress amid threats against her person.

The hull grated bottom, and Elise glanced around in time to see Fitch reach his goal. With a great shout of victory he hurled himself, still striding, from the top of the low bluff directly into the path of the boat. Though his entry into the water raised a sizable geyser, Fitch paused only briefly beneath the surface before he came up spewing water and gasping for breath. He flogged about wildly with his arms, raising a white froth until he regained his senses and began to make some discernible progress toward her.

The boat lurched, and Elise turned to see Spence's huge hands grasping the stern. She tried to swing the oar, but it was too long, too clumsy, and much too heavy to be an efficient weapon. The rear of it caught on the mast and almost sent her tumbling overboard. After another rough jerk she glanced forward and saw a pair of hands grasping the gunwales, one on either side of the prow. Very slowly a straining, dripping, leering man heaved himself above it. With a brief whine of enraged frustration Elise started forward, intending to poke him away with the oar, but she staggered unsteadily as Spence flung a leg over the stern, inadvertently kicking the tiller. Now free of the restraining weight, the tiller flipped hard over, and the boat careened and teetered like some love-drunk walrus a-reel in euphoric bliss.

Elise clung to the oar and grasped a corner of the sail. Neither served her well when the boat teetered sideways into a growth of reeds. The tough, wet canvas slipped from her grasp, while the weight of the oar across her middle pushed her backward into the river. The shock of the icy water struck her, and it was only by a dint of will that she did not gasp in a lungful as she sank below the surface. Releasing the oar, she lashed out in blind desperation, trying to right herself in the water. Her head came up, and she sucked in wheezing breaths of air until the painful, icy shock ebbed.

Elise ground her teeth as she saw the pair of men

now standing fore and aft in the boat. They stared back at her in awe, as if frozen by what they saw. She could well imagine the sight she presented with a welter of broken reeds crowning her head, dripping strands of hair streaming down her face, and her once-crisp ruff draped around her neck like the much-bedraggled ornament of a woebegone sea nymph.

Though the water was only slightly deeper than the draft of the boat, the weight of her sodden skirts kept her from rising. She braced her feet beneath her and pushed hard, then grimaced in repugnance as she felt her once-dainty slippers sink into the slimy muck that covered the bottom. For her trouble, she gained only a half-crouching position, and with a snarl of rage she jerked an arm free of the tangled reeds and caught hold of the oar. Plunging the tip downward into the ooze, she braced herself against it and, with an effort, withdrew a foot from the mud, minus her shoe, and tried to step forward. The oar lost its footing, escaped her grasp and, like some vengeful prig, banged her across the head as it fell back to the surface. Elise's lips tightened with her mounting frustration, and she shoved the oar away angrily. Fitch caught the piece as it glided past him and copied her manner by sinking the tip firmly into the muck. Leaning it against the boat, he pushed the hull close beside her and kept his face carefully blank as he offered her a hand.

Elise's chin came up in a silent but eloquent snub and, managing to turn her back to him, she staggered from the muck, dragging her ponderous skirts with her as she left the river. Gaining solid footing, she set her jaw to keep her teeth from chattering as the two men pulled the boat ashore. Avoiding her baleful stare, they set about building a fire, then hung the cast-off drapery on a rope between two trees as an offering of privacy for the lady.

Elise used the makeshift chamber to doff her garments and found a hollow in a tree where she could hide her purse temporarily. The men spread her clothes to dry before the fire while she sought comfort in the warm furs. Spence bagged a hare and was soon roasting its cleaned carcass on a green stick above the flames. Bread, cheese, and wine were also provided, and though the rabbit was rather tasteless and dry, the victuals sufficed to soothe the gnawing hunger in her stomach. In a cool, stoic manner Elise relented enough to thank the men for her portion.

"Ye'd best rest yerself, mistress," Spence advised. "We'll be on our way 'gain come dusk."

Hardly enough time for her velvet gown to dry, Elise mused morosely. "What do you expect me to wear?" she demanded. "My gown is ruined! 'Twill never be the same! I've lost a shoe! Everything is still soaking wet!"

Spence stepped away briefly, then came back with a pair of hide shoes, a frayed woolen gown, and a coarsely woven cloak of the same cloth. "Here be somethin' for ye ta wear if ye've a mind ta put 'em on," he offered as he handed the garments to her. "Simple though 'ey be, 'ey'll serve yer needs an' get us past ta where we're goin' wit'out so much as a twitch o' a brow."

Elise's glare conveyed her lack of gratitude. She had no idea where they were bound to warrant her wearing such drab clothes, but she found nothing in his statement to suggest their destination would be among the establishments of the elite. She accepted the garments, knowing the foolishness of wearing a soaking-wet gown or trying to maintain her modesty with only the fur robes. She dried her hair by the fire, combing it out with her fingers and left it tumbling in loose curls. When her undergarments were dry enough, she returned to her makeshift chamber and made some adjustments to her farthingale, reducing it down to a thin, padded wheel into which she tucked her purse. She donned her petticoats, laced the bodice of the woolen gown, tying the cords tightly at her waist, and tucked her feet into the pair of hide shoes. The gray woolen cloak provided some warmth for which she was grateful, and she pulled the deep hood close around her face.

Night had not yet draped the river with full darkness when Elise was shaken gently awake. With protest she yielded the furs, allowing the men to make a comfortable place for her in the boat. "I'll catch my death ere long," she complained, "but do you care? Bah! A heartless pair of scoundrels, you are. I swear I will cry for vengeance upon your souls from my grave."

"Nay, mistress! 'Tis not true! We've been charged wit' yer safety, we 'ave, an' do cherish it above our own," Spence declared.

Elise gave him a dubious stare. "Well, Spence, I for one can attest to the fact that you've been lax in your duties, and ere I would hear the banshee's cry, I pray to have no more of your tender care, for my frail form cannot long withstand your mercies."

Spence could not find the words to soothe the girl's ire. She had much cause to feel offended, and he could not blame her for resenting them. His lordship had foresworn them to secrecy, and he could not go against that troth, though he was beginning to feel much like an ogre.

The best he could do was to prepare a cozy place for the girl in the boat. This he did, lining it with thick pelts and leaving the finest for her to use as a cover against the crisp night air. Her wet garments were rolled in another hide and tucked away in the boat, though he had grave doubts as to their future usefulness. He handed Elise in and took care as he laid the robes over her, for this was indeed precious cargo which had been placed in their charge.

Chapter 4

*T*HE SHROUD OF NIGHT still hung over the river as the craft slipped into the currents flowing through London. Elise awoke from a fitful drowse and saw dark towers and buildings drifting by on either bank. The small boat lurched and swayed as Fitch leaned against the tiller, steering toward the darker shadows. Spence paused in reefing the sail and glanced down where his charge lay warm and snugly nestled in her bed of furs. He saw the faint glimmer of her eyes as they swept the riverbank.

"Stay where ye be, mistress. Make like a wee, small mouse wit' nary a sound from yer lips. I'll be layin' this pole"—he patted the short mast—"down in a bit, so be mindin' yer head."

Sleepily Elise nodded assent and, as directed, avoided the lowering mast. Once all was secure, the men bent their backs and strained at the oars to row from shadow to shadow, much like a shadow themselves. A thin, ragged vapor drifted from the stills and backwaters along the river, partially obscuring their passage as they hugged the shoreline. With only the slow, rhythmic creak of the oars intruding upon the hushed stillness, they rowed past palaces both magnificent and declining. The slowly fading beauty of the Savoy was masked by darkness, but no gloom could hide the splendor of the houses of Arundel and Leicester. Beyond the Middle and Inner Temples, the riverfront degenerated into rough timber structures and shabby wharves. Here the men dug the oars deep, slowing the cock until it bumped gently against a landing where crudely constructed stairs gave access to the river. Her curiosity aroused, Elise sat upright and experienced a foreboding of doom as she saw where they had halted. Beyond the wharf was an area she had traversed in the guise of a homeless waif when she had gone in search of her father. It seemed logical that she should be brought here, for Alsatia was a refuge for every sort of renegade, murderer, vagabond, or strumpet. By the Queen's own edict, it had become an area exempt from any law or official who might be wont to carry out justice here and, as a result, it offered a safe haven for her abductors. In Alsatia the pair would be among their own kind.

Spence stepped across to the landing and, beneath the light of a dim-lit lantern, secured the painter around a heavy piling. Fitch followed more clumsily and then turned to help their hostage from the craft, but Elise snatched away from his reaching hands and shook her head angrily. For the moment she had no choice but to resign herself to being their captive, but she would not be an accommodating one.

"I shall see to myself," she hissed, keeping her voice low. She did not like being in this hellish place and knew the folly of arousing the curiosity of others perhaps more evil than the two she was with. When Fitch displayed his obstinance, she flared back in a rasping whisper, "I've no intention of being rudely mauled while you carry me where I have no wish to go. For the moment I'm your captive, with little choice but to follow where you lead, but I'll take naught but your hand. That is all!"

Fitch set his arms akimbo, as if he would give her

further argument, but her unrelenting look of defiance encouraged him to acquiesce and give only the assistance she asked for. Accepting his brawny hand, Elise caught up her skirts and leapt to the landing, taking care with her sore ankle. Spence kept a wary eye on her as he helped Fitch collect the supplies from the boat, but there was no need for caution. Elise had no intention of fleeing their custody while they were here in this foul place. Such an act would be tantamount to jumping from a boiling pot into the fire. Worse villains than Spence and Fitch roamed the shadows of this sin-bound district.

A bone-chilling dampness, imbued with musty odors, closed in about them in the form of an insidious fog. Elise shivered, feeling detached from reality by the dank, cloying vapors. She was totally at odds with her surroundings, and she found no security in the knowledge that not very far away, residenced in the old Whitefriars monastery, was the great vagrant army of the Beggar's Brotherhood. She had once dared enter its halls in her guise as a boy to make inquiries about her father, and there had found an odious order of diverse and devious artisans who were not above robbing graves or the gallows at Tyburn for their elaborate disguises. Among their members were the violent and thieving ex-soldier rufflers, the horse-thieving priggers, the soap-frothing grantners, and the dummerers who mutely mouthed and feebly gestured for their coins but in the security of Whitefriars told riotously ribald tales and slapped their sturdy thighs in high glee. The most ingenious were the caperdudgeons who were known for their outlandish trappings. The most frightening and grotesque sights she had ever witnessed was when one of these wretches strapped on a corpse's severed and shriveled limb so he could pose as a cripple. The sight had been enough to send her flying to a secluded spot where she had promptly relieved her nausea. Outside the city, the beggars traveled in groups of a hundred or more and were usually preceded by foreboding cries of "The beggars are coming! The beggars are coming!" Inside Alsatia one never heard the warnings nor really ever knew when it was safe to move about or what eyes might be watching from the shadows. Here roamed the dregs of society, and their hours were as varied as their crimes.

Seeming as nervous as she, the two men cast furtive glances along the riverbank before they hustled her up the stairs. Firm grasps on her elbow and skirt checked her flight and made her aware of their restraint as she was whisked down a series of narrow streets and passageways where the stench of offal nearly made her gag. She was taken through a maze of shabby buildings until they came to a tall, narrow, gable-roofed structure. A weatherworn sign hung above the doorway, identifying the place as the Red Friar's Inn.

They huddled in the deep gloom of the portal as Fitch peered up and down the street, then he raised his knuckles to lightly rap upon the oaken plank. Silence answered him, and, nervously licking his lips, he rapped again, this time a hairbreadth louder. Finally a voice from within gave response before hurrying footsteps approached the door. After a rattle of chains, a thump of a bar, and a loud creak of rusty hinges, the panel moved inward a slight degree, allowing a dim sliver of light to escape. A woman's face appeared in the opening above a candle, and she looked them over with eyes that were still dull and puffed from sleep.

"'At ye, Ramonda?" Fitch broached the inquiry guardedly.

The woman's stare moved from the man to slowly rake Elise. A lopsided, somewhat sardonic smile displayed brackish teeth, then her slitted eyes cut back to Fitch. "Aye, I remembers ye alright. Ye were the ones what brought 'is lor'ship ta me."

"Aye, 'at we did." Fitch cast a wary glance over his shoulder before he pressed closer to the door. "The master said ye'd give us shelter."

The portal swung wider, making loud protest in the still night, and Ramonda motioned them in. "Come in 'fore ye're seen."

Fitch tugged on the woolen cloak he grasped and received an unappreciative glare from his captive. "Come now, mistress," he coaxed pleadingly, anxious for her to obey without creating a scene. He was no more at home in this place than she was. "'Ere be vittles inside an' a place where ye can rest for a spell."

Flanked by the two hefty bodies, it was clear to Elise that she had no other choice. Holding the cloak tightly about her, she stepped through the narrow doorway and could hardly dismiss the close proximity of the men as they shuffled in behind her, nearly trodding on her heels in their haste. When they all were safely ensconced inside, the portal was slammed and bolted behind them to a duet of relieved sighs.

"No need for ye ta fret yerselves." Ramonda smirked as she handed a lighted taper to the taller man. "Ye're safe enough now."

Fitch and Spence were none too sure. Beyond the pale circles of flickering candlelight the common room remained dark and obscure. They knew not what form could fly out at them from the shadows.

Dying embers still glowed in the hearth, awaiting another stirring to life at morningtide, while the stench of stale ale, peat smoke, and sweat seemed to hang close above their heads, held there by the low ceiling.

Elise felt Ramonda's close inspection and boldly returned the same with eyes that were cool and distrusting. Here was a third face she was determined to remember, if ever there came a time for justice. The woman's age was somewhere beyond a score and ten, but she was still a handsome woman though evidence of a hard life was beginning to show in her face. A large shawl had been thrown over her nightgown, but the wrap was nearly lost beneath the wildly tossed, flaming-red hair.

"Ye're a young one." Ramonda voiced her own observations as if strangely disturbed.

Elise had seen the fine lines across the other's brow deepen into a troubled scowl and was quick to give comment, just in case Ramonda held any trepidations about her own part in this conspiracy. "That I may well be, madam," she retorted, "but I'm old enough to know you'll be hanged at Tyburn with this pair of louts if you plan to do me harm."

Sweeping her long, fuzzy hair casually over her shoulder, Ramonda banished any idea of a suffering conscience when she responded with a deep, throaty laugh. "No need ta get yerself in a stew, missy. Ye'll be taken care o' well 'nough, though 'tis a mystery ta me why ye're even 'ere. But then, I 'afta remember 'is lor'ship 'as a feelin' for gittin' even."

"And just who might this wayward lord be?" Elise queried, eyeing the woman closely. She was well aware that both Reland Huxford and Forsworth Radborne might desire revenge upon her, and though the prideful Forsworth had no claim to a title, he had always enjoyed putting on airs and thinking of himself as some exalted personage.

"I'll reckon ye'll be knowin' soon 'nough," Ramonda

answered with a confident air. Dismissing the girl with a flippant shrug of her shoulder, she beckoned them to follow as she made her way from the common room. Entering a passageway, she led the way up narrow, rickety stairs. It was a long, wearying climb which took them beyond the bowels of the place to a landing where they were warned to silence by their guide. Even Elise was fearful of making a sound as they passed down a long corridor with many doors, with no doubt many an unworthy taking his rest behind the portals. At its end, another door led to another steep staircase that demanded another long climb. Elise's ankle and legs were aching when they reached the lofty level, evidence of the stiffness her enforced confinement was imposing upon her.

Stepping ahead of them down a short hall, Ramonda entered a tiny room tucked beneath the gabled roof of the inn and set a candle on the table. As Elise and the men followed, the woman swept a freckled hand to indicate the barred window in the dormer. "The liedy'll keep 'ere well 'nough whilst ye tend yer business in the Stilliards."

Elise quickly took note that the tiny window had been secured with small pegs to prevent it from being opened from the inside, not only forbidding the escape of the occupant, but preventing any verbal exchange with passers-by. The tiny chamber was obviously intended to be her prison, albeit one which had been made relatively comfortable with a narrow rope bed, a chair, and a small table at which to dine. Nearby, a washstand held the bare necessities for a toilette, a basin and pitcher, a towel and a small chunk of soap.

"As ye can see for yerselves, she'll not be escapin'," Ramonda boasted.

Fitch tucked in his chin, compressing the folds beneath it as he expressed his doubt. "Ye'd better keep an eye on 'er just the same," he advised. "She's a crafty one, she is, an' canna be trusted."

Ramonda arched a querying brow as she contemplated the slender girl and the hulking man. When she peered closer, she noticed the bruise alongside his cheek and questioned in some amazement, "'As the lil' twit done ye ill?"

"Truth be, a shrew 'as better manners," Fitch complained without discretion. "'Twill be folly for 'is lor'-ship if he canna' curb her mischief."

"Aye, 'is lor'ship may well rue the day he told ye ta fetch her," Ramonda agreed, wishing fervently he would do so before it was too late to turn back.

"Come now," Elise coaxed jeeringly. "If you think I'll bring so much havoc to his poor lordship, whoever the rapscallion may be, why do you not favor him with a gift and set me free? Why, I'll even be generous and forget I've ever seen the three of you."

"'At'd set us ta a bloody war with 'is lor'ship for sure," the burly man observed.

Ramonda kept her eyes lowered, afraid her desires could be seen in them. The emotions of jealousy and hate were hard to mask when they roiled so near the surface.

Spence had remained silent through their comments, but now interrupted in a brusque tone, directing himself to Ramonda. "The girl'll need rest an' vittles. See ta her needs whilst we're gone, an' when this be done, ye'll be given the purse ye were promised ... if ye've done yer part."

Spence nudged Fitch's arm, and the men took their leave, closing the door behind them. Ramonda's demeanor turned venomous as she glowered at Elise. She would have gladly crawled on her hands and knees to serve his lordship, but now, having seen what a beauty he had captured, she knew he had asked too much of her. By helping spirit this girl out of the country, she would be sending another woman straight into his arms, a place where she longed desperately to be herself. Too many hateful emotions churned within her when she looked at—her mind formed the description derisively—the sweet, young thing. Hate. Envy. Jealousy. They were cruel barbs on a cat-o'-nine, tormenting her unmercifully and tearing into her heart and soul.

Oh, she knew how farfetched her own yearnings were. The probability of her infatuation congealing into any sort of close involvement with his lordship was simply nonexistent. The time he had spent at the inn was so brief, she knew he was totally unaware of her devotion. Yet that knowledge did not ease her pain.

Ramonda's disdaining gaze descended over the rough garb of the girl. Though the shabby gown was not what a lady might wear, the creamy skin, the regal bearing and carefully tended nails gave evidence of the girl's true station in life, and it nettled Ramonda sorely that she could never be where the girl was already. "'Igh-falutin' ye may well be, missy," she jeered, "but ye can bet life won't be so foin where ye're goin'."

"Where am I going?" Elise lifted a delicately sweeping brow in curiosity, hoping the answer would come, though at the same time knowing it would not.

Enjoying a small slice of revenge on her rival, Ramonda chortled, "Ta 'ell, maybe."

The younger woman responded to the jibe with a casual lifting of her slender shoulders. "I suppose 'twould be no worse than this place."

Ramonda's eyes narrowed into a glare. Revenge was not so sweet when her words were cast aside with a mere shrug. She was tortured by envy and wanted to wreak vengeance upon the girl for all the misery she was now suffering, but she dared not, knowing she could never endure the humiliation of his lordship learning of her deeds. In truth, if the blame could be cast elsewhere, she would even allow the chit to escape.

"I'm s'posed ta fetch ye some vittles," she announced sharply. "Would ye be wantin' some gruel now ... or later?"

The offer was unappetizing, and Elise declined with a bland smile. "I believe I can wait until later."

"Suit yerself then," the woman snapped. "I ain't gonna force no 'igh an' mighty liedy like yerself ta eat me gruel. It might spoil yer ap'tite for all 'at rich fare ye're used ta."

Too tired for further argument, Elise remained mute beneath the other's sneering regard, and finally Ramonda snatched up a candle and strode out, locking the door behind her. In much relief Elise sagged onto the cot, thankful there would be no physical abuse laid upon her, to which she would have to respond. It was not that she was afraid of the woman though Ramonda was at least half a head taller and outweighed her by a good two stone. It was just that she distinctly remembered the advice of the scullery maid's son, that if she could not avoid a challenge or a fight, then at least choose the time and place to her advantage.

Elise slipped the hide shoes from her feet and curled up beneath the coverlet. She had not realized until now the depth of her fatigue, for she felt totally drained and sorely in need of rest. Her eyelids sagged, and her mind began to wander aimlessly until sleep overtook her, then she drifted in a dreamless void that was bereft of all knowledge and awareness.

Of a sudden Elise found herself staring at the low ceiling, and she lay listening to the creaks and groans of the place as her eyes slowly searched the small cubicle for the cause of her disturbed slumber. The tiny flame of the candle burned steadily, then strangely began to dip and flutter, as if teased by a current of air. Elise's gaze flew to the door, the only source through which a breeze could flow, and there she saw the portal moving inward. Her heart began to flutter. She could only think of the countless doors she had passed downstairs, and behind each she knew not what.

Elise almost breathed an audible sigh of relief when Ramonda came through the doorway, but she lay without stirring, watching from beneath lowered lids as the woman crossed to the table, carrying in a trencher of meats and bread and a mug of some unknown brew. Immediately Elise's eyes flicked to the open doorway, and her heart began to race again. She saw a chance to escape, and she knew she must seize upon it without delay. Whatever the outcome, it was well worth the attempt!

Elise, that sprightly spirited one, did not hesitate another moment. Leaping to her feet, she dashed toward the door, giving Ramonda a quick shove as she ran past. Though she had meant to use all her strength, the action seemed to take only the briefest touch to send the woman stumbling with the food-laden tray into the far wall. Elise did not stop to question her own prowess, but flew through the portal and slammed it shut behind her. The key was still in the lock, and she twisted it in frantic haste to bar the passage of the other. Only then did she dare breathe and attempt to quell the trembling that had suddenly taken hold of her.

She swallowed hard against the dryness in her

throat and crossed hurriedly to the stairs. She was shaking as she began the descent, for she had no idea what she might encounter on the lower levels. She remembered only too well Ramonda's warnings to be silent on the second floor and prayed she would be able to pass down the hallway without being discovered.

Nearing the bottom of the stairs, Elise slowed her steps and cautiously approached the door. She pressed an ear against the wood to listen for any sign of activity beyond the portal and felt a dulling sense of disappointment when she heard shuffling footsteps and the muted voices of several men in the corridor. She waited, fervently hoping they would enter a room and leave her a way to escape. The footfalls came ever nearer, and her mind began to race, for she was now confronted with the likelihood of the men opening the door. A thousand questions assailed her. What was she to do? Where was she to hide? Where could she go when she could not even hope to gain the upper hall before the men entered the passage? Her eyes flew upward, measuring the distance in a swift glance. Impossible or not, it was her only option!

Her slender feet flew on the stairs, racing in time with her swiftly beating heart, but alas, the feat was beyond her ability. Before she had climbed half the distance, the lower door swung open, and if that was not enough to make her heart stop, then Fitch's cry of alarm was.

"Eh! 'At's her! She's escapin'!"

Thundering footsteps shook the weak and rickety stairs, and in rising panic Elise shot a glance over her shoulder. A tall, pale-haired stranger came up the stairs first, with Spence following close on his heels. Behind them, hurrying as fast as he could, was Fitch, toting a large chest on his back.

Elise forced every measure of strength she possessed into her frantic climb, but the long-legged stranger lengthened his strides and leapt up the steps three at a time, quickly overtaking her. A long arm stretched out and closed tightly about her thin waist, snatching her from her feet and pulling her back against a wide, solidly unyielding chest. Elise was not one to silently or meekly abide this rude handling of her person. Kicking her bare heels against the man's shins, she gave vent to a loud, indignant screech of outrage.

The scream reverberated within the narrow space, seeming to ricochet off the very walls, and was successful in raising Fitch's hackles. Of a sudden he could envision a large troop of snarling men charging through the lower doorway in a zealous quest to rout any and all strangers. Any common, decent-looking man could be bludgeoned into incoherency before explanations could be made and suspicions could be appeased. In growing apprehension Fitch glanced around to see if the door behind him was still shut, forgetting about the length of the clumsy chest. The piece bumped against the wall, jolting the handle from his grasp. He swept his arm about to catch it as he felt the weight of it slide down his back, but in the process he lost his balance. Helplessly teetering on the edge of a step, he saw the chest tumble noisily down the stairs, and a helpless, plaintive mewl escaped his lips a fraction of a second later as he followed its thudding descent.

A large hand clamped over Elise's mouth, stifling her cries before she was lifted from her feet by a sturdy arm. Against her struggles to escape, she was carried up the remaining steps and whisked effortlessly down the hall. At the small chamber door, the stranger stepped aside to let Spence unlock and throw it open. Ramonda whirled from the window where she had watched so expectantly and stared in roweling disappointment as the one she had hoped to see fleeing on the street below was hauled back into the room. Wildly tangled torrents of auburn hair masked the girl's face, but Ramonda had no need to see the creamy visage to be crushingly aware that her ploy had failed.

The stranger cursed suddenly and snatched his hand away from the sharp teeth that tested the flesh of his palm. He set the slender maid to her feet and then jerked back abruptly as her small fist swung around with vicious intent. Catching the fine-boned wrists, the man gathered them together and gripped them easily in one hand against her furious efforts to yank free.

Elise flung her long hair back from her face, sending it spilling down her back, and glared into the ice-blue eyes that fairly sparkled with humor behind a fringe of pale lashes. The man was dressed as wealthily as a lord, wearing velvet doublet and puffed breeches of dark blue corded with threads of gold. Slowly his gaze descended, sweeping boldly down the length of her and stirring forth a blush to her cheeks as his appraising eye paused momentarily upon her heaving bosom. When he looked into her face again, his grin had widened in obvious approval.

"Now I understand," he murmured as if to himself and, in a somewhat louder voice, introduced himself. "*Kapitan* Von Reijn of the Hanseatic League, at yur service, *vrouwelin*." His speech was curiously marked by the flavor of the Teutonic tongue. "Or if yu've a vish to be better acquainted . . . Nicholas, to yu and to my friends."

"You . . . you jackanape!" she snarled in rage. "Let me go!"

"Nein, nein." Captain Von Reijn waggled a long finger chidingly in front of her slim and winsome nose. "Not until yu are made safe behind a locked door."

Glancing at Spence, he jerked his head, sending the man out to help Fitch who was bumping his way back up the stairs. Shortly the frazzled Fitch entered the room, backside first, dragging the chest behind him.

"Step aside now," Spence bade from the other end. When his companion lumbered limpingly aside, he gave it a last hefty shove into the chamber.

Grimacing, Fitch hitched himself around to slam the door, and there he leaned, mopping the glistening sweat from his reddened face. His hat was oddly crumpled and from beneath its edges, his hair stood out on ends, as if he had been frightened by a screaming banshee on his flight down the stairs.

"Yur pleasure, *vrouwelin.*" Captain Von Reijn grinned as he released his captive.

"A curse on all of you!" Elise railed as she snatched away. She rubbed her wrists and sneered at the captain. "And you! For all of your fine clothes and fancy twisted tongue, you're no better than these blackguards who do your bidding."

"Of course," Nicholas agreed and chuckled at her darkening glare. "Ve are a very select group, are ve not?"

"Oh, indeed." Elise's tone clearly conveyed her sarcasm. "Very select . . . for Alsatia."

"Yur kindness overvhelms me, *vrouwelin.*" Nicholas swept her a flamboyant bow.

Ramonda sidled nearer the door, hoping to take her leave as inconspicuously as possible, but the Hansa captain suddenly bestowed his full attention upon her. "Vere yu not promised a purse for keeping this maid secure?"

"The lil' twit bashed me noggin," Ramonda charged,

rubbing her head. "Ye can sees for yerself 'at she's a witch. She waited 'til me back was turned an' 'it me from behind."

Elise tossed her head and scoffed at the twisting of the tale. "Well, me dearie," she mimicked, "the way ye left the door wide open, I thought ye were askin' me ta leave."

"Ye lie!" Ramonda shrieked, drawing an arm back to strike the girl, but the cold, deadly dare in the deep, jewel-blue eyes made her pause. Though the twit was not heavily muscled, there was something in those eyes which promised dire recompense if she was attacked. Fitch had found cause to be wary of the girl, and in view of that fact Ramonda thought it unwise to test her fortitude. Rather, it would be better to let the matter cool, and hopefully all would be forgotten before it was reported to his lordship.

Captain Von Reijn had raised no hand to halt the threatening blow, but watched the two women with amused interest until Ramonda's gaze faltered and finally lowered in defeat. He chuckled softly as the woman turned her back to the smaller maid and began petulantly picking up the food from the floor.

Reaching down to the chest, Nicholas loosened the hasp and lifted the arched lid, then frowned as he ran a hand over the wooden interior. "Unfit though it be, it vill have to do."

In mild curiosity Elise peered into the interior of the piece and asked with rampant scorn, "For your treasure, milord?"

The captain chuckled at her gibe and returned a question to her. "Vhat is yur guess, *vrouwelin?*"

Elise plucked at the clothing she was presently wearing and remarked with satirical snideness, "I can hardly believe you brought it to accommodate my vast wardrobe."

"It is neither for my treasure nor for yur raiment," he replied, "but yur conveyance to my ship."

Elise laughed in a derisive display of humor until she realized he was serious, then she stared at him agog. "Sir! You are either daft or well-besotted! Come, let me smell your breath, for I would know which it be."

"I am quite sane, *vrouwelin*, I assure yu," he stated. Suggestively he caressed the end of a belaying pin which he had tucked in his sash. "And though I am not one to mistreat a lady, yu will go vhether avake or sleeping. The choice is entirely yurs."

Elise raised her brow in an arrogant arch and met his gaze squarely, trying to dominate him as she had Ramonda. The captain's gaze never flinched or wavered, though his lips twisted slowly upward. His interest in this fetching, but troublesome, wench was growing apace with his admiration of her undauntable spirit.

The longer Elise stared, the wider his grin became until it was she who turned aside in confused discomfiture. Noticing the food Ramonda was gathering on the trencher, she found an excuse for delay. "I have not eaten for some time," she protested. "Indeed, 'twas so long ago I am hard-pressed to recall just when it was."

Eagerly Spence held up a finger to interrupt. "Why, 'twas last eventide, mistress, by the river . . ." His memory came swooping back in vivid detail, and the mental image of himself being dragged end over end behind the boat brought a crimson stain to his face. The blush deepened when the captain bent a stare of wide curiosity upon him.

Fitch was every bit as eager to please. He seized the trencher from Ramonda and, setting it on the table, lifted the bread. Dusting the small loaf off against his well-stained jerkin, he placed it on the rumpled napkin, then, with the cuff of his sleeve, he carefully wiped several particles of grime from the hunk of cheese before he laid it beside the bread. With a sheepish smile he held out the food to her.

Elise stared at his offering in mild repugnance, and it was the captain who finally took it. He gathered the four corners of the napkin and, with deft fingers, knotted them together before presenting the bundle to her.

"My apologies, *vrouwelin*. The hour grows late, and I must return to my ship before dawn. If yu are of a mind, yu may dine in yur sedan."

"Am I allowed to know where you are taking me?" she asked coldly. "And why I must be carried about in this thing?"

"'Tis a matter of precaution. No one vould think it amiss if ve place a chest aboard my ship, but if ve vere to carry aboard a struggling damsel, it might arouse unvanted interest."

"And then?" she demanded, as an oppressive feeling of doom descended upon her. Ships were for sailing, either to other towns or to other countries. The question of her destination was paramount in her mind and burned to be spoken. "Where are you taking me after I reach your ship?"

"I vill tell you our destination after ve set sail."

"But you intend to take me from England, do you not?" she pressed.

"That is correct."

"I'll not go!" she cried in a rising panic.

"Yu have no choice, *vrouwelin*. I'm sorry."

Elise bestowed on him a glare of such heat and intensity it should have reduced the Hansa captain to cinders, but Nicholas merely inclined his head toward the chest again in an unspoken directive and awaited her compliance with a firm, commanding stare. Grinding out a stream of mumbled threats, Elise slapped the bundle from his grasp, sending it flying, and stepped into the chest. She rapped her knuckles on the hard wooden sides and cast a derisive sneer toward her small audience. "Faith! You've provided such comforts, I may not survive the journey."

"Entschuldigen Sie," Nicholas apologized, sweeping a quilt from the cot. He folded the piece and laid it over the bottom, then tossed a pillow atop the heap. Cocking a brow, he crossed his arms and stared down at her expectantly. "Anything else, *Englisch*?"

Averting her face, Elise sniffed primly and reluctantly lowered herself upon the quilt. The hide shoes were placed in her care before the captain squatted beside the chest.

"Now, *vrouwelin*, I vould ask yu to give me yur solemn oath..."

"You *are* daft!"

Nicholas ignored her interruption. "Give me yur vord yu vill not attempt to alert anyone's attention to this chest, and I vill refrain from using a gag and ropes to bind yu. For the most part yur cries vill not matter, but should there come a moment, I vant yur assurance yu vill remain mute until ve are safely aboard my ship. It vill be more bearable for yu if yu are allowed some freedom."

"Again, what choice have I?" she asked bitterly. "You could let this thing become my coffin if you so desired, and what objection could I make?"

"None," he answered simply. "But I vould make a pledge to yu in return to see yu safely aboard my ship as long as yu keep yur vord."

Her eyes were cold as steel as she looked into the pale blue orbs that rested upon her. "I have a care for my life, sir, and 'twould seem I must give you my oath to preserve it." She inclined her head stiffly. " 'Tis done then. You have my word."

Gently pressing her head down, Nicholas lowered the lid, and as her limited space darkened Elise took note of several patches of light where small holes had been bored through the chest to allow for the passage of air. At least she could take some solace in the fact that the first intent of these miscreants was not directed toward snuffing out her life by suffocation.

The hasp was secured with a lock, and Spence and Fitch looped ropes about the chest to form a sling of sorts to enable them to carry the cumbersome piece with more ease down the stairs. Nicholas quickly opened the door and made certain the way was clear before moving aside. Spence stepped to the front of the chest to bear the weight, while Fitch guided its passage from the rear, and together they slid their burden to the top of the stairs and peered down the flight as they considered the task at hand. Fitch was understandably concerned after his recent experience. He wiped his sweaty palms against his jerkin and, seizing the handle, lifted the chest on end with a single heave, then immediately clapped a hand over his mouth as he heard a loud thump and a muffled screech of pain followed by a lengthy string of unintelligible words. The tone was hot enough to convey the girl's rage, and with a great deal more caution they proceeded down the stairs.

On the lower landing Captain Von Reijn slid past the two men and, with belaying pin in hand, opened the door a crack. Once again he made sure the passageway was empty before he moved aside. Receiving his nod of assurance, Fitch and Spence snugged the ropes across their shoulders and, lifting the chest, steadied it between them with their hands.

Elise could feel their short, jogging steps as they

hastened down the hall and eventually out the door. There was a pause on the cobbled thoroughfare and a swoop upward, ending in a head-jarring thump as they lifted the piece to a higher elevation. Elise started in surprise as the ropes were dropped across the top, and from the rattle, jolt, lurch, and sway, she guessed the coffer was being pushed in a small handcart. Her suspicion was further borne out by the erratic path they wove amid much hushed and urgent cursing and hastily given directions. At the complete mercy of the men, she could only wince at the bumps and brace herself against the sides as she tried to avoid more serious damage.

There was a hurried plunge, first downward and then level, and for a short distance the cart moved along speedily, then suddenly, without warning, the wheel fell into a rut, bringing the conveyance to an abrupt halt. The chest had no such restrictions. It lurched forward to a sudden accompaniment of anxious shouting, and for a breathless space of time it seemed to Elise that her world teetered on the brink of an unknown precipice until the chest finally settled back into the cart. Hearing the loud, audible sighs of the men and a nearby splash, she decided it was better for her to remain ignorant of all that had just transpired. A brief vision of the coffer sinking slowly into the dark, ebon depths of the Thames reinforced her relief.

Once more the chest swung upward, and then with much wheezing and short, halting steps it was carried down a walk that sounded hollow beneath their footfalls. The movement ceased with a final jolt as the chest was placed aboard what Elise assumed was a small craft, possibly the same boat in which they had sailed into London. She heard the slow lap of water against the sides and, a moment later, the steady creak of oars as they pulled away from shore.

It seemed like hours elapsed before the thump of wood on wood and the muffled exchange of voices intruded into the silence. The chest was tilted from side to side, then a wrenching sound came as it was hoisted upward, seemingly into the very heavens. When it was lowered again, the chest was put through another series of gyrations, which left Elise braced rigidly against the interior. At long last it came to rest upon a solid floor, or so it seemed to Elise until she heard a slow creaking, such as a large ship might make as it lay anchored in the main stream of the river. Once more the chest was lifted by the men, but this time the passage was short and in a moment or two a heavy door closed behind the party. After a few fumbling thumps against the exterior of the chest, a thin shaft of light appeared as fingers slid beneath the lid and lifted it.

Elise raised a hand to shield her eyes from the un-accustomed glare of a lantern that was held close above her. Beyond its light she could see the dark shapes of the three men who bent over her and, be-yond them, the low-raftered ceiling of a ship's cabin. The men seemed incapable of movement as they stared down at her, yet her own vituperation over-shadowed everything else. With an angry grunt she managed to heave her shoulders up and twist an arm beneath her. Her legs refused to comply as she fought to extract herself from the restrictive space of the cramped chest. Brushing tumbled tresses from off her brow, she raised a vengeful glare to blatantly accuse each of them.

"If *ever* I should chance upon any or all of you being flogged to the bare bone"—she spat the words out in a half-monotone that singed the ears of those who listened—"I would ransom my most precious possessions to serve tea and scones to your tormentor, so he might be well refreshed and wax eager in his labor."

She levered herself upward, but her numb legs remained twisted beneath her. It was Nicholas Von Reijn, most bright of mind and perception, who moved first to assist her. Spence was a half-measure behind him, and Fitch eagerly pushed forward to lend aid. Before Elise could accept or reject their assistance, she was almost assaulted by the sudden plethora of helping hands, all seeking to pry her free at the same time. She was nearly plucked from her composure before the captain brushed the others aside. Placing a strong arm beneath her back and sliding another underneath her knees, he lifted her from the chest and stood her gently to her feet.

The awakening circulation in her legs was comparable to the sharp, stinging prickles of a thousand needles, and as Nicholas released her from his firm grasp, Elise teetered unsteadily, as yet unable to stand alone. Quickly he slipped an arm about her shoulders and half-supported her against his broad chest.

"Yur pardon, *vrouwelin*." His warm breath brushed her cheek. "Here, let me help yu."

Elise was abruptly aware of his overzealous assistance and the crush of his brawny arm about her. It brought to mind a possible reason for her capture, and a sense of panic overtook her. With a screech she flung up her arms, thrusting herself away from him, and staggered back a few stiff-legged steps until she came up against a desk. A gnarled oak staff leaned against it, and as she struggled for balance, her hand brushed the smooth knob of the weapon. Or so it became for her. With a defiant snarl she snatched the stick and brandished it, sweeping a wide, wicked arc in front of her, setting them all back upon their heels. Disheveled, ragged, and filthy, Elise braced herself against the desk, looking very much like a savage woman with her auburn hair straggling in long tendrils across her face and a smudge darkening the tip and side of her nose. Her eyes blazed defiance at her three stout-hearted foes, and in the same half-snarl, half-monotone she warned them all, without distinction for rank.

"Sirs ... or gentlemen ... or worthless scum of whatever gutters you sprang from, listen well, I bid you. I've been most poorly used and abused these hours past. Mauled and pawed! Trussed up like a roasting goose!" Her outrage gained ground as she listed the offenses. "Tossed over a shoulder like some common baggage! And thence, against my will, taken from my home and brought here to this ... this ..." Her eyes swept the cabin in search of a name to lay to the place wherein she now found herself and left the sentence hanging for want of an answer. Her gaze blazed afresh. "For this deed, perhaps some of you will soon be rewarded, but I warn you ..." She waved the cudgel threateningly. "If I am so rudely touched again ..." —her eyes pierced the captain through—"or violated in any fashion, I swear to you that your payment will come at once, be ye Grand Duke of England or surly knave! And though I may die in the levying, I shall extract a dire tax from any who dare lay a hand to me!"

Strangely none of the men seemed to doubt her efficacy. Indeed, they had every reason to believe her, for the maid had already proven herself an uncommonly tenacious example of womanhood.

Captain Von Reijn's heels came together with a loud click, and he bowed briefly as a deep chuckle rumbled in his chest. "Again I must beg yur apologies, *vrou-*

welin. I had no hint of yur frailty and only sought to give aid."

"Frailty, indeed!" Hefting the staff, Elise turned it slowly in front of her. "I will show you frailty, the sort from which you will beg relief. You may slay me here and now, whether by blade or halberd." Her eyes marked the two weapons hanging on a wall, then a feral gleam began to burn in their blue depths as her gaze settled on the three. "I only know I have had enough of this abuse and I will tolerate no more! Now do your worst or be done with it altogether!"

Elise's small, firm chin jutted as she clenched her teeth against a shudder. If they were truly desperate men, she had just invited her own demise.

"Belay yur fears, *vrouwelin*," the Hanseatic captain attempted to reassure her. "I svear to yu ve are all svorn to yur velfare, to see yu safely borne on a voyage vhich yu may in due time view to yur benefit. Ve vill give yu our service and protection until ve deliver yu into the hands of the one who arranged yur capture."

"Protection!" With scoffing laughter Elise rapped the end of the staff against the floor. "Oh, pray thee, saints above! Should I receive protection such as this much longer, I might yet succumb. Yea, I would rather have a pack of slavering wolves at my heels than the lot of you seeing to my care! *Protection? Service? Bah!*"

Her challenging stare dared any of them to repeat the vow, but stubbornly the captain tried again. "Vhat-ever vas done, *vrouwelin*, vas not carried out vith malicious intent. I say once again ve are at yur service. Do yu have a need ve can attend?"

"Aye, that I do, Captain! My most urgent need is to be gone from here and on my way home!"

"Unfortunately, *vrouwelin*"— the humor returned

to the captain's deep voice—"that is one service ve cannot perform, at least not yet."

"Then the next pressing need I have is to get the lot of you *out of my sight!*"

Von Reijn nodded in compliance to her wishes and jerked his head at the other two who gladly made their departure. He made to follow, but paused at the door a moment, lifting a large brass key from his pocket.

"Until ve are out of sight of land yu must stay here." He waggled the key before her gaze. "Of course, the door vill remain locked until that time. And unless yu fancy being lost on the North Sea vith me and my crew, I vould urge yu not to disturb anything here. Since mine is the only cabin aboard fit for a lady, I must beg yur indulgences now and then in permitting me to fetch my charts and instruments. Be assured, *vrouwelin*, I vill respect yur privacy as much as can be managed."

"I will believe that only when I'm given a latch to bolt the door against your untimely intrusions, Captain," Elise returned in sharp distrust.

"I vill announce my presence vith a loud knock, *vrouwelin*," he stated. "That is the best I can allow."

"You are so kind, Captain." Her oversweet, jeering tone belied the compliment.

Nicholas ignored her sarcasm and touched his fingers to his brow in a casual gesture of farewell. "I must bid yu adieu and be about my duties, *vrouwelin*. Once ve have put England to our backs, yu vill be permitted to come up on deck. *Guten Abend, vrouwelin*."

Chapter 5

*T*HE SHIP PLUNGED into a deep trough and, with its chunky bows, blew twin flumes of spray aloft where they were seized by the near-gale force of the nor'wester and whipped across the decks with vengeful verve. Elise gasped as the stiff, water-laden gusts struck her and penetrated to the very marrow of her bones. Clinging cautiously to the rail, she struggled up the gangway to the quarterdeck where Nicholas Von Reijn stood with his hands clasped behind his back and his feet spread wide to brace against the pitch and heel of his vessel. He favored her with only the briefest glance before he turned back to watch the binnacle over the shoulder of the helmsman. Elise gathered the coarse woolen cloak closer about her and sought out a place near the stern where she would be out of the way and hopefully out of sight and mind of the captain. She had had enough of being a prisoner, and at least on deck she could feel some sense of freedom, though she soon realized the price would be a heavy sacrifice of comfort. For the time being, however, she blinked against the salt spray and averted her face from the wind, refusing to yield to the elements.

Captain Von Reijn scanned the straining masts and billowing sails high overhead, then stepped away from the helmsman. Carefully inspecting every line and spar of his ship, he strolled the reeling deck as if he were quite at home on the high seas. His sturdy legs stayed well beneath him as he moved with a slightly rolling gait, and by the time he passed near Elise, she knew the rhythm of his bold strides, for his heavily booted footfalls came with uninterrupted regularity until he halted beside the rail.

Though she huddled in her woolen cloak and seemed unmindful of his presence, Elise was sure his eyes had settled upon her. In truth, she felt divested of the simple wrap and everything beneath it. His unrelenting regard touched off a quickening temper, and amid the gathering storm of emotion she tossed a glance over her shoulder, only to find that he was squinting into the sails. Vexed with him, she jerked back, wondering if she had truly imagined his hawkish stare or if he was just adept at concealing where his eyes had been.

Elise stiffened as his footsteps drew near, and when he halted beside her, she looked around with a piqued frown and found him giving her a slow, impassive scrutiny.

"All is vell vith yu, *vrouwelin*?" he asked, and his voice, just loud enough to be heard above the wind, was deep and smooth.

Elise met his inquiring regard with eyes that had turned dark, steely gray to match the cold and turbulent sky overhead. "Captain!" She raised her nose only the slightest degree to convey her vexation, then set her jaw with determination as she plunged onward. "If you had one whit of honor or decency in you, you would turn this vessel about and return me to England." Her smile was tight and bereft of any warmth. "Any part would do. I can find my own way home."

"My apologies, *vrouwelin*. I cannot do that."

"Of course not," she sneered. "You would lose the

coin you have no doubt been promised." She stared out to sea for a moment, braving the icy spray upon her face, then lifted her gaze once more to the pale blue eyes. "You've not yet taken me into your confidence, Captain, and I am most curious to know where we are bound. Is it some dark secret to be forever withheld from me, or will I be allowed to know your destination? Were I to guess, I would say we are bound for some Hanseatic port, considering you are part of that league."

Nicholas acknowledged her statement with a slight dip of his head. "And yu vould guess rightly, *Englisch*. Once ve cross the North Sea, ve vill sail down the mouth of the Elbe River to the port of Hamburg vhere yu vill, in time, meet yur benefactor."

The cold wind whipped her cloak unrelentingly, but Elise suppressed any shivering reaction as she asked with a hint of sarcasm, "Would he be a German like yourself, Captain?"

"Perhaps...perhaps not." Nicholas shrugged indolently. "Time vill tell you all, *Englisch*."

"Aye, and time will see the lot of you hanged for the scheming brigands you are," she retorted.

"That, too, remains to be seen," he murmured with an unaffected smile. Sweeping into a shallow bow, he took his leave of her and returned to stand beside the helmsman.

Elise would have tossed a glare at his broad back, but a chill blast drew a shudder from her, and she huddled deeper in her cloak. Its warmth was evasive, and she had to clench her teeth to keep them from rattling.

The ship chewed on along its halting course, gaining the northern reaches of the channel. The wind stiffened and became nearly unbearable. Elise suffered the open air until each icy spray made her gasp for breath and every frigid draft of wind sent the cold piercing through her, leaving her shuddering in bleak discomfort. At times stubborn to a fault, she was quickly learning the necessity of yielding to wisdom and common sense. The folly of a foolish course was not beyond her comprehension, and with each passing moment the remembered comfort of the cabin grew more inviting. Logic and reason could no longer be denied when her feet and hands grew numb. Trying to control her haste, she left the deck and stumbled through the passageway to the cabin. The door slammed shut behind her as the ship lurched into yet another swale, and she leaned against the wall to steady herself, savoring the draftless warmth of the quarters as she slowly dragged the sodden cloak away from her. Never in her life had she been so cold, and in her mind it was just another mark against the one who had perpetrated this offense.

A large, leather-bound chest had been carried in during her absence and now rested near the narrow bunk. What use it would serve aroused her suspicions, for she recalled with a shudder another cask of comparable enormity in which she had been rudely transported. Finding it securely locked, she huddled beneath the heavy quilts on the bunk and awaited that time when she would learn of its function.

The midday hour approached, and a quick rap came upon the door, but before she could answer, the ship lurched forward and the cabin boy stumbled through, struggling to keep the tray he bore from spilling. He bobbed a quick apology, then, mumbling something in a foreign tongue, placed his burden on the table.

Elise pointed to the chest, sure that he had brought it in. "What is this and why is it here?"

The youth shrugged to denote his lack of understanding and offered a name to aid her. "*Kapitan* Von Reijn."

His reply assured that her questions would have to be answered by the one he had named, a fact which Elise had already surmised. The lad gave her an inquiring look, and in return she gave him a nod of dismissal, allowing him to beat a hasty retreat.

A savory aroma wafted from the table, drawing her to the tray the cabin boy had brought, but the small, covered dish was ignored as she noticed a pair of pewter bowls and a like number of utensils, indicating she would not dine alone. She could only think of one person who would have the affront to invite himself to share the noon victuals with her, and that, of course, was the good captain himself.

A sudden anger took hold of her. "Methinks that wily jackanape is sorely addled if he expects to find me a willing companion."

A brisk knock intruded and, reluctantly bidding entrance, Elise turned stoically, knowing who it was before the portal swung open. Her reasoning proved correct. Nicholas entered, sweeping the fur cap from his head.

"Aarrgh! This vind vould have us battling the North Sea before the morrow," he rumbled, doffing the fur-lined, salt- and spray-bespeckled coat he had worn on deck. Giving it a shake to dislodge the droplets, he hooked it over a peg beside her cloak and approached her, rubbing his hands briskly together to encourage the flow of circulation through his icy fingers. Her stare was as frosty as the North Sea they sailed, and he regarded her with a humorous twinkle in his eyes as she confronted him with arms folded squarely across her chest and a look of stubborn defiance on her face.

"Do you have a need in this cabin?" Elise questioned him bluntly.

"It crossed my mind," Nicholas responded jovially, "that ve could share the victuals prepared by my cook ...a lover of fine foods like myself. I believe *Herr* Dietrich has prepared something very special for yu. A stew vith oysters from yur *Englisch* Thames. I should like to partake ... if yu have no objection, *vrouwelin*."

"I can hardly *insist* that you leave," she retorted. "I can only *hope* that you do."

"After ve eat, eh?" Nicholas chuckled, ignoring her testy reply. He crossed to the table where he ladled the oyster stew into two bowls, placed them at opposite ends, and then tore off portions from a small loaf of bread. He casually gestured to the place across from his own.

"If yu please, *Englisch*. I assure yu, I vill not bite."

Elise bristled as she heard the laughter in his voice, and their eyes locked in a challenging battle of wills. "If you're suggesting I'm afraid of you, Captain"—she managed a brief, tight smile—"let me assure you that I consider you a blustering buffoon, to be mainly ignored. And as you may have guessed I have no wish to dine with my captors."

"If yur choice is to starve, then so be it." He folded down the tops of his thigh-high boots and lowered himself in a chair. Contemplating her stoic demeanor, he braced an elbow on the table and thoughtfully crossed his lips with a finger. "If yu vould decide othervise, *vrouwelin*, I'd rather savor yur company and have yu join me ... at yur leisure, of course."

It was impossible to ignore the delicious aroma drifting from the table, but through dint of will Elise held to her place while the Hansa captain satisfied his hunger. A short time later she felt some chagrin as she watched the cabin boy clean away the dishes, leaving no crumb for her to savor.

"Vhen the evening vatch is out, ve vill shorten sail for the night and stand off a bit from the vind," Nicholas informed her, letting his gaze rest upon her again. "Dietrich enjoys preparing a small feast for the evening meal. I shall expect yu to join me then."

Elise's chin came up in a gesture of unswerving tenacity. If he meant her to be obedient to his requests, then he was again mistaken. "I pray you command no special favor for me, Captain," she replied crisply. "I am quite hearty and fully understand that I am a prisoner here."

"Hearken, *vrouwelin*." Nicholas held up a hand to stem her words. "It is my own pleasure I seek. The enjoyment of good food is my second passion, and I only ask yu to share it vhile ve endure ... *ach!* How do yu *Englisch* say ... a common misfortune? *Ja?* This journey does not require me to be uncomfortable, and toward that end"—he rose, wagging a finger against her reply—"neither should yu."

"My very presence aboard this ship fills me with indignation," she retorted. "I know not what awaits me, and I find no encouragement from your simple prattle. I've been snatched from my home and thrust aboard this ship with no guarantee I will see the end of the voyage. A common misfortune, you say? Pray tell me, sir, lest I should be blind, where do you suffer ill fortune? It seems a most singular experience to me."

She stood before him with arms akimbo, a vision of fire and beauty. In spite of her mean garb she was a sight to warm any man's blood, and his eyes passed over her, taking in every detail where the woolen gown molded itself to the swells and hollows of her womanly curves. It was a scrutiny Elise might have expected from any man, but in this case she could hardly dismiss it, considering she was his prisoner and she had no place to flee for safety should he seek a closer inspection. His brow furrowed into sharp creases as he turned his attention to the gray haze of sea and clouds beyond the gallery windows, as if he struggled with some inner turmoil, then he stepped past her. Going to the chest, he dug two fingers into the pocket of his leather doublet and removed a large key which he plied promptly to the lock. Lifting the lid, he dropped to a knee before the piece, then paused and, with eyes narrowed in careful contemplation, considered her again from head to toe.

"*Ja! Ja!* Yu be of the right size, I think. Ve did good."

Subduing a mild curiosity, Elise passively observed him as he took two large bundles wrapped in cloth from the chest. He placed them on the floor beside him, removed another of a slightly smaller size, then a fourth one which was even smaller. Dropping the lid, he rose and went to the bunk where he spread the bundles for her benefit.

"Yu vould no doubt be more comfortable vearing these clothes this evening, *Englisch*, and it is my vish yu do so." Abruptly he stepped away. "*Ach!* I cannot stay a moment longer. My duties call, but I vill return vhen darkness comes."

He tugged on the hat, outfitted himself for another tour on the deck and left, slamming the door behind him. Elise was intrigued, and she teased herself for only a moment before she opened the two larger packages. In both she found a treasure of carefully folded, royal blue velvet garments, in the first a cloak of rich beauty fully lined with silver fur, and in the second a gown trimmed at the neck with a white ruff edged with silver lace and long sleeves puffed at the shoulders and intricately embroidered with silver thread. Another bundle contained undergarments, a hooped farthingale, chemise, and delicately worked petticoats, while the fourth held a pair of silken slippers of a shade to match the gown. To be sure, the garments were far richer than anything a prisoner could expect.

Elise smoothed the soft fur and stroked the blue velvet with her hand, caressing it almost in a daze as a sudden longing came over her. Though only a scant few days ago, it seemed like ages since she had soaked in a perfumed bath and enjoyed the luxury of fine clothes such as these.

A harsh frown suddenly creased her brow as she remembered the captain's scrutiny, and she began to fold and wrap the garments again. She did not know his purpose, but there had to be some reason for these gifts, a reason she would not likely care for. He could quite easily take her by force; there was no question of his greater strength, but if he carried some hope of persuading her to be a willing and ardent companion by giving gifts of delectable foods and rich clothing, then in that too he was mistaken. Her favors were not to be purchased for any price.

The hour of darkness drew nigh, and the masts and yards above the cabin creaked heavily, as with a changing stress. Gradually the incessant rolling of the ship eased, and Elise knew that Nicholas Von Reijn, true to his word, had altered the course to run the ship with the wind more at its heels. It would not be long now before he would make an appearance.

The cabin boy came in to prepare the table for the evening meal, adorning it with fine linen, enamel-handled knives, silver dishes, and stemmed goblets of the same. When the service was prepared, he busied himself laying out a feast of poached pigeons with gooseberries, marinated salmon, and a small assortment of side dishes. When the lad fled the cabin, leaving her to await the coming of his master, Elise grew tense with the prospect of what the evening might bring. Of course, with his love of food the good captain would not dawdle overlong with the meal close at hand. He would be coming soon, and with each moment she grew increasingly aware of her predicament. If she refused to yield to him, he could easily resort to force, and there was not a single seaman aboard the vessel who would protect her from him. Even though Fitch and Spence made an appearance now and then, their attitude was one of pure distress at the motion of the ship. Nor could she have considered them helpmates had they been of stronger fortitude. As far as she could determine, they obeyed Von Reijn's commands explicitly and would not dare interfere if he ordered them out of his sight.

Despite her usual tenacity, Elise felt unprepared for the approaching battle and more than a bit fearful. The advice of the scullery maid's son was not in the least bit applicable to her dilemma. The overwhelming strength of her opponent was an obstacle she could never surmount, no matter the time and place. She could only rely on her wits, and she feared those were badly frayed from worry.

A sharp rap sounded on the portal, and Elise paused a moment to gather her poise. Smoothing the rough woolen fabric of her gown, she took up a stance near the desk where the staff would be close at hand and, breathing slowly and deeply to prepare herself for the battle to come, faced the portal like an heroic felon awaiting the attack of a fierce and mighty foe. At her summons, Nicholas swung open the door, but halted in the doorway as a piqued frown vexed his brow. He deliberately perused her from head to toe, making it obvious that he was annoyed with her refusal to wear the gift of clothes. "So, *Englisch!* Yu have decided to portray the poor, beleaguered captive."

"Forsooth, Captain! Am I not exactly that?" Lifting her chin with recalcitrant spirit, Elise dared to meet his ominous scowl.

Nicholas stepped into the cabin, quite dashingly garbed in fine clothes. Over a dark brown velvet doublet stitched with golden threads, he wore a rich, fur-lined chamarre of the same cloth. Tiny cordings of silk and gold finished the slashes of his short, padded breeches, and beneath them he wore close-fitting hose and low-topped shoes. His rich clothes presented a heavy contrast with her attire, and had she been the sort to regret her refusal of his gifts, Elise might have felt at odds with her own appearance, for she looked very much like a pauper in the presence of a prince.

"And do yu intend to leave me to dine alone?" he questioned gruffly.

Elise could see no reason to starve herself. "I shall be glad to join you for dinner, Captain."

"Wunderbar!" Nicholas exclaimed and swept into a brief bow before her. He offered his arm to escort her to the table, and she allowed him to assist her to a chair. They entered the meal, and it seemed the captain's attention was fully occupied for several long moments while he appeased his appetite. Elise picked at the delicious morsels that filled her plate, wondering when the storm of debate would begin. She had had occasion to witness the captain's harsh verbal reprimand of a bumbling seaman and, though she had not understood a word of his harangue, she had felt no envy of the lad. It had seemed doubtful to her at the time that the youth would ever make the same mistake again.

Needless to say she expected the worst when Nicholas slid back his chair and regarded her for a long moment with something of a puzzled air. "Yu are not a prisoner here, *Englisch*," he began in an almost lecturing tone, and Elise raised her nose a slight degree to silently convey a difference of opinion. "I yield to yu the comfort of my quarters and, vithin reason, the freedom of my vessel." He reached out and fingered the sleeve of her gown. "And yet yu insist on portraying yurself as the vanquished one, poorly dressed and ever vary of my intent."

The eyes of sapphire blue rested on him steadily as Elise rigidly maintained her position of stilted aloofness.

Softly he questioned, "Is it possible that yu do not like the clothes?"

"On the contrary, Captain," she responded in coolly measured tones. "They are very beautiful, but as yet you have not stated what the cost will be." She paused for effect. "No doubt such rich garments have a price I can little afford in my present circumstance or perhaps one I'm not willing to pay."

Nicholas stared at her, a frown troubling his brow, before he made use of the finger bowl of rosewater to wash his hands. "If yu know I am of the Hansa, then yu must also be avare that our merchant captains take a vow of celibacy until they have attained a certain measure of vealth."

"Vows mean little to some men," she replied. "Though you may say you're an honorable man, I've seen little evidence of that. I do not know you, but I know what you've done."

He pursed his lips, considering her answer, and then presented a different argument. "Yu have misunderstood my intent, *vrouwelin*. The gifts do not come from me, but from yur benefactor. He has borne the cost of the clothes, and is it not right that he should repay yu for the gown yu lost after yu vere seized?"

Thoughtfully Elise ran the tip of a slender finger over the rim of her goblet as she pondered aloud. "I've been curious as to the reasons for my abduction and have wondered if my captivity has anything to do with my father. Could this be possible?"

Nicholas lifted his wide shoulders to convey his lack of knowledge. "Vere I to guess, *Englisch*, I vould venture to say *ja*, but I cannot know for sure vhat is in a man's heart. Yu are a prize vorth taking, thus it vould not be uncommon for a man to be so smitten."

"Smitten?" Elise's brows gathered in deepening confusion. "Of what do you speak, sir?"

"Do yu find it so amazing that a man can be enamored vith yu, *vrouwelin*?"

"Aye!" she responded crisply. None of the suitors who had vied for her attention had seemed anxious enough to possess her by these methods.

"Believe me, *Englisch*. 'Tis a simple enough matter."

Elise met his gaze and was puzzled by the strange, almost yearning look in the light blue eyes. If this was passion she saw, then it had a softer look than she had ever seen before. Averting her face, she answered stiffly. "After what I've suffered, I would think the man who ordered my abduction harbors a deep hatred for me."

Nicholas chuckled softly. "*Nein*, that is not so, and I vould not take yu to him if I thought his intent vas to torment you."

"Why do you delay in telling me who he is?"

"His lordship vished his name withheld until he could explain to yu himself. He thought it best that yu did not form a hatred of him before he could defend his motives."

"I assure you, Captain, he has failed," she stated bluntly. "Whatever name he bears, the hatred will run as deep."

By morning, the wind had slackened somewhat, but a frigid coldness had settled down upon them with more intensity, as if to punish them for their audacity in daring the North Sea with winter nigh upon them. Not willing that anyone should think her soft or frail, Elise returned to the quarterdeck the next morning. Her nose and cheeks quickly reddened, and though she sought a place to keep her hands warm, her fingers once again grew numb with the cold.

Nicholas approached her as he had the day before, and as he stared down at her, his lips slowly spread into a grin that softened his own wind-reddened face. "I commend yur mettle, *Englisch*. 'Tis said for a seaman to sail the North Seas after Martinmas is to tempt God. I say for a lady to brave the decks in this veather is to find a voman vorthy of a sea captain."

Elise gave him a coldly quizzical stare. "Are you proposing, Captain?"

Nicholas shook his head with a laugh. "*Nein, Englisch*. Though yu are a temptation, I am honorbound."

" 'Tis good then! 'Twill spare you my rejection," she returned caustically. Without further word or excuse she moved away, leaving Nicholas staring after her in some amusement. Despite her drab gown, she strolled the decks with the dignity of a great lady, giving no indication of her discomfort, which he knew had to be considerable.

"Good spunk, *Englisch*," he murmured to himself.

That evening when Elise prepared herself for the evening meal, she took into consideration the fate of her own clothes and donned the blue velvet gown. It seemed only fair that the man responsible for the loss of her own fine clothes should replace them. She had suffered enough abuse because of him. She might as well enjoy a few of the luxuries he could provide.

Paying a compliment to the clothes, she garbed herself with care and dressed her hair in an upswept coiffure, making use of a silvered tray as a looking glass. If she had any doubts as to her appearance, they were quickly dispelled when Nicholas entered the cabin. His smile widened, his eyes glowed, and as he stared at her he slowly nodded his approval.

"The gown suits yu, *vrouwelin*."

"'Tis a rich piece," she commented, for want of something better to say. She did not know how to react when Nicholas looked at her with such warmth. "My benefactor, as you call him, must be very wealthy to afford such clothes."

Nicholas chuckled softly. "He has yet to receive the bill."

Elise raised a querying brow. "Were not the clothes his idea?"

"Certainly his, but he left the details to me since he vas pressed for time." The captain shrugged. "I only asked a seamstress to fashion something very varm and beautiful for a lady using the skins I acquired trading vith the Easterlings from Novgorod. They have closed their ports to the Hansa, but now and then I manage to strike a bargain vith one of their ship captains. The clothes vere the dressmaker's creation. I did not specify a limit on the cost."

"Perhaps my benefactor will be angry with your extravagance."

"One look at yu, *vrouwelin*, vould banish even the slightest irritation."

Elise allowed a moment of silence to pass as she studied the Hansa captain. He was a man of considerable knowledge and did not seem to have the characteristics of one who lightly joined himself to a company of brigands, especially for the purpose of kidnapping a helpless woman. She was curious to know what had prompted him to do so. "As merchant captain of this vessel, you must reap a great profit from your voyages."

"Perhaps a token or two," Nicholas answered with a noncommittal shrug.

Elise responded with a short, incredulous chuckle. "You would probably be more truthful if you said a fortune or two."

"The Hansa are dedicated merchants," Nicholas responded, wondering what she was leading up to.

"So I've heard—and as you say, they are sworn to a single life until they acquire wealth." Elise slowly raised a brow as she inquired, "Have you a wife, Captain Von Reijn?"

Nicholas shook his head as a smile touched his lips. "I have yet to obtain that status in life."

"Just the same, I perceive you have a fatter purse than you admit, a condition which suggests you do not need to resort to common thievery or kidnapping for your substance. Therefore I would assume your price is high, and for your part in this abduction you will undoubtedly be paid very well."

Nicholas brushed aside her statement with a careless wave of his hand. "'Twas but a favor for an old friend, *Englisch*, naught else."

"If you can be bought for a price," she persisted, ignoring his denial, "how weighty a purse would it take for you to change your allegiance and return me to England?"

A burst of laughter erupted from the Hansa captain, and though Elise's expression grew coldly brittle, the sound of his amusement ran its course until it finally dwindled. Nicholas grinned at her and, with a shrug, spread his hands apologetically as he responded. "I gave my vord to a friend, *vrouwelin*. There is naught else I can do but keep my troth."

"What does the keeping of one's troth mean to a brigand?" she asked in annoyance. She moved away from him while his eyes, shining with humor, followed her. "You talk honorably of your pledge, Captain, but is that pledge honorable? Is there such great esteem among villains that you can boast of your own repute even while cutting the purse from your victim's sash? Or spiriting away a captive to other climes?"

Nicholas opened his mouth to interrupt, but Elise pivoted on a heel and held up a hand, halting him abruptly.

"Give me leave to speak my words through, Captain. Since you have obviously grown calloused about your deeds, my attempt to reason with you and point out the error of your ways will no doubt prove futile. Nevertheless, I ask to be heard. You have made a pact with the devil, and I am caught in this trap with you as the gatekeeper. Innocent though I be, I will be plunged into a dark pit of that unnamed villain's making while you boast of your honor. Well, sir, your integrity has the foul stench of barbarism. You and your black-hearted accomplice have set yourselves to do mischief of the most wicked kind, and you are as guilty as he for carrying out his bidding."

"I cannot plead my cause," Nicholas admitted with an accommodating smile. He was intrigued with the way her eyes flashed when she was provoked. "I am guilty as charged."

Though she had hoped to sway him by the logic of her words, Elise now realized she had failed. He was a man who had set himself to a task, with full knowledge the deed was wrong, and apparently felt no chagrin.

Nicholas considered her statements in thoughtful reflection, wondering if the future would prove his actions as vile as she had claimed, or if he would be fully redeemed in her sight. Though placed at his mercy for this passage of time, she seemed as yet undaunted. She continued to conduct herself with a proud grace that conveyed an inborn dignity, an unquenchable verve, and a resilience that few men could lay claim to.

He gently plucked at her sleeve, like a small, wayward child trying to make amends. "Yu may have me flogged if in a year you regret this voyage," he murmured softly. "I trust it vill prove to be of benefit to yu as well as to my friend."

Elise stared into the warmly shining eyes and finally, after a lengthy pause, moved away. Nicholas released his breath slowly, fighting an ever-growing desire to comfort her and pledge his protection as her champion and suitor. He was beginning to understand how a man could be so taken with a woman he could forget honor and a troth fairly spoken.

Chapter 6

*T*HE SHIP ENTERED the mouth of the Elbe, and as lookouts watched for sandbanks and ice floes, Elise stood on deck, anxious to see what she could of this land wherein she would be held prisoner. Mostly she saw marshes and lowlands until the banks began to rise on the north. A frosting of white mantled the trees where the heavy mists of the prior evening had formed crystalline trappings of ice. Along the shores, a jagged upthrust of giant ice shards traced the water's edge, and where the ground was protected by trees, a blanket of snow remained. An occasional flurry drifted down in the hushed silence of the still day, more as a reminder of the season than any real threat of a storm.

Finally the ship approached the quay at Hamburg, and seamen rushed aloft to reef the sails and secure the lines. The cold air penetrated Elise's threadbare garments as she waited with Fitch and Spence for the ship's landing and the signal to disembark. When word came, she crossed the gangplank first, with Spence and Fitch following close behind, each grasping an end of the chest her new clothing had come in. As she stepped to the dock, Elise felt the weight of the captain's gaze and turned back to stare up at him as he watched from the rail. He inclined his head slightly, which was his only parting gesture, and Elise responded in kind, somewhat confused by his stoic manner. He had been most distant with her since the night she had asked him to take her back to England, and except for the brief occasions when he had been in need of a chart or some such item, he had kept himself away from the cabin. Not that she mourned his reticence or his aloofness, for he had never given her any choice in accepting or rejecting his company. It was just that he had seemed to enjoy the exchanges before that particular evening, and she was curious as to what had made him change his mind so abruptly.

Elise and her two escorts merged with the bustling activity of the docks. All around them vendors hawked their wares in a language she could not understand, while eager merchants haggled for the cargoes that had been brought in, yet the lightly falling snow muffled the variety of sounds and seemed to bring a softer note to the cloudy day.

Fitch had taken the lead through the milling throng and now faced her with an explanation. "I gots ta go an' fetch a key for the manor 'ouse 'is lor'ship rented for ye. Now be good an' give me yer word ye'll wait 'ere wit' Spence 'til I return."

Elise raised a sharply questioning brow. "If Spence is to remain, is it not reasonable to assume that he will catch me if I try to escape? And who in this foreign place would I plead shelter from if I did manage to escape? I've no knowledge of this jargon these people speak."

Fitch thought upon her answer, then finally accepted her logic. Leaving her to the other man's care, he hurried off down a street.

A vendor of cooked meats had built a small fire beside her cart for the preparation of her wares, and its cheery flames promised the warmth Elise was seeking. Drawn to its heat, she stretched her icy fingers toward the fire, and almost immediately a jolly, rosy-cheeked woman greeted her. Speaking to her in a foreign tongue, the vendor pressed her to take a short wurst on a stick. Elise was reluctant to refuse the purchase, for fear she would be forced to leave the fire, and she looked pleadingly to Spence who had set her chest down nearby. He seemed happy to comply and laid a coin in the hawker's eager hand. That one received it with a jovial *"Danke, danke!"* and handed Elise the juicy tidbit. She fetched another for Spence and it was promptly consumed. Encouraged by his appetite, the woman pressed him to buy another and chortled in glee when he consented. Elise leisurely nibbled her own sausage, more interested in savoring the heat of the crackling fire than the meat, though it was a new and succulent taste for her.

They had more than enough time to finish several sausages as they waited for Fitch to return. Indeed, Elise was beginning to wonder if the man had lost his way, but finally she caught sight of him trudging slowly toward them. From his doleful expression, she could swear he bore the weight of the world upon his shoulders.

" 'Ere be a change in plans," he announced glumly when he halted beside them. "We'll be puttin' up at a different place north o' here. We'll be needin' mounts ta take us . . . an' supplies ta see us through 'til 'is lor'ship comes."

Spence frowned in sudden bemusement. "But 'is lor'ship said he rented a manor 'ouse right 'ere in 'Amburg an' put out coin for it."

A long, wavering sigh slipped from Fitch, seeming to deflate his spirits even more. " 'Ans Rubert said the 'ouse's been taken. 'Tis no longer 'vailable."

Spence peered at his companion closely, but the man would not raise his gaze. With a snort of irritation the taller man held out his hand for the purse. "I'll go an' fetch the 'orses an' supplies meself whilst ye wait 'ere wit' the girl."

Fitch mutely nodded and, with another laborious expelling of breath, lowered himself onto a stack of firewood. He dropped his chin into his cupped hand and was in such a state of despair, he was oblivious to the peddler who persistently urged him to try her sausages. It was only when the aroma wafted beneath his nose that he came to an abrupt awareness and eagerly dug in his jerkin for a coin.

It was some time before Spence returned. What he acquired from the waterfront livery made Elise doubt his capable judgment of horseflesh. The saddles and tack were worn relics of an era long past, which might have also been a way to describe the four small horses. The beasts were short-legged and shaggy with long winter coats, and they plodded slowly along with no apparent ambition to move any faster. The food and provisions procured from shops along the quay and gathered into bundles upon their backs would not have been a wearisome burden for an ordinary steed, but the two geldings on whom they had been laid wheezed and labored under the strain, as if the weight was far beyond their ability to carry.

Having grave doubts as to the strength of her own nag, Elise settled herself gingerly on its back, then caught her breath as the rising winds sent shivery blasts coursing beneath her woolen cloak. Catching the flaring garment and tucking it securely around her, she huddled within its warmth upon the sidesaddle and prodded her mount with a thumping heel until the animal reluctantly followed Spence who led the procession on his steed. Bringing up the rear, Fitch held the lead rope of the packhorses as he kept a wary eye upon their charge.

The short caravan traversed the winding streets of Hamburg, crossing stone bridges that spanned canals and narrow waterways until they gained the outer limits of the city, then they traveled north along a wide road that led them through a thick forest. Though it was early afternoon, low leaden clouds continued to dull the western light and deepen the gloom beneath the trees. Spitting snow stung their faces, leaving traces of white upon the mulched leaves upon which they trod. Eventually they came upon a path that was wide enough for a cart, but only a little better than a worn rut. Without word or nod Fitch turned his horse onto the trail. Climbing gradually from the lowlands, they picked their way through the thinning forest and around large tumbled rocks which became increasingly more plentiful.

The wind whistled over a low ridge that buttressed the hill and wailed a mournful lament as it passed behind them through the trees. The sorrowful sound seemed to echo the dismal mood of the three. The men were only slightly more knowledgeable of the terrain than their hostage, and from the questions exchanged between them, it was apparent the three of them shared a common curiosity as to where the path would end. As for Elise, she was anxious to know where she would be imprisoned, in what house, hall, dungeon, or fortress she would eventually find herself.

They topped the ridge, and to Elise's amazement she found that their path led to an ancient castle nestled on a low bluff a short distance away. Gray and bleak as the wintry sky overhead, the outer walls rose from a jumbled pile of jagged rocks near an elbow of an ice-crusted stream and were themselves breached in several places. Dry tufts of withered grass randomly pierced the clumps of snow that covered the rampart. A low bridge constructed of stout timbers provided access across a moat to the dark, gaping maw of the gatehouse where a rusty portcullis hung askew over the upper part of the entrance, held there by one chain that still secured a corner. A wooden gate lay in a broken heap across the passage and was covered with a fresh dusting of snow.

Picking their way around the fallen gate, the three passed through the gatehouse and entered the courtyard. Elise found little to assuage her anxieties. The storehouse and barracks had all but collapsed against the west wall. On the east stood a dilapidated stable, to which Spence led the packhorses. The main keep was still intact at the juncture of the east and north walls, but most of the shutters and some of the windows on the second and third level, along with the steep slate roof, were in sore need of repair. A few windows stood open, as if to welcome the birds that fluttered about them.

Fitch stared agog at his snow-bedecked surroundings. Finally he dismounted and approached the maid, seeming reluctant to meet her gaze. Without word or excuse he helped her down and followed at a distance as she climbed the front steps to the arched doorway of the stone keep. The large, heavy portal gaped open, offering little protection from the blustery winds that whipped about them. Peering into the gloom of the inner chambers, Elise moved cautiously inward. She had no knowledge of what creature, human or otherwise, might be lurking within the shadows of the great room, and she was alert to any sudden movements as she descended the pair of steps that led from the entrance. No ferocious beast sprang upon her from the darkened corners of the hall; there was only the assailing attack of her senses by the filth of the place. Decades had apparently passed since the castle received the care and attention of a human hand.

Huge, grayish shreds of long-abandoned cobwebs hung from the darkly timbered, rough-hewn trusses that braced the ceiling. The webs spanned doorways, corners, and other nooks and crannies, while tiny droppings gave evidence of the comings and goings of small rodents. As Elise moved about the room, her skirts raised dust from the long, tapering ridges of dirt that stretched across the stone floor, marking where strong drafts had long invaded the hall. A large table lay on its side in front of the huge hearth, and several benches were piled in a jumbled heap beside it, some broken in pieces as if used to feed a fire of a more recent time. The soot-coated interior of the open hearth bespoke of a lengthy age of roaring blazes and smoldering coals. A brick oven had been built close against the side of the inner wall, indicating that the area had been utilized as a kitchen. A large iron kettle still hung on its bracket above the ashes, and from a beam overhead assorted pots and utensils hung, covered by a thick mantle of dust.

Stone stairs ascended in a flight to the second floor and were buttressed by stout wooden balustrades on either side. A landing existed on the upper level and led to another flight of stairs.

"A poor camp," Elise sighed wearily, "but at least 'twill give us some shelter against the wind." She faced Fitch, who had paused behind her. "How much farther is it to your master's house?"

"Yer pardon, mistress," Fitch mumbled shame-facedly. "I fear this be the place."

"The place?" Her brows came together in confusion. "What do you mean? Where are we?"

Fitch glanced about in wry repugnance and was well aware that this was no fit shelter for even one night, much less a place where a fine lady should have

to live. "Faulder Castle, mistress. This be where the
agent said 'twas ta be found."

Elise's bewilderment did not diminish. She found it
difficult to understand the significance of his words.
This tumbledown keep could not possibly be where
they were going to live. "Are you saying"—her tone
was flat and frigid—"we'll have to stay here in this . . .
pigsty?"

The servant hung his head and scrubbed a toe
across a mound of dirt. "Aye, mistress. At least 'til 'is
lor'ship arrives."

"You jest!" Her voice was weak, and she could put
no force behind her words.

"Yer pardon, mistress." Fitch dragged off his hat
and twisted it worriedly in his hands. He cleared his
throat, as if his words were wont to stick there. "I
fear 'tis no jest. This be Faulder Castle for sure."

"You really cannot expect me to stay here!" Elise
cried incredulously. She was suddenly bone-tired,
weary, and racked with despair at the thought of having to search out even meager comfort in such a den.
"'Tis not fit for swine!" An outraged anger began to
burn within her and gave her words a stinging disdain.
"Though your lord and master is wealthy and powerful enough to command the loyalty of the likes of you
. . . yea, even the captain of a Hansa ship . . . not to mention how many others . . . will you now tell me he
cannot provide better than this for us? Must we make
our home among the vermin?" She flung a hand toward the tiny-footed tracks tracing across the mounds
of dirt and then looked about her in sneering contempt. "His humor must be supreme to send us to
this pile of wreckage. I vow this hovel has to be the
leavings of Charlemagne or some such lord who
roamed these lands in eldritch times."

Fitch wrung his hat in his hands as he sought to

excuse his master from blame. " 'Twas none o' 'is lor'-ship's doing, mum. 'E paid rents for a manor 'ouse in 'Amburg. 'Twas the agent, 'Ans Rubert, what made the mistake. 'E heard we'd been shipwrecked an' gave the 'ouse, the very same 'at 'is lor'ship paid for, ta 'is poor bewidowed sister."

Elise gnashed her teeth in roweling vexation. "And I suppose the good Hans Rubert gave you this keep for a mere tuppence."

Fitch hung his head and mumbled in agreement, as if reluctant to talk about the matter. "Aye, at least a tuppence."

Elise set her hands on her hips and flared, "Then, my good man, you have paid a tuppence too much!" She swept her arm about in a gesture that encompassed the interior. "Look around you and tell me, if you can, how anyone can exist in this filth."

Fitch crumpled the poor hat between his pudgy hands as he tendered a question for an answer. "May'ap if it were given a good cleanin'?"

Elise gaped at him in stunned disbelief and finally arched a delicate brow as she asked, "What say you, Fitch? Are you offering your services? Will you bend to your hands and knees and scrub the floors until they gleam? Will you repair the door? Scrub the hearth?" The man backed away in great discomfiture under her barrage of questions, but Elise followed, persisting. "Will you mend the windows and peg up the shutters, sweep the chimney, dust the rafters, and braid new rushes into mats to warm these stone floors?"

Fitch halted abruptly with the wall to his back and waved his arms helplessly as she pressed closer. " 'Ere be little choice, mistress. 'Til 'is lor'ship arrives, we 'aven't the coin ta rent a finer house . . ."

"Did you not receive the difference in rents from

Hans Rubert?" she asked, already perceiving the answer.

Gingerly Fitch shook his head. "Nay, mistress, 'Ans Rubert said 'is lor'ship owed him a debt, and he wouldn't discuss the matter wit' a servant. I 'ad ta take more coin out o' me purse ta pay 'im for this, an' 'twere the best I could afford, what wit' havin' ta buy supplies an' all for us."

Elise glanced about her in growing dismay. For some strange reason she had held a vision of a wealthy hall wherein she would find a bath, a good meal, a private chamber, and a down-filled tick upon which to rest. She had been unable to sleep during the night, knowing they would soon be docking. The long wait in the cold after the hustle of the landing and the wearisome ride had done nothing to ease her discomfort. "'Twould seem we have little choice indeed," she murmured dejectedly, then sighed in doleful spirit. "On the morrow we must make an accounting of what coin you have left and what needs be done first. As for tonight, we will have to make do with what little comfort we can find."

"A mighty task ta be sure, mistress," Fitch commented dismally.

Elise shivered as a chilly draft swept through the hall. "A fire would help and perhaps something to block up those windows that cannot be closed."

"Spence is settlin' the horses. I'll go an' fetch some wood an' bring in the supplies, then I'll see what's ta be done ta mend the windows an' shutters."

The servant hurried out, and Elise lifted her gaze toward the higher level, wondering if the upper chambers were in any better condition than the hall. Taking up her skirts, she slowly mounted the stone stairs until she reached the second level. There a short hallway jutted off from the landing. The floor consisted of only two rooms, a tiny one as would be suitable for a lady's maid and a larger chamber. The portal of the latter stood slightly ajar, allowing a shaft of light that filtered in through the windows to pierce the gloom of the hall. The hinges creaked in rusty protest as she pushed the door wider, and in sharp repugnance she brushed aside the cobwebs and entered. Within the bedchamber the floor was covered by a thin layer of dirt rather than variegated ridges. The light was afforded by several tall, narrow windows whose lower panes of octagon-shaped colored glass cast variegated hues into the room. A few stood open, allowing birds and persistent drafts to enter, while beyond them the sagging shutters flapped and rattled in the wind. Crudely chiseled beams supported the ceiling and from these, thick cobwebs swept downward, gracing the canopy of a bed that was closed in by solid panels of deeply carved wood at the head and the side against the wall. Tattered shreds of a feather mattress was all that remained to cover the rough planks of the box. Another canopy of sorts, constructed of copper and wood, sheltered a large, circular copper tub, which stood in the corner between the fireplace and the windows. Its once-elegant hangings were now merely long shreds of rotted cloth which fluttered in the errant breezes. Deeply carved buffets, chests, armchairs, and armoires completed the furnishings that were untouched by anything other than dust and time.

Elise could well surmise that the distance and difficulty of getting to Faulder Castle had, at least for the most part, discouraged the ransacking and pillaging of the place. It was the neglect of years that had been the worst culprit in the destruction.

A pair of low stools, thickly crusted with dirt and grime, squatted before a large fireplace at the end of the chamber near where she stood. On the same wall, nearest the door, a huge tapestry hung from ceiling to floor, covering a section of wooden panels. A grayish layer obscured the needlework, and Elise reached out to examine it to see how well the fabric had withstood the ravages of time. Her hand raised a thick cloud of dust from its surface. Noticing a tasseled cord hanging beside it, she tugged on it, curious as to its purpose. The cord refused to yield to her small inquisitive jerk, and finally in exasperation she gave it a mighty yank. A screech of rusty nails tearing loose from dry wood suddenly splintered the silence, bringing her head up with a snap. Without pause the tapestry, the rod on which it hung, and the carved wooden valance that covered both began a majestic descent as one mounting after another gave way, spilling a billowing cloud of choking gray dust in advance of their ponderous fall.

Elise gasped and stumbled back, barely noting the doorway that had a moment earlier been hidden by the tapestry as the weight of the cloth brushed heavily against her. In the next instant the air was filled with a growing swarm of small, chittering, black creatures that flitted about her head in swift, staccato swoops and dives. The horror of the attack seized her, and she gave vent to an undulating scream as she twisted this way and that, seemingly forever confronted by their darting flights.

Rapidly thudding footsteps sounded in the hall, and Fitch burst into the chamber, the heavy splitting axe he carried held at the ready. It was apparent he had come to do battle with whatever fierce assailants the lady had encountered, be it bear or wolf...

"Bats!" he bellowed as he skidded to a halt in the middle of the room, which incidentally was within the center of the swarm of bats. As a hundred dread stories of the evil creatures welled up within his mind

he swung the weapon with mighty sweeps and let out a roar in blood-red tones. "Fly, mistress! Get yerself safe! I'll 'old 'em off!"

The broad axe head fairly whistled as it cleaved the air but amazingly very little else. The skirt of Fitch's jerkin flew out as he spun on a single foot, raking the weapon around again in great swooping strikes.

'Twas Elise's good fortune to have fallen to the floor. From there she lifted her gaze and realized that her defender, in order to keep these fierce beasties from his eyes, had the latter tightly clenched. Recognizing her plight, Elise remained crouched as she crept to the doorway. When her breath returned, she noticed Fitch had gallantly cleared the room of the winged creatures and with such astounding success that no sign of the bats remained, neither sundered wing nor splintered body. She called out to that mad dervish with the axe. "Cease your attack, Fitch! You've won the day!"

The man halted abruptly with his feet braced wide and the axe still at the ready, then he teetered as his eyes rolled wildly in his head. When he finally steadied himself and was certain no enemy remained, Elise deemed it safe to rise and dust off her skirts.

"Look, Fitch! They've fled you as demons would an avenging angel."

"Aye, mistress," he panted between gulps for breath. "An' well 'ey would. I must've slain"—he searched about for evidence of his destruction and was somewhat confused by the lack of same—"at least a . . . 'undred or so . . . ?"

"Aye, Fitch!" Elise laughed as the man wiped his sweating brow and leaned in puffing exhaustion against the haft of the axe. "But I fear the power of your blows has flung them all out the windows." She gave a nod toward the panels of leaded glass. "For the sake of caution, you'd best latch the windows against their return. We would not want them to visit us again."

"Ta be sure!" Fitch agreed heartily, and swiftly applied himself to the task, closing and securing all windows to prevent any future threat of their entry.

"This corner will have to be given a thorough cleaning," she observed, indicating the filth the bats had left. Indeed, it promised to be a monumental task. The dung would have to be scraped from the walls and floor before the corner could be washed with stiff brushes and soapy water and the chamber pronounced fit for occupancy. As for the tapestry, it would take a more careful cleaning.

Surreptitiously Elise contemplated the paneled door that had once been hidden behind the tapestry. She was most curious as to where it might lead, but allowing Fitch to notice her interest in the portal would only defeat her purpose, if indeed it might later provide a way of escape. It would be much better to investigate its secrets when she was alone.

Alas, Elise's thoughts were not entirely unique. Espying the same portal, Fitch made his own mental notes. It was to his benefit to establish a strongly fortified haven so his lordship would not have to question him later, and toward that end he formed the opinion that the door would have to be somehow secured, just in case the portal led to a secret passage and the lady would entertain ideas of leaving the castle at some later date.

Elise stepped into the hallway and swept her gaze upward, wondering what the higher chambers would offer for accommodations and just what she might find there. She was not yet ready to face another such adventure as she had just experienced and chose to invite an escort. "Come," she bade Fitch. "Be my guard while I explore the rest of the keep. Should we have occasion to meet other beasties, I would prefer your strength closer at hand."

Fitch straightened his jerkin and preened a bit at her words of trust. "Aye, mistress," he agreed heartily. "'Tis best we stick together."

Willingly Elise followed the man up the wooden stairs which turned in long flights to an upper-story hall. To the left, the corridor held to the outer wall where arrow slits had been strategically placed every few yards or so in the solid stone. On the right the hallway led as it did below to a pair of doors, the larger of which sagged from its hinges. The smaller opened onto a room obviously meant for a servant. Its stark furnishings and tiny dimensions were hardly much bigger than a dressing room or a privy.

Fitch tried to appear casual, but Elise noticed that the axe preceded him as he poked warily at the sagging door to push it wider. Tentatively thrusting his head through and finding no immediate danger, he put a shoulder to the thick plank and heaved the portal aside to allow Elise easy entry. Apparently these had once been the lord's chambers, for the quarters were comprised of a huge bedchamber, a dressing room, and a privy. The bedchamber might have once been habitable, but a gaping hole in the roof allowed a large expanse of sky to show through where the tiles gaped awry. Snow had accumulated in a small mound on the floor beneath the opening, and its icy form bespoke the chill that hovered in the chamber.

Elise surveyed the room and commented wryly, "Considering my choices, I shall take the bedchamber below for my own. Perhaps your lordship has a penchant for the crisp air of this clime, but I do not."

Fitch's mouth sagged open as he was struck with the sudden realization that there were no alternatives and that his lordship would be highly displeased with the chambers. Lost in deep thought, he made no move to follow Elise as she turned to go. Instead, he mumbled as much to himself as to her, "Me an' Spence'll 'ave ta fix 'at roof just as soon as we can."

Elise's small, tight smile readily conveyed her lack of concern for his lordship. "Other repairs will have to be done first to make this place livable for us," she pressed. "Since your master is not expected immediately, the roof can wait. We have need to place ourselves in comfort first."

Fitch cast a worried glance at the hole, unsure of where his own priorities should be, but Elise gave him little space to dwell on the matter.

"First things first," she reasserted. "Come along. We've much to do before you get back to this."

Reluctantly he followed her down the hall, but grumbled to himself, quite bemused as to just when this small, slim snip of a girl had taken charge of the household.

"We'll start with the sweeping, dusting, and scrubbing. Hopefully there is enough light left to aid us in making some improvement to this place before night befalls us."

The woolen cloak billowed out around her, swirling up small puffs of dust on the stairs as Elise began her descent. She moved so swiftly, Fitch was hard-pressed to keep up. When she halted suddenly, he nearly trod on her heels and accomplished a sideways, skittering jig to keep from doing so.

"Is there a serviceable well from whence to draw water?" she asked.

"Aye, mistress. In the courtyard 'ere be one. An' another in the stable."

"Good," she replied. "We'll need a fair flood of the stuff to clean this heap of stone." She spoke to him over her shoulder as she again hastened her descent. "We'll need supplies! Whether you find, make, or borrow them! Brooms! Buckets! Soap! Rags!" Each word seemed to jolt from her as she took a step downward. "And capable hands! But yours and Spence's will have to do for the time being."

Elise swept past the hall near the chamber she had claimed and continued on down the stairs. "There was a kettle here..."

And what Fitch and Spence recalled of the rest of that day was nothing more than work, work, work!

Chapter 7

*E*LISE WAS WAVERING near the brink of complete exhaustion when she retired that evening. Her limbs felt so heavy she could hardly manage the climb to her bedchamber. She had thrown herself into a frenzy of activity as she sought to improve their state of circumstance before the fall of eventide. Little progress had been made, and considering the monumental task laid out for them, their efforts that afternoon were comparable to scratching a stony surface with a green stick. For the moment she felt defeated, and when the door of her chamber was securely closed behind her, she collapsed weakly to her knees before the hearth and stared into the flames in a dull stupor. Tears glistened in the heavy lashes as memories of her father came stealing upon her, and the agonizing questions roiled up. Was he in some prison? Was he being tortured? Was he even alive?

She closed her eyes, spilling the overflow of tears down her cheeks, and from the dark recesses of her mind a vision took shape, that of her father pacing the length and breadth of a dark cell. Around his ankles and wrists he wore bands of iron, and his face had a gaunt, ravaged look about it. His clothes were torn and filthy; his once-costly cloak was pulled close about his shoulders as his only protection against the cold. With vacant eyes he stared at the blank stone of the

opposite wall while his lips moved slowly in unintelligible words.

Elise dropped her face in her hands and began to
sob out her heart. She wanted desperately to be gone
from this place, to have her father free, and to be at
home within the comforting security of his arms. She
was afraid for him, and she was tired of being snatched
about, poked, and degraded. She had had her fill of
captivity, from that which her cousins had inflicted
upon her, to the greedy, grasping, and questionable
hospitality of her uncle, and now to this latest farce
of misguided, misdirected miscreants. Her youth
yearned for a lighter, gayer side of life, of an adoring
father advising her on no more important matters than
caring swains who passionately quoted sonnets and
urgently whispered declarations of undying devotion.
She longed to let her feet fly to the steps of unending
measures, galliards, and lavaltos. She wanted to smile
and coyly lower her eyelids in a flirtatious moment.
For once in her life, she wanted to act as if life was
made just for her and the world was at her feet waiting
to be recognized, with her father standing in the back-
ground, nodding his approval.

Alas, it was not so, and might never be!

Her sobs slowly eased, and she lowered her hands
and raised her head to stare through brimming tears
at the filthy chamber. They had swept the floor,
washed the wall, and cleaned a spot large enough for
her to lie on a pile of furs in front of the fire, but this
was reality, this cold, dirty, barren place of pervading
musty odors and chilling breezes which whistled
through every crack and crevice. And she was here,
not on some soft, high throne served by a legion of
anxious suitors. Her father was either being held a
captive somewhere or he was dead.

Her surroundings presented Elise with the cold,

hard facts of her present state, and she realized if she yielded her thoughts to dreaming dreams of another world without first bettering her plight in this one, she would be forever caught in the bondage of defeat and would never progress. If she wanted a softer life or one filled with glory and excitement, she would have to work hard to attain it, for it was not free, nor easily garnered.

Taking firm command of her emotions, Elise sat back upon her heels and brushed the tears from her cheeks. A long, calming sigh escaped her as she continued to peruse her surroundings. With a few minor repairs, a thorough cleaning, fresh ticking for the bed and a bolt of cloth or two, the chamber could be made into a rather pleasant room. All she would need herself was a great deal of strength, wit, and patience to see it changed.

In the morning Elise's newly formed resolve nearly crumbled as she stared at the unappetizing fare of hard bread, salty meat, and sticky porridge. It was the latter's reluctance to leave the spoon that persuaded her to reject Fitch's offering. When she mentioned the possibility of hiring a cook from Hamburg, the servant shrugged lamely and opened his mouth to explain, but sensing what he would say, Elise waved away his answer.

"Never mind," she sighed glumly. "You needn't tell me. There's not enough coin in your purse."

The man gave her a woeful smile. " 'Tis sorry I be, mistress."

" 'Tis sorry we all will be if one of us doesn't learn to cook in the very near future. I've managed servants for several years now, but cooking I've never done."

Fitch and Spence exchanged inquiring glances and both answered in the negative, lending little hope for the possibility of a palatable meal any time soon. Elise heaved a long, laborious sigh and nibbled on a crust of bread. She was beginning to hope his lordship would make haste to come ere they all starved to death.

"Just when will this lord, earl, duke arrive?" she questioned. "Where is he now, and why was he not here to take care of these money matters?"

"'Twas a matter o' importance 'e 'ad ta attend ta, mistress. 'E'll be along in a few days."

"A matter of foul deeds, no doubt," Elise mumbled. She wrinkled her nose in repugnance as she tried to rub a soiled spot from her woolen gown. Perhaps it would have helped her mood if she had been given other garments to wear while she cleaned the keep. Her choices were limited to the dress she was wearing now and the rich blue gown. She refused to ruin her fine clothes at such dirty labors, but the woolen gown was becoming nearly impossible to bear.

"'Tis certain we've a need ta go back ta 'Amburg," Spence declared. "We've precious few supplies ta see us through another day."

"'Tis certain we've precious few coins ta buy 'em wit'," Fitch reminded him emphatically.

"We'll 'ave ta find a merchant what'll trust 'at 'is lor'ship will pay when 'e comes."

"An' what if 'Ans Rubert spreads a tale 'at 'is lor'ship is lost at sea? Betwixt ye an' me, Spence, 'ow much do ye think we're worth?"

"We'll have ta at least try!" Spence argued, emphasizing his point by thumping his fist into his palm. "No good in thinkin' 'ey'll be sayin' nay 'til we ask 'em."

The need for the journey was fully realized, and a full host of problems reared uniformly ugly heads. Spence neither trusted Fitch to go and find a merchant with a sympathetic ear with whom they might beg credit from, nor did he think him capable of staying behind and watching the girl. If Faulder Castle was an example of his dealings, he would need a guide in the matter of haggling, and as to his performance as a gaoler, their hostage had already proven herself of far quicker wit.

Fitch had his own doubts about his companion's abilities, considering the bony nags he had acquired. "'Tis certain ye've no eye for horseflesh."

"Wit' scant few coin," Spence flared in his own defense, "what else could ye expect after ye wasted 'is lor'ship's purse on this pile o' rock? 'Em beasties were the best we could afford!"

"May I make a suggestion?" Elise asked sweetly as she listened to their heated debate. Somewhat wary, the two men gave her their full and undivided attention. "If you'll allow me to go with both of you," she proposed, "I might be of some assistance. Though I have no knowledge of the German tongue, I do know something about the manners and affairs of titled lords and their ladies. 'Tis a simple fact that if you seek credit, you'll not find it as a pauper."

Immediately rejecting the idea, Fitch resolutely shook his head. "If she escapes, what will 'is lor'ship do ta us?"

"What will 'is lor'ship do ta us if the roof's not mended?" Spence railed. "I say she's right. We aren't the ones ta go beggin' for credit."

"Ye know how crafty she be! An' how'll we explain if she tells the townfolk she's been kidnapped? She'll 'ave all o' 'Amburg down 'pon our heads."

"Why would the townfolk even care? She's English."

"An' lovely as any maid 'ere be!" Fitch pointed out, firm in his argument. "Someone could take a likin' ta her an' steal her away from us."

"I still say she goes," Spence replied firmly. "We'll

just have ta keep an eye on her ... an' a *closer* one on the menfolk."

Fitch threw up his hands in a dramatic display of defeat. "She'll be the death o' us! Mark me words! If the merchants don't 'ang us, 'is lor'ship very well might!"

Fitch's doubts increased by leaps and bounds when their charge came down the stairs elegantly bedecked in the blue velvet gown and cloak. Her auburn hair had been parted in the middle and smoothly combed in a rather sedate coiffure that allowed only a few, softly curled tendrils to escape the knot coiled at her nape. In all, she looked the part of a young mistress of a great house, while he saw nothing that resembled the dirty, hardworking maid who had kept pace with them since their arrival, hauling, cleaning, scrubbing, and mending.

The trip to Hamburg did not seem as long to Elise this time as it did when she had first traversed the winding path to Faulder Castle. Perhaps what lightened the mood of the journey was the prospect of seeing civilization again and being able to communicate with people. Though there loomed an enormous problem in being understood, at least she was not being kept totally a prisoner, and who was to say what opportunity for escape might be presented while she was in the port city?

Even before they arrived at the market square Elise caught a tantalizing aroma wafting from a nearby inn. The morning fare had not set well on her stomach, which was now protesting its abuse.

Fitch lifted his nose in the air and sniffed like a starving hound picking up a scent of a wounded goose. There was no need of any verbal exchange between the three of them, for with common accord they turned their mounts toward the inn. Each seemed anxious to be the first one there, and after dismounting, the two men huddled together to count the coins in his lordship's purse.

"Why, 'tis true! We've barely 'nough coin ta see us through 'til 'is lor'ship comes," Spence said in some surprise after tallying the coins. "'Ow much did ye give 'Ans Rubert anyway?"

Fitch's cheeks flamed a bright red as he flapped his arms in outrage. "An' would ye be tellin' me how much ye laid out for 'ese foin an' mighty steeds we arrived on? 'Tis clear ta me ye were taken for a fool!"

Spence let out an offended cry. "Och, man! Ye callin' the kettle black, are ye now? If ye'd insisted 'Ans Rubert give us the manor what 'is lor'ship rented, 'ere wouldna've been a need for mounts. As 'tis, we've wasted most o' 'is lor'ship's purse on supplies."

"I'll take no more o' this!" Fitch flung out a hand to indicate the inn. "Ye take the mistress inside and I'll stand out 'ere in the cold an' look after 'ese unworthy nags!"

"Ah, no ye don't! Ye won't be doin' 'at ta me! I've no mind ta hear ye moanin' an' complainin' 'bout how I took me fill whilst ye starved ta death in the cold."

The two men were standing nose to nose, jabbing each other on the chest with a forefinger and were so intent upon besting the other in their disagreement, they failed to notice Elise slipping away on foot. She had seen the masts of sailing ships at the end of the lane where they stood and took advantage of her escorts' diverted attention.

Her hopes spiraled upward as she neared the wharf, but for the sake of caution she slowed her step, casting an anxious glance about her for Captain Von Reijn. His ship was still being unloaded, but if he was aboard, she hoped he would not notice her in the bustling activity of the quay. Passing between the vendors' booths and carts, she carefully considered the vessels in dock. Only a few larger ships were taking on cargo, while other vessels rested like slumbering giants alongside the piers and jetties. She adjusted the hood over her head, unaware of the interest she had stirred among the sailors and merchants. Very few ladies walked the dockside alone unless they were after making a coin or two, and this one looked most enticing. She was young, beautiful, and finely dressed, which readily conveyed her cost. It was apparent that she was not for the likes of common seamen, but for those men of means who could afford such tidbits.

An aging, white-haired captain standing a short distance off nudged the elbow of a younger man who stood beside him, bringing that one's attention around to bear upon the girl. The ice-blue eyes widened in surprise at the sight that greeted him, then took on a humorous twinkle. Giving a murmured excuse, Nicholas left the elder and pushed his way through the crowd of men who were gathering. He had hoped he would be successful in thrusting aside the memory of her beauty, but when he halted behind the lady, he was amazed what her nearness did to him. He was a man four years past a score and ten, but this slip of a girl started his pulse leaping as if he were but a yearling hart in his first rut.

Nicholas removed his hat, uncovering the thatch of pale hair, and spoke the address softly, as if it had become a special name for her. *"Vrouwelin?"*

Elise gasped as she whirled about, and she stared at him awestruck, unable to believe how pitiful her luck had been. To be discovered by Captain Von Reijn, of all people!

Nicholas tilted his head to the side as he peered down at her, and a slow smile curved his lips. "Could it be that yu've escaped yur captors and are now considering possible vessels for yur passage home?"

Angrily Elise glanced away, presenting her profile to him. "You would hardly believe me if I told you nay, so why should I answer you at all?"

"Precious few ships vill be leaving vith vinter coming nigh upon us, *vrouwelin*."

She tossed him a glare for his unwelcome information and, lifting her nose in the air, stared stonily into the distance.

The captain ignored her lack of verbal response and queried, "Vhere did yu leave Fitch and Spence?"

The small, pert chin briefly rose to designate a direction. "Down there arguing over which one of us was going to eat."

Nicholas raised a brow in curious question. "Is there a problem?"

"Nothing that a fatter purse and better cooks would not solve," she retorted. "His lordship, bless his soul, left the managing of his purse to a pair of slackwits. They have precious little coin left to last until his return, and neither of them have any talent as a cook."

"His lordship's credit is good with me," Nicholas offered. "Vhat do they have need of?"

"Everything!" Elise replied laconically. "Beginning with a place to live!"

A soft chuckle shook the broad shoulders of the man. "It can hardly be as bleak as all that. I'm vell acquainted vith the manor his lordship rented. 'Tis a very fine place."

"Ha! The only place we're in is Faulder Castle, and that is far from town and not so fine!"

"Faulder Castle?" A moment passed as the captain's amazement slowly ebbed, and then he heaved a hearty guffaw of amusement. "So, Hans Rubert has gone and done it! Stung his lordship behind his back, he did!

Vell, he'll soon see the folly of his greed. His lordship vill not take kindly to this."

"*If* he ever returns," Elise jeered.

"'Tis good to see yu again, *Englisch*," Nicholas stated, salving his longings by letting his gaze feast upon her beauty. "And I vill make a bargain vith yu. *Ja?*" His voice lowered and the Teutonic roots rode heavy on his turn of vowel. "If in the spring yu still insist upon returning to England, I vill take yu home on my ship."

Elise's surprise was evident as she faced him. "Do you promise on your word of honor?"

Nicholas smiled. "*Ja*, I pledge my troth to yu that I vill do this thing."

"And what will you charge for the voyage?" she queried carefully.

"I've no need of yur money, *vrouwelin*. Yur companionship vill be payment enough."

"I'm able to pay," she replied stiffly. She disliked making any compromise that would indicate a willingness to accept his attentions. "I've no need of your charity."

"Keep yur money, *vrouwelin*, or better yet put it vhere yu might receive some usury vhile yu're here."

"And who would I look to for that?" Elise scoffed. "Hans Rubert?"

"I have a feeling Hans Rubert vill be having some difficulties in the days ahead. *Nein, vrouwelin*, I vill do such a service for yu, and to prove that yu can trust me I vill even use the contents of my own purse until there is a profit. Just tell me how much yu vish to invest."

Elise studied him a long, thoughtful moment and decided he could be relied upon to be honest, at least in the matter of her wealth. From inside her cloak she withdrew a leather purse in which she had placed a third of her wealth. The remainder was securely tucked beneath her farthingale. "Here are fifty gold sovereigns to do with as you may. In one month I shall expect a return of my investment at a goodly gain. Is that too short a time, Captain?"

Nicholas tossed the bag in his hand as if judging its weight, then his lips slowly curved into a smile. "It vill be enough time, *vrouwelin*. In fact, I already know who has a need for it."

"Cap'n Von Reijn!" The shout drew their attention to Spence as that one ran toward them waving his arms. He was followed closely by Fitch who chugged along behind and grinned in bold-faced relief.

"Ye found her!" Fitch declared the obvious with glee. "Oh, sainted mother! I nearly lost me wits when I see'd she'd taken off." He grasped a handful of Elise's cloak firmly in his pudgy fist. "She won't 'scape us again. I'll make sure o' that. We'll keep her locked away 'til 'is lor'ship comes, 'at we will."

Elise cast a jaundiced glare in Fitch's direction, displaying a lack of appreciation for his statements. By rights his flesh should have withered beneath her glower, but he seemed oblivious as he accepted a weighty purse from the captain.

"This should take care of yur needs until his lordship returns," Nicholas said with a grin. "I'm sure the matter of Faulder Castle and Hans Rubert vill be settled very shortly." He turned to sweep a bow before Elise. "*Goten Tag, Englisch.* Yu vill be hearing from me in a month's time."

A smile lifted the corners of Elise's mouth, and she inclined her head to acknowledge his statement. "A month's time then, Captain."

Chapter 8

*T*HE FRONT PORTAL burst open with a mighty gust of wind, and amid a swirling haze of snow a tall, cloaked figure swept inward as if borne by the force of the blustering gale. White flurries whirled about him in a frenzied eddy, blowing into the hall before the door could be slammed against the violence of the wintry night. The man swept the hood back from his head and faced the hearth where Spence and Fitch gawked back at him in surprise. His thick, pale-streaked hair had been clipped short, and the beard that had once adorned his bony jaw was no longer in evidence. For a moment the pair seemed incapable of movement, then with a dawning recognition they leapt to their feet, nearly overturning the trestle table at which they had been dining, and scurried across the room to welcome the man.

"Lord Seymour! We barely knew ye wit'out yer beard," Fitch choked through a mouthful of charred rabbit he had been struggling to swallow. Grimacing, he gulped down the mass and continued more clearly. "Ta be sure, m'lord, 'tis relieved we are ta see ye! Rumors had it ye'd been lost at sea." Feeling the ominous weight of the Marquess's close perusal, Fitch self-consciously averted his face to hide the red scrape that marred his cheek. "At least, 'at was what we'd been told."

A tawny brow jutted up in sharp curiosity when Spence, the bearer of a large lump upon his brow and a blackened swollen eye, stepped close to receive his lordship's snow-dampened cloak.

"What is this?" Maxim queried, shrugging out of the garment. "The pair of you look as if you've been beset by a band of rogues. Have you been scuffling over some pittance of an argument again? Or can it be that the two of you have foolishly tried to hold this tumbledown keep until I was here to claim it? God's truth, it would have been better had you let it be taken. 'Tis a sorry place indeed and a poor excuse for a shelter. Why are you here and not at the manor house I rented?"

Anxiously wringing his hands, Fitch explained with a lame shrug. "We went ta fetch the keys from 'Ans Rubert, m'lord, just like ye said ta do, but the agent said he'd heard y'ed been drowned at sea an' gave the place ta his newly widowed sister."

"And the purse I gave him to hold the house in my name?" Maxim's voice sharpened with irritation. "Where is that?"

Unable to meet the sharply probing green eyes, Fitch retreated, making a hasty descent of the pair of steps. "'E gave me no coin, m'lord, but said this castle was ours for as long as we wished ta stay."

"The devil, you say!" Maxim thundered and pressed forward, causing the men to stumble back in nervous trepidation.

"We hadn't a ken what ta do, m'lord!" Spence rushed to allay his lordship's rising temper. "'Twas no fit place ta bring a liedy, ta be sure, but 'til Captain Von Reijn gave us a purse, we had precious few coin with which ta pay the rents on a better place."

"I shall attend to Hans Rubert in my own good time," Maxim promised. "'Twas well that Captain Von

Reijn met my ship when it came into port and gave me directions here. Otherwise, I would have never found you. The captain offered no explanations. He only told me there was a problem. Is this the extent of it?" A frown of concern touched his face. "What of the lady? Is everything well with her?"

"Aye, m'lord." Fitch rolled his eyes toward his companion as if reluctant to speak on the matter of their charge. "We can assure ye she's both hale an' hearty."

"Aye, 'at she be," Spence eagerly agreed. "The young mistress be as chipper as the first light on a spring morn."

"Then what has happened that the pair of you show me bruised and swollen faces?"

The two quickly directed their attention elsewhere, one to brush the snow from the cloak he held and the other to hold up a hand invitingly toward the hearth.

"Come warm yerself 'fore the fire, m'lord," Fitch cajoled. "We've vittles ta share, though I canna say they'll be ta yer likin'." He lumbered across the room to drag a large, tall-backed chair to the end of the table where the Marquess could be near the warm hearth and beckoned him to draw near.

Maxim was suspicious and observed his men closely, wondering what they were trying to hide. They were about as nervous as children caught in some mischief. "Well?" he barked. "Have your tongues grown lame? I would know what has happened here."

The two jumped in sudden alarm, and the fretting Fitch was the first to relent. "'Tis the young mistress, m'lord. She took us ta task 'cause we locked her in her chambers an' wouldn't let her out."

Maxim laughed at the very idea. "Come now, I would hear a better tale than that." The possibility that such a display of temper could come from the mild and meek beauty he had known would not settle down in his mind, yet his men seemed very sincere about the matter.

"Truly, m'lord, after she tried ta escape from us in 'Amburg, we brought her back an' bolted her chamber door ta keep her from runnin' away," Fitch explained. "Why, the way she let on, we was a-feared she'd taken on a devil."

"She set 'pon us in a rage, she did," Spence joined in. "A-heapin' curses on us an' throwin' everythin' she could a lay hand ta. Fitch, 'ere, was bringin' her a servin' o' vittles when she laid a piece o' firewood alongside 'is 'ead an' tried ta scamper out the door. An' meself, sir. She poked me in the eye when I caught her an' then slammed the door on me 'ead when I took her back in her chambers. 'Twas clear she wanted no part o' being locked up."

"And the lady? She was not injured in all of this?" Maxim's urgency demanded their answer be the truth.

"Nay, m'lord!" Spence was anxious to deny the possibility. "She's just a bit put out wit' us, 'at's all."

Maxim was sorely tempted to dismiss their story as wild exaggerations, but by rights he could not do so until he had a chance to delve into the matter. This tale of violence did not match with his vision of the fragile beauty he had known so well.

"I shall see to the lady myself." He crossed the hall and leapt up the stairs two at a time, displaying an impatience to appease his curiosity. On the second level he strode down the hall and halted before the thick oaken door. A light frown flitted across his brow as he noticed a heavy latch had been attached to the outer face of the portal to prevent it from being opened from within. Again his recall of a delicately formed, brown-haired maid cast the need for this restraint totally at odds with his perception of one who was serene and pleasant to be with. Had he missed something in his earlier observations?

There would, of course, be no explanation to salve his confusion until he questioned the maid. He rapped his knuckles lightly against the plank. "My lady, are you robed? I would have a word with you."

Silence answered his plea, and after several repeated attempts to obtain her response, Maxim lifted the latch and pushed the door open. The chamber appeared empty, and he stepped within to have a look around.

"Arabella? Where are you?"

Elise had pressed herself against the wall behind the door and had been well-prepared to launch an attack upon this foolish mortal who had dared enter her chamber. She had frozen when the warm and vibrant voice stirred memories of a darkened stairway at Bradbury Hall, and she stepped from hiding, lowering the small hearthside stool she had intended to smote the visitor with. Though the man was now dressed in the manner of a wealthy lord and the beard was gone, there was no mistaking the handsome rogue.

"What the deuce...?" A sharp frown quickly creased his brow as his eyes came upon her. "What are you doing here?"

"'Twas you!" The sapphire-blue eyes fairly flashed with sparks of indignation. "'Twas you who bade them take me! And all the while I thought ... aarrgh!"

In the next instant the stool was hauled back and swung with all the impetus of her outraged fury behind it. Maxim jerked back to avoid the clumsy weapon, and though he stared in utter amazement at the seething girl, the stool came around again with the same dire intent. The need to disarm the maid seemed of vital importance to his continued good health, and he reached up, plucking it easily from her grasp.

"Where is Arabella?" he demanded sharply. His eyes swept quickly to every corner of the chamber, but the one he sought was nowhere to be seen.

"Arabella, is it?" Elise snarled the question venomously. So! He had bade his men to fetch Arabella, and they had caught her instead. Her fair lips curled with contempt as she continued. "No doubt Arabella is wherever a good wife should be found ... at her husband's side ... most assuredly in England."

"In England?" The door of Maxim's understanding burst wide, igniting the fires of his rage. He recalled this vixen all too well. When he would have rushed to Arabella's side to soften the shock of her abduction with an explanation, the meeting with this wench and her recognition of him had necessitated a change in plans. Now she was here, where his former betrothed should have been, a fact which he was certain the girl was somehow responsible for, whether by design or misfortune. "Why are you here?"

With a flippant shrug Elise flung a hand toward the door. "Ask your men. They were the ones who took me."

"They were instructed to bring Arabella here," he informed her brusquely. "What are you doing here instead?"

"You dim-witted buffoon!" Elise railed back. "Can you not hear me? If you would have the answer to that question, seek out your henchmen! That simple pair of dolts were waiting for me in Arabella's chambers. The next thing I knew I was being carried off!"

"I'll throttle them with my bare hands!" Maxim ground out. Spinning on a heel, he stormed from the room, flinging the door wide. His voice thundered ahead of him as he leapt down the stairs three at a time. "Fitch! Spence! Dammit, where are you?"

The two had left the hall and were about the same distance from the front portal when his shout halted them. Scrambling back, they hit the opening at the same time, somehow managing to wedge themselves into the narrow space. A cacophony of loud curses and clamor arose from the entrapped pair before they managed to extricate themselves. Gasping for breath, they hastened back to the Marquess who had paused in the middle of the hall. With fists braced firmly on his waist, he fixed them with a dark, ominous scowl that fairly sundered their feeble attempts to smile. His voice began as a low thundering rumble. "Do you know what *you've done*?"

The pair stumbled back as the last words were blared at them, and they looked at each other in wary confusion. The soft whisper of footsteps compelled them to lift their worried gazes to the girl who slowly descended the stone stairs. The smile that curved her lips was one of sublime pleasure, as if she anticipated what was forthcoming. What venom had they stirred in the maid's heart that she should countenance their comeuppance?

The two glanced between his lordship and the girl and were quick to note the absence of the blissful smiles of lovers reunited. The Marquess was genuinely enraged, there was no doubt. Those green orbs fairly burned with rage, while the muscles twitched tensely in his lean cheeks. By long association they knew that small movement boded ill for all concerned.

Glancing over his shoulder at the girl, Maxim made a request in a tightly controlled tone. "Would you be so kind, madam, as to tell us who you are."

Elise continued her leisurely descent with all the aloof dignity of a great queen. "I am Elise Madselin Radborne." Her voice, though soft, was given resonance by the echoing chamber. "Sole descendant of Sir Ramsey Radborne, only niece of Edward Stamford, and first cousin to his daughter, Arabella."

The servants' jaws went slack, and they gawked at Elise as if loath to believe what she had just announced. They turned in lame appeal to the Marquess, realizing at last the reason for his wrath. He was staring at the girl, as if he too were surprised by what she had revealed, but that well-kindled emotion of anger had by no means diminished when he faced his men again. He inquired in a growling whisper, "Now do you understand what you've done?"

"Please, m'lord," Fitch entreated. "We didn't know!"

"You should have made sure!" Maxim's sharp tone sliced through the room. "Did I not tell you what she looked like..."

"Aye, an' we were sure 'twas this one."

"Brown hair, I said!"

Fitch lifted his hand as if to draw his lordship's consideration to the long, tumbling tresses that fell over the girl's shoulders. "An' is this not brown, m'lord?"

"Are you blind, man?" Maxim roared. "Do you not see 'tis red?"

Squeamishly Fitch tested his lord's patience again. "Red-brown?"

"Gray eyes! Not blue!"

Making no further attempts to reason with the enraged man, Fitch sidled behind his companion-in-folly, allowing him to give answer.

"'Twas easy ta make a mistake, m'lord," Spence offered. "The chambers where ye told us ta go were dark, and though we waited, this one was the only lady what come. 'Ere was no one else, m'lord."

"You were told to take Arabella!" Maxim bellowed,

this time startling the girl as well as the pair. He flung his hand to indicate Elise who stood frozen upon the last step. Of a sudden, she understood why the two servants had been so apprehensive about provoking his lordship. By his mere presence he could dominate a room and, now in a towering rage, he claimed their undivided attention. "Instead you have saddled me with this half-crazed chit!" he continued harshly. "And she is useless to me! Edward Stamford loves his riches too well to be concerned about her disap—"

Impertinent as always, Elise dared to interrupt his ranting. "You can send me back."

Maxim stared at her as if astonished by her suggestion, then his face clouded again with darkly brooding anger. "Believe me, madam, if it were at all possible I surely would, but I fear your return is entirely out of the question at this present time."

"If you're afraid I'll reveal where you are or that you were the one responsible for my abduction, I promise to keep my silence. My word is good."

"I've been accused of murder and treason against the crown, Mistress Radborne." His tone had taken on an edge of sarcasm. "I rather doubt that you could besmirch my character more than it is already. Consider further, madam, that Elizabeth has no authority here, so you see I'm quite safe from the axeman's blade."

"You have no need of me here," she cajoled. "You've said as much yourself. I'm useless to you. Please let me go."

"Nevertheless, madam, you will remain."

Elise stamped a small foot in frustration. "You must let me go! I have to return and find my father! He may be lying somewhere wounded ... or worse! And I am the only one who has a care to seek him out. He has need of me. Can you not understand?"

"I'm quite aware that Sir Ramsey Radborne was taken," Maxim commented. "If you be his daughter in truth, then I must also tell you there was a tale that he was placed aboard a ship which later sailed from England. If that is true, 'twould be useless for you to return there in search of him."

Elise stared back at him aghast. "Where would they have taken him? And for what reason?"

"Anywhere in the world," Maxim replied laconically.

"I'll not stay here!" Elise blurted out, close to tears. How could she hope to find her father when she now had to search the entire world for him?

"For the moment you have no choice but to accept my hospitality," Maxim said, turning aside with a small nod. "My apologies."

She flew across the room and tugged at his arm until he condescended to face her again. He gazed down at her with sardonic amusement, and beneath that scornful smile there grew within Elise a strong desire to rake her fingernails across those handsome features.

"Your misguided cohorts snatched me from my uncle's house," she snarled. "They locked me in a chest and brought me to these decaying ruins. Now you mewl and beg my pardon. Well, m'lord Murderer, I say your lame apology is not enough recompense for what I've suffered!"

His brow arched upward in curious question. "And what amends would you have me make, madam?"

"I cannot rest until my father is found. Don't you understand? At least in England I'd have a better chance of finding someone who knows where he was taken. You must take me back posthaste."

Casually he shrugged his wide shoulders. "Impossible."

Elise gnashed her teeth at his blunt answer and raised on tiptoes to deliver her threats full in his face. Her eyes flashed with fiery sparks as he responded with a mocking smile. "Sir, I would warn you to take care! You'll not have a moment's peace in this dung-heap while I'm here! I'll make your life so miserable you'll regret the day you issued orders to have Arabella seized. Though my cousin may have been willing to give you love and companionship, I'll give you naught but hatred and contempt. Your waking will be to the cries of the banshee, and when darkness comes, you'll long for the rest you'll never find."

Maxim responded with a dubious chuckle. "Come now, maid," he chided. "You're far too fragile to give your threats substance." He watched the face so close to his own turn livid with rage and laid a gentle, consoling hand upon her shoulder. "Still your anger, and think on what you say. I've bested men twice your size on the field of battle. 'Tis foolishness for me to consider defending myself from so tender a foe."

"Nevertheless, my lord," Elise whispered in spitting tones of venom as she flung aside his hand. "I'll torment you until I'm set free!"

Realizing she was completely serious with her threats, Maxim could only marvel at the girl's tenacity. Never had he met a wench so full of fight and spirit. "Be reasonable," he cajoled with a chuckle. "If you pester me overmuch, I'll have you locked away again, and neither of us . . ."

"Over my dead body!" Elise snatched back an arm and let it fly toward his grinning visage. It was caught before it met its mark and held in an effortless vise.

"Now see how foolish your threats are," he admonished almost gently. Against her repeated attempts to snatch away he turned her hand over and briefly considered the fine-boned wrist. "Why, if I

were a true judge, I would say you're … ah … rather
puny … as maids go."

Hardly one to stand still for this disparagement,
Elise once again drew back a hand, but as she tried
to deliver a blow to his head, he ducked, at the same
time swooping an arm about her hips and lifted her
up high against him. With a strangled gasp of outrage,
she clutched his shoulders for support, horrified that
he could be so familiar with her person. The limp
woolen gown did little to preserve her modesty, and
against her buttock she was crushingly aware of the
bold placement of his hand. Its warmth singed her
through the single layer of cloth and set her cheeks
to flaming.

"What say you, maid?" Maxim leaned his head back
to look up at her, settling his gaze momentarily upon
her rapidly heaving bosom before he smiled into those
snapping sapphire orbs. "Who be the fox and who be
the hare? Surely I could gobble you for a morsel. A
delicious one, too, I would think."

Elise issued no feminine protests, but deliberately
softened her manner. If she could not best the rogue
by mightier brawn, then by wit and womanly wiles
she would do the service. Leaning close with a coy
smile, she feigned a warming that could have stripped
away any man's defenses, but for Maxim, it had a
devastating effect. He was a man who had bound himself in the honor of betrothal vows, and after that,
there had been long weeks of recuperation from his
injuries. The slender, meagerly clad body sliding
against his as he loosened his restraint and the soft
breasts brushing his face nearly snatched his breath
as the womanliness of her flicked awake his long-
starved senses. Her mellowing took him completely
off guard and allowed her to catch the tip of his ear

firmly between her teeth. Like a spiteful shrew, Elise gave the lobe a solid yank.

Maxim's sudden yelp coincided with her release, and she jumped away, swift as a frightened hare, and darted across the room to place herself behind the table, there to glare back at the Marquess as he held his bloodied ear. Her attack had had the same effect on him as a bucket of icy water. It did nothing to cool his temper.

"Catch me if you can, fox," she taunted, tossing her head and laughing at him. She feigned a look of sympathy. "Poor cub, did I hurt you overmuch?"

Incensed by the mischievousness of this little minx and intent upon teaching her a lesson about men that she would not soon forget, Maxim approached her as he would some untamed prey that threatened any second to bolt and run. Elise eyed him warily, waiting until it seemed that all he had to do was reach out and take hold of her, then she whirled away, avoiding his grasp with an agility that surprised him. As she danced away, she snatched a long-handled warming pan from a peg above the hearth and, with all of her strength, brought it around. He ducked to avoid the vicious swing, but he did not count on her letting it go. In its flying descent, the thing caught him smartly alongside the head.

"Cease, you vixen!" His bellow gave her impetus as he tossed aside the pan. He was sure she had meant to spill his brains.

Elise sprinted in earnest toward the stairs, aware of the jeopardy she was in.

"M'lord! Spare the lass!" Spence cried, his hands almost a-blur in a twisting frenzy.

Maxim was thoroughly enraged and ignored the servant's plea as he leapt after the girl. Fitch and Spence stumbled after him in hasty but uncertain pursuit, not knowing what they could do to halt him should he become violent. They had never faced such a dilemma, for his lordship was usually quite well-mannered in the presence of the ladies. Still, they had both tasted the spite of this slender maid and could well understand how his temper could have been tested beyond restraint. In truth, she was a rare challenge to any man, whether lowborn or of noble birth.

Elise passed a standing candelabrum beside the balustrade and, with a strength born of desperation, swept it around behind her as she fled. It toppled to the floor in front of Maxim, catching him across the shin in its descent, and sent him sprawling upon the lower steps. In great perturbation, he raised himself to see the girl's skirts flick out of sight on the higher level. A door slammed from that vicinity, and the sound of an inside bar dropping into place reverberated throughout the keep.

"M'lord! Be ye hurt?" Spence questioned anxiously, trying to grasp the Marquess's arm and haul him to his feet. He was greatly relieved that circumstances had not necessitated the use of force to subdue his lordship.

"Get away!" Maxim snarled and brushed aside the servant's hands. Pushing himself upright, he tossed a glare toward the upper level, rankled by the fact the girl could remove herself from any confrontation by the simple barring of her door. In truth, she was not as helpless as he had first imagined. No mere rabbit she, but a vixen through and through.

Tugging at his damaged ear, Maxim bent a scowl upon the two who stood watching him. "So! What do you have to say for yourselves?"

"What can we say, m'lord?" Fitch replied, nervously stroking the sides of his ponderous belly. "We made a dreadful mistake, 'at we did, an' if ye've a mind ta cut off our 'ands, we'd be deservin' h'it."

"Spence?" The Marquess raised a brow as he awaited that one's answer.

The taller man scrubbed a toe over the stone floor, thinking how a week or so earlier it had been thickly covered with filth. If not for the girl it might have remained so. "I feel a great burden in me heart for the young maid, yer lor'ship, 'specially with us makin' a ragged mess o' everythin'. Why, if ye were o' a mind ta give me leave, I'd like ta be the one ta take her back an' restore her safe and sound ta her uncle's care."

Maxim considered the man a long moment, recognizing the heartfelt plea and the longing to right a wrong. "There's another problem that prevents me from letting her go back."

"What be that, m'lord?"

"Her father was kidnapped, and 'tis my belief that she would be in grave danger if we returned her to England before he is set free. She has no one there to give her protection other than Edward, and I know what kind of goat he is."

"Then, ta be sure, m'lord, we must hold her for her own safety."

"Precisely."

"Will ye not tell the girl o' the danger?"

"Would she believe me?"

"Nay, m'lord, but she'll hate ye for keepin' 'er 'ere."

Maxim lifted his broad shoulders in a brief shrug. "I've borne the hatred of fiercer foes than she."

Fitch cocked an eye toward him in dubious doubt. "Humph! Just wait 'til ye gets ta know 'er. Ye might change yer mind. I can't say as I've ever seen such a bloodthirsty wench."

Maxim smiled ruefully as he rubbed the knot on his head. "You have a point there, Fitch."

"But what o' yer betrothed, m'lord?" Spence pressed.

After a long moment of solemn musing Maxim heaved a sigh of resignation. "Lost to me, 'twould seem. I cannot go chasing back to England for her. In this, Edward has been victorious. He has his daughter, my properties, and Reland's wealth to add to his coffers. 'Twill be many months ere I can return to confront him."

"Aye, m'lord, 'ere be times when plans go awry," Spence sighed in sympathy. "But on occasion, when all be said an' done, 'tis almost as if a wiser hand has held the reins. If Fitch an' meself, by our bumblin', have served ta keep the girl from a greater danger, then I'll be proud o' the deed for her sake, but sorry for yers."

Maxim remained silent. He could not argue with the wisdom of the man's words, but logic did not ease the dull ache in his heart. Slowly he began to mount the stairs, the soles of his boots grating against the stone as he instructed, "Bring food and ale and a basin of water to my chambers, then leave me be 'til the morrow. I've need of a good night's rest upon a fresh pallet..."

"Ah...yer pardon, yer lor'ship..." Fitch called, once more apprehensive.

Maxim paused on the stairs and half turned to await the servant's words. He sensed there was more to be told to him, and from the man's hesitant manner, he would wager he would not find it pleasing.

"Ah...we...ah...set ta cleanin' the keep right away, m'lord. We scrubbed the floors in the hall an' the stairs, an' spent some time makin' the mistress's chambers fit..."

"Go on," Maxim encouraged, wondering what the servant's roundabout discourse was leading to.

"Well, yer lor'ship, we were so busy"—Fitch stroked his belly again in nervous agitation—"we had no time ta tidy up yer chambers."

Maxim stared at his man in some irritation, yet he knew he could suffice with only a clean pallet to lay his weary frame upon. "'Twill have to wait 'til the morrow then. All I want is some sleep."

"Ah, yer lor'ship . . ." Fitch continued squeamishly.

The muscles in Maxim's cheeks began to twitch. There was something of a more serious nature that the servant was not telling him. "What is it, Fitch?"

"Ah . . . well, ye see, m'lord . . ."

"Get on with it!" Maxim snapped. "What's wrong?"

"The roof!" Fitch blurted. "We haven't repaired it yet."

"And what is wrong with the roof?" Maxim barked, growing vexed with the man.

"She's got a 'ole in 'er the size o' a large kettle, yer lor'ship. 'Tain't likely ye'll find much comfort up there in the lord's chambers. Would ye not rather take yer rest down 'ere by the fire where 'tis warm?"

Maxim fixed cold green eyes upon the man, and his countenance held no more warmth than his voice. "How long do you think 'twill take you to repair the roof and make my chambers acceptable?"

"Oh, 'twould be no more 'an a good day's labor ta mend the shutters an' the door. Ye see, m'lord, it won't close, an' then there'd be another day or two, mayhap three, ter patch the roof. An' 'at's not takin' inta account the cleanin' an' scrubbin'."

Maxim slowly retraced his steps downward. "I'll sup by the fire, but before I retire, I will expect my chambers to be made adequate for a night's lodging, even if you have to hang hides to protect the bed from the snow and cold. If you fail, you will spend the winter in the stables with Eddy. Do I make myself clear?"

"Indeed, m'lord," Fitch hurried to assure the Marquess. His mind had already begun to race, taking account of all that needed to be done. There was not a moment to spare. "I'll set ye out a trencher o' meats an' be about it."

"Never mind. I can serve myself. You have precious little time as it is."

"Aye, m'lord," Fitch heartily agreed.

Spence was already running to fetch a broom and a bucket. He had no desire to be a stable companion of Eddy's all winter long. True enough, there was a room with a hearth and chimney behind the stables, but he did not think his lordship meant them to have such comforts if they failed at their task. He was not sure what this frigid northland would be like in the months to come, but he had come to favor the warmth of a well-stocked hearth and a well-stuffed pallet to soften a night's sleep.

Chapter 9

ELISE PUSHED BACK the fur robes, allowing the crisp, cool air that flowed through the chamber to touch her face and shoulders and, with its fresh and frigid touch, to banish the last lingering traces of sleep. The chill draft raised tiny bumps on her skin and turned her breath into vapors of frosty white. The cold penetrated until a sneeze threatened, and though she held a slim finger beneath her nose, the urge grew stronger. She sucked in air in little gasps, and coming upright in bed, she gave vent to a series of small, but forceful, eruptions that left her red-eyed and sniffling.

"A pox on that blackguard!" She collapsed back upon the bed in petulant displeasure, wondering how the great lord of this dilapidated keep was faring in his lofty bedchamber. She had heard him pass on the stairs near her room the night before, and thus far this morning had not heard him descend. It was only right and just that he should suffer more than she, for it was his blundering folly that had caused her to be seized and brought here. He deserved to feel the bite of this wintry morn in such a way that he would never forget. Indeed, if the roof collapsed upon him and left him bruised and battered amid a pile of timbers and planks, she rather doubted that her desire for revenge would be adequately appeased.

Tugging the fur robes close beneath her chin again,

Elise curled up beneath their warmth. The rain and snow and slush of the previous day had frozen into a coating over the windows that glistened and twinkled with the light of the dawning sun. The brilliant orb failed to warm the chamber with its rays, and though Elise contemplated leaving her cozy haven to dash across to the hearth to lay fresh kindling and logs upon the glowing coals, she delayed the torture, wishing fervently there were servants to come and build a fire. She had always been rather self-sufficient in the matter of her own needs, or so she once had thought, but that had been before coming to this northern clime. She now realized that servants provided for a multitude of comforts, both reasonable and frivolous. Stoking up a dying fire, cooking delicious meals, carrying pails of water for a bath—these were but a few services she had once taken for granted, but now, with the absence of such, she sorely felt the loss. It was just another reason to protest her captivity, and although she could fend for herself quite adequately, she would make sure in the future that Maxim Seymour heard a multitude of complaints from her on the lack of household help.

She had many more woes to express to him. Not the least of these was the fact that she felt and looked the part of a wild woman turned loose upon the world. The woolen gown was hardly recognizable as a garment a woman might wear, much less a lady.

"All because that lame-witted, love-smitten swain takes it into his head to seize his light-o'-love!" Her eyes narrowed into slanted slashes of piercing blue. "He will pay, and dearly so.

"And as for suffering abuse!" She aired her grievances to the room. "The Radbornes should have taken lessons from that lout! By foolish folly he has far outstripped my cousins' carefully devised strategies on the techniques of torture. 'Twill serve him right to endure the thrust of my revenge."

Stifling another sneeze with a slender finger, Elise rose to sit on the edge of the bed. When the urge passed she ran a hand over her arm, feeling the roughness where the chill-bumps rose upon her flesh. Pulling one of the still-warm furs around her shoulders, she considered her predicament. When she undressed the night before, she had foolishly left her clothes on a chair near the now-cold hearth, a fact which now offered her little comfort since it was a goodly distance from the bed.

Tentatively she stretched out a foot, but snatched it back from its first contact with the cold stone floor. Once again she bolstered her courage. After all, it would not be a lasting torment. Gritting her teeth and steeling herself against the frigid air, she dropped the fur and leapt from her snug cocoon. Snatching up her clothes at a run, she made a whirling dash back to the bed and dove under the furs until she was once more cozy and warm. The bundle of clothes was cold against her naked flesh, but under the protection of the covers, she began to don them until at last she was fully garbed. Rising like a fabled bird from its nest, she lifted her face to catch a warming ray upon it and sat back upon her heels. She combed her fingers through her snarled hair, bringing its long, shining length to the best semblance of order she could attain without a brush or comb. A more careful grooming would have to wait until she could heat water for a bath and move about the room in comfort. She did not relish washing in cold water, and it was so chilly in the room she was sure that ice crystals had formed in the bucket of water Fitch had brought upstairs for her the night before.

Elise paused as a sudden thought struck her, and

she almost leered at the wooden pail as her mind began to race. If ever she wanted to make a man take heed of her threatening words and come to the realization she could not be easily dismissed, then surely there was a way to gain that one's undivided attention. Her last glance at the lord's chambers had assured her the door still hung askew and could not stand as a barrier to her now. If that high and mighty lord was still asleep, then she might deliver her first assault upon that fortress of pride and manly power.

Slipping on her soft hide shoes, Elise hurried to the hearth and tested the water in the pail. It was sufficiently cold to rouse even the soundest of sleepers from the deepest of slumbers. Taking up the bucket, she went to the door where she paused and pressed an ear against the panel to listen. Hearing nothing out of the ordinary, she carefully lifted the inner bar and stepped out into the hall. The loud snores of Fitch and Spence drifted up from below, reassuring her that all was well, at least from that vicinity. The lord's chambers might be a different matter entirely.

She waited and listened, but no sound emitted from the lofty rooms, and with careful step she began her ascent. Her heartbeat was far from steady as she left the stairs and tiptoed to the doorway of the master's chamber. Hardly daring to breathe, she peered past the broken planks into the room where shafts of pale wintry light filtered in through the windows and down through the opening in the roof. Beneath the hole a wooden tub had been placed to catch what it could of the snow that drifted in.

A tent of sorts had been hung over the wooden canopy of the bed as protection against the drafts. Apparently it afforded some comfort, for within the huge, ornately carved structure lay her adversary sound asleep and completely at her disposal. His handsome face was turned toward her with darkly lashed eyelids closed in slumber. A fur robe covered him to the waist, leaving his upper torso bare, and even in rest, his strength was evident, for the muscles in his shoulders and arms flowed in lithely bulging lines. Thickly curling wisps of a light brown hair covered his upper chest and narrowed to a thin line that trailed beneath the fur pelt. Several old scars marked his chest and shoulders and gave clear evidence that this was a man who had frequently faced the challenge of his enemies and had lived to speak of it.

For the sake of caution, Elise made sure the path to the doorway was clear, knowing it would be necessary for her to flee unhindered and with all possible haste once she emptied the bucket on him. The pace of her heart began to quicken as the moment approached, and her nerves wavered unsteadily. Fitch and Spence had shown their dread of the man; was she a fool to rouse his ire?

Stubbornly she resisted the doubts. It was what the rogue deserved—every feeble bit of her revenge. The bed was near and so was the opportunity. She did not waste it. Taking a shaking lip between her teeth and raising the bucket, she let fly the contents.

The icy water came out of the pail in a solid stream to snatch the unsuspecting man brutally awake. Maxim caught the liquid torrent full across his face and shoulders and, with a hoarse gasp, sat bolt upright. An enraged snarl emitted from his lips and increased in volume as he swung his head once to clear his vision and fixed her with those piercing green eyes.

Elise had paused perhaps one second to savor his reaction, but her delay made her question her own wisdom in doing so. She stumbled back as he flung aside the pelts that covered him. The shock of seeing that totally naked and purely masculine form nearly paralyzed her. It was not a sight she had planned on viewing. Indeed, the possibility of glimpsing such manly nudity had never even entered her mind . . . but the vision of a golden Apollo leaping from his bed was instantly and forever forged upon her memory. However, this was no god made of marble; this was a flesh and blood man, living and real, bold and masculine, and he was *enraged.*

Elise whirled in fear of her life and barely heard his feet hit the floor over the loud drumming of her heart. If she did not manage to reach the safety of her chambers before he seized her, she had grave doubts as to her continued existence. In a desperate attempt to delay him she swung the empty pail behind her, letting go the rope handle. She knew her aim hit true, for the evidence was provided by a pained grunt and an awkward stumbling which ended in an ominous thud and a loudly muttered curse. Elise did not dare glance around to see what damage she had caused, but concentrated every measure of her strength on gaining desperately needed ground in her quest to escape.

Her feet flew as she ran into the hall and, swinging around the balustrade, half-stumbled, half-slid down the stairs. Her heart kept pace, and when the Marquess picked up the chase once again it raced faster still. She could hear him behind her, closing the distance with each running stride he took, and with an anxious gasp she bolted through the door of her bedchamber and whirled, slamming it closed behind her and dropping the bolt into place. Panting for breath, she leaned against the portal, shaking in relief. She was safe! But just barely. With a surprised start she stumbled away as the flat of his hand slapped hard against the planks of her door, and she heard his softly growled threat.

"I'll tear this door from its hinges, wench, if you ever do that again!"

Though grateful to have the barrier between them, Elise did not put much faith in its strength and refrained from giving a retort. It seemed foolish to challenge an irate man when it was highly probable he could accomplish whatever he threatened to do. It was wiser by far to let his temper cool and prick him again when the element of surprise was in her favor. Whatever transpired, she would be more wary of the man in the future. This one was neither slow of wit nor a stumbling laggard, and she neither enjoyed feeling his breath upon her nape when she had to escape, nor being frightened out of her wits.

It was past the noon hour before Elise finally found enough courage to leave her chambers. She was hoping the Marquess had taken leave of the place and was halfway down the last flight of stairs before she realized he was sitting at the end of the trestle table. A half-filled trencher sat before him, giving evidence that he had been taking his meal before the warmth of the hearth, but when she halted on a step and stealthily began to retreat, his deep voice broke the silence of the hall.

"Come join me, Mistress Radborne," he bade coldly and held up a hand to indicate the place at the opposite end of the table. "I have a need to see you before me rather than to feel you at my back."

Reluctantly Elise continued her descent, sure that she could hear the knelling of her approaching doom. His stoic gaze came upon her as she left the stairs, but she refused to betray her trepidation. Regally she went to the table and, receiving no offer of assistance from him, slid stiltedly into the massive armchair that awaited her at the far end. His staid manner attested to his displeasure, and he studied her at great length as the silence filled the hall.

"I understand, Mistress Radborne, that you may be a little vexed with me..." he finally stated, but his tone was dark and foreboding, like that of a judge pronouncing sentence upon a felon.

As was her wont, Elise rose to the challenge and laughed scoffingly. "A little? Pray tell me, my lord, what is your understanding of the word? By little, do you actually mean a flood when you say a little water passed through the town? Or perhaps a great calamity when you mention a little problem?"

"I shall correct myself." Maxim gave her a crisp nod and obliged her by becoming more precise. "I understand you are greatly vexed with me."

"Even that would be a gross understatement of the facts," Elise rejoined flippantly. The warming fire seemed to give her courage, and she returned his unwavering stare unflinchingly.

Maxim acknowledged her reply with a bland smile. "I believe I can safely assume that you think I'm a loathsome, despicable beast for having put you in this predicament."

Her eyelids dipped briefly to convey her partial acceptance of his statement. "Until I can find a more appropriate description of my opinion of you, your statement will have to suffice."

Again Maxim gave a nod of acquiescence. "'Tis evident that neither of us have any great love for the other, but I fear we are both caught in a trap which cannot be easily resolved. I cannot send you back for obvious reasons, and you are not content to stay. Therefore I would suggest we make the best of this foul predicament and come to terms."

"The only way I will make a pact with you, my lord, is when you agree to send me back on the next available ship. Otherwise, I shall make no parole."

Maxim met her gaze squarely. "Nevertheless, I desire to live at peace within the walls of my own house..."

"Then let me go!"

"I do not relish the idea of a war raging between us and battles being constantly waged..."

"You need not hold me prisoner here!"

"I consider myself a gentleman..."

"An opinion held entirely by you, sir, let me assure you."

"...Having regard to the welfare of gentle-born ladies."

"As you have so appropriately displayed by having me abducted from my home?"

"A mislaid attempt to halt a gentlewoman's marriage to a titled ruffian..."

"Tell me, my lord, are you kin to Reland? You bear a strong resemblance to him in both manners and character."

"And you, Mistress Radborne, bear a strong resemblance to a vexatious twit!" Maxim blurted, then paused in some irritation, angry with himself for allowing her to effectively needle him.

Elise calmly murmured, "You can always let me go."

"I cannot!" He slapped his hand down upon the table. Why was she so stubborn?

Elise's smile displayed no hint of warmth. "Then we are at war, my lord."

"Elise..." Maxim softened his voice, seeking a different approach through the thick mire of their disagreement. The use of her name made his opponent raise her brows in silent question, but he pressed on, ignoring the challenge in her stare. "The Elbe is already icing up, and the North Sea is treacherous with the advent of winter. Have a mind for your own safety when you consider leaving here now. Even the best of seamen bide their time until the weather begins to warm."

"Is not a journey by land to Calais possible? From there I could take passage aboard a ship bound for England."

"A long and dangerous trek across land this time of year. I can neither take you nor allow you to be taken."

"So kind of you, Taylor." She stressed the name to ridicule him for his earlier use of it. To come into her uncle's house in the guise of a servant with the intent of stealing away the squire's daughter was a contemptible act for any man to commit, whether he be rogue or nobleman. She would not let him forget it.

"Maxim, if you please," he corrected tautly.

A falling log on the fire sent a shower of sparks flying outward onto the stone hearth and gave relief to the tense moment. Maxim rose and went to lay several more pieces of wood on the blazing heap, then turned to her, dusting his hands. Elise avoided meeting his gaze, having taken in the full measure of his appearance as he fed the fire. Though not flamboyantly garbed, he was most attractively groomed in clothes that seemed to accentuate his manliness. The sleeves of his dark green velvet doublet and the puffed trunk hose were adorned with lined slashes, the edges of which were finished with silk cordings. The crisp white ruff of his shirt was worn close and high about his neck. Similar touches of stiffly starched white showed beneath the silk-corded cuffs of the well-fitting doublet. That garment displayed the width of his shoulders and narrowed along his ribs to fit his trim waist. Though he wore thigh-high boots over dark stockings, she had briefly glimpsed the muscular strength of those long legs and had found no flaw there.

Elise squirmed in sudden discomfiture. His handsome appearance made her feel very much like a small, dowdy mouse perched on the edge of a huge chair. The frayed woolen garments she wore presented her at a disadvantage, and her resentment overflowed the rim of her pride as his gaze casually perused her. She could well imagine her drab appearance in the cast-off gown, and she came out of her chair in an angry huff.

"I'm sure your apologies would have extended to the ridiculous if Arabella had been here in my stead, though I truly doubt such a faint spirit would have survived the ordeal, and surely if she had she would have hated you forever. Indeed, my lord, your crimes against her might have been far greater had you succeeded in netting the right hare. As 'tis, you and I have been tied together like a pair of spitting cats and, at present, are unable to get loose one from the other. You stand there like a grand lord of this woeful place, while I must wear this miserable garb"—she flicked a sleeve in repugnance—"and hear you prate about your inability to send me home. I tell you in truth, sir, that you have no more regard for a lady and her feelings than the wood you just tossed into the fire."

"Surely you must know there's a hue and cry for me in England," Maxim rejoined. "Should I return now, I would be led straight to the block."

Folding her arms across her breasts, Elise turned her profile to him with her nose lifted in the air while her toe tapped a self-satisfied tattoo on the stone floor. "As you should be," she chided. Of a sudden she broke the pert stance and, spinning on a heel, continued around with a wide-flung slashing gesture of her hand. As she faced him, a steady flow of subdued frustration and anger showed in her flashing blue eyes and tight-lipped snarl. "'Twould be expected of a rudely

masked highwayman or a crude barbarian from the
north, but here we have"——she measured the length
of him with an upflung hand——"a *lord* of the realm, a
mannered *gentleman,* no less, and a rightly branded
murderer and a traitor to his queen!"

Maxim glowered blackly at his tormentor. He had
never known a woman who could so effortlessly set
him on edge.

"You would have had your vengeance through the
souring of a poor bride's happiest night," Elise accused, "and through the snatching of that damsel, thus
and the same, shaming her rightful groom. Yea, I praise
the virtue of justice! Your villainous plans were set
awry. Your hired henchmen blundered heavily in the
performance of their duties, and thus, 'tis I who must
suffer the stones and arrows of this most outrageous
farce.

"Do I humble you overmuch, m'lord?" Elise sim-
pered mockingly as she took note of his darkening
scowl. "When I beg for my return to England, do you
set my request beyond the range of your perverted
plans? Or will you suffer me to stay forever in this
cold and drafty prison?"

Maxim growled beneath his breath, swallowing a
most unlordly chain of curses that he was tempted to
shower upon this upright and outright example of
womanhood and the whole tribe of her sisters. It was
bold in his mind that a monk sworn to chastity would
never be forced to suffer the bitter sting of this feminine venom. Arabella, on her worst day, seemed only
a churlish girl by comparison. Indeed, her fragile
beauty was far more favorable in his memory than the
bolder hues of this viciously spitting vixen.

Maxim crossed the hall like the enraged giant
of some ancient fable. It was poor timing on the part

of Fitch and Spence that they chose to enter from outside at that precise moment, but when they came face to face with his lordship, they shuddered in sudden worry as he paused before them in a visible temper. When he spoke his voice had the heavy-toothed snarl of a saw.

"If you do nothing else while I'm gone, see to your charge and, on threat of your life, fix the door of my chambers..."

Elise had followed him to the base of the steps and stood listening, her hands folded demurely and on her face a look of such innocence a meeker virgin would have been put to shame.

"...that I might spend a restful night free from the attentions"—Maxim jerked his thumb across his shoulder—"of this sorely injured maid.

"And you!" He whirled sharply to confront Elise. She raised a brow and waited with a sweet smile of unerring sincerity. "'Twould not be taken amiss," he sneered, "if you would assist these hapless creatures and make some use of your time. For the good that is done here, we shall all share."

He made as if to go, having properly vented his spleen, but Elise stopped him with a delicately upraised hand, seeming the very spirit of virtue. "Oh, my lord, I cannot, for you see I'm a prisoner bidden to contain myself in yon bedchamber and forbidden to venture forth lest I worry my guards."

Maxim was ready to throw up his hands in despair. The wily wench turned every word against him! Grinding an unspoken retort between his gnashing teeth, he swung away and snatched up his cloak, but before his long strides reached the door he heard her voice raised in further admonition.

"'Twould be advisable, my lord, if you would fetch from town at least a cook to prepare a decent meal, if not a maid or two to tend the quarters properly. I fear your men are somewhat less than adequate with their household duties."

Her last word was oddly punctuated by his attempt to slam the thick portal behind him. The door was wrenched free of its worn hinges and raised a thick cloud of dust as it crashed to the floor. Maxim mumbled a few threatening comments under his breath and closed his cloak against the crisp bite of the wind and the icy sleet that accompanied it. He crossed to the stables, and a few moments later, when he thundered across the courtyard on the back of the black steed, his men were still struggling to lift the door into place.

Hans Rubert had remained in his small waterfront shop past the time of the usual closing at noon on this particular Saturday, having found a need to make several entries in his journals. He was perched on a high stool before the tall desk and was carefully plying goose quill to parchment when a chilling draft swept his back, and the slamming of the front door made him aware that a customer had entered. One could never be sure about the purpose of clients in this vicinity, and he let his hand rest on a stout oaken cudgel as he swung around on the stool.

His visitor was a tall man, and though his face was hidden by the lowered hood of his cloak, he seemed somewhat familiar. The man stamped snow and icy slush from the soles of his fine leather boots, and Hans Rubert slid from the stool, more at ease with the man's bearing and finely tailored clothes.

"I beg your pardon, *mein Herr,*" he began. "Is there something I can . . ." His voice trailed off as the fellow raised his head and full recognition dawned.

"*Herr* Seymour!" The words were snatched from a

throat that was suddenly dry and parched. The green eyes of the other met his with a deliberate coldness that sent chills up and down his spine.

"Master Rubert!" The voice was low and its flatness might have warned Hans of more to come, had he not already been atremble with fright.

"I...um...*jaaa!*" The agent's mind raced. "I was not aware that you were in Hamburg, *mein Herr!*"

The Marquess ignored the man as he peeled a pair of leather gloves from his hands and shrugged out of the cloak, spreading it over the back of a nearby chair. Small beads of perspiration dappled Rubert's upper lip by the time Maxim deigned to face him.

"I paid you a healthy advance for half a year's rent on a town house worthy of the name. A thousand ducats, I believe." The words rumbled from deep within his chest. "But to my surprise I arrive to find my people ensconced in a draft-riddled, vermin-infested pile of stone."

"Faulder Castle?" Rubert's tone seemed to portray his amazement, and he frowned as if bemused by the Englishman's description. "Why, the last time I was up there..."

Maxim answered brusquely, squelching the man's attempt to justify his deeds. "I'll warrant the last occupants died in the Crusades."

Hans's excuse was silenced by the other's challenging statement. He saw a dwindling profit and began mentally rearranging numbers in his head as he sought another course of reasoning. "Of course, *mein Herr,* you must recall that our terms were such that if you could not claim the place before the turn of the year, I was not to be held responsible, and there were rumors of your having met with a disaster."

Maxim took a step toward the man, and Hans scurried to put a long table between them. The Marquess rested his knuckles on the piece and leaned forward, his gaze so intent as to fairly pierce holes in the other's head. "I must admit you did not come to me well-recommended." He paused and Rubert tried to swallow a persistent lump in his throat. "However!" The smaller man twitched at the word as if it stung. "I am aware that perhaps a year or so now past, certain members of the Hansa sought properties in another town and paid an agent a handsome sum to obtain the same for them. When they sought to claim the estates they discovered no payments had been made and that their agent was nowhere to be found. The Hansa are a vengeful lot, not given to merely pursuing the law. Had they word of where this man could be found, I fear they would be ill-met to bear the affront and would seek him out with dire intent."

Despite the coolness of his shop, Rubert took out a kerchief to mop his glistening brow with a trembling hand. The man had a most persuasive way about him.

Maxim's voice lowered and took on a confidential note. "I care no whit for the Hansa. They are for the most part cruel and heartless money-grubbers. Had I knowledge of an honest man who caught a handful or two of their coin I might be greatly loathe to spread word of him."

"I . . . I . . . I . . . of course, *Herr* Seymour," Hans stammered. "I am, as you say, only an honest man."

"My men paid more than enough in rents to buy Faulder Castle and all of its lands."

"It shall be so!" Hans agreed quickly and, searching in a cabinet for a paper, finally found the deed and hastily put his seal and sign upon it, sprinkled sand to blot the ink, and handed it over. "There!" he chortled. "The place has been a blight since I bought it. I'm glad to be rid of it! It is now yours."

Maxim took the deed, scanned it, and lifted it to

gently blow the sand off its surface before folding the parchment and tucking it within his doublet. "As to the advance on the town house..."

"Refunded, of course!" Hans gulped. "I rented the place to my ailing and widowed sister...only after hearing tales of your demise, of course," he hastily added. "I could hardly, in all honesty, keep a double rent."

Maxim nodded slowly, and the agent withdrew from behind the desk an iron-bound, wooden coffer from which he counted coins to some length, scooped them into a bag, then scribbled a receipt. When Maxim had signed the latter, Hans slid the heavy bag across the table.

"A refund in full, *Herr* Seymour." He smiled broadly. "As promised. Is there something more?"

Maxim hefted the bag, then dropped it within his purse. He donned his cloak and pulled on his gloves. "I find it a pleasure doing business with a man who knows the value of...uh...an honest way."

Hans Rubert let out a long, quavering sigh and finally summoned enough courage to ask, "Then the Hansa will never..." He swallowed heavily.

Maxim tossed him a brief salute. "Not from my lips," he assured the fellow and, with the closing of the door behind him, was gone like a gust of wind.

Hans slowly climbed onto his stool and sadly turned back several pages in the ledger to make a brace of corrections and significantly lower totals on a later page. A long sigh wheezed from him as he glumly closed the book. The skin of his teeth had been sorely tested this day, but his quick wit and honesty had brought him safely through, albeit somewhat poorer.

Maxim picked his way across the slush-covered thoroughfare and entered a smoke-filled room of an inn. He barely had time to shake a crusting of wet

snow from his cloak before a jovial voice bellowed
from a corner.

"Ho, Maxim!"

Seymour wiped his stinging eyes with the back of
a hand and pierced the hazy gloom to espy Nicholas
Von Reijn indulging his second passion at a well-laden
table. Maxim waved a casual acknowledgment before
he swept off his cloak and spread it over a pair of wall
pegs to dry. Stripping off his gloves, he strode across
the room to the warm hearth and stood for a long
moment, savoring the heat of the roaring fire as he
rubbed the chill from his hands. Finally he crossed to
Von Reijn's table and, raising a hand for service, spun
a chair into place directly across from the captain.

"Ich mochte Branntwein, fraulein," he ordered
when a plumpish, sweating young girl with a daringly
low-cut blouse arrived. He sat down and leaned back,
tilting the chair on its hind legs. *"Eins heiss Krug,
bitte."*

"Ja, mein Herr. Danke." The girl bobbed a quick
curtsey and, with a swirl of skirts, was gone.

Nicholas Von Reijn watched his companion for a
moment as he chewed on a well-spiced leg of mutton.
If he were a man to judge, he would be of a mind to
say there was something troubling his friend, for the
man seemed lost in thought and a harsh frown creased
his brow as his gaze roamed absently about the room.

Abruptly the merchant captain decided his friend
needed a confessional. If not, then his own curiosity
was sorely piqued. He laid down the well-gnawed
bone and, pushing back the platter, carefully wiped
his mouth with a large linen cloth after politely stifling
a stentorian belch with the same.

"Maxim?" Receiving no response, Nicholas repeated the name, somewhat louder. *"Maxim?"*

The Marquess turned with a questioning brow

raised, but the serving girl arrived to place a steaming stein of mulled brandy on the table before him. She lowered her tray and waited suggestively.

Somewhat vexed at the untimely interruption of the maid, the Hansa captain uncharacteristically tapped his own purse and frowned her away. Maxim nodded his thanks for the other's gratuity and sipped from the tankard, savoring the warmth of the brew in his mouth and the heat of it in his belly. A dapple of honey and spice floated on the surface and sent a pungent aroma through his head as he inhaled.

"It is miserable outside, *ja?*" Von Reijn nodded in answer to his own question. "A bad day for a long ride."

A noncommittal grunt came from Maxim as he wrapped his hands around the warm stein and let his gaze roam the room again. He vaguely recalled the icy chill of his long journey.

Nicholas pried on. "That old castle is cold and drafty on a day such as this. The inner rooms are probably comfortable..." He let the last word hang in a half-question, but Maxim missed the bait and only nodded in distant response as he sipped again from the mug.

Nicholas Von Reijn, seaborne merchant of the world, knowledgeable in seven languages and privy to the subtle nuances of cultures and manners necessary to conduct successful trading voyages, summoned all of his skills to draw out his distracted friend. "*Ja, ja!* But the girl, she is most comely, is she not?"

The slow nodding suddenly halted. The brows gathered darkly, and the green eyes smoldered as if with a well-kindled rage.

Von Reijn waited a space. Had he breached the reluctant dam? He was about to plunge on, even more boldly to the point, when the front legs of the other's chair slammed down. Maxim leaned across the table, his manner now intense and urgent as he braced on his elbows. A veritable torrent burst forth.

"Women! Bah! I vow to you, good friend, that fearsome gender is the vexation of all mankind! They have set their minds to bring us all to our knees in groveling despair. There's no reason to their logic! Nor a whit of fairness or justice in a score!"

Maxim's words only brought confusion to the captain's well-ordered mind. He spread his hands and, with a worried smile, sought to wring some sanity from the affair. "*Ja,* but yur *Liebling* . . ." He hurriedly corrected himself. "Yur betrothed . . ."

Maxim's fist slammed into the table. "By damn, I *am* a responsible man, and 'tis a soreness to me that my men took the wrong woman, that Arabella remains with her husband, and that her cousin was brought here in her stead!"

Incensed with his tirade, Maxim did not notice that Von Reijn, who dared not voice the words aloud, still moved his lips to form the question, "Wrong voman?" The captain's eyes widened, and he slumped back in his chair to stare with jaw aslack as his companion raged on.

"Ah, poor Arabella, delicate and gentle to a fault, left to perform the biddings of her father's avarice. In sadness she was set to wed much against her will and bade to place herself beneath the plunging flanks of that lusting stud . . . while I, quite ignorant of the mistake, rushed upstairs to receive my betrothed and was set upon with fury by a harpy bent to drink my blood and leave me rent to the bone. A vicious wasp! With naught a tender word, she has set herself to sting my soul at every turn!"

Maxim had no care that Von Reijn by now was rigid in his chair. The captain's face was red, and though his lips were clamped tightly shut, his belly jerked with the effort of subduing his mirth. Oblivious to the other's struggles, Maxim slapped his hand upon the table and fastened an angry but unseeing gaze upon his companion who bowed his head and, with a napkin, made haste to wipe away the tears that were streaming down his cheeks.

"I vowed to that snippet that I could not, for her own safety, see her sent back with the seas raging with storms, but she has set herself to be a thorn planted deeply in my side to ever pain and prick me until she is plucked and gone from sight. She intends to see her own ends met while strewing mine to willy ned and back. She cannot understand my head is forfeit if I venture to return."

Von Reijn took a long draught of wine and managed to control his spasms while Maxim calmed and likewise serviced his brew.

"Ah ha!" Von Reijn's mirth almost came out again, but he lowered the glass with care, studious of face. "I see yur plight, Maxim. But tell me, vat of this damsel? Who is she? Surely one so comely and so fair of..."

"*Comely?*" Maxim almost barked. "*Fair?* 'Tis in my mind a slavering wolf upon the moor would cause me less concern. Verily I say, 'tis only safe to venture near that one with blade half-drawn and shield at the ready if you value the wholeness of your skin." He sipped from his mug and, with his improving mood, felt his hunger grow apace. He seized a chop and took a bite before he noticed the remaining question in the captain's eyes.

"Elise Radborne is her name." He waved a chop and took another bite. "Cousin to the Stamfords. Arabella must have left her chambers for some reason, and this wench was there when my men, not knowing one from the other, wrapped her up and brought her here." His frown grew sharp once again. "What should I do with the chit, Nicholas? She sets me on edge, and though I would be much relieved to see her gone, they would lift my head from my shoulders if I ventured back to England."

Nicholas shrugged. "The answer seems simple enough if yu be fond of yur head, my friend. Yu must endure her presence for at least a time. But tell me, Maxim." He scarcely could control his eagerness as he approached the subject of his first passion. "Since yu have no fondness for this ... ah ... person, perhaps yu vould not be against this lady enjoying the companionship of a ... ah ... em ... as you English say ... a suitor?"

"What say you, Nicholas?" Maxim straightened and stared aghast at his friend, thinking him daft. But then, who was he to dictate a man's fancy? "You would pay court to such a one as she?"

Nicholas hunched his shoulders against the other's scorn and dipped his head aside with a half-cocked grin. "I find the lady ..."—he toyed with his glass—"... most delec ... ah ... I mean ... most comely. She has a strong spirit assuredly ... as vell as a certain grace. She vould be a challenge to a man vith skill and patience."

Maxim snorted. "I have no say. She is hardly my charge. If she would have you, then I would say good riddance. Mayhap 'twould distract her vengeance from me. I can only wish you luck and good fortune should you chance upon her meaner side."

"It is good," Von Reijn half chortled. He sat back and, spearing a pickled plum with his dagger, nibbled at the morsel. "Vill yu be returning tonight?"

Maxim glanced at the front door. Outside the wind howled and the snow swirled like a maddened dervish, dulling his desire to leave, but it could not be helped. "I suppose I must," he sighed, "'ere she turns that pair of knobblies into stone."

Von Reijn chose a roasted apple and, after skinning it, delicately stripped the sweet, tender flesh away. "'Tis plenty enough here to eat, my friend, and yu should be vell-stocked against that journey. Be my guest." He set a platter of roast duckling squarely in front of him and rubbed his hands in anticipation. "I svear," he laughed, "the whole of yur tale has brought my hunger to an edge again."

The two ate in silence for a time, savoring a variety of meats and tastes. When Maxim could eat no more, he washed down the last bite with the dregs of his brandy and declined a plate of thinly sliced beef. "No more, I pray you. No more. I shall slumber in the saddle as it is, despite the cold."

The captain held up a hand to delay his friend. "Then vhile I have yu disposed as my guest"—he swallowed a bite of duckling and washed it down with a glass of wine—"I beg yu one more favor. Vhen yu see the maid, Elise, vill yu inform her of my intent to call upon her this Friday next? About the noon hour I vould expect. I shall of course bring a light repast vith me. I've heard the food there is somevhat lacking."

Maxim laughed and, rising to his feet, clapped Von Reijn on the shoulder. "'Tis your own shattered hopes you will bear, I fear, but I shall risk my welfare and bid the girl to be prepared for your visit." He reached into his purse and pulled out the leather pouch of coins. "I shall settle my debt with you as one would a dying friend. You may not survive the trauma."

Nicholas returned a pained frown to him. "Yu do not allow me to gain much interest on yur debts, Maxim. Now I vill have to invest the monies elsevhere to fetch the amount of coin I guaranteed."

"I see no difficulty," Maxim replied, counting out the money. "You will now have more money to invest elsewhere."

The Hansa captain heaved a sigh. "Nay, no difficulty. I can easily sell a portion of my investment in another captain's voyage. It vould no doubt bring a better return, but I rather think it vill not bring as much delight."

"Delight?" Maxim queried, giving his friend a curious look. "Who is it that invests in my venture?"

"Give no heed to my ramblings, my friend," Nicholas bade with a chuckle. "Just remember me to the maid."

When Maxim returned to Faulder Castle that evening, the hour was close to midnight and all was silent and still, save for the low, rumbling snores of his minions who slept soundly on their pallets near the hearth. He quietly barred the repaired door behind him and made his way stealthily up the stairs. Before ascending to the third story, he moved quietly from the stairs and went to stand beside the maid's door, there to listen for a long moment. He could not hear even the faintest breath of a whisper or movement. Curiously he reached out to test the door and found it firmly barred from within. He nodded thoughtfully. It was as he had surmised; the wench would be ever cautious of her safety while he was about.

Continuing his ascent to his own chambers, he found there the welcoming warmth of a well-banked fire awaiting him. A goodly supply of wood had been laid up for him on the hearth, and a small kettle had been brought to warm the water now filling a nearby bucket. His gaze lifted, and to his surprise he found that his men had effected a repair to the roof through the use of a stable door secured in place to cover the hole. Even as he looked, light flurries drifting down through the firelight indicated they had not been altogether successful. Beside the hearth the wet furs had been laid out to dry, and upon his bed a fresh pallet temporarily stuffed with straw had replaced the sodden one. This brought to mind his need for security, and after spreading his cloak and doublet before the fire, he inspected what his men had done toward that end. Huge brackets had been placed on the inside of the frame, and a beam hewn down to size was propped nearby. With a rueful grin, he dropped the bar in place and slipped wedges behind it to tighten it. It would take a series of mighty blows to break it down, and he could now consider himself safe from the antics of that slender young maid.

Satisfied as to his safety, Maxim pulled a bench close to the flames and slowly worked the sodden boots from his feet, placing them where the warmth of the hearth would slowly dry them. The addition of a few logs soon had a cheery blaze crackling, and he strode about the chambers, loosening the ruff of his shirt. He was still restless to a fault, and he investigated the privy and dressing room, noting that his men had brought up his chests and made use of the pegs on the walls, but he found nothing there to occupy his roaming mind.

Returning to stand near the fireplace, he reached out a hand to brace against the wall and was amazed when a portion of the wooden paneling gave beneath his weight. The area was cast in deep shadows behind a jutting corner of the stonework that formed the chimney and hearth, but tracing his fingers downward, he explored a joint and found a small latch cleverly wrought of iron hidden beneath a raised portion of wood. Lifting the same, he pressed until the whole panel moved inward, opening onto a small, dark room. Seizing a stout candle, he lit it from the fire, then returned to the panel, pushed it wide, and stepped within. Lifting his tiny torch high, he saw that he was in a narrow space tucked between the back of the fireplace and another wall. The cubicle tapered to an end not far above his head, and no more than a pace away from him, a steep narrow stairway curved downward. He felt for the dagger he wore at his side and, confident with the presence of the weapon, eased his curiosity by following the passage downward. The stairs were sturdy and firm, and his stockinged feet made no whisper of sound. He had gone the distance of a full floor when the stairs ended abruptly in a short passageway. There, warm stone on his right jutted up against the boards of a wall where a single door offered the only exit.

Maxim found a small latch securing it, much like the one above. He tugged, and the door gave beneath a light touch. Though he had opened it no more than the breadth of a hand, he found himself much bemused, for he was standing at the threshold of the chamber belonging to his charge, one Elise Radborne.

The fire on her hearth had burned low, and the lady herself was sound asleep beneath several furs spread upon her bed. He pushed the door wide and, in his stocking feet, crossed the room with noiseless tread. Lifting the candle high, he looked down upon her, feeling as if he had chanced upon a victory of sorts. Her long lashes lay like dark shadows on her fair cheeks, and her soft lips were slightly parted as she breathed long and slowly in deepest slumber. Her hair formed a dark, tumbled halo over the pillow, over which an arm rested in a flawless ivory curve above her head, leaving her shoulder and the higher, swelling curves of her bosom naked to his gaze. He allowed his gaze to linger on her face and the tempting fullness of her breasts, as one who had chosen to savor a special treat. She was more woman than child, to be sure.

He leaned slightly closer to study her more carefully. In sleep the lass seemed harmless, indeed most innocent with her delicate features and creamy skin.

"Perhaps Nicholas," he mused, "has seen more of what I could not."

She possessed an uncommon beauty, certainly more vivid and lively than that of the translucent paleness of Arabella. Where that one evoked a vision of ivory and lace, this one seemed to exude the very essence of life. Both women, by their striking and stirring comeliness, were set well apart from others. Invariably they would be easily noted in any crowd.

Maxim passed to the hearth where he carefully laid fresh logs on the coals, then silently withdrew, taking note that the latch on her side of the door had been removed. Seeing the adjustments, he entertained a glimmer of hope for his henchmen. When, several moments later, he closed the door of his chamber behind him, he found a small stick of firewood in the pile and, as a precaution, wedged it tightly against the latch to prevent the panel from being opened from the other side. On the morrow he would remove the barrier, for it was to his benefit to keep the passageway a secret, at least for the time being.

He stoked his own fire, then arranged the furs on his bed, doffed the remainder of his clothes, and sought a warm spot to indulge his slumbers. A knowing smile curved his lips as his thoughts turned back to the vision he had just seen, and he drifted into the arms of Morpheus, no longer dreaming of Arabella.

Chapter 10

*T*HE DAWNING SUN burst upon the land, sending long streamers of light shining across the vast empyrean. In the eastern sphere the morning sky was bathed in spectacular hues of magenta pinks and dulled to a dark grayish-blue on the western horizon. Puffy white clouds with gilded edges seemed to glow with a luminescence of their own as they drifted near the sun's face. Against such splendor the dark silhouette of the hilltop dwelling stood out in bold relief, like some slowly decaying sentinel. Its dulling presence could easily serve as a reminder to the world that man's attempts were all too frail and fleeting against the contrast of more heavenly and eternal creations.

Maxim opened a frosty panel of octagonal leaded glass to view the radiant panorama. He relished the zesty tingle as the crisp morning air caressed his naked body and washed the last dregs of sleep from him. He stretched his right arm upward, then winced slightly as the muscles twitched in his back, a frequent and painful reminder of his most recent wound.

A chill breeze wafted over him, eliciting a shiver and prompting him to pull a woolen mantle around his shoulders. He leaned out, letting his gaze range far and free before bringing it inward to the courtyard and its tumbled structures. A bleak smile curved his lips as he surveyed his newly acquired domain. Nearly a week had passed since his confrontation with Hans Rubert, but he was by no means the richer for his purchase. To say that he had come down in the world was putting it mildly; by the Queen's own decree he could lay no claim to his wealth or title. If ever he would be allowed to return to England as rightful lord of all he had once owned, he would first have to present evidence of his innocence to Elizabeth. Just how he might go about that involved more than merely setting his mind to the matter, for it did not promise to be a simple task.

Maxim could hear the animals nickering for their morning grain and knew that Fitch and Spence were moving about in the stables. His gaze drifted elsewhere, moving along the path that led beyond the main gate. Piqued by a sudden curiosity, he dropped his eyes downward alongside the keep to the windows just below his. If the little vixen was up and about and bent on some chicanery, he saw no visible evidence. The lead-glass panels were tightly closed against the wintry chill, but even as he watched a window opened and the maid appeared with only a fur pelt wrapped about her and that hanging loose and low around her bosom. As she tossed a bucket of dirty water into the courtyard below, he was rewarded with a brief flash of creamy white and rosy-pink breasts, fully naked to his gaze.

She lifted no slightest glance upward, but withdrew and closed the window again, ignorant of what she had given him. He rubbed his icy hands together, as much in glee as in need, and chuckled to himself, feeling a new vitality with which to meet the day. At least now, when he played the challenging hector, he need not think of her as a rude child in need of a thrashing, but could derive pleasure sparring with a wench who was both comely and curved.

Whistling a frolicsome melody, he closed the window and placed a kettle of water to heat over the fire. He washed and carefully shaved the light stubble from his face, then garbed himself casually in suede trunk hose, dark stockings, and a fine white linen shirt. He donned a soft leather doublet over the latter piece and tugged on thigh-high boots, then stepped to the door.

Quite cheery of mood, he left his chambers and made his way downstairs, noting as he passed the hallway near the girl's chamber that her door was now standing ajar. A dull clank of copper kettles drew his notice to the hearth as he descended the last flight of stairs. There he found his charge attending the morning meal. He had for the last several days stayed away from her as much as he could, rising early to hunt or to roam his newly acquired lands and the surrounding territory. For the most part she had also kept her distance, remaining in her chambers or the other end of the hall when he was about. Thus, this morning, it was almost as if he was seeing her afresh and with clearer vision. She was without a doubt a most comely maid, and even clothed in the rough woolen gown, she would have done much to shame women in far richer garb. A thin strip of frayed cloth gathered her hair in a Grecian style on top of her head, leaving the softly curling length falling in freedom past her shoulders. Such a display of rich auburn tresses could fuse a thousand impressions into a single thought in a man's mind, and that was how she might look robed only in the glory of her hair. For a moment his mind paused as he regarded the treasure he had recently viewed from his window. Once, in Florence, he had chanced to see Botticelli's *Birth of Venus.* He had admired the artist's talent in creating his subject, but now the memory of that lifeless goddess was brought to vivid life by this more refined and exquisite example of womanhood.

" 'Tis pleasing to see you have taken my advice and applied yourself to some meaningful duty," he needled. "I was sure you could if you would only put your mind to it."

Elise faced him, and her eyes sparked with well-fired irritation. The desire was in her to tell him how hard she had worked to clean this pile of stone, but if he was so blind and lamebrained not to see that his men needed a strong example and a firm guiding hand, then she would let him stew in his own stupidity.

Dropping hands to slender hips in a petulant stance, Elise gave as good as she got. "What ho! The good master of the house has at last deemed to grace us with his presence this morning. Did you sleep overlong, my lord? I swear I saw the rising of the sun some hours ago."

"Perhaps one, if that," Maxim replied pleasantly.

"Well and good! And here be a feast for you, all prepared to meet your royal favor." She stepped to the kettle, slopped porridge into a bowl, and dropped the wooden piece with a dull thud on the table before his chair. She smiled tightly. "Your pleasure, my lord."

"You are most kind, maid," he countered with a shallow bow. "And indeed, most fair to look upon. I swear, if the ladies at court were to espy your raiment, they would rush out en masse to the clothiers. Your gown fair bedazzles the eye."

His light mockery touched off a fuse of indignation within Elise. "Aye, they should! As witness to the generosity of my lord." She swept a slender hand to indicate his long form as he lowered himself into the chair. "Look how he denies himself that others may enjoy his wealth and protection. Why, his clothes must be worth no more than..." A long, heavy knife cleaved the air and chopped off a chunk of bread from the loaf that lay on a wooden tray near his arm, drawing a surprised start from him. Maxim turned an incredulous stare upon her, certain he would have lost a finger had he been a hairbreadth closer. Elise smiled with half-lidded eyes that boldly locked with his until, heaving a casual shrug, she finished, "...a few gold sovereigns, at least."

Maxim snorted and ignored her for a moment as he tasted his morning fare, then he glanced at her again, curling his lip in repugnance. "Your talents as a cook are indeed lacking, maid," he berated. "Perhaps a bit of salt will help."

"Certainly, my lord." Elise took the bowl from him and faced the hearth. When she stepped back to the table again, she placed the wooden piece carefully in front of him. "Is this more to your liking?"

Maxim caught a tantalizing scent of freshly washed woman as she leaned close, and his eye, drawn to her bosom, saw where the gown gapped away from her to tease him with a brief, but tempting, view of porcelain-perfect skin. The effect of sight and smell was rather disruptive, and he stirred in sudden discomfiture as his blood began to warm.

Elise straightened and, in some surprise, saw that his eyes had followed her movement, as if reluctant to leave her cleavage. Her color heightened, and snidely she asked, "Considering a replacement for Arabella, my lord?"

Maxim scoffed, not willing to give her any quarter. "'Twould be an impossible task for you to accomplish, my girl, so you needn't inflate your vanity overmuch." Smug with his answer, he lifted a spoonful of porridge to his mouth and sampled the portion, then grimaced in sharp distaste and quickly gulped a long draught of water from his cup.

"Is that enough salt, my lord?" Elise questioned in overstated sweetness. Indeed, sweetness was not what she was feeling toward him at the moment. She was rather regretful that she had not whacked off his finger along with the bread and then rubbed salt in the wound.

Glaring at her, Maxim came out of his chair and, snatching up the bowl, dumped the contents into the fire where it fell upon a log and hissed and bubbled in an obnoxious white glob until it began to char and smoke. He ladled another portion from the kettle, added a tiny pinch of salt, and returned to his chair.

Elise felt the weight of his steely stare and turned aside as he began to eat. Seemingly quite innocent, she began to putter about the hearth, straightening this and washing that. Taking up a broom, she busied herself with sweeping the floor, and for a moment she worked diligently, picking up stools and setting them aside as she brushed beneath them. A frenzy seemed to seize her, as if she became completely engrossed in her labors. At first, the dust rose in small puffs before the broom, but the faster and harder she swung the thing, the higher and wider the dirty cloud became. A billowing, dusty haze soon roiled up around her, becoming more pronounced until it engulfed the table. The Marquess choked suddenly and brought the flat of his hands down hard upon the plank. His bellow of rage nearly shook the rafters.

"Cease, witch!"

Elise obeyed, but directed her gaze over her shoulder and bestowed upon him a look of cool contempt. "Does my lord find displeasure in my work?"

Maxim coughed, waving his hand before his face in an effort to clear the air of dust, and stabbed his finger toward the opposite end of the table. "Sit yourself down, wench!"

"Witch? Wench? Witch?" Her slender nose lifted primly, while her eyelids lowered to partially mask the deep blue orbs that stared at him in aloof disdain. Her eyebrow jutted upward in a piqued quirk. "My lord, you speak to me?"

"Aye!" Maxim barked. "And all like you, be they bitch, witch, wench, or lady!" He spread his hands and glanced upward with an impatient supplication, a gesture Elise would not let pass without comment.

"No good to look there for help, my lord. I declare your copemate is in the nether direction just waiting to roast your foul carcass."

Maxim peered at her with a jaundiced eye, then slowly shook his tawny head as if sorely grieved. "I told Nicholas, but he would not listen."

"Nicholas?" Elise's curiosity perked.

"Aye, Nicholas." Maxim nodded. "He asked if he could pay court to you."

"Really!" Her tone had definitely sharpened. "And did you give him leave to do so, my lord?"

"He will be arriving today near the noon hour."

It was Elise's turn to come out of her chair and slap the table with the palm of her hand. " 'Twas so good of you to give your consent, *Master* Seymour!"

"I gave him nothing save the best of advice," Maxim answered casually. "I have no authority to say him yea or nay, but bade him seek your answer for himself. In all honesty I warned him against doing so and to don cuirass, helm, and buckler if he was intent upon the matter and valued his skin at all."

"Oh, you . . . !" A fiery brightness came into the jewel-blue eyes, while her lips tightened to a pinched whiteness. "You dare bandy my name and abuse my repute with your cronies! *Oh!*"

Her fists were clenched tightly with rage as she, unable to bear his mocking grin a moment longer, spun on a heel and beat a retreat toward her chambers. But if that gawking fool thought the battle won and done with, he was to pay a heavy price for that presumption. She paused on the first flight of stairs and requested rather sharply, "Could you send Fitch and Spence up with some buckets of water? Plenty of them! I am in a mood to try that copper tub in my chambers."

It was shortly before the noon hour when Maxim, having returned from another ride that encompassed the borders of his newly purchased lands, passed his chamber windows and, from there, caught a glimpse of Captain Von Reijn's small party coming along the trail toward the castle. He opened a panel to have a better view and chuckled at the sight that greeted him. At times Nicholas had a penchant for being flamboyant, and this matched his best. His attire was as rich as any king's. Indeed, the heavily embroidered chamarre nearly bedazzled the beholder as its gold threads twinkled in the sun. The fur lining apparently kept him from feeling the chill, for he rode his mount as if it were a fine spring day. He grasped the reins in one gloved hand and rested the other fist on his hip where it held the fanciful coat open in such a way as to reveal doublet and puffed trunk hose of dark crimson velvet. His plumed toque sat jauntily upon his head, and even from where he stood, Maxim could see a costly gold chain adorned with flashing gems hanging around the man's neck.

Mounted guards wearing chest-plates of polished brass rode fore and aft of the captain, and the halberds they bore marked their intent to defend him from any miscreant who would try to waylay him. Following behind the threesome came a rather rotund servant who led a packhorse weighted down with all manner of bundles, casks, and cases. His own steed was loaded down not only with his considerable weight, but with copper pots and a wide assortment of paraphernalia that clanged and clattered as they approached.

"Behold, the suitor cometh," Maxim observed with an amused chuckle. Leaving his chambers, he made his way downstairs and went outside to await his guests. He stood on the top step in a bold stance, feet spread wide, and fists resting on his hips, while the brisk wind ruffled his close-cropped hair. The Hansa captain had approached the seemingly lifeless pile of rubble with a look of distaste, and when he espied his host, he spurred his horse into the van and led his party across the moat.

"Maxim!" Von Reijn called in buoyant greeting. "How fares the day vith yu, good friend?"

"Sweetly," Maxim rejoined. "The morning has graced me with many pleasurable sights to woo the eye."

"*Ja*, it vas a beautiful sunrise, I must agree." Nicholas nodded, then glanced about him at the tumbledown wall and structures. "Though 'tis hard to imagine how yu could enjoy any view from this pile o' stone."

"A man never knows where he might behold marvelous wonders. Why, it could be right beneath his very nose," Maxim remarked, with a mind toward the sight that he had glimpsed from his own windows that morning.

"Not in this place!" Nicholas stated with conviction.

Maxim laughed and descended the stone steps. "I see you have chosen to ignore my warnings and have ventured forth on this hazardous quest of yours. While you are still unmarked and whole of limb, set your feet to ground and come warm yourself before the hearth."

Nicholas slid from the saddle and tossed the reins to Spence as the pair of servants came running to assist the guests. The captain slowly turned full circle as he surveyed the courtyard, its crumbling stonework and the sagging roofs of the outbuildings. "I had at least hoped to find some shelter for the horses."

" 'Tis there." Maxim directed the man's attention toward the stable. " 'Tis solid enough and out of the wind. Behind it there's even a room with a hearth where your men can find respite. Fitch will see they are given food and a cup or two of ale to stir the blood."

"Not too much of the ale," Nicholas advised. "They must be alert for the trip home tonight."

The portly man seized an armful of pots and pans and rattled and clanged his way into the keep, as Maxim's amused gaze followed him.

"I've brought *Herr* Dietrich, my cook, to assure a vorthy repast for this eventide," Nicholas explained. "I'm sure there are some here who vill be happy to hear that."

"Anything is better than salty gruel," his host grunted dryly. "I have had my fill of it this past week."

Nicholas chortled and approached with a hand held out in friendship, and Maxim clasped it in a warm, amiable welcome.

" 'Tis a heavy escort you keep for only an hour's ride out of the city," Maxim remarked, inclining his head toward the guards.

"A man cannot be too careful." Nicholas winked as he confessed, "In truth, I thought it might impress the lady."

"I was inclined to hopefully regard it as protection against the lady," Maxim quipped and then chuckled as the captain paused in sudden confusion.

Clapping his guest on the back, Maxim escorted him up the steps and into the hall where Nicholas strode about in some wonder, looking much like the late Henry the Eighth of England. He set his feet wide apart and, drawing back the rich coat, settled his fists on his hips. "*Ja,* I can understand vhy the townfolk never came up here. They believe this castle is haunted, and by the looks of it ..."

Fitch skipped a step near the entrance and stumbled headlong into the back of his companion who had stopped dead in his tracks. The captain's words had won their full and undivided attention, and as they righted themselves and carried several bundles to the cook, who had taken charge of the hearth, they cast cautious glances about the hall, as if they now expected some unseen specter to fly out at them from the shadows.

"It is a dark and foreboding place, to be sure," Nicholas continued. "It abuses the term *castle.*"

"Actually, you've arrived after some improvements have been made," Maxim replied with a lopsided grin. "Think of what it must have looked like when the girl first came."

The Hansa captain snorted. "It is hard to imagine it looking vorse."

The Marquess directed him toward a grouping of chairs set apart from the hearth. "Come, my friend. Rest yourself."

Stripping off his gloves, Nicholas dropped his rugged frame into a chair and leaned forward. Bracing an elbow on his left knee and resting a fist on the other, he peered intently into the face of his host. "Vell, man? Vhat say yu? Is the girl agreeable?"

Maxim responded with a noncommittal shrug. " 'Tis hard to say, Nicholas. She has a mind of her own and does not confide in me."

"But yu told her," the merchant captain pressed.

"I did."

"And she said nothing?"

"Nothing that would indicate her intentions."

"Ach!" Nicholas slapped his gloves against his thigh in frustration. "This damnable uncertainty! It gnaws at me!"

Maxim stepped to a nearby table, splashed a small amount of mead into a tankard, and handed it to the distraught man. "Here, this will bolster your courage."

Von Reijn accepted the offering and gulped it down with one toss of his wrist, drawing his host's dubious regard. He beckoned for more, and Maxim raised the flagon to splash more liquid into the mug.

"I've never seen you so wrought up over a wench before," he observed, and settled into a chair beside him. "I remember when you came to my estates to scour the countryside for any young, eligible ladies in attendance. You did not limit your attentions to any singular choice then..."

"Come now, Maxim," Nicholas chided as the corners of his mouth twitched with humor. "Yu know I'm a blessed saint."

"Have a care, Von Reijn!" Maxim grimaced. "You may bring lightning bolts down upon our heads, and I bid you keep in mind this is the only roof I have at the moment."

"Vhat are yu suggesting?" Nicholas challenged, feigning outrage. "I demand an explanation."

A tawny brow lifted in deep skepticism as a smile played about Maxim's lips. "I know of the vows purportedly taken by the members of the Hanseatic League, but there are many of the Hansa who have their own definition of those vows, that in secret they are naught but lusting roués bent on the conquest of every comely wench who captures their eye." He shrugged. " 'Tis none of my concern whether you are chaste or chastened. You've been a rogue from the cradle, and I feel some responsibility for having brought the girl here. I know you are no innocent."

"Vell, neither are yu!" Nicholas blustered.

Maxim smiled pleasantly. "I've never laid claim to that fact."

The ice-blue eyes flew to Maxim as the gentle taunt met its mark. "A foul cut," Nicholas protested in good humor. "Yu destroy my reputation."

"An impossible feat since you have done that yourself. Besides, I only challenge your claims between thee and me, friend."

Nicholas waggled his head, accepting the other's rebuke. "Between thee and me, friend, I admit to being something of a rascal."

A slow smile turned Maxim's lips. "I've known that for some time."

"But the girl, she is different from most. She has touched my heart."

Maxim almost came out of his chair with a derisive snort. "Have a care for what you give into her hands, I bid you, Nicholas. If you offer your heart to that maid, she will rend it to hash in a thrice." He well remembered his torn ear. "She is a spiteful and spirited wench."

"Have I not sailed vith her across the North Sea?" Nicholas pointed out in hot defense of the girl. "*Ja,* she has spirit, I vill agree, but spiteful? *Nein!* She is only fighting for her freedom. Vould you not do the same?"

"I would at least listen to reason."

"Is it not reasonable for the girl to vant to go home and to insist she be taken? The act against her vas *un*reasonable."

" 'Twas a mistake," Maxim agreed helplessly. "Had my men taken Arabella, I'm sure she would have been satisfied to stay."

"Did yu ask her?"

The simple question set Maxim to glowering. "I intended to." He lowered his gaze and swirled the mead in the bottom of the mug. "I meant to the night of the wedding. I wanted to soothe her fears at being taken from Bradbury." His face came up with an angry slant to the brow and a tight set to his lips. "I was forestalled in that endeavor by a chance meeting with Mistress Radborne and her recognition of me. It seems from the very first she has been ever underfoot and always in the way."

"Ja!" Nicholas chortled loudly. "I heard about yur escapade at Bradbury Hall. Yu bearded Edward properly, and in yur own hall!" He laughed again. " 'Tis been bandied about that Edward now sleeps behind a locked and guarded door. Yu have put the fear of shadows into the good squire." He dissolved into tearful guffaws again, and it was not until he sobered under Maxim's disgusted glare that he continued. "Mayhap yu have roamed too boldly and far afield, and that is the reason yu find the girl so much in yur path."

An angry snort came from the Marquess. "From the very first she has thwarted my cause."

"Vhat exactly is yur cause, Maxim? Vhat prompted yu to do such a thing? Vas it love for Arabella, or yur desire for revenge against her father?"

"I only meant to allay the consummation of the wedding until..." Maxim clamped his jaw and frowned sharply, uncomfortable with the other's prodding questions and his own defense. "Good Lord, man, do you think I'd have sought Arabella as my wife had I not cherished her above other women?"

Nicholas leaned back and considered his friend thoughtfully. "From vhat yu've said of her"—he almost chewed on the words as he mulled over the possible reasons in his thoughts—"she is both beautiful and soft-villed. It vould seem such a voman vould be a logical choice for yu to marry. She vould be pliant, not given to high spirits or rebellion, nor vould she make unreasonable demands." He paused until he gained the other's undivided attention. "Yu said often enough that yu had a need to acquire a vife and family in order to carry on the name. Vhat I'm vondering, my friend, is vhether you chose Arabella with yur mind or yur heart. And then, once betrayed by her father, did yu seek her out of spite, or vas there in truth a burning passion yu felt for the lady?"

"I'm sure a veritable dynasty would have sprung from our loins," Maxim ground out in useless, but dogged, determination.

"Yu cannot blame the damsel for looking to another. Yu vere supposed to be dead."

" 'Twas Edward's eagerness to seize another fortune that forced her to wed Reland," Maxim insisted.

"Come now, man," Nicholas gently prodded. "Yu vere little more than a dead man vhen yur men brought yu to my ship. 'Tis to Ramonda's credit she kept yu alive for the voyage, but 'twas most of a month before yu could walk. Give Arabella yur sympathy," he urged. "She vas in all likelihood much pained by yur death and longed for the bliss of vedded life. Yu should be glad yu're alive to seek some other voman to varm yur bed."

"I *am* grateful to be alive!" Maxim exclaimed. "I'm very grateful that Spence and Fitch were in a boat hidden beneath the bridge, as we had planned for my escape. They have most assuredly proven their loyalty to me and have served me well, down to the saving of my life. 'Twas a wry twist of fate that they had never set eye on Arabella, an oversight I now regret, but you needn't think me despondent to the point I do not appreciate being alive!"

Nicholas paused a long moment, then murmured

in hushed tones, "If yu value yur life, my friend, I vould caution yu also on another matter."

His host looked up and, in curious wonder, waited for him to continue.

The Hansa captain complied. "Yu have met Karr Hilliard, a high master of the guild?"

Maxim inclined his head to indicate a positive response. "On my return voyage from England, he made himself known to me. You probably know it was his ship I was sailing on."

"Karr Hilliard owns many Hansa ships, and he is most serious about profit. He is an agent of the Hansa until the next Diet in the summer, vhen he vill probably be elected again. He is easily the richest and singly most powerful person in the league."

Maxim remained guarded. "He bade me call upon him should I venture to Lubeck." He reached inside his doublet and withdrew a waxen seal with the imprint of a signet on it. "He gave me this to gain entry to his presence."

Nicholas took the seal and examined it before reaching a finger into his shirt and pulling out a gold chain to which was attached a brass stamp. The face of the stamp was smaller, but similar to the signet. "It is a seal of the Hansa. Every Hansa captain has one and is svorn to keep it on his person at all times." He handed the waxen image back to Maxim. "That one vill open many doors for yu. The size bespeaks its importance. I neglected to tell yu that Karr Hilliard is also the most dangerous man yu vill ever know. He has ordered men to go under the axe on the merest suspicion. In Lubeck his power is absolute, and he is far more dedicated to the cause than I, my friend. Surely I have not been a fine example of the Hansa. I have felt no great need to seclude myself from the vorld around me or to maintain the secrecy that the league guards so jealously. Vhen I apprenticed as a youth in the Hansa, I slept in unheated and unlighted *kontors* as did other lads, seven or eight of us to a room. I even survived initiations that killed others, and in all of this I formed my opinions apart from the league. Karr Hilliard is of the sort to be vary of; he is one of the first to take part in the rituals to initiate our youth . . . and he has killed some because he extended their trials beyond the limits of reason. He is a mean-spirited man, and it has come to my attention that he has been making inquiries from Lubeck as to yur reasons for being here in Hamburg."

"Why should he be interested in me?" Maxim inquired as he lowered his eyes to stare into his mug.

"He hates vhat is happening to our ports and trade," Nicholas stated. "Ve are slowly being squeezed out of existence. A hundred years ago ve vere the masters of trade from the Baltic to the Mediterranean. Now ve are fighting to survive. Elizabeth is against the presence of our *kontors* in England, and Hilliard has taken offense. He has already lost two ships to that pirate, Drake."

Maxim momentarily raised his gaze. "Aye, I've heard as much. Bound to Spain, they were. It seems Philip's seizure of English grain ships in the Basque ports this summer gave the Queen cause to outfit her sea dog for raids against the Spanish."

"Drake has likevise become a menace to us since his return to sea! He loves to tweak the noses of the Portuguese and Spanish, and now he is tweaking ours!"

"Look you, I've no great love for Elizabeth myself after the injustice that was done to me," Maxim replied. "But face it, man, the Hansards have nearly throttled English trade for the past two or three hundred years because of their vast monopolies.

They've paid no tolls or taxes in England for at least that long. Ever since King Edward the Third borrowed from the league and pawned the royal jewels, English merchants have had to suffer even in their homeland. By Edward's decree, the Hansa reigned supreme for a time, but whenever English seamen ventured into Hansa ports, they were cast into prisons and treated as unwelcome vermin. Perhaps Elizabeth is remembering the ninety-six English fishermen who were captured off Bergen, bound hand and foot, and then thrown into the sea by members of your league. Whatever ill feelings she might have toward the Hansa, 'tis Spain she has come up against."

"My friend, do not let Hilliard hear yu say such things. He vill have yu arrested as a spy. Even here in Hamburg the Hansa once took a hundred and fifty foreigners and beheaded them as pirates. Should I tell yu that yu vill suffer the same fate if yu tread unvarily with Karr Hilliard?"

Maxim scoffed, "If I were a spy, do you think I'd have been so close to death when I was taken aboard your ship and brought here to Hamburg? If I had come to fulfill a mission, then Elizabeth's men almost spent my life ere the deed was performed."

"My friend, I vould be the first one to deny yu are vorking for Elizabeth, but Karr Hilliard is nevertheless a dangerous man. If he could arrange it, he vould put Mary on the throne to see his own ends met." Nicholas paused a moment, reluctant to continue, but he knew the threat to his friend and could not silence his concern. "The Throgmorton assassination plot vas of great interest to him. He is no doubt interested in forming a similar plan to eliminate Elizabeth."

"Does he know I've been accused of treason?" Maxim asked carefully.

"*Ja*, he knows, and I think that is vhy he is interested

in yu. He may vant to buy yur services."

"He need only ask, and I will tell him what he desires to know."

"Hilliard is also a careful man, Maxim. He is vary of foreigners, and he vill sniff you out vell ere he takes a chance."

Maxim swept his hand about to indicate the hall. "Do you detect any guards lurking in the shadows, ready to pounce on any who might wander in? I am destitute; my wealth has been stripped from me. What have I to defend?"

"The most precious possession yu have, my friend. Yur life."

Maxim sipped the mead in silence, and it was a long space of time before either of them spoke. Growing impatient, Nicholas glanced toward the stairs and waved a hand in that direction.

"Yu say the girl is in her chambers? Does she know I've come?"

"Her windows overlook the courtyard. She could not have missed your arrival. She is no doubt testing your patience."

Nicholas flung himself from the chair. "I vill go and fetch the maid!"

"I would advise against provoking her," Maxim muttered into his cup. He took a sip of the mead and raised his gaze toward the stairs, detecting some slight sound from the middle chambers. His smile was brief and his words mocking. "Behold, the fair damsel has finally deigned to grace us with her presence."

Nicholas whirled in obvious eagerness and, with long strides, crossed the hall to await the girl. Maxim watched in detached amusement, curious as to what the vixen would wear to greet her guest. Although he had directed funds for the purchase of clothes, he had thus far seen no evidence of any finer attire than the soiled woolen gown. From the bucketfuls of water the men had carried to her chambers, he could only surmise that she would at least be clean.

Maxim continued to address his attention to the stairs until a silken slipper first came into view beneath a blue velvet hem. As she stepped fully into his range of vision, he braced an elbow on the wooden arm of the chair and settled his chin between his thumb and forefinger, a subtle way to keep his jaw from falling agape. He observed her sweet and gracious greeting to Nicholas, and the thought came to him that they had housed a changeling in their midst, for here indeed was the winsome lass Nicholas had glimpsed.

Elise laid a slender hand upon the captain's arm and allowed him to escort her across the hall. This time Maxim rose to his feet to give her the benefit of his manners, but she all but ignored him as she verbally admired the wealthy dress of their guest. "Faith! I am overwhelmed by your handsome appearance, Cap—"

"Nicholas," the pale-haired man eagerly insisted.

"As you wish . . . Nicholas," she murmured pleasantly, and gave a small nod of acquiescence. "You do me honor."

Maxim rolled his eyes in wide disbelief. The wily wench had a glibber tongue than any serpent in Eden!

"I came here to ask a most pertinent question," Nicholas blurted. "And if yu are of a mind, I vould have the answer now."

Elise sank into a chair in chaste silence, sweetly attentive to his words. Nicholas's enthusiasm was brimming over as he dragged his own armchair around in front of her and leaned forward to take her hands into his. "My dear Elise . . . I've never met a vo-man who intrigued me more . . . and I've reached such status in the Hansa, I am free to court whom I vould . . ."

The corners of Elise's mouth lifted prettily as she teased, "Why, Nicholas, I seem to remember that you wished to avoid any mention of your state of wealth while we were aboard your ship. What has changed?"

Nicholas cleared his throat and shot a glance over his shoulder at Maxim, who was now lounging with his feet stretched out before him on the floor and an arm braced upon his chair. At present their host appeared highly entertained by their conversation, for he eyed them with the interest of a curious hawk, seeming to hang on each word for any tidbit he might glean from it. After another grumbling deep in his chest, the captain faced the lady again and confided, "Maxim informed me last veek that yu vere not his betrothed."

"Had you asked me that aboard your ship, Nicholas, I would have told you I didn't even know the man," Elise pointed out. "But you were so intent upon keeping the identity of my abductor a secret, you did not allow for the possibility of a mistake. This awful tragedy might not have been carried to such extremes if you had spoken up."

"I had no reason to think Fitch and Spence had made such a blunder," the Hansa captain carefully explained. "Believing yu belonged to another, I struggled to remain as impersonal as possible." Pausing, he glanced down and brushed his thumb against the soft, smooth flesh of her hand. "I failed abjectly."

Elise glanced at Maxim and felt a whetting irritation with the man. Behind Nicholas's back, he raised his hands and, in a mocking fashion, silently clapped them together, applauding her performance. Her eyes narrowed and snapped in loathing disdain. What she wouldn't do to wipe that smirk from his face!

"Nicholas?" Her voice was soft and honey-coated, and in eager response the captain raised his gaze to probe the depths of the sapphire orbs. "Lord Seymour spoke of your desire, and I am pleased to have such a gentleman call upon me."

Her statement really made the green eyes roll, and the tawny head took up the movement upon the tall back of his chair. Maxim averted his gaze briefly and then turned back to her with a brow sharply cocked to accentuate his exaggerated expression of profound skepticism. He responded to the girl's perturbed glare by shaking his head in mute, but rankling, disapproval.

"I brought yu a gift," Nicholas announced. He left the girl and rushed across the hall to seize a long bundle Spence had carried in. Hurrying back, he untied the large, cloth-wrapped, cylinder-shaped roll and spread a luxurious Turkish rug for her consideration. "For yur chambers to protect yur feet against the chill."

"Oh, Nicholas, 'tis a rare and beautiful piece you gift me with."

"For a rare and beautiful lady," he murmured.

"I'm overwhelmed by your generosity. It grieves me that I've nothing to give you in return."

"Yur companionship is a gift I vould greatly cherish."

Maxim rose from his chair, displaying some annoyance with the couple. "I've listened to the pair of you mewling and caterwauling long enough," he stated testily. "I shall take Eddy out for a ride, and I have no idea when I will return."

"No need to hurry back," Nicholas responded, welcoming his departure. "Ve shall be adequately entertained in your absence."

"I'm sure you will!" Maxim replied, making no effort to disguise his sarcasm. He strode across the hall, mounted the pair of steps, and took his leave through the massive portal. The slamming of the door punctuated his departure and brought a sweetly voiced and well-disguised jeer from Elise.

"Poor man. He is still brooding over Arabella." Her attention returned to the Hansa captain as that one settled himself in his chair. "Tell me, Nicholas, how goes my investment?"

Maxim returned late that evening to find Fitch and Spence seated back to back upon a bench before the hearth. Each watched his half of the hall with a wary eye and with a cudgel held at the ready, just in case a phantom wraith should be wont to wander about, but when the lord of the keep pushed open the front portal, they started up with frightened cries and made ready to defend their post.

Maxim was not of such a mind to believe in ghosts, but their loud wails of fright nearly raised the hackles on his neck. "Cease!" he barked. "You'll wake the dead!"

"Beggin' yer pardon, m'lord," Fitch apologized, and tried to gulp down his trepidations. "We was afearin' the dead was already awake."

"There are no ghosts here!" Maxim stated emphatically, snatching off his gloves. "If you so desire you can sleep in the room behind the stables while I'm here, but when I'm away, you should remain in the hall and lend whatever protection you can to the maid during my absence."

"Aye, m'lord."

The servants gathered their pallets and cudgels and made haste to depart the great room, fleeing across the courtyard with coattails flying. Slowly Maxim crossed the hall and began to climb the stairs. He was chilled to the bone after his long ride, and he had to suppress a persistent shiver. Dragging the flap of his cloak across his chest, he draped it over his far shoulder to close it more securely against the drafts that flowed through the keep.

A wavering light shining from the second level aroused his curiosity, and he stepped away from the stairs to peer into the shadows of the short hallway. Elise stood in her doorway, silhouetted against the firelight that radiated from her chamber hearth. A fur pelt was wrapped around her shoulders, leaving the skirt of her lace-trimmed petticoat showing beneath. Her small, slender feet were bare against the stone, and he had no doubt they were as cold as ice.

"What is wrong?" he questioned, moving toward her. He could see that she was shaking and wondered if it was entirely due to the drafts. The candle she clasped illumined the worry in her eyes as she stared back at him.

"I had a dream," she whispered, and glanced about her as if trying to sort out reality from fantasy. "I dreamt I saw my father being hauled up a chimney. The smoke was so thick he could not breathe, and they left him hanging there to torture him."

Maxim reached out to brush back a curling wisp from her cheek. "Nicholas has been telling you tales of the rites of the Hansa..."

Lifting her gaze, she stared up at him in confusion. "Is that something they do?"

A long sigh slipped from Maxim. "Their rites of initiation are supposed to be well-kept secrets, but Nicholas does not always follow by the rules. He thinks of himself as something of an outcast. He is much offended by what the brotherhood does sometimes, yet he feels a certain loyalty to them, too. His mother is a Netherlander and lives in Lubeck. His father is dead now, but once he was a high master in the league." Maxim paused for a moment as he searched the troubled blue eyes and continued distantly, "Someday I expect Nicholas will break with them.

"But you are chilled," he observed as a shudder shook her. He reached out a hand and pushed her chamber door wider. The flames in the hearth had burned low, and the invading shadows crept ever closer to its dwindling light and warmth. "If you'll allow me, madam, I will add more logs to the fire for you."

"As you please," Elise answered quietly, and went to perch on the edge of a tall-backed chair that was drawn up close to the fireplace.

Maxim doffed his cloak and, watching her with close attention, laid it over the back of a companion chair that stood nearby. Self-consciously Elise covered one bare foot with the other as she felt his perusal. She could not imagine what he had found of interest, but the color crept into her cheeks as he took in every detail of her from head to toe. She was greatly relieved when he directed himself to the task of rebuilding the fire.

Going down on one knee before the hearth, Maxim stirred the reddened coals, laid kindling on the glowing heap, and then placed several logs upon the growing flames. "There, that should chase away the chill."

"Lord Seymour . . ." Her voice was small and quiet in the room.

"There's no need to be so formal, Elise," Maxim assured her as he looked at her askance. "I've no real claim to a title anymore."

"A situation no doubt caused by my uncle."

"You've probably heard the story many times," he responded. "I need not explain."

Elise folded her hands in her lap and swept her gaze

about the room until he bent to poke at the kindling, then her eyes wandered back to him, drawn by a growing curiosity. The feeding flames curled upward around the rough bark of the logs, casting a golden glow upon his crisply chiseled profile. She could not remember ever having taken such close and careful note of a man before, and to her recollection she had never seen one who so epitomized her vision of the Apollo of ancient fables. The question burned to be answered. Could such a man be a murderer? "I've heard many tales about you, my lord, and I often wonder what is true."

Maxim laughed shortly and, looking up at her, braced an arm across a leather-covered knee. "Are you suffering qualms at being alone with me because you think I'm a murderer?"

Elise lifted her chin a notch as his words pricked her ire. "I'm not afraid of you."

"Nay . . . I doubt that you are." He slowly nodded as he contemplated the regal set of her jaw. She had more mettle than any maid he had ever known. "At least, you've never shown any indication that you are."

"Well?" she pressed.

"My dear Elise." He addressed her as if beginning a lecture. "On occasion I've had to take up my sword and kill a man in the performance of my duty, whether it was as protector of the Queen or in some alleyway where my own life was threatened, but I pray you believe, fair maid, that I've never murdered anyone, especially in my own house. I had just arrived home that evening to dress for a banquet that was being held in honor of Arabella. I was told by a servant that an agent from the Queen awaited me. When I went to meet the man, I found him lying beside the fireplace. It looked as if he had just fallen and struck his head, for he bore an ugly wound across his brow and there was blood on the mantel, but later it was discovered that he had been stabbed. That has caused me considerable confusion, for when I first tended him there was no sign of any such wound. In fact, he was alive, and I was about to summon help when I heard a noise from the loggia and ran out to see who might be hiding outside. My meeting with the agent was meant to be private, but Edward later told the Queen that he saw me there with the agent. To have done so, he would have had to have been the one hiding on the loggia."

"Are you saying my uncle came in after you left the agent and then stabbed the man? I cannot believe that. Uncle Edward would never kill anyone! He's much too fainthearted for such a foul deed."

Maxim chuckled at her honesty. "I thought so, too, but he obviously witnessed the fact that I was there. Why would he accuse me of killing the man if he were all that innocent of the deed himself?"

"Do you hate my uncle because you think he blamed you to cover his own crime? It certainly seemed your intent to kill him when I left the hall."

" 'Tis not my desire to see Edward dead. At least, not yet. I would like him to suffer the humiliation of being found out a liar, a thief, and a coward. I cannot swear he murdered the agent, but his guilt will be found out, I've no doubt."

"Even if you must arrange it?"

"For the present, Edward is safe from me." Maxim raised a brow at her. "Perhaps you should be grateful for your uncle's sake that I cannot go back to England."

"I'm no blood kin to Edward," Elise admitted thoughtfully. "My mother was an orphan, left as a wee babe on the Stamford lands."

"Your character shows me vast improvement with that knowledge." A grin twitched at the corners of his lips. "There may be hope for you yet."

"And what of Arabella?" Elise countered. "Did you see any hope in her, being his daughter?"

Maxim responded with a wayward smile. "I could never understand how Edward managed to sire so splendid a creature."

The warming heat of the fire touched Elise's cheek, and for the first time that evening she felt a comfort and security she had not known for some hours. Surreptitiously she observed the man again as he stretched long, thin fingers toward flames that flickered ever higher, and she wondered distantly if his presence in the keep had anything to do with her feeling of well-being. Was she so dubious of Fitch and Spence's protection that she would find safety in the company of a rogue lord?

"Nicholas knows how to give good gifts," Maxim commented as he nodded toward the rug lying on the floor beside her bed. "He will spare no coin to see you happy."

"I've been told that your coins purchased the gown I was wearing this afternoon..." Elise raised a lovely brow and needled as she asked, "Or should I accept the gift as replacement for my own clothes that were ruined during my capture?"

Ignoring her sharp jab, Maxim lifted his gaze to the frayed woolen gown hanging from a peg. "Is that the only thing you have to wear around here?"

Elise straightened her posture to display a haughty mien and gazed at him from her chair, as if she were a queen looking down upon her subject. "Do I detect a slur against my wardrobe, my lord?"

A snort of derision expressed his opinion adequately.

Feigning sorrow, Elise placed a delicately boned

hand over the fur pelt covering her breast. "I'm wounded to the quick."

Maxim's brief glance swept along the contour of her face, taking in every detail of it. The girl was not only comely, but she had wit and humor, which in truth Arabella had seemed at times to lack. A slow grin tugged at his lips. "I shall address you to a clothier's on the morrow. There you may select several gowns to fit your needs. The dressmaker knows of me and will take the order on account until you receive it."

"I'm overwhelmed by your generosity, my lord."

Maxim caught the sarcasm in her statement and lifted himself to his feet. "I've overstayed my welcome, it seems. The air grows chilly once again."

The hearth gave off more warmth than it had all day, but Elise shrugged pertly, ignoring his subtle meaning and the green eyes that rested upon her. "As you please, my lord."

Taking up his cloak, Maxim stepped to the doorway, but paused there to glance back at her. "You'll need slippers and shoes to keep your feet warm. There's also a shoemaker in Hamburg where you may acquire what you have need of."

"Will I be going with Fitch and Spence?" she queried innocently.

"Indeed, no!" Maxim answered with a short laugh. "You'll have them locked up in a goose cage within moments of your arrival. I shall do the honors myself."

"Am I then to be presented as your prisoner? If that be the case, you can hardly expect me to abide a fitting while you're present."

"You needn't fear, madam. I shall be elsewhere. I'm sure the dressmaker knows how to keep you well enough."

Elise slumped back in her chair and frowned petulantly. What kind of woman was this dressmaker any-way that he could be so confident about leaving her?

Maxim turned to leave, but she bade him pause once more.

"A moment, I pray you, my lord." She twisted her thin fingers worriedly as he faced her. "I should like to announce that I've hired a cook for us."

The handsome brows gathered into a suspicious frown. "Indeed? And where did you find this cook?"

"Nicholas allowed me to have his."

"No doubt after much sugar-coated pleading on your part!" Maxim snapped, and wondered why his anger was so easily roused. "Nicholas would not let his cook go to me without a promised sweetmeat, which you seemed ready and willing to give him . . ." His voice sharpened with the accusation. "Even while I was here!"

"You're only afraid of the coins you might lose," she charged with a flippant toss of her head. "You do not consider we might have starved to death waiting on *you* to find us a cook! I think Nicholas conveyed a most compassionate trait in allowing *his* cook to come to work for *you.*"

"You think!" Maxim barked. "Why, you can't even see that Nicholas means to have you . . ."

"As his wife!" Elise finished sharply, flinging herself from her chair. Instinct told her that he would say otherwise.

With ponderous steps Maxim strode back to her until he stood close before her. He leaned down slightly until his eyes fairly blazed above her own, and as he gave her answer his reply built to an angry shout. "You mean as *his mistress!*"

Her own eyes flashing, Elise pushed with all of her strength against his hardened chest, but Maxim re-mained obstinately stubborn and the best she gained was the loss of her wrap which slid from her naked shoulders. Even so, the proximity of such an outrageous fiend made her oblivious to her own appearance as she slowly pounded his chest. "Get out!" she demanded. "Be gone from here!"

Maxim's eyes swept downward to where the delicate chemise molded itself to the full curves of her bosom. The soft, pale peaks strained against the gossamer thinness of the garment, making him aware of her womanliness. The fact that she could so casually reveal herself to him made him inexplicably furious. Was she such a bold wench then? Unchaste? Wanton? If she displayed such a lack of modesty with him, what treasure would she allow Nicholas to view?

His ire was quickly surmounted by a swiftly growing passion which only heightened his anger. His cheeks tensed as he struggled against his needs. Still, the hot blood flowed into his loins and started his pulse pounding in his ears. He had seen her in the early afternoon as a properly groomed lady, all soft and warm and beautiful, and he had found her stirringly appealing. Now here she was a fiery, sultry vixen who whet his appetite no small degree. Her breasts gleamed with the luster of pearls, luminescent where bathed by the firelight and darkly shadowed in the deep valley between those pale orbs. He was suddenly possessed by a raging desire to seize the wench and ease his long-starved passions with her.

Clenching his teeth, Maxim leaned closer until Elise's entire vision was filled with his snarling face. Even then he had to steel himself against violence as her heady fragrance invaded his being and wafted through his senses. "Do you think me a bloody eunuch, wench?" he questioned harshly. "Cover yourself before I spill your virgin blood!"

Elise's breath caught in a shocked gasp, and she

stumbled back with flaming cheeks, snatching the fur robe around her shoulders. Only then did she dare raise her gaze, shamed by a rebuke that made her painfully aware of her own carelessness.

Maxim still glared at her as he battled his desires. His lean nostrils flared above tight lips, from whence came harshly rasped words. "I went to England for a bride, and if not for you, I would have had me one, willing and warm. Now I have a man's need roiling in the pit of my belly, and unless you be wary, madam, you will find yourself serving my needs. I'm not one to abuse a lady so, but now that Arabella is forever lost to me, any wench will do." His steely green eyes bore into her. "As you may be aware, madam, many a belated vow has atoned for a gentleman's ravishment of a reluctant maid."

He turned sharply and stalked from the room, leaving Elise staring after him in awed amazement until the fires of her own rage ignited into unparalleled fury. Following in the path of his footsteps, she went to the door and slammed it closed.

How dare the man threaten her with rape! She dropped the bar in place across its plank.

Did he think her some easy strumpet to abide his crude exercise of rutting manhood? She paced to and fro in front of the hearth.

By heavens, he would hear from her on the morrow! She would chastise him with a volley of verbal attacks that would rend that strutting cock to the core of his conceit!

Chapter 11

*T*HE FORMER MARQUESS sat the back of his horse with his hands resting on the high pommel of the saddle. Below the wooded bluff whereon he had paused, a river meandered peacefully between ice-crusted banks. On the far shore, patches of snow sparkled between growths of evergreens, and now and then a small, furry creature could be seen scurrying about in a perpetual search for food.

Maxim raised his head and watched a small flock of birds flit and swoop on the airy rushes of wind above the vale. Beyond their darting flights the sky was an azure blue. Only an occasional cloud scudded past to cast its shadow upon the land as the southerly breezes blew warming gusts through the treetops and out across the snow-bedecked meadows and forest glades. Maxim's gaze ranged far and wide, but he saw little of what met his eyes, for his mind was turned inward upon a memory. He had seen sapphire eyes alight with fire and auburn tresses cascading in glorious splendor over a scantily clad bosom, and the visions of her beauty haunted him. He was a man snared by a trap of his own making. The heat of a lengthy abstinence had thrust him to the very brink of restraint, and only by dint of will had he hauled himself back from that abrupt precipice, crushing the urge to sweep her into his arms and carry her to her bed. The fact that he had reacted with such intensity and threatened her with rape left him struggling with a painful chagrin.

Maxim forced his meandering thoughts to a more agreeable subject, his once-cherished betrothed. Now there was one who by her sweetness and quiet reserve merited his attention! No one argued that Arabella, by nature, was the epitome of a genteel lady and a serene beauty. His mind had always found succor when he sought out the memories they had made together, and he almost relaxed as he waited for his tensions to dissolve. Instead, he found himself grasping for images of her soft, gray eyes and the silken curl of her light brown hair. The visions were vague and indistinct. The curve of her lips escaped him. The shape of her nose and the curve of her chin shifted in a confused blur as he tried to evoke her visage. A weak smile of acquiescence was all he could recall of her response when he had presented his case for marriage to Edward. The memory stirred nothing in his breast, let alone in his loins. What eldritch wisdom had Nicholas been privy to that had allowed him to sense this pallid reaction, while he had himself been convinced that a raging passion, worthy of the risk of death, had goaded him? Was it for revenge alone that he had sought Arabella's abduction, as Von Reijn had suggested?

Cautiously, as if he sought to pluck a red-hot coal from amid the glowing embers of his mind, Maxim tested the accuracy of his recall of a momentarily glimpsed view of lustrous breasts nestled in the careless cover of a fur wrap, and pale peaks erect with a chill. His will betrayed him, and his memory expanded to a broad spectrum of visions that came at him from every quarter of his mind. He could see his charge's lips drawn tight in a sneer, then soft and gently parted as she slumbered. In his mind her russet hair spread out like a dark halo over her pillow. Her lashes rested like soft shadows on her cheeks or were flung wide, fringing deep blue eyes that smoldered dark with anger. He could imagine the set of her tensed jaw as she berated him and the slender column of her throat, from the lobe of her ear to a pale shoulder and the soft roundness of her breasts as she stood boldly before him and answered his objections, point for point.

Maxim cursed beneath his breath as he realized what those impressions extracted from him. Anger and frustration spiraled upward with the awareness of his desire. He fought against this burgeoning attraction that left him both outraged with himself and shaken by its swift encroachment into his life. Who was this waspish maid to be ever in the way, ever testing, ever trying his patience, ever thwarting him? He had no need for her to entangle his mind with her winsome looks and softly curving form. He was a man without a country, an outcast to the world, and before he could claim his worth and his place in society again, he had to set his affairs in order, or perhaps die trying. He had no time to be preoccupied with cravings that left him rutting after a reluctant and headstrong minx. Like a small, vindictive snipe, she would only turn on him again, rejecting any advance he would make.

The black stallion pranced in sudden apprehension, seeming to sense his master's vexation. Maxim touched his heels against the trembling flanks, and the animal leapt forward in an abrupt release of energy. The steed stretched out into an easy canter that swept away the troubling turmoil that roiled in Maxim's mind, and for a time they followed the level ground at the top of a bluff. The ridge lowered, and they passed through a widely spaced copse of evergreens. The stream, released from the steeply confining barrier of the cliffs, lent its overflow on the low far shore to form a marshy pond where tall, ice-bound rushes twinkled and glittered beneath the bright rays of the sun.

Slowing Eddy to a walk, Maxim deliberately directed his attention to the hunt. He nudged the stallion across a shallow expanse in the frigid water where a series of ripples gave evidence of a rocky base that would permit a crossing. Upon gaining the far bank, he dismounted and tied the steed beneath an ancient oak which spread its barren branches across a narrow glade. Slipping the bow from across his back, he braced the end in a soft-booted instep and, in one easy motion, strung the weapon. He nocked a blunt birding arrow and, with practiced, silent tread, made his way toward the pond where a muted gaggling gave evidence that a flock of late geese were feeding in the open water at the edge of a growth of reeds. Drawing the bow, he sent the arrow unerringly on its way. A gander took the blow, flopped once, and slowly spread its wings to float in still repose upon the surface of the breeze-riffled water.

Maxim retrieved the goose, tied its legs with leather thongs, and secured his prize behind the cantle. A movement in the trees across the stream caught his eye, and as he scanned the low brush that bordered the bank, a stag in its third season or so stepped out, cautiously surveyed the area, then lowered his head to drink from the river. Streams of light from the mounting sun lit the mists of the icy glade, seeming to bring each color and sound to the perfect pitch of excitement. Maxim went down upon one knee and, setting an arrow with a sharp broadhead to string, took the shot from beneath Eddy's neck. The stag coughed with the impact as the shaft pierced his heart and leapt forward, then crumpled to his knees and collapsed, felled in one swift stroke.

Maxim considered his fallen prey, musing in rueful reflection. If not wary, he could be taken down by the cruel arrows of that enticing little vixen. Indeed, she would lead him about by the nose as she did that great oaf, Von Reijn, and where would he be but cast upon the rocky crags of frustration's shore and left to flounder on the reefs of despair?

Elise drummed her fingers against her hips as she stood with arms akimbo in the great hall. She had primed herself to lay the sharp side of her tongue upon the pompous pride of the lord and master of this crumbling keep, and was raked with peevish disappointment to find him gone.

"And where has Lord Seymour hied himself this early morning hour?" she demanded of Fitch.

" 'Is lor'ship's gone a-huntin', 'e 'as. Gone out ta fill the larder wit' fresh meat for the cook," the man replied. He had been around the girl long enough to sense when she was annoyed about something, and in an effort to lighten her mood he pointed out the fact of their much-improved state of circumstance. "Aye, ye can be sure whilst 'is lor'ship is 'ere, we won't be starvin'. An' for yerself, mistress, the master 'as bade me tell ye 'e'll be takin' ye ta 'Amburg when 'e comes back 'round the noon hour. 'E asked for ye ta kindly be ready."

"As his lordship commands," Elise returned with ill-feigned meekness.

Her testy reply made Fitch wary of testing her disposition. He hastily made his excuses and took his leave, seeking out the security of the stable. There, he began to groom the lady's horse as his lordship had bade. Hopefully, by improving the nag's appearance, he could lift the maid's spirits and thereby prevent another confrontation between his master and his charge.

Elise had no immediate desire to return to her chambers or to garb herself in finery. It would be a while yet before the Marquess returned, and she felt in need of a short respite in which she could detach herself from the keep and roam the hillside at her leisure.

Her dream of the previous night came back to haunt her as she donned her cloak. She could not place any degree of reliance on the meanderings of her mind, nor could she accept any part of the dream as truth until she could delve into the matter. She had no real evidence that her father had been seized by the Hansa, yet the chance of such a coincidence happening was well within the realm of possibility, for he had gone to the Stilliards frequently in the months prior to his abduction. She would have to keep an attentive ear and eye upon those cities she visited, in the hope that she would glean some small bit of knowledge about her father.

Pulling the woolen hood of her cloak over her head, Elise stepped out onto the front stoop and looked about. Though the sun was shining brightly, reflecting off the windows and patches of crusty snow, blustery winds chilled the air and gave strong evidence of the crispness of this early December morn. Slowly she descended the steps and made her way across the courtyard. No hue and cry was raised as she crossed the bridge, and once past the moat she followed a path along its edge where the castle wall gave protection from the frigid blasts of air.

On a sun-swept hillock Elise paused, seeing her way barred by thick brambles and briars. Clumps of snow weighted down the dense thatch of grass growing beneath the thorny bushes and she could see no sign of a trail though her gaze ranged far afield. Finding no haven to tempt her progress, she turned back upon the path, but a sharp prickle against her ankle made her pause. She lifted her skirts to pluck the thistle from the top of her hide shoes and flinched as the tiny barb pricked the flesh of her finger. She stared at the tip of the digit as her mind began to roam along a devious course, and a slow, wicked smile began to grow and widen. Of a sudden she wondered how the mighty lord of the castle keep might react if he found spiny barbs in his bed. Oh, what sweet revenge she could extract from him, and there would be no need to place herself in jeopardy or to suffer any qualms about him overtaking her in her flight to safety. She would be securely ensconced in her chambers with the door well-bolted and braced against his intrusion.

Laughing aloud, Elise raised her skirts, unfastened a string tie, and shook herself out of her petticoat. The quickest way to gather the burrs was to whip a cloth over the grass and bushes, allowing them to attach themselves to the piece. It was certainly a less painful method than picking them separately. In no time at all she had gathered enough to meet her purpose, and she wrapped the undergarment into a ball to protect herself from the discomfort of the tiny barbs as she hurried back along the trail. She must hasten now. Maxim could return at any moment.

Once more Elise crossed the courtyard and assured herself that both Fitch and Spence were out of the keep before ascending to her chambers. Fetching the comb Maxim had deigned to give her from her chambers, she continued her climb to the third floor. Stripping the furs from the bed and turning back the sheet, she set herself to her labors. Carefully she combed the burrs from the petticoat and shook them over the coarse ticking of the mattress, liberally covering the surface. When this was done, she spread the sheet and replaced the furs exactly as they had been.

Tiptoeing stealthily to the door, she assured herself that the passage was clear before she left the lofty chambers. It was time now to get ready for the trip to Hamburg, and she wasted no moment in her haste to do so. Her mood had taken on an impish bend, and she was quite happy and pert when, some time later, Maxim rapped on her chamber door.

"I'm coming," she promptly called and, catching up her cloak, swung open the portal. She paused as his eyes swept down her, taking in every detail, and a curious, questioning quirk lifted her brow as he met her gaze. "Next time you undress me, my lord, at least leave me my shimmy," she chided. " 'Tis rather drafty in the hall."

"I was merely admiring the gown," Maxim excused. And all within it, his mind accused.

"I realize you intended the clothes for Arabella," Elise needled, deliberately setting the spurs to him. "But under the circumstances I'm sure she won't mind, since she has a husband to buy her such costly garb."

Maxim scowled harshly. It disturbed him to be reminded of Arabella, but strangely it was not for reasons he might have expected. His feeling of guilt goaded him. It was as if he had turned his back on every commitment he had ever made to Arabella—and yet, it was she who had accepted another on the very heels of his purported death. When he thought back upon it, she had not mourned his loss for very long at all.

Maxim directed a curt nod toward the stairs. "Shall we go?"

Hurrying past him, Elise swept down the hall and

began her descent, leaving Maxim to stare after her in some confusion at her haste. His easy strides brought him swiftly to her side, but Elise dared not glance at him for fear he might glimpse something akin to admiration in her face. He looked quite dashing and debonair in leather-trimmed green doublet and trunk hose, and though he was the one whom she had the most cause to hate, she had to admit he was probably the most handsome man she had ever met in her life.

"Allow me," Maxim bade at the front portal as he took her cloak. Settling the fur-lined garment upon her shoulders, he reached past her to swing open the door and executed a brief but courtly bow.

Elise was taken aback by his gentlemanly display, and felt a certain unease when faced with the gallant side of his nature. It was far easier to remain aloof and distant when he ranted and raved. She swept through the portal with a small nod of gratitude and paused on the stoop in a place where it was protected from the probing winds. Maxim followed a moment later, having donned a cloak, and descended the stone steps.

Fitch was waiting with Eddy and gave the reins over to his lordship, then ran back to fetch the lady's steed. In response to a gentle nuzzling Maxim rubbed the stallion's velvet-soft nose affectionately. He paused as his fingers traced small, raised weals on either side of the animal's nose and leaned back slightly to carefully examine the pattern of scars. Four thin lines ran together, such as a small, furred creature might make in an attack. "What is this?" he asked as if questioning his steed. "What have you tangled with, old boy? You look as if you've run afoul of a cat."

Eddy rolled his eyes, and Elise felt them pause on her for an accusative moment. She shrugged off the idea of the mute condemnation and, pulling on a pair of gloves, made her descent. She glanced around as she heard Fitch coming with her mount and stared in amazement at the sight that greeted her. The short, squat, shaggy white mare she had dubbed "Angel" would certainly have been a shameful palfrey for any lady of quality to claim, especially when brought in sharp contrast to the powerful black steed, but now, with a festive array of tiny bells and colored rag ribbons twined through the stiffly rebellious white mane, the mare looked utterly ridiculous.

The sight broke Maxim's demeanor and elicited a burst of uproarious mirth from him until he caught sight of Fitch's puzzled expression. Immediately he squelched his laughter as he realized the man had probably labored most of the morning in an effort to groom the mare and make it presentable for the lady.

Elise's indignation had been sparked by Maxim's amused guffaws and she might have vented her rage right then and there if not for the fact that Fitch had thought he was doing a kind service for her. She could not abuse his tender heart in such a fashion. It was the not-so-noble lord she wanted to wreak her anger upon, and she settled a withering glare upon that one before graciously extending her hand to the bemused servant.

Elise seated herself upon the decorated nag and adjusted her cloak and gown for a moment before accepting the reins and quirt from Fitch. Applying the short whip, she encouraged the animal to its fastest pace and rode forward without even a brief glance toward her escort. The small hooves clattered across the bridge before the heavier hoofbeats of Eddy's bold trot were heard behind her. Chuckling as he passed her, Maxim took the lead and then slowed the stallion to match the plodding gait of the mare. Now and then he turned in his saddle to take in the sight, and his laughter would echo back from the hills.

The winds died down, as did finally the sounds of his lordship's amusement, and with the sun high in the sky, the day warmed to a most comfortable degree. The snow became wet and the path softened beneath Eddy's hooves. Elise's short-legged steed splash-plopped along in the deeper tracks, and with each step the small hooves threw up splatterings of muddied snow until the lower belly and legs of the mare were no longer white.

The tinkling of the tiny bells echoed in the hushed silence of the hillocks and forests as they passed along the trail. It was not an unpleasant sound, and Elise found her irritation easing by slow degrees as she began to enjoy the outing. Though Von Reijn's heavy escort had brought home to her an awareness of the dangers that might abound when traveling this far from the well-used paths, a strange security suffused her which made her wonder at its source. Perhaps she had faced too many threats of late and grown contemptuous of them all. Or could it have been the presence of her companion that eased her qualms?

A stout English bow and a quiver of arrows were slung behind his saddle. A sword hung from his side, and there was an alert readiness in his manner and the bold erect way in which he sat his horse. That black beast in himself was enough to stir caution in the stoutest of hearts. The great hooves lifted and fell with ponderous regularity, yet with an ease that only hinted of a fair turn of speed.

Elise focused her attention more closely upon the man, and though he seemed at ease, she saw his head turn slightly as he scanned each bush, copse, or thicket where danger might lurk. If a bird flushed, his eyes followed it. If a branch moved, he assured himself it was only the wind. She pondered on his silence and the attitude he displayed. He seemed quite responsible about her safety and comfort and glanced about often to assure himself of both.

Elise almost cringed at the remembrance of the burrs beneath his sheet, but she shrugged off the brief pang of conscience. He was due much more than she was able to deliver him. To be certain, when taking into account what she had suffered because of him, she should listen with eager ear for his reaction.

After a time Maxim halted and pulled Eddy aside. When she drew abreast, he paced her for a moment. "All is well with you, Elise?" he queried solicitously and, at her nod, questioned further, "You're warm enough? And comfortable?"

Elise inclined her head again without comment.

" 'Tis well then, but if you should have a need, just call out." As if on his own accord Eddy resumed his position in the van.

"Amazing," Elise sighed to herself as she watched the pair. Horse and man seemed like one, but when Reland had ridden the stallion his commands had usually been accompanied by a heavy-handed sawing on the reins and a pronounced flogging of the heels. Frequently the Earl had equipped himself with spurs and heavy gauntlets and, for an excuse, had cited Eddy's high spirit and reluctance to obey. He had preened and smirked in self-satisfaction when he gained the awe of those who would listen. "Takes a brawny man with a hand of steel to keep a big one like this in check."

Yet here was one who belied Reland's harsh hand by a light touch on the reins. He never affected a spur, and yet the horse almost danced beneath him as if eager for his weight and companionship. "Should he bend that gentle touch to a lady, such a one would no doubt be anxious to respond," she mused with a hint of mirth. "Except for me, of course." She mentally denied the possibility. "I've had enough of rags and ropes and chests and such. I would not be so susceptible."

She lifted her gaze from Eddy's flowing tail to the broad square shoulders of the man atop him. "Maxim seems more at ease facing danger," she pondered, "than confronting the likes of a simple maid. If he could only understand my..."

Her mind ground to a halt. *"Maxim?"* 'Tis the second time today I've thought of him like that. How so? Do my musings betray me? Is there in this heart a softening for the man?"

Tentatively Elise formed a vision of herself richly gowned and he, wealthily attired, entering some majestic and courtly chamber with her hand upon his arm. In her mind she heard the hushing of the crowd as all eyes turned to see and the low murmur of the ladies as they admired her escort with glowing eyes. A flood of emotion washed through her, tinging the blue of her eyes with a subtle green. She knew her answer before a blush filled her face with warmth and, afraid to entertain it further, flung the thought from her mind before it blossomed into words.

In some embarrassment Elise retreated from the illusion and shifted her eyes away to follow the flight of a small flock of birds from a bush. She deliberately recalled the abuses of her person and polished each incident with care until she felt the familiar, now-welcome heat of anger and resentment rise up within her again. Only a wee, small voice from deep within her mind warned her to take care. This impassioned hatred would take careful tending to survive, and she dared not dally overmuch in her musings if he was to receive his just reward.

They gained the outer limits of Hamburg and a few moments later entered into the bustling activity of the city. Maxim rode beside her through the slush-covered streets, and finally they came to a halt in front of a group of small shops. Elise had a deep reluctance to dismount for fear of ruining her slippers and soiling the hem of her gown. Yestereve's snowfall and the warmth of today's sun had left the streets well-mired with melting muck. At the present moment a pair of tall chopines would have greatly eased her dilemma. Yet there was little choice left her but to dismount as gracefully as she could manage. She could hardly plod barefoot across the thoroughfare.

Elise delayed as long as possible, searching for a dryer place to dismount, and lifted a somewhat worried frown to Maxim when he stepped around the head of the mare.

"Are you in need of assistance?" he asked with an amused smile.

Her countenance turned quizzical. "Are you offering it?"

"Aye, that I am, madam."

Her dismay faded. "Then I gladly accept."

Maxim swept the toque from his head and made a gallant leg. "Your servant, fair maid." His white teeth flashed in a sudden broad grin, then he settled the hat jauntily upon his head. Slipping one arm behind her back and the other beneath her knees, he plucked her clear of the saddle. Catching her high against his chest, he took several tottering steps backward as the thick mud sucked at his boots.

Elise caught her breath and closed her eyes tightly, expecting to be immersed into the well-churned slush at any moment, then the world settled and all was still. Cautiously she opened her eyes to find the green ones staring into her own at a very close range. Maxim plumbed the sapphire depths with a leisured thoroughness until she realized that she had locked both her arms tightly about his neck in her panic.

Seeing the warmth flood over her face, Maxim nodded ever so slightly and, in a soft voice, embarrassed her further. "My pleasure, madam, I assure you."

Elise brought her right hand from around his neck, but there was no place to rest her left arm except around his neck. She could feel the stavelike firmness of his muscular ribs against her and the rock-hard steadiness of his arms. Unbidden, a vision from an earlier morn stirred in her mind, and beneath his regard her face reddened perceptibly.

They reached the door of the shop, and Maxim's arm twisted beneath her as he lifted the latch and nudged the portal open with a shoulder. Stepping inside, he lowered her to the floor with a prolonged gentleness that set her senses to reeling. She glanced away for a moment until by sheer dint of will she regained her composure, piece by shattered piece. 'Twas the same old haughty stare she meant to bend on him when she faced him again, but that too faded as he pressed a sizable purse into her hand.

"This should see you reasonably attired for the moment," he murmured.

Though Elise searched his face, she could read nothing in it to stir her resentment. Absent was the satire and scorn she had expected. In truth, his smiling eyes were soft and almost tender as he cupped the hand holding the purse between the two of his.

"For the time being I must bid you contain yourself to whatever the purse will allow until I am able to afford a richer wardrobe for you."

"You need not waste your coins on me, my lord," Elise responded, regaining her aloofness. "As your prisoner I hardly expect to be favored with gifts."

Maxim folded his hands behind his back as he bent a pointed stare upon her. "Unless you have some penchant for selecting the outlandish, I trust the new gowns will not be a waste. In any case, the choice will be yours to make and bear the consequences of. Almost anything will be better than that rag you wear about the castle. I would see you better gowned than that."

Ponderous footsteps came from the rear of the shop, and Maxim turned to greet the large woman who came into view. *"Guten Tag, Frau* Reinhardt. *Mein Name ist* Maxim Seymour. *Ich sei Freund mit Kapitan* Von Reijn..."

"Of course!" the dressmaker answered in crisp English, and chortled exuberantly as she continued. "How good it is to meet you. Captain Von Reijn spoke to me some time ago and said he thought you would be coming in."

"Von Reijn's foresight is unlimited," Maxim returned graciously. "He's a man who knows quality, and you came well-recommended."

A blush of pleasure suffused the round face. Madam Reinhardt, a true Englishwoman at heart, had been a widow for some three years now and though the number of her years was increasing, she had not grown so old to be oblivious to the charm of a well-spoken English gentleman, especially one whose handsomeness compelled most women to stare in fond appreciation. "The captain is most kind, sir, as you are." She swept a hand about to indicate the cloak and gown Elise was wearing. "I remember when Captain Von Reijn ordered these made. 'Tis a joy to see them so well-displayed."

"Having seen such evidence of your talents, madam, we have come to enlist your aid in the matter of other gowns. You will take care of my charge's needs?" Maxim inquired.

"Certainly, sir. Is she your..." Curiosity prompted the question, but proper decorum made her hesitate. It was a foolish woman who ruined a chance at profit by an unchecked tongue. Still, the pair made a most attractive couple, and she had always been intrigued by affairs of the heart.

"In my care for the moment." He cleared his throat and examined the detail of a nearby fabric. "She was ...ah...inadvertently separated from her uncle, through no fault of her own, of course." He turned and, taking the widow's hand, gave her such a smile that she began to recall the more tender moments of her own marriage and completely forgot the subject at hand. "For her own protection," he continued in a low voice, "I would prefer the young lady remain here with you, until my return."

"Indeed, Master Seymour. There is always a threat on the streets for a lovely young lady if she is not properly escorted."

Maxim dared not face his charge to receive the accusing stare she no doubt would be tempted to give him. "Then you understand the necessity for keeping watch over her. She can be quite willful at times."

"Certainly, sir. You need not worry."

"Good, then I will take my leave." He faced Elise, whose brows were slanted downward with a sharply piqued frown. She made it apparent that she disliked the way he cautioned the woman. "Be a good child while I'm gone," he admonished, leaning down to place a light peck upon her cheek. He felt her stiffen as he laid a hand upon her arm. "I shall return as soon as possible."

"Oh, I'm sure we can manage quite well without

you, my lord," Elise assured him. "There's little reason for you to hurry."

"To be sure, sir," Madam Reinhardt agreed. "Take your time."

Maxim bestowed a doubtful stare upon Elise and was uneasy with the innocent smile she gave in return. He opened his mouth to speak a word of caution, but closed it again, deciding that he would only add tinder to whatever mischievous flame burned behind those deep blue orbs.

Elise tucked Maxim's purse into her own as the door closed behind him. Removing her gloves, she watched him lead Eddy and the bedraggled mare away, leaving her no way to flee the shop but on foot. "Always suspicious," she mused. "A body would think he wants to keep me his prisoner."

She faced Madam Reinhardt abruptly. "I would send a message to Captain Von Reijn. Do you have someone who can go?"

The widow clasped her hands tightly together to keep from wringing them. There was a no-nonsense firmness in the younger woman's voice that somehow boded ill for Master Seymour's wishes. "I . . . I suppose I can send the neighbor boy . . ."

"Good! I shall pay whatever is reasonable." Elise shrugged out of her cloak and laid it across a chair while Madam Reinhardt wallowed in a quandary. Elise saw the indecision in the woman's face and laughingly laid a calming hand upon her arm.

"Madam Reinhardt, the matter is really quite simple. Although Lord Seymour is my . . . uh . . . guardian of the moment, Captain Von Reijn holds my moneys on account, and if I'm to pay for my clothes, I must contact him. Please send the boy and let us get on with the selections."

In relief Madam Reinhardt hurried from her shop

to find the boy and, with a promise of a small reward, sent him on the errand. She returned to find her customer already making selections of material from a private collection that was kept in a cabinet near the far corner of the shop. Realizing she had left the armoire unlatched, the dressmaker set up a renewed fretting, for the fabrics which the girl was closely examining were some of the finest and most expensive in the shop. To be sure, only her wealthiest patrons could afford such raiment. Doubtful of the girl's ability to pay, the woman brought out several bolts of less costly material. "I'm sure these would be lovely on you, my dear."

Graciously Elise looked at everything that Madam Reinhardt placed before her, but with each, shook her head in firm decision. "These are more to my liking," she said at last, indicating the fine silks, plush velvets, and rich brocades closeted in the armoire. "Is there some difficulty with these fabrics?"

"Why, my dear, the cost alone poses a problem! These fabrics are worth a great deal! Are you sure you can pay?"

Turning aside, Elise withdrew a pouch from beneath her skirt and counted out a small stack of sovereigns. "This will serve as a deposit for what I would order from you," she assured the woman. "Captain Von Reijn will affirm that I'm capable of paying for the rest."

The dressmaker hefted the heavy coins in her hand, feeling the soft touch of gold. She turned aside momentarily to test one between her teeth, then breathlessly counted out the coins, flipping them over with a finger. They were all new and unshaved. She raised her gaze in amazement. "A deposit? Why, these would pay for a pair of gowns made from such cloth."

"I know full well what the coins will buy, madam,

but I have a desire to be outfitted in a better manner. I've been negligent of my attire of late, and I mean to correct the condition posthaste." She leaned forward with a coy smile and murmured confidentially, "You see, I'm being courted by a brace of wealthy suitors, and as you may be able to understand, I cannot portray myself a pauper in their company, lest the pair become wary of my sincerity."

Her statement was true for the most part. Nicholas was wealthy and desired to court her, and although her clothes had always been of a fine quality, she had been rather conservative about her selections in the past, buying only what she had deemed necessary and, even then, dressing in dark shades and subdued styles. She now felt a desire to change that pattern and laid the reason primarily to a need to be adaptable to any occasion that might arise in her search for her father. Certainly if Nicholas introduced her to any of the more influential members of the Hanseatic League, her gowns should be of a quality worthy of the moment. Who could say what information she might gain through such a meeting?

She had other more personal reasons for a change, reasons she found harder to put a finger to. Arabella had always given great attention to her own appearance, which fact had never bothered Elise before, but the remembrance of the Marquess's casual taunt and denial of her ability to be a fit replacement for her cousin gnawed at her, and though she had no feelings save hatred for the man, she felt a rankling need to make him eat his words. It goaded her that he could dismiss her so easily as someone unworthy of a man's devotion. He had made it quite clear that he wanted her to serve his baser pleasures, but for his cherished one, it seemed he reserved that honor for very few women.

Madam Reinhardt's enthusiasm grew apace with her imagination. Such a comely maid would be able to attract a whole flood of eager swains, and it was not farfetched that she should win a wealthy gentleman as her husband. It was understandable that if such a match took place, the man would want to keep his young wife well-clothed, which could possibly mean future profits for her small shop.

"Do you think yourself capable of the task?" Elise questioned in a gracious tone.

Frau Reinhardt drew her large frame up in a proud manner. "There is no finer seamstress in all of Hamburg and abroad."

Elise smoothed her hand down the front of her gown. "I can see you are talented, madam. I've no qualms about that, only your ability to finish the gowns before the end of the month. 'Tis so short a space, but I have naught else to wear for this advent season."

"I shall give the matter my full attention," Madam Reinhardt promised. "Although I may not be able to deliver all of them to you in so short a time, depending on the extent of your order, you'll not be left wanting."

"Then, madam, I will enlist your services."

"You'll not be disappointed, my dear, I assure you."

"Good, then we should get started," Elise suggested. "I have other shops to visit..."

"But Master Seymour...he said you should stay here..."

A chuckle of amusement came from the girl, denying the possibility. "You may follow me if you so desire, madam, but I intend to furnish myself with shoes, hats, and other accessories before this day is done. I shall not be hindered from that purpose."

Meekly Madam Reinhardt folded her hands and gave

no further argument. The girl made it clear that she would not be easily dissuaded from her course of action. In truth, one might be tempted to have pity for the poor souls given such a task.

It was several hours later when Nicholas Von Reijn was found. He answered the summons immediately and after searching several shops through which Elise had left a trail of happy proprietors, he finally found her carefully selecting a fine leather for a pair of lady's boots. The shoemaker was ecstatic with her order and eagerly agreed to have the boots made posthaste and sent out to Faulder Castle to be properly fitted.

Nicholas hid a smile as the man bestowed grateful kisses upon the slender fingers. "Yu've brightened his day considerably, *vrouwelin,*" the captain commented later as he left the shop with her. He plucked at the fur trim of her cloak as he teased. "And here I had thought at last vas a voman who could hoard her vealth and never spend it on trifles."

"Trifles! Of what do you speak, Nicholas?" she protested. "Except for what I have on, I am bereft of all my possessions. Were I to refrain from these purchases, I would soon be without a stitch to wear!"

Nicholas tilted his head in museful imaginings. Now there would be a sight he would walk the whole continent to view. "Maxim is responsible for yur velfare. Let him provide vhat yu need."

Elise's jaw tensed with stubborn insistence. "I shall purchase my own clothing without his help. Which reminds me . . ." She dug in her purse and withdrew the one Maxim had given her. "I should like you to invest this sum also at a high rate of interest collectible within a short period of time. Will that be possible?"

Nicholas spread his hands in dismay. "I've spoiled yu, *vrouwelin.*"

A pretty smile lifted the corners of her lips as Elise

laid a hand upon his arm. " 'Tis true, of course. I never hoped to gain what you have given me for my investment. I perceive you've been far too generous, and if you choose to deny me now, I'll understand."

"Deny yu?" he murmured warmly, covering her hand with his. "If yu ask for my heart, I vould not say yu nay, my dear Elise. I vould give it gladly."

Elise withdrew from him and folded her hands together. The glow of adoration she saw in the pale blue eyes made her feel uncomfortable, and she was not sure why. When Nicholas had visited Faulder Castle, she had been strangely exhilarated and had even encouraged his attentions, but she had also felt a driving desire to wipe the taunting smirk from Maxim's lips by showing him that another man could desire her as much as he had ever desired Arabella. Her enthusiasm had waned when Maxim stormed out of the keep, as if the warmth of her response had been sparked by his challenging presence.

Nicholas escorted her from the shop and again Elise faced the dilemma of the slushy mud. "His lordship has taken the horses and left me afoot. I'll surely ruin my slippers if I try to cross the street."

"No need for yu to fret, my dear. I'll fetch a sedan to see yu safely to the inn," Nicholas offered. "There ve may dine together vhile ve avait Maxim's return."

"You are a soothsayer, Nicholas," Elise declared with the warmth of laughter in her voice. "I'm simply faint with hunger."

"Vhat, vith my cook?" Nicholas rejected her claim with a loud chortle. *"Nein! Nein!* If anything, *vrouwelin,* yu vill grow more hearty." His eyes twinkled as he waggled his head and playfully tried to judge her shape beneath her cloak. "On second thought, I shall fetch *Herr* Dietrich back home. He may ruin the sights of vhich I've grown so fond."

"For shame," Elise rebuked with a coy smile. "You talk more like an undisciplined rogue than any monkish Hansa sea captain."

"Ach! Yu have seen my colors, and vhat shall I say yu now? That I am a fair judge of *frauleins* and yu are the best of the lot?"

"Are you a fair judge?" Elise queried, humor curving her soft lips. "Or have you taken pity on a poor girl who has been stolen from her home?"

Setting his thumbs into his jeweled belt, Nicholas laid his head back and hooted to the heavens. "And have I not eyes in my head to see for myself that yu're the finest bit of vomanhood to grace my company?"

Elise felt her face grow warm with a blush as she glanced about at the townspeople who had paused to stare and gawk at them. The Hansa captain certainly had a way of commanding attention with his booming voice. "Shall we go, Nicholas? I fear we've become a curiosity among the townfolk."

" 'Tis the rare gem they see that attracts them," Nicholas vowed. "Her beauty steals the heart of every man who glimpses her."

Elise responded with a soft chuckle. "Then tell me, Nicholas, why does his lordship hate me so?"

"Bah, he is blind. He yearns for vhat he cannot have and overlooks the treasure vithin his grasp. I vould teach him the vay of vomen had I the time, but I fear it vould be lost on such a stubborn fellow."

Chapter 12

*T*HE GLOOM OF LATE AFTERNOON had deepened the shadows in the common room of the inn, and to ward off the approaching darkness many candles had been lit just as the fire in the huge hearth was stoked to hold back the chill. Maxim had no need of the added illumination to find Von Reijn's table. Even had it been in some area other than the usual, the captain's bellowing laughter drew his notice like a beacon on a stormy night, or more fitting, like the challenging cat-calls of a victor with the spoils. His search for Elise had drawn him through a series of shops in which she had left a trail of purchases which exceeded by nearly thrice the purse he had left, and to be told that she had been escorted through the last few by a most attentive Hansa captain had further chafed his temper. He might have accepted her purchases more graciously had they been a matter of simple indulgence, but the suspicion weighed bold in his mind that she had indulged in a sweet revenge by playing him for a fool and overrunning his allowance for the sole purpose of despoiling his credit and destroying his repute with the merchants of the city. Now here she was enjoying the company of one who yearned to lay the world at her feet.

Maxim's irritation mounted when he passed a small gathering of people and caught sight of the couple seated together at the captain's usual table. Nicholas played the doting swain as he leaned near that charmingly coifed head. The girl's hair had been parted in the middle and then braided into two long lengths before being coiled upon her head to make a comely crown of rich auburn. Feathery wisps had escaped the sedate style to curl in coy abandon around her temples and nape. With the soft candle glow on her face and the firelight at her back, framing her in a warm halo and shining through the thin haze of tendrils, she was the very vision of soft femininity. Maxim remembered the delicate scent of her when he had carried her in his arms that very afternoon, a fragrance that now had to be wafting through Nicholas's senses and tantalizing his imagination.

"Good eventide," Maxim greeted brusquely as he halted beside their table.

"Maxim!" Nicholas cried jovially and rose to grasp Maxim's shoulder in warm greeting. "Ve vere vondering vhere yu had gone." The Hansa captain swept his hand about to indicate a place at the table on his left. "Come! Come join us, my friend."

Ignoring the invitation, Maxim stared down at the girl as he drew off his gloves. His eyes held no warmth to soften the moment, and Elise, feeling his glowering regard, was confused by it. She thought she had never seen his eyes so cold and angry before. He dropped the gloves on the table beside her and, doffing his cloak, settled himself in a chair on her right.

"You must be famished, madam," he commented dryly, rubbing a finger reflectively across his chin. "Every shopkeeper that you visited informed me that you have been most diligent in your labors. And such praises!" He laughed derisively. "I've never heard the like. A fine and comely young lady with excellent taste, they all declared. She has chosen only the best ... every last piece of the best!"

"Oh, surely, my lord, I left something behind." Elise voiced her taunt sweetly as she recognized the reason for his dark mood. "I could not have been *that* extravagant."

Maxim's reply was tensely spoken. "We obviously hold a difference of opinion on the matter. In truth, 'twill have to be discussed when we have more privacy. 'Twould hardly be fitting to air our differences before strangers."

"You speak as if we were more than strangers ourselves, my lord, and have endured a score of years of marriage," Elise needled, and continued with a flippant shrug, not willing to ease his disposition. "I'm sure Nicholas has heard you rant and rave before, and since you coaxed him to take part in your nefarious abduction, 'twould appear the two of you have shared a multitude of diverse and devious plans. I would think a small disagreement is to be expected among kidnappers and their victims. Such tiffs would hardly shock the good captain."

The muscles in Maxim's cheeks flexed with his growing irritation. "I realize now I should have been more cautious of your shrewish bend. Instead, I trusted you ..."

Elise disguised her gibe with a soft, beguiling smile. "Was it not right that I be given as much as you intended to bestow upon Arabella? Did I not suffer as much ... or more?"

The green eyes flashed with fiery indignation. "Do you think I've denied you a like comfort?" he demanded, struggling to control his ripening temper. The little witch had the ability to goad him far beyond reasonable limits. "If that was your cause, then you have far exceeded the boundaries. I gave you what I could afford and nothing less!"

"Come now, Maxim," Nicholas chided. "The girl has been fair..." His words were abruptly silenced by a sudden, sharp nudge against his shin, the sort a lady's slipper would deliver with the force of a quick kick. He glanced at the maid to receive a brief, warning frown and realized she wanted nothing said of the vouchers he had issued assuring that she was capable of paying for what she had ordered herself. He casually continued with a crooked smile. "I'm sure ve vill all enjoy her purchases."

"No doubt you will!" Maxim snapped, somewhat amazed by the rancor he felt toward a man who had been a close friend for a number of years. It was an experience that was now happening with more frequency, and though he knew the source from whence it sprang, the realization of his growing animosity surprised him. It kept apace with his deepening interest in the girl, and try as he might to refrain from putting a name to it, it had the moldering stench of jealousy.

Leaning back in his chair, Maxim accepted a mug of ale from the serving maid who had brought it at his bidding. He tossed out a coin, and she left as he tasted the foamy brew. Dabbing the corner of his mouth with the back of his hand, he bent his regard upon Elise. Of all the women he had known, she was the only one who had ever turned his emotions upside down. While he wanted to have his revenge for what she had done to him this day, there was still within him that throbbing desire to know her in the most intimate of sharings. "My charge has declared she'll have her vengeance upon those who've done her ill, and I vow she has near picked me to the bone this day." A bleak smile lifted a corner of his mouth as he directed his gaze toward his friend. "You should be wary, Nicholas. She may see us all hanging from a gibbet before she's through."

"Only you, my lord," Elise assured him almost pleasantly, meeting those dark, challenging emerald eyes that watched her with unswerving tenacity. "You are the *one* responsible for my abduction! You are the *one* who should bear the penalty!"

"Are you saying that Nicholas's life is safe with you?" He paused to receive her slow nod and then questioned her more harshly, "But if mine fell into your hands, it would be forfeit?"

In taciturn eloquence Elise turned away from him, allowing his mind to dwell upon whatever doubts it might choose.

"What is this?" Maxim queried, contemplating her coolly reserved demeanor. "Have I offended you?" He received a quickly tossed glare from beneath dark lashes and scoffed at the idea that she disliked the conclusion he had drawn. "Come now, maid, tell me 'tis not true, and see if I'd believe you. You've promised to torment me at every opportunity, and have you not done just that?"

"True enough," Elise admitted loftily.

"Then why should I think otherwise?" he pressed.

"You may think whatever you like, my lord. I cannot govern your thoughts, and far be it for me to tell you what you should think of me."

"Your actions provide proof of your intent," he prodded in a relentless effort to draw her out. " 'Twould be foolishness to think otherwise."

"Foolishness is a state each man achieves by himself, as you have so amply demonstrated, my lord. No argument is profitable against it."

A burst of laughter escaped Nicholas as he fell back in his chair. He roared at the rafters in high mirth, content to witness her rebuttal of the Marquess. It was rare to see any young lady so zealous in her disdain of his lordship. It was the usual wont of the fairer gender to throw themselves at the man and beg for his favors while promising him all of theirs. None of those adoring creatures had ever understood the true complexity of the man. Maxim was one who preferred the challenge of a difficult chase, a hard-won tournament, and held no esteem for trophies easily gained. Indeed, Nicholas mused as he considered the ever-warring pair, if his friend were not so caught up with the idea of Arabella and his errant gambit, this girl would be a prime candidate for the hunt. It would behoove a man who was smitten with the girl to keep reminding the Marquess of his lost love so he would not recognize the rare prize that was within his reach.

Firm of purpose, Nicholas approached the matter of Maxim's lost love. "I've heard that Reland and Arabella vent to London a few days after the vedding and that she ordered a complete new vardrobe for her appearance at court. I've also heard it cost him a small fortune." He smiled. "One that he vas vell revarded for, I'm sure."

Elise lifted a finely arched brow to meet Maxim's stare and delivered her reproach in a softly spoken comment. "At least Reland knows how to treat a lady."

Maxim snorted in contempt. " 'Twould provoke you much, my dear Elise, if I were to imitate that clod's manners." A sneer grew on his lips as he continued. "I dare say the man would ride a maid down in a romantic frenzy, then demand her gratitude for his attention."

"Do you declaim a man's reputation in his absence, my lord?" Elise questioned in a guise of innocence. Though his comment was very much her own opinion of Reland, she would not give him the satisfaction of hearing such a confession from her lips. "Have you spied upon the man to know his failings, or are you so confident of your persuasive ability with women that you can set yourself as judge?"

Maxim laughed briefly. "I hardly need to spy upon a man to plumb the depths of his callousness, but as to the other . . . yes!" Bracing an elbow on the table, he leaned forward until his eyes met hers and, with unrelenting conviction, held them in the meager light. "Had you been witness to Reland's boasts, fair Elise, you'd know he cares no wit for a lady's pleasure, only his own. What man can boast if he leaves his love still yearning?"

Nicholas fretted as he watched a slight frown of bemusement touch the maid's brow, drawing a smile from the other. It was obvious she had no idea what Maxim was talking about, and Nicholas worried that her naïveté would so intrigue the man that he would be wont to test her knowledge . . . or the lack of it.

Nicholas welcomed the distraction as large platters of meats and vegetables were laid out before them. The feast would have sated the most rampant cravings of a starving man, and the Hansa captain rubbed his hands together in deep anticipation, showing an enthusiastic impartiality for each and every dish. Not so the Marquess, whose attention never ranged beyond the auburn-haired girl.

"Come, Maxim," Nicholas coaxed. "There is plenty for all."

"To be sure," Maxim agreed as he considered the feast. "But I would rather sup at home."

"At home?" Nicholas's brow jutted up in wide wonder. "Yu speak as if yu're becoming attached to Faulder Castle."

" 'Tis far better than some hovels I've sheltered in and no worse than many others. There's a hearth to warm me, a secure bed, and enough of a roof to give me shelter."

Elise coughed to clear her suddenly restricted throat as his words brought to mind the trap she had set for him. For an ever-so-brief moment her conscience tormented her far more than any discomfort he would likely experience, but her surge of compassion faded with the judgment that it was but a tiny portion of what he actually deserved. Beneath the questioning regard of the two men, she swallowed daintily and, with a smile, resumed her meal.

Nicholas went back to his argument to forestall any attempt Maxim might make to rush the girl through the meal and drag her away. "I shall be offended, my friend, if yu refuse my hospitality. Here now"—he handed Maxim a wooden trencher—"I bid yu enjoy vhat is before yu, and stop dreaming of vhat is far-off. There is far richer fare here."

Maxim relaxed back into his chair and considered the other's advice, reading more into it than Nicholas intended. It was not so difficult to forget what had been left behind in England when the sights were so appealing close at hand. "Your wisdom amazes me, Nicholas," he stated. " 'Tis meet that I should enjoy the meal with you." He took a slice of suckling pig on the trencher and extended the invitation he knew the captain was waiting to receive. "You will of course come and sup with us at Faulder Castle when you have time."

"Of course!" Nicholas eagerly accepted the suggestion, adding to it an invitation of his own. "I shall be visiting my mother in Lubeck next month. As my mother vould deem it inappropriate for Elise and I to travel alone, I hope yu vill consider serving as our escort, as yu, Maxim, are the only likely choice."

"I can think of nothing that might prevent my

going," Maxim replied. "Perhaps the trip would allow me to visit Karr Hilliard while I'm in Lubeck."

"How many lives do yu have left, my friend?" Nicholas queried in dubious wonder. "Yu've already crossed the valley of the dead once, and may I remind yu that it vas by the bare skin of yur teeth. How long vill yu scorn death before yu admit yu are only mortal?"

Elise laid down her fork, having somehow lost her appetite. It was impossible to believe she could feel any concern for a man who had caused her to be forcibly taken from her home, and yet the serious tone of warning in Nicholas's voice filled her with an inexplicable dread.

Maxim chuckled softly and made light of the other's concern. "Come, come, Nicholas, you spoil the meal with your gloom. We have much to be thankful for."

"*Ja*, that is true. I am indeed a fortunate man." His eyes settled on Elise with a warmth that Maxim did not miss nor mistake the significance of. It was obvious the captain was becoming increasingly enamored with the maid. Nicholas laughed and slapped his hand on the table. "And yu, my friend, are establishing a new vay of life here in Hamburg, and yu are obviously grateful to be alive. As yu say, ve have many reasons to be thankful."

"And all is well," Maxim mused aloud, thoughtfully regarding Elise. She had become introspective, and he wondered where her mind wandered, if it retraced the path of her capture or raced along on some other memory she held dear. "What say you, maid? Do you have cause to be grateful?"

The blue eyes came up to meet his, and there was a long moment of silence as she searched the dark, translucent green for the mockery she was sure would be there. It was not. Instead, she found an honest query and a quiet deference to her right to have an opinion on what mattered most to her. "I appreciate being alive," she answered softly. "But living isn't the sole reason for one being grateful; one can be miserable being alive. 'Tis the heart that determines what value one places on the ability to breathe and live. The secret depends neither on the fame nor the fortune one has achieved. 'Tis possible for the poor to be happy and content with their meager fare, while some who are rich seriously contemplate death as an escape. The secret is in the heart."

"A veritable sage," Maxim commented in wonder. He was amazed that one so young could have so much wisdom. It passed through his mind that in his courtship of Arabella he had never been profoundly touched or impressed by the vastness of her understanding. "And what burns in your heart, maid? What will you make of your life and where are you going?"

"I've a desire to find my father and set him free," she replied quietly. "I'll not rest 'til that is done."

"You do not mention your own desire for freedom," he pointed out.

Strangely, her freedom had ceased to be the most pressing need in her life. It was only when she thought of rescuing her father that it became a goal that had to be reached. "I answered your question," she said. "You already know my feelings on the matter."

Nicholas was uncomfortable with the way the pair excluded him from their conversation, albeit unintentionally. It was almost as if they were becoming oblivious to his presence. He took a sip of wine, mulling various choices of topics to regain their interest, and cleared his throat sharply to draw their attention. "Ja, yu can bet this veather vill be changing come the morrow. It is not often this varm so close to the end of the year."

Maxim remembered his manners and directed the subject to one wherein the captain could be more at ease. "What hear you from the sea captains, Nicholas? What do they report is happening in the world?"

Nicholas lifted his shoulders in a casual shrug. "Vord travels slowly this time of year, my friend, but I have heard that vith the fall of Antverp, Elizabeth has agreed to send a sizable company of men under Leicester to help the Dutch provinces. After the assassination of Villiam of Orange, Farnese has become a venging dragon for Spain and poses a threat to England. Elizabeth has refrained this long from declaring var on Spain, yet she continues to play her games vith Philip, setting her ships to snip his purse strings behind his back. Her Sea Dog vanders in search of Spanish vessels he can plunder, vhether near or far. Her recent treaty vith the Netherlands is bound to bring England and Spain into open conflict." Nicholas chuckled as he continued. "The Spanish have reason to fear vith that voman on the throne of England. She is a crafty vench, to be sure."

Thoughtfully Maxim traced the tip of his finger around the rim of his tankard. " 'Twould seem Philip will eventually grow tired of the struggle with the Dutch. The conflict has been dragging on for at least a score of years or better."

"Ja, he and his *Inquistitores* tried to keep the Calvinists out of the Netherlands after his father gave him rule over the provinces. The Spanish reign has been a continuing battle there ever since, but daily the causes for var grow broader and more intricate."

"You cannot be too fond of the Spanish with your mother being Dutch," Maxim observed.

"Ach! My mother hates them! Seven and ten years ago her brother vas executed by Alba and his Council of Blood. It does not sit vell vith her that the Hansa

continue to trade vith Spain." He grinned lopsidedly. "If not for her love, I vould be an outcast in my own family."

They finished their meal with only an occasional word spoken, and when Maxim pressed for their departure, giving the excuse that it would be far too dangerous to travel any later, Nicholas took charge of the situation. He ordered a pair of his men who sat at a nearby table to go along as escort. He would take no argument from Maxim and let it be known that his real concern was for Elise. Maxim could do naught but shrug in submission and follow along as the captain escorted his lady to the door.

Receiving their captain's command, the pair of men went promptly to obtain mounts for themselves and to fetch the Marquess's horses which had been left at a livery. They returned and were waiting with the animals when their captain and his lordship stepped from the inn. Elise paused at the door to contemplate the stiffening slush, once again faced with the prospect of ruined slippers. She did not glance up until Nicholas gave a low whistle of appreciation.

"Ja, Maxim, yu've got yurself a fine mare there . . . a real beauty, she be."

A vision of the dumpy white steed came to the fore of Elise's mind, prompting her to look up in some doubt of Nicholas's sanity. To her amazement she found the two men admiring a dark liver-chestnut mare. Her faith in Nicholas was abruptly restored, for the beauty of the mare was immediately apparent. Large, expressive eyes were well-set in a gently contoured face, and beneath the flowing mane the long neck arched gracefully. She was a tall, high-headed animal with straight, fine-boned legs. To be sure, she was of a quality quite appropriate for any lady's palfrey and a far cry from the dumpy white beast she had dubbed Angel.

Maxim took the reins and led the mare to Elise for her inspection. "It may please you to know I've sold the other horse and have bought this one for you to ride. She is a fit mount, do you not agree?"

"Truly, my lord," Elise answered in wide amazement. She could not understand why he had sold the stocky little mare when it amused him so to see her riding it, but to buy such an elegant mount for her purposes seemed out of character. A new sidesaddle and accoutrements had also been purchased.

Elise lifted her gaze to his, unable to tap the wonder of his gift, and murmured with a smile, "I'm taken aback, my lord. I did not expect you to do such a thing. Thank you."

Captivated by the beauty of her gentle smile, the first she had ever bestowed upon him, Maxim was reluctant to drag his attention from her, but as Nicholas moved forward to assist her in mounting, he stepped away, presenting his back to them. He adjusted his own saddle and slowly stroked Eddy's neck as the low murmur of their voices reached him. His mind was bombarded with a score of visions of the man kissing her cheek or the slender fingers in farewell and looking into those wondrous blue eyes with the same adoration he had exhibited in the inn.

Of a sudden Maxim was motivated by a roweling desire to be on his way. Gathering the reins, he swung into his saddle and faced the pair, impatient to be gone.

Nicholas took the obvious prodding in stride and gently squeezed the small hand in silent adieu. Solicitously he tucked the cloak over Elise's skirts before moving away. "Now yu keep a vary eye out for trouble," he cautioned Maxim. "I vould see yu both again."

Maxim lifted his hand in a casual salute of farewell and, with a light tap of his heels, nudged Eddy into a slow, high-stepping gait. The girl turned briefly to wave farewell to the lone figure standing in the street, and then settled herself for the long ride to Faulder Castle as his lordship fell in on her right.

The night was still. No slightest breeze stirred the air. It was as if the whole world held its frosted breath. A full moon rising above the hills gave the world a silvery hue dotted with black shadows in places where its light could not reach. Tall trees with thick boughs laden with mantles of white stood stock-still as the snow made a squeaking sound beneath the plodding hooves of the horses. Elise gathered her cloak close about her face and huddled in its warmth, aware that Maxim held the stallion in check beside the mare. That well-muscled beast was wont to prance and flag his tail like a randy cock in a courtship dance. It took a firm, steady hand to keep him under control, and yet Maxim did it with an ease which could have only come from a practiced skill.

Some distance away Fitch settled his bulk in a niche between the well and the stone watering trough about halfway between the main gate and the door of the keep. Earlier he had watched the long winter twilight deepen until the sky became a tapestry of star-bejeweled black velvet. An orange moon had risen eerily above the hills and had paled as it climbed the ebon ether. It was a time he had dreaded most, the coming of night and the rising of the spirits from their graves.

On the matter of ghosts Spence had accepted the premise that if they existed at all, they were limited to the keep, and so he had wrapped himself in secure innocence and snuggled beneath a pile of furs in the stable quarters. He was soon reaping timber with sawing snores that challenged the mightiest, but not so Fitch. That one had drawn the evening watch, and his thoughts plowed a slower furrow of reason as he pondered a wealth of tales that drifted up from his memory to haunt him. Anxious to vacate the keep after *Herr* Dietrich retired, he had hurriedly banked the fire in the hall, secured the doors, then upon venturing outside had seized an oaken branch as tall as himself and as thick as his forearm. Patrolling the courtyard, he had seen no wraiths or shades. Still, his imagination had thwarted his attempts to remain calm and stalwart in the face of the ever-elusive foe. Elongated shadows, cast by the brilliant moon, stretched across the courtyard and his hackles prickled with the idea that in each a specter could be lurking. He glanced up at the stone structure of the castle keep that towered over him like a dark giant and, with a shudder, gathered several pelts close about his shoulders. Whether his quaking was attributable directly to the cold or some inborn fear, he could not say, but he kept a wary eye upon the portal to see if anything unseemly issued forth.

The night was crisp, but the covering warm. Fitch's eyelids grew heavy as the night aged. His head nodded, jerked erect, then sagged again to stay as the staff slowly fell across his lap. His sleep was uneasy, his dreams filled with all manner of wraiths evoked by childhood stories and overheard recountings of much-exaggerated tales.

Torches were set in sconces on either side of the door, and they cast forth a welcoming light into the night, guiding the returning party into the compound. The clip-clop of hooves was muffled by the cushioning snow until they reached a point near the well where water had frozen over the ground, leaving the way slick and treacherous. There, the sharp crunch of

Eddy's massive hooves breaking through the icy crust echoed in the courtyard, sounding much like the cracking of bones.

Fitch's eyes snapped open at the sound, but his mind was still encumbered with the dregs of Stygian dreams. Four cloaked and hooded wraiths astride night-hued steeds loomed before him like some evil horde emerging from the bogs of hell. Their long shadows reached out over him and wavered eerily in the torchlight. Certain that he was about to be seized and slain by the ebon sprites, he let out a wail of pure terror and heaved himself to his feet. Caught between the well and the trough, the forgotten staff resisted the sudden upthrusting movement for a space, then popped free and sailed high into the air as Fitch's feet clawed at the frozen ground. His rapid effort to run yielded amazingly little progress until he tripped and measured his ponderous bulk on the ice in a grunting slide. The descending staff rattled to the frozen ground directly in front of Elise's startled steed, then rebounded in a bouncing, zigzagging advance upon the mare. The animal danced away in wide-eyed panic, jerking the reins from Elise's hands, and though the slender hands grasped the flying mane, the frightened mare was ready to fly.

Barking out a sharp command that brought Fitch to his senses, Maxim whirled the Friesian about and pressed him close against the mare, forcing her to yield ground. Her front hooves left the ground as she began to rear, and he swept out an arm and, with effortless strength, plucked Elise from the saddle. The mare pitched and bucked her way to freedom until one of the guards caught the trailing reins and led her back, soothing her with softly spoken words.

Maxim caught Elise close against him, feeling her tremble as she looped her arms tightly about his neck.

The fragrance of the auburn tresses filled his mind, and for a brief moment he yielded to an urge to savor the tantalizing scent more fully by turning his face into her hair.

"Are you all right?" he whispered, moving his lips closer to her ear.

Elise nodded and lifted her head to stare into the shadowed green eyes for a long, perplexed moment. Without comment, Maxim nudged Eddy closer to the stoop. Fitch, chagrined and eager to redeem himself, rushed to lend Elise assistance, apologizing anxiously for the trouble he had caused. Her slippered toe touched the step, and Maxim's arm slid free of her waist as she stood to her feet. He held the stallion to his place and waited until she raised her gaze to his. In the flickering pool of yellow torchlight their eyes met and locked for a long, quiet moment, then his voice seemed to reach out and caress her. "You will grace my dreams tonight, fair maid. Rest assured."

Elise's confusion deepened and, not knowing what to reply, fled quickly into the great room. Her feet flew on the stairs, and she burst into her chambers with naught but one thing on her mind. The burrs! If ever she regretted an act, then surely it was this thing that she had done to his bed. How would she face him again once he had suffered in her trap? It would have been better had he not been so generous with her. A ride home on the back of that unworthy white nag would have strengthened her desire to see him punished.

Carefully Elise laid the bar across her door, securing the room from any possible invasion. Dragging off her cloak, she paced back and forth in front of the hearth, fretting over what might happen in the lord's chambers. It seemed an eternity before she heard the distant creak of the balustrade and the scrape of a booted foot on the stairs. It would only be a matter of time now before she would hear Maxim's enraged snarl and possibly the pounding of his fist upon her door. She waited in tense silence, listening to the sounds of the keep. Her fingers were icy cold, and a persistent chill made her shiver. Though she added more wood to the fire, she could find little warmth that would ease her trembling. Time dragged by, and she began to slowly undress. Chill-bumps rose along her flesh as she slid naked beneath the furs, and for a long time she stared at the ceiling, waiting and wondering why she had not yet heard a movement or thunderous outcry from the loftier chambers.

Maxim had slipped off his boots and, in a restless mood, paced the corridor of the upper hall, glancing now and then through the arrow slits into the darkness beyond. He had no desire for sleep. His thoughts ranged like hunting birds of the night and could find no place to roost though they wandered far afield. From every corner of his mind he was assaulted by visions of Nicholas and Elise together. Perhaps he should stand aside, he told himself, and let Von Reijn carry out his courtship unhindered. Had he not expressed his own lack of interest in the girl and given taciturn approval to the swain? Yet with each passing hour he was aware of a growing reluctance to see her wooed by another man. He found it rather bewildering that he was overtaken by a burgeoning urge to reserve that right for himself alone.

Frowning in discontent, Maxim braced a hand against the stone wall and peered through the long, narrow opening of an arrow slit. A cloudy haze, pushed by a rising wind, drifted across the face of the moon, dulling the sky to a blackness bereft of stars. He found no ease in the shades of night for his pensiveness and once again took up his aimless strolling.

He was as one caught on the twin horns of a wild dilemma. He could not tolerate the idea of his best friend paying court to Elise. Neither could he justify his own approach as a suitor. He knew that in her mind he was her abductor and chief traducer, the villain in her life. The situation as cast by fate had to be endured until some unforeseen happening would free him of the onerous task.

Nay! Maxim paused in reflection, considering his own part in her abduction. 'Twas not an event cast by the winds of fortune! He had devised the plan himself and lent it the credence of a fool, allowing it to be executed in error and to be finished in mutual frustration.

The moon continued its flight across the ebon sky, heedless of his conflict, and gave no notice when he made his way to his chambers. There was only the whisper of his footsteps in the silence of the empty hall. The fire had all but gone out on the hearth when he entered his chambers, and he took a moment to heap kindling and fresh logs upon the glowing coals before he began to undress. Garbed only in close-fitting hose, he stood before the warming fire with legs spraddled apart, as if he braced against the rolling heave of a quarterdeck. His thoughts took up the chase again as he lifted his gaze toward the paneled wall wherein was hidden the secret door. A vision of his charge lying asleep in her bed came back to him in meticulous recall. She would be lost now in the depths of slumber with her hair flowing over the pillow and her silken lashes resting upon the pale skin. It was a sight a man could hold dear.

Moving to the bed, Maxim braced a hand high upon the carved wooden canopy as his mind roamed boldly to sights he had never seen. Whenever the woolen gown had clung to her form, he had been most attentive, and now-remembered glimpses came together to form a mental image of her lying undraped upon his bed. Her slender body was soft and womanly, her breasts temptingly round and pale-hued, and the long legs trim and sleek.

Shaking his head to thrust away the disturbing thoughts, he took several deep, slow breaths to cool his warming ardor. He rubbed a hand over his bare ribs and glanced about him, half-expecting to see her in the dark shadows of his chamber. Deliberately he turned his thoughts away and prepared his bed, flipping back the top sheet with the furs. He sat on its edge, determined to put her from his mind long enough to allow sleep to come upon him, but he knew it would be a difficult task. She was like a sweet intoxicant that coursed through his senses, awakening his very soul.

Maxim heaved a frustrated sigh and fell back upon the bed with arms upraised. Of a sudden his eyes widened as a thousand needle-sharp pricks cleared his mind, and he came out of bed as swiftly as he had fallen upon it. Turning in confusion, he whipped back the bottom sheet and swept his hand over the feather tick, frowning as some of the barbs stuck to his palm. He held his hand up where the firelight could provide more illumination and picked a sticker from his flesh. Holding it between his fingers, he cocked an eye toward the door.

"So! The little minx has not yet given up her games," he mused aloud.

A desire rose up within him to confront her with what she had done right then and there, but he paused and a smile slowly spread across his lips as he thought of a better way. Carefully he replaced the sheets and furs until the bed once again looked undisturbed. Taking a fur-lined cloak from the dressing room, he wrapped it about him and dragged the huge, high-backed chair to the edge of the hearth, where he settled within it. Leisurely he propped his feet up to the warmth. He could play the game as sharply as any fox and slumbering here in easy rest was tantamount to confounding the she-hound hot on his trail.

Morning dawned, and Elise came awake with a start, realizing that somewhere during the night she had fallen asleep listening for the loud explosion of Maxim's temper. Obviously he had not come downstairs to beat upon her door. So now what was she to do, and what should she expect of him? Was it even safe for her to leave her chambers?

Clasping a fur about her naked body, she ran across to the hearth, poked at the coals with a rusty old sword she had found in the keep and then laid a handful of splintered wood upon them. Tucking the lower edge of the pelt beneath her, she knelt upon the stone and bent down to blow life into the dying embers. A thin trail of smoke curled upward from the heap, then a small flame appeared and fed with ravenous delight upon the dry kindling. She laid several dry logs upon the burning sticks, then sat back upon her heels and watched the hungry flames licking up in frenzied haste. The warming fire took the chill from her, and she began to brush out her long hair until the silken tresses tumbled in loose curls around her bare shoulders. In her mind she saw cold, accusative green eyes staring into hers, and she slowly lowered her hands upon her lap to gaze in dismal dejection into the dancing flames. If only Maxim had not purchased the mare for her . . . if only he had not lifted her from the frightened steed and comforted her against him . . . if only he had not spoken to her so warmly at the front stoop . . . perhaps she would not be so tormented now by what she had done.

A persistent clapping of a shutter drew her to the windows, and she laid her brow against a pane of glass to stare out upon the wintry day. Gray clouds scudded across the eastern sky, chased by the howling wind that swirled through the courtyard like a venging wraith, slapping shutters and scouring the frozen earth of all debris. The skies promised a turbulent day, but the coming storm would be no worse than the one brewing between her and the master of the keep.

Fitch came into view as he left the keep, and a sudden gust of wind took his hat and led him on a zigzagging chase across the compound. With a sigh Elise returned to the hearth, seeking the warmth that had not yet reached to the far corners of her chamber. She prepared herself for the day, donning her usual drab clothes, and dolefully went downstairs.

Herr Dietrich glanced up with a jovial smile of greeting as she crossed to the hearth. *"Guten Morgen, frau. Wie geht es Ihnen?"*

Elise returned a hesitant nod to his inquiry. What she knew of the Teutonic tongue was enough to fill a thimble. "Good morning, *Herr* Dietrich."

The cook bobbed his head in acknowledgment and continued plying a ladle to his various pots and kettles, eliciting savory odors that both tempted and tantalized. It had occurred to Elise that *Herr* Dietrich's presence in the hall might offer the safest haven for her since he was loyal to Von Reijn, and for that reason Maxim might be wont to temper his arguments in front of the man. Reluctant to stray too far from that dubious comfort, she puttered around the table.

The moments lagged in their passing, and her nerves tightened until they were as taut as the gutstrings of a harp. Elise waited for some indication from above that would warn her of Maxim's approach, and started at every noise in the castle, sure that he was coming until the sound became distinguishable as something else. Finally she sank into a chair at the far end of the table where she would be well out of Maxim's reach, and silently reviewed half a dozen possible replies to whatever accusations might be forthcoming when he joined her. One by one she dismissed them as inadequate. He would reject her attempts to placate him and dash her efforts beneath a stern rebuke.

A shutter, flapping open with the force of the wind, brought her almost out of her chair, for it sounded like the slamming of a door. With repetition the noise betrayed itself. Folding her arms, Elise braced back into the corner of the large, tall-backed chair, steeling herself for that moment she dreaded. At last an upper door creaked and closed softly, then leisured footfalls were heard on the stairs making their descent. Elise closed her eyes as she listened. The sound was a portend of her approaching doom.

Herr Dietrich did not notice her distress as he placed a small, steaming tankard of cider, spiced with rosemary and sugar, before her. Thankfully she clasped cold hands about the warm mug and gave a tentative smile up at the man, not knowing the words to convey her appreciation. Her look of gratitude was enough, and the man returned to his hearth, humming a rousing melody to himself.

"Good morning," Maxim bade from the stairs, and when Elise glanced up, she found his smile warm and pleasant. Strangely his eyes were void of that steely-cold anger that could pierce her like the sharpest blade.

"Good morning, my lord," she replied, giving the usual odd twist to the title that made it more of a slur than a compliment. She regarded him warily over the top of her mug as he strode with purposeful stride across the hall. He halted beside her chair, and cautiously she set the cup on the table. Though she folded her hands primly in her lap, she was well-poised to flee should he threaten.

"You look rested, Elise. Did you sleep well?" he questioned in gracious concern.

"Aye, my lord. Very well, thank you," she murmured. Casually he reached out and brushed a curl over her shoulder. Her heart gave a sudden double beat as his hand dropped upon her shoulder, and though it rested there with the lightest touch, it seemed to pin her inescapably in the chair. Carefully she asked the question that burned to be spoken. "And you, my lord? Did you sleep well?"

Growing thoughtful, Maxim folded his arms across his chest and lifted his gaze to the rafters before he looked down at her again. "Well enough, I suppose, considering..."

Elise steeled herself for his next words. It would not surprise her if he shouted them in her ear.

"My mind was restless." Maxim gave the excuse smoothly. "And I sought out a chair near the hearth. Alas, the late hour overtook me, and 'twas there I spent the night."

Relief was hardly what Elise experienced when he stood so close. "Was there a reason for your restlessness, my lord?"

Lifting a curl, Maxim bent forward to test the fragrance of it and murmured with a slowly widening grin, "I was thinking of you, fair maid, as I promised."

Her gaze swept upward abruptly to meet his, and

she stared at him in astonishment, wondering what game he was playing. "Me, sir?"

Dropping the silken tress, Maxim chuckled and moved to the opposite end of the table where he accepted a mug of cider from the cook. He settled in his chair and replied as he raised the cup to his lips, "I was worrying about what I would have to sell to pay for the clothes you purchased."

"Oh." It was a very small word, spoken in a very small voice imbued with disappointment. Slowly Elise let out her breath and was surprised to realize she had been holding it at all. The possible cause astounded her. Had she truly believed he would express some softening of his feelings for her? "You need not trouble yourself overmuch, my lord." Her reply, tainted with the slightest note of regret, was cool and aloof. "I have no further need of your coin for what I have purchased."

It was Maxim's turn to be confounded. "How so?"

" 'Tis simple enough." Elise flipped her hand in a curt, backward gesture, as if to end the discussion. "I have enough of my own to pay for the remainder."

Maxim stared at her in bemusement. He could not say just what he had done to change her mood, but she had adopted that same defiant mien she had displayed upon his arrival from England. He realized that whatever ground he had lost in this discussion, she had gained.

Herr Dietrich slid a trencher of food before his lordship and placed another of the same but with smaller portions in front of Elise. Folding his hands beneath his long apron, he stepped back and waited for the fare to be tasted. Each took part in the repast, breaking the morning fast with a light sampling of the delicious sausages, raveled bread, and crisp fruit tarts before bestowing well-deserved compliments upon the cook.

"Delicious!" Elise assured the man with a buoyant smile. "Thank you."

"Es gut," Maxim agreed. *"Danke."*

Herr Dietrich's smile broadened, and once again he nodded his head with enthusiasm. Then he grew serious. Drawing a deep breath and squaring his ponderous shoulders, he forced out the reluctant words. "Tank yu, mad-am . . . sir."

Elise laughed and applauded her approval, and a pleased *Herr* Dietrich returned to his many tasks, leaving Maxim to resume the conversation. He did so with a perplexed frown.

"You say you have enough coin of your own to pay for the clothes, but how could you have been carrying such wealth on you when you were taken?"

Though Elise lowered her gaze and turned away to let him view her profile, it seemed her nose raised just a snip to convey her lofty disdain. "I've been aided by a friend," she replied, knowing with keen feminine discernment what erroneous conclusion he and his hunting logic would come to. Let him feed upon that bitter meat, she mused in smug silence, and tendered no further explanation for his comfort.

Von Reijn! The talons of Maxim's reasoning sank deep in the lure. It could only be him! An outright gift? Or in return for . . . ? Maxim's mind rebelled at the thought, and he struggled with himself as a mighty gorge of rage rose within him. "You seem to be quite fond of Nicholas," he prodded rather tersely. "But I wonder if you'll be content as the wife of a Hansa captain."

"I cannot see why that should be any concern of yours, my lord. I'm sure you're far too involved with Arabella to care whether or nay I'll be satisfied with my choice for a husband. You may have had me kidnapped from my home, but no one appointed you my guardian."

"I feel a certain obligation."

"Your obligation to me is to see me returned to my home as soon as possible and to provide for what nourishment and necessities I've need of while I'm here as your prisoner. Beyond that, my private life is none of your affair." With that Elise rose and, bobbing a brusque curtsey, left him glowering into the leaping flames on the hearth.

Chapter 13

*T*HE WIND HOWLED like a venging fury against the stone walls of Faulder Castle, probing each crack and gap until it seemed that its icy breath intruded into every chamber and hall. Elise shivered as the frigid drafts stole what warmth the hearths could provide with their roaring fires. Though she gathered a woolen wrap about her shoulders, her fingers were chilled and beneath her skirts her slender feet grew numb with the cold. From the upper reaches of the place there came a repeated slamming as if a stubborn shutter would not latch, then she heard Maxim's voice raised in a bellow of command as he directed a shout from a window to the courtyard below. 'Twas a brief moment later when Spence and Fitch came stumbling through the front portal on a hefty gust and, spilling their burdens noisily on the floor, threw their combined weight against the door to shut out the stubborn, snow-ladened gale. Both were wrapped in pelts for the short trip from the stables, and beneath a thick mantling of fluffy white they looked more like hoary creatures from the far north. The two men paused briefly near the hearth to spread their outer robes where the heat would banish the crusting of ice and snow, then Fitch again gathered a saw and an armful of planks, while Spence hefted a wooden box full of nails, hinges, and other fittings weighted down by a pair of hammers. As he passed Elise, Fitch bobbed a hasty "Good morn'n, mistress," and continued on his way without pausing for an answer. Clutching their tools and lumber, the pair clattered and rattled their way up the stairs, vying in a constant joust for leadership until at the narrower section of stairs Fitch forged into the van and, heedless of the verbiage Spence heaped upon his back, led the way to the master's chambers. There they found his lordship standing with arms akimbo and feet braced apart behind a narrow veil of falling snow. A sharply jutting eyebrow quickly conveyed his irritation as he slowly raised his gaze toward the ceiling where their makeshift repairs were being torn apart by the strong gales. Without word or excuse they set to their labors in earnest haste, this time getting assistance and direction from the master of the keep.

While the men labored, Elise addressed herself to the task of cleaning, with the idea of using it as an excuse to gain entrance to Maxim's chambers. She worked diligently in the lower rooms, sweeping, dusting, and scrubbing the furnishings, stairs, and floor. The midday hour came and went, and as she waited for the men to leave the upper chambers for the noon repast, *Herr* Dietrich passed her with a tray laden with food, squelching her plans to secure entrance to the room while they were gone.

Much later, as she poked ragged pieces of cloth around the windows to stop the persistent drafts in her own room, she despaired of ever finding the upper rooms empty, for the men continued through the late afternoon with their labors. As the hours aged, it became obvious that if she did not remove the spiny barbs from Maxim's bed before he retired for the evening, she would spend another night in anxious turmoil, wondering when he would discover them and explode in anger.

She left the windows, having done as much as possible to stem the flow of frigid air that seeped through the cracks, but she was still very much aware of the strong drafts that persisted in the room. When she searched out the flow of air, she discovered a cold waft coming from around the door which had once been hidden by the tapestry. Her past attempts to open the portal had been futile, and another testing of the door assured her it was quite soundly latched from the opposite side. Whatever held the door closed was sufficient to keep her out of the passage, but failed to hold back the drafts.

Since directing her attention to improving the state of the keep, she had taken much care cleaning the tapestry. She knew the piece was heavy enough to act as a barrier against the cold air, but whether or not she was strong enough to lift it in place by herself remained to be seen, for it was no light cloth to be sure.

By dint of will Elise dragged the rolled tapestry to the base of the wall where it was to be hung. Thence began the epic struggle of slight maid against monstrous tapestry. It seemed whenever she lifted the top, the bottom end was beneath her feet and if she stood far enough away to avoid trodding upon it, she had not the strength to lift it. Finally she had the whole of it draped over her, and its weight nearly bore her down. She braced her hip against the wall and, with the weight thusly suspended, managed to lift one end of the bar into its bracket near the juncture of the wall and timbered ceiling. She worked backward until she had the other end of the bar firmly within her grasp, but it did her little good, for it came nowhere near its wooden cradle high above her head. She assessed her predicament with some frustration. If she let the whole bar down, the other end would slip or the tapestry would cascade down upon her. A chair stood near the hearth, but, like the tapestry, it was a weighty thing. If she could somehow manage to reach the chair and drag it close, it would serve as an answer to her dilemma.

Easing away from the wall until the engaged bracket creaked with the strain, Elise held firm to the end she had within her grasp and then stood on one foot, reaching out with a slippered toe and stretching, stretching until she snagged the chair's leg. Flushed with her victory, she drew it close by slow degrees, then, with quick bumps of her hip, pushed it against the wall. She panted for a moment, then took a fresh breath and climbed onto the seat of the chair, while the ominously huge and burdensome tapestry almost brought disaster at several junctures. In a last surge of determination, she thrust upward, then ground her teeth in despair as the bracket flopped loosely and turned awry when she tried to lift the bar over the last curve. She rested for a moment to catch her breath again and wiped her glistening brow on an upper sleeve. She was so close, she was loath to let the whole thing fall and start over again.

Elise rubbed her brow again against the sleeve of her woolen gown, then froze as she heard a light chuckle behind her. Her arms trembled with fatigue, but she managed to twist far enough around to see over her shoulder. Maxim, garbed casually with his shirt hanging open to the waist, leaned lazily against the doorjamb. Even as she looked, his gaze swept upward from her well-displayed ankles, past the curve of her hip where the limp woolen cloth clung to her buttocks, along the slimness of her waist and finally rose to meet her accusing glare.

"The door was ajar," he explained with a shrug. "I heard the . . . ah . . . struggle and wondered if all was well with you."

" 'Tis not! So don't stand there grinning like a fool! Come and help me!" The last was a desperate plea as she feared at any moment she might collapse under the strain.

Maxim was there without pause, stepping onto the chair behind her and reaching up to take the rod from her trembling grasp. He held it easily in one hand while he twisted the bracket into alignment with the other, and though Elise felt almost smothered by his nearness, she still sought to help and lifted a fold upward to ease the weight. He was so close he seemed a part of her, and to remain calm and quiescent while their bodies touched was without question the most difficult task she had ever had to perform.

Maxim leaned forward to drive a loose peg home with the heel of his hand, and Elise warmed as she was made boldly aware of his chest pressing against her shoulder and the light caress of his loins against her buttocks. The heady smell of him, a clean masculine scent, shot like tiny hot darts through her senses and evoked a rush of pleasure that flooded through her. She had never experienced such heat, and though it was completely foreign to her, it was at the same time strangely exciting. He paused, and after a moment she glanced around to find his attention riveted downward over her shoulder. Following his gaze, she discovered the bodice of her gown gaping away from her bosom, displaying a generous portion of her full, blushing breasts.

Elise snatched her arms down and, in a bit of temper, continued the movement with one elbow, driving it into his hard ribs, then, like a fairy sprite, she snatched away and leapt to the floor, jerking her skirts free of the chair. Had the tapestry, man, rod, and chair ended in a tumbled heap, she would have considered it a well-deserved justice.

"You're a lecherous lout! A true roué of the first water!" she accused with flaming cheeks. "I must be on guard at every turn! I cannot trust you!"

The bracket held as Maxim lowered the rod into its cradle, then he turned with a wayward grin and stepped lightly to the floor. He slid the chair back to the hearth and came to stand before her, settling his hands on his hips. "My dear Elise, 'tis not a matter of trust. I've made no advance upon you, but what you display I'm more than willing to view. 'Tis the same with most men when they have a chance to admire a comely maid so wonderfully made."

"You spy upon my person like a rutting hind!" Elise cried. She was very conscious of his height and, where the shirt sagged open, the crisp furring of golden hair that covered his muscular chest. She was stirred by the manliness of him, which played upon the womanliness of her, but she crushed the wayward feelings behind a determined frown. Clenching her fists tightly, she lambasted him further. "You do indeed need a wife to ease your lusts upon."

Maxim's mouth twitched with barely bridled humor as he arched his brows in mock surprise. "Is marriage then your proposal, fair maid?"

Vibrant sparks flared in the blue eyes as Elise gasped in outrage. "Certainly not!"

Chuckling, Maxim shrugged and crossed the room, waving a hand over his shoulder. "You have only to ask, and what you seek will be done."

"I did not suggest that you wed me!" she ground out with an angry snarl.

Maxim peered back at her with a twisted grin. "I was referring to such tasks as what might be performed here today, but if you have a need, I suppose I might consent to wed you, considering I've compromised your reputation by having you brought here."

"You, sir, would be the last person I'd exchange vows with!" she exclaimed. "You're . . . you're despicable!"

"Perhaps." Casually he traced a finger along the molding of the door. "But I would know how to treat the woman I was wed to."

Elise scoffed at his statement. *"How?* By carrying her off to your chambers and refusing to let her go? She would be as much of a prisoner as I am now or what you intended Arabella to be!"

"I'd be a most attentive husband," he assured her with a warm twinkle in his eye. "And you, fair maid, would not oft be in want of a companion on a long winter's night."

"Are you suggesting that I would be lonely married to Nicholas?" she asked incredulously.

"Nicholas would be a good husband to you . . . when he is in port," he replied casually.

Elise cocked her head to the side and peered at him dubiously. "And can you assure me you would be ever at my side?"

"I cannot promise when fate might decree otherwise, fair maid, but when duty does not demand my attention, I would seek you out in all haste and eagerness."

Elise looked away in the guise of impatience, but she was confused by his words, the glow in his eyes, and the warmth of his voice. How could she believe he would be an ardent husband to her when they both knew he was in love with Arabella? But then, a man had no need to be in love with a woman to take his pleasure of her. 'Twas all he wanted, nothing more.

She turned back to give further argument and was surprised to find him gone. He had left without a whisper of a sound. In his absence the silence seemed to shout at her, and there was within her a desire to have him back with her. To be sure, their arguments were far more titillating than conversation with the four walls.

"What is he about?" she mused. "Does he only seek to make a mockery of me?" She threw an accusative stare toward the door. " 'Twould no doubt amuse him greatly to woo and, should I yield, use me, then put me aside when his humor has run its course." Thoughtfully she rubbed the tip of a forefinger behind an earlobe. "I'd rather not play the simple fool in his frolic. Nay, 'tis ever true that the game is far, far sweeter when played by two."

Still, she was disquieted. All the places where they had touched still burned as if she had been branded by the flaming heat of his body. How could Arabella have forgotten the excitement of this man's presence and accepted so soon after his purported death the bullish attentions of Reland Huxford? Where was the woman in Arabella that she had not mourned the loss of such a man for at least a decade or more?

Elise kept to herself and remained in her chambers for the rest of the day, even refusing to go down for the evening meal. She did not trust her jumbled thoughts to withstand the barrage of soft persuasions Maxim could heap upon her. She might well succumb like any weak-minded maid bent on self-destruction.

A lame excuse sent down by Spence soon brought the master of the keep knocking on her chamber door. "Spence reports you ill," Maxim called through the portal in response to her inquiry. "Have you need of a physician?"

"Heaven forbid! I'd sooner die in peace than be

poked and prodded by a quack who cannot understand a word I say!"

Maxim folded his arms across his chest and smiled.
At least the maid had strength for her usual shrewish
retort. "I shall send *Herr* Dietrich up with a tray of
food for you," he said, and leaned nearer the door as
he questioned, "Should I have him find some scales
of a dragon or a root of a hemlock for you to boil in
your cauldron, my lady?"

Maxim could well imagine the lass glaring at the
door with feet spread wide, arms akimbo and blue
eyes flashing as she gave him two for one in reply.

"Aye! Bring me that and more! Eye of newt! Tongue
of bat! Heart of mourning dove! Touch your ears, my
lord! Do they lengthen? Feel your nose! Is it growing
long and furred? Do your hands and feet take on a
likeness of hooves? Does a mule's tail cleave your
buttocks? Witch, indeed! Were I one of those, you
would even now bear the markings of your asinine
wit! Get thee hence, Sir Brute, ere I set my pot aboiling
in the faintest hope that some such deed could be
brought about."

His reply came softly through the door. "I am well-
assured then, fair maid, that you are once more found
of fair health and good temper."

After an amused chuckle all was silent, and Elise
knew he had gone from her door. His absence did
not lessen her irritation.

"Witch, am I!" she fussed as she snuggled down
into her bed later that night. "I vow 'twould serve
him right to feel the sharp pricks of the barbs this
night." Despite her words, she spent a sleepless night
in restless tossing, and though the winds howled and
swirled about the castle in a merciless eddy, she could
lay her thoughts to naught but the agonizing memory
of Maxim's touch and, if not that, then the expected

eruption of his rage when he discovered her trap.

Morning came, and though Elise listened long and carefully for the scrape of footfalls on the stairs before she eased the door open, she was much taken by surprise when she left her chambers and found Maxim leaning against the wall near the stairs. To all intents and purposes, it seemed as if he awaited her.

Immediately on the defensive, she slowed her approach as she eyed him with some apprehension. Any moment she expected to be taken to task for what she had done, and braced herself for the assault of words. Strangely a wide smile broke upon his countenance.

"Dreadful poor luck," he sighed and shook his head sympathetically. "You becoming sick."

Elise quickly averted her gaze from his probing eyes. "I'm in very fine health now."

"Are you sure?" he persisted, stepping near. Placing a forefinger beneath her chin, he lifted it and considered her closely as he turned her face from side to side to assess her color. "I hope the storm didn't keep you awake."

"Somewhat," she replied stiltedly. She had given little notice to the turmoil outside when the one on the inside held her attention. "Did you . . . ah . . . sleep well, sir?"

"Alas, no. After we made the repairs to my roof, Fitch laid so many logs on the fire, I found it too warm in my chambers. I took a pelt and slept in the hall. I could have sworn the man was trying to burn the whole forest in my hearth."

Elise brightened inwardly at the thought of another day's reprieve. Perhaps there would yet be a chance to whisk away the burrs before they were found. "I'm sure Fitch thought he was being helpful," she offered, and continued lamely, "He overdoes it sometimes."

"Aye, 'tis true. The man means well, but I'll have a care henceforth and lock my door to keep him out."

Elise's hopes were momentarily dashed, but she plucked up her spirits as she ventured, "I was going to try and clean your chambers. I'm sure after yesterday's repairs the rooms are in need of a good dusting."

"Fitch straightened everything last night so you needn't trouble yourself."

" 'Tis no trouble at all, I assure you."

"Nevertheless, I cannot allow it. You've been ill, and I'll not see you take to your bed again."

It seemed futile for her to argue with him, and for the moment she accepted defeat. In the next days, however, Elise began to have her suspicions. No man in simple day-to-day life could have as many excuses for avoiding his bed as Maxim Seymour appeared to have. She could more readily believe he was biding his time until it met his mood to seek vengeance upon her.

Outside the frigid stone of Faulder Castle, the storm raged on. The winds swept the snow in soaring arches from the tops of the walls, and only narrow paths were etched out in the drifted courtyard, laboriously shoveled where necessity dictated.

Elise anticipated another such excuse when she ventured downstairs on the fourth day, and she sat with a sweetly sympathetic smile as he voiced it, then replied, "How sad it is, my lord, that you've been so far removed from your bed this week. Why, the way you're avoiding your pallet, one would think you've formed an aversion to it."

"True, it's given me little ease of late," he agreed thoughtfully. "No doubt I've grown restless being imprisoned here by the weather."

"Aye," she sighed. "Captivity has a way of wearing

on one. 'Tis certain the captain will not be coming today as he intended." There was only the slightest note of disappointment in her voice.

Maxim stared at her long enough to gain her attention. "On the contrary, madam, Nicholas *will* be coming," he informed her bluntly, then strode to the front door and threw it open to observe the day. Though the leaden sky still hung low and ominous, it was void of the white, drifting flakes, and the wind had calmed to a bare shade of its former fury. Slamming the door closed again, he came back to the hearth and warmed his hands before the fire. "Aye, you can be certain at this very moment Nicholas is on his way."

"How can you be so sure?" Elise was more than a trifle skeptical, considering the storm had covered the ground with a thick layer of snow and the north winds had added a frosty nip to the air. "Surely the man has more sense than to venture forth on a day like this. Why, the storm could rekindle at any hour."

Maxim considered her for a lengthy moment, then approached the table. Setting a booted foot atop the bench, he braced an elbow on the raised knee and deliberately rested his chin in the supported cup of his hand. There was a devilish twinkle in his eyes and a smile of the same ilk played about his lips. "I will wager the man will be here ere the sun has tipped the noon hourglass."

Elise's mind raced as she considered his challenge, and she was loath to give it weight.

"I will wager," he continued in the same measured tone, "a night in my bed..."

Elise waved a hand to halt him as she saw his ploy. "I'll accept your judgment," she interrupted curtly. "In fact, if that be the case, I should hasten to make myself presentable." She seized the excuse and spun on a heel, calling out, "Fitch! Spence!" When the larger one came running, she hurried to instruct, "I would have a bath at once. Bring hot water to my chamber . . . and some cold to temper it. And hurry!"

Her feet tapped a quick patter on the stairs, and Maxim's laughing eyes warmly followed the rich display of shapely ankles. He silently observed the pair of servants, once loyal only to himself, as they rushed to draw water from the huge kettle kept simmering on the hearth and hie it to the lady's chamber. When Spence came through the hall with a yoke bearing two buckets of cold water, the lord of the castle smiled in amusement and bade Fitch to fetch another, causing that one's brows to jut upward, for the servant knew his lordship had already indulged in a bath earlier that morning.

When all was prepared, the bolt was thrown on the lady's door, and a loud scrape gave witness that a heavy chair was used to further bar the portal. The yeomen watched in amazement as Maxim hefted the last brimming bucket and began a stealthy climb of the stairs. The pair sighed in audible relief when he passed Elise's door and continued on to his own chambers, then they settled themselves to begging slices of freshly baked bread from the cook.

"The wily knave," Elise fumed to herself as she slid deeper into the copper tub. "He thinks to play me for a fool and set upon me at a moment to his advantage."

Safe within the security of her chambers, she leaned forward, savoring the warm currents as the water swirled around her. After a long moment of pure enjoyment, she readjusted the thickly coiled knot upon her head, catching it a bit higher, and began to generously lather her neck and shoulders with a large bar of scented soap, a luxury she had purchased on her last trip to Hamburg. She lay back again and closed her eyes as the liquid warmth washed away the suds and banished the last chills from her body.

It was a splendorous respite, and Elise heaved a deep sigh, moving slightly in the tub to send fresh swirls of water across her...

An ice-cold droplet splashed upon her breast, eliciting an astonished gasp from her. Her eyes flew open, and she found herself staring at the underside of an oaken pail even as another drop formed at its edge and plunged downward. Her gaze went beyond the bucket and focused on the smiling face of Maxim Seymour.

Immediately Elise recognized the vengeance he intended to extract and, in a swift movement, bent forward, giving vent to an anguished shriek as she flung her arms over her head in full expectation of an icy drenching. She waited... and waited... Opening her eyes and lifting her gaze, she saw that he had lowered the pail and was staring down into the water. One downward glance told her that the soapy water was clear enough that he could see all that he desired to see.

Crossing her arms before her, Elise bestowed upon him a most indignant glare. *"Well?"* she snapped. "Did you come to gape or to take your revenge?"

His teeth flashed briefly in a mocking grin. "My fair Elise, I fear the sweetest flower of vengeance oft fades in the moment of its blooming and becomes a bitter brew. Such beauty is not to be abused lightly, and mercy has its own rewards, not to mention the merits of wise restraint or simple compassion. The opportunity is reward enough. The burrs are stripped and in the hearth."

"Oooohh!" His mocking pity was worse than the chill draught he had offered. Her hand anxiously sought the bar of soap with mean intent. "You gaping jackanape! How dare you intrude upon my bath!"

Maxim chuckled at her rage and countered with humor. "A lady's bath is as private as a man's bed. Methinks the punishment befits the crime."

A shrill mewling of rage parted her lips and grew from clenched teeth as her fingers sought the soap. She raised her arm, heedless of her rudely strained modesty as the water swirled beneath her rosy breasts. With a chuckle Maxim gave her a casual salute of farewell before he leapt across the room, kicked the chair aside, and slammed open the bolt. He ducked just in time to avoid the flying missile which careened off the jamb and flew astray, but as he glanced back he gained a most delightful glimpse of a thoroughly enraged Elise and temptingly round breasts fully naked to his gaze.

"If your bath needs cooling, my pet, feel free to use the bucket," he quipped and gallantly blew her a kiss. Elise snatched up a bottle of scented oils from a table beside the tub and drew back her arm to let it fly. Maxim jerked open the door and ran through it, letting the panel intercept the flight of the vial as he slammed it closed behind him.

Elise pushed back into the tub, creating a wave that threatened the limits of the rim, and folded her arms in a frightfully spiteful temper. Her lips formed words that scarcely complimented the lord of the keep. The insults were growled through grinding teeth as she gave vent to her pique, and the loosely bundled hair twitched as she jerked her head this way and that in her venomous oration. At long last she calmed enough to rise from the tub, and absently she began to towel herself dry before she recalled having seen Maxim kick aside her barrier and unlatch the door.

Her eyes flew to the tapestry and widened as she remembered the door concealed behind it. "The prowling beggar! I should have been more wary!"

Chapter 14

THE SUN HAD LOWERED behind turbulent gray clouds, but at dawn it had made a brilliant appearance, bringing a welcome respite from the bleak haze that had for the past days enveloped the hilltop dwelling. Nicholas had ventured forth as Maxim had anticipated, having made his way with an escort of horsemen through the snowy drifts and bringing with him gifts of needlework, thread, and a sewing frame for Elise and, for Maxim, a keg of fine aged brew. Elise had been sweetly attentive throughout his visit which had lasted several days. She had hung upon his every word, though behind his back she had been coldly tolerant of his host who regarded her with unswerving fascination. Whenever Maxim was about, she could feel his gaze upon her, and it seemed whenever she glanced his way, her intuition proved to be true. His stare was sometimes questioning, sometimes puzzled, or just thoughtful and penetrating, but whatever his mood, he could hardly be ignored. And though Elise had vowed to remain aloof and pay him no heed, she had fairly groaned in frustration over her own failure in this endeavor. If it had been his purpose to unsettle her, in that foray he was successful.

Nicholas had said his farewells at the front portal, assuring her that the next time he came out, it would be with a conveyance that would take them to Lubeck.

Despite his verbosity, she had had difficulty following his words, for she had been far too aware of Maxim standing a short distance behind her, watching her unrelentingly.

It was later that same evening, after the meal was concluded, that Elise bade Spence to stoke the fire in her bedchamber. In Maxim's presence she bade the servant to put a latch on her side of the hidden door, appeasing her sense of outrage some small degree until she met the glowing green eyes. She settled with her gifts in the solitude of her chambers, leaving Maxim staring down the long length of the table at her empty chair. Long ago he had enjoyed the privacy of a quiet evening alone; now he found his loneliness oppressive. He had become accustomed to the maid's company and even though much of their time was spent sparring, he realized he enjoyed every moment that was shared with her.

Herr Dietrich had tidied up after the meal and then sought his bed, while Fitch and Spence, having sensed that all was not well between his lordship and the lady, dared no comment as they set to their evening chores. As Fitch readied the master's rooms for the night, Spence made a last pass through the hall with an armload of firewood destined for the lady's chamber.

Maxim quickly contemplated his choices. He could spend the rest of the evening alone or he could seek out the maid's company. He did not pause in making his decision, but immediately rose from his chair. From force of habit, he caught up the sword that was kept close at hand during the evening hours and, ascending to the second level, followed Spence to Elise's door. There he leaned a shoulder against the doorjamb while the servant stacked wood on the floor beside the raised hearth. A pair of candles burned on the table beside Elise, casting their soft glow upon her face. From where he stood, Maxim could not see the blush that suffused her cheeks as he watched her; he only knew that she had become a sweet nectar he craved to savor.

A lengthy silence dragged out between them as she stretched a linen cloth snugly over a tapestry frame. A tawny brow arched in wonder as he questioned, "Are you intent upon spending the evening alone, or do you mind if I join you?"

The slim nose lifted to indicate her pettish mood as she returned to him a cool stare, absent of smile. "You may do whatever pleases you, my lord. I can hardly tell you where you may go in your own house." She glanced about her chambers and shrugged as she added, "Such as it is."

Spence hurriedly took his leave, casting a worried look over his shoulder as his lordship strode past him. The coolly reticent maid peered askance at her visitor and beyond that tall, muscular frame bathed by the golden light of the fire, she looked small and slight. It was in Spence's mind that Lord Seymour had always conducted himself as a proper gentleman while in the company of ladies, and though the pair were ever at odds, he had to trust the man would not lose his temper with the maid as he had the first day of his arrival.

A smile played lightly about Maxim's lips as he dragged a high-backed chair closer to the hearth and settled into it. "I see you've not yet forgiven me."

"I was not aware that you desired forgiveness, my lord," Elise answered stiltedly. "You obviously considered your actions well-warranted."

Casually he waved a hand. "At least I spared you the full thrust of the icy water."

"Humph!" Dismissing his logic, Elise concentrated

on sorting the colored threads and tying them loosely to the top of the frame. For a moment her lovely brows gathered as she came upon a tangled snarl, and a curious light softened the green eyes as Maxim followed her movements and expressions with close attention. Whether vexed or not, she created a most appealing vision of domestic tranquility. The aura of the scene settled on him with a heightening awareness. There was much pleasure to be found in her presence, and the realization came upon him that even with the present rift between them, he enjoyed being with her more than any woman he had ever known. The memory of Arabella had faded to no more than a mere shadow in his past, and he knew that if this one ever opened her arms in welcome to him, he would be hard-pressed to remember any other.

Trying to bridge the gap between them, Maxim made several attempts at drawing her into a conversation, but Elise met his forays with stubborn silence until he finally abandoned the effort. It was obvious she was in an introspective mood and would play the offended damsel until it met her whim to pardon him.

Scourged by her slanted glower, Maxim leaned his head back in the chair and stretched out his long legs, crossing them at the ankles as he rested a booted heel upon the raised stone hearth where the heat could warm his feet. Laying the sheathed sword across his thighs, he folded his arms and closed his eyes, drawing to mind details of that moment when he had stood above her bath and gazed down upon her nakedness. Even if she refused to talk to him, it was not his wont to seclude himself in his chambers or return to the hall, at least not yet. There was more pleasure in seeing her fume than seeing her not at all.

Elise continued separating the threads as she surreptitiously contemplated the man whom she had come to regard as her tormentor. Here was the man who had set his henchmen upon a fool's errand. Here was the man who had called for her abduction and been responsible for all the discomfiture she had suffered. Here was the man who had brought her to a foreign land where she could scarcely understand the simplest of greetings, and had boarishly intruded upon her bath to seek his revenge. And yet, it was his presence that stirred a thousand jumbled dreams in her mind and awakened her to a strange excitement whenever he looked at her.

Slowly the realization dawned that Maxim's breathing had grown deep and regular. Though she knew Nicholas had kept him up for most of the past nights and he had not been allowed much sleep during the captain's visit, the idea that he could be so blasé as to slumber in her presence further aggravated her mood. She felt wounded by his casual dismissal of her. She was offended, incensed! And the more she considered his crisply chiseled features, the brighter glowed the coals of her resentment until small, snapping sparks began to flare in her eyes. Her mind railed at the insult.

Setting aside her needlework in growing vexation, Elise came to her feet and strode across the room behind him, gathering a shawl closely about her shoulders as a cold draft found her. "The simpleton can hardly be a lord," she thought shrewishly. "Look at him! He finds his comforts in the crudest hovel, as if he had never known anything better."

Elise pivoted slowly around and surveyed the dimly lit limits of her bondage. Tall shadows wavered upon the walls and ceiling as a tiny flame dipped and danced upon the tip of the taper. The remains of a log settled in the fireplace, sending a shower of sparks up the chimney. The flames dwindled, and it was as if a sneaky, insidious chill encroached upon the darkening chamber to seek her out.

"Pompous oaf!" The words escaped her taut lips as she snatched the shawl tighter about her. She went to the hearth and, seizing a brace of logs, tossed them upon the glowing coals. Eager young flames licked feverishly at the dried wood, and she stepped onto the hearth, turning her backside to the heat as she raised her skirts. As she warmed herself, she took meticulous account of him, until now never having been availed of the chance. Above the turned-down tops of his boots she considered the long, lean, muscular thighs and allowed her gaze to leisurely wander upward over the padded and slashed breeches covering his narrow hips. There was no question that he garbed himself well and with subtle taste, not following the custom of others of his same gender who selected lavishly embroidered costumes and bejeweled codpieces that made it seem as if the wearer was flaunting his manhood . . . or making much ado about nothing, Elise mused wryly. But then, in all truthfulness, she could not judge this man in want of anything. Of face and features, she had seen no match for his handsomeness. Of stature, he walked among the tallest and could be the stuff of any girl's dreams.

Elise mentally shook herself as she realized where her mind was wandering. Taking firm hold on her emotions, she stiffened her spine and hardened her heart. This man had to be confronted once and for all!

In a vixenish, spiteful bent, she lifted a foot and swept Maxim's from the hearth. She smothered a gasp and stood transfixed by the speed of his reaction. His feet snapped back and hit the floor. A thin whine of steel rang sharply in the room as the scabbard went clattering across the floor, and a wicked, winking light danced along the naked blade as Maxim came to his feet. Glancing to each quarter of the chamber, he found no other threat than the slender maid. He straightened and tossed aside the sword as he stepped squarely before her. Though she stood on the raised hearth, Elise found herself meeting his eyes on a level with her own.

"You wished a word with me, madam?" His voice was soft, but flat and void of feeling.

Elise could only wonder at his mood as she struggled to recall her own rage. Perhaps sweet reason was the best course to take with him. "Have I your full attention now, my lord?"

"The fullest I would lend to any maid," Maxim avowed. A corner of his lips lifted roguishly. "You may well rue the day I bend it all to you." His eyes pinned hers and held them until her cheeks flushed with color. "I've known a few fine ladies whose manners might have been better honed by a stint of discipline across my knee. Though I've never raised a hand to any of them, at times I've been sorely tempted."

"You draw the line of propriety most thin, my lord," Elise observed with bravado. "You threaten to see me chastened for my offense, yet you abuse the privacy of my person and my chambers as if you have a right as lord and master of this keep."

Maxim noted the pulse beating in the long curve of her throat before his gaze dipped downward to where the gown molded itself to the ripely swelling breasts. Meeting her gaze again, he queried with an uplifted brow, "Did you not do the same and unleash your attack upon me while I slept?"

Elise tossed her head with a flippant air and paced back and forth along the edge of the hearth, unaware of the vision she gave him with the firelight outlining her slender form and turning her hair to a lustrous flame. She came back to stand close in front of him and tilted her head to the side as she considered his handsome visage. "Do you in truth yearn to lay the flat of your hand to me as if I were some wayward bratling?" Her fingers plucked at the ties of his shirt and casually caressed his chest as she tested her womanly wiles upon him. She was curious to see if he would be as susceptible as Nicholas to a gentle touch or a word. "Have I abused you so?"

Maxim had learned to be wary of this maid and eyed her carefully, wondering what she was about. "Aye! And abuse it was, I vow."

Her eyelids lowered coyly as she averted her face a slight degree, allowing him a view of her saddened countenance. "Is your agony unbearable, my lord? Do you wish to lay punishment upon my hide 'til your anger is spent?"

This was not the vixen he had come to know, and though Maxim felt the pulse start to leap and throb within his veins as the maid leaned against him, he was cautious of being led into another trap. Aware of the teasing pressure of her soft breasts against his chest, he fought an urge to clasp her to him and smother her questions beneath hot, fervent kisses. He gave answer in a hoarse whisper. "I've never wished to do you harm, Elise."

"What say you now?" She straightened as if he had stung her and her eyes flashed with rage. "Then in your tender, mitigated ministrations, my lord, I have been sorely used!" Her small fist struck him squarely in the chest, and he stumbled back a step, amazed at her sudden change. "Did you not have me abducted from my uncle's home, my lord? Did you not have me hauled through the dregs of Alsatia, tossed into a

moldering box, carried willy-nilly across the seas to a foreign land where I'm held as a prisoner among strangers?" Alighting from her perch, she followed him and thumped his chest with the doubled fist as she continued her barrage of questions. "Have I not been made your slave?"

Maxim tried to retreat, but was halted abruptly by the bed at the back of his legs. He sat down heavily, and still his antagonist gave him no quarter. She followed between his spraddled legs and pressed her finger upon a spot above his heart, her sharp nail digging into his flesh where the shirt fell open. She ground out her words in short phrases as if she were lecturing a simple child.

"What think you that I am, sir? A soldier of the realm? Forsooth, I am not on a foray in the field, nor do I wax fond of this pile of stone wherein you seem to feel at home! I'm as hearty as the next, but I do not like the cold seeping through the cracks and crevices of every chamber. I huddle in my bed each morn and dread the leaving of it." She calmed and spoke in a softer voice. "In truth, my lord, I would prefer a bed of warmth and safety and, were it possible, a woman to help with the cleaning."

The slight, shadowy form moved away from him, and in a subdued, wistful vein Elise stared into the waning fire for a long moment. At long last she faced him again, and Maxim was surprised to see the shine of tears in her eyes.

"I do not ask for the rich comforts you would have provided your dearest Arabella," she murmured, her anger spent. "I've made no further demands that you send me home before the spring. I would only ask that we try to live at peace while we're imprisoned here together in this place. I am weary of the battles, and though I know you would prefer sweet Arabella at your side, neither of us can remedy the mistake that has been made."

Embarrassed by her own outpouring, Elise moved to stand beside the open door. "I bid you take your leave now, my lord," she said in a small voice. "May you sleep well."

Maxim rose to his feet, a veritable flurry of thoughts coursing through his brain. Catching up the sword, he sheathed it and approached the door where he paused beside the maid. Words evaded his grasping tongue, for any denial of his feelings for Arabella would have seemed a crude ploy. Reluctantly he left the maid.

The hinges squeaked slightly as Elise closed the door behind him, and heaving a sigh, she leaned her brow against the smooth surface of the wooden panel as the solitude of the room pressed down upon her. At the moment she felt very tired and utterly alone. It seemed that whenever they were alone together, she always ended up acting the vindictive shrew. She was unable to pass even an hour's time with him without getting into a fray. It was as if he set her at odds with herself.

A dim gray light marked the coming of morn, and Elise came abruptly awake as a door opened and closed somewhere in the keep. Thrusting her nose above the furs, she noted the leaden skies. She dreaded the thought of more snow, for the hilltop keep was becoming a fortress of white, impenetrable by all but the most hearty. She dragged her shift and gown beneath the covers where she pulled them over her head. Thus garbed against the cold, she rose and slid her cold feet into the hide shoes. Wrapping a shawl about her shoulders, she scampered across the room and hastened to restore the nurturing warmth of a fire.

A short time later, her face and hands pink from a scrubbing and her hair gathered in a heavy, coiled knot upon her head, Elise left her chambers and made her descent of the stairs. Her manner was one of soft contrition at the fury she had unleashed upon his lordship. Indeed, she was reluctant to face him as she recalled the fist she had driven into his oak-hard belly. "What must he think of me?" she groaned in misery. "Arabella would never have done such a thing!"

Spence was seated on the raised hearth eagerly eyeing *Herr* Dietrich as that one took out fresh buns from the oven that was set in the wall close against the fireplace. As she approached, the smaller man jumped up and hastened to pull out her chair from the table. It was rare to see Spence without his companion, and Elise made mention of the fact. "I say, Spence, you seem to have come out without Fitch. Is he well?"

"Don't ye worry 'bout him none, mistress. 'E an' 'is lor'ship went ter 'Amburg 'fore sunup, 'ey did."

Behind the cook's back, the servant snatched up a roll from the iron planch and scampered away, just in time to avoid a ladle Dietrich swung at him. Tossing back a grin at the petulantly frowning cook, he settled on a squat stool on the far side of the table, out of harm's way.

"Hamburg?" Elise's voice was fraught with dismay. Had Maxim finally taken exception to her abuse and left the keep? "Will he be coming back . . . I mean, will they be returning soon?"

"I don't rightly know, mistress. 'Is lor'ship ne'er said a word ta me 'bout 'at."

"I guess it really doesn't matter," Elise sighed, and gave a small laugh. " 'Twill give me some time to myself."

Spence never noticed her distress as he eagerly consumed the stolen bun. "Aye, 'at's likely what 'is lor'ship was thinkin' when 'e left ye here."

Elise braved a smile. "He'll be lucky to return without running afoul of the weather. The gray sky bodes ill."

As if in compliance to her words, a thick fog settled over the countryside that afternoon, obscuring the distant hills until they became vague, dark shapes. At times they disappeared altogether, consumed by a mass of whitish gray. Gazing out from her windows, Elise had an eerie feeling that she and the keep were marooned atop a mist-shrouded pinnacle set apart in a faraway universe and she would never again know the comfort of England and home. With an effort of sheer will, she shook off the dismal gloom and busied herself with a vigorous cleaning of Maxim's chambers. She straightened his dressing room and smoothed the velvet doublets beneath her hands as she placed them in neat order. Though the tiny room was not what one might call cluttered, it undoubtedly belonged to a man who was used to leaving such matters in the hands of servants.

Every now and then Elise would catch a faint melody drifting up from below where *Herr* Dietrich lent his voice to song. From the stables Spence added his own harmony to the tune with a vigorous hammering. The sounds reassured her, and yet the hours since Maxim's departure grew long, and it became a labor to fill them. She was puzzled by the feeling of emptiness that pervaded the keep, as if his presence gave life to the structure. Though she struggled to deny the evidence of her own emotions, she was beginning to realize she had grown accustomed to his company and actually missed him when he was gone.

It was late afternoon when Spence appeared at the front portal. He seemed anxious as he hurried across the hall to fetch his long bow and a quiver full of arrows.

"What's wrong?" Elise questioned in sudden apprehension.

"No need for ye ta fret, mistress," he assured. " 'Ere's just some strange voices on the trail, an' I thought we'd best be wary, what wit' thieves and vagabonds known ta roam 'ese 'ills."

Motioning for *Herr* Dietrich to lower the bar across the door behind him, Spence slipped out and ran across the courtyard. As the cook made the hall secure, Elise raced upstairs and, opening her chamber windows, watched Spence mount the rampart beside the gate. She heard a distant creaking and a rattle of many hooves coming up the snow-packed trail, then a muffled call, hardly the sort of sounds a pair of riders would make. Whatever sort of brigands roamed these barren hills, it was obvious the castle's lone defender would need help against their attack, for it seemed they were coming with force.

Over the top of the crumbling wall she could see the vague, darker line where the ridge crested and indistinct patches where the lighter path crossed it. A dark shadow moved in the mists, becoming the ghostly form of a man on horseback. Behind him another appeared, little more than a grayish haze in the fog. A larger apparition came behind them, taking on the shape of a cart drawn by a team of oxen. A second conveyance followed.

A small gasp escaped Elise as her eyes returned to the lead steed and she recognized his prancing gait. When she saw the tall, straight form of his rider, she realized by the telltale beat of her heart that she felt more than mere relief.

"Maxim is home!" The thought burned through her consciousness and warmed her with joy.

Catching up her skirts, Elise raced from her chambers. In a thrice she was down the stairs and lifting the heavy bar away from the front portal. By the time she reached the stoop, Maxim and Fitch were in the courtyard. Behind them came a cart loaded down with barrels, crates of chickens, and a pair of small cannons. On the seat beside the driver sat a large, squarely built woman, wrapped in a hooded cloak. The other cart was heaped with wooden planks, two large chests, bolts of cloth, feather ticks rolled and wrapped for protection against the elements. A trim, neatly dressed older woman had taken a place beside the driver and clutched a tapestry-covered case upon her lap. Following in the wake of the crude conveyance came a veritable entourage of animals: a lone cow, a small flock of sheep driven by a lad carrying a tall staff and a shaggy-haired dog that scampered along beside the youth.

Maxim dismounted and tossed the reins to Fitch before he turned and approached the stoop. Drawing off his gloves, he paused before her. "As my lady commands." With a grin he swept a hand to indicate the strangers. "Masons and carpenters to help mend the breaks, a woman to clean for you, another to ply a needle for a time where needed, animals to keep us in good supply of food and a lad to tend them."

Elise was overwhelmed. "But how could you afford such comforts?"

"Nicholas advanced me moneys against the holdings of the Marquess of Bradbury," he answered with a rueful smile. "Some would name him foolish, but he obviously trusts that I'll be restored in good graces with the Queen."

"And what of Edward and his lies?" she murmured.

He reached out and brushed a wayward curl away from her cheek. "Of late, I've thought little of the man. Perhaps the fire of my hatred is waning in the pleasurable presence of his niece."

She felt a flood of warmth toward him, and yet when he was so handsomely clothed in fur-trimmed cloak, velvet doublet, and fine leather boots, she could not ignore the fact that her own rough garb was base and crude. She scrubbed self-consciously at her cheek where his fingers had touched, spreading a smudge of dirt that encrusted it as she replied hesitantly, "You've outdone yourself, my lord, and been most generous."

The two women were directed toward the stoop by Fitch, who was having difficulty keeping up as he struggled with their cases. As the pair mounted the steps, Elise retreated into the hall and held the door for them. The older woman smiled graciously, but no lady of quality ever put on so many airs as the larger one. She paused several paces beyond Elise to glance about with contempt at the interior, then she turned to peruse the maid with an equal amount of disdain.

Fitch was faced with the challenge of getting his bulk and the baggage through the portal at the same time. He mounted several abortive attempts before making an advance sideways. Even then, when he squeezed through, it was like a cork bursting free from a fermenting flagon of wine. No matter how hard he tried to hold them, the trunks and cases flew helter-skelter.

"Oh, look vhat yu've done, yu clumsy oaf!" the woman of bovine proportions scolded. Her words were marked with a faint German accent, and she gestured imperiously for Elise to give Fitch assistance just as Maxim entered.

"Don't dawdle, girl! Help the man, and then show the dressmaker and me to our rooms!"

"Nay, mistress!" Fitch cried in an anxious dither,

shaking his head at Elise. "Do not trouble yerself!"

"Mistress?" Raising her brows in sharp skepticism, the newcomer looked Elise up and down, bringing the blushing heat of humiliation to that one's cheeks. Beneath that haughty stare of disapproval, Elise could find no suitable reply, aware that her appearance would have matched a scullery maid's rags.

Maxim made the introductions: *"Frau* Hanz, this is your new mistress ... Mistress Radborne."

"Then ..."—the woman paused, her dark eyes passing down the worn, woolen gown disdainingly—"she is not the Marchioness?"

Maxim felt a prickling of irritation as he noted the derisive smirk on *Frau* Hanz's broad face. Her expression left little doubt to the conclusions she had drawn. "You were hired as housekeeper here, *Frau* Hanz, and your duties will be to lend yourself to whatever Mistress Radborne sets forth for you. If you're displeased with that arrangement, you may leave come the morrow. I shall have my man take you back."

The housekeeper stiffened at the softly spoken rebuke, and it was a long moment before she answered. *"Entschuldigen Sie, mein Herr.* I did not mean to offend."

"Take care in the future that you avoid doing so," Maxim replied, and gave a brusque nod to Fitch. "Show the women to their rooms."

In the silence that followed their passage, he contemplated Elise who appeared frozen by the exchange. " 'Tis difficult to find good servants in so brief a time," he murmured as his eyes softly caressed the downturned face. "If you're not satisfied with *Frau* Hanz, she can be dismissed."

Realizing the threat of her crumbling composure, Elise stiltedly bade, "I must beg to be excused."

Before Maxim could reply, she pressed a knuckle

against her trembling lips and fled toward the stairs. He stared after her, his senses dulled by confusion. He had seen the hurt in her face and was able to understand it, yet for some reason he felt as if she had cast him as the villain in all of this.

Running after her, he caught up with her on the third step of the stairs and pulled her gently around to face him. Her eyes, spilling a wealth of tears from the lashes, refused to meet his gaze. " 'Tis no simple annoyance I see," he whispered. "What's wrong?"

"You . . . you shame me, my lord," she sobbed softly.

"What?" The word burst from his lips before he could halt it.

Elise flinched at his retort, and her teary eyes lifted to search his face. "Do you not ken what she thought of me?"

Maxim accepted the blame without argument. "I know I have compromised your good name, but short of exchanging vows, Elise, I can make no further amends than what I've already made. *Frau* Hanz can be sent away as easily as she was brought here. All you need do is give the command."

"She looked at me . . . as something loathsome." Elise stared down at her clothes and plucked distastefully at the frayed woolen gown. "And she had a perfect right to. I . . . I look like . . . a . . . charwoman!" She sniffed and wiped the back of her hand shakily across her cheeks as the words stumbled out between intakes of breath. "How can I face any servant you have brought here, much less go to Lubeck with Nicholas looking like this?"

Maxim frowned his displeasure. So that was it! Nicholas! She wanted to look her best for the man. "You took moneys from him for the clothes. What have I to do about that now?"

Elise lifted her hands in earnest appeal. "I came here

with moneys of my own hidden beneath my skirts, and those I gave to Nicholas to invest for me. I've never taken anything else from him. Nor have I taken anything of yours. The purse you gave me was taken to the exchangers for benefit of usury. Nicholas can make full account of it all, every last coin."

Maxim folded his hands behind his back and gazed down at her, his face enigmatic, as if he held a secret and would draw it out until the last moment. "Women," he murmured softly. "I'll never understand the breed. They cause me great trouble and even greater bewilderment. You could have explained, yet you allowed me to think you'd take moneys from both of us."

"Give me leave to go to my chambers before *Frau* Hanz returns," Elise pleaded miserably. "I would not have her see us together like this."

"I pray you delay a moment more, Elise, while I'd make you aware that when *Frau* Reinhardt thinks one is deserving of her attention, that one also takes on a high priority." He noticed her brows drawing together in confusion and allowed himself a small smile. "Except for the last fittings, the gowns were ready and have been brought along. Were I you, maid, I would hie myself to my chambers and make ready to receive them . . ."

A sharp intake of breath interrupted him, and in the next instant Elise was stretching upward on the tips of her toes and flinging her arms around his neck. Locking them fiercely about him, she drew his head down, amazing Maxim who was pleasantly taken aback by the swift, soft brush of her lips against his cheek.

"Oh, thank you, Maxim. Thank you," she whispered against his ear, and before his arms could close about her narrow waist, she had slipped free and was flying up the stairs.

"*Frau* Reinhardt sent the seamstress along to see the gowns properly fitted," he called after her and, a moment later, heard the slamming and bolting of her chamber door.

Maxim retraced his steps downward and crossed to the hearth where he stretched his hands toward the heat. The memory of Elise's radiant face warmed him more than any fire, and the idea of making a temporary home of Faulder Castle was settling comfortably within his mind. Until a time came when they could return to England, the keep would be a nurturing haven for both of them.

Elise came awake suddenly, her body bathed in cold sweat. The remaining dregs of a nightmare, in which she had seen her father imprisoned in a dark, foreboding place, lingered in her mind. His hands and feet had been shackled with long chains, which had clanked in a slow, plodding measure as he trod the cold, stone floor with bare, bony feet. The boundaries of his prison cell were marked with bars of iron attached to a stone wall. A pair of eyes, of mammoth proportions and as transparent as a thin veil, overlay the vision, and the impression that they had stared with a deep, troubled longing straight at her had wrenched her from the depths of slumber.

Restless now, Elise left the comfort of the soft, downy tick and pulled the clean, sweet-smelling sheets and furs into place behind her to preserve what warmth she could for her return. She slipped a long velvet robe over her naked body and donned a pair of slippers, giving little heed to the luxuries she now enjoyed. What did they matter when her father could be suffering terrible hardships?

The fire had burned low, and she placed a few more logs upon the glowing coals before tugging a chair close and propping her feet upon the raised hearth. The nightmare had left her mind cast awry upon the vast, barren steppes of some foreign place, and though she searched hither and yon, she could find no comforting home for her thoughts to rest.

Finally she forced herself to review the past weeks with meticulous detail and deliberation, and memories of Maxim quickly overshadowed the gloom. In both manner and charm he had outdone himself, and as a suitor he had been irresistible. He had cajoled, pampered, teased, and delighted, leaving her feeling wonderfully alive. For the first time in her life she was being courted by a man who was mature enough to know what he was about and to be assured of himself and his powers of persuasion. A light brush of his lean fingers upon her arm or a cheek could evoke sinuating waves of pleasure and leave her giddy with delight.

The advent season had come and gone, and servants and highborn alike had feasted well. Even *Frau* Hanz had given a chuckle or two as they listened to the wildly humorous stories told around the hearth as each took their turn to entertain. In private Maxim had gifted her with a bejeweled box and, with a soft husky voice, had urged her to keep it solely for the hearts she had won. Elise remembered only too well the soft, warm feelings she had experienced when he graced her slender fingers with a kiss.

For a time they had been kept busy at separate tasks, she with instructing the housekeeper on her duties; he with directing the carpenters toward the repairs that needed to be made. The seamstress had been enlisted to sew draperies for the bedchamber windows and new hangings for the beds, heavy enough to keep out the drafts. Rugs had been placed over the stone floors in areas where they were most wont to sit, and woolen lap robes were furnished for the chairs.

Elise's own chamber had taken on a feeling of coziness with the draped velvet on the windows. The new bed-hangings added an inviting warmth to that haven, and it was almost a pleasure to curl beneath the downy comforters as she drifted off into the arms of Morpheus. Even in its shadowed corner the copper tub now gleamed after a thorough polishing.

A growing feeling of security was settling down upon her because of the improving conditions outside the keep. No longer did Elise need to fear the coming of night. The small cannons which Maxim had brought back now graced the front walls, and the portcullis, which had been made serviceable by the addition of linked chain, could be lowered at nightfall behind the newly repaired gate.

Still, Elise found the passing weeks had chafed hard against her emotions. The many hours she had spent with Maxim within the narrow confines of Faulder Castle had begun an erosion of the once-solid wall of her defense. His warm and gentle manner was beginning to bring about a change in her, a change which boded ill for her weakening will. She was very much a stranger to the growing yearnings that assailed her and more than a little cautious of the desires that enflamed her. Never in her life had she felt the smallest urge to seek out a man's company, as she now was inclined to do with Maxim. She enjoyed being with him and being the recipient of his attentions. He seemed casual enough about touching her, but to be so familiar to respond in kind was a yearning she had not yet appeased. She had been totally amazed by the attack on her senses the morning she had come upon him bereft of a shirt, and she had been hard pressed to drag her eyes away from that lithely muscled expanse. From simple to sensuous, her mind was ever wont to wander when her hungering eyes touched upon the man. She had memorized every shape, every swell, every bulge, every leanness, every firmness, every flowing muscle that had all been wonderfully combined to create that tall, handsome torso. Quite often her lashes would flick down, brushing burning cheeks as she tried to hide her growing fascination, but her imagination refused to halt on the outer garb of the man. She had seen all, and wanton maid that she was, all was what she desired to see again.

Stepping away from the hearth, Elise slowly paced about the chamber. Her longings were by no means a singular problem, for Maxim had made it known that he wanted her as a man wants a woman. But she had refused them both, crushing down the cravings, cindering them beneath the firm heel of her restraint. Still, the longings came back to haunt her, and, such as now, she could not find the soothing comfort of rest.

Her eyes turned as if compelled to the tapestry. She now had a suspicion where the doorway led, and a deep curiosity began to grow within her as she stared at the piece. What better time for her to explore this mystery than when Maxim was asleep and he would know naught of her wanderings.

She lit a taper and, with purposeful intent, slipped beneath the work of art, holding it a safe distance from the burning candle. She was determined that nothing would dissuade her from her resolve, not even the bats that had once inhabited the shadows of the tapestry. Gently she slid back the latch that Spence had affixed to the door and, thus freeing the panel, carefully opened it.

Lifting the candle high to banish the darkness, Elise

stepped into the passageway and moved cautiously beyond the fireplace wall to the steep, narrow stairway. Gingerly testing each step, she made a slow, careful ascent. At a small landing she found a door with a neatly worked latch positioned low on the right side. She set the candle down where it would give her light and cautiously turned the latch. The panel swung smoothly without the slightest sound, and as she stepped over the threshold, she caught the slow, steady breathing of the slumbering man who occupied the bed. The low fire cast more shadows than light, while the heavy velvet hangings held the darkness secure within the bed.

Elise's nerves stretched taut as she crept to the canopied piece. There was no mistaking the tousled tawny head of the lord of Faulder Castle. He lay on his left side, facing away from her, and the fur pelts barely preserved her composure, for they provided only a meager covering over his narrow hips. An ugly, purple scar marred the smooth symmetry of his back, lending her an understanding of those brief times she had seen him grimace and stretch, as if some twinge of pain plagued him.

A sudden pang of compassion stirred within her as she thought of the agony he must have suffered when Fitch and Spence dragged him from the murky depths of the river and then spirited him away in the dead of night to the inn in Alsatia. Nicholas had said he had been close to death, and the whole of England had been persuaded that he had died. It greatly pleased her that he had not.

Elise held her breath as he stirred restlessly in his sleep and rolled onto his back. A long sigh slipped from him as he flung an arm up over his head and turned his face slightly away. Though she dared not move or breathe, her eyes wandered where they would, while a warming blush suffused her cheeks at the forwardness of her inspection. Slowly her gaze passed down the furred chest and lean waist and moved on to the firm, flat belly with its light tracing of hair. A dark shadow of a scar traced upward across his ribs from his left side, and curious to know the extent of it, she leaned over the bed as her eyes followed the line of it.

Of a sudden long fingers closed tightly upon her arm, and Elise gasped in sudden alarm as she found herself being swept down over the man. Maxim rolled to his side, pulling her full against him, and held her there with an arm clasped close about her slender waist. For a stunned moment Elise stared with widened eyes into his shadowed face, while the firelight etched his dark form with a golden light, tracing along the side of his head, the square, muscular curve of his shoulder, on downward over a naked flank to where the open skirt of her robe covered his leg. She saw the gleam of white teeth beside her, and even in the darkness, she thought it had more the twist of a lurid leer.

"What? No pail of icy water to drench me?" His voice was soft and deeply laced with humor. "What say you, maid? Have you brought aught to rend me to my pallet?"

"Let me go!" Elise gasped. She laid a hand to his naked chest to push herself away and struggled to rise.

"Not yet, I think," Maxim whispered, bringing around his left arm to fold it beneath her head. He raised slightly on that member until his shadow covered her, and he lowered his head toward hers. Elise flung her face aside, but he forced it back as his arm curled about her head, and she was imprisoned in a gentle vise that refused to let her go. Deliberately he took his time, touching kisses as light as thistledown upon her lips, insidiously stirring her woman's passion. Her trepidation began to fade and her qualms were sundered beneath the onslaught of his persuasive gentleness. By slow degrees his mouth parted and began to pluck the sweet nectar from hers in soft caresses, sipping deep, slowly sampling until she began to feel almost heady with the strong intoxicant of his kisses. His fervor mounted with her advancing response, and his tongue became a flicking firebrand as his mouth consumed hers with a hunger that would not be lightly appeased. A soft sigh slipped from her as his lips wandered down the slender column of her throat. Her dressing gown fell away from her naked breasts beneath his searching hand, and Elise caught her breath at the flaring pleasure evoked by the warm wetness of his mouth and the flaming strokes across a softly pliant peak.

A log fell in the fireplace, sending a burst of crackling sparks flying outward from the hearth and startling Elise to her senses. Her eyes flew open, and with a sudden heave, she pushed the naked man away and scrambled over him to escape the bed, not caring that her modesty paid the total price as the skirt of her dressing gown flared wide. With urgent haste she fled the chamber and slammed the portal behind her. She seized the lighted tallow, and her rapid descent of the stairs made the tiny flame dance crazily atop the wick until it was nearly doused by the swift current of air. She plunged through the lower portal, secured it well, and flung aside the tapestry. Setting the candle in place, she knelt before the hearth, trembling and shaken, but it was not the coldness of the room that left her so. It was the realization of where their passion had led her.

A soft scratching on the hidden panel snatched her

breath, and she heard the subdued plea.

"Elise? Open the door."

Slipping beneath the tapestry, she braced her brow against the panel. "Please, Maxim, go away."

"I want you." Though but a whisper spoken against the panel, it seemed like a shout in the darkness that enveloped her. "I need you."

Despite the coldness beneath the heavy cloth, a fine dew of moisture covered her skin, and her hands shook as she clutched them to her trembling mouth. "Go away, Maxim. Leave me be. Forget that I ever came."

His brief, scoffing laugh attested to the difficulty of that feat. "Forget that I've a heart that will not slow? A hand that will not cease its trembling? A man's lust that is not quenched? Would you have me seek out another to sate it?"

"No!" The answer burst from her lips before she could halt it, and she began to sob. Her heart ached with the sudden threat of his words, but she could not yield to the driving urgency of their passions, not when there was much yet to be spoken between them.

Chapter 15

*T*HE HANSA CAPTAIN had arrived at Faulder Castle in his usual buoyant spirits, and settling his gaze on Elise, had thrown his arms wide and lavishly praised the maid on her appearance. "Oh, ho! Vhat have ve here? A fair damsel grown more radiant in these northern climes? Pray tell, vhat has done this thing? Can it be the new gown she is vearing?" His light blue eyes gleamed as he perused her. "*Nein*, I think it is more than that. I vow the frost in the air has set a sparkle in her eyes and a bloom upon her cheeks." He leaned near with a teasing leer. "Truly, *vrouwelin*, if I did not know better, I vould think yu are happy here."

"And had I no better ken, Captain Von Reijn, I would think you were endowed with the wayward tongue of an Irishman," Elise parried with a beguiling smile and laid a hand upon his sleeve. "Truly, this cold weather does bring a blush to the cheeks, and your good company a warmth to my heart. We bid you welcome to Faulder Castle."

"Yu are as gracious as yu are beautiful, *vrouwelin.*"

Maxim could do naught but silently agree with the captain's observations. It seemed with each passing day Elise grew more exquisite in her beauty. This evening she looked exceptionally striking dressed in a black and gold matelasse' gown she had donned for the benefit of their guest. A ruff of stiff gold lace adorned her slender throat, and beneath it hung a most recent gift from the Hansa captain, gold chains intertwined with pearls and starred with tiny jewels. Heavy strands of auburn hair had been coiled intricately and dressed high upon her head, lending her a regal countenance that seemed to awe even *Frau* Hanz.

Maxim was intrigued by every aspect of Elise's character and appearance. He found her totally engaging and easily understood how she captured the attention and imagination of both her suitors, though he stood mute and reluctantly reticent while the other man zealously wooed her. It was not a role Maxim greatly cherished. To play the disinterested bystander and ignore the painful proddings of jealousy as Nicholas freely claimed her company was an extremely difficult task. Had it not been for his own foolishness in giving the man permission to court her, he would have pressed his own suit with great fervor.

"*Herr* Dietrich has spent the day creating a feast for your pleasure, Captain." Elise swept a hand toward the table invitingly. "It awaits only your enjoyment."

Nicholas hooked his fingers in his jeweled belt and grinned. "Someone has read my mind."

Elise laughed brightly. "There was no need, Captain. We know of your great love for food."

The meal was entered, and the time passed amiably. Much later the three left the table and found their own place of relaxation as *Frau* Hanz cleared away the last of the wooden trenchers and *Herr* Dietrich prepared a tray of sweetmeats to serve with tankards of mulled wine. Nicholas retired to a huge chair, while Maxim remained near the table, half-sitting, half-leaning against its sturdy planks. From there, he observed the graciousness of his charge as she served the spiced wine, which, to his irritation, also seemed the desire of the Hansa captain.

"Yu are an exquisite and unmatchable beauty in yur new gown," Nicholas extolled. His pale blue eyes sparkled with pleasure as she danced around in a slow circle before him, and he cocked a wondering brow at Maxim who remained carefully stoic while his gaze rested on the maid. "I don't know if I should trust her here vith yu much longer, my friend. Such a tempting sight vould vear hard on any man."

Elise met Maxim's stare with a challenge in her eyes and could not resist a taunt. "I doubt that his lordship even notices I'm alive. He's far too involved with his memories of Arabella."

Nicholas drained his mug and rose to refill it. "Maxim has not lived in this northern clime long enough. Cold nights have a tendency to varm a man's heart and make him more appreciative of a maid closer to hand. It . . . ah . . . becomes a matter of survival . . . though for certain, his lordship has proven he has a vill to survive."

"Do we not all share that inclination?" Elise inquired with a cryptic smile.

"Of course, *vrouwelin!*" the captain agreed. *"Am Leben bleiben!* 'Tis an urge so strong in some men, they vill sometimes ignore the call of a drowning man to guard their own lives." He splashed more of the mulled wine into his mug and gazed thoughtfully into the distance for a brief moment before facing them again. "No one knows a man's true mettle 'til the challenge comes. When faced vith danger, some turn tail and run, while others stand and fight. I've always considered myself a fighter, vith many a brawl to advance as evidence, but I've also fancied myself a lover of life and ladies. God only knows vhat I vould do if faced vith certain death. So vhere is truth to be found until that hour of testing?" He raised an arm to indicate the Marquess. " 'Tis different vith my friend. He has faced the foe and bested him."

A wry grin curved Maxim's lips. "I've also fled to preserve my life. Indeed, you could say the guards very nearly ended my life ere I escaped their tender care."

Nicholas leaned back in his chair and entwined his fingers over his chest. "I see yu make light of yur valor, my friend, and jest over yur escape. Yet very few have escaped Elizabeth's guards and eluded their search and then lived to banter over the whole of it."

"And you make much ado about nothing." Maxim shrugged casually. "Besides, whatever repute I once had serving Elizabeth, I've now lost. I've been stripped of home, honor, and possessions."

"Stripped of home and possessions, perhaps." Nicholas considered his host with a thoughtful smile. "But I think not honor."

"I fear my charge would disagree with you," Maxim commented dryly, directing his gaze again to the maid. "She is of the belief that there's no honor among thieves and other sorts of vagabonds."

"To be sure, my lord. Pirates, brigands, and kidnappers have no more esteem than the foulest scum." Elise slowly approached the table as she teased him. "But then, since I cannot speak from experience as to the lengths a man will go for love, I may in time learn what goads a man and alter my opinion. As you have already clearly demonstrated, you'd do much to have Arabella at your side." With gracefully veiled deliberation and a touch of boldness, Elise reached for the platter of sweetmeats *Herr* Dietrich had placed on the table, brushing so close to Maxim that her skirts half covered his booted legs. Lifting coyly questioning eyes to meet his stare, she dared to goad him.

"Your devotion to her was the reason for her planned abduction, was it not, my lord?"

Maxim felt the prodding of her words and, at the same time, the pulsing of his blood as her nearness tantalized him and struck sparks in his mind. In the past days he had come to realize she could, with no more than a look, a touch, or a smile, awaken his lusting desires more effectively than any woman he had ever known, while seeming oblivious to what she did to him. Or was he being too kind to believe that she had not been born with the wiles of a temptress?

Elise eyed him quizzically as she gently taunted, "Lost your tongue, my lord? Cannot speak? Offended?"

Maxim slowly grinned as a rather wicked gleam glimmered in the green eyes, but no words broke his lips.

"Oh, you *are* in a peculiar mood," she observed.

His brow crinkled lopsidedly, betraying an amused skepticism. "Strange that you should be saying that to me."

Elise responded with a soft laugh and a flippant toss of her head. "I really don't know what you mean, my lord," she said in a guise of innocence. Holding forth the tray, she offered him the delicacies. "Would you care for a sweetmeat?"

Maxim caught her gaze and held it, making no attempt to select a tidbit as he kept his arms folded across his chest. He knew she had a propensity for being mischievous. What he had to determine was whether she was trifling with him for the sport of it, or if she was following the immortal pattern of a lovesmitten maid by doting on a suitor she had come to fancy. Her sincerity would bear testing. "Most assuredly, madam. It has been my craving for some time now."

Elise carefully tended her reaction, feeling a delicious warmth suffuse her. His eyes plunged to the very depth of her being, and his subtle meaning did not go unheeded. Softly she queried, "Which should it be, my lord?"

"Whatever you've a mind to give me. 'Twill be the sweetest," he murmured, and his voice was like a caress, stirring forth a blush to her cheeks. Though his statement was simple enough on the surface to escape Nicholas's attention, it was made highly suggestive when combined with the casual boldness in his gaze.

Elise selected a tiny fruit tart and held it up as an offering. Again Maxim made no move to take it. Instead, his eyes continued to burn into hers, then he leaned forward slightly and opened his mouth to receive the morsel. She raised it to his lips, and her heart quickened as she set it between his teeth and felt the soft flick of his tongue against her finger as his lips closed upon it. It was the most stealthy of caresses, yet it made her doubt her wisdom in playing her girlish games with him. He was no naïve lad to be encouraged and then held at arm's length by a teasing shake of the head. As evidenced by her previous encounters with him, he was capable of reciprocating in a most provocative way.

"I'm forgetting our guest!" Elise stated breathlessly. She snatched her gaze away from those entrancing green orbs and stepped quickly away, managing to laugh as she faced Nicholas with the trencher of sweetmeats. "What is your delight, Captain? A sweet confection?"

With thoughtful care Nicholas made his selection and consumed the morsel with his usual relish. After a moment he faced his host with a sly smile and raised his tankard. "Though yu may still grieve over yur loss of Arabella, my friend, I for one am most grateful that

yur plans vent awry. Had they not, I vould never have
known Elise, and that vould have been a great misfortune for me. As to yur folly, my friend, may it in
time bring yu as much pleasure as it has brought me."

Maxim lifted his cup in response and inclined his
head briefly in acknowledgment of the toast. "May
providence be kind to us all."

Nicholas tossed down the wine in a single turn of
his wrist and, setting aside the empty mug, sighed in
what seemed smug pleasure. "As a matter of fact, providence has been most kind to me of late." Drawing
forth a small, wilted sprig of greenery from his pocket,
he held it up and twirled it by the stem for their
benefit. "Give heed, my friends, to vhat I managed to
acquire from an Englishman visiting Hamburg."

Elise moved closer, looking at the twig in curious
wonder. "But what is it?"

"Mistletoe," he answered simply.

Elise's bemusement was hardly sated by his matter-
of-fact reply. "Whatever is it for?"

"A multitude of things, I've been told." Having
gained the curiosity of his companions, Nicholas made
a show of tying a ribbon around the stem. Stepping
onto a bench, he secured the colored band around a
wooden beam, and arranged the sprig so it would hang
free. Alighting from the perch with a broad grin, he
folded his arms across his chest as he met the perplexed stares of the two. "The Druids claimed the
mistletoe had great medicinal value, especially as a
remedy for poisons."

"The very idea, Nicholas!" Elise scolded, taking offense. "You cannot possibly be concerned with being
poisoned here, especially after stuffing yourself on
Herr Dietrich's cooking."

"Not in the least, *vrouwelin*," he assured her. He
swept his hand upward toward the twig as he ex-

plained, "Actually, vhen one stands beneath it, the mistletoe can offer a most exhilarating experience."

Elise moved beneath the sprig and eyed the captain with marked dubiety. "Are you sure you haven't been taken in by a charlatan, Nicholas? I detect no change."

"You'll not be disappointed," Nicholas assured her. "Why, Pliny the Elder wrote of its benefits many long years ago." He paused to ask in curiosity, "By chance, do you know of him?"

"Are you sure he even existed?" she countered with humor. "Perhaps his existence was as airy as his claims."

Maxim strode forward leisurely. "Oh, the man lived all right...about fifteen hundred years ago. His adopted son was a consul of Rome around the turn of the first century."

Nicholas acknowledged the other's reply by touching his fingers to his brow in a brief salute of admiration. "Yu know yur history vell, my friend."

Maxim casually dismissed the compliment. "The letters of Pliny the Younger were often used by my tutors for an historical insight into Rome. Yet I must confess my lack of knowledge concerning the mistletoe. Surely if its merits were so enormous, they'd have been well-documented by now."

Elise settled her arms akimbo in chiding amusement. "And then perhaps I would know what to expect."

Nicholas approached her with a grin as he gave a reply. "How can yu know vhat to expect if yu've never experienced anything like it? 'Tis understandable that truth gets bound up in superstition. The Druids have largely contributed to a great number of tales. For instance, a most pleasant custom of kissing under the mistletoe gave rise to the idea that such an occurrence leads inevitably to matrimony. Vould yu give heed to

such claims if I vere to kiss yu?" Giving her no chance
to think upon his question, Nicholas took her into his
arms and bent an avid kiss upon her lips, oblivious to
Maxim who started forward in sharp displeasure, then
caught himself. Releasing her, the captain met her
astounded stare with a grin. "A most revarding experience for me, if not yu, *vrouwelin,* but vould yu
consider that ve are now betrothed?"

Breaking away with an embarrassed blush, Elise
crisply admonished, "Certainly not! I'm quite capable
of making a decision of that sort on my own, without
being duped or tricked into a trap . . . which you deliberately laid for me."

Nicholas executed a flamboyant bow before her.
" 'Tis a sweetmeat I can take to my pillow and dream
of, *vrouwelin. Ja,* the hour grows late, so I must urge
yu both to seek yur pallets if ve are to leave for Lubeck
before dawn. Ve vill need our rest. I bid yu both *Gute
Nacht.*"

With a casual wave to Maxim, Nicholas strode
across the hall and made a rapid ascent of the stairs.
Shaking her head at the captain's antics, Elise watched
his flight until she became aware of Maxim stepping
close behind her. She held her breath as long, lean
fingers slid along her arm, taking her elbow in a gentle
but unyielding grasp. Her pulse quickened, and she
turned to find Maxim regarding her with a strange
and inscrutable smile.

"We must honor tradition, must we not?" he queried softly. With an upward glance, he drew her attention to where the mistletoe hung above their
heads, and then his face lowered and his parting lips
moved upon hers in a slow, deliberate caress that
denied her resistance and sapped the strength from
her limbs. Her thoughts whirled in a reeling eddy, and

evoked all the yearnings she had experienced once upon a time in his bed.

His mouth left hers, and Elise sighed as if coming out of a pleasurable dream. She opened her eyes and stared into the lean, handsome face so close above her own. It filled her vision, neither retreating nor advancing until she raised up on her toes and flung her arms tightly about his neck. Maxim was taken back by surprise, but the experience was immensely gratifying. The kiss that she gave him created a slowly mushrooming glow inside his head, having the same effect as a strong brew. His arms tightened about her narrow waist, and he tasted fully of her warmth and passion. He could feel her soft breasts pressed tightly against him and, beneath the fabric of her gown, the stiff ribbing of her stays as his fingers slid over her back.

From somewhere near the hearth a loud "Humph!" was expelled with derisive contempt, and Elise snatched away from Maxim in sudden embarrassment. She had forgotten there were servants present to witness their kiss.

The green eyes swept coldly over a broad shoulder, picking out the offender. *Frau* Hanz felt the chilling coldness of Maxim's glare, while *Herr* Dietrich clucked his tongue in sharp disapproval of the housekeeper.

Gathering her dignity, Elise coolly directed her gaze toward the woman. "*Frau* Hanz, I've been somewhat disappointed in your performance here. I've made a list of things you should do while we're away. Upon our return, I shall expect to see them completed. Otherwise, you'll have to find employment elsewhere."

If *Frau* Hanz expected some word to come from the master of the keep that would demonstrate his authority and override the girl's order, she was to be greatly disappointed. By maintaining his silence, Maxim gave his approval to the ultimatum. Finding no help there, the woman faced the girl, her back rigidly bolstered by her pride. "Vhatever may be yur vish, mistress."

"Then we understand each other," Elise replied in a gracious tone. "Yet there's still a matter which needs be discussed."

Frau Hanz fixed the younger woman with a stony stare. "And vhat is that?"

"Your manners," her mistress answered bluntly. "They're detestable."

The stiffly sprung disposition of the woman remained intact as she sniffed haughtily. "I've always tried to conduct myself in a manner becoming my station, mistress. I'm sorry if yu've taken offense."

Elise calmly met the housekeeper's frigid stare. "I would advise you to consider how you might improve upon them while we're away. If you refuse to see the need for such, we'll have to let you go."

"Ve?" *Frau* Hanz bestowed a questioning stare upon the Marquess. "My lord, is this in agreement vith yu?"

He almost smiled. "Of course."

"Vell!" The word came out in a huff. "I suppose if I've no other choice, I must comply vith the vishes of the mistress, else find myself discharged."

"That would seem the case, *Frau* Hanz," Maxim agreed.

Frau Hanz inclined her head ever so slightly in acknowledgment of the directive. "If that is all, my lord, I should like to get back to my duties...so I might make myself of use."

Maxim looked to Elise for approval, lending strength to her authority. She responded with a small dip of her head, acknowledging and appreciating his support.

Frau Hanz went back to her labors, and it was hardly a moment later when she took out her spite on *Herr* Dietrich by sharply instructing him in his work. The man was not of a mind to take untutored criticism and the argument that ensued was both loud and demonstrative. Skillets and pots were slammed down amid hotly voiced exclamations shouted in the Teutonic tongue, and the portly man became so incensed that he pressed close to the woman and waggled his forefinger beneath her nose in a threatening manner.

"What have I done?" Elise lamented.

Maxim chuckled. "Never fear, madam. *Herr* Dietrich is capable of defending himself."

"I hope so." She heaved a rather dejected sigh. "It might be wise if I left now. I may be tempted to send *Frau* Hanz back to Hamburg on the morrow."

"Think no more of her," Maxim advised. "She'll have some time to think while we're away. If she shows no improvement by then, she'll be gone."

"Then I'll bid you good night, my lord." Elise smiled up into the warmly glowing green eyes. "I shall see you again ere the morn breaks."

He honored her with a finely executed bow. "May the bliss of evening lull you gently to sleep, sweet maid."

Several moments later Elise fell into bed with a dreamy sigh escaping her smiling lips, and she hugged the pillows close against her naked bosom, while memories evoked strange hungers in her loins. She had felt the bold caress of his mouth upon her breast, and ever since, the remembrance of the deed persisted in her mind, intruding into her thoughts even while she was with him or, more disturbingly, when they were with Nicholas. Whether or nay he sensed the reason for the blush that came into her cheeks, she could not say, but sometimes when he looked at her with those smoldering eyes, she was almost certain he was remembering the same event.

Her dreams were filled with fantasies and she found herself being swept up in strong, sturdy arms. At first a haze of confused visions swirled about her, and for a breathless moment the need to escape them pressed down upon her. She struggled in sinewy arms as a ruddy face and pale blue eyes filled her mind, then as if by a miracle the skin bronzed and the eyes darkened ever-so-wonderfully to a deep emerald green. Her heart soared as she waited for the kiss that would fill her with an ecstasy of bliss, and for parting lips to move upon hers in a questing search for an answer. The answer came, and though her mind meandered through the dark caverns of sleep, she knew what it was. Love had come stealing into her life, and she would never, ever be the same.

Chapter 16

*F*LUFFY FLAKES DRIFTED to earth in a soft, downy flight, nestling cozily on wide-spreading boughs of lofty evergreens and covering the hillocks and vales with mantles of white. Beside a gurgling, half-frozen stream a russet-hued doe raised her dripping muzzle and tested the air with flaring nostrils. Her long ears flicked to and fro as a faint, distant tinkling invaded the hushed stillness of early morning. The tiny bells rang with silver clarity through the forest, forewarning the rapid approach of a foreign presence through the wilderness. A shout and the muffled drumming of massive hooves further attested to the intrusion, and the hind bounded off in a zigzagging flight through the trees, wary of this unwarranted invasion into her domain.

Soon a foursome of huge steeds entered the glade, drawing behind them a conveyance that closely resembled a long, wooden box. Three more horses were tethered to the rear of the ornate sleigh, and the high, bold gait of Eddy kept easy pace with the matched four-in-hand. The blue, red-lined, hooded cloaks of the six horsemen who rode as escort brought flashes of color to the wintry shades of the forest. Their garb was typical of Captain Von Reijn's penchant for the ostentatious.

Indeed, Nicholas delighted himself in the game of impressing the maid, and no small attention had been given to detail in accomplishing that objective. He had commissioned the building of the luxurious vehicle to accommodate the travelers in grand style, using as a loose example a coach which the Earl of Arundel had introduced in England several years back. In summer the conveyance could be affixed with huge wheels or, as it was now in winter, with runners faced with iron straps to enable the contraption to glide easily through the snow or over the ice.

The interior was even more impressive. Ornately carved shutters could be either opened wide to catch the intoxicating breezes of the warmer months or closed against the frigid blasts which were wont to buffet the box in winter. To further muffle the drafts and hold out the chill of the wooden sides, velvet panels had been sheared on rods and hung within the interior. A wealth of small pillows and fur robes were strewn over the heavily cushioned seats, assuring a cozy and comfortable ride. Warming pans rested in brackets on the floor between the seats where the passengers could share and enjoy their heat.

Ever thoughtful of food and the accoutrements of dining, Nicholas had a small, collapsible table made that could be positioned between the seats when the need arose. For the combined pleasure of all he had brought along a wide variety of wines, while *Herr* Dietrich had stocked several baskets with sweet and succulent sustenance.

To be sure, whether in fine food, elaborate appointments, or rich attire Nicholas was never to be outdone, not even by Elise who, after taking note of Maxim's rather austere chest, had felt almost extravagant in the inclusion of two of comparable size. However, the captain's four enormous, leather-bound cases, distinguishable by his initials emblazoned in the center of a filigreed shield, had done much to reassure her.

From the onset of the journey Nicholas had taken on the authority of host and arranged the seating to his advantage, placing himself beside Elise and designating the opposite seat for Maxim. The captain enjoyed his much-presumed claim on the maid and instructed her on the history of the Hanseatic League, beginning at its conception when a band of German merchants had united for the purpose of protecting themselves against lawless buccaneers and other miscreants. He continued on through three hundred or so years of the Hansa's growth, relating vivid stories of their powerful reign as merchant kings in foreign ports and on the high seas. More introspectively, he mused aloud on the weakening or closing down of their strongholds on the Thames, in Novgorod, and with the Danes, and grew pensive as he lent himself to questioning their future.

"At times, *vrouwelin,* I vonder if there is not the faintest stench of our forthcoming doom vafting on the breezes and ve are too proud to catch the scent of it."

Sensing his decaying mood, Elise wiggled on the seat and stretched her slippered feet toward the warmth of the covered coal pans lying on the floor between the two seats. Sitting forward, she sought to catch his downcast eye and drag him from his doldrums. "Tell me, Nicholas, are there ever any prisoners held for ransom by the Hansa?"

Nicholas leaned back in the seat. "We've taken hostages here and there, mainly for offenses against our league." Growing suspicious, he raised his gaze and peered at her. "Do yu have someone in particular in mind?"

"Of course," she answered readily. "My father made

several trips to the Stilliards before he was kidnapped, and there was much speculation about the possibility of his seizure by members of the Hansa. I cannot help but wonder if some of those tales are true."

"Usually ve are traders of goods, *vrouwelin,* not of men," he replied.

Elise pressed him further, reluctant to be put off so easily. " 'Twas rumored that my father traded many of his treasures for Hansa gold. Would not the idea of a coffer full of gold be of interest to someone in the league?"

"Of course, there are always those who are seeking riches, but since I've heard no such tales myself and know of no one who has, I fear I cannot help yu... as much as I vould like to, *vrouwelin.* If I could somehow restore yur father to yu, I vould no doubt vin yur love forever, and that vould be a prize I vould greatly cherish."

"Who would know then?" Elise persisted, ignoring his inclination to turn the conversation elsewhere. "Whom should I ask?"

The captain swept a hand toward Maxim, brushing her question off with a wayward grin. "Perhaps my friend can assist yu in this matter. He has his spies."

Maxim promptly raised his gaze and gave the man a highly skeptical look. "Your humor escapes me, Nicholas. What spies do you speak of?"

"Vhy, Spence and Fitch, of course," Nicholas answered jovially. "A pair of the most crafty, to be sure. Yu sent them to spy out Arabella, and they came back vith this jewel of a maid. If they vould do like favors for me in the future, I vould urge yu to send them out again on such an errand. Give them the task of finding Elise's father, and who knows vhat they'll bring back."

"I dare not trust them again." Maxim settled his

shoulders in the corner of the seat and warmly considered his charge. "I'm still trying to straighten out my life after their first adventure, and I'm not sure I can handle another surprise of such magnitude."

The corners of Elise's lips lifted enticingly. "Do I hear the laments of a coward, my lord?"

In challenging question, the green eyes fixed their stare upon her and glowed with warmth. "And have I not a right to be? You nearly unmanned me, madam."

A gently scoffing chuckle escaped Elise as she leaned back into the cushions. "You portray yourself as an innocent, but we all know you deserved every bit of it."

"An arguable statement," Maxim protested. "Indeed, I was certain my men had gone to the far ends of the earth to find such a gifted tormentor." He raised his hand to indicate the beauty whose face radiated her happiness. "No ordinary maid, this, but one well worthy of any game. Truly, I doubt that even Arabella could have created such stimulating diversions."

Elise tossed her head in sudden perturbation and spoke before she thought. "Arabella is far too timid for a man li—" Realizing how Maxim might interpret her statement, she halted in some confusion, not knowing how to finish. "I mean . . . you . . . ah . . ."

Maxim did not miss her hesitation and pounced on her words with eager delight. "A man like me? Is that what you were about to say?"

She busied herself by tucking a fur robe about her lap in an effort to draw his attention from her reddening cheeks. "I only meant that you seem so . . . ah . . . bold . . . at times."

Maxim had held some qualms about the trip to Lubeck, knowing he would be sorely tested while Nicholas pressed his suit, but he saw in Elise's warming behavior some glimmer of hope for a much more pleasurable journey. "And do you think a bolder maid would be better suited to me?"

"Who am I to say, my lord?" She posed the question as if astounded by his inquiry. "I've known you only these few months past, certainly not long enough to give an accurate judgment."

"Still!" He stressed the word, denying her attempt to escape his questioning. "You've formed an opinion, and I'm most interested in hearing your views. 'Tis apparent you think Arabella and I would not have made a proper match, but you don't say who would be a better choice for me." He regarded her closely as he asked, "Would someone with your temperament be more appropriate?"

Elise opened her mouth to spurn his suggestion, but no words issued forth as she struggled with the denial. How could she disclaim what she felt?

"Nein, nein," Nicholas insisted, coming to her rescue. He was beginning to feel uneasy with the turn of conversation and her delay in answering. For many years he had witnessed a series of women from every realm and state in life settling their attention on Maxim. Whether the man had been aware of it or not, he had nevertheless stirred the hearts of many a maid. It would not be strange if the girl also became susceptible, and that was the matter that concerned him. "Yu are a man strong of mind and purpose, Maxim. A meek maid vould better serve yur needs and be submissive to yur dictates. Understandably Arabella vould have been the best choice for yu."

"And what of you, Captain?" Elise queried, rather irked by his statement. How could he say that Arabella, an ambivalent and indecisive maid, who seemed void of any fervent emotions, would complement his lordship more than she? Oh, nay, Elise thought with surety, Maxim would be better suited to a fiery wench than any frail and fearful mouse. Thoughtfully she tilted her head as she contemplated the captain. "What sort of maid would be good for you, Captain? One of sweet temper and melancholy eyes?"

"The answer is obvious, *meine Liebchen*," Nicholas replied, dropping a hand upon hers.

Maxim's brows raised sharply as he looked at Elise, but she did not dare meet his gaze. She was afraid he would see the discomfort she was presently experiencing. She felt a painful chagrin for having ever encouraged Nicholas. Where once she had used his attentions to tweak Maxim's nose, she now only wanted to be friends and nothing more. Yet she was hesitant about broaching the subject and was most perplexed as to how she might wisely dissuade him, for he seemed most intent on courting her.

Maxim wedged his shoulders deeper into the corner and directed a stony stare out the window. His mood had definitely darkened, and though he observed the passing countryside, his mind churned in a continual turmoil of conflicts. For many years Nicholas had been his friend, but this rivalry that was growing by leaps and bounds between them could well endanger their longstanding camaraderie. He wanted to see Elise cool the captain's ardor, as much to break the shackles of this damnable reticence he found himself bound by, as to banish that foul, green viper, Jealousy. That loathsome serpent raised its ugly head every time the man approached her, and Maxim found it hard to suffer in silent agony as the sharp fangs sank ever deeper.

The travelers paused at the noon hour to give the horses a rest and to take nourishment from a well-supplied larder. A fire was built in a sheltered glade, and after a brief stroll to stretch their limbs, the drivers and guards settled near the warmth of the flames to appease their hunger while their captain and his guests enjoyed a more private repast in the conveyance.

'Twas shortly after the meal when Nicholas excused himself and strolled off into the woods to clear his head, having liberally imbibed from a flagon of wine. In his absence Maxim openly watched Elise until she could no longer ignore his unwavering stare. "My lord? Have I grown warts of a sudden?"

"There's a matter which has troubled me overmuch of late, madam," he informed her bluntly. "And I would have it out."

Elise's curiosity was greatly piqued. There was an intensity in those fiery green brands that clearly conveyed the depth of his concern. "You have my leave to speak of whatever plagues you, my lord. Have I done aught to offend you?"

Though Maxim had mulled the words over in his mind, he plunged ahead with the recklessness of an impatient suitor and answered in a sharper tone than he had intended. "The only offense I must contend with is your delay in telling Nicholas that you're not in love with him."

Elise stared at him aghast, astounded by his attack. "My lord, you speak boldly of a matter which has seemed to amuse you in the past. How is it that you know my emotions ere I express them?"

"As I've already explained, madam, I'm a man well-primed to take a woman to wife . . ."

"Any woman, my lord?" she queried, but the sweetness of her tone only enhanced her portrayal of the skepticism she felt. He had already stated that after losing Arabella, it did not matter what wife he took for his own.

Ignoring her jibe, Maxim pressed on. "I would know if I'm a fool."

"Have I the ability to reassure you that you're not?"

"Aye, madam! You do! By telling me that I have not imagined what your kisses say to me. You play with me as a woman tempted with desires of her own, and I move ever closer to that time when I shall break the bonds of restraint and take you to my bed. If you don't intend for this to happen, whether as my mistress or as my wife, then give me the word now and I will make no further demands that you talk with Nicholas. For mercy's sake, don't lead me on like you do him."

"And what of Arabella, my lord?" Elise dared to remind him of his once-professed love. "Have you no lingering fondness for her?"

Maxim leaned forward, bracing his elbows on his knees as he spoke intently. "She's nothing more than a vague memory. Truly, her face has become obscure in my mind. Now I see only yours."

Elise's heart warmed, and her elation would have caught her up in a whirlwind of bliss and swept her on to immeasurable heights, but she was cautious. He had not spoken of love, only of desire, and that was not sufficient. She wanted his heart, his mind, and his passion for herself alone and would not be content if she had to share his love with another woman. "It could be nothing more than a passing fancy, my lord," she chided. "Here today, gone come the morrow."

"I'm no fickle youth, madam," he avowed sharply. "I know my mind."

"But do you know your heart?" she argued. "You were so positive you were in love with Arabella, and now you say she's all but forgotten. Can you pledge a troth to me that I'd be of greater worth to you in years to come?"

"Madam, you have no ken of my thoughts, what my feelings were toward Arabella."

"What are you saying? That you were not in love with Arabella?"

There was a reluctance in him to answer her prodding, for it would only make him seem more of a villain in her eyes. He chose his words carefully. "I've an aversion to anyone taking what belongs to me by force. When I look back upon my anger toward Edward, it comes to my mind that I meant to avenge myself more than anything else."

His answer heightened Elise's curiosity. "That was not what you told me before. Indeed, I was sure your love for Arabella was the cause for my abduction."

Maxim cursed beneath his breath. This damnable arguing was chafing sorely on his patience. He wanted her, and he was frustrated because she refused to believe him. He tried another approach, one of reason. "Madam, I'm offering to give you my protection and my name, such as it is. Would it not be a logical decision for us to marry? After all, I arranged for your abduction and, in so doing, have compromised your name and reputation."

"You hated me once, remember?"

"Never!" Maxim denied.

Elise ignored his astounded mien and returned to him an injured air. "I was sure you did."

Maxim answered in exasperation, "To enter into a union that is well-suited to both of us, do you need to examine my heart so closely that you must rend it from my chest? Are we not both alone in this world? I've no family, and you very few whom you can trust. We cannot say what has happened to your father. If for naught else but shared comfort and companionship, will you not accept my proposal?"

Elise fought against the logic of his words. She wanted something far more out of marriage than a union which seemed right or sensible. "Are you sure of what you want, Maxim?" she asked quietly. "Mayhap there'll come another in your life whom you'll want more than me." She ignored his light scoff as she continued her argument. "And you may want to marry her."

"Madam, I've never met another woman—" he paused for effect as he leaned forward to fix her with an intense stare—"who is as exasperating as you are!"

Having fully expected him to make protestations declaring his desire for her, Elise opened her mouth several times, completely at a loss for words. In a huff, she finally settled back into the seat with an injured comment. "If you find me so aggravating, my lord, why should you even bother asking me to become your wife?"

Maxim's mouth twisted in a lopsided smile. "Because I've never wanted a woman more than I want you."

Placated, Elise sat for a long moment in thoughtful silence and finally responded. "Your proposal has come upon me suddenly." She spoke with measured care, not because she was unsure of herself, but because she felt a need to be cautious of him. With his stirring good looks, he would always be confronted by women who wanted him and would do anything to have him, if naught else but to take him into their beds for no more than an evening or an hour. And how could she manage to hold him against such odds? Oh, truly, she would have gladly yielded him an affirmative answer if only she could be sure that in time he would not find another and come to regret their marriage. "Before I can give you answer, I must know truly what my own heart would say."

The green eyes conveyed Maxim's disappointment. "As you wish, Elise, but . . . I beg you . . . have a care. My emotions are rent asunder when I stand aside and watch you being courted by another man."

"I will take care, my lord," she murmured softly, understanding only too well what jealousy would do to her.

Feeling a need to be out in the cold air where she could think clearly and rationally, she reached for the old hide boots. "If you'll excuse me, my lord. I'd like to take a walk outside."

"The snow has blown into drifts," Maxim observed, glancing from the window. "You'll likely ruin the hem of your gown if you try crossing them."

"There's no help for it," she replied, taking up the boots. An earnest need had arisen, and though she fretted over spoiling her new clothes, she could not travel the rest of the day and not seek relief. "I'll only be gone a few moments. Perhaps the damage will not be too severe."

Maxim knelt before her and, taking a boot from her grasp, slipped it on her foot. "I doubt if these will suffice to keep your feet warm."

"I dare not wear my new ones."

"If you must go out, let me assist you," he urged.

"If you will, my lord," she murmured with a smile.

Removing her other slipper, Maxim rested her stockinged foot upon his thigh as he prepared her boot. The contact warmed her pleasantly, and though it might have been a small service he performed, for Elise his ministrations gave evidence of the sort of man he was. He had fought his battles and faced the foe, yet he was not without a gentler side. His solicitousness brought home the realization that the two of them had grown quite compatible in the past weeks. Little services performed one for the other had drawn them into a unity that had been both comfortable and immensely satisfying. Perhaps she was a fool to demand all the answers at once. Though he might not love her, if he could be the kind of caring husband she needed and wanted, it was a very practical reason for them to come together. Perhaps in time love would find its way into his heart.

Maxim raised himself to his feet and reached out to take her hand. Pulling her from the cushioned seat, he brought her hard against him and for a long moment held her as his eyes searched hers.

"Tell me you don't feel what I feel when I hold you." His voice possessed a rich timbre that could, by itself, start her pulse leaping in her veins. The assault on her senses seemed to advance threefold as he leaned forward, and she caught the clean, masculine scent of him. She could hear, smell, and feel him; she needed only to taste him, and even that experience seemed near as his lips hovered over hers. "Tell me you don't tremble when I touch you," he whispered huskily, "and then try to tell me you don't want me to make love to you."

With a gasp Elise raised her head to stare at him, knowing that she should be offended by his words. The denial was ready to be spoken, but the only words that stumbled from her lips were confused and faintly chiding. "You shouldn't talk to me that way, Maxim."

His eyes burned into hers, and he read the truth of her desires as he searched the sapphire depths. "Why? Are you afraid to hear the truth? You need loving, madam." His nostrils flared as his eyes blazed with fiery passion. "By damned, madam! 'Tis my torment that I want you here and now!"

He was too close! She could not breathe!

Snatching free, Elise stumbled to the door, but Maxim was immediately behind her, taking her hard against him. His hand slipped beneath her cloak and clasped her breast as he pressed his face into her hair. His hoarse, ragged breathing sounded loud in her ear, then with a low growl of frustration he tore away and presented his back to her.

"This is humorous," Maxim jeered derisively over his shoulder. "I've had you close beneath my hand for these many weeks past, and though you roused me to heights I could not endure, I did not try to force you. The moment we're away, my wont is to throw up your skirts and set upon you like a rutting stag." He looked down as he ground out the words. "Truly, with less clothes you'd have surely served my pleasure."

Elise's heart would not stop its chaotic flight, but she whispered unsteadily, with all the dignity she could muster, "I should be most glad for your help through the snow, my lord."

His head snapped up, and he looked at her in surprise. He saw her troubled profile and knew that she was genuinely upset, but not with him. Stepping past her to the door, he looked back and found uncertainty clouding her eyes. He sighed mentally, feeling chagrined. There were times when he forgot that she was very young and she had no real knowledge of men or the lusts that goaded them. "The fault is mine, Elise," he assured her gently. "You did nothing that was deserving of my rudeness."

Alighting from the coach, Maxim paused a moment to let the cold air cool his mind. The guards were huddled near the campfire, talking and warming their hands, but when he reached up and swept Elise into his arms, he could feel the stares of the men come full weight upon them. Nicholas had made his claims upon the girl obvious to everyone, and it would not be long before word reached the captain of this encroachment.

Elise laid her arms about his neck, but when Maxim looked at her, her flitting gaze portrayed her shyness and a reluctance to meet his eyes. He could not blame her, for he had acted no better than that pompous oaf, Reland.

He trod through the rolling, motionless waves of white until he reached a still, silent clearing surrounded by a copse of evergreens. Only a light layer of snow covered the ground within the shelter of the trees. It was a place of peaceful enchantment, where green boughs glistened with a heavy frosting of white, where the snow squeaked beneath the feet, and where spirits soared as high as the birds that flew near the treetops.

Suddenly Maxim chuckled, feeling a need to lighten the moment, and whirled about in a circle, snatching Elise's breath as he clasped his arms close about her. When he halted, she pressed her brow to his temple and, dizzy with delight, breathed out a plea. "Oh, please, my heart is spinning as fast as my head."

"And thus I would have you swoon from my kisses, fair maid," he murmured, turning his face to hers until their lips were nearly touching.

Unconsciously Elise threaded her fingers through the short-cropped hair that lay on his nape. "Are you so sure of your mastery over me, Maxim?"

"I'm certain of naught but your firm hold over me," he avowed softly. "Would that you could feel the same."

Elise felt the threat of blurted-out confessions and commitments that had not been thoroughly considered hovering near the tip of her tongue and spoke with more than a wee vein of truth. "Methinks I would do well to use caution when considering life with you, for I would be ever-fraught with the fear that you would whisk away another young maid to your palace far afield." She chuckled. "There also looms a threat that you might be tempted to give Spence and

Fitch the task of carting me off to some other foreign port to be rid of me. Should that ever happen, I vow to see you drawn and quartered ere my revenge be sated."

"The deuce you say!" Maxim gave her a quick toss into the air, eliciting a gasp. When his arms closed about her again, his grinning face pressed close above her own. "Perhaps I should be wary of your intent?"

"As much as I should be wary of your purpose," Elise rejoined. Once again feeling her defenses weakening, she pressed a hand to his chest and pushed herself away until she could look him squarely in the eye. "Now behave yourself, foul fellow, and my good behavior will stand. I would have a moment of privacy from you and all mankind."

Maxim slowly grinned and jerked his head toward a thick growth of trees. "Might you consider that secluded spot sufficient for your needs, madam?"

"You are uncompromisingly bold and brash," Elise accused.

Maxim rubbed his nape against her soft fingertips as she unconsciously teased the curling ends of his hair. "I've naught to offer you but myself, fair maid," he breathed warmly, touching her brow with his lips. "Flawed though I be, 'tis all I have."

An incredible warmth enveloped Elise's heart as she searched his eyes and found a strange sincerity there. They stared at each other so long it seemed the world had ceased its motion. Then a shout from the camp echoed through the forest, shattering the spell.

"Maxim? Elise? Vhere are yu?"

Maxim let her legs slide beneath her until her feet reached the ground, and though her cloak, skirts, and petticoats were twisted askew, Elise became conscious of the presence of a booted knee between her own and, ever so boldly, a large hand sliding over her breast. She found no desire in herself to pull away, and Maxim battled his own mounting desires as he forced his hands downward to her narrow waist. Reluctantly he set her from him, and as she appeared somewhat befuddled, he bent and swept down her rumpled skirts until they swung free of his leg. Behind him he could hear Nicholas thrashing through the woods.

As if she were naught but a wooden doll incapable of her own movement, Maxim took Elise by the shoulders and, turning her about until she faced the thick growth of trees, gave her a gentle shove. "Go tend your needs, madam. We've been found out."

Cooling his mind and his body, he watched her enter a thicket and then faced Nicholas as that one charged into view.

"There yu are!" the captain exclaimed, puffing from his swift advancement through the deep snow. It was obvious from his haste that he had been informed of their exit from the coach. He halted and glanced around in confusion when he realized the one he sought was not in sight. "But vhere is Elise? I thought yu vere together."

Maxim indicated the lone tracks leading into the trees. "She'll be back in a moment."

Nicholas contemplated the small footprints, then twisted around to consider the pair of furrows opened through the drift, recognizing one as his own.

At his pointed stare, Maxim shrugged casually, hating to make an excuse, but knowing that any other declaration would have to come from Elise. "I could hardly leave the maid to struggle through the drifts by herself. She was reluctant to ruin her hem, and I offered her assistance."

Feeling some annoyance at the other man's boldness, Nicholas snatched the fur collar of his chamarre up close around his neck. "I could have performed the service just as vell."

"You were attending your own needs," Maxim reminded him. "And the lady was in distress."

The captain was hardly placated. "Yu needn't vait for her. I can escort her back to the coach."

"As you wish," Maxim replied and swept his hand before him in a brief gesture of obeisance.

A piqued frown touched Nicholas's brow as he stared after the man. The uncertainty of where he might now stand with Elise made him question his wisdom in asking Maxim to act as escort. He was not a fool to underestimate the magnetism of his lordship or the man's attraction to women. It was just that he had sensed a great measure of security while the pair waged their battles and aired their complaints against each other. He had not even questioned the sincerity of their emotions, for they had good cause to hate each other, and he had certainly never expected a softening of their hearts.

Elise suffered a moment of disappointment when she returned and found Maxim gone and the Hansa captain awaiting her. She could find no solace for the sudden feeling of guilt that assailed her in his presence, and though she was reluctant to admit her love for Maxim, she knew she had to dissuade the captain from further involvement. She searched for the words that would gently sever whatever ties that had formed between them. Esteeming his friendship, she wanted to compose a rejection that was both tender and suitable, but she found nothing that seemed adequate, and for want of something better she gave comment on the weather. "It doesn't seem to be snowing as much now."

Nicholas peered upward into the hazy gloom and made his own conjecture. "It vill continue for a vhile longer, I think." Tugging a glove more firmly over his hand, he lowered his gaze to her. "I'm here to carry yu back to the coach, *vrouwelin.*"

"Oh, but there's no need, Captain," Elise assured him hastily. She was reluctant to have him perform such a service for her, especially now when she was seeking to find a way to turn aside his affection. "I'm quite sound of limb."

"I vould not see yu ruin yur gown in the snow," Nicholas argued, advancing a step.

A soft rustling sound came from the growth of trees behind the captain, drawing their attention to the recently formed path, then a snuffling snort intruded into the stillness of the forest. Elise watched through the trees until she spied Maxim coming toward them leading the huge black steed, Eddy, behind him. When she saw him, she experienced a burgeoning relief that gave evidence of where her affection was solidly centered.

"The men are ready to leave," Maxim announced as Nicholas met him with a sharply questioning stare. "They're wondering whether to ride on ahead to patrol along the road or to stay with the coach. I believe they're waiting for your direction."

In some frustration Nicholas faced Elise. It was not the manner of a gentleman to seize a maid in a rush and carry her back to a camp full of men who would likely make much of the matter. After all, their curiosity had already been aroused by her rather noteworthy exit from the coach. Nor could he again press the advantage of being the only escort available when Maxim's presence prevented such a claim. Thus he had to yield the day to his lordship when that one offered to take the girl back on Eddy.

"We'll ride beside the coach for a space," Maxim threw back over his shoulder as he lifted Elise to the back of the steed. A broad, flat saddle accommodated the pair of them as Maxim swung up behind her.

The animal flagged his tail and pranced sideways for a moment, making the captain retreat to a safe distance. Nicholas clamped a bridle on his growing irritation and kept his silence, realizing that any invitation for the maid to wait and ride with him would appear provoked by an overly possessive nature. Still, when Maxim tapped his heels against the steed's flanks and set him into an easy canter, he was sorely tempted to act the outraged suitor, for the maid fell back against that sturdy frame and there she stayed within those encircling, protective arms as they rode back through the trees.

Maxim's arm tightened about Elise, tucking her closer against him as he whispered close to her ear. "I was fraught with jealousy when I thought of another holding you close, even for such a service as carrying you back to the coach. I had to come back for you."

Elise laid a hand upon his arm, tempted to confide in him that she had been much relieved that he had returned for her. "Nicholas has become a good friend. I would not see him hurt."

"If you love him, Elise, then tell me, and I will go away." Maxim's voice rasped in her mind. "There needs be no word of explanation. But if what I sense is true and there is something growing between us, then a kind word spoken to him now is better than a belated apology. That, my dear, would lend the same effect as a full broadside from a large carrack upon a small cog."

Chapter 17

*T*HE RIVER TRAVE and the battlements laid out by Hansa burghers several centuries prior had made Lubeck an easily defended port. Before the walled city, the stout twin towers of Holsten Gate stood guard, its guns visible and ready to challenge whatever enemy would dare approach. Set beneath a sky inflamed by the lowering sun, the city gleamed like a multijeweled brooch, its steeply jutting rooftops and the lofty pinnacles of its churches reflecting the dwindling light and piercing the gloom with shards of radiant color.

"Lubeck! *Unser aller Haupt!*" Nicholas exclaimed as they approached the gates on horseback. "Head of us all! Queen of the Hansa!" He grinned at Elise who rode beside him on her mount. "She is a jewel, is she not, *vrouwelin?*"

"Truly," Elise replied in much admiration and awe.

Once past the Holstentor, Nicholas led the way through a confusing maze of streets and finally brought his troop to a halt before a large, timber-supported house. Inside the structure a young man pressed close to a lower window and peered out. A smile quickly broke upon his face as he caught sight of the approaching entourage, and he disappeared in an instant. Hardly a moment's pause later, an upwelling of excited cries issued forth from the dwelling as the front door burst open to spill forth two women and the youth, all waving and calling out vociferous welcomes.

Nicholas slid from his mount and, spreading his arms wide, roared out a greeting. Rushing forward like excited children, the women gave glad cries and flung themselves into his embrace, while their young companion, of an age near, clapped the captain eagerly on the back. For a moment Nicholas seemed lost in a veritable tangle of reaching arms and clasping hands.

"Nicholas's family appears to be as exuberant about life as he is," Maxim observed with a chuckle as he lifted Elise from her mare. Setting the maid to her feet, he paused a moment to stare down at her as his eyes conveyed a volume of wondrous things. Though his outward manner was most decorous, she read the heat in his gaze, and it was like being hit with a full volley. An invading weakness began in the pit of her belly and spread like quicksilver through her veins. On its heels was born an exciting warmth that embraced her whole being. If she wanted to, a wayward thought slyly tempted, she could call him into her bed and have done with these childish pangs that left her hungering for something more. He could teach her all there was to know about...

Elise mentally shook herself, amazed at where her thoughts were leading her. With such suggestions flowing into her mind, she would be hard-pressed to resist his arguments. Her defenses would crumble like towers of sand, and passion would be allowed to range where it would.

Curbing what seemed to be a rather ribald wandering of her imagination, Elise took a secure hold of the arm he offered and strangely felt a growing ease with his nearness. When she remembered that Arabella had rejected the manly favor of this one for wedlock with a boorish clod, she could only wonder if the woman was made of stone.

"Arabella was a fool," she breathed, hardly aware that she had spoken.

"Madam?" Maxim frowned at her in dubious wonder. "Whatever brings Arabella to your mind?"

Elise released a soft, quavery sigh. "I doubt if you would really understand, my lord. 'Twould take a woman to fully fathom my thoughts."

"You're being most elusive," he accused with a grin.

" 'Tis the way of women, my lord." She cast a sidelong glance at him as her mouth curved upward. " 'Tis our only defense."

"I'll probably never know what goes on in that fine and lovely head of yours." His hungering eyes caressed her face, prompting a blush to rise to her cheeks before she carefully lowered her gaze. His words came to her as a whisper. "Perhaps you do not completely share what I feel toward you..."—then his voice deepened as he continued—"but I can teach you many things..."

Elise's head snapped up in surprise. He had penetrated so deftly into the pattern of her own musings, she was pricked by a sudden fear that he could read her mind. It was an immense relief to her when a young, fair-haired woman, of about a score or so years, separated herself from the welcoming party and approached Maxim with an exuberant smile.

"You must be Lord Seymour," she greeted in crisp, fluent English. "Nicholas has told me so much about you I've been most anxious to meet you. I'm his cousin, Katarina Hamilton..." She paused and, giving a quick shake of her head, laughed as she corrected herself. "Actually, our mothers were very distant cousins, which makes us"—she chuckled again as if the thought delighted her—"barely even kin."

Maxim responded debonairly, showing a fine leg as he swept into a courtly bow. "The pleasure is mine, *Fraulein* Hamilton, I assure you."

"And this must be Elise," Katarina surmised, assessing the beauty of the younger woman. Though it gave her heart little ease, she could clearly see why the captain had become infatuated with the maid. "Nicholas wrote and said he would be bringing you here for a visit. Did you have an enjoyable journey?"

"Quite enjoyable, thank you," Elise responded graciously, realizing her moment of panic was safely behind her, at least for the present. "I'm much relieved to be able to converse with someone. I was afraid I'd not be able to understand a single word that was spoken."

"It must be difficult living in a foreign country when you've no knowledge of the language, but you seem to have fared well. You've obviously been well-protected by Nicholas and Lord Seymour."

"Once upon a time I was sure I was watched too closely," Elise quipped as she tossed Maxim an accusative glance. He inclined his head briefly to acknowledge her genteel barb, but Katarina frowned, somewhat bemused by the remark, and Elise rushed on to forestall any inquiry by presenting one of her own. "But how is it that you speak English so well?"

"My father was an Englishman who chose to remain here after he married my mother," Katarina readily explained. "My brother, Justin, and I were little more than children when my mother died, and when my father passed on much later, Nicholas's mother took us in and treated us as her very own." She lifted her slender shoulders in a casual gesture. "It has been dreadfully boresome since Nicholas left. I must confess I've been most envious of you."

"Of me?" It was Elise's turn to be bewildered. "How so?"

"Why, to be surrounded by so many handsome men has to be the fantasy of every maiden in the world. I'd leave Lubeck in a moment had I such an escort, but as you see, I'm naught but an aging spinster."

"Katarina! Vhat vill Lord Seymour t'ink of yu?" The plumpish, white-haired woman who had greeted Nicholas came forward on his arm. Claiming Maxim's gaze, she slashed her hand back and forth as if to erase all that the younger woman had said. "*Nein! Nein!* Yu must not take to heart Katarina's vords, *mein Herr*. She know not vhat she say."

"Oh, but Katarina has alvays spoken her mind quite vell," Nicholas interjected, his eyes glowing with humor.

"And yu!" The ancient jerked on his sleeve as she scolded, "Shame on yu for encouraging her! Yu put ideas in her head effer since her poor *Vater* vas killed and she come to liff vit' us. If yu vere not my son, I vould bar yu from t'is house!"

Justin was eager to join ranks in teasing the elder. "*Ja,* if not for Cousin Nicholas, Katarina and I would be a pair of blessed saints. He fills our heads with such wild notions, we cannot help ourselves."

"Bah!" the old woman scoffed. "The two of yu haff no need for ot'ers to put vayvard t'oughts in yur heads, Justin Hamilton. Yu make t'em vell enuff on yur own."

Justin grinned as he reached out to gently tweak the elder's nose. "You shall ever be our conscience, *Tante* Therese, especially since your eyes throw sparks when you're angry!"

"Keep to yurself, young man," she warned direly, but her chuckle dismantled her rebuke as she slapped his hand away. "Yu not so big t'at I cannot take yu 'cross my knee."

Nicholas laid his arm around his mother's shoulders and gave her an affectionate hug. *"Meine Mutter! Es ist Wonne sehen Sie."* He placed a kiss upon the white head. *"Ach,* but I'm forgetting our guests." He raised his hand to indicate Elise who was delighted with the good-natured bantering of the family. "Mother, these are two of my very good friends, Mistress Elise Radborne"—he swept his hand onward to the one who stood beside the maid—"and Lord Maxim Seymour."

"How goot of yu to visit us," Therese declared, and fondly patted Elise's hand. "Velcome to our home, *Fraulein... mein Herr."* Beckoning to them both, she bade cheerily, *"Bitte, Kommen Sie ans Feuer... Kommen!* Come varm yurselves by the fire." Lifting the hem of her skirts, she led the way into the house. Passing quickly through the hall, she directed a maid-servant to help the guests as they entered, and clapped her hands to signal another two to begin setting out a feast in an adjoining hall. With quick and kindly attention she watched over the gathering as cloaks were doffed and boots were wiped clean.

Katarina tugged playfully on Nicholas's fur-lined cloak as he moved past her. The captain paused, torn between the need for replacing Maxim as the gallant who was at present helping Elise off with her boots and a desire to answer the impish challenge sparkling in the blue-gray eyes of his cousin. He postponed his first objective and yielded to the temptation of the taunt. Sweeping off his cloak with a flamboyant swirl, he flung it over Katarina, enveloping her completely within its voluminous folds. In an instant an uproar of guffaws, shrieks, and muffled threats filled the hall as Katarina gave vent to promises of dire recompense to a brutish cousin. She tried to escape the heavy wrap, but Nicholas swooped her up with unbridled gusto and, tossing her over his shoulder, turned to leer at Elise.

"Remember vhen ve first met, *vrouwelin?*"

Laughing at the captain's antics, Elise balanced herself with a hand on Maxim's shoulder as she slid a slender foot into the slipper he held. " 'Tis an event I shall never forget."

Therese had paused behind the English couple to take careful heed of the Marquess's solicitations. Now she bustled past the two in her haste to reach the melee. Snatching a broom from a maid who had been sweeping up the loose snow, she came around and applied it with merciless force to the rear of her son, drawing a feigned wail from him.

"Sie Scheusal! Sie Schuft!" she scolded, and just in case her son had forgotten his native tongue in all of his travels, she repeated the same in English. "Yu monster! Yu rascal! Let her go, or I vill make yu t'ink yu got hot coals in yur britches!"

Scampering out of harm's way, Nicholas set his cousin down and continued on the run as that one flung off the fur wrap and gave chase. The game shifted swiftly when Nicholas darted between a pair of servants and, with a hand on a post, swung himself around to abruptly face the one following. Roaring loudly, he opened his arms to catch her, assuming the posture of a ferocious beast. Katarina squealed in glee and did a sprightly turnabout with skirts flaring wide. Nicholas gave chase, and in an attempt to escape the girl flung herself around the laughing Elise who was just about to step into the other slipper Maxim held. In the course of the evasion, their hips collided solidly.

"Ooh!" Katarina flung over her shoulder as Elise teetered precariously on one foot. Immediately abashed by her foolery which now promised to end in disaster, Katarina whirled with a hand clasped over her mouth.

Maxim had been squatting on a heel before the maid as he watched the capers of the other couple over his shoulder, but when he heard the soft gasp above him and glanced up just in time to find Elise tumbling down upon him, he fell backward on his haunches and raised his arms to catch her, but it was too late. She sprawled upon him, landing in a most undignified heap squarely between his outflung limbs. Her full skirts covered them both and displayed a rare amount of petticoat and stockings, to which the gentlemen in the crowd gave particular heed. Horror-struck, Elise braced up on an arm and found herself staring into Maxim's amused visage.

"My sweet, I'm overwhelmed by your ardent attention," he assured her in affected surprise.

Though he spoke in a barely breathed whisper, to Elise he might as well have screamed the words. In sudden panic she struggled to rise, far too aware of their suggestive posture and the wanton direction of her earlier thoughts. In her haste to escape, her hip rolled across his loins, eliciting a look of shock from the prostrate man.

"Madam, have a care!" he warned softly, and grinned as he prolonged her discomfiture. "You threaten our future."

"Oh, hush!" she begged in a fearful whisper. "They'll hear you!"

Nicholas was no less anxious than Elise to separate the tangle and came quickly to her aid as she renewed her struggles. Slipping his hands about her narrow waist, he lifted her as easily as he would a doll and set her to her feet. Elise hurriedly straightened her skirts as she cast a furtive glance at Maxim. He knelt again with an arm braced across a thigh, and the

wicked leer he bestowed upon her promised uni-
maginable recompenses.

"Forgive me, Elise," Katarina pleaded almost shyly
as she stepped forward. "I didn't mean to knock you
down."

"Of course you didn't," Elise assured the woman as
she nursed her own sorely bruised dignity. "I fear it
was my fault, what with blocking a busy hall."

"Nonsense!" Katarina blushed as she shook her
head. "I was terribly thoughtless, but as you see . . .
we've always been a trifle wont to behave like a tribe
of heathens at times."

"Heavens, how you do offend!" Justin interjected
in feigned aloofness. " 'Twas thee and your renegade
cousin the ones at fault, my dear. Surely not I! I am
most refined." His pompous airs abruptly vanished
and he did a quick sidestepping dance to escape the
swishing broom as Therese scurried toward him.

"I t'ink yu're the vorst!" she declared.

Nicholas chuckled, content to let his mother discipline the youth, and gave a hand to Maxim, pulling
him to his feet. "Perhaps I should make apologies for
our conduct. As yu can see for yurself, ve are somevhat
unrestrained."

"I found the incident most . . . ah . . . instructive."

"I vas vondering about that." The captain looked at
him with skeptical humor. "Or did I imagine that
twinge of pain in yur face."

Maxim slowly smiled. "My only regret is that I had
so many witnesses. I'd have enjoyed the event far
more with less of an audience."

Nicholas's grin grew pained. "I vas prodded by
some fear of that."

"I'm sure our trafelers are hungry," Therese surmised. "If yu vould like, ve eat now, *ja?*"

The Marquess glanced about as he asked the captain, "Is there some place where I might tidy up? After traveling the whole day, I feel somewhat less than presentable."

"*Ja*, I vill show yu to yur rooms." Nicholas jerked his head to indicate the stairs. "The servants vill bring up yur baggage vhile ve dine."

"Perhaps *Fraulein* Elise vould also like to freshen up." Therese posed the suggestion, looking questioningly at the young maid.

"I'd like that very much," Elise responded, still feeling the heat of a blush in her cheeks.

"Nicholas can show yu to the guest room." Therese raised a brow of inquiry to her son as she asked carefully, "I give *Fraulein* Elise the guest room. Is t'at all right?"

The captain carefully masked his reaction and inclined his head in a brief nod. To voice any objection to Elise and Maxim being sequestered entirely alone on the same level would have clearly demonstrated a lack of trust, which for pride's sake he was most reluctant to express.

Together the three climbed to the uppermost level of the house with Nicholas leading the way. When they reached the third floor, they passed down a wide hall where wooden floors gleamed from a recent polishing and small-paned windows twinkled, reflecting the candlelight from the porcelain sconces. Maxim glanced toward the end of the corridor and made a mental note as to what direction the window faced as he paused with Nicholas outside a massive door. The captain swung open the portal, unaware of his guest's divided interest, and swept a hand inward as an invitation for Elise to enter the well-warmed and lighted chamber.

"I shall return for yu in a moment, *vrouwelin,*" he announced.

Carefully avoiding Maxim's gaze, which she was sure could be quickly joined by that same lecherous grin she had seen earlier, Elise responded with a mute nod. Moving inward, she closed the door behind her and drew a long breath. If she had heretofore managed to keep down a vivid blush as she climbed the stairs, it now came upon her with a heat that warmed her breasts. Though she knew the idea was ridiculous, the question still plagued her. Was there some intimacy in that awkward tumble which the others might have seen? Or which a keen-minded person might have been able to perceive? If not, then the shock of that encounter was entirely her own, for she was sharply aware of the battle that raged in her mind. Her fantasies had sprouted wings and were now wont to soar recklessly from one wild and lucid imagining to another. Paramount in her musings were memories of Maxim as he had appeared to her on that morning of her first attack, and she found herself wondering what it would be like for a woman to be freely and intimately familiar with a man like that and what it would be like to be able to claim such a magnificent specimen entirely as her own.

Stepping away from the lady's room, Nicholas led Maxim down the hall to a large suite of rooms wealthily appointed with fine furnishings. Shelves lined the wall in a small antechamber and were weighted down with countless leather-bound volumes. A large desk and stately chair of Spanish origin stood before an ornately worked armoire where a multitude of rolled parchments jutted from keyholes.

"These vere my father's chambers vhen he vas alive," Nicholas informed him. "Justin took over these rooms after learning that none of the rest of us like the climb. He enjoys his privacy up here . . . and of course, my father's books and maps. Perhaps he vill be a great scholar someday. But enough of that. Vhile yu're here, my friend, these chambers vill be at yur disposal. Justin vill be bedding down in a small room near the kitchen."

"I need nothing this grand," Maxim protested. He had not missed the subtle exchange between the captain and his mother, and though he relished the idea of his proximity to the maid, he was also aware of the temptations which he himself would face being so close to her. He thought it wise to avoid them rather than abuse the Von Reijns' hospitality. "A small room will meet my needs just as well."

Nicholas shook his head. "*Nein,* my friend. My mother vould be offended if I placed a guest in that tiny little closet. Justin is vell-acquainted with the nook and does not mind being occasionally displaced, considering he claims the largest chambers in the house for most of the time."

Maxim mentally shrugged and, by his silence, accepted the chambers and the potential pitfalls of being ensconced near the maid. Deliberately turning his mind from Elise, he directed his thoughts toward other less fascinating, but equally important, matters. His restraint would be best nurtured by diversion, of that he had no doubt.

Stepping to the window, he pulled aside the drapery and peered out into the thickening shades of night. "I must take care of some business while I'm here in Lubeck, Nicholas," he commented over his shoulder. "Will I disturb your family if I come and go as I please?"

His host frowned slightly, wondering what business this particular stranger would have in Lubeck. "Yu are free to roam as yu vill, Maxim, but be varned. One can get lost easily here in Lubeck. The streets are a puzzle no stranger has easily solved. If yur vont is to vander beyond the doors of this house, yu should have a guide. Othervise, ve may never see yu again."

Maxim acknowledged his advice with a chuckle. "I'll take care."

"If there is someplace vhere I may escort yu..." The captain let the offer hang unfinished as he waited for an answer.

"I'm sure you have affairs of your own to give heed to. Mine are not so important. 'Tis an affair of no real significance, merely a minor curiosity about the city."

"Vhat say yu then?" Nicholas inquired, rubbing his hands together as he felt the invading chill of the room. He was not satisfied with the other's casual rejection of his suggestion, but he could hardly keep the man a prisoner either. Besides, his absence might move Elise to more readily accept the attentions of one who doted on her. "Are yu almost ready to dine? I'm famished!"

"I shall wash and be down directly."

Nicholas crossed to the door and there paused to glance back at Maxim. After several unsuccessful attempts to state his concern, he finally blurted out the question, "Yu vouldn't be so foolish to seek out Karr Hilliard vhile yu're here, vould yu?"

A contemplative demeanor accompanied Maxim's reply. "Oh, I might consider it. I've been most curious about the man."

Nicholas threw up his hands in exasperation and faced the Marquess to make his point more clearly. "Karr Hilliard is dangerous, Maxim. Far richer men than I fear him. Please! Have nothing to do vith him. Only by avoiding him vill yu manage to survive."

"I don't intend getting myself killed," Maxim protested, brushing aside the other's worry with an abortive laugh. "Believe me, I have many wonderful things to live for."

"If yu ask me, yu take too many chances vith yur life," Nicholas muttered, and continued in a dismal vein. "No one can blame Arabella for not confirming yur death before she ved another. It vas too easy to believe that yu vere." With that, the captain strode out the door, slamming it behind him.

Mulling over the other's comments, Maxim went to where he had seen a low cabinet equipped with pitcher and basin. Thoughtfully he poured water into the bowl and began to wash his hands. When he no longer could hear voices in the hall or footsteps echoing on the stairs, he took up a lone candle and returned to the window. Parting the draperies again, he passed the lighted taper back and forth in front of the night-darkened panes. He repeated the motion several times, then blew out the tiny flame. In the velvet shades of night he watched and waited until from close beneath a distant roof he saw a like response.

When Maxim returned to the lower chambers, Therese stepped forward to direct everyone into the dining hall. "Katarina, vhy don't yu escort Nicholas to his place and sit beside him vhile I get to know our guests. I vould be interested in hearing vhat *Fraulein* Elise and *Herr* Seymour haff learned from t'eir trafels."

Taking Katarina on his arm, Nicholas approached Elise with a broad smile. "If by some miracle there are finer cooks than *Herr* Dietrich in the vorld, *vrouwelin,* then they're here in my mother's house." He held up a hand as if to attest to what he was about to declare. "Yu cannot imagine vhat yu are about to experience."

"Will it be anything like the mistletoe?" she asked, then chuckled in delight as he tried to shame her with a dubious frown. "You've made me wary, Captain. I'm not sure I can trust you anymore."

"I giff yu good advice. Nicholas never to be trusted,"

Therese confided in a loud, rasping whisper as she leaned past her son's arm. "Katarina vill agree vit' vhat I say. He is not goot boy."

"I pray you, *vrouwelin*," Nicholas pleaded. "Give these vomen little heed. As yu can tell, they enjoy roasting my carcass over a hot fire."

"The idea sounds intriguing and I've no doubt it would be a most delightful pastime," Elise teased. "I shall be tempted to try it sometime."

Nicholas groaned in mock agony. "Vhat have I done by bringing yu to this madhouse?"

"You've enlightened me, Captain," she rejoined, bestowing on him a most charming smile. "No longer will I think of you as a formidable captain of the Hanseatic League who has long been separated from kith and kin, for I perceive that you carry your loved ones close to your heart whether here or abroad."

Therese's eyes shone with pleasure as she eagerly nodded. "*Ja!* It is so. Nicholas alvays remember us vherever he go."

Chapter 18

*T*HE MOON ROSE HIGHER in the star-bedecked ebon sky as the midnight hour drew nigh. A snow-laden mist, swept in by the cold night air, drifted down Lubecher Bucht from the Baltic to slowly engulf the city beneath a salt-tainted blanket. Maxim Seymour paused outside the door of the Von Reijn house and carefully scanned the empty streets that converged on the one where the house stood. Drawing up the hood of his cloak, he selected a forward direction and set off with purposeful gait. He hurried along for several blocks, then, turning a corner, ducked into the nearest alley to wait silently for a space. Once certain that no one followed, he continued on his way, his long strides rapidly devouring the distance. After a short passage of time, he halted in the shadows of a narrow lane and surveyed the area he now found himself in. Across the street the Lowentatze loomed tall and dark on the indistinct border of the waterfront, rising to a height of four stories before reaching its gabled, steeply pitched roof. A weatherworn sign which hung from an iron bar identified the place as the inn he sought, bearing the red letters of the name in a curved arch above a single paw print of a lion.

The erstwhile Marquess cast another cautious glance along the thoroughfare and, assuring himself that it was deserted, made haste to cross the distance.

Pausing beside the door, he listened for a moment, but no evidence of habitation issued forth. He slipped within the hall, then pressed back into the darkness that enveloped the entrance. Only a few candles illumed the common room, which was empty save for a spindly lad who earnestly plied a straw broom to the rough-hewn planks of the floor. The boy was bent to his labor and gave no sign he was aware of another's presence.

Maxim reached out and tugged at the lanyard of a small brass ship's bell that hung on a post near the entrance. The clangor seemed loud and strident in the silence, yet the lad gave no heed as he continued moving a growing pile of dirt and trash across the stubborn floor. Maxim jerked on the lanyard again, and this time a grumbling voice answered from somewhere beyond the first level.

"Ja! Ja! Ich kommend!"

The sound of slow footfalls drifted from the bowels of the inn, then a huge, stoop-shouldered man came to stand in the doorway at the rear of the common room. Peering toward the entrance, he ambled a few paces closer, then paused as he spied the insistent intruder.

"Bitte, kommen Sie naher," the innkeeper bade, beckoning to Maxim invitingly. *"Wir haben leider sehr selten Gaste bei uns."*

"Actually I'm not a guest," Maxim answered, and saw the man's eyes grow suddenly wary and a slight bit fearful. Maxim fished a coin from the pocket of his jerkin and, with the flick of his finger, set the single gold sovereign spinning on the top of a nearby table.

"Sprechen Sie Deutsch?" the man asked guardedly, making no move to take up the coin.

"I was given to understand that you spoke English," Maxim countered.

The innkeeper's eyes regarded him furtively from beneath beetled brows, as if by dint of will he would read what was in Maxim's mind, and yet he gave no hint of a yea or a nay.

"Ist jemand da, der Englisch spricht?" Maxim queried, glancing around for evidence of another on the premises who spoke English.

"Wie heissen Sie?" the rotund man finally inquired.

"Seymour ... Maxim Seymour."

The man lumbered forward until he reached the table and, picking up the coin, inspected it closely until satisfied one side bore the face of the English queen and, on the opposite side, all the markings which identified the stranger as the one he had been told to expect. A grin widened his lips and he flipped the coin in a high arch to Maxim who caught it with a sweep of his hand and swiftly pocketed it.

"Well, milord! I guess ye be the one, alright." The innkeeper chortled as he relaxed. "Me name's Tobie."

Maxim glanced at the boy and posed the question, "What of him?"

"Aw, don't ye be troublin' yerself 'bout him none. The lad has no hearin' an' is gifted with a simple way of mind. 'Tis safer that way."

"What of the men I'm supposed to meet?"

"Master Kenneth an' his brother come up from Hamburg 'bout a week ago an' said 'at a gentleman'd be arrivin' soon. When I saw yer signal, I fetched 'em here. 'Ey're upstairs waitin' for ye."

"What of your other guests?"

"Ah, precious few there be, milord. None of 'em's the sort what would give heed to anythin' a body does here. 'Ere be me friends, more or less."

Thoughtfully Maxim contemplated the innkeeper. *"Sie Sprechen sehr gut Deutsch,* Tobie. How is that you speak it so well and abuse the English language so poorly?"

Tobie hooked his fingers in his rope belt and rocked back on his heels as he pondered the question. "Well, milord, I figgers it's safer lettin' those what would think me an ord'nary common English bloke. A high-up lord like yor'self'll likely lose yer head o'er this, but meself, sir? Well, I'm thinkin' maybe 'ey won't use me as an example . . . if'n ye knows what I means, sir. I says 'tis better ter be a little safe than dead sorry."

"You can hide behind your churlish tongue if you choose, my friend, but if worse comes to worse, I rather doubt anyone will take time to separate the classes. We'll all be lined up and executed as quickly as they can drop a headman's axe."

Tobie grimaced and rubbed his throat, as if already feeling the sharp blade. "Yer words ain't a mite comfortin', milord."

"The truth rarely is."

Maxim slipped quietly into the Von Reijn house and moved with silent tread up its stairs and through its halls. He paused a moment at the open portal of the chambers he had been given, feeling as if something was out of place. Slowly his eyes swept the length and breadth of the antechamber, carefully probing the darkness. The fire had burned low in the hearth, and all that remained of the logs were broken pieces of charred wood glowing red and black on a bed of gray ashes. The dying coals created no more light than a tiny aura of red and gold, hardly banishing the shadows in the hearth, much less the chambers. In the night-shaded room it was difficult to discern fact from fantasy. The furnishings were merely ghostly shapes and indistinct blurs that had taken on a slightly blacker hue. A tall-backed settee which stood before the hearth was the only thing even remotely distinguishable, only because it was partially silhouetted against the glow of the coals. He could detect nothing that seemed out of order, but a feeling nagged at him that he was not entirely alone.

Closing the portal behind him, Maxim swept off his cloak and laid it over his arm as he made his way into the adjoining bedchamber. As in the anteroom, the log that had once blazed in the hearth had diminished to little more than a charred strip of burning embers.

Tossing the cloak over the back of a chair, Maxim approached the massive four-poster and touched a spark from a tinderbox to light a taper on the bedside table. The glow spread, illuminating the chamber, and for a moment he considered the huge bed, anticipating the comfort he would find between its feather ticks and fluffy quilts. The comforters were invitingly turned down to reveal sun-whitened sheets edged with hand-tatted lace. It was the fresh scent of them that reminded him of Elise when he had watched her spread a sheet to dry over a large shrub in the courtyard. Other, more savory memories came to mind, but he banished them, lest they rend what was left of his meager slumber.

Maxim sighed and dropped wearily to the edge of the bed and began tugging off his thigh-high boots. When he rose again, he had doffed his doublet and shirt and was garbed only in the narrow-fitting, waist-length stockings he sometimes wore instead of the padded breeches. He shivered as an icy chill swept his naked back, reminding him of the dwindling warmth of the dying embers.

Soon he had rekindled a blazing fire in the hearth. It radiated a welcoming warmth across the room, and though his eyes swept to every corner, he did not discover the reason for his mild disquiet. Returning to the antechamber, he lent himself to a similar task of stoking up the fire there. Kneeling before the hearth, he raked the live coals together and laid on fresh kindling and seasoned logs, bringing to life again a cheery fire that soon crackled, sizzled, and hissed in warm exuberance.

Maxim rose to his feet and stared for a long, contemplative moment into the growing flames, enjoying the heat as he reflected on the recent information he had gleaned this early morningtide and the plans which the three of them had made. He would have little time to press his courtship of Elise while they were in Lubeck, and that gave him no pleasure, for his absence would give Nicholas the advantage of seeking her out.

A long sigh intruded into his thoughts, and he turned in surprise, wondering who had come into the room. His eyes quickly scanned the shadows near the door, finding no evidence of another's entry, then a slight movement caught his attention, and he dropped his gaze to the settee. There, curled in sleep beneath a fur throw, was the one he had come to desire. Her face was barely visible above the dark covering, though her hair spread out around her in loosely curling tresses. Its deep, auburn hues were set aflame by the rich glow of the fire whose light reached out to touch her delicate features. The heavy brush of silken lashes lay on cheeks rosy and fair as her softly sighing breath slipped through temptingly parted lips. She stirred, turning her profile upward as she flung an arm over the fur covering, and his breath caught and held as the bodice of her robe fell open, revealing a most enticing view of fully ripened breasts. The plunging neckline teased him as it threatened to slip away entirely from the creamy flesh and bring to his starving gaze the pink, pliant peaks. Though the sight inflamed his passions and started the blood coursing through his veins, Maxim could not convince himself that she had braved his chambers for a lover's tryst. If he knew the maid at all, he would say her reasons involved her father.

As if in response to his musings, the long lashes fluttered slowly open, and when she turned her head on the small pillow, he found himself gazing down into the sapphire depths. She stared at him calmly, as if her thoughts were readily at her disposal and not dazed by the confusion of slumber.

"I wanted to talk with you ... so I waited ..." Her gaze passed slowly down his naked chest to the narrow stockings that clung boldly to the manliness of him. He made no attempt to hide evidence of his arousal, which prompted Elise to check her own appearance. With flushed cheeks she gathered her robe together and hurriedly explained, "I must've fallen asleep."

She swung her legs over the edge of the settee and would have fled from the room in painful chagrin, but Maxim eased her embarrassment by presenting his back and throwing another log into the fire.

"Why did you come?" he asked over his shoulder.

Her voice was small and timid. "Nicholas said you might be the one to help me find my father ..."

Maxim laughed briefly. "Nicholas has a way of thrusting aside your questions by deliberately intimidating others. You can't believe everything he says."

"I know he was making light of it all." Elise twisted her thin fingers in roweling disquiet. What must Maxim think of her for having sought him out in his chambers dressed as she was? She should have fretted less about pleading for his help and given more heed to her state of *deshabillé.* Now he could only be repulsed by her apparent forwardness. "I should not have come," she mumbled timorously. "And yet, I thought you would be the one to help me."

"Actually . . ." Maxim paused a moment, wondering if he should encourage her. "I spoke to a man a short time ago . . . he might've been mistaken . . . but he thinks he saw a man who could've been your father."

Elise came to her feet, her courage returning as her hopes burgeoned. "Where?"

Maxim waved his hand in a casual gesture and went to pour himself a shallow draught of mild wine. "I don't know if you should give the matter much heed, Elise. The man wasn't sure if it was your father."

She quickly crossed the space that separated them, and Maxim faced her as she laid a hand on his forearm. "But it might've been, Maxim. It might've been."

"I'll certainly make other inquiries . . ."

"Was he seen here in Lubeck?" she queried anxiously.

Maxim took a short sip of the wine. "The man I spoke with said he was at the dock one early morning when an Englishman was escorted by members of the Hansa down the planks of a ship . . . in chains."

"Then Nicholas might be able to help us find . . ."

"Nay!" The word was issued firmly, and Maxim stared down at her as he spoke, as if to instill in her the importance of leaving Nicholas out of the matter. "You cannot involve him, Elise."

"Involve?" She repeated the word in confusion and, searching for his meaning, carefully questioned him. "Do you mean he cannot be trusted to help us?"

Maxim shook his head, very much in a quandary over how he should explain. The last thing he wanted to do was to paint the captain as a villain in her eyes. To suggest that the man was capable of such a thing might seem a deliberate defamation of his character, especially while he was waiting for Elise to make up her mind.

Setting aside his goblet, Maxim gently took her hands into both of his as he compelled her to understand. "Nicholas is my friend, Elise. He's also a member of the Hansa . . . as his father was before him. Despite his denials, the law of the league has become his way of life. If he had to choose his loyalties, I've no idea to which side he would go. I say 'tis better not to force the issue. If we confide in him, we may regret it. If we keep him uninformed, he'll not be tempted to give us away."

"Then how may I learn if it was truly my father who was seen?"

"Give me time, Elise, and I promise you I shall find out what I can."

A gentle smile curved her lips as she gave him an answer he did not expect. " 'Tis strange that I have come so far from home to find the ones I love."

His eyes searched hers for evidence of her meaning, and almost hesitantly he inquired, "Should I take encouragement from your statement?"

"I give you leave to think what you might, my lord," she murmured warmly.

Maxim bent toward her and spoke earnestly, pressing for an explanation. "You open wide the door of my imagination, madam, and I am already a man tormented by my lusts. What say you, have you an answer for me?"

"Lest I be tempted to appease my own inquisitiveness, my lord," she replied with amazing candor, "I think marriage would be the lesser of many evils."

With a sudden smile Maxim slid an arm about her narrow waist and pulled her close. His boldness knew no bounds as he spread a hand over the curve of her buttock and pressed her hips tightly against his loins.

Elise held her breath, totally conscious of his lightly veiled passions as he brought her chin up with a thin knuckle. His green eyes seemed to glow into hers as he whispered, "I'm most eager and willing to appease whatever curiosity you have, madam."

He would have swept her into his arms, but Elise laid a hand upon his naked chest and, with the lightest touch, restrained him and his ardor. "I pray you give heed to where we are," she pleaded. " 'Twould not be right for me to give myself to you and shame Nicholas in his mother's house."

"This thing between us is too strong, Elise," he whispered hoarsely. "How can I stop when the desire overwhelms me?"

"Promise me you will." She sighed tremblingly.

Maxim slipped his fingers through her hair and cupped her head between his hands as his eyes plunged to the depth of the sapphire orbs. Then his parting lips descended, seizing hers with a passion that took her breath away. Never had she known such fire, such heat in a kiss. It was wild and deliciously wanton, divesting her of the innocence of maidenly dreams while it sowed the seeds of sensual pleasure. His open mouth slanted across hers, greedily seizing what she would give, and she gave all, holding nothing back. His arms wrapped tightly about her, fitting her close against his hardened, near-naked frame, and a searing heat began to build in the depth of her body, arousing yearnings that were completely foreign to her. She was aware of the manly feel of him and of a growing urgency to press even closer. Her breasts ached to be touched, and beneath the pressure of his muscular chest the pliant peaks warmed in eager anticipation as the bodice of her robe began to separate. His passion was a brand that ignited a flame within her, and it threatened to consume her. She could not think of stopping now...

It was Maxim who, bound by his word, finally snatched back with a frustrated groan, but his nostrils flared as he fought the urge to take her into his arms again. "Sweet mercy, what have we wrought?" he rasped. Tormented by his hungering need, he watched her gather the bodice of her robe together. She was timid now, unsure, and it was all he could do to hold himself in check and not reassure her with his passion. "I cannot be content with a kiss like that," he whispered. "It sets my mind ablaze for want of more." Reluctantly he stepped away. "I cannot endure being alone with you and not making love to you. I must bid you leave ere good intentions be rent asunder."

Like a silent wraith Elise moved away, drawing his gaze as she went. When the door closed behind her, he turned with tensed jaw to stare into the fire. On the morrow he knew what he would do. Of that, he had no doubt.

Chapter 19

Nᴵᴄʜᴏʟᴀs ʜᴀᴅ sᴛʀᴜɢɢʟᴇᴅ with a strange feeling of foreboding since his arrival in Lubeck. Something was afoot with the Hansa, he sensed, or more correctly, with Karr Hilliard and his small band of followers. With that one's authority reaching into the uttermost ranks of the order, the whole league could be swayed and maneuvered by the man's ambitious schemes, and who could stand against his power?

A messenger had come to the Von Reijn house summoning Nicholas to a meeting with Karr Hilliard, causing the captain much concern as he expected the matter had something to do with Seymour. It was no great secret that Hilliard despised the English queen and would do whatever he could to bring about her fall from power or even her demise. It was further apparent from his interest in Maxim that Hilliard had hopes of enlisting the Englishman in his cause. If Maxim refused Hilliard's proposal, he could be easily dispatched, perhaps to the pleasure of Elizabeth. If the two reached a mutual accommodation, then Maxim would no doubt serve as scapegoat for whatever offense should take place. Either way, Maxim would lose his life, and since he seemed blind to such possibilities, what was a friend to do?

The black-glazed brick turrets of the Rathaus seemed to pierce the morning sky high above Nicholas as he passed through its arched portals. He quickly mounted the stairs that led him to the chambers that Karr Hilliard, on occasion, claimed for himself. He handed his toque and cloak to a barrel-chested man of medium height named Gustave, well-known among the Hansa as a personal attendant of Hilliard's, whatever the duty entailed. Shrugging his chamarre straight on his shoulders, Nicholas entered the room where the huge man awaited him.

"Guten Morgen, Kapitan," Hilliard bade as he came forward to greet his guest. He was a large, extremely corpulent man who walked with the rolling gait of a seaman, yet when taking his girth into account, Nicholas had trouble envisioning him moving in any other manner. His hair was lank and straggly and was somewhat lighter than the brown leather of his boots. His eyes were a weak gray beneath thickly protruding brows adorned with a brush of wispy brown hairs. The sagging bags which underlined his eyes were no more complimentary to his face than the loose, hanging jowls that seemed to flap and sway with his movements. Though there had been those to doubt Hilliard's agility or strength, Nicholas had seen him descend upon a pair of sailors who had once questioned his authority. The man had caught each head in a beefy hand and brought the two noggins together with enough force to crack their skulls.

"Guten Morgen, Herr Hilliard," Nicholas returned the salutation decorously.

A smile slowly spread across the heavy lips, displaying a set of badly stained and crooked teeth separated by wide gaps. "It is goot of yu to come so soon."

"Yur message appeared urgent."

"There vas indeed a matter I vished to discuss vith yu." Karr Hilliard waddled to the hearth and lifted a steaming kettle as he peered inquiringly at Nicholas. "Some tea, *Kapitan?*"

"Of course, *mein Herr.*" With a nod of gratitude the captain accepted the refreshment, then sipped the spiced brew, finding the addition of a dapple of mead much to his liking.

Not so the company. Nicholas came to a definite conclusion as he considered the man. He owed Karr Hilliard nothing at all.

Hilliard settled again in his chair and clasped his hands around his ponderous belly, giving the captain a lengthy perusal. He had known Nicholas for some time, and though he had never had cause to doubt him, the man's attitude was one of casual nonchalance, as if he were one of the few who were undisturbed by his reputation. Hilliard's brows beetled menacingly. It was a foolish man indeed who ignored the importance of his superiors. "Vhat do yu know of the Marquess of Bradbury?"

"There *is* none at the moment." Nicholas took a small draught from the steaming mug and held it in his mouth a moment, savoring the taste of the tea before swallowing. "The title has been stripped from the one who bore it, *mein Herr.* As yet there has been no other named to replace him. Of course, the English crown is notoriously slow on these matters."

"Yu bandy words vith me, Nicholas," Hilliard accused jocularly. "Yu know I speak of Maxim Seymour. I believe he is a friend of yurs."

"Oh, that one." Nicholas wet his lips in anticipation as he refilled his mug. "He's been my friend for some years. I used to visit his estates, and he has oft taken passage on my ship. Ve have emptied many a keg together."

"Vere yu not the one who brought him here to Germany?"

"Indeed, it vas aboard my ship that he escaped. Yu can say he did not care to sustain the fickle attentions of her royal majesty's headsman."

Hilliard digested these tidbits only briefly before moving on to a more pertinent matter. "I understand the man vas accused of treason."

"Ja, mein Herr." Nicholas blew into the mug to cool the tea. "He vas accused of conspiracy vith the Scottish Mary and of laying down a royal agent."

"And they say he escaped from a troop of royal guards who vere taking him to the Tower." From the tone of his voice it was clear Hilliard found this hard to believe.

Nicholas replied with a light smile. *"Ja."*

"A man of arms then?"

The captain slowly nodded. "That, too." After taking a sip, he proceeded to enlarge upon his statement. "But not that foppish dueling kind. His knowledge and skill are born of battle, and his blade vill ever end a fight in the quickest vay possible. He has even captained a ship of his own." Nicholas shrugged and tasted the tea again before continuing. "Vere he bound to the sea in spirit, he vould perhaps rival Drake himself."

A low growl sounded in Hilliard's throat. "Now there's a raving fop! A dandy of the first vater!" His jowls fluttered and the gray eyes took on a distant look as he mulled over the information. Of course, everything he had heard this evening was nothing more than a confirmation of what he already knew. When he spoke again he laid bare the meat of his inquiry. "And vhat allegiance does Seymour still bear to this Elizabeth of his?"

It was Nicholas's turn to be wary and thoughtful. He took another leisurely draught and, setting the mug down, folded his hands over his stomach. "I hesitate on this," he began carefully, then locked Hilliard's gaze with his own. "I vill tell yu vhat I know. Maxim Seymour is not a man of loose allegiance. Indeed, to the contrary, he vould as soon die for one he has called friend, yet not foolishly so. In such a case I have no doubt he vould arrange to take many vith him. As an enemy I vould respect him. As a friend I cherish him. Still, he has been injured deeply . . . in estate, stature, honor, dignity . . . and, I think, not lastly, in spirit. He chafes for vengeance and has need of income. He has considered lending his talents to Villiam the Vise and the Hessians. As an officer, he vould command a healthy stipend." Nicholas nodded in agreement with himself. "And he vould be vorth every jot and tittle of it."

This time Hilliard's jowls fluttered only slightly as a calculating gleam came into his eyes. "Then yu think he vould lend out as a mercenary?"

"It is his own thought," Nicholas replied. "He has some moneys . . . some investments England cannot touch, but they dwindle rapidly. Yet I think in truth his heart begs a return to England, and should Elizabeth fall or fail, I think he vould seek his home."

Maxim climbed the stairs three at a time and, gaining the level of the uppermost floor, crossed quickly to Elise's door, whereupon he snatched off his toque and gloves and rapped lightly upon the sturdy planks. A soft call begged for a moment more, and after only a brief delay, the portal was opened to reveal Elise, clad in a gown of midnight blue, struggling to fasten a cuff. A warm glow of admiration brightened the emerald eyes as Maxim gave her a lengthy perusal, and the smile that followed his close examination attested to his fervent approval, drawing a blush of pleasure to her cheeks.

"Fair maid, your beauty is like the sun gracing this frozen land with its warmth and brilliance," he avowed gallantly, sweeping an arm across his chest and bowing low in a courtly manner.

Though the gown was subtle in its adornments, the vision she created in the wearing of it was both regal and stunning. The huge puffed sleeves were fashioned with rows of midnight blue velvet ribbon and narrow silk ruching whose iridescence changed from dark to a silverish blue. Tightly stitched tucks diminished the bulk of the sleeves at the wrists, where they ended beneath crisp, lace-edged cuffs. The ruche-edged stomacher displayed the slimness of her waist, and below it, voluminous iridescent blue skirts were distended over a rolled farthingale. The wide, pleated ruff was trimmed with costly lace and was slightly elevated in back to complement her beauty. Beneath a saucy, feathered cap that sat jauntily upon her head the auburn tresses were dressed elegantly high.

"At last!" Elise exclaimed with a smile of triumph as she closed the difficult fastener. She twirled in a tiny pirouette to show off her new gown to him and then, rising on her toes, brushed a kiss upon his cheek. "Oh, Maxim, I feel so wonderfully alive this morning!"

"Aye, my love," he agreed, bringing her close within his embrace. "You do indeed feel wonderfully alive in my arms."

She laughed gaily and then grew serious, leaning back in his arms. "Madam Von Reijn gave me the message that you would be taking me for an outing, but you gave her no hint of where we are bound. Have you received some word of my father? Are we going to talk with someone who has information about him?"

Maxim chuckled. "Does it seem impossible, my charming little goose, that I may want to spend some time with you alone? Though the vows have yet to be spoken over us, between thee and me, my love, you are now my betrothed and my promised bride. 'Tis my desire to be with you and know that you are mine."

Her lips took on an upward curve and made no reply, though her eyes, in tender delight, spoke volumes.

"However"—a grin widened his lips as he continued—"I have made arrangements for you to meet with Sheffield Thomas, an Englishman who was here about the time your father was taken. After you've spoken with him, you can make your own judgment whether or nay it was your father he saw. I'll be fetching him here later this evening, but for now, we must be on our way. I intend to spend the whole of the afternoon with you."

"But where are we going?" she queried eagerly.

Maxim folded his hands behind her waist and, tilting his head to the side, contemplated her a long moment before he countered with a question of his own. "What if I told you I was taking you to a place where you will have to make a choice?"

Elise was as curious as a little child. "What kind of choice?"

"That, fair maid, you shall know soon enough." He lowered his lips to hers and leisurely savored the sweetness of her response. The kiss quickly warmed in intensity and could have easily led to other pleasures, but he drew back with a sigh, regretting that time and wisdom denied the opportunity. "If we stay much longer," he murmured, pressing another kiss upon her mouth, "I'll lock the doors and have my way with you."

Gently she laid the back of her fingers alongside his cheek. "You'll find me most willing, my lord. I'm look-

ing forward to the day the nuptials will be spoken and
I'll be your wife in truth."

"'Twill be a fair day indeed," he whispered.
"Though the winds may frost your fingers and redden
your nose this day, we shall enjoy our hours together."
With a smile he set her from him. "Now fetch your
wrap, my love, and let's be off ere I carry out my
threat."

With his help Elise donned the fur-lined cloak given
to her on the sea voyage and tucked her hand within
the security of his arm as he led her from the room
and down the stairs. As they descended she felt the
pride of being at his side. Even when casually attired
Maxim was a most handsome man, of that fact there
could be no dispute, but this morning he was garbed
in fine apparel: a taupe velvet doublet, puffed trunk
hose of the same hue, and a rich burgundy chamarre
lavishly embroidered with gold threads around the
high, stiff collar. The scrolled design of the elaborate
needlework broadened as it traced down the front
and around the hem. The garment was lined with fur
and rivaled any Nicholas had ever sported.

Therese stood at the front door to bid them farewell, and though her smile was kindly, the small, worried frown that flitted across her brow gave an
indication of her concern. "Take yu care on the streets
not to get lost."

Sensing that her anxieties were born in areas other
than what her words conveyed, Maxim took the aged
hands within his and smiled down into the pale blue
eyes rimmed by wrinkled lids and a thin smattering
of pale lashes. "You needn't worry, *Frau* Von Reijn. I
have a care for Nicholas, too."

Her head, crowned with bands of pale, yellow-white
braids and wispy tendrils, slowly nodded, as if accepting the true meaning of what he said. In what

seemed like acquiescent resignation, she clasped her hands together before her waist and watched them depart.

The horses were saddled and waiting, and Maxim lifted Elise to the back of her mount before carefully tucking her cloak around her. Swinging up on Eddy, he reined the stallion close to the mare, and together they set off on a leisurely jaunt down the cobbled thoroughfare.

The day was brisk and cold with a wintry wind that rushed through the city, stirring the crisp air and bringing a rosy bloom to Elise's cheeks. It was some time later when they halted outside a modest church and Maxim swung down from his mount. Bidding Elise to wait, he entered the structure and returned a short moment later. Sweeping off his toque, he halted beside her mount, seeming as hesitant as a young lad with his first love.

"Elise . . ." The name came from his lips in a yearning whisper, as if he found the matter too difficult to address.

"What is it, Maxim?" She was sweetly attentive, watching him with adoring eyes.

"Last eventide . . . I asked you if you would give me answer . . . and to my everlasting pleasure, you said yea." He turned the hat in his gloved hands and, for a moment, seemed uncertain. "Elise, I would know now if you did speak true . . . for I have waiting inside a man of the cloth who has consented to marry us this very moment . . . if you will but agree."

Wonderment filled her at his manner. Maxim was so strong and manly, always so self-assured, she would never have guessed he could ever show such incertitude with her, especially when she had already given him a reply. Perhaps their union meant more to him than she had realized.

A growing smile gave him her answer, and Elise reached out her hands to lay on his broad shoulders, encouraging him to lift her from her mount. Taking her in his arms, Maxim held her close against him, as if relishing the moment and the light of love he saw in her eyes, then joy came and swept them along with it. He set her to her feet and caught her hand. Elise laughed as they dashed into the church and responded warmly when Maxim paused to press an ardent kiss upon her lips. Smiling into her eyes, he led her into a small rectory where a monk gave them a jovial greeting before leading them to a spartan chapel.

Elise followed, oblivious to the sights, the sounds, and the smells that were not a part of them, and yet completely aware of everything that transpired between them and even more mindful of the man who knelt beside her. As the vows were exchanged, binding them together, his long, brown fingers clasped hers in an unspoken communication of commitment. In fascination she observed the play of knuckles, bone, and muscle across the back of his hand where golden hairs gleamed with the sheen of the soft candlelight. Her own hand looked pale and small within his, and there she silently vowed it would rest as a symbol of her trust.

The priest announced them one and presented a parchment for them to sign. Elise stood close as Maxim took quill in hand and scrawled his name boldly across the piece. Perhaps it was the budding realization that he was now her husband that made the moment seem so wonderful and yet so excitingly strange. When she thought back on the circumstances that had brought about this event, she could hardly believe they were now wed. Once, she had been certain that she hated him.

"If ever I should return to England," Elise whispered

close against his shoulder, "I shall have to speak with the Queen. She does not judge a man rightly if she declared you guilty of all the crimes laid against you."

The rosy glow in her face conveyed her confidence in him and in her future with him. Perhaps he had been selfish to take her to wife when so many things were as yet uncertain, but he could not chance losing her. Indeed, Nicholas's increasingly zealous courtship had brought home to him just how much he wanted her for his own. "The thought comes to mind, madam, that Elizabeth would tell you that you are blind to your husband's faults."

Elise answered with puckish spirit. "I shall instruct her differently, I think. Indeed! My father earned some merits attending the Queen's duties. Should she not in turn give an ear to the daughter of one of her loyal subjects?"

Maxim laid an arm about his bride's shoulders and brought her close against his side. "She should indeed, my love, and I believe you are just the one to tell her."

He moved aside, allowing her space at the tall desk to accomplish the signing of the parchment. The letters flowed gracefully from the tip of the quill and ended in a flamboyant flourish, giving evidence of her elation. Their eyes melded, and so intent were they upon the other, they hardly noticed when the monk sprinkled sand across the drying ink and took the documents away. They were lost in a world of their own as Maxim lowered his lips to hers and sealed their vows with a kiss.

Farewells and words of gratitude were spoken before they took their leave. A blustery wind whipped their cloaks and snatched their breath with its crisp chill as they ran from the church. Maxim swept his young bride into the saddle and then snugged the fur-lined wrap close about her as he spoke.

"There's an inn nearby where we might dine"—a slow grin curved his lips upward as he continued—"and pass a few moments alone together."

Elise smiled through a blush, unable to find an appropriate reply while her heart quickened with a new excitement. The opportunity to be alone had seemed so far away, she had not dared to hope for even a few moments of privacy while in Lubeck, but then, she should have known that Maxim would make the time happen. He was just that sort of man.

Some moments later they entered a small, but neat, establishment a short distance away, where Maxim made inquiries for a room. The innkeeper was somewhat in awe of his wealthily garbed guests and begged a moment to prepare suitable chambers. A serving maid hurried to place a proper meal upon the table Maxim indicated. It was a small trestle table set between rough-hewn benches with tall, solid backs that protected them from the curious stares of the other patrons.

"To our marriage," he whispered as he lifted his goblet of wine in toast.

With a glowing smile Elise raised her glass and entwined her arm with his. "May it be nurtured by love..."

"And many children," he added softly.

Staring into the eyes of the other, each sipped the wine and ended the salute with a long, slow kiss. Maxim sighed as he pulled away slightly. "I'm impatient to make you my wife in truth."

"Only a few moments more," she breathed with a warming blush.

"When each moment seems like a year, my lady, 'tis hard to wait."

"My lady?" Elise marveled at the sound of the address.

"Yea," Maxim affirmed in a whisper, squeezing her fingers. "Lady Elise Seymour and, should ever I regain my title, the most lovely Marchioness of Bradbury. Until then"—he brought her hand to his lips—"my love."

Her cheeks brightened with a fresh glow of color. " 'Tis the last I prefer above all others, my lord . . . to be your love . . ." Tentatively she tried out the title. ". . . my lord and my husband." Her eyes drank their fill of his handsome features. "Never did I dream when I was snatched so rudely from England that I would come to bless that day."

Maxim gave her a wayward grin. "Never did I imagine when you dumped that pail of icy water on me that I would come to be thankful you were taken instead of Arabella. An overwhelming desire to lay my hand boldly to your bare backside was not born of lust that morn, my love, but rather another kind of passion, the sort that yearns for vengeance."

With sparkling eyes Elise reached up to press a kiss upon his lips. " 'Twas only your just due, my lord," she teased. "Your plan to capture Arabella was not of a gallant mien."

" 'Twould seem that a far wiser hand than mine guided the events of that night."

"To think I once hated you," she sighed.

"And now what think you of me, fair maid?"

"I think, my lord," she murmured, "that I have grown very fond of you."

"Fond of me?" Maxim peered at her dubiously. "Is that what I've seen in your eyes, or is it something more? What other passion beats within your breast, my lady? Shall I test it?" Beneath the covering of her cloak, he laid a hand boldly high upon her thigh and then cocked a brow at her in quizzical skepticism. "Like other men, madam, I'm completely mystified at the lengths a woman will go to hide those parts which would nourish a lusting eye and a roaming hand. Here I am a husband newly wed, well-warmed, and most willing, and I find my wife bound up in far too many petticoats and farthingales."

Elise laughed softly and looked up into his gleaming eyes. She could not even tease him by pressing a breast against his arm, for the stiff corset restrained her curves too well. "Perhaps you should confine your rutting lusts to our marriage bed and restrain yourself from fondling me in public?"

Maxim brushed her nose with the tip of his finger and grinned. "You've many things to learn from your husband, my lady, and one of those is his desire to handle you when the moment is ripe. The bed is most convenient, but there are other places where bliss may be found. For instance"——his lips replaced his finger to bestow a kiss upon her brow—"I have visions of making love to you beneath the wide-spreading limbs of a tree with your eyes giving back to me the blue of the sky."

Her burgeoning emotions were softly displayed in her eyes now as she gazed at him with all the adoration of a woman in love. "My lord, I would welcome your attentions in whatever hovel, castle, or field we may find ourselves in. And as you have guessed, I have grown more than fond of you. Indeed, my lord, I have fallen in love and to such a degree that my heart would surely break should you ever cast me aside."

His thin fingers brought her hand to his lips for a kiss. "Never fear, my love. That time will never come."

The front door burst open, aided by a gust of wind, and Maxim leaned forward to peer around the solid back of the bench as a heavy stomping of boots near the portal gave a good imitation of an invasion. Though there was a small crowd of men there, he saw only the one who stood in the fore.

"So! There yu are!" Nicholas's booming voice filled the confines of the room, making Elise almost choke on her wine. Though she could not see around Maxim or beyond their own small nook, she clasped a handkerchief to her mouth in horror and stared at her husband as he leaned back and breathed an angry curse.

"How did he find us?" she whispered frantically.

"I don't know," Maxim growled through gritted teeth.

Nicholas paused to doff his cloak and gloves and to hang the larger garment on a peg, then strode forward with great gusto. As if in response to Elise's question, he chortled. "That great oafish Eddy vas refusing to be led into the livery as I passed the inn, and I thought to myself, 'Ah ha! My friend is taking a few victuals. I vill join him and relieve his loneliness...'"

Elise wanted to sink below the table as she heard his footsteps halt beside them, and for a brief passing moment she could not find the courage to raise her gaze to his. She wished she had had the presence of mind to slide away from Maxim to lessen the shock of their discovery, but it was too late to think of what she should have done. It was enough for her to find the resolve to meet those flaring blue eyes.

"I think yu not so lonely after all, my friend," Nicholas observed tersely.

"Would you care to join us?" Maxim offered in quiet, good manner.

The captain's brows lowered ominously as he settled himself upon the opposite bench, and he glared his anger at the Marquess who made no attempt to smile.

It was not a moment Maxim would have chosen to tell the man of their marriage, yet it seemed there was naught else to do. Forming the words in his mind, he would have set himself promptly to the task but for Elise warning him with a small shake of her head. It was then that he turned his head and noticed the men who had served as their escort during their journey to Lubeck taking places at a nearby table. There were at least half a dozen of them, and being countrymen one and all of the good captain, he had no reason to doubt with whom their sympathies would lie should an argument ensue. Maxim did not consider himself a coward even in the face of so great a threat, but he had the welfare of his young bride to think of.

The men watched with interest as the captain braced his arms upon the planks and glowered at his companion. "Vould yu kindly tell me vhy yu are here vith Elise?"

"Is it not obvious?" Maxim waved a hand to indicate the food. "We're sharing a few morsels."

Nicholas snorted in contempt, hardly satisfied with the other's answer. "Vhat else did yu plan to share? A bed?"

Maxim relaxed against the straight board planks at his back, but his eyes took on the glint of hot steel. "You defame the lady mightily, my friend, and though I know your plight I scarce can abide such insults. 'Twas I who drew Elise out this day, and thus 'tis I who must stand to her defense." He felt the light touch of her hand upon his thigh and saw her chin lift slightly as her pleading eyes begged him to let her have the responsibility of Nicholas's enlightenment. He mentally bowed to her request. "There is nothing here but the most honorable of intents. I remind you to have a care for Elise's repute and gentle your accusations, at least until I return her home and am free to settle this dispute with you in private."

"I shall escort the lady home myself," Nicholas gritted out. "It is vhere I'm going now. And yu . . . my friend"—he stressed the last two words with a sneer—"may keep yur appointment vith Karr Hilliard, and may God have mercy on yur foolhardy soul."

"Karr Hilliard?" Maxim gazed at the captain questioningly.

"He asked me to send yu to him," Nicholas answered coldly. "If he does not kill yu"—he ignored Elise's sharp gasp as he continued—"then I may try." He flung up a hand to indicate the guards. "I have no need of their help."

"Would you care to set an hour for our meeting?" Maxim inquired almost cordially. "I would not want to miss it."

"If yu survive the meeting vith Hilliard, ve can meet on the morrow . . ."

"Why so late? Why can we not settle this matter tonight?"

"I have a meeting at the *kontor* this evening," Nicholas answered tersely. "Othervise I vould accommodate yu."

"And this appointment with Hilliard? What time is that to take place?"

"About four."

Maxim rubbed his chin thoughtfully. "I was to meet a man this evening. He might have word of Elise's father." He met her worried stare briefly before turning back to the captain. "Is there a way the meeting with Hilliard might be postponed?"

"Hilliard vaits for no one. Either yu keep the appointment, or yu vill lose the opportunity, such as it is."

A sigh of resignation slipped from the handsome lips. "And just where is this meeting to take place?"

"In Hilliard's varehouse near the docks." Nicholas handed over a small piece of parchment upon which he had hastily drawn a map. "This is vhere yu are to meet him."

Maxim studied the map briefly and then gathered up his gloves from the table. "I've just enough time to escort the lady home ere I must leave again."

Angrily Nicholas slammed his fist upon the table. *"Yu vill not take her home!"*

Though Elise blanched at each word of the captain's outburst, Maxim just smiled blandly and jerked on his gloves as he rose to his feet. "I'm afraid you must order your guards to keep me from doing so, my friend. I brought the lady here, and be damned, I shall take her back!" He gestured Elise from the seat and, when she rose beside him, settled her cloak about her shoulders. She glanced at Nicholas in anxious trepidation, afraid of what he might do, and was thankful that, save for a flurry of disgruntled snorting and muted cursing, he chose not to make a further scene.

Maxim drew Elise with him toward the door and paused a moment beside the innkeeper who had wisely held his silence when the other man had intruded into the privacy of their small table. Pressing a few coins into the man's hand, Maxim spoke a quiet word to him in German, then took his leave with his bride.

"We must hasten," he murmured, laying an arm about Elise's shoulders as they walked swiftly toward the livery. "I must hie to my appointment with Hilliard."

"You'll be in danger, Maxim." She searched his eyes pleadingly as he halted beside her and took her hands. "You may even be killed. Must you meet with Hilliard?"

"I've no other choice but to go, my love. Believe me, I would that our wedding night be something other than this. I set my plan to spend this afternoon alone with you. It seems fate has set my intent awry. Were it of less import, I would stay at your side, yet I can only beg you to have patience and to rest assured that I will not long be denied the joy of making you my wife in truth." He bent to her lips and, having no care of who watched, kissed her heatedly to seal his pledge. Then, taking her hand into his, he continued on toward the livery.

Maxim tightened the girth of her saddle and lifted Elise upon the back of the mare, but as she reached for the reins he caught her gloved hand and pressed his lips upon her fingers, silently praying that he would return to keep his vow.

Chapter 20

MAXIM PAUSED in the dark shadows at the bottom of the stairs and carefully assessed his surroundings. The stairs, which might take him threateningly close to danger, began only a short space away and ascended to a short landing which led toward another flight and many more beyond. He leaned back against the wall and drew in a long, deep breath, slowly steeling his nerves. The man he was about to face was at the height of power in the Hanseatic League, at least until the Diet met in the spring. The members, wildly diverse in origins, resources, and opinions, had not seen fit at their last meeting to dispense with their debates and cast Hilliard from their midst. Unless something unforeseen took place, there was no reason to hope the man would be replaced this year either. By their altercating and brooding silence, the voting body sanctioned their delegate's authority, giving tacit approval to his brutish methods. Hilliard had been successful as a merchant captain, and was now even more so as an "enforcer" of the contracts, laws, and agreements of the Hanseatic League, most of which he interpreted as he saw fit. His power was absolute; he answered only to the Diet and then only in premise.

Laying his left hand upon the hilt of his sword to keep it from swinging wildly, Maxim leapt up the stairs, taking them two at a time. He had donned more sober garments after he returned Elise to the Von Reijns' home and belted on his sword, anticipating the worst. If his marriage to Elise was to be terminated by his death ere the night was out, he was at least determined to fight until the bitter end.

Gaining the upper landing, Maxim turned to take the second flight and, in his progression, swiftly advanced to the third level. Giving no pause, he crossed the last landing and turned the latch of the only door that confronted him.

The portal swung wide, and a densely muscular man paused in the placing of charts in a deep armoire and half turned to face the door. Seeing Maxim, he closed the cabinet and dusted his hands officiously as he approached.

"Do yu vish somet'ing?" His voice was soft, not quite effeminate, yet was belied by a sense of ruthless strength embodied in the strong shoulders and bulging arms. The sinewed hands that folded into each other seemed to rest patiently as the man awaited an answer.

"Maxim Seymour, at your service. I believe *Herr* Hilliard is expecting me." Maxim delved into the pocket of his doublet and, producing the impression of the seal, passed it casually to the man. The examination was careful, and when the blue eyes lifted again from beneath pale, fringed brows, they had lost their curiosity and conveyed at least the guise of respect.

"I am Gustave, *Herr* Hilliard's . . . personal scribe." The pause was almost imperceptible. Still, it was effective in giving the impression that there was a vast range of titles and duties from which he could select. "Come in."

Maxim tucked his gloves beneath his belt and obeyed the directive, briefly considering the large, solidly muscled hands. To entertain the idea that they were capable of making short work of a man's life was hardly a foolish notion. Indeed, he thought, they were probably very adept at performing such a deed.

"May I take yur cloak?"

Maxim laid the garment over his own arm, denying the man's request. If he had to leave in a rush, it was better to be prepared for a long flight through a frigidly cold night. At the man's deepening scowl, he shrugged and gave the excuse, "I'll keep it beside me if you don't mind. I took a chill coming here, and I may have need of its warmth."

"I vill tell *mein Herr* yu haff arrived." Gustave crossed the room and, barely opening a door behind a desk, slipped his barrel-chested frame through the narrow space, yielding the guest no glimpse of the adjoining room.

Maxim turned slowly about as he considered the room wherein he found himself. It was both plain and ordinary, yet strangely messy. Sheaves of manifests, bills of lading, and other documents lay atop a long chest of drawers, which no doubt were filled with more of the same. Though the documents seemed very much in disorder, Maxim guessed that any disarrangement of them would be easily detected.

The sound of heavy footsteps approached the portal through which Gustave had passed, and promptly the door was swung wide by the man. *"Mein Herr* vishes yu to vait in here for him."

Maxim passed within, and when Gustave indicated a chair, he draped his cloak over the back of it and settled his long frame within its cushioned comfort, carefully arranging his sword beside him. Gustave retreated into the adjoining room, and the door closed behind him. Though Maxim waited to hear the grate of a key in a lock, none came. He almost breathed a sigh of relief, but knew the folly of counting his blessings too soon. The contest of wits was only about to begin and would in the end determine whether he left at a leisurely pace or fled for his life.

Leaning his head back, Maxim let his eyelids sink half-closed as he surveyed the luxury that surrounded him, yet every nerve tingled as he sensed that he was being closely observed himself. The chamber was a complete contrast to the former one. Wherever the eye touched, there were rich momentos of a lifetime of travel. Every piece of furniture, every drape, every rug or cushion was of the finest quality and bespoke the prominence and wealth Hilliard had attained. A warming fire crackled in a fireplace adorned with an elaborate marble mantel. Nearby, a large chair, covered with dark leather, stood behind a monstrous desk of rich, satiny woods. This was obviously the apartment of a man of means, for the chamber exceeded the luxury of many a royal office.

When the moments had drawn out into a long, quiet space, a door opened with the barest whisper of sound and Karr Hilliard deigned to make his entrance. He waddled forward to greet his guest. "Ah, Lord Seymour! So goot of yu to come."

Cocking an eyebrow in haughty question as the enormous bulk of humanity known as Karr Hilliard halted squarely before him, Maxim rose in good manner and responded in kind, "So good of you to ask, *Herr* Hilliard."

Hilliard's chuckles seemed to set his enormous bulk aquiver. "I vas vondering if yu vould remember me."

"How could I not? You are lord of the Hansards, are you not?" The slight twisting of his lips could be read as a smile, but only Maxim knew of the derisive sneer he hid behind it.

"Yu honor me, Lord Seymour, but I am hardly a

king. I am vhat yu vould call a common peasant in England." As if he thought he deserved more acclaim, however, he paused a moment to allow some protest and was disappointed when none came. He heaved a sigh. "I am merely a servant of the league."

Maxim offered a small token of what the man sought. "Then a servant who has gained much respect."

"It is true," Hilliard readily agreed. "I am one of the more successful delegates of our Diet."

"None dare question the truth of that statement," Maxim declared, knowing he split a fine hair between truth and insult.

His ego much placated, Hilliard chortled in good humor and gestured Maxim back into his chair. As the younger man settled his tall frame between the ornately carved arms of the stately chair, Hilliard moved his ponderous bulk across the room to a cabinet of sorts built within the space of a window. Inside the compartment, a tapped barrel had been laid within a frame. A wooden grating, the kind that would cover a ship's hatchway, was used as part of an outer cage around the opening. The whole of it was shielded from the elements by oiled canvas which could either be raised or lowered from the inside. The cabinet, subjected to the cold outside, allowed for the chilling of the keg as well as the pewter mugs stored beneath it. When firmly latched, the doors prevented any drafts from invading the chamber, while it kept the heat from reaching the keg.

The High Lord Merchant King of the Hansa, or so Hilliard thought of himself, waddled forward with a frosty tankard filled to the brim with foaming ale and held it out to his guest. "Vould yu care to join me in a cool libation, *Herr* Seymour?"

"I'd be so inclined, *Herr* Hilliard. Thank you for your

offer." Maxim accepted the cold brew and took a long draught, finding it much to his liking.

"*Kapitan* Von Reijn met vith me this morning," Hilliard informed him, settling his own huge mass into a stout chair. Opening his mouth in the manner of a fish, he sampled the ale from his mug before he continued. "He told me of yur desire to hire out as a ... mercenary?" The last he posed as a question, as if uncertain as to the accuracy of the term.

Maxim responded with a lazy nod. "I've considered it."

Hilliard assessed him for a long moment, as if trying to read the depth of intelligence behind the handsome face. "Have yu made any definite plans toward accomplishing that goal?"

Maxim paused as he was about to take a sip and glanced at the man. "And if I have?"

Hilliard laughed shortly, setting his jowls aquiver. "Unruffle yur feathers, *Herr* Seymour. If I pry, 'tis for a reason. It vould be of great interest for me to know to vhich country yu vould sell yur services."

" 'Tis a matter of logic," Maxim answered simply. "It would of course be whatever country offers the largest purse."

"Nicholas told me of yur need."

Maxim curled his lip in derision. "I'm not a pauper yet, so I can afford to bide my time."

Hilliard sensed that he had pricked the man's pride. Perhaps *Herr* Seymour was closer to poverty than he let on. "What if someone *vere* interested in obtaining yur services and could offer yu much gold, vhat say yu? Vould yu hear him out?"

"I would be a fool not to." Maxim returned a level stare to the shadowed gray eyes that probed at him.

"Vould it matter to yu vhich country hires yu ... or vhich yu vould have to set yurself against?"

Maxim scoffed lightly. "If my friend Nicholas has not yet told everything there is to tell about me, perhaps I should enlighten you, *Herr* Hilliard. I'm a man without a country, and what loyalties I once held have indeed been wasted. I now serve my own pleasure."

The watery gray eyes narrowed as they watched the Marquess closely for any glimpse into his character. "Vhat of Elizabeth? Do yu owe any allegiance to her?"

A sneer distorted the handsome shape of the manly lips. "By her hand I have been stripped of my title, my estates, and all my possessions." Maxim lashed the words out in caustic venom. "Now by your gauge judge what loyalty I should give her?"

"Vere it myself, I vould give her none."

"Precisely."

Hilliard traced a long, dirty fingernail thoughtfully around the rim of his mug. The Marquess's reply was crisply spoken, and if one were to consider his poor state of circumstance, it was possible to believe the man had set himself staunchly against the English queen. "I vould ask yu rather bluntly, *Herr* Seymour. Vould yu entertain the idea of going back to England under the rule of Queen Mary?"

The reply was cautious. "If she would return my title and properties to me."

Hilliard hunched forward in his chair, propping his massive arms upon his own flesh as he carefully chose his words. "Have yu thought of helping Queen Mary escape?"

Maxim's abortive laugh strongly hinted of his doubt. "And what miracle would bring about such an event? I'm but one man. What can I do alone?"

"Be assured, *Herr* Seymour, yu vould not be alone. Ve have people in England who vould help yu. But then, there are others who think it vould be easier to assassinate Elizabeth first before setting Mary free."

"What are you proposing?" Maxim asked harshly. "Helping Mary to escape? Or murdering the Queen?"

Hilliard's eyes avoided Maxim's for a moment. He seemed to ruminate over the last question, and his manner waxed anxious, as if he were uncertain of his course. Then he steadied his purpose and, after a moment of thought, ponderously heaved his corpulent mass from the chair. He passed to where large, glass-enclosed shelves, laden with books of all sizes, shapes, and forms, covered an entire wall. He paused for a space, and when he glanced back over his shoulder, his eyes were filled with a new light, one mixed with avarice and a strange, evil lust.

"Come." His head jerked to enforce the command. "I vish to show yu something." Behind the bulk of his body, his finger pressed an unseen latch, then he pushed against the case, and to Maxim's amazement, it began to move slowly and without a sound. A door appeared behind the bookcase, and Maxim followed the wide form of his host until they reached a high, narrow walkway protected by a rough-hewn rail. Lanterns hung from rafters near the walk, creating islands of light that shone into the blackness. The cavernous warehouse stretched out almost into what seemed like oblivion and was stacked with endless wooden boxes, crates, bales, and barrels. Moving spots of light gave evidence of a slow patrol of guards, armed with axes and pikes, bearing lanterns.

Hilliard waited, allowing Maxim to take in the sheer immensity of the place. When the younger man finally faced him with a brow raised slightly in question, the Hansa lord grinned in greed-inspired glee. "Yu see before yu that vhich vould purchase the ransom of several kings or, more simply, several kingdoms. Indeed! Some of it has." He pointed to a portion along one side. "There are spices, teas, and silks from Cathay." His finger jabbed again. "There are tapestries, carpets, and sugared dates purchased·from the emirs, beys, and sultans who reign beyond the Black Sea. Over there..."—his arm swung to another dark mass below them—"a recent acquisition of furs, amber, and honey from the Easterlings and the ports along the Baltic."

He faced Maxim and his grin bared his uneven teeth again. "My ships bring cargo from all corners of the vorld, and I send desired and much-needed items to other corners of the vorld...for a healthy profit, of course." His face darkened as some vile thought beset him. "Or at least I do when that bastard, Drake, lets me vend about my business. That is vhat the Hansa is about. Just a band of honest merchants seeking to make an honest profit vhere it can."

Maxim followed the man back to his apartment, wondering about the black-hearted means and the thousands of dead who paid for this particular Hansa master's profit.

"And now," Hilliard continued angrily, "that bitch Elizabeth plays her clever games of innocence vhile she sets Drake and his sea dogs to ravaging those of us who have labored to build our trade." He almost threw his body into the chair where he drooped his shoulders and leaned forward over his massive paunch. Beneath beetled brows, his eyes gleamed with an evil light. "There are others, mind yu, who are like-minded and who vould see an end to her high-flown ways." He slumped back against his chair as if exhausted, and his manner became one of weedling and pleading. "Vhy, I have been threatened myself. I dare not inspect my own properties in the Stilliards, lest I be set upon and cast into prison for offenses I'm innocent of. There's no justice in that black heart of Elizabeth."

Maxim resumed his seat, mentally dismissing the man's avid protests as bold-faced lies. He laid a finger on the hilt of his sword. "If you fear Elizabeth's trickery, then why have you allowed an armed Englishman in your presence? Are you not wary of my intent? Could she not have sent me?"

Hilliard rested his elbows on the arms of the chair, making a steeple of his pudgy fingers as he smiled knowingly. "I take some assurance in the fact that yur life vas nearly spent at her command, Lord Seymour. Still, I'm a cautious man." He raised his hand toward the wall behind his guest. "Vould yu care to look behind yu?"

Maxim sat forward and looked around. A large painting in an ornate frame had been moved aside slightly, revealing an opening in the wall behind it. Maxim remembered the cabinet into which Gustave had been storing charts and knew its placement was just about right to allow for surveillance of the room through it.

"Gustave has had a crossbow vith a heavy quarral resting twixt its thighs directed toward yur back ever since yu came in. Had yu laid a hand to yur blade, yur friends vould never have seen yu again." He nodded pensively. "Even in vinter, the river carries most flotsam into the sea and disposes of it nicely."

"And, of course, Gustave is your most loyal servant," Maxim remarked.

"Assistant vould be a better vord." Hilliard smiled smugly. "He has a penchant for dispensing vith my adversaries. Yu understand, of course."

"Your precautions have been well-noted, *Herr* Hilliard," Maxim replied, leaning back in his chair again. "However, as yet my question remains unanswered.

Which is it to be, an assassination or an escape?"

"Vhichever is convenient." The gray eyes took on a gleam above a sly smile. "Though I dare say the obvious. Even if Mary vere allowed to escape, she could not become queen 'til the other is done avay vith or her supporters rally around her to make her queen. 'Tis certainly to your benefit that Elizabeth be killed."

Maxim sneered in contempt at the man's suggestion. "Aye, and the moment I set foot in a castle where Elizabeth is housed, I'd be arrested and then taken to the Tower to await my long-delayed execution. Forgive me, *Herr* Hilliard. I'd rather keep my head than lose it on a block. A bag of gold is no good to a dead man."

Hilliard carefully posed the question. "Vhat if someone vould help yu get into the castle and, in so doing, could assure that yu vould not be seen?"

"If you have such a one in the castle, then why would anyone have need of me? Your man in the castle could slay the Queen and escape undetected."

Hilliard leaned back in his chair with a disgruntled sigh. "Therein lies the crux of the matter. A lady-invaiting could hardly bear the sword of a man."

"Nay, but she could bear the poison of an asp." Maxim leaned forward, peering into those shadowed gray eyes as he pressed the man. "Come now, Hilliard. If you have someone that close to the Queen, then your deed is done. You have no need of me."

"I vish it vere that simple." Hilliard set his jowls trembling as he shook his head in disgust. "The lady vill not do it. She is loyal to the Queen, and should yu gain entry, she vould have no knowledge of vhat yu intend."

"Then why would she allow me to enter the Queen's apartments at all?" A frown troubled the noble brow as the Marquess tried to understand the reasoning behind the man's plan. "Why would she trust me enough to allow me entrance?"

"She is but a vorthless pawn..."

"Why would she let me in?" Maxim persisted.

The weighty shoulders heaved upward. "She is aging and has simple thoughts of love..."

"And?"

For once in his life Hilliard realized he faced a man whose will was at least as strong as his. Despite the power he claimed to have, he found himself squirming beneath those flaring orbs of emerald green and almost whined as he gave answer. "The vench has a lover..."

Maxim fell back in his chair and smiled slyly as he pressed his own fingertips together. "And, of course, the maid would not think her lover capable of such a dastardly deed." The green eyes glimmered and then narrowed into a glare. "Then, pray tell, why do you not pay her lover to assassinate the Queen?"

Hilliard almost jeered in disdain. "That fellow is valuable in his vay, but he does not have the heart. He vould murder on the sly, but not vhere there's danger."

"He is a coward then." Maxim bluntly supplied the word the other seemed unwilling to use.

Noncommittal, Hilliard waggled his head, setting his jowls to swaying.

Watching the other closely, the Marquess baited him. "A German should have more daring."

"A German vould! But he is naught but an English-bred veakling." The protruding lips curved downward, giving evidence of Hilliard's dislike for the one mentioned.

Maxim urged him on. "And you dare not vex him

lest you lose your accessibility to the Queen. Perhaps you even pamper him."

A low snarling growl grated in the thick throat. "I've done that, though it has no doubt cost me a fortune in gold. Indeed, I'll never know vhat I've lost..."

Maxim sipped his ale as he mused on the man's ramblings. "Gold is a hard thing to come by. Only a fool would let it out of his grasp."

Dejectedly Hilliard slumped forward again, as if in great sorrow. "It vas mine...or nearly so, but that misbegotten whoreson threatened to break off vith the lady. I had no choice but to give in to his demands."

"You obviously need the man to keep the lady pliable to your plans," Maxim surmised. "Yet I sense that you would see the death of him if you could."

Hilliard drew his lips back in a sneer, showing his dark, gaping teeth as he made a twisting motion with his two hands. "If I could," he swore between hissing intakes of breath, "I vould do the deed myself."

Maxim witnessed the gesture and could almost imagine the loud snap of his own neck breaking within the grip of those beefy paws, yet he was set to a course and he would not falter from it now. "Tell me, *Herr* Hilliard. Do you have any definite plans to assassinate the Queen? Or is this some hopeful dream of yours that will never come to pass?"

The gray eyes flared with instant anger as Hilliard detected a tone of ridicule in the Englishman's voice. "Fear not, *Herr* Seymour, I've my plans, and they vill be carried out. If not by yu, then another."

"And what is the sum you offer?"

Hilliard smiled smugly, nestling his large head into the fat folds of his shoulders. "Vhy, yur estates, yur vealth, and yur properties, of course. Are they not enough revard?"

Maxim drained the last dregs of his ale and rose from his chair. Taking up his cloak, he looked down at the man. " 'Tis a sufficient reward if you can guarantee it."

"Assassinate that Tudor bitch and free Mary Stuart from prison, and yu shall have it all."

"I shall of course need a small purse to tide me over until I can make arrangements to return to England." Maxim smiled blandly. "You may call it a demonstration of your faith in me."

Hilliard waddled out of the room and came back with an iron-bound chest. Maxim recognized it as a larger but very similar version of one Von Reijn owned, which the captain called his testament. Producing a key from his coat, Hilliard plied it to the lock and withdrew a small purse which he tossed to his guest. He made a waxen impression of his seal and gave it to Maxim. "This vill help identify yu should there come a need, though there are few in England who have not heard of the Marquess of Bradbury."

"Will your man be contacting me? Or should I seek him out myself?"

"He vill contact yu shortly after yur arrival."

Maxim stepped to the door where he paused a moment. "Should Nicholas make inquiries about our visit, I would take it much amiss if you tell him of this matter. He fancies himself an expert on Maxim Seymour. I choose to keep him uninformed."

"He shall be told nothing."

Maxim gave a crisp nod of farewell and took his leave, releasing a long sigh of relief as he departed the company of Karr Hilliard and his man, Gustave.

Chapter 21

*T*HE SUN SLOWLY FADED to an indistinct glow in the western sky, silhouetting the tall spires and sharply pitched rooftops against the horizon. It seemed as if the winds paused to take breath, allowing a still, breathless dusk to descend, but soon, wafts of air stirred from the north, bringing a bitter cold that sucked away the last dregs of warmth the day had managed to instill. The sky darkened from a bloodless gray to a featureless black, then a dust-fine snow began to fall. Inside every pane of glass an intricate and ever-varied pattern of frost began to form, spreading its crystals in an intricately elaborate array. The air grew brisk, and the white bearding deepened on every surface that would hold it.

A weak gust found its way between the solid rows of buildings and became a snow eddy that danced its dervishlike, whirling step up the middle of the empty street in front of the Von Reijn house, there dissolving abruptly in a puff of white that slowly settled with the rest. The only evidence of its passing was the obliteration of tracks and paths left previously in the deepening, fluffy snow.

Elise drew away from the small window in her chamber, and the frost made haste to cover the circle she had wiped clear. The delicate, weblike tracings that formed before her eyes entranced her for a moment, then the glass trembled as another blast of air shook it. A low murmur moaned in the rafters as a rising wind took up a playful chase across the acute angles of the roof and eaves.

Elise heaved a lengthy sigh of her own and began to pace the narrow confines of her room. Outside, the swirling gusts swept the snow into the streets, whipping the flakes into frenzied flight until a thick haze of white obscured familiar thoroughfares. Anxious worry assailed her fortitude as the wind mounted again to a relentless wail, as if a band of banshees flitted about the rooftops in fruitless searching. Nicholas's grim comments had left her feeling a deep dread of a man she had never met. Karr Hilliard apparently had the power to dispose of Maxim in whatever fashion he might deem appropriate, and, in so doing, would steal every joy from her life. She could not hope for reassurance until Maxim returned, and even then, there would be Nicholas to be dealt with. She had made the decision to approach the captain herself and tell him of their marriage, but as yet any clear opportunity had eluded her, for he too had avoided returning home.

The shutters continued to bang, while every gust of wind seemed to shake the very foundation of the house, and still Maxim did not return. She stayed close to the window, clearing peepholes in the frost as she searched the encroaching storm for any glimpse of that tall, broad-shouldered form she longed to see. The mere sight of him could set her heart leaping with joy, but alas, the moment of elation did not come.

A sudden clattering clamor rattled across the roof, followed for a space by silence, then a splintering crash came from the street below. A freshening, howling wind shook the manse with renewed vengeance and sent Elise, in carefully controlled flight, to the hall below where she found both Therese and Katarina intent on the stitches of their respective tapestries. Justin entered the room only a step behind her.

"The wind must have blown a tile from the roof, *Tante* Therese," he remarked.

Therese carefully plied her needle to a stitch. "T'at noise scare the vits out o' poor Elise!" She paused to press a hand over her own swiftly beating heart, and then, regaining her aplomb, shook her finger at the amused Justin. "Tomorrow yu go up t'ere and make sure no more come down."

"Ja! Ja! I giff t'em good scolding, too."

"Humph." Therese raised a brow at him. "Maybe I show yu how first, *ja?"*

"Nein, Bitte," he pleaded with a laugh, raising his hands wide in a posture of yielding. "You've instructed me well enough."

Satisfied, Therese returned to her sewing as Justin approached Elise, who had taken up a stance near the front window and was trying to penetrate the thick veil of snow that enveloped the street.

"You needn't trouble yourself so about Nicholas, Elise. He knows this city as well as he knows his ship."

Though Justin misread her concern, Elise managed a smile for his gentle assurance. It was not that she was unconcerned over the possible plight of the Hansa captain, but the danger to Maxim seemed far more real and imminent. As the moments passed, the burden of her distress grew more insufferable.

Justin bent closer to a crystal pane and scraped clear a larger peephole as a vague shadow took on the appearance of a cloaked form. The man leaned into the gale-force winds as he approached the house, slipping and sliding as he fought against the powerful gusts.

"Ho, there! I believe we're about to receive a guest

who has braved the elements to seek us out." Justin caught Elise's silent query and read the restrained anxiety in her furrowed brow. A sharp pang of pity made him return to the glass. He strained to make out the figure, moving from pane to pane to get a better view, then he straightened and shrugged as he gazed down at her. " 'Tis only a stranger, Elise."

She sighed and, clasping her hands together, glanced at the timepiece on the table. The hour was approaching eight, late enough for Maxim to have finished his meeting with Hilliard and returned.

"Open the door, Justin," Therese bade, "ere the poor man freeze to death."

The young man hastened to the entrance and swung the portal open just as the fellow was about to apply his knuckles to the wooden planks. The startled man gaped at Justin for a moment with his fist raised, then, somewhat embarrassed, he cleared his throat and assumed a more dignified stance. Pushing aside the snow-covered hood of his cloak, he made known his objective.

"M-my name is S-Sheffield Thomas, sir," he stuttered through cold-stiffened lips. "I-I've c-come to speak with M-Mistress Elise Radborne about a m-matter. Lord Seymour sent a message that he had a matter of great import to attend to with Hilliard. I assumed he'd meet me at my inn afterward, but he didn't come, and I thought perhaps he might've come back here."

"Lord Seymour is not here at the moment, but Mistress Radborne is. Would you care to come in and warm yourself by the fire while I fetch her?" The man entered and Justin took his cloak and then led the guest into a small antechamber where a warming fire greeted him. "If you'll wait here, I shall tell Mistress Radborne you've come."

Sheffield drew a large handkerchief from his blanchet as the young man left him and applied it to his red, bulbous nose. Upon hearing footsteps, he lifted his watering eyes to the doorway where a slender, feminine figure moved with grace through the haze that blurred his sight, taking on a beauty he had not recently beheld. The man hastily dabbed his kerchief to his eyes until he could focus clearly, and was amazed to find the vision incredibly real.

"Good sir." Justin hid a smile as the fellow snapped his mouth closed. "May I make you acquainted with our guest, Mistress Radborne?"

The aging, bald-headed man managed to bend his frost-stiffened body in a brief bow. "My pleasure, mistress. My pleasure indeed!"

"You have information for me, sir?" Elise questioned softly.

Her voice, though fraught with tension, reminded Sheffield of a spot in England near his home where a wee brook tumbled melodiously over a rocky bed deep in a small, mossy glen. Indeed, he was half a mind to think he was dreaming the moment. After all, the icy winds were so numbing, he might have passed into paradise without realizing it. "Yea, mistress. Lord Seymour asked me to speak with you about an incident which I witnessed some months ago. I understand he is not here."

"He was detained," Elise murmured, struggling to ignore her worries. This stranger could have news of her father, and through him she might learn information of her sire's whereabouts. It should have been a moment of hopeful anticipation for her, but she was ill-met to dismiss her concerns for Maxim so easily.

Justin closed the door and invited the man to take a chair. "Mistress Radborne has asked that I stay and witness. Be that acceptable to you, sir?"

"Certainly." Sheffield declined the chair and edged

closer to the fire as he faced the other occupants of the room. Folding his icy hands behind his back where they would catch the heat, he began to speak. "I'm an English merchant. Some time ago I brought me ship to Bremen and continued on to Nuremberg and the fairs at Leipzig to trade for merchandise from afar. Karr Hilliard bade me come to Lubeck and view his precious wares ere I returned to England. Thus I came to Lubeck a full season and a half ago to trade with the man. I had amassed a rich cargo and had such treasures that kings would have vied for the opportunity to own them. I was sure Hilliard and I would strike many a bargain, but alas, me ship burned at anchor the night after I off-loaded a few samples to show him." He waxed slightly morose. "I lost me captain and a full dozen seamen left to guard her. Well-armed the lot were too, but come morning, there was only the charred stubs of a mast jutting up out of the water. The harbormaster had to haul it over and rip the hull apart with grappling hooks to clear the area, choice spot that it was." A light syrup of derision dripped from his words. "Not a scrap of her timbers looked familiar." He jabbed a finger into the palm of his other hand to emphasize his point. "And not a shred of all that finery has come a-bobbin' up this whole time since. 'Twas as if the brigands stole away me ship and burned an empty hulk in her place."

Suddenly lost in thought, Sheffield turned to stare into the fire and spread his hands to warm them for a long moment before he wheeled about again and continued as if no time had elapsed at all. "The next morn the rest of the crew was roused from a drunken stupor in a scurvy alehouse and could speak naught of the night before. Few there be who could drink them blokes under the table. Still, when I questioned the burgomaster o' Lubeck, he rattled off excuses so swiftly, he made me head swim. He claimed to have looked into the matter, but as yet no sign of me ship nor me men has come to light." Sheffield's tale continued to captivate his audience. "I've learned to speak the jargon more ably since, and here and there I've overheard stories of English sailors chained in irons and forced to walk the plank of one o' Hilliard's ships." He shrugged, and his eyes grew distant again. "When I try to question anyone about it, they sidle away and talk no more of it."

"I'm sorry to hear of your losses, Master Thomas," Elise said kindly. "But what has this to do with my father?"

Master Thomas started to answer her, then coughed and spoke in distressed tones to Justin. "Prithee, sir. Me craw be parched and raw. Would you have a wee draught to ease the blistering of the cold?"

"Of course." Justin nodded and moved from his place behind Elise's chair to a sideboard where he rang a small bell. A moment later a maid bustled in, bearing a wide tray which in turn bore, to the guest's dismay, a steaming pot and a triplet of cups. Justin smiled as he noted the man's disappointment and, after pouring half a cup, liberally enriched it from a flagon he took from the sideboard.

Sheffield eagerly accepted the proffered brew and, after sniffing its steaming essence, sipped long and loudly. "Ahhh," he sighed. "The heat"—he paused pointedly—"does wonders for the throat." He sipped again and returned the empty cup to the tray after another statement of pleasure. In slightly more fluid tones than before he continued his tale. " 'Twas some months ago I gots the idea to watch Hilliard's ships as they came into port or took on cargo, just by chance there would be something of me own wares I would spy. In so doing I saw a strange happening, which at first I was sure involved one of me own men."

Elise sipped her tea and tried not to think of Maxim dealing with such a man as Karr Hilliard. Sheffield's account gave her thoughts no ease at all.

"Hilliard's great ship, the *Grau Falke*, had just arrived from the Stilliards in London," Sheffield recounted. "From a safe distance I watched until I saw a man bound and chained with as much weight as he could carry being escorted from the ship."

"And the man whom you saw was an Englishman?" Elise questioned carefully.

"Aye, mistress."

"How do you know?" Justin inquired.

"Later I was in an alehouse, and I recognized one of the guards. After buying the bloke a few ales, I asked about the man." Sheffield chuckled as he enlivened the story. " 'I heard ye had a mutiny,' I says to him, and the fellow near cuts me down with his eyes. ' 'Tis all abuzz and about,' I says. 'Why, ye brought one o' them beggars back to be hanged...or so's I heard,' I says, not wantin' to let on 'at I was spyin' on the ship.

" 'Ye heard ill,' he spat in his funny twisted tongue. 'There be no mutiny on a Hansa deck. Never been, never will! 'Twas just some English bloke Hilliard caught a-spyin' in the Stilliards.'

" 'Aye,' I says, 'ye'll bring Drake and his dogs down 'pon ye, takin' an Englishman from his own sod like that.'

" 'Bah,' he sneered, gathering up his coins." Sheffield waxed rich in his mimicry of the guard. " 'T'ey neffer know he's gone.' The man would give me no more and left me."

Elise sat forward on the edge of her chair, encouraged by his tale. "What did you notice about the man who was shackled? Was he tall? Thin? Dark-haired?

Even-featured?" To each of these Sheffield nodded, and her hopes strengthened. "Tell me, by chance did you notice if the man was wearing a large ring of onyx and gold on his first finger?"

Sheffield paused a moment in thought and finally shook his head. "That I cannot say, mistress. He was chained with his hands before him, but as far as I can remember he wore no ring at all."

Elise's shoulders slumped slightly as she struggled against the grip of disappointment. The ring would have been a sure way of identifying her father, but now she could not be certain who the man really was.

"Surely they would have taken such a ring from him," Justin pointed out.

"Of course," Sheffield agreed, wanting to see again that spark of hope he had briefly glimpsed in the sapphire eyes.

"If my father is truly here . . . and if he is still alive"—Elise spoke the words slowly as she fought the invading grayness of doubt and uncertainty—"then the only likely place he would be is somewhere in the dungeons of the Hansa."

"Nicholas might be able to help find him," Justin offered.

The deep blue eyes lowered cautiously. Maxim had warned of any attempt to involve Nicholas, and she had to be careful, lest she give Justin some encouragement in that endeavor. "Is there anything more you can tell me, Master Thomas?"

"Nay, mistress." Sheffield sadly shook his head. It fair broke his heart to disappoint her. "I wish I could fill your sails with a sterner wind, but I fear what I've given you is precious feeble indeed."

"Had you given me a gale, sir, I'd have followed it to the ends of the earth." Elise straightened and met his gaze directly. "But to what end?" Her hand flipped from side to side. "Is he here? Is he there? I've followed my quest in a dozen different directions to no avail. Do you give me a new one? Surely I'm no worse than I was before, and you give me some hope that he is near." She slid her hand beneath a fold of her gown, then withdrew it and extended her closed fist to him. In some bemusement Sheffield stared at it and raised questioning brows. "Here, take this," she encouraged, her fingers opening. " 'Tis something for your time and trouble." The sovereign seemed overlarge in her small hand. "For venturing forth on this miserable eventide."

"Ah, nay, mistress. You do me shame. 'Twould be ill-done, indeed, were I to take even a farthing for laying a father's hand to his daughter's. What I've given you is naught but the dregs of the smallest hope. You've shared your warmth and I've listened to the sweetest English tongue since me own good mistress passed away. I bid you good eventide, mistress and kind sir. I'll be about my way."

Justin let the man out and came back to lean against the doorjamb of the chamber portal. Elise sat staring into the fire, hardly aware of him regarding her. He contemplated the slight tugging of small, white teeth against a bottom lip and the rubbing of one slender thumb against the other as she clasped her hands together. He could almost see her mind struggling against a flooding tide of helpless frustration.

"What are you thinking of, Elise?" The question was quietly spoken, barely reaching across the space between them. He had grown fond of the girl since her arrival and wanted to see her happy.

Elise looked up at him and for the first time discovered beneath that facade of carefree gaiety a young man filled with concerns. She laughed softly in an attempt to hide her own. "There are times, Justin, when a woman must keep her musings to herself."

Justin watched her turn away, and there was no further indication of her restlessness as she folded her hands demurely in her lap, though he could well surmise she was dissecting piece by piece the information Sheffield Thomas had given them. Becoming deeply involved in his own ponderings, Justin moved past her chair to stand before the hearth and stare into the frolicking flames. "Once more," he mentally sighed to himself, "Hilliard's repute takes on the blacker shade of midnight ... skulduggery, theft, and piracy. Indeed, what shallow right has the man to lay an acid tongue to Drake's deeds? What Drake has gained in battle on the high seas, Hilliard has acquired through treachery and murder."

It had been as evident to Sheffield Thomas as it would be to any who had to confront the same problem. Hilliard, through the Hansa, held sway and power over the officials of free Lubeck. There was no use to seek justice through that course. Long ago Justin had come upon that truth. Visions of a hangman's rope bending Hilliard's neck or a headsman raising an axe above his large head had faded when he realized the futility of such dreams, but another aspiration had come in their stead. With each passing day the desire grew stronger within Justin to see Hilliard's ponderous jowls quivering with fear as his blade slid keenly beneath the man's breastbone to sunder that evil heart.

Elise roused from her musings to consider Justin for a quiet space, somewhat reluctant to break into his ruminations. He stood in a gallant pose, his weight on one leg, his other knee slightly cocked, his hands folded behind his back. She could see no trace of the flippant, jesting youth, for now he seemed taller, broader of shoulder, and more of a man than a moment before.

Briefly she glimpsed a slight twist of a satisfied smile curving his lips, and then she recalled his sudden interest when Sheffield Thomas had mentioned Hilliard. It came to her that Justin's performance as callow youth would effectively divert the attentions and suspicions of his elders, which left him free to roam and wander where he would. He had a remarkable knowledge of the Hansa, at least locally, and of Karr Hilliard, certainly more than could be explained by mere passing fancy.

Before her thoughts could bear the fruit of a question, Justin faced her and, with a show of casual interest, spoke in a most solicitous tone. "Why do you suppose Maxim went to see Karr Hilliard? Would it have been to inquire after your father?"

Elise met his gaze with a shrug, meaning to play the simple youth herself as she struggled not to show her distrust. "Perhaps, but I cannot say with any certainty that his visit was for that purpose. He gave me no reason, nor did I feel he needed to."

Justin saw her sniff lightly and regard the back of her hand in silent reproof. He smiled behind the hand that rubbed his cheek, realizing he had touched a tender chord. "My pardon, Elise, I meant no unkindness." He pressed on as if musing. " 'Tis just that Hilliard only gives his time and his favors to those who might be of benefit to him. What has he to gain from Maxim?"

"Very little, I would imagine," she replied cautiously. "Maxim can lay claim to neither his properties nor his wealth. He is virtually penniless, and as far as I know, he is quite free of allegiances save that of restoring his honor."

"And yet Hilliard has called upon him. 'Twould be

unlike the man to invite Maxim into his lair for the single purpose of answering inquiries about your father. Nay, there must be something more."

Elise arched her brow, feeling the prick of his prying. If he was suggesting that Maxim was in league with such a man, the brash youth was about to be set back upon his heels. "Perhaps you'll enlighten me, Sir Justin. You seem to know Karr Hilliard quite well yourself. What would you say was his reason for bidding Maxim come?"

Justin settled in a chair across from hers and, propping his elbows on the wooden arms, musefully folded his fingers together. He observed her haughty, but guarded, manner for a long moment before he gave answer. "Of late, Hilliard has been ranting about Drake taking his ships and of Elizabeth giving the man letters of marque condoning piracy on the high seas. Now Hilliard beckons an Englishman to his chambers? Of course, he is a deposed lord . . . but he is familiar with the English court. I ask you in turn, Elise, what would your judgment of such a meeting be?"

Elise lifted her chin, taking offense as she chafed at the direction of his reasoning. In a tightly controlled voice she inquired, "How is it that you know Karr Hilliard so well, Justin? How can you draw such conclusions unless you are closely familiar with the man?"

Justin was aware of her advancing disdain and smiled blandly. He had been impressed, even infatuated by her beauty from the first moment of their meeting, but he had also sensed a strong attraction between the maid and the Marquess. Her reaction supported his suspicions that she doted on the Englishman, but the questions remained. Was this man, by his reputation an accused traitor, involved in something far worse than either of them could imagine? "I know Karr Hilliard because I've observed him closely for some years now. There were circumstances linking Karr Hilliard with the death of my father. Indeed, I believe either he or his henchman, Gustave, was directly responsible for my father's murder."

The shield Elise had begun to raise as protection against his probing questions lowered with the enrichment of knowledge. "Then you understand my worries."

"Very well, I'm afraid." Justin gazed down at the floor as he fought back a thickness in his throat. His father's death still troubled him even after these many years. "Hilliard has rare use for living Englishmen. Whatever Maxim's intent, he treads on dangerous ground."

Fretting openly now, Elise wrung her hands as she wrestled with her imagination. "You mean he could be lying dead somewhere?"

"They found my father stuffed in a wine vat," Justin informed her morosely. His curiosity still persisted, for he could feel no sympathy for a traitor and a murderer. Why was Maxim interested in Hilliard and what did he have to interest the Hansa master? "Sheffield Thomas will likely find himself in a similar situation if he's not careful. Who knows what fate awaits Maxim?"

"Speak no more!" Elise cried, springing to her feet. She glared at him through mounting tears. "Do you take delight in frightening me when I know not where my cherished ones are? I cannot bear it!"

"Mercy, Elise," Justin soothed as he went to her. He would have laid his arm comfortingly around her slender shoulders. "Forgive me. I did not mean to be cruel."

"What am I to do?" she sobbed, moving away from his intended embrace, as she drew perilously near to that dark, rank cavern of utterly consuming fear. "Nicholas said there was a Hansa meeting this eventide. Surely Hilliard has plans to be there and would be done with Maxim by now."

Justin dropped his arm and stepped to the fire, stung by her unspoken reproof. This Maxim was a bold enough fellow with the maid, but what were his true colors? Except for Nicholas's ramblings, he knew nothing of the man and felt a sharp pang of jealousy at Elise's unflagging faith in him. Another thought pricked his consciousness. Hilliard was often disposed to calling a meeting at the *kontor* for no apparent reason except his own gratification. He indulged himself in the idea that his power was that of some exalted sovereign and the Hansa masters the subjects over which he reigned. At times he would boast of his schemes, while veiling them in such a way as to portray a feigned innocence. He often sought tacit approval from the local masters on diverse matters, stroking their ego while he cleverly disguised his real intentions. If a stir was later raised for an evil deed done, then he could simply declare that he only acted as a Hansa agent and under their express direction. It could even be his wont this eventide to bring before the Hansa some excuse for hiring the Englishman. All one had to do was discern the dark side of his reason.

A brief bow to the maid accompanied his plea, "Will you excuse me, Elise? I must venture out for a time."

"But where are you going?" she questioned anxiously. Surely no sane man would venture out on such a cold night unless the matter was of considerable urgency.

Justin paused as he considered what his answer should be. He could not tell her of his need to penetrate the *kontor* or that somehow he meant to confront Maxim and lay bare the roué's intentions. Thus he gave her in varied form what she had given him earlier. "There are some things, my dear Elise"—his smile was brief and stiff—"a man should not tell a woman."

Elise listened to his footsteps in the hall as he made his way to his temporary chamber, and she turned back to stare into the flickering flames as a small frown flitted across her brow. The premonition was strong within her that his leaving was not meant for Maxim's good. He had made it obvious he distrusted her husband. Perhaps, the thought intruded, he even intended to do him harm.

Elise flew from the room and, catching up her skirts, raced up the stairs in something less than a genteel fashion. She knew what she was about, and she would not be stopped. Whether she was right or wrong about Justin, she had no choice but to follow and find out what he was up to. She had seen a chest of his old clothes in the bedchamber Maxim was using and had every intention of putting a few of the garments to use.

Hurriedly Elise doffed her clothes and hid them in Maxim's chest. She bound her breasts as flat as she could by wrapping a wide cloth several times around her chest and pulling it tight. She hastily slipped into a loose shirt and dragged a woolen tunic over it. Two layers of heavy stockings and a pair of loose breeches would help obscure the womanly curves of her hips, while banning the cold. Stuffing her loosely coiled hair beneath a leather skull-shaped hat, she drew the ties securely beneath her chin and knotted them tightly. Her worn hide boots served her purpose well and, with woolen rags tucked inside, would keep her feet warm and soften her step.

The sound of a door opening into the next room gave Elise pause, and she listened in frozen stillness as the floor creaked slightly beneath the careful steps of an intruder. It was surely not Maxim, she thought. He had no reason to sneak into his own chambers.

Carefully she crept to the portal separating the two rooms and eased the door ajar, just wide enough to peer through. Her breath caught in her throat as she saw a man, an ancient one with stiff gray strands of hair jutting from beneath his toque. Then he turned and set a candle on the table, and she recognized the familiar profile of Justin outlined against the dim light. A dark ruby stain covered the left side of his face from temple to jaw, and from it, tufts of gray hair seemed to grow. A thin stubble of a beard now seemed to darken his chin and upper lip. The latter he held twisted in a perpetual sneer. When he moved there was a slight stiffness and limp in his left leg. His manner and gait were far removed from those of a sprightly youth, for the disguise had added many years beyond his own.

Justin removed a wooden testament from the armoire and set the small chest on the desk. Slipping a key from his coat, he plied it to the lock and lifted the lid. With a sigh he plucked the knotted ends of a slender cord from the box and lifted the string until a bronze-hued seal twirled free of its confinement. For a moment he stared at the disk, then, tossing it in the air, caught it within his grasp and with a wide flourish swept a woolen mantle over his shoulders and departed the room.

Elise snatched a shorter cloak from Justin's chest and made haste to follow. She tiptoed to the landing and, from there, saw him flitting down the stairs. Her softly booted feet moved swiftly on the steps, and as she reached the second landing she paused in flight, catching the low murmur of voices drifting down the hallway from Therese's room. Quickly she pressed back into the shadows as Katarina stepped from the elder's room and crossed the hall to her own chambers. Elise breathed a sigh of relief and peered over the balustrade in time to see Justin glide noiselessly to the front door. After a quick glance out and about, he was gone before the latch clicked home behind him.

Cautiously Elise made a similar descent and carefully approached the door. Slipping out the portal, she stood in the dark shadows for a moment as she scanned the street. The wind had died, and there was no sign of Justin except for the faint tracings of footprints trailing away from the house in the fresh snow.

Elise had ventured into Alsatia and the Stilliards enough to be wise in passing unnoticed through the streets of a darkened city. She flew along like a night sprite, hot on the trail of her prey, the old hide boots making only the barest whisper of sound in the soft snow. Wary of being seen, she proceeded cautiously, running to corners and peering around them before venturing forth along another street. And still, it seemed Justin remained far ahead of her. The only evidence of his passage were the tracks left in the snow. Then at last she glanced down a street and saw him pause and glance about before ducking into another alley. She rested and counted slowly to five, then sprinted across the street and into the alley.

Thus it went. Fox and hound. Ever onward, always cautious. She knew not how far they had come, but surmised it to be a goodly distance. She had no idea where they were or why he had chosen this particular direction, but for the sake of her own peace of mind, she could not lose sight of him now, or she would be forever lost in the night-bound city.

Her worst fears were realized when she came out of a dark alley and realized the trail in the snow had ended. In sudden panic she glanced around her, wondering where Justin had gone. Anxiously she retraced her steps, finding several narrow paths that meandered away from the lane, but none held evidence of recent use. It was as if he had vanished in thin air.

Her heart caught in her throat as she became aware of a trio of shadows entering the alley, blocking her retreat. She stumbled backward, searching for a place to hide, then suddenly a hand reached out, closing over her mouth, and she was hauled backward into total blackness. In a panic she struggled to free herself, but an urgent whisper hissed in her ear.

"Make no sound! There's danger for us here."

The voice was Justin's, and her trembling eased as she relaxed against him. The three approached, and in breathless silence the pair waited, not daring to move, frozen by fear of discovery. The lead figure paused with arms akimbo in the center of the alley and presented a most magnificent and fearsome figure against a distant light. His clothes and those of his cohorts were unfamiliar to her. A long sheared lambskin coat was snugged about his lean waist with a wide leather belt, from which a sheathed sword hung. The collar was pulled high behind his neck, and in front the stiff flaps fell open to reveal the crisp banding of a dark tunic. Lambskin trimmed the lower part of his hat, but the woolen top was folded to one side where it was fastened with a bejeweled clasp. The slightly flared skirt of the coat reached lower than mid-calf and covered what appeared to be voluminous breeches of the same length stuffed into the tops of black boots. His features were hidden in the deep shaded night, but Elise thought she could see the shadow of a long, dark mustache drooping over the corners of his lips and a scar running down his cheek.

The man seemed to listen for a space, then moved on. She heard the soft crunch of his boots against the snow as he passed the spot where the pair of them crouched. Elise eased ever-so-carefully back into the darkness that surrounded them and slowed her breathing. Her lungs ached for want of just one deep gasp of air, but she kept as still as a mouse waiting for the cat to leave.

The man reached the end of the alley, and there paused as the other two joined him. From there, they strolled from the alley onto a wider thoroughfare. In the silence that followed their passing, Justin released a deep sigh of relief, as if thankful to have the trio well beyond them.

"Easterlings from Novgorod," he informed her in a hushed whisper. " 'Tis rumored there's been a whole order of them here for the last several weeks. I've seen only two or three now and then at the *kontor*. They're fierce men and keep to themselves mainly. Even Hilliard is afraid to approach them. 'Tis said these are boyars who were once exiled from Novgorod by Ivan when he laid waste to the city some years ago. Since the czar's death last year they are openly seeking to reestablish their power in Novgorod. The Baltic ports are anxious to resume trade with them and are leery of offending them." He inclined his head toward the tallest figure. "If that one is not a prince, I'd be surprised. He looks as if he might have fought his way out of Novgorod."

"Where are they going now?" Elise whispered.

"To the communal hall of the *kontor*... no doubt to watch and listen." The insinuation was subtle, but whatever these men were about, if Hilliard intended to speak of a certain Englishman, he wanted to be there to hear.

"Is that where you're going?" she queried.

Justin pulled her to her feet. " 'Tis my intent, but I cannot leave you here alone, and I have no time to take you back. What am I to do with you?"

"Can you not take me with you . . . or leave me to follow as before?"

"You'll never get into the *kontor* alone, and if I leave you, someone might take you for a spy." Justin rubbed his hand across his brow as he chafed in indecision, then the thought took hold. What better place for the maid to learn of Maxim's deeds than from Karr Hilliard himself? "I seem to have no choice but to comply." He nudged her arm. "Come on."

The two of them ran to the end of the alley where they crouched again to watch the three Easterlings approach a massive structure faced with a rather stark front and broad steps leading to a large portal. A huge guard stood before its doors, and even from her place of hiding, Elise thought she detected the sentry's almost fearful respect of the tall Easterling who mounted the stairs first, for the guard hurriedly straightened and motioned the man and his companions inside with only a brief glance at the seal that was displayed.

"The guard is usually much more thorough when he inspects my seal," Justin sneered sourly. He glanced aside at Elise. "If any should ask, say you are Du Volstad's apprentice, but keep your hood over your head and your eyes down whenever someone looks at you. You're not very convincing as a boy."

Elise lifted her nose in an aloof snub. She could tell him a thing or two about disguises. For instance, the one he had created for himself was immensely effective in distorting his appearance, but to her way of thinking it was rather repulsive and would probably, for that reason, alienate most people.

The last thing Justin wanted was for the sentry to see the maid's face clearly. It was far too feminine a visage to survive a close inspection. Thus, for the benefit of the guard, he played a part as the seal was presented. The roar of shouts and boisterous merry-making drifted from the hall, and it was to Elise's painful chagrin when she tried to peek through the doors that Justin cuffed her, albeit gently. Showering her with verbal abuse in fury-garbled German, he booted her across the posterior, nearly sending her through the entrance headfirst, all to the amusement of the guard who nodded in approval. That one barely glanced at the seal, much less the maid, as he ridiculed the quality of the new generation of apprentices.

Rubbing her backside, Elise glared at Justin's back as he led the way into the crowded, lantern-lit hall which was full to overflowing with men. The odors of roasting meats, smoke, sweat, and strong ale assailed her as she reluctantly hung her cloak beside Justin's. Daring nothing more than flitting glances, she kept her shoulders hunched and stayed close behind him as he merged with the crowd. There was much feasting and quaffing of ale at crowded trestle tables, while other men gathered in large, noisy groups or mingled in more sedate and much subdued ranks.

On a higher platform a group of portly men sat at a long trestle table. Though she had never seen Karr Hilliard in her life before, Elise immediately recognized him as the one who resided in the largest chair in the middle. He wore his rank, power, and authority with a casual arrogance. A massive gold chain hung about his neck and supported his badge of office, the full shield of the Hanseatic League. A short distance away a man with a barrel chest seemed to hold himself apart from the activities as he watched over the hall. His stance gave evidence of one who had been given much authority in discouraging all who would intrude upon the council, and specifically upon that one known as Karr Hilliard. The sword at his side, the curved dagger in his belt, and his hand resting upon the latter lent strength to her observations.

A bedlam of clashing cymbals, loud laughter, and the chant of men counting captured Elise's attention, and she raised on tiptoes to look past broad shoulders, finding beyond them a lad of an age close to her own weaving ponderously between two rows of shouting, stout-armed men brandishing short, multi-tongued lashes. As the youth stumbled past, the masters applied their straps to his back with gusto and hooted with merriment as he forged staggeringly onward toward the end.

Elise ducked away from the sight of his torn and bloodied shirt, sensing that this was some sort of ritual to prove the worthiness of an apprentice. She prayed fervently that she would not be caught in such a trial. To be sure, more than her stamina would be tested.

Wary of being discovered, she made herself as small as possible behind the heavy-shouldered bodies that formed an impassible barrier around her. Nervously she glanced through each breach and opening that appeared in the human wall to assure herself that she was safe. She suffered a moment of panic, realizing she had lost sight of Justin, and though she searched her limited range, she could find no sign of him. In her quest to find her escort, however, she spied Nicholas absorbed in a solemn conversation with a group of Hansa masters. He seemed pensive, even angry, and she wondered ruefully if his disposition had anything to do with her. A moment later a broad back blocked her view of him, and she stepped carefully around in a small circle as her eyes probed in other directions.

Though the hall was dark and smoke-filled, she found the tall Easterling standing across the hall with his companions. He had doffed his coat but the hat had remained. Beneath it, a dark tunic hung loosely from broad shoulders to a lean, belted waist. Amber stones studded the metal links of the belt, and the sword he had worn outside his coat was now strapped around his hips. The man stood like a prince, straight as a rod with shoulders erect. Elise could not help but stare, though as yet she had been unable to see his face as clearly as she desired, but the long, drooping mustache and almost slanting darkness around his eyes set against swarthy skin gave him an almost Mongolian caste. Yet . . . not quite. She could not lay a finger to it, but even in the darkened hall, she was struck by a feeling of familiarity. It would not have astounded her to have found a likeness of him in one of her own well-aged, girlish fantasies.

Elise suffered some alarm when she felt the increasing pressure of large, sweating bodies closing in all around her. Several more huge forms intruded into her meager space, and she glanced around in sudden apprehension, realizing that she was blocked in on all sides by men who towered well above her. She wondered wildly what had set her upon this foolish course, and she clutched a trembling hand over her heart, wanting desperately to be gone from the place. Indeed, if she ever escaped, she might be tempted to dispense with her masquerades forever and live out the rest of her life as a loving and mild-mannered wife.

A rude elbow caught Elise in the middle of the back, and a grunt of pain was wrenched from her as she was shoved full force into the back of the man in front of her. That one stumbled a step forward, then, turning with a snarl, swung a well-aimed cuff to the side of her head. Elise saw stars and staggered in a momentary half-stupor.

"Ach! Dummkopf!"

The words echoed in her ears as if from down a

long hall, then a rough hand caught her arm in an iron grip. She tried to wrench free, but her struggles only incensed him, and muttering something in an unknown tongue, he shoved her before him across the room until they reached an open spot. The hall blurred as she was swung in a wide circle around her captor, then with a sneering chortle he let go, sending her sailing into a small group of masters. An older man, of an age about three score, reached beneath her shoulders to lift her up, and she thought he might rescue her from the oafish brute. Alas, the man only chortled and tossed her back into the waiting arms of her tormentor. That one roared with laughter and shook a many-tongued lash above his head while he held her by the scruff of the neck and shook her, none too gently. All at once there was a rending tear as the woolen tunic and the shirt beneath it was ripped open down her back. In the very next instant the hall was filled with the most horrendous feminine scream that the Hanseatic League had probably ever heard. Abruptly the place went silent, and all faces turned toward her in questioning wonder. She struggled mightily to keep the falling garments in place, but the smooth creamy shoulders seemed to catch the gleam of the meager light. Suddenly Elise found herself staring into the pale blue eyes of Nicholas Von Reijn. They widened and his jaw sagged as a slow dawning occurred. The small face, bound about with leather, was too familiar, but his mind stumbled in confusion in a wild, frantic search for reasons. Why was he seeing Elise garbed as she was? And why, by heavens, in this place? His mind was cauterized by sudden doubts. It was as if there was a part of him that wanted to rescue her, but in so doing he would be disassociating himself from the Hansa. He stood frozen, unable to move, as he wrestled with his conscience.

The burly master seized the slender arm again, and Elise was spun around to be subjected to his piercing, searching eyes. His free hand tore the skullcap from her head, spilling forth a bounty of auburn hair before his eyes. A sharp intake of breath gauged his surprise, and he bellowed in ear-splitting tones, *"Was ist das? Eine junges Madchen?"*

Karr Hilliard came to his feet with a lunge and, leaning halfway across the table, braced his upper torso on his trunklike arms. *"Eine Fraulein?"* His face darkened to an apoplectic red as his searching glare found the slender girl. Roaring out a command, he thrust a finger in her direction. *"Egreifen ihr!"*

Incited to action against this blatant intrusion into their domain, the men moved en masse to take her, and Elise suffered a wave of prickling, sickening horror as she saw herself being torn apart by the venging masters. Painfully conscious of her solitude in the midst of the crowd, she clamped her jaw against the trembling that beset it and by dint of will set herself to the confrontation, refusing to yield without a fight. She drove a small foot into the belly of the man who held her and gained her freedom as he doubled over in pain. Flinging an arm backward across another's throat, she struggled forward, ducking and twisting in a frenzied effort to escape the hands that snatched and grasped for a hold. Piece by shredded piece, she yielded the shirt and tunic to stronger hands until she was left with nothing more than a few thin scraps hanging over her bound breasts. Vaguely she became aware that Justin had launched an attack with a bludgeon at the outer edge of the tumult, but his attempt to reach her was ineffectual against so many. Elise almost sobbed as fingers painfully raked her bare shoulder and slipped downward to catch her arm in a steely vise. She was snatched around, and a bloated, mottled face pushed forward to fill her entire vision. Suddenly there was a bright flash in front of her eyes, and magically a thin line of oozing red droplets appeared on the man's cheek. His reaction seemed slow and sluggish as his eyes stretched in horror and an undulating squeal of pain issued from the widening cavern of his mouth.

The tip of the rapier dipped again, this time more slowly to allow the eye to follow. It pressed threateningly into the thick rolls of the man's throat, bringing him gingerly to the very tips of his toes as his eyes searched askance for the one who held the weapon. Elise's own gaze flew in amazement along the shining length of steel, up a black-garbed arm and finally reached the face of the tall Easterling. A gasp was stillborn in her throat as she recognized those translucent green eyes which bore into the man. It was Maxim! And there was a sneer in his voice as he spoke to her captor.

"Wenn du deine Freunde heute nicht zu deinem Begrabnis einladen wilst, wurde ich vorschlagen, dab du die Dame so schnell wie moglich freigibst, mein lieber Freund."

The man complied, having no wish to make mourners of his friends, and ever-so-carefully raised his hands away from the maid as his eyes moved downward warily to the blade. Afraid to move lest the point prick a vital vein, he stayed very still, only daring to watch as the maid obeyed the beckoning motion of the Easterling's free hand. She slipped behind the tall man, and his two companions finished the protective circle around her as they raised their swords at the ready.

There was a surge forward as the Hansa masters answered the invitation. Swords rang from scabbards, and the Easterlings' blades sang, weaving a web of protective steel about the maid, nicking here and stabbing there, setting the masters all back upon their heels. With swords slashing, they bloodied more than a few.

Watching the fray, Nicholas cursed himself for his lack of action in rescuing the maid, and then roused himself to a belated determination that he would not allow Elise to be taken by the Hansa, or the Easterlings. He plowed his way through the churning body of men, tossing aside any who stood in his way. Masters tumbled helter-skelter beneath the wrath of this aggressor as he seized one after another and threw them from his path. He grabbed a sword from one of his last victims and raised it in earnest, preparing to meet the attack of the tall Easterling, then he halted in astonishment as he met the flaring green eyes.

"Maxim!"

"What say you, Nicholas?" Maxim's low, rasping tone challenged him. "Do you seek to kill me, too?"

"Ah, damn yu!" Nicholas growled in frustration. He didn't need a seer to tell him he had lost this game of hearts to a more worthy opponent. "Get her out of here!" he cried, thrusting his sword upward.

Maxim met the feigned jab with his own blade and sent the other's sailing. Even as the blade clanged to the floor another sturdy figure stepped to the fore. The Hansa masters moved back in shuffling haste as Gustave clicked his heels together and lifted his straight, two-edged rapier in a salute to Maxim.

"So! Ve meet again, *Herr* Seymour," he greeted in derision, having observed Nicholas's recognition. "I am sure *Herr* Hilliard vill be interested in knowin' it is yu, but I vill tell him shortly." Gustave smiled confidently as he swished the long blade before him in a series of zinging X's. "Yu vere a fool to expose yurself for the *fraulein*. It vill mean yur death."

The hall reverberated with the sound of clashing steel, and Elise smothered a frightened gasp as Maxim stumbled back a step beneath the forceful assault. The Hansa masters nudged each other and grinned with amusement as they widened the circle to allow Gustave more room and the sole privilege of deciding this contest. It had been well-confirmed on a number of occasions that among his other talents, Gustave was a very adept swordsman. They had no doubt that he would handle this upstart Easterling with ease.

Cringing in trembling fear as she watched Gustave's thrusting and slashing advance, Elise wondered if Maxim would be able to defend himself, much less gain the advantage. It seemed his blade was ever blocking, parrying and then riposting, but would it be enough to withstand Gustave's strong, aggressive attack? The man continued to strike and lunge with a rather haughty arrogance, forever pushing Maxim back. The masters, anxious to watch the fight, stepped around the small band, clearing a path for their retreat.

Elise became aware of Nicholas taking Justin's arm a short distance away and, after a murmured comment, pointing toward the entrance. The younger man seemed to gain some enthusiasm from the captain's words and began shoving his way toward the door. He seized their cloaks and the Easterling's coats from the rack and was directly behind them when Elise saw him flit through the portal. Lifting his head, Nicholas fixed his eyes upon the two men who were on either side of her and frowned at them as he jerked his head toward the door. Elise knew the signal. They were to escape with her. Now!

"No," she moaned as one of them caught her arm. "I cannot leave without Maxim!"

"Please, madam," the urgent whisper came close

above her ear. "We must get out now . . . for your husband's sake!"

Shaking her head as she sobbed, Elise struggled against their attempts to pull her away. "No, I won't! I cannot desert him!"

Quickly Maxim tossed a stern command over his shoulder. "Go, woman! Get out of here!"

Elise gave no further argument, but reluctantly obeyed his directive and allowed the men to draw her toward the door.

Gustave smirked as he delivered several slashing assaults upon the ever-present blade of his opponent and gained more ground as the other retreated. "Yur *liebchen* may go, *Herr* Seymour, but she vill not escape. Nor vill yu. Yur end is very, very near."

"Perhaps, *Herr* Gustave. But then, you could be mistaken." After a glance behind him to assure himself that his companions were within close range of the portal, Maxim settled himself in a comfortable stance. With an ease and subtle finesse he had not thus far displayed, he launched his attack. No longer did he block and parry, but now his blade began to threaten. A flicker of surprise touched Gustave's countenance as he found himself repeatedly twisting away to avoid the thrusts. The sudden suspicion that he had only been played with set his heart thudding a new rhythm. His blade was forced to move ever faster to safeguard his defense, and when one tardy movement answered a lightning slash, he felt the tip of the other's rapier lay open his cheek.

" 'Tis but a small trophy, Gustave. Nothing to fret about," Maxim assured the fellow.

Elise had paused a moment in the doorway to watch and was struck by the change in the flavor of the duel. Maxim was now master of the game, and he played with his opponent as a cat would tease a mouse. It was as if his retreat had only been a well-executed maneuver to get his companions safely to the entrance, and though she had been slow to grasp it, Nicholas and the others, in turn, had picked up on his ploy.

"My lady, I must urge you to leave." The plea came as her arm was taken. "Lord Seymour would not wish you to see this."

Elise shivered from more than the cold as she stepped through the doorway, sensing that Gustave would not survive what would follow. Justin was already on the steps below, having dispensed with the dozing guard, and wrapped a cloak about her bare shoulders as she quickly descended.

Inside the hall sweat dappled Gustave's brow as the clever blade became a blur of movement, reaching ever inward to breach his defense and deliver painful snips and cutting pricks. His clothes were snagged and bloodied by the relentless assault, and he grew increasingly weary. He saw an opening as his opponent leaned in to attack and with a snarl, raised his arm and swung the sword with all of the strength in his arm. With a clang that echoed in the hall his blade was halted, and he saw the slightest of smiles flit across Maxim's lips before the straight blade slid down his own and the point dipped toward his chest. It seemed only a quick, sharp pain in his ribs, but a heavier twinge told him the blade went deep. Very deep.

Maxim stepped back and nearly half of his blade was covered with a dull, dark red. Gustave staggered back a step and stared down in horror at his chest and a slowly spreading blossom of red. His breath seemed locked within the cavity, and though he raised his blade, he stood stock-still. A low murmur rippled through the communal hall, and in the dwindling light he saw his opponent back away with his sword raised to threaten any who would interfere. His breath freed, and Gustave filled his lungs with a deep, gurgling wheeze. The blade fell from his numbing fingers, and he lifted his gaze to stare at the tall, princely garbed man, then his eyes dulled and he collapsed forward to the floor.

Maxim retreated quickly as the awestruck crowd stared at their fallen champion. He took a last step and was through the door, slamming the massive portals behind him. He twisted the heavy hasp into place, knowing it would not hold the throng at bay for very long, but it would allow him and his companions a short space in which to flee.

The guard had roused to awareness and staggered in a daze to his feet, just in time to catch the solid hilt of Maxim's sword squarely on the point of his chin. With a waning sigh, he sagged again to the step, where he lay unprotesting as Maxim leapt over him. Justin swung his arm to encourage Maxim to hasten down the stairs, but that one needed no such invitation. Thrusting the rapier in the scabbard, he raced down the steps, his long strides taking them three at a time. He soon joined his companions and caught the lambskin coat Justin tossed at him. He did not pause in the donning of it, but jammed his arms through the sleeves as he ran. As he passed Elise, he caught her hand, and she fairly flew at his side as he took the lead.

Justin yelled from behind and when Maxim glanced back, the younger man pointed toward an alley they had not traversed before. They raced into its dark security as a loud crash shattered the stillness of the night, marking the fall of the great door of the *kontor.* Shouts filled the night as the league's members charged over the fallen barrier, leapt down the stairs, and spread out in different directions.

"This way!" Justin whispered urgently and gestured down another narrow lane. "We'll lose them quicker if we go this way."

The darkness deepened as the torch-lit area of the *kontor* was put well behind them. The five of them went like dark spirits in the night, silent shapes flitting through shadows, an occasional crunch of frozen slush the only sound to mark their passing. They dashed headlong through the twisting, winding streets of Lubeck, traversing through an endless maze that would end where only Justin knew. Elise made a gallant effort to match the longer strides of the men, but finally she could go no further. In a dark alley she took a few last faltering steps and sagged wearily against a rough stone wall as she gasped for breath. Nearby Justin stumbled to a halt and braced his hands on his knees as he fought to control his own labored breathing. Maxim went on a few steps to see what was at the end of the alley and then came back to lean against the wall beside Elise.

"What say you, Sir Kenneth?" He panted the hushed question as he peered through the darkness at one of the men. "Do you have a ken where we are?"

"That I do, my lord." The knight responded in an equally breathless and subdued voice. "And I've a mind what you're thinking, and I do heartily agree. 'Tis best we split up."

"Then take Sherbourne and go. I'll need Justin to show me the way out of here. I'll see you later at the keep."

Sir Kenneth stepped forward and, reaching out toward the other in friendship, clasped arms with Maxim. "If there should be such a thing that one of us should not arrive at the castle, let it be known that I consider it an honor working with you. Good night to you." He touched his fingers to his brow in a salute to Elise. "The pleasure has been mine, my lady. I wish you and Lord Seymour long life."

"Thank you ... for everything," Elise murmured softly. As she watched the two men sprint from sight, she sighed forlornly, feeling as if she had made a blundering mess of everything.

Justin had been most attentive as he witnessed the farewell. Sir Kenneth's comments had much bemused him, and now he peered through the meager light at the couple, desiring an explanation.

Maxim gave the younger man no time to launch a barrage of questions, but took Elise's arm and led her further down the alley, leaving Justin staring after them with a perturbed frown.

"Why did you come?" Maxim whispered, propping a hand beside her head as she leaned back against the wall. "What made you don these clothes and sneak into the *kontor?* Had you no ken of the danger? Hilliard despises women, especially English women."

Elise glanced toward Justin and then dropped her gaze, feeling foolish and ashamed. Her presence had endangered his life and those of his companions, and any explanation now seemed feeble. "I was worried about you. I wanted to assure myself that you were all right and no one was going to harm you."

He leaned forward ever so slightly, and his voice was like a soft flutter against her ear. "My love, I swear to you, your face was ever before me, and my one desire was to return to your arms and spend this night with you as your husband." He straightened and, doffing his coat, handed the garment to her. "Hold this a moment, my love, and I will give you my shirt."

Elise smoothed the lambskin admiringly beneath her hand, afraid to ask him why he had garbed himself the way that he did. "I almost didn't recognize you."

A soft chuckle came through the shirt as Maxim pulled it over his head. "Madam, I very nearly didn't recognize you."

Maxim tossed an inquisitive glance down the alley toward Justin. Sensing the younger man's curiosity, he stepped around to block his view of Elise as she doffed the cloak. Shivering from the cold, she drew the shirt quickly over her head and breathed in the clean, manly scent of her husband as she settled it into place. Again she sought the warmth of the mantle, and only then did Maxim motion for Justin to join them.

"We must go," he urged. "Hilliard will not rest until we are found."

"But where can we go?" Elise asked. "We cannot go back to the Von Reijns'. 'Twould mean danger to the family, and will Hilliard not search the inns and taverns for any strangers?" It was a poor night indeed to try and find a place to hide, she thought, shivering as a slight breeze wafted beneath the folds of the cloak.

A look of dawning lit Justin's countenance. "I know of a place where 'tis safe for you to hide." He beckoned them to follow. "Come, I'll take you. No one will think of looking for you there."

Maxim was not sure whether or not he trusted the sly grin the younger man wore, but he obeyed the directive, not willing to reject the plan ere it was made known.

The mists thickened as they neared the wharves, and the silence of the night gave way to the low creaking of lofty masts and ice-bound hulls protected by heavy beams at the waterline. The three approached the pier cautiously, glancing all about, then Justin encouraged them to hurry as he skittered along the icy quay in front of them. Enveloped in the shadow of night, he crouched beneath the largest vessel in the area and, with a grin, pointed upward to her name. It was Hilliard's *Grau Falke*!

Chapter 22

*I*T SEEMED A WORLD APART from reality, one frozen by time and the elements, where ice-shrouded yards and masts bore no resemblance to earthly shapes, but took on ghostly forms and strange sculptures where the freezing spray and foam had been swept by the northern winds. A fine dusting of snow covered the deck of the four-masted carrack, treacherously masking a thick layer of ice. Rooted well beneath the planking, tall masts thrust upward into the belly of the night sky, losing their tops in a haze of flurries and murky darkness. Long, bearded icicles hung from the yards, spars, and standing rigging, and from those clinging to the latter came an incessant clicking as the crystals were stirred by the plucking fingers of passing breezes. The sound wafted through the silence like the frozen claws of some savage wintry beast a-prowl on the deck. Blending with the eerie melody, a distant and almost imperceptible grinding and popping drifted from the river where open water met the insidiously encroaching ice.

Maxim led the way carefully across the deck with Elise following close behind and Justin bringing up the rear. The slippery footing demanded caution, for a wrong step could end in a bone-jarring fall. As if befriending them, the gentle gusts blew their cold breath across the surface, promising to sweep away all evidence of their passing. As they entered the companionway Maxim reached back a hand and took Elise's fingers within his grasp to lead her carefully through the darkness. But even as they exercised caution, the coldness of the interior made it unlikely that even a watchman was aboard.

They moved ahead in the darkness, but came to another abrupt halt when Maxim's head struck a tallow lantern hanging from the rafters. Muttering a derogatory comment about shipbuilders being abnormally short, he yanked the fixture down and, despite his discomfort, smiled in the dark as he heard Elise's soft voice close beside him.

" 'Tis obviously a singular problem, my lord," she teased. "I've never been bothered by it myself."

Reaching a finger inside the lantern, Maxim fished out a small tinderbox as he quipped, "Madam, I assure you I considered it fair reason to give up sailing the seas."

He finally struck the wick alight, and the tiny flame sputtered in the breeze that wafted through the hall, then the small door was closed and the light grew stronger, touching their surroundings with its meager glow.

"You jest, of course," Justin whispered in amused curiosity. "Sailing on a ship has been a dream of mine, but I would not join the Hansa to do it."

"I spent a few years at sea," Maxim remarked casually. "In fact, I even commanded a small galleon for a space. Alas! Her majesty's navy was not for me." He cocked his head to one side and gave a smile of gentle recall. "My parents enjoyed their life together. I intend to share as much of my time as possible with my wife." His eyes warmly glowing, he glanced at Elise and found the sapphire orbs mirroring the tiny candle flame. More than that, they shone with a loving light of their own to fair bedazzle him.

Maxim raised the lantern as they progressed down the hall. Pausing beside a door on his left, he pushed it carefully open and entered what was soon judged to be a small galley set just forward of the master's cabin. All the accoutrements of a chef hung from a bar secured above a table. A huge, open-faced hearth, consisting of three walls and a flooring covered with brick, was located at the far end of the narrow space. A large kettle hung on a spit above the charred remains of several logs. Overhead, a grating of iron allowed a place for the smoke to escape, but was now covered with a hatch. On the interior of the hearth, on the wall nearest the main cabin, hung an iron door. When Maxim opened it and looked inside, he found the reverse of a similar portal securely fastened on the far side of the hearth wall.

They continued down the companionway toward the main cabin, and the door creaked slightly as Maxim pushed it open. Even without the aid of a lantern, the stern gallery windows would have allowed enough illumination from the snow-shrouded night to verify that the compartment was empty save for its rich appointments. To assure that no leakage of light reached the world beyond the cabin, the pair of men made haste to pull the heavy velvet draperies across the windows.

Shivering, Elise glanced about at the luxury that abounded in the spacious compartment, but it was of little comfort. The cold had penetrated so deeply into the ship, it was like an icy tomb, bereft of even the smallest warmth.

" 'Twould seem Hilliard is not in the least fearful of anyone stealing from him," Justin commented laconically.

"Aye," Maxim agreed. "Should any dare, I've no doubt justice would be swiftly served by the burghers of Lubeck."

" 'Up on the yard, hang that *Schuft!*' they'd cry," Justin sneered. "How I yearn to hear such a cry and see Hilliard swinging by the neck from a masthead."

"He may someday, or better yet, have to face the axeman's blade," Maxim replied in distant thought as he glanced toward the bunk. Rich furs promised an abundance of comfort, even from the cold, but the presence of the young man precluded any hope of the marriage vows being consummated.

" 'Tis obvious you're not working for Hilliard," Justin stated, his curiosity desiring appeasement. "Are you a spy?"

"A spy for whom?" Maxim scoffed. "Please! Lend no gilding of the cavalier to what I did. I am a man without a country."

Maxim shunned further questions as he searched the bulkhead, starboard of the door through which they had entered. Rich wood paneling covered the walls of the cabin save for a space perhaps an arm's-span away from the portal. There, an iron skirt protected the flooring beneath a small black door set in brick. Lifting the latch, he opened the portal and found, as he suspected, that it opened into the interior of the galley hearth.

"Clever man, Hilliard. He designed this ship to have a small private galley nearby to serve his own gluttonous appetite and has even provided a way for us to get warm while enjoying his fine accommodations."

"Do you think you should light a fire?" Justin asked, fretting at the thought of discovery.

"W-we cannot s-stay here without one," Elise stuttered through chattering teeth. "I'm f-freezing."

"As long as we leave before daylight, I doubt there'll

be anyone moving around the quay to notice," Maxim replied. "I see no reason to be further discomforted."

"I must leave you for a time," Justin informed them, and became aware that the interest of the other man centered on him. "When Hilliard realizes you're the one who killed Gustave, you can expect this city to be turned upside down until you're found. I mean to return to *Tante*'s house and pack up your chests so you can put Lubeck well behind you ere morningtide. If you tell me where your two friends can be found, I'll have them ready the sleigh and hold it at the edge of town until I can bring you your mounts and lead you through the city."

Maxim braced his arms akimbo as he peered at the other closely. "Are you so trustworthy then?"

Justin drew himself up to full height and, with anger blazing in his eyes, laid a hand on the hilt of his dagger. "I've played the fool and fop for the benefit of the Hansards for some time now," he said through rage-whitened lips. "I've roamed this city in a dozen guises and tweaked the masters' beards a score and more times. I'll not stand here and have my honor questioned."

"Calm yourself," Maxim warned. "Anger has a way of making a fool of a man."

"Have I served you so ill this eventide that you still doubt me?"

"You've served us all well," the elder man admitted. "But you've much to learn of responsibilities..."

"Indeed?" Justin fairly sizzled with outrage. "How so?"

"For example"—Maxim allowed himself to show a little irritation—"by bringing Elise into the communal hall when you knew it was dangerous for her. Be damned! Had anything happened to her I would have called you out..."

"Maxim, please listen," Elise begged. " 'Twas my fault, truly. I followed him, and had he denied me, I'd have tried to enter on my own."

"Aye, madam, but you'd never have gotten past the guard without a Hansa seal, which Justin undoubtedly has . . ."

"Which reminds me," the youth interrupted, fixing Maxim with an attentive stare. "How did you manage to get in?"

The Marquess returned a stoic mien to the younger man. He could find no reason to tell, but then, with the deed well behind them, no harm could be done in appeasing the other's curiosity. "If you must know, I told the guard we were traders from Novgorod and had been personally invited by Karr Hilliard himself. It helped considerably to show the man a document impressed with Hilliard's own seal."

"So! That is why you're dressed the way you are." Justin nodded as he began to understand the Englishman's reasoning. "You knew the guards would easily accept your statements as truth because it would be something Hilliard would readily do to gain the Easterlings' trade." His eyes narrowed as he sought further answers. "But how did you get the clothing?"

"I've made a few friends in my years of travel," Maxim rejoined. "Having themselves acquired an aversion to Hilliard, they were willing to assist me."

"It must have been some Easterling prince, the way you're garbed. I suppose you even speak their tongue." Though Justin expected the subtle probing to gain more answers, the sharp jutting of a tawny brow assured him he would gain no further information.

" 'Tis your choice, of course, whether to accept me as a trusted friend," Justin needled. "Or you can wait until Hilliard's men find you. If you return to the Von

Reijn house, you'll endanger all who are there, and I'll not allow that. Better you learn to trust me as I, this night, have come to trust you. I've no intention of doing a favor for the one who murdered my father, and if Hilliard did not do it himself, he gave the order."

Elise laid a hand upon her husband's sleeve as she issued a small measure of advice. "I believe he can be trusted, Maxim. He means no harm to us."

A nod and a smile acknowledged Justin's gratitude for her faith in him. "You're most gracious, Elise."

Maxim stared at the man a moment longer as if he would make up his own mind, then he spoke. "I choose to honor the lady's confidence in you, but should you prove anything less than trustworthy, I shall see that adequate recompense be delivered to your door posthaste. Mark my word."

"I understand explicitly, my lord," Justin declared. "I must admit I didn't hold you in the best esteem a few hours past either." A brief smile touched his lips. "I hope you have room for another guest at your castle. You'll need as many men as possible to defend it when Hilliard comes calling. I don't intend to miss the event."

Maxim crossed to the desk and, with quill in hand, scrawled out a note on a scrap of parchment. As he handed the piece to the younger man he asked, "Do you know the Lowentatze?" He saw the other nod. "They await word there." Maxim removed a small coin from his coat and gave it over with further instructions. "You'll give them the note and show them this coin with Elizabeth's face on it. They'll trust you then."

Justin tucked the piece away securely. "I shall not disappoint you."

"Good!" Maxim's voice carried a note of concern, for he had need to be wary, as had the knights, Kenneth and Sherbourne. They were virtually on their own until the ports came free of ice in the spring, and there were many others in his care who would suffer should Hilliard gain the upper hand.

Justin crossed to the door and announced in a lighter vein, "I shall remove the hatch and light a fire in the galley for you 'ere I leave." He paused at the portal to consider them with a hint of a mischievous gleam in his eye. " 'Twill be my wedding gift to you both."

Elise was taken back by surprise. "How did you know?"

A rather cocky grin traced Justin's lips as he tilted his head to the side in a mode of museful pondering. "I believe 'twas something Sir Kenneth said that made me wonder about you two, and then I sorted the rest of the puzzle out as we came here. Is it to be known when the vows were spoken?"

"It was only this morning," Elise murmured, taking comfort as Maxim's arm settled about her shoulders.

"Obviously you've not told Nicholas?" The last was presented as a question, and Justin waited until the maid answered with a slow nod. "Then be assured, fair Elise, that I'll not tell him either." He started to step through the door, but turned back again. "Of course, you know if Hilliard remains in power, you'll be in danger as long as you stay in this country. You should make arrangements to leave at the first possible chance, at least as soon as the ships can sail again. Perhaps I shall speak with Nicholas about the matter of your leaving. He'll no doubt be waiting to question me when I arrive home." He sighed as if he found the idea rather tedious. "In any case, be assured that Hilliard will not cease until he has salved his hurts. I've no idea what your business was with him, but you can stand assured that he does not take well to being played a fool, especially by spies." He smiled briefly as the other man's brows gathered into a scowl. "Though you deny it, my lord, I find no other explanation, but you can trust that I'll hold my silence. Also, I would warn you that Hilliard has his following. *His* spies are everywhere."

"I'll be careful," Maxim assured him. "And thank you for getting us here."

"I could say it has been my pleasure, my lord, but in truth I think the pleasure will all be yours."

Heaving a rather forlorn sigh that hinted of his own disappointment, Justin touched his brow in a farewell salute and left them, closing the door behind him. Maxim made the portal secure and set a kettle filled with small chunks of ice inside the hearth to thaw. He prepared the bunk as the sounds of Justin's footsteps came from overhead and then from the next room. He removed his drooping mustache and wiped most of the stain from his face. With the aid of a strong intoxicant, he freed his lips of the sticky substance that had held it in place. A short time later a blazing fire lit the interior of the galley hearth and spread its heat to the main cabin. Silence returned as Justin left the ship, but the couple hardly noticed as they came into each other's arms. Though the warmth was slow to push back the chill in the compartment, they doffed their outer garments and tossed them aside.

Elise giggled as she kissed the taste of brandy from her husband's lips. "I should be cautious," she sighed. "This might be a ruse to get me well into my cups."

"Give it nary a thought, my love," Maxim breathed as his open mouth caressed her parted lips. " 'Twould be my intent only if you were reluctant and I had debauchery in mind, but I mean to cherish the fullness of your response in this moment of coming together, this joining of bodies and hearts."

Elise stretched up on her toes and, looping her arms over his naked shoulders, teased him with a coy smile. "Perhaps you should remove the black from your hair and all the tan from your skin. Otherwise, I might think some strange man is making love to me."

"Afterward," he whispered, slipping his hands beneath her shirt and unfastening the wide cloth that bound her bosom.

A quick gasp answered his bold possession of the rounded curves. Her eyes sultry with passion, Elise moved into his embrace gladly. "On second thought," she breathed, her lips against his cheek, "I don't believe you mean to leave any doubt."

His mouth sought hers in a passionate frenzy, and it seemed an eternity passed before he broke away with a sigh, leaving her spent and breathless. As if he fought some inner battle on his own, he raised his head and stared down into the encompassing warmth of the sapphire blue. His own were aflame with fiery passion.

"I could lose myself in those pools, madam, and I'm hot to pursue the moment." He drew in a ragged breath. " 'Tis a mountainous task for me to hold you and remain tender and patient when my hunger for you has brought me to the brink of starvation."

"My lord, pray consider that I'm not a rose, nor nearly so delicate. You'll hardly bruise or crush me by holding me close or caressing me. I assure you, my lord, I'm quite hardy. And very inquisitive. Truly, my love, might it occur to you that I yearn for what is to come as much as you? I want to please you, and yet I'm a stranger to the knowledge I need and am seeking. Is it acceptable for a woman to pleasure a man?"

"Indeed!"

"Then teach me how to make love to you. Let me

know what is pleasurable to a man. Let me be your lover, replacing all thoughts of any other you might have once cherished." With a softly teasing, beguiling smile she plucked at the fastenings of the bejeweled belt that encircled his lean waist. When it was free and flung aside, she slid both hands slowly over his wide chest, marveling as she caressed the rugged firmness of the muscular expanse. She guessed by the expectant stillness with which he accepted her touch and the warming heat in the green eyes that he enjoyed the play. Encouraged to a bolder mien, she slid her hands around his ribs and downward from the small of his back as she pressed herself to him.

Warmed and intrigued by her response, Maxim slipped the shirt from her shoulders, and Elise freed it with a shrug. The garment fell to the deck unheeded as his lips trailed down the pale column of her throat. Her round breasts gleamed enticingly in the golden firelight, and raising his head a moment, Maxim drank his fill of their perfection. Gently cupping the soft, scented roundness within his hands, he bent and leisurely caressed them with his mouth, pressing wanton kisses over their warmth. Elise's head fell back as the fires raged in the depths of her body. A pulsing heat began to throb in her loins, spreading outward, reaching upward until she thrust out her breasts to luxuriate in the hot, flicking strokes. Her breath was wont to catch in ecstatic gasps, interrupting the quickening, shallow rhythm. She felt consumed by a pleasure that threatened to melt every fiber of her being and leave her naught but a quivering relic of herself. In truth, she was made of sterner stuff, but never in her wildest imaginings had she guessed the height to which a lover's touch could catapult her. Indeed, when Maxim began to pull away her clothing, a fever caught hold of her, and her fingers joined his until at last she stood naked before him. In turn she plucked at the lacings of his breeches, and she rubbed her breasts seductively against his chest as his hands explored downward.

Taking her with him to the bunk, Maxim sat down and tugged off his boots. Rising to his feet again, he freed the final cords that held the breeches in place and dropped the full-skirted garment to the floor. Surprise halted Elise's breath for barely a pause, and a sudden timidity made her raise her gaze to the slight, questioning curve that traced the handsome lips.

"Are you frightened?"

Thoughtful for a moment, Elise considered him with more boldness, plucking at the gutstrings of his awareness. It was as if rivulets of excitement pulsed through his body as she stared at him. Meeting his gaze again, she murmured through a soft, challenging smile, "Curious perhaps."

Since their first meeting Maxim had never ceased to be amazed and fascinated by the enticing blend of innocence and boldness he had seen in this young maid. Each trait was wonderfully intriguing, and he was never more aware of his infatuation than at this present moment, when they were about to enter the realm of conjugal intimacy.

Slipping a hand admiringly over her bare shoulder to the back of her nape, Maxim pulled her close and, lifting her chin with a knuckle of his free hand, pressed light kisses upon her lips as he gave her words back to her. " 'Tis all for the sharing, love. If you have a curiosity, then by all means satisfy it. I'm quite sturdy and most eager. Nor will I bruise easily."

Elise stretched upward to her toes and folded her arms around his neck. Maxim took her full against him, and holding her thus, he lowered himself to the edge of the bunk, at the same time settling her boldly onto his lap. His mouth blended with hers as his hands moved leisurely over her body. The sensations he aroused with his kisses and caresses, combined with the subtle pressure of his manliness, stumbled the evenness of Elise's breathing and set her heart beating to a new, frantic rhythm that suffused her with an expanding warmth. No chill could touch her, not when her husband roused her so completely.

A strange frenzy seized her, and the pain of penetration was but a brief discomfort that she forced back as she became aware of a driving need to appease a burgeoning, insatiable hunger. Maxim leaned back into the pillows and as she touched her lips lightly, almost reverently, to his chest, his hands settled to her hips. A whispered word brought eager compliance, and she began to move. Amazement etched her countenance as he met her strokes with vigor, and the budding, blossoming pleasure in her loins intensified and swept her on with the promise of still greater heights to reach. His hands stretched up to seize her breasts, and she flung her head back, spilling her long hair down her back and over his thighs as she arched her spine and made love to him with all of her heart, mind, and body. In the stillness of the cabin she could hear his hoarse, ragged breathing as his hands seemed to touch her everywhere. Then her world reeled out of control as a ravishing, rapturous splendor burst upon her. It seemed a thousand, twinkling lights flared through her body, touching off myriad scintillating flashes of ecstasy. She was woman; he was man. She was lady; he was lord. She was wife; he was husband. She was Elise; he was Maxim. Forever joined as one, they were, fused by the heat of their loins, joined by the love in their hearts.

A long sigh slipped from Elise's lips as she slowly collapsed upon the chest of her husband. For a long, blissful moment he held her close, kissing her brow, stroking her hair, and whispering words of love, then her body began to cool, and a small, shivering tremor shook her as the cold air settled on her back. Catching a corner of the fur throw, Maxim clasped her to him and rolled until he lay on top of her. A smile teased the corners of his mouth as his eyes gleamed down into hers. Though recently sated, he could feel again an awakening deep within his loins.

"Is your curiosity appeased, madam?"

Feeling the returning heat, Elise wiggled under him, deliberately arousing him as she slid her arms around his neck and breathed dreamily, "You've more to teach me, my lord?"

"You're not bruised overmuch?" he whispered with a brow raised questioningly.

Elise smiled up at him with sweet seduction as she teasingly decried, "My lord, I'm completely at your mercy."

Another flight was shared to the stars, and an eternity passed before Maxim grudgingly left the bunk. Pouring steaming water from the small kettle into a basin, he reached his arms toward the ceiling and stretched under the close, admiring attention of his bride, then he began to wash himself, removing the brown stain from his face and the flecks of blood from his body. Lastly he rinsed the black from his hair and then came to the bunk as he toweled himself dry. Abruptly Elise covered her head, giggling in delight as he shook out the wet strands above her, sending a shower of small droplets flying down upon her. Feeling his weight come upon the mattress, she lowered the fur to inquire, "Did you save some water for me?"

Maxim grinned askance at her. "Of course, my lady. I would not miss the pleasure of your bath."

Holding the furs over her breasts, she sat up and

leaned back into several pillows that were propped against the wall of the bunk. "My lord, I would reason with you a while..."

"Aye, my dear...?" His overeager tone readily conveyed a number of conclusions that he might draw upon.

"I cannot bathe in your presence," she stated timidly. " 'Twould be unseemly."

"Ah, but I've enjoyed your bath before," he bantered. "Would you deny me a husband's right to admire his wife?"

"Nay, my lord," Elise answered sweetly. "I would enjoy the sharing... after I've become more acquainted with... everything."

Maxim chuckled and leaned forward to lay a kiss upon her warm, responsive lips. "The fire needs be fed, my sweet. I'll be back when you've attended your needs."

He donned his breeches and shirt, then left the cabin. Elise wasted no time making use of the water he set out for her. Afterward, she wrapped a fur robe about herself and began rifling through the drawers of the desk in search of a comb. Suddenly, her eyes caught and held on a small leather pouch lying in a rear compartment of the drawer. The initials *RR* were scrolled across the front of the bag, the very same as her own father's purse. Lifting the pouch, she hefted it and thoughtfully felt at the bulge within. It had not the feel of coins, but...

Eagerly Elise shook the contents out into her palm and stared in awe as a prickling crawled up her spine. It was a large, ornate ring with an onyx stone cleverly wrought with gold. Trembling now, she took it closer to the lantern to examine it better. There could be no mistake. It was her father's ring!

A light rap sounded, and the door opened behind

her. Elise swung around to face her husband. "Maxim, look! My father's ring! It must've been my father Sheffield saw that day after all. But why? Why would Hilliard kidnap my father? For what purpose?" She shook her head in confusion. "Was it only for the gold my father had put away? Surely Hilliard has enough of his own."

"The man has no ken of the word 'enough,' my sweet. He is greedy beyond measure."

"This truly gives evidence that my father is being kept here somewhere."

Maxim shook his head as he drew her to the bunk. "Nay, my love, I think he has been returned to England."

"You mean set free? Is he there safe while I'm here worrying about him?" She clasped her hands before her and leaned her head back as if she prayed intensely for such a possibility. "Oh, if it could only be, Maxim."

"I fear 'tis not that way, Elise."

Maxim's heart went out to her as he saw crumpling hope replaced by disappointment. Through gathering tears she stared at him, waiting expectantly for an explanation. He sighed and, gathering her across his lap like a small child, slowly rocked her as she sobbed and spilled her tears against the side of his throat.

"If you tell me he is dead ... by God's truth, Maxim, I'll not accept it. I cannot accept it until I see his body myself."

"Truly, Elise, I do believe he is still alive," he cajoled, "but I don't think he's been released. Should Ramsey make the mistake of telling his captors where the treasure is hidden, it may mean his end. His continued silence is his only protection."

"He'll never tell," Elise stated with conviction as she gulped back her tears. "He'll never break. They may torture and torment him, but he's strong and wise."

"Then let us hope we reach England in time to gain his release."

Elise raised her head and searched her husband's face in wonder. "Do you dare return, my love?"

"I dare not stay here beyond the first advent of spring. Justin is right. Hilliard will learn who killed Gustave, if he hasn't already, and he'll come after us with an army of men."

"Perhaps it isn't safe to return to Faulder Castle."

"There's no place else where we can go, but rest assured I have made provisions to defend the castle, at least to a degree. Hilliard will not find vengeance easy, and, God willing, we'll turn the tables on him."

Elise nestled her head upon his shoulder again. "I trust you with my life, Maxim, and though I never thought I'd ever say it, I'll be glad to get back to Faulder Castle."

Maxim touched a kiss to her lips as he rose with her in his arms. Sweeping aside the upper layer of furs, he laid her within its warmth. In a moment he had doffed his clothes and slid in beside her. Wrapped in each other's arms, they did not care at the moment what transpired in the world beyond the *Grau Falke.*

A sense of wonder stirred within Elise's subconscious mind, rousing her to a comfortable awareness of Maxim's presence. A delicious warmth encompassed her, radiating from his strong male body that pressed close against her back. Long, lean, muscular thighs were tucked beneath her own, and an arm held her close as a large hand cupped her breast. She could feel his chest against her back, and the slow, warm tickle of his breath against her nape. All was very right in her world.

She nestled closer to her husband with a contented sigh, and a peaceful slumber suffused her again until she became aware of the slow, gentle stroking of his fingers over the soft peak of her breast. Light as thistledown his lips touched a spot on her neck and then dropped a kiss on her shoulder. Twisting around to face him, Elise luxuriated in the radiant warmth of the green eyes. No word was spoken between them, but in the meager glow of the firelight their eyes melded in unspoken words of love, gently searching and probing to the innermost thoughts of the other. Bracing on an elbow, Maxim rose above her and lowered his lips upon her waiting mouth to drink deeply of the sweet nectar of her response. Her senses awakened beneath the slow onslaught of his kiss, and she became aware of the boldness of his caresses and the fiery heat of his naked body. His lips moved across her cheek, and he brushed aside the curling auburn strands, freeing a path for his kisses to wander unhindered along her pale throat and on downward over her breast.

A distant sound echoed like a drumbeat in the stillness of the cabin, and Maxim raised his head to listen as his manner took on an instant alertness. The hollow sound came again, much like the slow, ponderous tread of someone walking on the icy deck. Throwing back the furs, Maxim grabbed his breeches and thrust his legs through them. Aware of the rapidly advancing footsteps entering the companionway, he leapt to his feet and quickly secured the garment over his hips. Snatching up his sword, he crossed to the portal just as a loud knock beat upon its planks.

"Be you friend or foe?" Maxim challenged.

" 'Tis Nicholas," the familiar voice answered. "Justin is vaiting vith the horses. I've come to fetch yu."

Flipping the latch, Maxim lowered his sword and

swung open the door, but cautiously retreated as the captain came striding boldly in. Abruptly Nicholas's face hardened when his gaze found Elise sitting in the bunk, clutching a fur throw over her naked bosom. Her hair was tumbled wildly about her bare shoulders, and though his glance searched the cabin, he could find no other place where Maxim could have slept. Indeed, the rosy blush of love still stained the creamy skin.

"Yu bastard!" Nicholas snarled, facing Maxim. Doubling his fist, he gave the other no chance to explain, but took a long step forward as he came around with all of his strength behind the blow. His knuckles met the solid jaw of the other, sending Maxim stumbling backward across the cabin. Elise's scream shattered the silence as the crumpled form came to rest on the floor beside the bunk. A-rage in dark, bitter jealousy, Nicholas watched her scramble forth, heedless of what she gave the fallen man as she adjusted the fur robe to settle it evenly over her shoulders. It was all too obvious to Nicholas as the maid knelt beside the dazed man that her singular concern with her state of undress was to ensure her modesty be preserved only with him. Maxim braced himself up on an elbow and tried to shake the fog from his head, and Nicholas's conclusions were reaffirmed as he crossed the cabin to stand over the fallen man and Elise made haste to cover herself with the fur throw.

"Get up," he growled down at Maxim. "I vant to give yu more of vhat yu deserve."

Straightening, Elise swung her arm with a snarled cry of unleashed fury, catching Nicholas low in the belly. He stumbled back, somewhat amazed at the forceful blow this slight maid could deliver. As Maxim propped himself against the wall and gingerly tested his jaw, she gathered the robe up high around her and faced Nicholas with a feral gleam in her eye.

"How dare you barge in here like some rutting stag, snorting and blowing hot! You interfere where you've no concern, Nicholas. 'Twas my intent to tell you more gently, but your boorish actions have abused my good temper. Yestermorn, Maxim and I were married." She ignored his sharp intake of breath as she continued to deliver her words crisply. "We meant no hurt to you, nor did we intend at the fore to fall in love, but it . . . it just happened. And if you think that Maxim has taken advantage of me, then let me assure you, sir, I know my own mind and what I want. I'm well-pleased to have Maxim as my husband, and I shall seek all ends to make him a good wife . . . as I would have with you, had we taken vows together." She paused a moment to gather her thoughts and continued in a calmer vein. "I owe you many apologies for my delay in telling you that my interest had turned elsewhere. Maxim bade me to give you the news some time ago, but I decried the hurting of you. I see that this was awry, for I've indeed brought you deeper pain, and for that I am sorry. To the very depth of my heart, Nicholas, I *am* sorry."

A long, heavy sigh seemed to deflate Nicholas's good posture. "I could have guessed this vould happen," he muttered. "Yu vere ever together, but I thought to overcome it."

He raised his hand in a lame gesture toward the door. "Justin has brought some clothes for yu both. I'll fetch them, then ve must be on our vay. I'll ride vith yu as far as the city limit, and there say my farevell. I must be assured of the velfare of my mother and Katarina ere I leave for Hamburg. Justin has convinced me of yur need to leave the country at the first possible chance. I vill make arrangements to leave as soon as the ice allows us to sail. Vhen I am ready, I vill send a messenger to bid yu come."

"Will you truly help us to escape, Nicholas?" Elise queried worriedly. At his nod, she contemplated him closely. "And your loyalty to the Hansa?"

"Perhaps, my dear Elise, there needs be a change in the hearts of the masters." He voiced his musings carefully. "Long ago, the league banded together to protect themselves from pirates and other harpies. Now it seems to protect a pirate in our midst. It vill take some time to think it all through. Perhaps in my concern for my own comfort, I deliberately turned a blind eye to vhat Hilliard vas doing. It vas easier not to interfere."

With a grimace Maxim came to his feet and carefully straightened to his full height behind the maid who gave herself to tending his bruised face with a cold cloth. Maxim winced as she found an especially tender spot and, over her head, tossed his friend a disgruntled frown. "You nearly broke my jaw."

"I intended to," Nicholas retorted with an amused smirk. "Now ve are even. I never could best yu vhen ve pitted our skills against each other. Gustave vas a fool to think he could defeat yu. I knew vell enough vhat yu vere doing, and I saw no need to interfere."

"I noticed! Once you knew who I was, you didn't burden yourself at all," Maxim needled. "I was beginning to suspect that you had turned against us completely."

"Be damned!" Nicholas snorted in contempt. "If not for me getting yur clabber-headed companions out, yu vould still be there trying to herd them through the door."

"Who are you calling clabber-headed?" Feigning offense, Elise snapped the question over her shoulder and gave him a dressing-down. "Watch your tongue, knave, or I shall give you a good lashing with my own."

Nicholas chuckled as he stepped through the portal, leaving them both with the assurance that all good humor had been restored.

The captain returned apace with a large bundle which he tossed to Maxim, then he left again advising them that he would wait outside until they were ready. Elise welcomed the sight of feminine apparel and silently blessed Katarina and Therese for having had the presence of mind to send along all the necessary stays, farthingales, stockings, and garters to make her toilette complete. By the time she managed to don the intimate garments, with Maxim pausing at intervals to answer her distressed pleas for assistance, he was fully dressed.

" 'Twould appear, my lord, that you've given serious study to the private attire of women," she observed as he laced her stays. "Should I consider that you've acquired the art by repeated practice?"

Maxim laughed and dropped a kiss on her bare shoulder. "I shall never tell, madam, but many's the time I've taken off your clothes . . . in my mind."

"Lecher!" she accused with a coyly flirtatious smile over her shoulder.

"Aye, madam, when it concerns you." He knotted the cords of her stays and then turned her around in his arms. "Now give your husband a kiss to last him on the journey home."

It was a deep, blissful exchange filled with stirring passion, but such a small sampling left them craving for more. With a sigh, Maxim gathered his wife's velvet gown from a nearby chair and, lowering it over her upflung arms, swept the skirt down over the petticoats. Lifting her hair aside, Elise waited and then shivered in tingling delight as she felt his warm hand slide over her shoulder and slip within the top of her chemise to briefly capture a soft breast. She leaned back against him, encouraging the fondling as his other arm, moving up from her ribs, folded around her and claimed the other breast over the cloth of her bodice.

"I'll be most anxious to reach Faulder," he breathed against her ear. "Such tender ground needs be explored more leisurely."

Elise laid a hand over the one within her chemise. "I think I shall always crave your touch, my lord, knowing what delight it brings. 'Twill also be a test for me to wait for that moment we can make love again."

"Nicholas waits us, and we have delayed long enough," he whispered. "Fetch your father's ring, and let us be off. The sooner we leave, God willing, the sooner we'll be home."

Maxim escorted Elise to the dock where Nicholas and Justin were waiting with the horses. He swept her onto the back of the mare, and then giving the excuse that he had forgotten something aboard the ship, bade the two men to start on their way with Elise. Worried, his bride watched him over her shoulder as Justin led the mare down the street.

Moving swiftly, Maxim returned to the galley and, with a long-handled iron scoop, dragged a burning log onto the wooden flooring. He made haste to roll another from the hearth and, dragging it down the companionway, tossed it into the hatch that opened over a deep hole where scraps of hawse, rope, and splintered spars littered the deck below. He smiled as he backed to the door. If there was naught else to incite Hilliard to come to Faulder Castle, then surely the burning of his ship would bring him flying in haste to search out the man who had set fire to it. If all went well, the Queen of England would have her revenge.

Chapter 23

*L*EADEN GRAY CLOUDS hovered low over the hilltop rise of Faulder Castle as the strong, snow-laden gusts whipped savagely across the barren trail. The horses strained through the deepening drifts, drawing behind them the long sleigh into which Elise had retreated to escape the driving winds. A glance outward assured her they were approaching the moat, and though the haze of white was nearly impenetrable she saw the vague shadow of the portcullis moving slowly upward. The muffled, hollow sound of the horses crossing the timbered bridge was followed a moment later by the equally subdued shouts of Maxim as he reined Eddy around and directed the men across the courtyard. Fitch and Spence were there to halt the team of horses, and as Sherbourne and Justin swung down from their mounts, Kenneth lent his assistance to the servants in getting the team and the other mounts stabled. The men squinted against the heavy flurries and had to shout to be heard above the strengthening gale.

Elise pushed open the door of the coach to find Maxim already there. Snowflakes studded the two days' growth of whiskers covering his lower face, and beneath the deep hood of his cloak she could see that his brows and lashes bore a hoary frosting of white. His jaw was clamped rigid against the frigid winds, and his face was pinched and pale. He could speak no word as he lifted her down. Elise sensed his need to find warmth and, slipping her arm behind his waist, lent him support as they moved toward the keep. Close on their heels came the huddled figures of Sherbourne and Justin as they sought to protect themselves from the bitter winds and the blinding snow. The thought surfaced in Elise's mind that they had reached the castle none too soon.

Maxim opened the portal, and the handle was promptly snatched from his icy fingers as the wind caught it and flung it crashing against the inner wall. A cloud of white swirled around them in frolicsome freedom, scattering snowflakes far into the hall as it pushed them inward on a hazy swell of billowing white. The portal was closed, and Elise turned her worry toward Maxim, who leaned in silent agony against the wall. Carefully she eased the frozen gloves from his hands and, as she tried to gently rub some circulation back into them, she tossed a searching glance about the hall, catching sight of a familiar bovine figure a short distance away.

Frau Hanz had halted at their intrusion and was incensed at the rapidly disintegrating neatness of the area wherein they chose to doff their white-crusted garments. Yet she dared not voice her complaint, for she remembered only too well what the mistress had said before her departure. With her hands folded before her, she held her tongue behind the grinding teeth of her annoyance.

Elise spoke with some urgency, commanding the housekeeper's attention. *"Herr* Dietrich does not understand English well enough for me to tell him what I want. So speak with him and instruct him to prepare trenchers of food to be sent upstairs. These men have traveled hard from Lubeck and have need of a rest. They're nearly frozen and need care. And tell him to heat plenty of water for their baths. His lordship can bathe in my room. The others may have his old chambers."

"*Ja, Fraulein.*" *Frau* Hanz started to cross the hall, but was halted as Elise gave further orders.

"And when Spence and Fitch come in, tell them to move his lordship's clothes and chests to my chambers. Our guests will be sharing the upper rooms while they're here. See that fresh pallets and cots are brought in from the quarters in the stables."

The woman's dark brows rose sharply. "But vhere vill his lordship be sleeping?"

"Why, with me, of course," Elise answered and, giving the servant no further notice, turned back to her husband.

A thousand disparaging titles rushed through *Frau* Hanz's mind, all accusing the maid of the vilest traits. It was what she had known all the time! The English strumpet was plying her favors on his lordship to glean what she could from him. She was not deserving of any display of respect. Indeed, if not for the Marquess, the little trollop would see a good measure of her contempt.

Now, with her earlier suspicions confirmed, *Frau* Hanz felt a renewed superiority as she considered herself well above the harlot. The girl had no rightful place in a great house and could not be a proper mistress to servants who dismissed her as common. And they would surely learn of her deeds, *Frau* Hanz silently vowed.

Elise failed to notice the disturbance in the kitchen as she bent her full attention to Maxim. *Frau* Hanz set her barbs into the cook and ordered him about as if she were the rightful mistress of the house. The housekeeper had decided the man needed to show more respect for her station and was dispensing commands with an authoritarian demeanor.

"Come upstairs, Maxim," Elise entreated. "You can warm yourself by the fire while a bath and food are being prepared."

A strong gust of wind burst into the hall as Fitch swung open the door. He scampered quickly in with Sir Kenneth close behind him. The pair struggled a moment with the willful door and finally gained the advantage, pushing it closed.

"Fitch, will you show these men to his lordship's chambers?" Elise bade. "And make sure there's plenty of firewood on hand upstairs. They'll need to thaw out and bathe and eat before settling down."

Eager to help, Fitch gave his attention to the guests. "Come along now. We'll see ta gettin' ya settled in upstairs, just like the mistress said."

The servant was ready to sprint upstairs, but the men followed at a much slower, much more painful pace. The winds had risen sometime after noon, and it seemed with each passing hour the snow had deepened while the gusts strengthened and grew more crisp. They were completely exhausted, and so cold they could hardly move.

Maxim slowly eased up the stairs as Elise lent him what support and assistance she was capable of. In the chambers upstairs, he carefully lowered his shivering body into a chair near the hearth, and immediately Elise was there to wrap a fur throw around his shoulders. She knelt down before him, and he winced slightly as she eased the boots from his feet, but he took heart, reassured that he still had feeling in his toes.

Elise stripped the snow-dampened garments from her husband, then gently rubbed his chilled skin, now and then dropping an anxious kiss upon his chest, his arm, or his hand until at long last he seemed to revive and respond. Tucking the fur around him more securely, she moved away to pour a strong draught into a tankard and then knelt before the hearth to warm it with a searing iron. A brief glance upward assured her that some color was returning to his skin.

"You must be feeling better." Elise voiced the hopeful conjecture with a tentative smile.

"The storm almost did me in," he admitted, unable to subdue an errant shiver. "During the last miles I began to wonder if we would make it."

A wavering sigh slipped from her as evidence of her pent-up tensions. "Hilliard will find it hard to follow."

"Aye, 'tis true. If this storm keeps up, he won't be able to get through until spring."

"My heart shall tremble in fear when he comes."

"I plan to be ready for him, my love. I don't intend to make you a widow for at least a score or more years yet."

Elise braved a smile as she rose and handed him the mug. Pausing beside him, she lifted a hand and smoothed the long wisps of hair that tumbled free from the loosening knot. "I begin to understand how Justin feels."

Maxim scraped a hand across his bristly chin. He was so tired he could barely lift his arms, and chagrined by his unkempt appearance. "This is hardly the way a new bride should view her husband. I must look a bit battle-worn."

"I love you," she whispered, slipping to her knees before him. "And I don't care how you look. My only concern is how you feel. I could not bear to lose you."

Maxim's movements were slow and leisured, as if a rare bird had come to perch on his arm. This woman he had taken as wife was indeed a unique rarity. She could be tender and timid, wild and wanton, serious and sober, happy and hopeful, all the things that a living and loving woman could be with a man, and in the short time he had come to know her he realized how good she was for him and how fortunate he was that Fitch and Spence could not tell red hair from brown.

Speaking no word, he loosened the coiled knot and stroked her hair as it tumbled around her shoulders. In some fascination he watched the brightly gleaming strands eagerly curl around his fingers, and it was as if a slow dawning came upon him. He had said the words before, but now they came upon him with a deepening realization. He really did cherish and love her more than his own heart.

A light rap sounded upon the portal, and the spell was broken. Elise moved away as Fitch answered Maxim's inquiry, and the servant was given leave to enter. Shoving a shoulder against the panel, he came hurrying in with two pails of steaming water. He dared a brief glance at the couple as Elise prepared to shave his lordship, but he kept his face carefully blank. When he had emptied the pails into the copper tub, he paused before his lordship's chair.

"Ye'll be proud ta know, milord, 'at Spence an' me's been behavin' ourselves, 'at we have. 'Ere's been nary a squabble 'twixt the two o' us. O' course, 'at's not sayin' we ain't 'ad a spat or two wit' 'at fat old crow, *Frau* Hanz. She sticks me in the craw some'in fierce, but 'at's neither here nor there. How's it been with yerself, sir, an' the mistress? Ta tell ye true, sir, we weren't 'pectin' ye back so soon, an' me an' Spence was wonderin' if'n ya might've 'ad some trouble."

"Trouble is a rather mild way of putting it," Maxim remarked as Elise carefully plied a blade to his lip.

"But as to the mistress and myself, we were married a brace of days ago in Lubeck."

Fitch's face lit up like a candle, radiating his pleasure. " 'At's real good news, milord." His eyes wandered around the room as the idea settled comfortably in his mind. It was perhaps the best thing that had happened to his lordship in some time, and even if it had been brought about by the loss of a title and possessions, the lady was well worth the price. "I ne'er gave it much mind 'at ye'd be speakin' the vows with the mistress, but ye made a fine choice, milord, 'at ye did."

Elise threw a smile at him over her shoulder. "Thank you, Fitch."

"Milady, 'tis a pleasure ta serve ye, 'tis," he vowed with a sheepish grin. Giving them an enthusiastic bow, he sidled nearer the door. "I'll be tellin' Spence right away, 'at I will," he said. "Just as soon as I fetch ye more buckets of water, milord."

The door slammed closed behind him, and in the silence of the keep they could hear him scurrying down the hall.

" 'Twould seem that Fitch approves of the match," Maxim observed, pulling his wife close to bestow a kiss upon the soft mouth.

Elise lost herself in the adoration she saw in his eyes. "He's probably overjoyed that we won't be fighting anymore."

Several more buckets of water were brought in, and as Fitch hurried out to fetch the last of them, Maxim rose and followed Elise to the copper tub where she poured cold water into hot and swirled the liquid about to blend the two. Dropping the fur, he eased himself into the steaming bath and was just beginning to relax when Fitch bumped the door open again and hastened across to the tub with another pair of brimming buckets. Elise poured in more cold as Fitch added the hot, and then scooping up a pitcher-full, she let it cascade down the well-muscled back.

A deliberately loud clearing of the throat drew Elise's attention to the door, where the housekeeper waited with a tray of food. *Frau* Hanz could hardly contain a sneer as Elise directed her toward the hearth.

"Just leave the food there by the fire where it will stay warm. His lordship and I will eat after his bath."

"I didn't understand that yu vanted to eat vith his lordship, *fraulein.*" The woman stood staunchly rooted to the floor, making no move to enter the chamber. She found the idea of a woman closely attending her lover's bath in the presence of others most offensive, and in no slightest way would she consider chancing a more intimate view of the naked man. For the moment it gave her delight in subtly hinting that it was not the place of common women to eat with their betters. "I vas t'inkin' yu vould vant to eat yur vittles downstairs in the kitchen."

"You were mistaken, *Frau* Hanz," Elise declared crisply. The arrogance of the woman sorely grated on her good humor.

"Then is it yur vish, *fraulein,* that I bring up another tray?"

"Of course!" Elise flung with growing exasperation. "And be quick about it. Oh, and tell *Herr* Dietrich to heat more water. I'll be wanting a bath after dinner."

Maxim saw no reason for the extra bother and offered with a grin, "You needn't wait, my love. There's plenty for sharing now."

Frau Hanz drew herself up with a shocked gasp and, marching a few steps forward, slammed the tray down on the nearest table, then whirled in a huff, offended by this sordid debauchery she was witnessing. Muttering to herself, she strode down the hall in a spiteful temper. As sturdily built as they were, the walls and floor seemed to shudder in her wake.

Fitch tried to keep his lips under tight restraint as her ladyship scolded his lordship with a shaming look, but the urge to laugh nearly got the better of him.

"You shock the poor woman, Maxim," Elise chided, but her eyes conveyed something far different than her concern over the housekeeper.

"I'll be going now," Fitch announced abruptly, catching a pointed frown from his lordship. At times the Marquess had a deliberate way of pinning a stare that prompted one to hasty action. On the way out he closed the portal securely behind him.

"Now, my lady..." Maxim laid his arms on the rim of the tub and leaned back as he fixed his eyes upon the comely form of his wife. "We have all the time in the world, and we need not be afraid of the long, cold night ahead. So come favor your husband by gracing his bath with your presence. My blood is quickly warming beyond my control."

With a seductive smile Elise lifted her arms and fastened her hair again in a knot. She left him for a moment to latch the door and set the tray before the fire, mentally taking note that there was more than enough to share between the two of them. She perched on the edge of the bed to slip off her hide shoes and then raised her skirts, giving him a lengthy view of slender thighs and calves as she rolled down her stockings. Piece by discarded piece, Maxim was teased with each fresh view of her body until she stepped over the edge of the tub. His burning gaze stroked slowly down her nakedness as she stood before him, then she lowered herself into the water and came willingly into his arms. Enjoying the wet, slippery feel of their bodies pressed together, he kissed her with all the leisured thoroughness of a man in no hurry.

Another knock intruded, and Maxim raised his head with an impatient frown. "Who beats upon my door?"

"*Mein Herr,* I haff come vith another tray of vittles," *Frau* Hanz answered through the thick planks. "Vould *Fraulein* Radborne vish me to bring it in now?"

"Go away," Maxim commanded. "We're busy now."

"But *Fraulein* Radborne said for me ..."

" 'Tis *Frau* Seymour now," Maxim corrected sharply.

On the other side of the door *Frau* Hanz clutched a pudgy hand to her throat in shock. Surely his lordship had better sense than to marry that baseborn snip of a girl! Seeking affirmation, she dared to test his patience again. "*Mein Herr,* do you mean that Mistress Radborne ... is now ... *Frau* Seymour ... ?"

"Woman, must you have it stated more clearly?" he thundered. "She is now Lady Seymour! Now go away and leave us in peace! I've no wish to be disturbed until I bid you come. Be gone with you!"

"As yu vish, my lord," *Frau* Hanz meekly returned, her voice quavering slightly. It was a sad day indeed when one of highborn nobility stooped to bestow his name on a common guttersnipe.

"Lady Seymour," Elise repeated with a dreamy sigh. Looping her arms around her husband's neck, she twirled a finger around in his tawny hair. "I like the sound of that."

"Aye, my lady," he breathed as his open mouth caressed the pale throat. "No other woman would have honored the name so well."

In curious wonder her blue eyes searched his. "Not even Arabella?"

" 'Tis you I love, Elise, and no other," he averred, and was rewarded by the radiance he saw in her face.

* * *

A haze of relentless white obscured the dawn as the storm continued to rage across the land, but within the warmth and security of what was now the master's chambers, the couple cared little about the howling tempest, for the bliss of the moment was almost tangible. They lay abed, luxuriating in the unhurried calm of the morning. It seemed an eternity since they had been allowed time to enjoy each other's nearness and to become intimate with the intricate nature of each other's character. Their voices were soft and hushed, the pace leisured as they shared the same pillow and spoke of a thousand different things: their hopes, their dreams, their yearnings, their past, present, and future. Snuggled beneath the covers, Maxim rested on his side with an arm folded beneath his head, while Elise lay on her back with her legs propped casually over the hard, manly thighs tucked close beneath her own. Their hands were entwined, and as Maxim nibbled, teased, and kissed the slender fingers he held, she watched him with love shining in her eyes. It was a beginning of a marriage, the laying of a sturdy foundation, a solid structure that could be built upon and enhanced by the pleasures of life, to stand firm against the buffeting storms and trials that would no doubt seek them out. It was a gentle melding of two lives into one.

The hour was approaching noon when Maxim finally escorted his wife down to the hall and, beneath the brooding stare of *Frau* Hanz, crossed the room to join their guests.

"Welcome to my humble castle," Maxim heartily bade, and chuckled as they answered his humor with hoots and guffaws.

"By faith! I swear the splendor rivals any palace of the Queen of England," chortled Sir Kenneth.

Elise moved to the trestle table where a most inviting feast had been laid out. To gain the attention of the men, she clanked a knife against a pewter goblet and called to them gaily, "Hear me, good gentlemen. Be kind to this old keep. Someday you may find yourself well into your years, perhaps even jeered at for your doddering ways. Turn your minds from the tumbling ruins of this place. Think no more of the rattle of shutters, the squeak of hinges, or its decaying face, but rather, come break the fast with us and please your palates. Let us make merry this morn, for we have not only singed the whiskers of one Karr Hilliard—"

Elise started in surprise as a clanging clamor nearby rent the tranquillity of the hall, and she looked in some amazement at *Frau* Hanz who stared down agog at the iron kettle she had dropped. The pot gyrated in lopsided circles on the stone floor until it finally settled into stillness, leaving a ringing resounding in everyone's ears. The housekeeper awoke from her trance and reached down to seize the handle of the wayward pot, not daring to meet the gaze of the one who stared.

With a brief nod of gratitude, Elise pressed a slender finger to her temple. "Where was I? Oh, of course! Karr Hilliard! We have indeed singed the whiskers of Karr Hilliard, but this storm has gifted us with enough snow to save us from his pursuit. Take heart, my good fellows. We've the rest of the winter to enjoy each other's pleasure and the delicious foods prepared by *Herr* Dietrich." Graciously she indicated the widely grinning man before she boasted, "Why, his talents would gain us the envy of the English queen herself."

"Here, here!" Sir Kenneth drank down a long gulp of wine and blustered a moment as he wiped his heavy mustache and prepared his own speech. "We've trod close to heaven's gate to view the loveliest angel that ever graced these eyes." He raised his pewter goblet to her. "To the most lovely Lady Seymour, who though but a fragile maid herself, dared tweak the nose of the Hansa masters."

The men drank the toast, and then Elise added one of her own. "And here is to the men who rescued her. May they have long life, every one . . . and be ready to dash a dozen more dragons to the winds."

Frau Hanz looked with contempt upon the jocular group, but she would wisely hold her tongue. The time would come when she would make sure that these poor feeble Englishmen reaped the revenge of Karr Hilliard.

Chapter 24

THE STORM RAGED on for one day less than a week, and then the seventh day dawned bright and bitter cold. Had an eagle braved the frigid, airy heights, he would have been hard-pressed to mark the site of Faulder Castle, save for the dark plumes of smoke that seemed to flow from the peaks of snowy mounts. Several leagues to the north, the free city of Lubeck fussed for a quartet and more of days as she turned her skirts inside out in search of the dastardly culprits who had committed murder and mayhem within her confines. When word reached Hilliard that his ship was on fire at its winter slip, he had raced to the dock and let out a howl of indignant rage as a shudder freed the blazing carrack from the ice-bound anchorage. A look of deadly purpose had come into his eyes as he watched his vessel sink into the river. Only the smoking stubbles of her masts were left jutting forlornly above the blackened muck floating on the surface, a grim reminder of what once had been a swift and mighty ship. With a driving fury he had vowed to see the ones responsible chased down and put to death.

A dark haze had lingered over the city long after the huge billowing clouds of black had been doused, but by the time the second Sabbath had passed, the city had nearly forgotten the intruders and returned to business as usual. Not so in the Hansa *kontors.* The halls resounded with the enraged bellows of one **Karr Hilliard** who fumed at the fates, cursed the climes, berated the snow for being snow, the ice for being ice, the wind for being wind, and roundly vented his agitated spleen with a fine eye for equality on any who came within earshot and many who simply misjudged the range. Masters and merchants who found it necessary to visit his offices crept in and promptly hastened out, for the Hanseatic agent was wont to lash out with tongue or heavy fist at any who ventured within reach of either. Pity those who gave him the slightest provocation.

The winter passed on spavined, leaden feet for those in the league. Each week, each day . . . Nay! Each hour was counted by many an anxious eye upon the sands that trickled with agonizing languor through the glass. But in snowbound Faulder Castle the days flew past with fleet-footed alacrity. The comfort and contentment of its occupants seemed boundless even while the storms raged outside. The delicious aromas of *Herr* Dietrich's cooking wafted through the keep, while the sounds of activity and the murmur, laughter, and gabble of many voices brought a warmth and vitality to the place. The camaraderie of all—save one—helped quicken the flow of those same tiny grains of time, and though all were aware of the coming conflict, it was a period well-marked with pleasure and fine rapport.

None doubted that Hilliard would come. The man would not let the affront pass without a fierce reprisal, and in preparation of that day, tactics for their defense were discussed, crossbows tested, swords and daggers oiled and honed, and proposals presented for the making of new weapons. While the weather remained inclement, the men tested their fighting skills against each other, and the hall rang with the clash of steel and boisterous shouts as they gave themselves over with wit and enthusiasm to the martial games. Though careful to maintain a safe distance, Elise eagerly watched their play and added her laughter to the clamor. The fact that she was there to witness their feats seemed to encourage the antics, and the younger men were especially committed to winning her light-hearted praises. Maxim felt no need to worry when Justin and Sherbourne displayed a courtly dash and daring for her benefit, for he was secure in the knowledge that she was entirely his. Ofttimes Justin was made the brunt of Kenneth's pranks in their competition, mainly because of his youth, but he accepted the teasing good-naturedly and gave more of the same in return.

It was usually in the quiet of the evening when the men withdrew to a more private area of the hall to plan their defense and strategy, secluding themselves well away from the straining ears of *Frau* Hanz. It became Elise's habit to retreat to the bedchamber to await her husband, and at times her soft, lilting voice would drift in song through the keep as she plied her sewing skills to her tapistry or, if need be, to mending the men's clothing. The airy strains seemed to calm the men, and they responded to each other in murmured voices, reluctant to argue when bathed in such contentment. Maxim neither took note nor did he especially care that the same sweetly melodious voice which soothed him could, with the very same notes, grate roughly on the ears of one *Frau* Hanz. The housekeeper's brows often gathered in stern concentration as she bent her attention to whatever task was at hand, and her lips would move in silent vexation as she made dire vows to herself or to some venging, unknown god.

Herr Dietrich, on the other hand, waxed jovial and

was given to low-voiced accompaniment. If the melody was light and lively, he kept time by tapping a spoon on a pot lid or moving his feet in a shuffling dance that matched the rhythm. At times, he would catch Maxim's amused contemplation and would grin in response and waggle his head happily as he lauded the beauty of the voice.

When the slashing winds and blinding snow finally spent their fury, the men shoveled paths through huge drifts, gaining better access to the surrounding wall, stable, and the tumbled ruins of the barracks and storehouse. They searched through the rubble until they found, in rough form, most of what they needed for the making of new weapons. They tore away wooden planks and piled heaps of it in protected places where it would remain dry. Small pieces of iron were thrown into barrels and the bulk of it stored near kegs of black powder. Their frugal confiscation stripped the outbuildings to stout timbers and bare stone, for they left no corner untouched.

Sealed jugs of lard were found in the cellar of the storehouse and were emptied into huge iron vats in the middle of the courtyard. The pots had been hung on iron frames fashioned by Spence, and roaring fires were built beneath them until the contents were melted down. When the kettles cooled, heavy lids were settled into place over the pots to keep out the moisture. There they were left for another day's heating.

With Spence assuming the duty of smithy in the stable, blades for lances, arrowheads, and heavy quarrels were fashioned. It was Spence's empathy with animals and a foreboding of the northern climes that had goaded him to make several trips to Hamburg for forage and hay while the master was away in Lubeck. Thus, while the storm had raged, all remained snug and warm in the stables. Now each night the ringing of iron and the roaring of the furnace drowned out the contented munching of the animals and lulled the lad who tended them to sleep.

In all of her maidenly dreams of requited love Elise had never once imagined that a remote castle, built on a barren bluff and caught in the depths of an ice-bound winter, could provide such a sublime haven. Many evenings she curled in Maxim's arms while he sat in a chair before the blazing hearth. Wrapped together in a thick fur, they solved the problems of the world in soft voices punctuated by long moments of silence. When the fire burned low and the chill drove them to bed, they burrowed deep within its warmth and passed such nights...Oh! They were far beyond any fantasy an innocent maid could have conjured.

It was inevitable that morning would break upon the land, and so, marked by the aging of one day into a week, a week into a month, another season would come. It was a lament of Elise's heart that time could not stand still. For once in her life she dreaded the advent of spring.

A brace of fortnights passed, and the castle remained secure from all outside interference. In the frozen world of white beyond its gates, there was a hushed stillness, as if this faraway hinterland and all of its inhabitants held its breath in expectant dread of the furor yet to come. An occasional breeze rattled the limbs of the trees, shaking free a fine dusting of snow that glittered iridescently in the shafts of sunlight streaming through the barren branches. Small birds flitted though the treetops, seeking seeds and frozen berries. A squirrel was seen sitting in the crotch of a tree, while below him a lone stag cautiously approached the slow, dark trickle of water that marked the first thawing of the river.

The days gradually warmed beneath the climbing sun as the harshness of winter dwindled to a mere shade of its former self. A shiver crept along Elise's spine as she watched the dust motes that danced a leisured ballet in the bright rays shining in through the thick, wavy glass of the windows, where the drapes and shutters had been opened wide. Maxim had built the fire high in the hearth before hot water had been carried up for a bath, then after partaking in a connubial lavation, he had left Elise to luxuriate in the warmth while he had toweled himself dry and dressed. After a lengthy kiss and another admiring caress of soapy, wet skin he had departed the chambers, giving the excuse that he wanted to exercise Eddy for a while. Though there was no outward reason for a chill, Elise shuddered as a cold knot of dread formed in the pit of her stomach. She realized only too well that a careful patrol of the area was beginning.

A long, pensive sigh slipped from her as she slid down into the tub, and her eyes moved sadly about the chamber as her mind brought back in careful recall the events of the past months. Since leaving England she had become a woman in more ways than one. She reveled in the stirring immensity of her love, for it satiated her heart to overflowing. Maxim fulfilled every facet of her far-reaching aspirations of a loving, considerate, and gentle husband, and yet there was a passionate sensuality about him that sparked the hot blood within her. He could, with a look, start her pulse leaping, but there was no need for him to be so purposeful. Her eyes could settle on his back and warm with desire as they wandered admiringly over his manly frame, especially if that form was bereft of garb.

A smile lifted the corners of Elise's lips as she leaned her head back against the rim of the tub. Deliberately she summoned to the fore of her mind an image of those wide shoulders, the muscled ribs, the narrow hips, and the long legs that bulged with the play of rippling sinews as he moved. When a man was as well put together as Maxim was, it was rather hard for a young wife not to admire her own husband. A lop-sided grin would slowly twist his lips whenever her stares betrayed her curiosity, and he would approach her with a purposeful gleam in his eye, interrupting many a toilette. His gentle guidance and instruction were every bit as exciting as those moments when his own rutting quests swept her into a whirlwind of frenzied passion.

Of a sudden Elise's eyes flew wide and she sat up in some astonishment. Canting her head, she raised her hand and slowly counted on her fingers. Could it be possible? She counted again, more carefully this time. Was it really true?

Foolish mortal she to doubt it! Beware the bed and the craving lusts of a man! Or so went the warnings of many an old dame to a virginal daughter. But where love abounded, there was pleasure to be had in all things ... even in this small, cherished blooming of life.

A secretive smile traced across her lips as she remembered numerous occasions when their love might have brought this small miracle into being. No exact determination could be made to single out the moment, but then, there was no need. Each memory was worth keeping.

Another week slipped past at the same idyllic pace, and as the days lengthened the men ventured out more. They rode beyond the gate to patrol the countryside and sometimes to hunt. Their careful vigil extended to posting a guard near the gate, and Spence and Fitch took turns to make the place secure from all intruders.

One early morn Elise came down to the kitchen to find that the men had already taken their victuals and had withdrawn to the courtyard. She was sipping tea before the kitchen hearth when the front door burst open and the sound of running footsteps claimed her questioning attention. Her apprehensive stare halted Sir Kenneth in his tracks.

"Your pardon, my lady, I...ah..." The man stammered in confusion as he searched for an appropriate excuse for his haste and finally took himself firmly in hand. "I didn't mean to disturb you, my lady. I only wanted to fetch my buckler and sword."

Elise's thoughts gathered in a dark cloud of worry as the ogre, Hilliard, came to mind. "Is aught amiss? Is..." Her tongue froze on the name. "Is someone coming?"

"No need to fret, my lady," Sir Kenneth attempted to assure her. " 'Tis naught of import. One of the small nags is missing, and *Frau* Hanz is nowhere to be found. 'Twould seem she has fled the fold. His lordship is saddling our horses. We only mean to follow the tracks for a ways to see...well, to see what state the road is in."

Elise read more in his pause than the knight had meant to convey. "Do you expect trouble to follow *Frau* Hanz's leaving?"

Sir Kenneth cleared his throat and returned a noncommittal answer to her inquiry. " 'Tis best to be wary in any case, my lady."

"Of course," she agreed. "And there is indeed cause to be cautious of *Frau* Hanz. I fear she was never one of us."

"His lordship's sentiments exactly, my lady," the

man conceded. "He was expecting her to leave and allowed for the possibility."

Elise absorbed the information in silence, aware that her husband seldom missed a detail. Before their trip to Lubeck, he had been totally indifferent to the woman...but his caution had become apparent shortly after their return. Whenever *Frau* Hanz had drawn near enough to listen during his discussions with the men, he had deliberately changed the topic or pointedly fell silent until she left. It became a matter of rote, when he called the men to private council in his bedchambers, that either Fitch or Spence would be posted outside the door to guard against possible eavesdropping. If there was naught but one thing Elise had come to realize about her husband in their brief time together, then it was surely the fact that he was not a man to be taken lightly. His confrontation with Gustave had given vivid evidence of his quick cunning and agile wit, and possibly the thing that made him even more dangerous to his enemies was his courage to carry out feats of daring with both aplomb and finesse, usually to the surprise and utter distress of his adversaries. Considering his capabilities, Elise concluded with some pride, perhaps it would be more appropriate to pity the foolish ones who were eager to challenge him.

"You needn't worry yourself about Hilliard, my lady," Sir Kenneth assured her, intruding into her thoughts. " 'Twould take better than the likes of him to outwit your husband. Mark my word, my lady."

His tender assurances brought a soft smile of gratitude to Elise's lips. "I shall be glad to, Sir Kenneth. And thank you."

" 'Tis always my pleasure, my lady."

He left her and raced up the stairs two at a time and, a short moment later, returned to take his leave of the keep. A rattle of hooves on the bridge and the clanging clank of the lowering portcullis gave evidence of their departure from the courtyard.

In the silence of the hall Elise recognized her own easement of tensions. It was rather encouraging to think she would not have to endure *Frau* Hanz's glowering frowns and sour disposition any longer. Her spirits soared apace with the release as the day aged, and with renewed enthusiasm, she bundled herself in a warm cloak and tugged on the old hide boots. Sherbourne gave her a brief argument at the gate, but at her sweetly voiced pledge to go no further than what was safe, he yielded and cranked the wheel that lifted the heavy iron grating.

Beyond the bridge, Elise wended east along the wall where the reflected sun had cleared a narrow path in the snow. A soft southern breeze brought a light, evasive essence of spring to her nostrils, and she pushed back the hood of her cloak to let its gentle warmth caress her face. For a time she stood bathing in the invigorating brightness of the sun and was about to walk on when a spot of color near the base of the wall caught her eye. Small green leaves had sprouted in a crevice, protected yet warmed by the sun. And in the midst of the green . . . Elise knelt to see it better. Aye! 'Twas a white flower, so tiny as to be almost apologetic for its brazen presence. Tugging off her glove, she reached down and carefully plucked the bloom.

Once, long years ago, she had gathered wildflowers to braid a crown of many colors to adorn her father's dark hair. Her mind drifted back in sweet recall and teased her with random shards and scattered glimpses of another time and another place. A haunting recollection came winging back of a narrow beach buttressed with towering cliffs that were themselves punctuated with caves. Eternally lapping waves washed over the beach, and an exhilarating sense of freedom filled her as she remembered racing barefoot along the stretch of sand as a child and her father giving chase. A memory drifted back of misty moors dotted with wooded crests, a large cottage, and tumbled ruins whereon they had sat and leisurely pondered the gamboling clouds high above. He had loved that place, and many were the times he had encouraged her to go back just to wander the moors, to explore the caves as she had done when she was a child, to enjoy the damp breezes on her skin, and to sit upon the stones. It was strange that in the last couple of months or so before his abduction his urgings to go back to their cottage and to that place of sweet, remembered dreams had grown stronger. He had even made her promise to return there upon his death, to take possession of her mother's portrait that had for years hung in the house, and do all the things they had done when they had been together.

Elise lifted her head as if she heard a voice speaking to her from the past. It seemed to echo in her mind. Go back. Go back. Go back. Go back.

A shout rang out from the tower, capturing her attention, and she turned her head as another answered from afar. Shading her eyes against the reflected light of the snow, Elise scanned the road until she caught sight of a pair of mounted riders racing along the path. Her heart quickened with excitement as she recognized the tall, familiar form of Maxim on the back of the stalwart steed. Lifting her skirts, she raced back over the rough ground along the wall. The low rumble of horses' hooves echoed from the bridge as it was crossed, stilling the trilling song of a nearby bird. The drumming seemed to reverberate within Elise's chest, filling her with excitement, and as the men rode into the courtyard she quickened her pace and raced across that same wooden expanse.

Maxim reined Eddy about as he heard the light patter of running feet behind him. Having cautioned Sherbourne to keep a close eye out for Hilliard, he was surprised to see Elise coming across the bridge. His first instinct was to reprimand the knight for allowing her to venture out alone, but as his wife neared, Maxim's heart fairly leapt within his breast at sight of her dazzling, disarrayed beauty. Rosy-cheeked and breathless, with her hair spilling in glorious color down her back, she was an unforgettable and unreproachable vision. He could think of no harsh rebuke when faced with such beauty.

Maxim's feet struck the ground, and he swept off his helmet, letting it fall to earth as she flew into his arms. Catching her close, he swung her about in a circle until she laughed aloud in dizzy glee. Halting, he searched out her lips, heedless of any who watched, and the couple passed a long moment in rapturous stillness ere she came to earth again.

Sir Kenneth lifted his visor and wiped the back of a gauntleted hand across his mouth as he watched the pair. Feeling a strange blend of envy and amusement, he could not help but think that even with the loss of title and lands, the Marquess was a most fortunate man.

Maxim released his wife, and her arms slowly slid from his neck. He saw her eyes grow sad as she raised a clenched fist between them and gradually opened it to present a small white blossom. When she lifted her gaze to meet his, he saw the smallest trace of fear beneath the sadness.

"Spring has come," she whispered forlornly. "Can the beast be far behind?"

Maxim removed a leather gauntlet and traced the

back of his fingers along her cheek. Resting his hand upon the coolness of it, he caressed the corner of her lips with his thumb. "We were on Hilliard's ground in Lubeck, my love, and still we won the day. Here"—he nodded toward the narrow road—"he must come on ours."

Chapter 25

SOUTHWESTERLY BREEZES swept the northern climes and brought a sweet, wet promise of spring to Faulder Castle. A pair of days passed, bringing a tumultuous thunderstorm that washed the slopes with a heavy downpouring. Even as night settled hard and stygian black over the land, thunder continued to rumble in the distance. An occasional flash of lightning lit the roiling clouds and the surrounding countryside with its blinding brilliance. It was a night of threatening violence, and Elise, brushing her hair near the hearth, started suddenly in alarm as a bolt of sizzling brightness transformed the dark shadows of the bedchamber into a ghostly white. In the next instant an horrendous crack rent the silence, sending her flying from her chair. Fretting now, she paced the floor in anxious worry, wondering if the road would again prove impassable. Fitch and Spence had managed to cart their trunks and possessions to Hamburg where Nicholas was preparing his ship to sail, but after their return, it seemed the very heavens had opened lofty floodgates to unleash a veritable torrent of water upon the land. The occup   of the castle were once again held prisoner by the elements, for the rains threatened to sweep away any who would foolishly traverse the deeply rutted muck of the road. They could only console themselves in the fact that if the rains kept them from getting out, they also prevented Hilliard from getting in.

The waiting wore heavily upon all, and their nerves stretched taut. Maxim fretted as he watched the days sundered beneath the pounding rains and relentless storms. He eyed the glass and marked the time of each passing hour, seeing naught but a dwindling hope for his wife's escape.

Finally the sun broke free of the clouds, and its warmth seemed to spur the men into a frenzy of activity, and though Elise had thought they waited only for the road to dry, the men hardly considered the lane now as they worked to ready the wall and castle for the attack that was expected. The dried wood they had previously stored was now piled in a long, continuous mound at the base of the outer wall. Fresh kindling was stacked beneath the kettles of rendered fat, and supplies of arrows, quarrels, rocks, cannonballs, kegs of black powder, and barrels of small, broken bits of jagged iron were taken to the wall. The recently repaired outer gates were drawn closed and a thick bolt of iron laid across them before the portcullis was lowered into place behind them, on the courtyard side.

Elise was in the bedchamber when a sudden, sharp explosion rattled the windows. Her heart filled her throat as she raced to the shutters and threw them open. Half-expecting to see Hilliard and his troop of cavaliers charging along the lane, she witnessed instead a small geyser of mud and debris just settling to earth on the top of the ridge. Her searching gaze found Maxim standing on the wall, crouching over the breech of a small cannon. Sighting along its barrel, he gave directions to Justin and the two knights as to where it was to be positioned. Gradually they moved the piece until he was satisfied with its new sighting, then the cannon was reloaded and relit. The weapon barked again, and once more a dirty plume leapt upward, this time in the middle of the narrow lane.

A cheer went up from the men, and in jovial spirits they applied themselves to another reloading. Maxim bent to sight the gun again, and once more the new position was tested. Thus it went until the road was marked every twenty paces or so with broad, muddy smudges trailing almost to the end of the bridge. When satisfied the cannon was well-laid and ranged, the men crossed to the other wall adjoining the gate to perform the same task with the companion gun.

Elise considered what the men's efforts had brought about since the departure of *Frau* Hanz, and the realization began to settle down in her mind that they were working more zealously to fortify and defend the place than arranging for their departure. Escape no longer seemed their concern.

Later that evening, as she waited for Maxim to join her in their bedchamber, she heaved a deep sigh of fretting impatience. Though she had only seen Hilliard at the communal hall, she had heard enough from Maxim and the men to know that the agent would not be satisfied until he had seized and slaughtered all of them, even if he had to pluck every last stone from Faulder Castle in his quest. To imagine now that their small force could stand their ground and take on the impact of his assault made her heart tremble within her breast.

Feeling her anxieties building up, Elise danced in a series of small circles, swirling the skirts of her robe high and wide as she swept about the room. She halted her dance with a little gasp when her eyes lit on her smiling husband. He was leaning against the closed door where he had, for the last moments, enjoyed a rich display of pale, slender thighs.

Maxim dropped the latch into place, locking the portal behind him, and strode across the room to take his wife in his arms. His parting mouth covered hers in a long, thorough kiss that sapped all the strength from her limbs, then, much to her surprise and disappointment, he caught her hands and stood back. He gazed into her searching, questioning eyes as if he longed to memorize every detail of their beauty. At last, with a heavy sigh, he set her free and turned away, but immediately he faced her again. This time a strange look of reluctant sadness showed through the otherwise determined mien he had assumed.

"There's a matter of grave importance I wish to discuss with you, my love." An odd, husky tone had invaded his voice, hinting of his troubled mind.

Elise stared at her husband in some puzzlement over his manner, sensing the matter to be of a serious nature. "You have my leave to speak, Maxim. What troubles you so?"

Chafing over his difficulty to forge ahead into the straight, bare facts of their predicament and thereby strip her of all hope of escape, he looked away and scrubbed a hand over his chin. He was unable to find the right opening that would soften the shock of what he was about to say. Tentatively, he approached the subject. "My love, believe me when I tell you that my intentions were to see you taken to Nicholas's ship and then to the safety of England . . ."

"See me taken?" Elise grasped hold of his words, and when she spoke, her tone was thick with emotion. "You planned awry if you thought to send me away from you, my lord." Her voice betrayed her crumpling composure. "How can I leave you when you're the very reason my heart beats?"

Maxim saw the rush of tears in her eyes and reached up a hand to cradle her cheek as his thumb wiped away the moisture that trickled down its delicate smoothness. "It fair rends my heart to see your tears, my love. Yet it troubles me even more to tell you that the time for flight has passed. If we go now, Hilliard would catch us on the open road, and we'd have no defense. He must come to us and fight on our terms."

"How can so few hold off so many? We know now since Nicholas sent word to us that Hilliard rode out of Lubeck with more than four score hired mercenaries. What are we to do?"

"Truly, we would have little chance of winning the day if that number enters the courtyard, but if I've planned well, 'twill cost the major part of Hilliard's forces to reach the wall. Therein lies the crux of the matter. Though my provisions were to see you safely away by now, it cannot be done, for the threat of Hilliard taking you is too great. You must stay here with us behind these walls, and in this matter I must beg your forgiveness."

Elise stared at him in wonder, beginning to understand that he was afraid for her and was strangely ashamed that events had not worked to allow for her departure. "Is this the thing that eats at you, my staying?"

"I thought I had planned well enough to see you gone by now, my love," Maxim confessed in a hushed whisper. "It pains me much to know that I've failed you."

"Failed me? What of the rains? The storms? Are you God that you can hold them back? Give heed to the truth of the matter. There was naught else you could do." She slipped her arms about him and dropped her head against his chest, feeling there the slow, reassuring thud of his heart. "Do you not ken my love for you, Maxim? Though the threat of death looms near, I'd never want to leave you."

Maxim reached a hand beneath her chin and lifted her face as his own lowered. "I was a stranger to love until you came into my life," he breathed above her lips. "Now my whole being is illumined with the joy of love, and I stand in much awe of what you've done to me. You are my life, madam."

His kiss was gentle and loving, but as it lingered, their emotions turned on a different path. A slow warming began to spread through their minds and bodies, and all thoughts of Hilliard were swept away as the velvet robe slid to the floor.

The dawning sun rose with dire crimson hues above the ragged shreds of clouds and spread its warmth across the land, forcing the last dregs of the morning mists to retreat to the lowest hollows, where with reluctant lassitude they would eventually evaporate. It was still in the sweet hush of early morn when the alarm rang out from the tower, shattering the tranquillity of the castle and snatching its occupants to their feet in quick response.

"Hilliard has come!"

Elise smothered a cry as Maxim leapt from the kitchen table and charged outside. She quickly ascended to her chambers where she threw open a window to watch what transpired. Near the middle of the road where it breeched the ridge, Hilliard came to a halt astride an outsized mount. On either side of him, his hirelings spread out in double ranks, preparing for an attack. Fitch and Spence scurried to light a fire beneath the kettles of fat as Maxim, with long, leaping strides, crossed the courtyard and climbed to the wall where one of the cannon awaited his attention. Sir Kenneth already manned the second gun, and as Sherbourne gave him aid, Justin came rushing to lend Maxim assistance.

Hilliard raised a white flag and, with a pair of mounted escorts, rode forward on his charger until he was within hearing distance of those on the wall.

"Lord Seymour!" he bellowed. "Give up this foolishness! Yu are out-manned and cannot hope to hold this fort against so great a number! I have four score men behind me! Vhat do yu have behind yu? A handful counting the vench? Give yurself up, and I vill allow the others to go free."

"Humph!" Justin scoffed. "That blackguard would hack us to death the minute the gates are opened, every last one of us."

"We bested you in Lubeck!" Maxim taunted. *"How many did you have beside you then? 'Tis my thought you have not come with nearly enough!"*

Hilliard's ponderous cheeks deepened to a mottled red as anger took hold, and he silently mouthed a renewed promise to crush Maxim Seymour's face beneath his booted heel. Spurring his mount around, he raced back to his army. Taking a position in the middle of the line, he lifted his arm high with a roar of command. A long moment passed as he wallowed in the power he exercised, then, sweeping his arm downward with a wordless howl, he sent his forces forward. His own mount danced with impatience, but the agent held him with tight restraint as he watched the two lines move forward toward the Faulder redoubt.

Sir Kenneth waited until the advancing line was almost to the ranging mark, then he dipped the lighted wick down to the fusehole. The spark lit and touched off a loud explosion that sent a large volley of iron pieces hurtling forcefully through the air. They landed in an eruption of earth, mud, and flailing bodies, and the knight shook his fist in triumph as he counted perhaps four or five men that had been taken out of action. Only one of the fallen rose, clutching his side where a jagged shard protruded, and limped back toward the ridge. Sherbourne hastened to help Kenneth reload, as Maxim lowered a flaming wick to the touchhole of his own cannon. He stepped aside just as the gun barked and recoiled on its trunnion. His guncrew of one leapt forward to swab and reload ere the smoke was cleared, and when the heavily laden vapors lifted, Maxim assessed the damage. It seemed as if a broad hand had torn a large gap in the line. A man writhed briefly in a muddied swale, then lay still. The whole attack had stalled, for Hilliard's warriors now stood in awed confusion. They had been prepared for shafts and spears, but they had hardly been prepared for life-sweeping bombardments of well-aimed cannons filled with scrap iron. The other gun barked its say again, and this time a leaden ball landed, spewing forth a large geyser of mud, rocks, and lifeless humanity. Another report of iron missiles came hard on its heels, shredding another section of advancing soldiers. As the devastation became apparent, cries of alarm rose up. The line wavered, then broke. Turning on their heels, the men raced back toward the ridge, shouting and wailing in fear.

Hilliard charged through their midst, flaying all he could reach with a lash and subduing them into stunned submission. Sir Kenneth, however, was just as intent upon hastening them on their way. He ignited a fresh fuse, and the cannon jumped, sending a ball hurtling toward them. Plummeting to earth amid their ranks, it raised a renewed outcry of alarm as it spewed up mud and gore, and the men scattered over the ridge.

A ricocheting shard of iron spun away, striking the shoulder of Hilliard's mount. Already terrified by the deafening roar of cannon, the destrier reared at the stinging blow and sought to rid itself of its burden.

It spun and bucked, alighting on stiffened legs, and Hilliard took flight, landing flat in a muddy puddle a full yard away. Flumes of liquid mud spewed up around him, eliciting loud guffaws and hearty laughter from those on the wall. It was a measure of Hilliard's stern constitution that marked his wallowing struggle to his feet, but by now, he was in such a high dudgeon, the soldiers realized they had as much reason to fear from him as from those on the wall. They had no cause to doubt for even an instant as he waved his musket that he would shoot any who fled.

A brief rest for the defenders of Faulder Castle ensued as Hilliard berated his men and silently corrected his own base assumptions. This Maxim Seymour was all that Nicholas had extolled him to be, and possibly even more. Only a fool would underestimate him a second time.

Archers gathered on the ridge to send their arrows raining down upon the castle yards. Shields were hastily brought to the fore to protect those manning the guns while Hilliard's men formed another charge, this time with a new intent. Now they advanced as individuals, spread out with several yards between them, and carried with them crude ladders to scale the wall. Justin and Sherbourne pressed near the wall and subjected the approaching force to the plinking attacks of arrows, but when one of the warriors fell with a shaft or a quarrel in his chest, another soldier would take his place.

The guns roared in earnest, yet each shot struck only one or two of the relentless horde. As the attackers crept closer to the wall, even Hilliard left the safety of the ridge and followed with several of his Hansa lackies. The advancing army progressed until the cannons overshot, and Maxim bade his crew to leave the guns and man the wall. The deluge of arrows ceased from Hilliard's camp, allowing the attackers to scale the stone barrier, but Fitch, Spence, Dietrich, and the stable boy came running with kettles of bubbling lard to discourage their climb. As Hilliard's forces braced the top of their ladders against the parapet and surged upward, they were welcomed with cascades of boiling fat. Agonized screams rent the air as the burned soldiers toppled from their lofty perches, but the cool earth beneath the ladders was no place to salve their hurts, for in the next instant a flaming wall leapt upward along the stone barrier as torches were tossed upon the piles of dry wood now sprinkled profusely with fat. Soldiers screamed in sudden horror as their soaked garments ignited, and they fled in panic, thereby fanning the flames that quickly consumed them.

Hilliard's presence rapidly diminished as a threat to the fleeing soldiers, for their pain was such that they almost welcomed a shot from his musket. The Hansa agent saw his forces crumpling around him, but he was wise enough to perceive that if he did not soothe their panic with a gentle hand, he would lose them en masse. He called for the soldiers to regroup beyond the ridge, and as they fled toward the safety it promised, the cannons commenced their destructive reports again, successfully striking where they would do the most damage.

As they waited Hilliard marked his time, bolstering the courage of the men he had left and rallying their spirits with promises of greater reward. He was himself devastated by their losses. He had come with more than four score men; now he hardly had a score capable of continuing the fight. Not only had his numbers been drastically reduced, but he found the swiftness by which they had been dispatched demoralizing. He chided himself for having listened to *Frau*

Hanz when she had foolishly derided the resources and capability of the castle's protectors. She had obviously been blinded by one more cunning than she. As for himself, he had been as much of a buffoon to accept her judgment.

Elise took advantage of the lull to reassure herself that none of their small number had been seriously hurt. The worst that had been done was to Sherbourne who had had an arrow graze his cheek. As she washed the wound and dabbed a poultice on it, she teased him that such a handsome scar would surely intrigue the ladies in England. Dietrich brought out food to nourish their bodies and tea, milk, and water to quench their thirst, and for a time they rested as they waited for another attack to begin.

It was early afternoon before the flames died down, leaving blackened scars reaching upward over the stone from the glowing ash heaps tracing along the front of the wall. The stiff, charred remains of several soldiers who had not been swift enough to escape the flames was a gruesome sight for those who had to face the prospect of scaling the wall. They could only wonder what this devil Englishman had planned for them next.

Once again the advancing army spread out along the line, this time moving so far apart that both Maxim and Sir Kenneth deemed it a waste to fire the cannons. The four of them took up crossbows, but even those became ineffectual when the enemy reached within close proximity of the wall, for the assaulting force managed to brace their ladders in sheltered corners and were soon climbing over the parapets.

Lances confronted those who succeeded, and Maxim thrust this way and that to dissuade the attackers, but it was already a foregone conclusion that his men would be seriously outnumbered in hand-to-hand combat. He hurled an order for his companions to flee to the safety of the keep, and as they obeyed, his blade sang free and bought him space to retreat. He leapt down from the wall and raced swiftly across the courtyard. The open portal welcomed him, and as he gained the safety of the hall, the panel slammed shut behind him, and a second later, the bar dropped in place.

Maxim caught up a ready bow and, jerking open the shutter of an arrow slit, managed to narrow the outside forces by at least three before the assailants blocked the opening with a well-braced plank. He caught sight of several men cranking up the portcullis of the gate and knew Hilliard would be in the courtyard soon. It would only be a matter of time ere the butt of a log would be smashing at the front door.

"Hilliard's men will shortly overrun the hall," Maxim announced as he faced the others. "Our retreat will be to the uppermost chamber. Now take heart, men, for we've not yet come to the end of our resources." He motioned for Sir Kenneth to provide the translation for the stable lad and the cook as he turned to Elise who waited on the stairs. Taking her close in his arms, he assured her, "Hilliard has not seen the last of my plans, my pet. We shall take him yet. Have no fear."

Elise passed a trembling hand along his soot-smudged cheek. "I feel no fear when you are near, my lord."

"The time approaches when we must deal Hilliard his just due," Maxim replied. "Take the boy up with you now, and watch for our coming. 'Twill not be long ere we join you."

Gathering her courage, Elise obeyed his directive and encouraged the youth to accompany her. The men took their places and braced themselves for the inevitable invasion of the hall. It was now only a matter of moments away. Dietrich hefted a heavy iron skillet and set himself to guard the stairs, while Justin grasped an axe and waited beside Maxim. Sherbourne, Kenneth, Fitch, and Spence completed the force of stalwart defenders, nocking arrows against their bowstrings a short distance from the portal.

Hilliard's harsh voice carried from outside as he ordered a troop of mounted mercenaries to bring a ramming log forward. Hardly a second later, the destruction of the door commenced. Beneath the force of a fourth blow, the bar splintered, and with the next, it broke in half, letting the panel swing wide. Arrows showered those who plunged through the opening first, crumpling the forward thrust of the attack. Those who followed did not even pause as they leapt over their fallen companions and surged inside to be met with blade, axe, and skillet. Maxim backed away from the portal, finding himself confronted by three of the enemy. He drove the boldest one to his knees with a kick to the groin, then eased the man's pain with his sword. In the next instant he blocked the thrusting attack of another's blade and gallantly stood against the two until one of them heaved a gurgling sigh and sank to the stone floor, clutching the haft of a spear which protruded from his chest. Maxim had no time to lend his gratitude to Sir Kenneth as another handful of men surged inside.

Though many of the enemy fell, Maxim and his companions were forced ever backward toward the stairs. Hilliard stayed at the rear of his men, hurling orders and sharp commands while pushing others back into the fray. When one of his Hansa cohorts caught a stroke from an axe across his belly and fled screaming, the agent coldly ended his flight with a powerful blow from a massive mace that he carried in his right hand. A sweep from a double length of chain which he clutched in his left sent the lifeless form tumbling away. Hilliard made it clear that he would countenance no retreat from this battle.

His act seemed to infuriate Justin, who leapt forward with a cry of pure rage. There was no one to shield Hilliard, and he took the force of Justin's attack with feet braced wide apart. The agent had outfitted himself for battle before entering the keep and barely moved under the impact as the axe careened harmlessly off his chest. A jeering sneer twisted Hilliard's heavy lips as he brushed the young man aside with a thickly padded arm. The spiked iron ball swished forward, intruding into the space rapidly vacated by the nimble youth. Dodging away, Justin bounced off the wall and quickly whirled to avoid another swipe from the murderous mace. As he came fully around, he had his weapon at the ready and did not miss a chance to take a slice at the distended belly. The padded leather doublet split beneath his blow, but alas, the axe met a barrier of steely stays hidden underneath.

Though Justin slashed and hacked with all the venging fervor of his years, his weapon was ever repelled by ball or chain. Hilliard became incensed at the gall of this lad and pressed his own attack with blatant force. When Justin swung with all of his strength at a perceived opening, Hilliard lashed out with the chain, wrapping the links tightly around the handle, just behind the head. He jerked hard, snatching the axe from the other's grasp and pulling him off-balance. Unable to catch himself, Justin stumbled forward, and a gleam of anticipated triumph brightened Hilliard's eyes as he recognized that one's vulnerability. The mace swept forward in vengeance, grazing Justin's shoulder with enough force to send him reeling backward into the stone wall. A cry of pain was wrenched from him, giving evidence to the depth of his injury, but as Hilliard stepped forward to finish his work, he was rudely jostled aside by the sprawling form of a soldier who had fallen victim to the Marquess's blade.

"You spineless coward!" Maxim chidingly called, deliberately distracting the agent from his goal. "When are you going to come forth and fight like a man? You hide behind your men and have not the courage you demand of others."

The heckling forced all thought of Justin from the agent's mind, and no further notice was given to the young man who stumbled toward the stairs holding his injured shoulder. Hilliard had locked his gaze on the one who had in the last months become a constant source of serious vexation for him, and all else ceased to matter. With a low growl the Hansa leader lumbered forward, elbowing his way through the press of soldiers. His grievances against the man could not be assuaged until he pounded him into a lifeless pulp. Desire to savor that revenge swept all caution from his mind.

Maxim leapt adroitly backward to miss the wickedly swinging mace and realized he not only faced Hilliard, but five of his Hansa compatriots. His thrusting, flashing blade protected him as he backed toward the stairs, and he was immensely relieved when Sir Kenneth and Sherbourne set themselves beside him. He felt the back of his boot strike the bottom step and as he lifted his foot upon it, Kenneth grabbed the tall candle stand that resided nearby and swung it around in a wide sweep, knocking noggins together and setting helmets awry with a vengeance, then he seized it by its base and thrust it forward like a ramming log against the stout form of Karr Hilliard. The rotund agent swept several of his men with him as he stumbled backward, and as they writhed in a confused melee on the floor, the castle defenders escaped up the stairs.

Reaching the highest level, the men raced down the hall to join the others in the chambers, which of late had been used by the three bachelors. The door was slammed shut and barred, and it was only then that the men stared at each other in sudden apprehension, for now it seemed that they would become sitting quarry when Hilliard and his troop broke down the door. Though none expressed their fears, each imagined a gruesome end...all save Maxim, who pressed an ear to the door until he could hear the thundering footsteps coming up the stairs. Turning to face the occupants of the room, he pressed a finger across his lips to silence them, then quickly crossed to the secret panel. Sighs of relief were joyfully expelled as he opened the hidden door. The wick of a candle was set aflame, and silently Maxim motioned Kenneth to escort Elise down the stairs. The Hansards were already pounding at the door and hacking at the sturdy planks with an axe, but Maxim took the time to push open the windows and shutters before joining his companions for the simple pleasure of confusing the enemy. Closing and securing the secret panel behind him, he swiftly descended the stairs until he reached the lower door where Kenneth waited with Elise. The knight gestured toward the chamber, and as Maxim pressed an ear to the portal, he could hear someone rummaging in the room. Careful not to make a sound, he opened the panel and saw the broad back of one of the mercenaries bent over a large chest. The intruder riffled through it, tossing the contents hither and yon, then as he draped a leather doublet over his shoulder, he paused and canted his head as if he heard some sound close behind him. Seizing his sword, he whirled to meet the presence he sensed was there, but it was only to meet his death with Maxim's blade piercing his chest.

The hall door was quietly closed and barred for the moment as the small group took account of themselves. All had survived, at least to this point.

A shout sounded from above, and a thunder of feet overhead announced the storming of the door. Hilliard's bellow of frustrated rage gave evidence of their lack of success. More thumping movement and mumbled voices drifted down as the soldiers regrouped for another charge.

"The door should challenge their efforts for a few moments yet," Maxim commented with a laconic smile. " 'Twas rebuilt to withstand the assault of an angry vixen."

His expression grew sad as he crossed to Elise. He took her hands in his and gazed deep into her eyes. "I've no time to explain, my love, but after we reach the courtyard below, you must ride out with Spence and Fitch. Dietrich and the stable boy will go with you while we hold Hilliard and his men at bay. Eddy should be able to carry the both of them, and Nicholas has said he would take the two horses across on the voyage."

"Maxim! What are you saying? I'll not leave you! I cannot leave you!"

Elise would have made further protest, but he pressed his fingers gently against her mouth to still her arguments. He blinked at the sudden wetness in his eyes and leaned down to press his lips to her brow. His mouth found its way to hers, and a long moment passed as he kissed her farewell, then, raising his head, he clasped her close to him, as if he would draw her into himself.

"I cannot go with you now, Elise. Please try and understand. You must sail with Nicholas." The muscles flexed in his cheeks as he fought for control. "I'll come later by way of a different vessel."

Elise clung to him as tears made wet paths down her cheeks. "But how will you get out of Germany if not by way of Nicholas's ship? No other Hansa captain will allow you passage, not when Hilliard has raised such a furor."

Maxim drew back to look down into her tear-streaked face. "Speak no word of it beyond this moment, my love, but an English ship will be coming down the Elbe River to carry us home."

"If that be true"—Elise's pleading eyes searched his face—"then why cannot I come with you?"

" 'Twould be too dangerous, and I want you safely away in case Hilliard wins the day here."

"Oh, Maxim, I cannot leave you!" she wept, flinging her arms about his neck in a desperate attempt to dissuade him. "Please don't make me."

"You must, my love," he whispered against her hair. "If we win the day here, there is still the march to the river to make, and if we're attacked in the open, we'd have no defense. Please go so I need not fear for your safety."

Reluctantly Elise murmured her consent, and Maxim turned to Sir Kenneth who waited beside the door. At his nod the knight carefully lifted the bar and swung open the portal. Thrusting his head out, he searched up and down the corridor, then, with a silent gesture to Maxim, stepped into the corridor. He was followed by Sherbourne who waited just outside the door as the others filed silently out of the chamber. The loud sounds drifting from the floor above masked their descent to the courtyard. There, Kenneth and Sherbourne dashed to the wall where they turned the cannons about, directing the gaping muzzles toward the front portal. The servants scrambled to the stables and, a brief moment later, dragged forth saddled mounts. *Herr* Dietrich climbed a brace of steps near the wall in order to mount Eddy, and the stable lad received the aid of his stout arm and was swept easily behind. Spence came at a run to lead Elise's mount around to her, and Maxim stepped close to hold his wife.

"Promise me you will come to me safe and sound," Elise begged him through her tears.

Maxim held her hard against him. "Guard my words carefully, madam," he murmured into her hair, "for I tell you this only to assure you of my most earnest intent to return to England." He drew away enough to meet her gaze, and as he spoke, he pressed her hands in prayerlike fashion between his palms. "If all goes well, my love, I mean to bring Hilliard back with me."

A shout from the windows high above marked the Hansards' entry into the chamber, and those on the ground looked up to see Hilliard and some of his companions leaning out the windows. There was a flurry of confused questions as the men searched the outer wall for some clue as to how the small group had executed a descent from so lofty a height, but their curiosity remained unappeased. Grinding his teeth, Hilliard followed his soldiers from the room, stepping over the splintered door and stomping his way down the stairs. He was of a mind to think the Englishman and his group had somehow grown wings.

Maxim lifted Elise to the back of the horse and slapped its rump to send the animal flying from the courtyard. Though he felt as if a heavy weight had just descended upon his chest, he ran to the wall to watch the small band of riders race down the lane away from the castle, then he turned to man the small cannon. He had little time to feel the sadness that was waiting to overtake him, for in a moment the remaining force of Hilliard's men came charging through the doorway to be met with twin, wide-sweeping, missile-spraying jolts from the two small cannons. It was a long time later when Hilliard finally raised a knobby pole upon which a white banner had been fastened.

Chapter 26

THE SHIP SEIZED a bone in her teeth as it filled its sails with deep gusts of wind. Though she was a stiffly laden vessel with a full cargo of copper, silver, dried cod, and Hamburg beer in her hold, her stalwart bows sliced through the turbulent gray sea with ease, making good time. Close above her white sails, dark clouds scudded past, chased by strong-winded zephyrs from the north. Now and then a spattering of raindrops slashed down upon the deck and were themselves washed into oblivion by the ocean spray that hurled itself over the prow. Sea gulls soared aloft on widespread wings and cried their strident song as they followed the vessel's progress around the Frisian Islands, then the topsails cracked like guns as the ship came off the last windward tack around the end of the isles. The helmsman caught the spinning wheel and steadied the rudder amidship, while the crew raced through the tops and along the deck to set more sail. The loudly bawled commands of the crew masters created a cacophony of sound that was discernible only to a seaman's trained ear. Slowly the Netherlands fell astern and the waters deepened as the ship headed out into the North Sea. The cries of the sea gulls ceased as the birds gave up their unrewarding vigil and sought food among the inshore shallows.

Elise shivered as the chilling gusts whipped her heavy woolen cloak and invaded the billowing hood to snatch her hair from its sober mooring. She had donned plain, warmly serviceable clothes, preferring to keep her better gowns and fur-lined cloak packed safely away. She had been wise in doing so, for she could feel a fine spray of spindrift upon her face as she stood by the rail and looked out to sea toward the distant horizon. England lay somewhere beyond that vague, grayish murk which blended sea with sky, but she could feel no joy at going home when her heart was still behind her. She had no assurance that Maxim was alive, and when the memory of the raging Hilliard continued to haunt her, she found herself confronted by a vision of her beloved lying dead at the feet of that bovine beast. Had she yielded to her anxieties and not waged a desperate battle to uproot the strong nesting instincts of her fears, they would have settled in her mind to completely rend her sanity. By dint of will and a tenaciously stubborn resolve, she kept reminding herself of her husband's prowess in battle and of his somewhat uncanny ability to turn every trial into a triumph.

Seeking a place beyond the reach of the mist, Elise climbed to the quarterdeck where Nicholas and the helmsman kept wary eyes on the binnacle. She was careful to maintain a discreet distance from the captain, and for once he hardly noticed her as he checked the heading and trimmed his ship. His voice was subdued but confident as he spoke to the helmsman, and with close attention the man followed his directions.

None could fault Nicholas's intelligence or his manners, Elise thought as she shifted her gaze starboard. It was evident that his men respected him, as did she, and though at times he had been somewhat reticent since their departure from Hamburg, for the most part he had been kind and solicitous toward her. She was certainly wealthier for having been acquainted with the man, for he had returned more than triple her investment. The real reward, however, was in knowing a man of such rich character, for he truly enjoyed life to the fullest measure.

He had been kind enough to vacate his cabin for her again, and whenever there was occasion to share the delectable cuisine prepared by *Herr* Dietrich, they exchanged congenial pleasantries and conversations, avoiding any mention of what might have been. There were times when Elise would catch him watching her, as if he shared her fears for Maxim with equal pain. At other times he seemed to struggle with the same restrictions he had placed upon himself during their first voyage together. She belonged to another; he had no intention of intruding or appearing forward, and yet when he had valued her beyond all other women, enough to want her as his wife, there was a tendency, or perhaps even a desire, for a truce or an understanding to be established between them so they might somehow glean a lasting friendship from the ashes of the past.

"Segelschiff! Viertel Steuerbord!" The shout rang out from the lofty heights above, and when Elise looked up, she saw the lookout high in the crow's nest of the mainmast pointing behind them to where a thin slice of land still darkened the horizon. A speck of white seemed to dot it, and though Elise could not understand what he had said, she knew the significance of that small spot of white. It was the sails of another ship!

Nicholas seized the kenning glass from the mate and whirled to face the stern quarter, bringing the spyglass up to his eye. For a long moment he peered through the elongated cylinder, and when he lowered it again, he wore a sharp frown of concern. He shouted brusque orders in rapid German, at which the helmsman quickly nodded, and then strode to the rail for another look through the glass.

"An English ship!" He spoke over his shoulder to Elise. "Sailing from the Netherlands."

"Is she ... one of Drake's ships?" Elise was almost fearful of asking, knowing what a confrontation with Drake would mean for Nicholas. By his own admission he was not as wealthy as Hilliard and losing his ship and cargo would prove a major blow for him.

Nicholas fretted in anxious worry. "That elusive devil! Who knows vhere he is now! He has been busy plundering Spain's vealth ever since Elizabeth gave him leave to sail again. From the Basque ports last summer, to the Cape Verde Islands and the Caribbeans this year, he flits about like a demon possessed. Santiago! Hispaniola! Cartagena! All have fallen beneath his guns! He vill make Philip a pauper yet! And all those who trade vith him! It vould be bitter irony indeed to fall afoul of him!"

"But surely he'll let you go free when 'tis realized you carry an English subject."

"Drake is hungry! He vill not stop to ask questions."

Nicholas stepped away and barked out orders which sent his men leaping into the rigging to set more sail. He keenly felt the need to wring every bit of speed he could from his vessel. Another shout sounded from the masthead, and almost as one, they turned to see another vessel off the starboard bow. The ship had moved within clear detail while attention was focused on the one astern. Even as they stared, a puff of smoke erupted from her bows and drifted downwind. A geyser of water rose several miles off, but the message was clear. Lay to! Nicholas had no choice but to reduce sail and bring her about, for he had not the guns with which to defend her against two opponents.

A short time later the English galleons, with their tall sail-shrouded masts looming large and imposing, came up on either beam of the smaller carrack. The larger of the two drew alongside, and grappling hooks were thrown over the rails to bring the two vessels together. The Hansa captain waited with jaw rigidly set as a boarding party came across.

The commander of the English vessel was a rather tall, handsome man. He introduced himself as Andrew Sinclair and greeted Nicholas almost cheerily, though that one glowered in mute rage at this offense. "Forgive me for delaying you, Captain," Sinclair begged, "but having just left the Netherlands, I was wondering if perhaps your ship is one of those which has been supplying Parma's Spanish troops." At Nicholas's look of outrage, he continued pleasantly, "If you are, I must warn you that I've no other choice but to seize your ship. Lord Leicester would not approve of your conduct and would most certainly take offense with me if I did not effectively discipline you."

Nicholas was not in the mood for such humor. "Yu have obviously taken note that my ship is laden to the maximum draught and, despite the fact that yur suspicion is false, have plans to seize vhat is in her hold on some inane pretext or another. If that be the case, *Kapitan,* then allow me to show yu vhat ve are carrying."

He spoke aside to his mate, and with a sudden grin, that one motioned for another sailor to follow him as he hurried away. As Nicholas and his guests awaited the return of the two, Elise felt the closely perusing eye of the English captain upon her, and when she dared to meet his stare, he readily returned a smile to her coolly questioning gaze.

Nicholas's eyes grew icy-blue as he took note of the Englishman's heightened interest in Elise. He might have yielded her to Maxim's bold claim, but he would be damned before he would allow the likes of this sea-bound roué to think she was there for the ogling.

Clearing his throat, Andrew Sinclair turned his eyes from the unspoken challenge in the maid's eyes and lifted his own aloft to the red flag marked with the white emblem of a tri-towered edifice flying overhead. "You are from Hamburg, Captain?"

Nicholas was mildly surprised at the man's knowledge of Hansa flags. "Yu are most perceptive, *Kapitan.*"

"We've dealt with Hansa vessels before," Sinclair informed him with a mild sneer. "I've learned to recognize their flags. Of particular interest to me are the plain red-and-white flags of Lubeck. They seemed to go in and out of Spanish ports with ease. If you haven't set sail from the Netherlands and you are obviously not going to Spain, just where are you bound, Captain?"

"England," Nicholas acknowledged crisply. "And beyond!"

Despite his attempt to cast his attention elsewhere, Sinclair returned his gaze to Elise. Her beauty had captured his interest so completely, he was hard-pressed to think of leaving the ship without first becoming acquainted with her or, at the very least, learning where she might later be found. "And what of the lady? Is she your wife?"

"She is an English subject returning to her home." Nicholas watched the other man carefully, wondering what mischief would come of his infatuation. "I've been given the pleasure of escorting her there."

"Indeed?" Andrew Sinclair digested the information

eagerly. "I would enjoy being introduced to the lady."

Nicholas debated the consequences of revealing Elise's association with Maxim. In England the sentiments against traitors were no doubt rampant with tales of more assassination plots against the Queen being bandied about, and when one considered this fellow's strong attraction for the lady, it was possible to imagine that Sinclair might seize upon any excuse to take her. Though he sincerely doubted that her father's name would be as well-known as her husband's, Nicholas offered it with emphasis, hoping to dissuade the other's zeal. "This is Elise Radborne, none other than the daughter of Sir Ramsey Radborne."

Sinclair recognized the name immediately. "Can she be the same Elise Radborne who was kidnapped from her uncle's house by the Marquess of Bradbury?"

Nicholas's face darkened, and he clasped his hands behind his back, refusing to gratify the man's curiosity. He had no way of knowing how widespread the reports were of Elise's capture, but it was obvious her abduction had started many tongues a-wagging.

The mate and the sailor returned from below deck, and together they heaved a barrel onto the planks. The English captain drew near to watch as they broke open the tops, and even from where she stood Elise sensed the Hansa sailors were up to some chicanery. She saw the mate grin and wink at Nicholas, and in a moment she understood their humor as the mate dipped a hand into the barrel and drew out a piece of dried cod which he waved tauntingly beneath the nose of the Englishman. That one faced away in obvious repugnance, eliciting the loud guffaws of the Hansa seamen.

"Ve have hogsheads of Hamburg beer, too, *Kapitan,* if you'd care for a draught," Nicholas offered with a chuckle, then nodded to where the pair of horses were closely confined between makeshift timbers. "Ve even carry a pair of nags, as yu can see."

"You may keep your fish, Captain, and your beer," Sinclair replied, disdaining the fact that he had been made sport of. There was, however, a way to wipe away the smirks of the Hansa seamen and perhaps win for himself the company of the uncommonly beautiful Mistress Radborne. "And please, let me not be remiss in thanking you for your hospitality, but I regret to inform you that you are under arrest..."

"Vhat?" Nicholas leapt forward a step to shout the question in the other's face and, in seething agitation, he slashed his hand back and forth as if to negate the other's statement. "Yu have no authority to seize my ship, at least not by any lawful means! I don't care if yu carry a missive directly from yur queen. This is not England! So if 'tis piracy yu have set yurself to, then let it be called that and naught else!"

Andrew smirked with lofty confidence, satisfied that he had turned the tables on the other captain. "You have aboard your ship valuable cargo...an English-woman, known to have been abducted by a traitor to the queen. How she came to be in your possession I cannot even presume to guess, but I've heard that her uncle has pleaded with the Queen to deal firmly with those responsible for her kidnapping. Though the royal sovereign still debates the matter amid the out-cry of the lady's kin, I'd be remiss in my duties if I allowed any opportunity to save Mistress Radborne to slip past unheeded. Therefore, I must insist upon your arrest. I shall put a crew aboard your vessel, and you and your men will be taken prisoner and held in irons aboard my ship until we reach England."

"This is an abomination of all the laws of the sea ...!" Nicholas protested. "I'm taking the lady home! Not kidnapping her!"

"There's not the least touch of truth in your claims!" Elise avowed, incensed that Andrew Sinclair could use her presence as an excuse to arrest Nicholas. "I bade Captain Von Reijn to take me home. Should he now be punished because he agreed?"

"If that be the case, madam, then I shall be happy to escort you to my ship, and Captain Von Reijn may have leave to go his way."

"Damnation!" Nicholas roared. *"I vill not allow it! I vould sooner be arrested than let her go vith the likes of yu!"*

"Nicholas, please." Elise attempted to soothe his rage. " 'Tis but a simple thing..."

"Yu have been placed in my charge, Elise, and I vill not see yu seized for my comfort." He drew her away and lowered his voice to a murmur as he spoke with firm conviction. "I failed yu once. It vould cause great conflict in my heart and mind to do so again."

"You needn't fret so about me, Nicholas. I can take care of myself..."

He shook his head in sharp disagreement. "Yu could not in the *kontor*; yu cannot here. If Captain Sinclair takes it in mind that he vants yu, yu cannot stop him! Who can judge if he is a gentleman in so few moments?"

"Spence and Fitch would go with me..."

The Hansa captain snorted in derision as he directed her gaze toward the two who had hunkered down near Eddy's small stall. Their pallor was tinged with a greenish hue, and beneath sagging lids their eyes were dull and doleful. Neither looked capable of handling themselves, much less the Englishman. If Nicholas ventured a guess, he would say both were presently battling an unsteady gorge. "The responsibility of yur safety was given me, Elise, and I cannot entrust it to another. As to that pair, ere ve veighed anchor both vere hanging their heads over the rail."

Nicholas's features hardened as he stepped back to the Englishman, and when he spoke, his voice held a caustic sneer. "Since England is my destination in any case, *Kapitan* Sinclair, I've no objection being escorted there by yu, but if yu intend to imprison me or my men ere ve arrive... or take the Lady Elise aboard yur ship, I must refuse yur hospitality... in vhatever fashion may become necessary." Sinclair opened his mouth and would have made protest, but Nicholas held up a hand to halt his threats. "Consider that yu have the ships to outdistance me and the guns to halt me should I be so foolish as to attempt an escape. 'Tis a simple thing to be escorted to England; 'tis not cheap to rebuild a splintered ship."

"Your point is well taken," Captain Sinclair conceded, recognizing the stubbornness of the Hansa captain. A confrontation would likely result in a bloody conflict, which, with the Englishwoman to bear witness, would likely result in a situation wherein he could be held to account. It seemed his course had been drawn for him, for he could neither blow the Hansa ship out of the water nor dismiss his threats against the captain without appearing the fool. "And your parole is accepted. I will lie off your windward beam with a broadside ready until we reach the Thames, then I will drop astern and follow after."

Stepping back, he gave Nicholas a crisp nod and, facing Elise, swept her a bow. "Until we meet again, Mistress Radborne."

With arms set akimbo and feet braced apart Nicholas observed the departure of the boarding party. He waited until the grappling hooks were dislodged and tossed across to the other vessel, then he strode the deck, issuing brusque orders to his men until they were underway again. He knew what lay in store for them in England, but it had become a matter of pride now. He would show this upstart Englishman that he could not casually issue threats of arrest without having them and his authority tested.

Chapter 27

*L*ONDON WAS INDEED a place of unrest. If not before, then surely after the Hansa captain and his men were arrested and carted away to Newgate gaol. And if not all of it, then surely the small portion at the quay where Elise set Andrew Sinclair back upon his heels. She gave him a fine sampling of her disfavor, venting her frustration at the outrageous injustice done in the name of protection. "You're not the keeper of my person and I decry any claims you make to that effect!" She only paused to take a breath as she further lambasted the astonished man. "Rather, you've portrayed yourself as a despoiler of honorable men! And I'll not rest until Captain Von Reijn and his men have been released from the gaol with your apologies! Believe me! 'Tis my most fervent intent to go directly to the Queen to see this affront put aright. And if I've naught but a final breath to speak it with, I shall most certainly seek that end!"

In a vixenish temper Elise snatched her arm away as Sinclair tried to escort her to a waiting barge and told him sharply, "I'll have naught from you but the release of Captain Von Reijn and his men! So leave me be!"

Lacking an adequate argument to soften the lady's anger, Sinclair gave her over to the boatman's care and waited in confused silence as Spence discreetly hired a seaman to take Eddy and the mare on to the stable at Bradbury while Fitch loaded the lady's possessions aboard. The pair took their places well aft of the indignant woman, daring nothing more than a glance or two at the suffering man. They both were given to fretting over the lengths a man would go to take an innocent man into custody and what such a one might do if he came across the Marquess. They were in agreement that it was good fortune indeed that Lord Seymour had not made the crossing with them, for there was no doubt in their minds that he would have been arrested and taken to the Tower posthaste.

It was some time later when the sailing barge halted at the river stairs belonging to the grounds and manor house of Sir Ramsey Radborne. The baggage was unloaded, the waterman paid, and the chests carried to the front stoop. Captain Sinclair had managed to inform Elise that her uncle was presently residing in the manor with his family. She accepted the news with stoic demeanor, but promised herself that on behalf of her husband, she would present her arguments to the Queen until Maxim was restored to honor and to the place he loved.

A feeling of anxiety plagued Elise as she approached the manse from which she had once fled in fear. Her last memories of her imprisonment blighted the happier times when she had lived within the security of her father's presence. Had circumstances been such that she could have foregone seeking an audience with Elizabeth, she would have traveled on to Bradbury Hall without stopping at the manse. Despite the protection Spence and Fitch provided with their presence, she was cautious about giving Cassandra any opportunity to seize her again.

The spacious hall was well-lighted, attesting to the

occupancy of the house. A low murmur of voices came from the great chamber, and for a brief moment Elise thought she detected the mangled speech of her uncle amid the chatter, but the words were too faint and blurred to be heard distinctly.

"Mercy! 'Tis the mistress!" The excited cry came from an elderly maid at the top of the stairs and did much to herald the newcomer's presence. "She's come home!"

Servants rushed from different parts of the manse until they neared the hall wherein she stood, then they came to stumbling, hesitant halts. From doorways, connecting halls, and behind large furnishings they watched her shyly, almost fearfully. There were more than a few who seemed distressed at her presence, and some who shook their heads in worry. None dared approach her, and much bemused by their reticence, Elise slowly crossed the hall, her hesitant steps echoing in the silence that now filled the place. The conversation had ceased in the great chamber, and now from all around her she was aware of being carefully observed. Finally, it was the tiny housekeeper, Clara, who hobbled forward to greet her.

In some relief Elise held out her arms to greet the ancient, remembering only too well that it was this small, thin woman who had repeatedly risked life and limb to help her during Cassandra's reign of terror. "Have I grown horns and a spiny tail of late?" Elise questioned in amazement. "What is troubling everyone?"

" 'Tis yer Aunt Cassandra," Clara answered in a hushed whisper. "She's livin' here wit' yer uncle now ... as his wife."

In wide astonishment Elise drew away to stare down into the small, wrinkled face of the old servant, hoping that she had misunderstood her. Surely even

Edward Stamford would not be so foolish as to take Cassandra to wife. "Tell me 'tis not true, Clara."

" 'Ere be no doubt, mistress," the diminutive house-keeper assured her. "Yer Uncle Edward an' yer aunt were wed shortly after ye were snatched away. The squire came here ta stay whilst he visited the Queen ta accuse the Marquess Bradbury o' yer capture an' ta press for his capture. Cassandra was probably a-eyein' the place waitin' for ye. She come up ta visit the squire, an' after settin' her eye on his riches, she must o' took it in her head ta stay on 'cause it weren't long 'fore they wed."

Perhaps more than anyone else, Elise was aware of the many faces of Cassandra. It was no great feat for the woman to ply her charms upon an aging old man. She was still beautiful enough to intrigue men of younger years, and a lonely widower would not have much of a chance to resist her.

Elise stiffened as she heard a soft, chiding chuckle behind her, and she turned to find the slender, shapely figure of her aunt silhouetted within the arched door-way of the great chamber. In the shadows behind her, Elise could see the jeering faces of her sons, among them the glaring dark eyes of Forsworth Radborne.

"My goodness, if it isn't our little Elise," Cassandra observed with smiling sarcasm, making no attempt to approach her niece. "Have you come back to pay us a visit?"

Finding herself face to face with her adversaries, Elise could not draw a deep breath into her lungs. It was as if someone had struck her solidly across the chest. All the frightening memories of yesteryear came back to assail her, and she was atremble with fear at the thought that it would all begin again.

Cassandra smirked in haughty pleasure, sensing her power over the girl as well as the hirelings. It was evident the girl lacked a strong defense, for the timidity of the Bradbury servants was typical of their earlier performance. Then they had fled in fear before her own strong display of authority. Considering their present lack of response to Elise's return, she had reason to believe they would crumble again beneath the heavy-handed demands she and her sons would exact from them. It would only be a matter of time before she would wrest the location of the treasure from the girl and establish the properties of Ramsey Radborne as their own.

Elise collected her scattered wits and formed a firm resolve to rout this well-attired caperdudgeon from her home as quickly as possible. Her swift departure would be for the good of all concerned.

Facing Spence and Fitch, who had not yet caught the gist of what was happening, she directed them to remain at her side, and then sent Clara off to tell the cook to prepare a meal for the three of them. While Cassandra looked on with amused condescension, she bade a pair of stout-armed servants to carry her chests upstairs to her chambers.

"But Mr. Forsworth is there," a young maid hurriedly informed her, as if the news would halter the command.

Elise raised a querying brow at the young beauty, sensing the maid had more than one reason to be knowledgeable about where Forsworth had bedded himself. If she knew her cousin at all, she would be inclined to think he was making use of the girl in a very sensual sense. "Then by all means," she instructed dryly, "strip the bed and pack up his possessions."

"But . . . but . . . where shall I take them?" The maid stumbled in bemusement and glanced toward Forsworth, seeking an escape from the dilemma she now found herself in. Having been only recently hired to attend the needs of the Mistress Cassandra, she was not acquainted with the extent of this newcomer's authority.

Elise's growing impatience with the unwise girl was detectable in her tight and humorless smile. "For now, just get them out of my chambers. We'll discuss where he'll be going very shortly."

Cassandra laughingly scoffed, "And who are you to advise where my son will or will not go? 'Tis his decision to make, not yours."

Elise briefly met the woman's challenging stare and answered her in a level tone. "Though you may deny my authority here, Cassandra, I'm still the only mistress of this house, and my orders will be obeyed forthwith. I need not seek your approval for anything I do here. Is that clear?" She disdained her aunt's smug smile and, with renewed irritation, turned upon the girl who waited in slack-jawed confusion. She saw a need to break through that one's daze and sharpened her tone. "Now go and do what I told you! And be quick about it!"

The maid dared no further question or delay, but bobbed a quick curtsey and fled, prompting the other servants to follow in hasty retreat. They saw an approaching confrontation between the mistress and her aunt, and they wanted to be well out of range when it erupted.

Coolly Elise faced Cassandra again, expecting some argument, but the woman and her sons stepped back to allow Edward to shuffle through the doorway. In the next moment Elise found herself stricken with shock. She could hardly believe the painfully thin, straggly-haired old man who now approached her was the same stout and blustering individual she had known all of her life. She was totally shocked to see how badly he had wasted away in her absence.

"Uncle Edward?" she inquired, seeking some affirmation that it was truly him. A small nod assured her, and she reached out to clutch his bony hand between both of hers. Further words seemed impossible as she stared into his face. Gone were the rosy, round cheeks and plump features of years past. The lackluster eyes were hollowed by the skeletal gauntness of his face, and were underscored with deep circles of a darkly translucent bluish hue. The darkness of them cast a sharp contrast to his pasty-white skin.

"Elise, me girl . . ." He made a brave attempt to smile, but the effort conveyed a frailness that was frightening. " 'Tis happy I am ta see ye back. Arabella needs yer company. She be a widow now . . ."

His statement stunned Elise anew, and with great compassion she gently embraced her uncle who choked back a sob at the demonstration of her affection. It was rare nowadays that he was given even a small outpouring of kindness, and he was much humbled by it.

"I'm so very sorry, Uncle Edward," Elise whispered. "I had not heard. Poor Arabella . . . she must be grieving sorely."

Drawing in a breath to steady his emotions, Edward tried to compose himself as he related the incident. "Reland was found floatin' in the river 'bout a month ago. He'd been out ridin', ye see. 'Tis me guess his horse spooked an' tossed him off. He must've hit his head 'fore he fell into the water an' drowned ere he could come ta his senses."

"Where is Arabella now?" Elise asked, raising her gaze to search the hall. "I would see her."

"She's gone to see some countess friend of hers," Cassandra answered from the doorway. "She won't be coming back until much later. The two of them are as thick as twins, but they don't do much though, just gossip."

Edward's face contorted suddenly as a spasm of pain seized him, and he clutched his belly as a dapple of sweat popped from his pores. Elise took his arm to assist him to a chair, but he shook his head, denying her help, and after a moment the wrenching agony eased. Finally, with difficulty, he straightened himself. "I'll be goin' upstairs ta bed now. I've not been a bit well lately, an' I'm so dreadfully tired."

"Uncle...I must ask you..." Elise delayed him a moment, and he waited for her to speak with a dulled gaze. She was almost fearful of asking, for he might confirm her suspicions and then the horrors of the past would be brought to the surface like a dead corpse uprooted from a grave. It was true enough that Cassandra had abused her, but there were other stories from her childhood that made her captivity seem almost gentle in comparison. Heretofore, she had pushed the tales to the back of her mind, not daring to let herself even think of them. "What has done you ill? When last I saw you, you were hale and hearty. What do the physicians say?"

"Humph!" Edward snorted in weak derision. "They scratch their noggins tryin' ta figger it out. The tearin' pain in me gut...it come upon me only a few weeks after you were taken. Me sweet Cassandra, she's been tendin' me ever since I became ill. The physicians gave me a nasty draught to take, an' me sweet wife assures me 'twill do me good...but I grow weaker..." He shuffled away, stoop-shouldered and badly shriveled.

"Poor child, it must be a terrible shock for you to see how Edward has wasted away," Cassandra commented, finally sauntering forward. She reached out to pat Elise's cheek, but her niece drew away in sharp distaste. The elder only smiled as she continued in overstated concern. "We've all been worried about him." She tossed a glance over her shoulder to receive the support of her brood. "We've tried our best to help him."

"We've done our very best," Forsworth agreed with a sly grin as he leaned a shoulder against the doorjamb of the great chamber. "None could fault us."

Cassandra shrugged indolently. " 'Tis unlikely he'll live out the year."

"I'm sure you've made preparations in advance of his demise," Elise retorted.

A smug smile traced the woman's lips. "Why, of course. Edward signed a marriage settlement with me the day we were wed. He agreed to pay all my debts upon the date of the contract, and, upon his death, to leave me his entire fortune and properties. I shall be quite a wealthy woman should he be taken, poor man."

Elise's own smile displayed her disapproval. "You will no doubt heartily encourage and cheer on that occasion."

" 'Twill tear me apart," lamented the woman, feigning a sorrowful demeanor.

"I'm sure," Elise jeered.

Cassandra tilted her head sideways as she contemplated her niece. "Why, dear Elise, I believe you've actually changed. I could even allow that you've grown more beautiful. Or is it that you've just matured."

"Hopefully I've grown wiser to your ways, Cassandra," Elise answered smoothly.

The woman continued as if she had not heard the remark. "There were such wild rumors about that rascally knave Seymour, 'twould probably be far-fetched to hope he did you no ill. Indeed, if his reputation is to be trusted, I'd be tempted to believe he made use of your captivity." Cassandra smiled as she saw the color rising to the other's cheeks and dug her claws in deeper. "A virile man like that with a young maid . . . Why, 'tis impossible to think that nothing happened."

Elise recovered her aplomb adroitly and gave quick riposte. "I wasn't aware that you moved in the same circles with Lord Seymour and could ascertain what he's really like. From what I've heard of him, he has always been very particular about his associates and friends, never acquainting himself with thieves and murderers."

"Humph! The man should've been hanged long ago for his offenses," Cassandra retorted, and smiled with undiminished confidence. "I'm sure the Queen will place a reward upon his head. Rest assured, my dear, he will hang."

"I welcome none of your assurances, Cassandra," Elise answered with a trace of a smile. "They're an offense to me."

The elder spread her hands in a guise of innocence. "I was just commenting on the Marquess," she excused herself. "Men like that deserve no compassion."

"I was treated with immeasurable care while under Lord Seymour's protection." Elise paced the length of the hall in thoughtful mood, and then faced her adversary with a meaningful stare. "However, I hark to a time in this very same house when I had good cause to fear for my life."

"Really, Elise, you should discipline your servants more severely," Cassandra admonished. "Their continued bungling can frighten anyone to death."

Elise had learned long ago the futility of arguing with the woman. Cassandra had the talent for turning every word to her benefit, and whatever her offenses, she would carelessly shrug them off and toss the blame elsewhere without feeling any remorse for wrongdoing. Changing her manner, she turned aside to Fitch and Spence and spoke in a voice clear enough for her aunt to understand. "Arm yourself with whatever weapon you may judge worthy and keep watch over my person at all times while this woman"—she paused effectively to mark the presence of Forsworth and his brothers, boldly adding—"and her kin are in *my* house."

"*Your* house?" Cassandra hooted in self-sustained confidence. "My dear Elise, must I remind you? You are naught but a mere maid and cannot inherit your father's estate without a grant from the Queen. There was no such settlement entitling you to his properties. Therefore, my sons are the only rightful heirs of any holdings of the Radbornes. They have full claim to everything you see and will surely take it as their own. Truly, my dear, as far as I can see, you are naught but a pauper . . . without home or possessions to claim."

Elise's lips lifted in a vague smile, but no warmth softened her eyes as she dug in the purse that hung from her belt. Producing her father's ring, she held it forth for Cassandra to see it clearly. "Do you recognize this?" She waited until the woman nodded hesitantly and then began a game that she was sure would reveal just what her aunt knew about her father's abduction. "Then you must remember that my father was never seen without it?" Again a slight inclination of the fair head prompted Elise to continue. "I offer this ring as evidence that I have knowledge of his whereabouts.

"My father is *alive!*" she declared emphatically and saw a look of consternation cross the beautiful, but aging, face of her aunt. The wary, confused expression gave evidence of Cassandra's innocence, at least in this matter of kidnapping. "And you can rest assured that he will not abide this appropriation of his properties by either you or your sons. Therefore, I'd suggest that you find other quarters to which you and your kin can hie to . . . as soon as possible."

"This is some trick of hers!" Forsworth declared, striding forward to glare at Elise. He had not forgiven her for the clubbing she had once given him, nor had he salved the wounds of his egotistical pride. "She is lying! Otherwise, Uncle Ramsey would be here with her!"

Elise challenged him with a barely tolerant smile. "You always were a bit slow-witted, Forsworth. Why do you not wait for my father to arrive? I'm sure he will give you the thrashing you deserve."

His dark eyes snapped with sparks of rage. "You lying slut! You go off to some hinterland and spread yourself for the pleasure of a traitor." He ignored the warning signs of ire chilling the blue eyes and pressed on like a raving fool. "You always wanted a man with a title. Now you've outdone yourself. What ho! A traitorous lord of the realm. A marquess, no less!" His sneer was filled with contempt. "By now, you're probably carrying his bastard whelp!"

The slap resounded in the hall, and for a brief moment Forsworth saw only a blurred haze before his eyes. Shaking his head, he cleared his stunned senses and, in a raging temper, hauled back an arm as he advanced upon the girl. Of a sudden he found himself nose to nose with Spence, who had imposed his bulk between the two of them.

"Ye'll not touch her." The man calmly denied the possibility. "Else ye'll regret it."

"You dare threaten me!" Forsworth roared, incensed that a common servant would dare interfere. *"Get out of my way!"*

Spence shook his head. He had been given orders

by Lord Seymour to see to the care of his lady, and that was what he intended till his last breath be drawn. "Me master said though it meant me life I was ta keep the mistress safe. An' ye'll not harm her whilst I'm at her side."

"Who has set you to such foolishness?" Forsworth demanded, backing away a step as Spence advanced a like measure. The taller man thumped his chest, causing him to stumble back even further, and in the face of such obstinate defiance, Forsworth lost some of his show of bravado. "Who would set a commoner against a lord?"

"Lord? Ha!" Elise scoffed, stepping forward again to face her cousin. She was unable to resist calling him down for his self-exaggerated importance. "If you're a lord, then I'm the Queen's cousin!"

"You . . . !" Forsworth snarled, and jabbed a finger at her as he threatened, "You will get what you deserve!"

"Oh, you're so brave with women!" she mimed, copying Cassandra's overly sweet tone, but her sneer belied the compliment. Elise saw the dark eyes narrow and responded to their piercing glare with an unleashed fury of her own. "Well, I, for one, will have no more of your abuse! Do you hear? No more torture! No more starving! No more beatings! This is my father's house, and I want you out of it! *Now!*"

Again Forsworth snatched back his fist and tried to deliver it full into her face, but much to his astonishment, he found his wrist seized by a man whose strength far exceeded his. It was not enough that he was so rudely confronted by a servant, but a step behind the tall one, the fat one pressed forward to make his presence felt.

"Me mistress says ye're ta go now, so ye'd best be on yer way," Spence instructed the arrogant scamp.

He raised his gaze as Forsworth's brothers came scurrying across the hall and immediately accepted the pistol Fitch shoved toward him. That one had had the presence of mind before leaving the ship to hide two such weapons beneath his coat... just in case there was trouble. It came sooner than they had expected. Spence deemed it a most appropriate time to make use of whatever help was at hand to dissuade the two, and since a pistol was most effective in deciding the outcome of this argument, he brought up the sights to mark the three brothers. "I'll make a hole in the first one o' ye what takes a step forward," he warned them gruffly. "An' I've little care who it be."

Cassandra tried to approach the pair, but Fitch was having no more of her than her sons. The bore of his pistol came around to face her. "Kindly keep yer distance, milady," he bade pleasantly. "I'd hate ta bloody me mistress's carpets."

"This is an outrage!" Cassandra strangled out in furious tones. She whirled around to face Elise. "I'm your aunt! Will you let these men threaten me?"

A bland smile touched the lovely mouth. "I seem to remember a time when you gave your sons leave to torment me. You're no blood kin to me, and if you were, I would disavow any knowledge of it. I give these men authority to do what they must to protect me from the likes of you and your sons. I've no ken how you seduced my uncle into marrying you, but 'tis obvious his health is now in a serious state... and since you make no attempt to hide your purpose, I can only believe the worst. Long ago, when I was young, I overheard the servants whispering about some strange happenings. One woman, well in her years and considered daft, rambled on incessantly about seeing you use poison on my mother and then on your husband." Elise saw her aunt start in surprise and a look of fear take hold of her features. "Now it seems that Edward is suffering sorely from your attentions. For what you've done, I'll see you taken before the magistrates of this land and tried for murder."

Cassandra drew herself up with shaky pride. "I'll not stay in this house a moment longer and be accused of such horrible deeds! 'Tis an offense I'll not stand."

"Aye! You'd best run!" Elise taunted, experiencing some relief at the idea. "Run for your life, for I will set the hounds on your heels, and as they take the scent of blood from a wounded hind and drive her to ground, so you will be cornered and brought down like a beast of the wild. Go! Get out of here!"

In a stunned daze Cassandra stumbled around and, with a weak jerk of her head, bade her sons make haste to follow. She had lost the haughtiness of the earlier moments and waxed eager to flee this venging, threatening minx who had gained from some source an unshakable resolve and now was proving a fierce and dangerous foe.

There was a fuss and furor as the Radborne family threw their belongings into chests and left the premises by whatever means available. In their absence the house grew still, as if it had taken a deep breath and expelled an invasive evil from its nooks and crannies. The servants wandered back to properly greet their mistress and in a spirit of relief hurried to prepare her chambers and unpack her belongings.

Exhausted beyond measure and with her emotions well spent, Elise could not find the energy to go to the hall and eat. She made her way to her chambers, where she slumped wearily upon the bed. Though Clara brought her a tray of food and helped her undress, she found no more than a few murmured words to speak ere she heaved a sigh and slipped into the comfort of the bed. The candles were snuffed, and for a time she watched the firelight from the hearth flicker across the ceiling, then her eyelids drooped as she drifted through a vague awareness. Dreams of Maxim invaded her slumber and cradled her with soothing comfort.

It was much later, sometime during the early hours of morning, when Elise came slowly awake again. For a time she lay listening, wondering what had intruded into her sleep, but nothing stirred, and all was silent and still within the manor. Her curiosity was little appeased, for she could find no cause for having been awakened.

Slipping on her dressing gown, Elise left her chambers and wandered down the hall to the rooms which Arabella had chosen for herself. A light rap on the door brought no response, and Elise entered, anxious to see if her cousin had returned and was just asleep. Shafts of moonlight streamed in through the lace panels draped over the windows, illumining a floor strewn with a veritable trail of discarded clothes. A fine satin gown lay near the gallery door, followed by petticoats and farthingale a short space away. Drawers of white fustian and stockings of silk were near the bed. The covers of that piece were drawn back and badly mussed, and each of the two pillows bore an impression, rousing Elise to embrace a strong suspicion that whoever had occupied the bed had not been entirely alone.

A prickling remembrance swept over Elise, and she quelled a feeling of apprehension as she faced the gloomy room. Though it was a different house and many months later, she was impressed by the similarities of that moment from her past. Once before she had gone to Arabella's room, expecting to find her cousin, and she had not been there. This time no culprits sprang from the shadows to seize her, yet there was something hauntingly reminiscent about her cousin's absence, except now the rumpled bed hinted of a possible visitor.

Bemused, Elise wandered back to her bedchamber and was about to doff her robe when a soft whinny made her pause. She fought a rush of apprehension as she ran to the gallery door. It would not be unlike Forsworth and his brothers to come back and do harm to those in the house. Carefully she pushed open the portal and slipped out onto the veranda. Keeping to the shadows, she moved silently along the gallery until the moon came out from behind a cloud, then she halted with her breath frozen in her throat. There, in the courtyard below, cast in a soft lunar glow, stood Arabella wearing naught but a light robe of thin transparency. Seated on a horse beside her was a fully garbed man. The hood of his cloak hid his features and draped his shoulders. As Elise watched, the shadowy form leaned down to meet the reaching embrace of the woman, and for a long moment the couple kissed. When the man finally straightened, he swept the hem of his cloak upward across his chest and braced a fist on his thigh, causing a sickening dread to invade Elise's chest. The man's movements reminded her only too well of the flamboyant mannerisms of Forsworth Radborne. Helplessly she watched as the man reached down a hand to bestow a soft caress along Arabella's cheek, then he nudged the steed with his heels and was gone with a clatter of hooves.

Cautiously Elise pressed back into the enveloping darkness as Arabella turned and approached the stairs. Fearful of moving lest her presence be discovered, Elise held her place, hardly daring to breathe as her cousin ascended the stairs. Only when the chamber door had been closed behind Arabella did Elise deem it safe to release a deep sigh of relief.

Elise's amazement found no end when Arabella came down to break the fast the next morning and portrayed herself as a grieving widow. Elise would not have denied the fact that her cousin looked the part, for the gray eyes were red, rimmed with dark circles, and her cheeks pale and drawn. Still, after witnessing the scene in the courtyard, Elise could only wonder why Arabella would even make such a pretense. She was much bemused when the woman fell upon her shoulder, and there she sobbed and lamented the loss of Reland.

"Did I not tell you that I was cursed?" Arabella gulped through her tears. "I tell you I'm beset by woe." She was quickly overtaken by a spasm of uncontrollable weeping.

Bemused, Elise patted the woman's back, not knowing how to react. "I understand Reland was out riding," she murmured quietly. "Was he alone?"

Arabella sniffed and drew back to dab a handkerchief to her slim nose. "We had gone out riding together, but he raced off, as he was wont to do, and I was left to find my own way home."

"Where did this happen?"

"Near Bradbury," the woman choked.

"A month ago?"

Arabella nodded hesitantly and pressed a pale hand over her bosom as her face threatened to crumple again. Elise's attention was drawn almost hypnotically to the necklace she was wearing, for she could not mistake it. Noticing where her gaze was directed, Arabella sniffed as she doffed the bejeweled piece. "It reminded me so much of you, Elise, I had to wear it." She laid it about the younger cousin's neck as she continued to sniff and cry. "When I returned to my chambers the night of my wedding, I found the strands broken and the pearls scattered across the floor. I nearly died when I realized you'd been abducted. I didn't know if you were alive or dead, so I had the necklace repaired, and I've worn it as a remembrance of you ever since."

"Thank you for having it repaired."

The woman dissolved into tears again, and her weeping continued on to such length, Elise despaired of being able to consume the morning fare without having it sour her stomach. The lamentations were beginning to wear heavily on her, and she longed to be alone again where she could calm herself.

Arabella wiped away the wetness that flowed down her cheeks and assumed a gallantly suffering mien as she eyed the younger woman surreptitiously. "How horrible it must have been for you. Taken by force like that. Everyone of course is wondering what happened."

"Actually, it was all rather wonderful . . . and quite romantic," Elise assured her with a poignant smile lifting the corners of her lips.

Arabella suffered a sharp pang as she noticed the distant look in the blue eyes. It seemed the girl was yearning for a lost love. "I've been wondering just who it was Maxim's men were after . . . and since you were taken from my rooms, I can only believe they made a mistake when they took you. Is that true?"

Elise was aware the woman waited for her answer with an eagerness that belied her deep grief, and with a small nod, she gave the reply that was expected. "His men were responsible for the mistake."

"I knew it, of course. Maxim was always so desperately in love with me, I did not doubt that he came back to fetch me. I suppose he was terribly disappointed when he found out that a mere girl had been taken instead of his own truly beloved." Arabella heaved a sigh as if sharing his imagined hurt. "Knowing him as well as I do, I think he was probably enraged."

Unable to deny the woman's statements, Elise averted her face to hide a hurt she could not confess. Perhaps she was too sensitive to the truth, but she was almost persuaded by the enthusiasm Arabella portrayed that the woman derived some bolstering of ego from the idea that it was she whom Maxim had set out to capture.

"No doubt Maxim has plans to return to make amends to me." The gray eyes traced the delicate, downcast profile of the other. "Did he mention when he would be coming back?"

"Maxim has been condemned a traitor," Elise reminded her cousin. "If he returns, he still has to face the threat of his execution unless the Queen pardons him."

"And if such a thing happens," Arabella murmured with a smile of anticipation, "I'll accept his offer of marriage."

Elise opened her mouth to reply, intending to tell all, but she slowly closed it again as she found herself assailed by uncertainty. Her bruised pride refused to lay claim to Maxim without first being assured that it was what he wanted. Once he returned to England and saw Arabella again, perhaps he might be reminded of his love for her and have cause to resent the vows he had made in Lübeck.

"If Maxim is alive, 'tis his plan to return to England," Elise informed the woman in a small voice.

Arabella pressed a trembling hand to her throat. "Is he in danger?"

"When has he not been in danger?" Elise countered.

"Tell me he is safe!" Arabella demanded in a breathless whisper. "He must be safe!"

Elise smiled sadly. "I cannot assure you of anything, Arabella, least of all his safety."

Chapter 28

WHITEHALL PALACE was a formidable structure with its thousand or so rooms, but the massive gardens, orchards, tennis courts, and tiltyard built during the reign of the late king were equally resplendent amid the color of the budding spring blossoms. Elise allowed herself a moment to enjoy the heady fragrance of the flowers as she climbed the stairs from the river, but it was not a day when she could savor anything for too long. Her audience with the Queen was only moments away, and though she struggled to attain a mood of tranquillity, the turmoil roiling within her had naught to do with contentment and peace. She had framed her words a thousand or more times in her mind, for she feared the moments ahead would see her spilling them in reckless disorder from her tongue.

She had taken some care to dress, for it was secretly rumored that Elizabeth loathed any woman who sported better finery than she. Thus she had donned a plain black velvet gown with a white lace ruff and allowed her only adornment to be the strands of pearls with their ruby-encrusted clasp. A pert attifet was worn over her carefully dressed hair, giving her a stylish, but somber, mien.

Nearly a week had passed since she had first requested an audience with the royal sovereign, and she was in a state of anxious fretting, wondering where Maxim was, while at the same time far too aware of where Nicholas was being kept.

She was escorted down long hallways, through arched doorways nearly twice as tall as she, and finally into an antechamber where she was to await her summons to the Queen's private chambers. Lord Burghley, Elizabeth's principal minister, came to inquire as to the nature of her visit, and Elise, hardly able to subdue the quiver in her voice, stated her cause. Satisfied with her answer, the man left her, and a short time later a lady-in-waiting came to fetch her. Elise composed herself as she was ushered into the presence of the sovereign monarch. She sank into a deep curtsey as the attendants were excused with a regal gesture, all except for the ancient Blanche Parry whose loyal service to the noble person of the Queen had begun when Elizabeth was but a babe.

"Come, stand yourself up so I can look at you," Elizabeth bade with authoritative dispensation.

In gracious compliance Elise straightened and submitted herself to the close scrutiny of the dark, grayish-black eyes, while permitting herself a like assessment. The Queen sat in regal splendor in a large, ornately carved chair close to the windows where the diamond-tipped pearl teardrops and precious jewels that adorned her flame-red wig twinkled with reflected light. The brightness of the hairpiece struck a sharp contrast to the startling whiteness of her skin. The forehead was of a woman two score, ten and two years of age, but it was high and proud, though nearly plucked void of brows. The nose was long and aquiline with little indentation across the bridge, and the gray-black eyes were keenly perceptive.

"You are Sir Ramsey Radborne's daughter," Elizabeth finally said and smiled pleasantly, putting the younger woman more at ease.

"I am Elise Madselin Radborne, your majesty, only child of Sir Ramsey."

"You are no doubt wondering why I've summoned you into my private chambers..." Elizabeth paused briefly to await a polite response and, when gratified, explained, "You've become somewhat of a curiosity among my councillors and courtiers. They're ever chittering about this one or that one, and on occasion, I like to indulge myself by keeping them uninformed while I'm made privy to the facts. 'Tis rumored you were kidnapped by Maxim Seymour, the Marquess of Bradbury, taken to Hamburg, and held as his hostage." Her long, tapering fingers, affixed with many rings, drummed on the elaborately carved arms of her chair, demonstrating her annoyance over the affair. "That rogue. I shall be enchanted to hear him talk his way out of this."

Elise wisely held her silence on the matter of their marriage, having heard many a tale about the Queen's venging reprisals against those among her nobility who had dared marry without her consent. Had Elizabeth not sent the Lady Katherine Grey Seymour to the tower for marrying without her permission and allowed the young mother to die in want of a pardon? Though the Queen had condemned Maxim to death, Elise still hoped for some leniency, some spark of regret that would move the woman to retract her order. It would be foolish indeed to jeopardize that hope by revealing news of their marriage. And if Maxim decided he loved Arabella more than she, a quiet annulment could be achieved better if the Queen had no knowledge of the marriage.

"Actually, your majesty, my abduction was a mistake unwittingly carried out by Lord Seymour's servants."

The slender hand slapped the wooden arm as derisive laughter filled the chamber. "And would you have me believe that to be true? You're no doubt smitten with the man if you seek to excuse his crimes."

"Lord Seymour is a handsome man. Any woman would be attracted to him," Elise confessed, and the Queen calmed and nodded in agreement, appreciating her honesty. "Nevertheless, what I say can be verified by my uncle, Edward Stamford. He was there in the hall the night Lord Seymour came to taunt him about stealing his properties from him with a lie."

"I've heard the Marquess's protests," Elizabeth acknowledged, unmoved by her guest's comments. "As yet, I've seen no proof of his innocence, but I have oft been reminded of his foul deeds by Edward Stamford."

"Edward has gained much by accusing him, and at this moment, your majesty, I cannot say whether Lord Seymour is alive or dead. Therefore I don't know if he's able to come to you with proof of his innocence, but I, for one, am certain he is guiltless."

The Queen sighed sadly. "If he's dead, then his secrets shall die with him, and his name will be stricken from my memory."

"I hope that he lives, your majesty," Elise murmured quietly.

The nearly hairless brows raised in the startlingly pale face, and for a moment Elizabeth presented an aquiline profile to her young guest as she considered a gold-trimmed cuff. "I understand you've also come to plead for the release of the Hanseatic captain whose ship was taken. Is that true?"

"Yea, your majesty," Elise answered quietly, sensing the monarch's disdain.

"How is it that you come to plead for the Hansa when 'tis rumored your father was kidnapped by the league?"

"Captain Von Reijn has a good regard for his English friends and is not guilty of any crimes against them. 'Twas Karr Hilliard who kidnapped my father."

"Are you in love with this Captain Von Reijn?" the Queen pressed.

Elise clasped her hands and bowed her head slightly as she murmured, "Nay, your majesty. He's but a friend."

" 'Tis rumored that Captain Von Reijn was also a friend of Lord Seymour . . . Is this true?"

Elise hesitated, but only briefly, feeling the penetrating gaze of the Queen upon her. It seemed the woman could read her very thoughts, and she dared not provoke her by avoiding the truth. "You've been well-informed, your majesty."

"Don't coddle me, girl!" Elizabeth snapped, startling Elise with her quick temper. "It has always been my aim to be well-informed."

Meekly Elise held her silence until the Queen's anger ebbed, and once again she was subjected to a lengthy perusal.

"What is that you wear about your neck?" Elizabeth queried, casually gesturing toward the piece.

Fervently hoping the pearl strands had not become an offense for which she would soon regret, Elise explained, " 'Tis a necklace that was found with my mother when she was abandoned as a babe."

Elizabeth raised her hand and beckoned Elise to come forward. When the girl complied, the Queen stretched out a hand and lifted the jewel-framed enamel to inspect the image more closely, then, turning aside, called for Blanche Parry to draw near. It was not until the aging woman stood before the Queen that Elise realized the elder was nearly blind.

"Is the Countess Dowager of Rutherford among those presently at court?" the Queen questioned Blanche.

The elder answered softly. "Nay, your majesty."

Elizabeth clasped her hands before her in her lap as she bade the woman, "Then tell Lord Burghley to send out a dispatch bidding Anne to come to the castle. I'm sure she'll be most interested to learn that she has a great-granddaughter living at Sir Ramsey's manor home."

"The Countess Rutherford?" Elise's mind flew in a flurry as the Queen nodded. "But how can this be?"

"Anne's daughter and grandchild... the latter undoubtedly being your mother... were seized and held for ransom. The Countess Rutherford was quick to respond to the abductor's plea and sent along the required sum. A short time later the daughter was returned... but without the child. It seemed they had been separated, and the woman who had been hired to tend the babe caught a fever. The woman died, unable to tell any where she had taken her, saying only that the girl could be identified by the necklace the child's mother was wearing when she was taken. The mother passed on with the pox some years later, leaving the Countess Rutherford to search for her grandchild. That was years ago, and now I must believe that you are the daughter of that missing girl."

Elizabeth waved a hand to indicate the necklace Elise was wearing. "That enamel you have hanging about your neck was taken from a portrait of the Countess Rutherford herself, which now hangs in that one's home. I've seen it myself and can verify that the enamel was copied directly from the original.

"I shall arrange for the Countess Rutherford to visit your home as soon as possible," Elizabeth continued. "She is as ancient as my Blanche here, but she has a good and valiant heart. I'm sure she'll be eager to make your acquaintance. She's alone now, without blood kin. And I'm sure you'll be a pleasure to her."

"I'd be pleased to know my great-grandmother," Elise murmured with restrained emotion invading her voice. A sense of elation, eager expectation, and contentment welled up within her at the idea that she had other, kinder, more caring relatives than the ones she was now acquainted with.

A light rap sounded on the door, and Blanche Parry went to the huge portal to admit a tall, bearded, dark-haired gentleman who crossed the chamber with some urgency. He made a show of obeisance before his Queen, then spoke to her in a confidential whisper as Elise stepped away with quiet diplomacy. When he straightened, Elizabeth lifted a hand to bid the young woman to approach and spoke aside to the man.

"Sir Francis Walsingham, you would be interested in learning that my guest is none other than Sir Ramsey Radborne's daughter. Elise has come to plead for the release of that Hanseatic captain who was taken."

The tall man faced Elise with some concern. "I knew your father personally..."

"Please, Sir Francis, I believe he is still alive... at least, I continue to hope he is. I cannot bear to hear you speak of him as if he were in the past."

"Forgive me, child." He came forward to take her hands in his. "I have despaired in his long absence from us and become doubtful of the mercy of his captors. I don't mean to be harsh."

"Sir Francis is most valuable as my Secretary of State," the Queen explained with a musing smile. "He has a passion for uncovering plots against my life..."

and I'm ever amazed at his findings. 'Twas in the *kontors* of the Stilliard one was purported to have spawned. Your father was set to uncover its source when he was seized."

Elise received the news in some amazement. "I was told he went there on a private mission to sell his possessions."

" 'Twas but a ruse to give him an excuse to visit their *kontors,* my dear. I've heard of this treasure he purportedly collected, but I seriously doubt its existence." Sir Francis clasped his hands behind his back and strode to the windows where he gazed out for a thoughtful space of time. "I've just now received word that there was, indeed, a plot against the Queen instigated in the Stilliards." He faced Elise and spoke with sincerity. "Therefore, I must plead with you to give up your cause for the release of this Hanseatic captain. 'Tis my thought the man deserves none of your charity."

"If a conspiracy was found to exist among some members of the Hansa, that does not mean all of the captains and merchants were involved." Elise appealed to the Secretary's sense of justice. "Captain Von Reijn helped us to escape Lubeck when Karr Hilliard and the Hansa were seeking to kill us. He has been a close friend of the English. If I allowed him to be executed or to rot away in Newgate without making an attempt to set him free, I could not live with myself. His only crime is that I was aboard his ship, and that is the only reason Captain Sinclair seized the captain and his ship. Forgive me, Sir Francis, for I can do nothing less than plead his cause. I'm convinced that Captain Von Reijn was unjustly taken and is being unfairly detained."

"Perhaps the man I have waiting in the antechamber will be able to clear this matter up. I'm sure you're acquainted with him, my dear, and will be relieved to know he is alive." He faced Elizabeth. "The gentleman is awaiting your permission to see you, your majesty. I thought you would want to do so privily . . . to decide his fate . . ."

"So! The rogue dares come lay his neck upon my blade and await my judgment, eh! . . . Or does he expect my pardon?" She waved a hand officiously. "Bid that scoundrel enter and let me hear him plead for mercy!"

Sir Francis swept her a bow and returned to the portal. Stepping aside as he swung it open, he announced grandly, "The Marquess of Bradbury, your majesty."

Elise's heart leapt for joy within her breast. Beside herself with both happiness and anxiety, she took a few halting steps toward the door, then, hearing the bold click of footsteps rapidly approaching the chamber, she forced herself to remain where she was, for fear the Queen might take offense at her greeting. Indeed, fear for her husband was the only thing that kept her from flying into his arms as he entered, for she thought she had never seen a man looking so wonderfully alive and so exceptionally handsome. He wore black trunk hose, stockings, low shoes, and a rich velvet doublet of the same hue. The dark clothes were accentuated by the crisp white cuffs and ruff of his shirt. Over the doublet he wore a cape of black trimmed around the collar and hem with embroidered silk threads. His skin had darkened to a golden tan, making his eyes seem more vivid. Those glowing orbs fastened on her as soon as he came through the door, bringing him to a surprised halt. Though no word passed his lips, she felt reassured by the warmth displayed in their depths.

Recovering his aplomb, Maxim turned to present

himself to the Queen. "Your majesty!" His voice rang clear as he stepped into a grand bow.

The royal monarch drummed her fingers in agitation and arched a bald brow over gleaming dark eyes. One would have had to be blind to miss the exchange between the couple, and though she could not plumb the depths or the real significance of it, the incident formed a tiny niche in her memory. She would seek the answer to it later. For now, she had other, more important matters to attend to with this man. "So, you rascal! You have returned as you said you would."

"Aye, your majesty, and better than I promised. I have spirited away from Lubeck the nurturing core of the plot against you. Karr Hilliard is even now locked away in Newgate prison, awaiting your decree."

"He has confessed to the murder of my agent?" Elizabeth questioned expectantly.

"Nay, your majesty, nor is he the one who murdered him," Maxim averred. "That man is an Englishman for whom I have no name, the lover of one of your ladies-in-waiting."

"The deuce you say!" she cried indignantly. "Well, we shall hear what my ladies have to say of this! I'll not tolerate such wanton behavior among my attendants!"

"The man will be identified," Walsingham promised her. "And imprisoned."

"Unfortunately he is also the one who holds Sir Ramsey captive . . ." Maxim informed them.

"Then we must proceed with more care." Elizabeth braced her chin reflectively between two pale, slender fingers and peered directly at Maxim. "Have you aught to suggest?"

"If you speak with your ladies, your majesty," Maxim began, "you may alert the man, though I was led to believe the woman has no idea she is being used."

"If that is the case," the Queen pointed out, "I'm sure when the delicacy of the situation is explained to her, the lady will gladly volunteer the information. I'm eager to know the identity of this traitor."

"If she is truly innocent, your majesty, would not her ire be roused against the man for his deception?" Maxim questioned. "And if she cannot control her resentment, she might unwittingly warn the man by a display of anger."

"Shall I imprison my ladies?" Elizabeth demanded sharply. "What are you suggesting I do?"

"Entice them to spread a tale that will draw the man into our trap," Maxim quickly answered. "Fill their delicate ears with a rumor that is sure to rouse the interest of the brigand, but let them not be aware of what they do. The information should appear to reach him by accident, merely the report of an over-heard conversation."

"And what rumor would you have me spill?"

" 'Tis my suspicion that the kidnapper is holding Sir Ramsey for the treasure he purportedly hid. If it should reach his ears that I know the whereabouts of the gold, the man might be tempted to seek me out and offer to exchange Sir Ramsey for ransom."

Elise moved forward, gaining the attention of the three. "And if he does suspect that you know, would that ploy help my father's cause or hinder it?"

Maxim's eyes softened again as they settled on his wife, and the promise of love, though it remained unspoken, was there to be seen in his face. "How would it hinder his cause, my lady?"

Elise stumbled through a hesitant nod as her cheeks warmed with pleasure. How could she successfully hide a love that was overflowing her heart? "If the kidnapper thinks you know, then he may decide he has no further use of my father and do away with him."

Maxim had thought it all out and was quick to reply. "The man would not be too hasty, for he would want to make sure of what I know first."

"Dare I suggest that Sir Ramsey may have told them already and been killed?" Sir Francis offered.

Maxim's mien grew thoughtful. "If the kidnapper cannot produce some evidence that Sir Ramsey is still alive, then we shall dispense with caution, gain his name from the lady, and have him arrested. However, if Ramsey is alive, and the brigand believes there's a large treasure to be had, 'tis my belief that he'll be anxious to keep him alive. I shall present my proposal in the manner of ransom. I think Sir Ramsey will be safe as long as there is hope of a reward and his captor believes 'tis to his advantage to keep him alive."

"The man will want to hide his identity," Sir Francis interjected.

"My task will be to disclose it," Maxim answered.

"Will you not be in danger yourself?" Elizabeth asked him.

"I shall do my utmost to safeguard my continued good health, your majesty," Maxim vowed with a smile.

"I'm sure nothing would give you greater pleasure than to seize the man who allowed you to suffer in his stead," Elizabeth returned musefully, then nodded her acceptance. "Proceed with your plans. I'll see that such a tale is spread among my ladies."

"And what shall we do about Captain Von Reijn?" Sir Francis asked the Queen.

"Captain Von Reijn?" Maxim was immediately attentive to the matter. "What has happened?"

" 'Twould seem Captain Von Reijn and his crew

have been arrested and thrown in Newgate gaol," Sir Francis informed him. "Captain Sinclair said the man might have been supplying Parma's troops in the Netherlands and perhaps is somehow connected with the kidnapping of Mistress Radborne here."

"I'm the only one guilty of that offense!" Maxim declared in a rush of anxious concern.

" 'Tis strange," Elizabeth responded sardonically. "Mistress Radborne said your men took her by mistake."

Ignoring a warning frown from Walsingham, Maxim boldly stated the facts. "They did indeed, your majesty, but my intentions were to take my former betrothed from her chambers before Reland Huxford could seal the marriage troth with her. As you're aware, before Edward Stamford came forward to accuse me of murder, his daughter and I were to be married." Maxim did not enjoy spilling out the truth in this manner. He felt sorely at a disadvantage, for he was likely to incur Elizabeth's wrath when he had all but salved it, but Nicholas had been his friend for many years, and that one's safety was paramount in his mind. "I sent my men to seize Arabella, but Mistress Elise Radborne was taken in her stead." He peered at Elizabeth from beneath his brows to determine the depth of her displeasure as he continued. "Later that same week, I bade Sir Francis to plead my cause for an audience that I could declare my loyalty to you and vie for a chance to prove that I was not the traitor I'd been judged to be."

Elizabeth threw herself from the chair and stalked toward Maxim with a feral gleam in her eye. "You came to me pleading your innocence when all the while you were guilty of this evil deed of abduction?"

"I thought I was in love with Arabella," he answered calmly, well acquainted with the woman's fiery temperament and its far-reaching effect on all who dared cross her. "Knowing I was guiltless of the crimes of which I had been accused, I hoped there would come a day when I'd be restored to your good graces." He paused in reflection. "I have since considered my actions and determined they were mainly done in malice toward Edward for the lies he told against me."

"Meaning?" Elizabeth railed, flinging herself in the chair again.

"Meaning I was mistaken when I considered myself in love with Arabella."

Elise had no time to experience the joyful relief which his answer brought her, for the Queen was quick to snap back in sharp irritation.

"Foolish man! You are not worthy of my pardon!" Elizabeth tossed up a hand to indicate Elise. "You had this child snatched from her home, and because of that, her name has been sullied ..."

"Your pardon, your majesty," Elise dared to interrupt. "If Lord Seymour had not taken me, I might not be alive today."

The gray-black eyes hardened to a dark flint hue as they settled on the young woman. She would brook no feeble excuse to interfere with her reprimanding of this man. "Explain yourself."

"I have kin who thought they could force the whereabouts of my father's treasure from me. I escaped from them after being subjected to their endless questioning and their mean and hideous torture. I've since learned that at least one of them is guilty of murder, and if not for the fact that I was taken by Lord Seymour's men, I'd most likely have been taken prisoner again by my aunt and held against my will until I breathed my last."

"One foul deed does not excuse another," Elizabeth retorted. "Lord Seymour made no effort to return you to your home or to restore your honor."

"On the contrary, your majesty, he has done just that," Elise said in a trembling voice, knowing well that she tested the woman's temper and chanced being thrown into the Tower for the crime of tenacity. "He has given me the honor and shelter of his name and has many times risked his own life to defend mine. I, for one, am most grateful that his servants made a mistake and, more than once, have considered my abduction a divine blessing."

"Humph! 'Tis evident, you silly woman, that you are in love with the scoundrel and will say anything in his defense," Elizabeth ridiculed her and turned her attention to the tall, tawny-haired man just as that one bestowed a tender look upon the girl. Though she witnessed a gentle meeting of gazes, the Queen sat back in the chair in some annoyance at the couple. They had set her to the task of debating the controversy of their actions in her mind, and she was weary of making decisions. If not for fear that Spain would turn upon England after crushing the gallant forces in the Netherlands, she would have left Philip to do the deed! She had procrastinated against taking action until at last her hand had been forced. Now when she was pressed to consider a more simple matter than the presently raging war, she was moved to resentment. Lord Seymour had not deemed it necessary to ask her permission to marry. Yet on the other hand, when she took into account that he had not been within close proximity to bide for her approval, she could be swayed toward leniency. By all that was right, he had to take the maid to wife to make amends for the wrong he had done. Still, he had shown a careless disregard for propriety and was not deserving of her forgiveness.

Dropping her arms on the chair, Elizabeth pointedly

asked, "What is this girl to you, Bradbury?"

Somewhat confused by the question, Maxim faced the sovereign queen and stated clearly what Elise had revealed. "She is my wife, your majesty."

"You married without asking for my consent?" she needled, but was quick to wave away his explanation. "What are your feelings toward her?"

"I love her," he admitted quietly, well aware of what his confession might mean.

Walsingham rolled his eyes back in his head, fearing he had just heard the death knell sound for the man.

"Love!" Elizabeth scoffed in caustic derision. "What do you know of love? One moment you adore one woman, the next, another? I liked you better when you were unmarried!"

Walsingham hid a smile behind a thin knuckle. 'Twas well-known that Elizabeth had long indulged herself in the audience of many a gallant and handsome blade in her court, and, though aging, she still had a most appreciative eye for a man of Seymour's good looks. She was by nature opposed to any courtier who wed.

"If I've risked my life many times over in service to you, your majesty, does that not prove the love and honor I give to you?" Maxim took heart as he saw the Queen's eyes lower in museful reflection. "If I'm willing to give my life to see Elise safe from those who would do her ill, does that not attest to my devotion to her?"

"You have given me good service," Elizabeth admitted. "And it caused me great pain to think you had betrayed me." She heaved a long sigh, at last coming to a decision. "I shall repent of my earlier decree, Bradbury. Henceforth, your titles and properties are restored to you and you may go with my blessings."

Elise gave a glad cry and would have thrown herself

in Maxim's arms, but she saw him hesitate and knew it was not over yet. Her heart trembled at her husband's daring, for he waited as the Queen breathed a soft sigh and leaned back in the tall chair. Relaxing, the woman closed her eyes a moment and rubbed her temple with her fingertips, then the dark orbs snapped open again and fairly pierced Maxim where he stood.

"Well! What more do you want of me? Have I not given you enough?"

"What of Captain Von Reijn, your majesty?" he softly questioned.

The Queen's eyes blazed as she stared back at him, then gradually they softened, and she gave a soft laugh. "When this is out, my repute for wise decisions shall be left in ragged ruins. Your tenacity has once again brought you your heart's desire, Bradbury. I shall give your friend pardon and restoration of his ship and cargo. Now leave me. I am weary."

Chapter 29

*E*LISE BREATHLESSLY PLEADED caution between gasps of laughter as Maxim pulled her along with him at a fleet-footed pace across the wide, well-groomed lawns of Whitehall. As they reached the river stairs Fitch and Spence rushed to greet their lord and clapped him eagerly on the back, displaying a joy and relief they could hardly contain over his arrival. Once the congratulations and felicitations were exchanged, Maxim extracted himself from their attentions and, sweeping Elise into his arms, hurriedly descended the steps and boarded the barge that awaited them. He stepped forward near the prow and, locking his wife in an exuberant embrace, fell back laughing into a cushioned seat. The soft, feminine giggles he produced by nuzzling his wife's ear and covering her face with eager kisses sharply raised the brows of the riverman's youthful assistant, who gawked in astonishment at the handsome couple. The master boatman was accustomed to a wide range of varied behavior from his wealthy patrons and brusquely urged the lad on about his duties whenever there was a lag. Fitch and Spence settled behind their lord, and after casting off the moorings, the two boatmen bent themselves to broad sweeps amidship until they levered the heavy craft out into the currents. Once the vessel began to swing, the master took himself aft to the tiller sweep while the lad labored to hoist the long single spar bearing the wide triangular sail. Soon the barge was slipping along nicely through the current and reached upriver at a fair pace.

Maxim yielded to an urge which had strongly tested his restraint since his entry into the Queen's chambers. He did not care that he had an audience of men and a most curious youth who was eager to spy upon them. What mattered was his craving to take his wife in his arms and kiss her at length and with a thoroughness that roused their hungering passion. He restricted himself only to the margin of propriety he deemed adequate when he pulled her across his lap and leaned over her, but it was enough to bulge out the eyes of the youth who watched from behind. It was a very long time before Maxim lifted his head, and then only slightly.

Elise's head swam from the heady intoxicant of his kiss and as her world reeled crazily under the starlit night, she sighed beneath his hovering mouth. "Your greetings have fair sundered my trembling heart, but oh, for such sunderings I've desperately yearned."

His breath was warm in her mouth as he touched light kisses to her parted lips, drinking in the sweet honeyed dew she offered. "I've come alive again," he breathed. "In your absence I fear I'm stricken deaf and dumb, as one cast with a spell. I thought my heart had stopped."

"If you could feel mine now, my love, you would know its rushing haste." Elise caught his hand as it moved to make the inspection and smiled into his shining eyes. "Later, my love," she promised in a soft whisper, "when there are not so many to see."

"They cannot see where my hand goes," he cajoled with a wayward grin.

"Oh, but they'll hear my sighs." She smiled and

raised a hand to caress his mouth with her fingertips. "I'd not be able to help myself. When you touch me, I become a woman possessed, and my frenzy is not appeased until we come together as one."

His glowing eyes plumbed the dark translucent depths of midnight blue as he promised in a softly rasped whisper, "I'll wait until that moment we're alone, then I'll tender you a lover's fete the likes of which you've never known."

"My heart quakes in expectation," she breathed in warm response.

Shifting his weight, Maxim relaxed back upon the cushions of the seat and snuggled her close upon his chest. With a wicked leer he pulled off her hat and tossed it aside. "Edward can leave Bradbury or stay, whatever you may see fit, madam. I would only claim my old chambers as our own."

"Edward is dying, Maxim. He's staying here in London at my father's house where he can be close to the physicians who are attending him. I think it's only a matter of time."

Maxim frowned in bemusement. "But the man was hearty enough when I last saw him. What has happened, my love?"

"I vow the mere act of marrying Cassandra would mean the wasting of any man." After a moment Elise realized her simple answer failed to enlighten her husband, and she went on to explain in more detail. "Long ago 'twas rumored among my father's servants that Cassandra poisoned my mother and then, later, her husband, Bardolf Radborne. As a child I didn't understand and later when I could, I passed the tales off as merely the delusions of a demented ancient. Now I am convinced the rumors were not fabrications. I've also come to think that before she even married Edward, Cassandra intended to poison him and had him sign a marriage settlement giving her the right to inherit everything he owns upon his death. Edward could never read very well and his understanding of the written word was ofttimes lacking. He was always cautious to let Arabella counsel him on the documents he signed, but I doubt she knows about it. 'Tis hard to believe that Cassandra gained those concessions from Edward while he was cognizant of what he was doing. He must have been well into his cups. Otherwise, he would have insisted that Arabella look over the document."

"The Queen's decree of restoration will disarm any attempt of Cassandra's to collect my properties."

"Cassandra knows the importance of legal documents only too well," Elise commented dismally. "My father left no guarantees for me, at least none that could be found, and ever since his disappearance, Cassandra has been trying to obtain his estates for herself and her sons, claiming that he is already dead. Should he be found so, I fear she'd have the upper hand. She's always had a good nose for wealth and a knowledge of how to get it."

"I shall ask that a royal warrant be issued for her arrest."

"The word is out that she has fled the country. Perhaps I should breathe a sigh of relief that she's gone, but I fear she will return one day and do us hurt."

"If they try, they'll be called into account for their actions. And if aught happens to me, my love, you should know that I've already given a document to Walsingham, stating you will become my heir, the Marchioness Dowager of Bradbury."

"I care naught for your possessions," she avowed emphatically. "All I want is you . . . and our babe."

"Our babe?" Maxim drew back enough to see her face. "What is this you say?"

Elise met his searching gaze with adoring eyes. "My body does joyfully nourish your seed, my lord. I carry your child."

Maxim pulled her close again and covered them with a light woolen throw to keep away the chill of the night. "I shall endeavor to fulfill your desire, madam, for surely, 'tis the yearnings of my own heart to live for you and our child. There is yet another head of this Hydra that needs be lopped off, but first I must search it out and restore your father to you."

A contented silence settled upon them as the barge wended along the river. Night studded the ebon sky with twinkling stars as a thin sliver of lunar brightness tore itself free of the rooftops of the city and climbed into the vast empyrean above. All was indeed right with the world while Elise rested secure in her husband's arms. She could feel the slowly throbbing beat of his pulse where her brow lay against the side of his throat, and she was lulled into a feeling of bliss she had not experienced since their parting.

Much later, they strolled hand in hand from the river's edge and entered the manor house of her father. Word was quickly passed that the mistress had arrived home with her new husband, the famed Lord Seymour. Every cranny, crevice, and nook seemed filled with curious eyes and eager faces as the couple crossed the hall. Having heard whispered rumors of the mistress's capture, they caught their first glimpse of the Marquess. Young maids were set atwitter by the notion that such a daring and handsome gallant would be housed in the manor, but their smiles drooped in disappointment when the word was given that his lordship would be taking his lady to his country estate when the morning came.

Maxim still struggled with feelings of anger and resentment toward Edward as he slowly mounted the stairs with Elise at his side. He braced himself for the moment of their meeting, but upon entering the sleeping man's chamber and seeing the frail form of what was once his adversary, it came to him that he need not have tried so hard. All the harsh angers faded to be replaced by the pity he had been reluctant to give. Compassion washed over him with a natural ease, releasing him from the bitterness that had bound him up for so many months now. An easy flowing peace untangled the knotted cords of his emotions, allowing him to clearly see how supremely he had been blessed because of the deceit of his enemy. If not for Edward's accusations, his life would have remained empty of the joy he now knew with Elise.

Astounded by the realization of his good fortune, Maxim laid an arm around Elise's shoulder and lifted her chin. His eyes glowed into hers as he drank deeply of the love he found shining there. "When all is said and done, my love, I must admit Edward did me a great service," he murmured in easy concession. "I found a treasure far beyond his ken . . . a woman worthy of all my aspirations . . . a fulfillment of my loftiest dreams."

"Seymour?" The strained whisper came from the bed, and they turned to gaze down at Edward. The invalid tried to raise himself in his much-weakened condition, but the effort proved too much for him. With a sigh of resignation, he collapsed back upon the bed and was much amazed when Maxim lifted him up and braced several pillows behind his back.

"I prayed you'd come . . ." the frail man whispered.

Maxim glanced back at Elise, who conveyed her own bewilderment by a small shake of her head. A light frown marked his brow, betraying his own confusion as he posed the question to the invalid. "Why would you pray for my return, Edward?"

"I've . . . a pressin' need ta clear . . . me conscience," the elder rasped in a weak whisper. "I cast the blame on ye . . . ta hide the evidence of me own doings. 'Twas meself who was responsible for the agent being killed."

"Do you ken what you say, Edward?" This deathbed confession was not what Maxim had expected. "How did you kill him?"

"Listen to me!" he gasped. "I did not kill him, but I was responsible for his death. If not for me, he might not've been slain."

"Explain yourself," Maxim urged. "I would know what happened that night."

The dulled eyes raised beneath sagging blue lids, and after a pause, Edward gathered his strength for the ordeal. His voice took on a nasal monotone, almost a whine. "I'd taken ta followin' Ramsey . . . ta see what he was 'bout. I'd heard rumors 'bout him hoardin' his wealth, an' I wanted ta see for meself just what he was a-doing, but the thought o' goin' inta 'ose nasty Stilliards sent shivers up me spine. So's I waited 'ere on the river an' watched 'til he come back to his barge . . . usually with a chest."

A long panic-filled moment passed as Edward tried to take air into his lungs, and he seemed on the verge of expiring. Maxim lifted him up to help him draw a deeper breath and held a glass of water to the colorless lips. Gulping down a draught, Edward nodded his gratitude and sank back weakly to the pillows. With more ease, he continued with his tale. "The Queen's agent noticed me a-waitin' 'ere several times, an' later when he come ta Bradbury ta speak wit' ye, he recognized me as the one what he'd spied. He faced me off, he did, an' accused me o' bein' in on the conspiracy ta assassinate the Queen. God knows that weren't true, but the bloke wouldn't listen. He grabbed me arm, hard like a tightenin' rope, an' snatched me 'round."

Edward's eyes seemed to plead from the caverns of their thinly fleshed sockets, begging them to understand. "I pushed him away an' his heel caught on a rug, an' he went down like a stone, hittin' his head on the hearth with a good, solid thump. He were bleedin' as much as a cut hen, he were, an' then I heard ye, Seymour, comin' down the hall, an' I slipped out onta the porch." Edward paused and stared at the quilt where his feet made twin peaks. He would not meet their eyes, but only nodded in distant contemplation. "Aye, 'twas meself what caused the deed ta happen."

"The man was alive when I knelt beside him," Maxim explained. "Why do you say you were responsible?"

"If we hadn't scuffled, or if I hadn't fled when ye heard me on the gallery, he might not've been stabbed later. He seemed a man well able ta care o' himself, an' surely after the deed was done...had you been there by his side...he'd not have been killed. Aye, I was the one responsible, 'at I was."

"If you're seeking absolution for the deed of murder, Edward, 'tis not your sin to bear," Maxim assured him. "You told a lie against me to clear yourself, but what you meant for evil has been turned to my good, so all is forgiven. I can only think that a far wiser hand than yours or mine directed the events, and I shall ever be grateful because it has happened."

"What'll ye do now?" the elder wheezed.

"The Queen has given my title and estates back to me. I shall be returning to Bradbury on the morn."

" 'Twould seem that I won't be livin' long enough ta enjoy it anyway." Edward heaved a deep sigh, relieved that his conscience had been cleansed on all accounts, and then he grimaced and clutched his belly with both hands. "Oh, Cassy . . . Cassy!" He rolled from side to side, and his voice grew strained with pain. "Where is me fair Cassandra? Why has she not been at me side these past days?"

"Uncle Edward." Elise laid a gentle hand upon his arm. "Do you not know what she's done to you?"

"Aye, I know it well!" Her uncle writhed in agony as a dappling of sweat broke from his pores. Rubbing his forehead with bony knuckles, he ground the words out through tightly clenched teeth. "She held me head ta her soft bosom when the knives o' hell tore at me belly. She eased me ailment an' even brought a good tonic for me. Aye! The tonic!" He raised a scrawny arm to indicate a small, dark green vial on the night stand. "Pass me the tonic, girl."

Elise lifted the tiny decanter to the light and watched the thick, yellowish ichor that swirled inside. She drew the cork and sniffed cautiously, then held it away, wrinkling her nose in disgust. Maxim stepped near and, removing the glass vial from Elise's grasp, put a finger over the opening, tipped it, and inspected the spot on his finger. Ever so lightly he touched his tongue to the drop. His mouth twisted in sharp distaste and, passing the tiny bottle back to his wife, he took a cloth to wipe it across his lips and tongue. He bent and took a close look at Edward's pallid face, noting the bluish tinge around the eyes, and examined his hands and the fingertips that bore the same hue.

"Whether or nay you were a student of Aristotle's works, or Pliny the Elder's, 'twould have made no difference, Edward. I doubt if you'd have known what I think this vial contains. The crystals that make this bitter vetch are sometimes found in the iron mines in Germany. I've heard that a few women have drunk a concoction of the stuff to make their skins pale and white, but 'tis a dangerous bane that can cause death."

"A pox 'pon the two o' ye! Me own sweet Cassandra would never . . . Why, she vowed 'twas the same tonic she plied on her first hus . . ." Edward's words came slowly to a halt as he considered the fate of her first spouse, and his jaw sagged. Even his simple mind caught the strings and wove them together. "But why?"

Elise laid a gentle hand on her uncle's arm and rubbed it consolingly. "Do you remember signing a marriage settlement with her the day you both were wed?"

The wispy brows drew together in a perplexed frown. "Vaguely I remember signin' me name to the nuptials, but there weren't no settlement between us."

"Cassandra claims she has such a document within her possession," Elise informed him. "You must have signed it without realizing it."

"What might it say?" he asked, painfully conscious that there had been times of drunken revelry from which he had awakened the next morning without any awareness of what he had done.

"It gives Cassandra the right to inherit all of your possessions," his niece answered simply.

"Be damned! She'll not!" Catching hold of Elise's arm, he struggled to rise. "I'll have no such deceit in me family!"

Maxim laid a hand upon the thin shoulder and pressed the man back upon the pillows. " 'Tis best that you conserve your strength for Arabella's sake, Edward. You'll need to draw up a settlement leaving her as the sole heir of your properties."

"Send me a barrister," Edward pleaded weakly. "An' be quick 'bout it." Then the elder frowned and grew thoughtful. "Why, I'll have nary a coin ta leave me daughter after ye take back yer estates." His brows lifted in a tiny shrug. "I needn't fret. She's got wealth o' her own. Reland left her all o' his lands an' treasures. He did well by her, 'at he did."

Maxim and Elise retired to her chambers, and the door was locked securely behind them. Leaning back against its planks, he brought her close within the circle of his arms and kissed her with all the fervor of his pent-up passions. His fingers freed her hair, and the silken tresses tumbled in loose curls about her shoulders. Her gown was plucked open and, along with her petticoats, was pushed with a rustle of silk to the floor. With a coy smile Elise lifted her arms beneath the curling auburn strands, raising them off her shoulders as she backed away from the lustful leer gleaming in her husband's eyes. While his hands made haste to rid himself of his garments, his gaze ranged hungrily over the full length of her. He anticipated the overflow of her swelling bosom from her chemise, and he could not help but admire those curving hips as she dropped the farthingale and strolled leisurely toward the lamp.

"Don't blow it out," he urged, tossing aside his shirt and doublet. "I've a desire to refresh my memory."

"Have you forgotten so much then?" Elise teased him with a sultry look as she slipped a silken arm from the lace strap of her chemise.

A wayward grin tugged at his lips. "Your image is forged on my mind forever, madam. Never fear that I'll forget you."

Stepping out of his breeches, he became the recipient of her warming gaze as she eyed the manly fullness beneath the stockings. With purposeful strides he moved to stand close before her. His eyes burned into hers for a long, intense moment before he reached up and tugged down the other strap. Leaning down, he touched his lips to the lustrous softness of her shoulder and drew a sigh of pleasure from her lips as his kisses descended with leisured slowness to her breast. The garment tumbled to the floor, and her breath stilled in blissful wonder as the warm wetness flicked across a soft peak, then she found herself being swept up in her husband's arms. The bed awaited, and their lips blended as he laid her beneath him. She welcomed his warmth within her and responded to his manly thrusts with all the vigor of a woman impassioned with the fullest measure of love.

The night was filled with similar adventures, and when the first light of morn came, Elise snuggled her head beneath a pillow and refused to answer the light rap that sounded on the door.

"Mistress? Be ye awake? Ye asked me ta rouse ye an' the master early so ye can be off ta Bradbury ere the morn is past. I've brought food for ye."

Elise's reluctant groan was muffled against the mattress, and Maxim gave a soft chuckle as he tossed a quilt over her. Donning a robe, he answered the summons himself and, accepting the serving platter from the maid, leaned a shoulder against the door to close it.

"Come, my love," he coaxed, setting the tray on the bed between them. "I'm anxious to be home. You can sleep in the barge on the way upriver."

He reached across and fondly patted the coverlet where it followed the curve of her backside. He smiled as his memory wandered back to the preceding hours, and his thoughts warmed with the images that drifted through his head. When it was the inclination of more than a few women to turn away from their conjugal duties with vague disinterest, Elise was proving herself as eager as he to explore the ever-expanding reaches of love. She was most comfortable with their intimacy, even displaying a trend toward boldness, which only heightened his desire and pleasure. Truly, no mere mistress could have captured his heart so deftly, nor so securely. He was totally infatuated with his young wife.

"Come, love, you must take nourishment after such a night just past," he urged teasingly. "There's marinated salmon, curds, cream, and banbury cakes." He leaned over and lifted a corner of the pillow to peek beneath it. One eye peered back at him through the tangled tresses masking her face. He laughed aloud when she groaned again and nestled deeper in the covers.

"For shame, sir," she muttered. "After following you in hot pursuit all night long, I've not the strength to dine, dress, and depart this place. I pray thee, be not so cruel. Let me slumber a few moments longer 'til I've regained my ambition. Am I not carrying your child? Does that not deserve some consideration?"

Maxim fondly caressed the roundness beneath the quilt again and grinned. "Your arguments have won me over. There's naught I can say against them. Therefore, madam, it shall be my very great pleasure to let you sleep until I get dressed. Would you be vexed if I called for a bath?"

"I'd enjoy it," she grumbled, pulling the pillow down again to shut out the morning light.

Maxim set aside the tray, choosing to wait until he could share the morning meal with her. Pulling the draperies closed about the bed to allow his wife some privacy, he bade the servants to bring up water for a bath and was soon enjoying the fruits of their labor.

Finally rousing herself to some awareness, Elise stumbled sleepily from the bed and approached the tub, brushing the long, curling strands back from her face. The beauty of her sleek, naked form bathed in the rosy glow of morning light commanded Maxim's undivided attention, and when she halted beside him to bestow a light kiss upon his lips, he was more than willing to have her stay a moment. Wrapping a wet arm about her, he held her there as he savored a more lengthy kiss.

Of a sudden and without warning, the hall door swung open, and an excited Arabella announced her presence with a flood of words spilling from her lips. "Elise, I just heard the news! My dear friend rode over bright and early this morn to tell me! Maxim is back..."

Her voice trailed off, and she stumbled to a halt as her attention came full upon the couple. Totally shocked by the scene that greeted her, she could only gawk in stunned confusion. Elise was too startled to move, and with a rueful grin, Maxim gave comment as he met Arabella's horrified stare.

"I think I should've taken more care to lock the door."

"What's going on here?" Arabella cried.

"What does it look like?" Maxim swept his hand about as if there was a need to direct her attention to what she saw. "I'm taking a bath, and my wife was about to join me."

"Your *wife?*" The woman nearly screamed the words at him. "But you loved me! Did you not come last year to take me back with you?"

"I did," Maxim admitted. "But my men took Elise by mistake."

Self-consciously Arabella dragged the top of her dressing gown closer over her bosom, for the nakedness beneath the long auburn hair brutally brought to mind a realization of her own thinness, which in the past months had become even more pronounced.

She could find no evidence to deny her rival's blooming beauty and was much relieved when Elise sought the covering of a robe.

Still, she stubbornly refused to accept that Maxim's love for her had faded because of a foolish mistake. "I'm aware of what happened, but I thought you would have honored your love for me and stayed true instead of taking ... this ... this ..."

"Be careful what you say, Arabella," Maxim warned with a gathering scowl. "The blame belongs to me, and I'll hear no slander against Elise. She was an innocent in all of this."

"Innocent?" Arabella scoffed, striding forward angrily. "Well, it would seem the innocent little slut fell willingly enough into your bed!" Her eyes touched upon his wide shoulders and dipped boldly into the water, seeking the full view of the man, for it was suddenly evident to her that beside the burliness of her late husband, Maxim Seymour would have seemed as handsome as a golden-skinned god.

Lifting a challenging brow, Maxim deliberately dropped a hand between his thighs and quipped, "Whatever you find, Arabella, already belongs to Elise."

His statement seemed to set Arabella off again, and she turned an accusing glare upon the other woman. "She stole from me! She took my place! She had no right!"

"What right have you to stand there and accuse us?" Maxim barked, growing incensed at her reasoning. Snatching up a towel to cover himself from her relentlessly searching gaze, he heaved himself up out of the water and wrapped the cloth about his hips.

Arabella stared at him slack-jawed. "But I was your betrothed."

"How quickly you forget, Countess!" He jeered the

title in contempt. "You're now the widow of Reland Huxford. You annulled whatever agreement we had between us by marrying him. You indulged yourself a day or less mourning for me and in a matter of a week's time were betrothed to him!"

"Your death was only one of many sorrows I had been through," Arabella lamented sadly. "I'm a woman tormented by misfortune! All my suitors lost to me by tragedies, and even now, my own father lies a-dying in his bed."

Maxim considered her a lengthy moment, gaining a new perspective into the woman's character. He remembered the many times she had deliberately drawn attention to the unusual number of tragedies she had had to endure, and her bent toward dramatics when others had expressed their sympathies to her or whenever anyone reminded her of her misfortunes had always bothered him. Oft were the times she had gained her way with her father by displaying a case of the vapors or a fit of depression, from which she had always been able to emerge in amazingly good spirits.

"I rather suspect you've come to revel in those tragedies, Arabella," he responded at last, "or at least the attention you've gleaned from them. I never saw you happier than when you were coddled and indulged through those times. You've a strange need for attention, but I'm no longer the one to appease it."

He took Elise within the circle of his arms and gave the shattered woman a level stare. "Whatever we had, Arabella, is now as dead as your suitors. Elise is the only woman I've ever promised to love 'til death do us part. 'Tis an easy thing to do with her. She'll be the mother of my children, and I'll give her honor every day of my life. Together we shall endeavor to forget that this encounter with you ever happened."

Almost in a daze Arabella left the room and wandered down the hall, leaving Maxim to gently close the door behind her. He shook his head, for even now he felt a sorrow for the woman. She did indeed have a craving in her life that no man could appease.

Chapter 30

*S*PRING HAD GRACED the grounds of Bradbury Hall with an abundance of flowers. They filled every garden and bordered every walk, lavishly spreading a vivid array of colors across the spacious lawns and in the carefully tended beds of the courtyard. From a distance the blossoms could not be thoroughly appreciated, nor could the air that was heady with their fragrance. Elise had been at Bradbury a week short a day, and still she delighted in venturing out to admire the beauty of the house and grounds. Though the manor had opened its doors to Nicholas, Justin, and the knights, Sherbourne and Kenneth, she still found an hour or so each morning to spend outside at some gardening chore or another. She donned skirts, blouses, and laced bodices that copied the simplicity of peasant garb, yet were themselves fresh bouquets of delicate spring hues. Wide-brimmed hats with long ribbon streamers not only framed the beauty of her face and complemented her gowns, but gave service in shading her creamy skin from the sun. To be sure, she drew more admiring glances than the flowers she tended.

Maxim was like a man slowly unwinding as the tensions that had oppressed him began to diminish and fade. His laughter came easier now and was heard more often. He pleasured himself in the good cama-raderie of his friends, in the loving attentions of his wife, and in the sheer joy of being home. Oft were the occasions when he strolled through the gardens with Elise. Usually when he was home, where one was seen, the other would not be very far away. Still, when some minor duty called him away, he would hasten back with an eagerness that set Eddy's hooves flying. Never having felt such consuming devotion stirring within his heart before, he luxuriated in the warmth of their uncommon companionship and was always impatient to resume their affair with love in the master's chambers.

It was on a Wednesday morn when a coach and four rumbled up the drive with an escort of two mounted riders. Elise was gathering flowers in a basket to make a bouquet for the house when the well-appointed, wagon-like conveyance and its accompaniment of horsemen came smartly up the lane to halt before the manor. A footman jumped down and, opening the door, reached up a hand to lend assistance to the elderly lady who emerged. She was white of hair, thin of frame, small of stature, and walked with the aid of a cane, but she was as elegant and well-garbed as any woman half her age and more. A crisp, lace-edged ruff adorned the deep green gown she wore, and a pert, plumed cap of the same hue sat jauntily upon her charmingly coiffured head. Her blue eyes were alert and bright, and as Elise approached, they settled on her with an eagerness that was unmistakable.

"I'm Anne Hall, Countess of Rutherford, my dear, and you are . . . ?"

In nervous excitement Elise bobbed a quick curtsey to the woman. "I'm Elise Seymour, Marchioness of Bradbury."

The blue eyes twinkled back at her. "I understand you have a necklace I should recognize. May I see it?"

"Of course, Countess," Elise replied and waved her hand to the heavy stout door of the main portal in gracious invitation. "Would you care to come inside?"

"I'd be delighted, my dear."

Elise hastened up the pair of steps and held the door open as the woman advanced with the aid of her cane. Pausing beside Elise, she smiled as she considered the oval face and then nodded as if she found the visage pleasing.

"You've a certain look about you, my dear, like the radiance of the sun sparkling through the leaves of a tree into a wooded copse. If I were to guess, I'd say you bring joy and light to those around you. You must make your husband very happy."

The delicate pink that graced the youthful cheeks deepened to a rosy glow, while a smile came timidly to the soft lips. "I hope so, my lady."

The aging eyes did not miss that glow of pleasure, nor the agile mind the significance of her answer. "I see you love him then."

"Very much," Elise murmured with fervent warmth.

The elder patted her hand in approval. "I need not ask if you're happy, my dear. I can see that you are."

"Yea, my lady."

"Call me Anne, dear." The woman gestured to the door with the hand that held the cane. "Shall we go in?"

"Of course." Elise laughed and escorted the Countess inside. Leading her into the great hall, she bade a servant to bring tea and refreshments, then ran upstairs to the master's chambers to fetch the necklace. It was in her rapid descent of those same stone stairs whereupon she had first recognized Maxim that she had to pause now and wait until her head stopped reeling. She would possibly never understand how Maxim managed to leap up and down their ever-turning length without quickening his breath or suffering some dizziness. He ascended them with a boldness that made her tighten her grip about his neck when he carried her in his arms, and at times she was sure he frightened her on purpose with the swiftness of his flight, for he was wont to chuckle in her ear as she clung to him.

The slight twinge of uneasiness she had suffered gradually passed, but it did much to drain the color from her cheeks. Upon her return to the great hall, the elderly woman showed some concern at her pallor and would have risen to give her aid, but with a weak smile Elise waved her back down.

" 'Tis naught but a passing queasiness," she assured her. "I tried to take the stairs too quickly."

"You are otherwise well?" Anne asked anxiously.

Elise nodded and draped the necklace over the back of her hand as she offered it to the Countess. Anne gasped as her eyes fell upon it and, bracing the cane against her knee, she carefully lifted the piece. Her fingers trembled as she removed a gold-framed spyglass from her purse and examined the jewel-encrusted enamel. After a moment, she clasped the necklace to her bosom with both hands and raised her eyes to the lofty ceiling as a blissful joy suffused her wrinkled face.

"At last!" she whispered as tears made wet paths down her cheeks. Blinking against the wetness, she smiled at Elise. "You say your mother was found with this necklace when she was but a babe?"

"That's what I've been told," Elise answered. "She was left in a basket at a chapel on the Stamford farm."

"This necklace belonged to my daughter," Anne confided with teary emotion. "You have the look of my daughter, and I can only believe that you are kin, the daughter of my grandchild who was stolen from us years ago."

Elise's smile brightened until the glow of it lit her whole face. In rich enthusiasm she informed the woman, "My father kept a portrait of my mother hanging in a cottage he owned some distance from here. I've already sent a man to fetch it for me. It should be here any day now. I was foretold that you'd be coming and assumed you would like to see what your granddaughter, Deirdre, looked like."

"Was that what they named your mother?" Anne inquired, and smiled as the girl nodded. "She was Catherine to us."

"I hope you'll be able to stay with us," Elise eagerly invited. "As long as you desire."

"I would be glad to stay for a while, my dear," Anne accepted. "I should like to get to know you better and that cannot be done so quickly. We've much to talk about."

The sound of approaching footsteps brought Elise to her feet with a happy announcement. "My husband is coming now. I should like you to meet him."

Anne chuckled lightheartedly and waved a hand to indicate Maxim's portrait that now resided on the wall beside the fireplace. "No woman who has ever been to court would miss the opportunity of acquainting themselves with such a handsome man as Lord Seymour, and I'm not so old that I cannot admire those fine gallants Elizabeth is wont to bring into her court. She has quite a discerning eye for handsome courtiers, you know."

Maxim laughed from the doorway where he had paused to listen. "Countess Anne, we meet again."

"So, you scamp!" she scolded with humor. "You've married yourself to my great-granddaughter. What have you to say for yourself?"

"That I'm a very fortunate man. I can understand now from whom she inherited her beauty."

The fragile eyelids lowered slightly to partially mask the shining blue eyes as Anne cast him a sidelong stare. "And what are you doing to carry on the family's tradition of bringing fine, beautiful babies into the world?"

Maxim tossed his head back and guffawed his mirth at the ceiling, prompting Anne to glance at Elise. The flush of color on the girl's cheeks and the embarrassed, hesitant smile assured Anne that what she wanted was already in the making.

"Stairs, pah!" Anne scoffed with amusement, then informed the couple, "I've a liking for girls, and plenty of them."

"We'll need at least a boy or two to protect the girls from the roués who'll be trailing hard and fast upon their heels," Maxim suggested with like humor.

Anne responded with a tiny shrug, agreeing with the logic of his reasoning. "One or two, at least."

Elise slipped within Maxim's embrace and smiled up into his eyes. "If we're to fulfill such ambitious plans for our family, my lord, you'll have to stay very close to home."

"My intentions exactly, madam," he assured her.

Spence returned with the portrait of Deirdre the very next day, and at Elise's request, the servant carried it upstairs to the anteroom in the master's chambers. Elise had planned to hang it above the mantel, and as Spence set about preparing the place, Maxim came in from a dusty ride across his lands. He wiped an arm across his brow and laughed as he saw the dirty smudge on his shirt.

"I'll have to wash ere I can even kiss you," he commented with a rueful grin.

"I was never of a mind to think a little dirt would hurt me," Elise rejoined with an expectant smile.

Maxim chuckled and stepped near enough to look down into those intriguing eyes. He tucked his thumbs into his belt and leaned his head down to savor the sweetness of her lips, then, after a long moment, drew away with a sigh. Over her head, he fixed Spence with a pointed stare, making that one stumble on the hearth.

"You have business here?" the Marquess queried in a tone that would brook no feeble excuse for a reply.

Elise laughed and, with a wave of her hand, dismissed the suddenly clumsy man. "Tell the servants to bring up water for his lordship's bath," she instructed, and as Spence hastened across the room she lifted a smile to Maxim. "Lord Seymour will help me hang the painting."

"Aye, mistress." Spence had paused long enough to receive her bidding and in the very next instant was moving out the door, reluctant to test his lordship's patience by staying a fraction longer than he had to.

"You ogre," Elise chided through her laughter as she met the dancing green eyes. "I think you enjoy sending everyone into a dither with those ominous looks."

" 'Tis a way of getting them out of my chambers when I've my mind set on other things."

"Such as?" His wife feigned innocence with coquettishly widened eyes.

"You know well enough." Maxim's perusal touched her everywhere, cindering her clothes with his burning gaze. His slow smile bespoke of his confidence. "Do you have any objections, my love?"

"Not in the very least, my lord," Elise assured him, reaching up on her toes to pluck another kiss from his lips, then, with a smile, she drew his eye to the canvas-covered painting. "Only a moment's delay I would beg 'til your bath be done. I'd have my mother's portrait hung ere I invite Anne in to see it."

"Let me wash some of this dirt off first, my pet," he pleaded above her lips.

As she smiled her acceptance and moved away, Maxim stripped off his leather doublet and shirt and tossed both garments aside as he strode into the bed-chamber. There he poured water into a basin, and, lathering up the soap in the water, began to wash his face, neck, and arms, then bent down to rinse himself. Reaching behind him for a towel, he felt Elise step close beneath his arm and faced her as she began to dry his face and shoulders with a towel. Her lips followed the passage of the towel and touched his moist skin with warm, caressing kisses. His eyes came slowly open to find a sultry heat burning in those jewel-blue orbs. He needed no other invitation. Pulling her close, he leaned back against a high stool and indulged in a long, passionate kiss. The stiff corps of her bodice refused to submit to his questing hand, and, with a wicked grin, he scooped the bulk of her skirts up to clasp her naked buttocks. Lifting her up high against him, he settled her astride.

"The servants will be coming with your bath," Elise warned in a breathless whisper.

"Aye, I know," Maxim lamented with a sigh, then he raised his head to grin at her. "Care to join me in a bath, my lady?"

Her glowing eyes promised him much. "That could be a definite possibility, my lord."

Elise's lips parted again as his mouth came upon hers, and it was a long moment ere she remembered her mother's portrait. When reason came stealing back, they reluctantly returned to the antechamber. While Maxim prepared the place above the mantel where the portrait would be hung, Elise carefully slipped off the protective canvas that covered it. Her eyes lit almost immediately on a rolled bundle of parchments secured to the back of the painting.

"What do you suppose these are?" She murmured the inquiry as she sank to a padded bench and slipped the bow that tied them.

Maxim stepped behind her and, leaning down over her shoulder, casually leafed through the parchments. With a curious frown, he took the documents from her and examined them more carefully, noting that each pertained to a specific piece of property. "Elise, do you have any idea what these are?"

"I've never seen them before in my life, Maxim. What are they?"

Dropping the sheaves into her lap, he sat beside her on the bench. "Why, my very sweet love, they're documents giving you the right of inheritance of all your father's properties."

Elise glanced down at them in wonder. Nothing of such import had been discovered since her father's disappearance. "Maxim, Cassandra and her sons searched high and low for these. They meant to destroy them if they could."

"Did they search the cottage where you sent Spence to?"

"They don't even know about it. My father preferred it that way."

"Obviously that's why he chose to hide them there. He probably considered they'd be safer at the cottage."

"But why didn't he give me some clue where he was hiding them?"

"Are you sure he didn't, my love?"

Elise paused in thought, remembering the urgings of her father to go back to the cottage after his death and fetch the portrait. "Perhaps he did, Maxim, and I didn't realize it. But are you certain about what these are?"

"Aye, my love. Very certain. Whether your father is alive or dead, I've no ken, but these documents are without a doubt a guarantee, signed by the Queen herself, granting Ramsey's plea to allow you the right of inheritance of his estates if he was killed in the performance of his duties. I'm sure Walsingham had something to do with arranging it all, since Ramsey was working directly for him."

"You're not jesting," Elise stated in wonder, amazed by the way her father had gone about securing the documents. Perhaps he had been more cautious of Cassandra than she had realized.

"Here, look at this," Maxim urged and traced his finger along the elaborately scrawled script of each designated property. "According to this, at the time of his disappearance Ramsey still retained possession of all of his properties, a house in Bath, his manor house in London, and the lands upon which he had built the cottage."

"But what did my father barter off in the Stilliards? There were so many rumors about him taking away coffers of gold. Even Uncle Edward said as much."

"I'm not sure, my love. Walsingham knew what he was about. And 'tis evident now that it was your father's will that you be provided for, and this is how he arranged it, by securing an agreement from the Queen. I can well understand that you were the light of his life, and that he wanted to keep you safe from Cassandra and her sons and those who would do you harm." He laid his hand where the stiff corps ended in a point over her stomach. "I'd do no less for my daughter."

Elise leaned her cheek against his arm. "I've been

thrice blessed in this life, Maxim," she murmured reflectively. "There was first my father, now Anne, and most dear to my heart, my husband. If the future holds such joys, I'll gladly meet each day that comes."

'Twas the following Friday when Maxim received a summons from the Queen, bidding him come to London. It seemed that one of her ladies-in-waiting had been found dead at the bottom of a long flight of stairs, and though there were no witnesses to say whether or not her death had been accidental, bruises of the shape and size of a man's fingertips had been found on her throat. The deceased woman was of an age two score and three years, and it was revealed by the weeping attendants that in the last year or so she had on several occasions slipped out to secretly meet a lover.

It was further reported to Maxim that at Newgate gaol, Hilliard had also met with a serious accident. It seemed that sometime during the wee hours of the morning his throat had been cut. None could aver who the culprit was, for the inmates had common cells and every one of them attested to the innocence of the other. Still, there were those who had more coin than usual to bribe the guards, and it was rumored that before the crime took place, a wealthy barrister who no one could correctly name, had come to the gaol to visit a common thief about an inheritance left to the brigand by a dead uncle. Word had it that the bequeathed sum had been delivered in its entirety shortly after Hilliard was slain, effectively squelching tongues that were eager to wag, if truly a bribe it be.

Elise remained at Bradbury, thinking it would be only a matter of a day or two ere Maxim returned. Anne was of uncommon comfort in his absence, for the bond that had quickly formed between the two women was forged with ties of kinship and heritage. After viewing the portrait of Elise's mother, there remained no smallest shred of doubt in Anne's mind that she had been the granddaughter who was taken. The resemblance was too close to dismiss, and the necklace by itself alone gave undeniable proof they were blood kin. Elise was jubilant over the matter. She had finally found the core from which she had sprung, while Anne indulged herself in watching the budding glory of her offspring.

Nicholas, Kenneth, and the other two men made their excuses after a trio of days had passed since Maxim's departure. They took leave of the manor as a foursome with different destinations in mind. Nicholas and Justin went back to the captain's ship to oversee the loading of new cargo, while Kenneth and Sherbourne returned to their respective homes closer to London. As they made their departure, each vowed with fervent troth that if ever Elise had need of them, she had but to send word and they would return posthaste, no matter the distance between them. Almost sadly she waved them off, knowing that she would see Nicholas and Justin only briefly before they left again for some other port, and the knights perhaps only a bit more ere they returned to their duties.

In their absence Elise gave herself over to longer hours in the gardens with Anne keeping her company. The two women laughed and talked, sometimes expressing their innermost thoughts, while other times just commenting on the weather or some other inconsequential matter.

It was early in the afternoon of the fourth day of Maxim's absence that Elise put shears into a basket and ventured to the courtyard with Anne. There she snipped off fading blooms and cut flowers for the house. About midafternoon she ceased her labors, doffed her hat and gloves, and settled at a courtyard table with the elderly woman to share tea and cakes. As they chatted, a faint, distant yipping persisted and finally commanded a pause in their conversation.

"Why, that sounds like a small dog," Anne commented as she held a thin hand to her ear to listen. "What do you suppose a dog is doing here on the Bradbury lands?"

"I don't know, but it sounds like it's coming from that maze of shrubs growing near the pond. Maxim showed me the place before he left." Elise rose and put aside her napkin. "I'll go and see."

"Take your shears, dear," Anne suggested. "The poor little thing might have gotten caught in a thicket or some such."

Dropping the heavy scissors into her apron pocket, Elise slipped through the sculptured hedge that bordered the end of the courtyard. She was led by the anxious barking across a lush greensward, and as she approached the place where large shrubs had been planted in a maze, she was encouraged by the nearness of the animal, for his whining seemed very close now.

Elise entered a long, narrow lane bordered on both sides by tall hedges, and at the very end of the aisle of green sat a small, male canine, barking and whining. As soon as he saw her, he leapt up and, with tail wagging, made a dash forward to greet her, but he was brought up abruptly by a leash that was attached to the collar he wore. The other end of the tether was caught somewhere within the shrub that grew nearby. Though the fluffy little dog jumped around and tried to get free, he could not break away. Sitting down again, he wagged his tail and whined forlornly, as if begging her to come release him.

Elise laughed and hurried toward him. "What are you doing here all alone?"

He cocked his head from side to side, as if trying to understand, and she ruffled his curling thatch vigorously behind his ears. "Never mind, little boy. We'll just take you home where you can romp as free as the wind."

She bent down to free him, then realized the ornate lead had been deliberately tied to a sturdy green stalk near the bottom of the shrub. She frowned in bemusement, unable to fathom why anyone would tether a dog in this place and why they would do so on Bradbury lands.

"You always were fond of those things," came a voice behind her.

With a gasp Elise whirled around as she came to her feet, of a sudden feeling much like a woman drowning... being sucked under by waves of overwhelming fear. She knew that voice only too well! It was one she had come to dread and hate more than any other. "Forsworth!"

"Why, if it isn't Cousin Elise," he mocked. "Imagine seeing you this far from home. I'd have thought that husband of yours would have built a tall, stone wall around the house to keep you safe."

Elise wasted no precious moment with words, for she was immediately aware of the danger to herself. She turned to flee, only to stumble over the dog who was bouncing eagerly at her feet.

Forsworth was a step behind. He caught her arm and whirled her around to face him again. His teeth showed in a savage snarl as he swept the backside of his hand hard across her cheek. "You won't escape me ever again, you bitch!"

Elise staggered in a white haze of pain for a frozen moment of time, then slowly her mind cleared and she glared up at him in renewed loathing as she wiped the back of a trembling hand across a bloodied lip. A multitude of disparaging titles tempted her tongue, but she held still, well aware that she trod on dangerous ground. This was no chance meeting. Forsworth had deliberately lured her away from Bradbury, using the dog as bait, and from the dusty condition of his leather jerkin and thigh-high boots, he had ridden a far distance to reach her.

"What is it you want, Forsworth?" Her tone did not conceal her repugnance.

The generous mouth twisted in a smug, self-satisfied smile. "Why, Elise, have you forgotten so soon?" he queried in feigned amazement. "I only want you to tell me where the treasure is."

"How many times must I tell you?" she gritted out. "I don't know where the treasure is! My father never told me where he hid it! There may not even be any for all I know!"

A heavy sigh gave evidence of his displeasure. "So it's to be that way again, eh? You and me. Arguing and fighting." He shook his head slowly, as if greatly sorrowed by the idea. "You know it will go hard for you this time. I'm not as lenient as I used to be."

She scoffed. "As if you ever were! You're about as deadly as a poisonous viper, Forsworth. Everyone should be wary when you slither from your slimy hole."

"Viper, is it?" he snarled. "I'll show you!" His long fingers closed cruelly around her upper arm, and he began to slap her, venting his desire for vengeance. The small dog quickly scurried beneath the shrub, where he whined and cowered in fear, sensing all was not right between these two.

Elise struggled to remain alert beneath the harsh battering. She tasted blood in her mouth and clenched her jaw against the painful blows, but still they continued, and she knew she would not be able to withstand much more without slipping into uncaring oblivion. Concentrating hard on the moment, she slid her free hand downward into the pocket of her apron. Clasping the heavy scissors in her fist, she snatched them forth and, with a forceful descent, stabbed them into the arm that held her imprisoned. With a pained yowl Forsworth stumbled back, holding his arm as he gaped in horror at the pair of shears that protruded from his shirt. A slowly widening ring of red spread outward from the wound, darkening the cloth. Grasping the makeshift weapon, he wrenched it out, giving a great cry of pain.

Elise had anticipated the need for swift flight and was already whirling, catching up her skirts. She forced every bit of strength she possessed into her quest for freedom. She heard the thrashing, stumbling advance of her adversary behind her and knew that if not for his pain, he would have overtaken her in a thrice. His muttered threats rang in her ears, and they only gave her impetus, for she could well imagine what would happen if he caught her.

She flitted about a corner, and her breath left her as she crashed headlong into another tall, solidly muscled form that blocked the lane. Her panic knew no reason as she cried out in alarm and struggled blindly against the one who now held her. She could hear the charging Forsworth behind her, coming ever closer.

"Elise?"

Once again she recognized the voice that spoke to her, and she jerked her head up with a gasp to find Quentin's face close above her own.

"What has happened here?" he demanded, frowning

sharply as he wiped his knuckles along her bruised cheek.

"Let her go!" Forsworth commanded, seizing her arm. "She's mine!"

Quentin brought a hand down sharply upon his brother's forearm, breaking his hold, and pulled Elise to safety behind him. When Forsworth tried to follow, he shoved a broad hand against the younger's chest and pushed him back. "Back off!" he barked. "You're not touching her again!"

"I'll beat her to a bloody pulp!" railed his sibling. "I've taken enough from that little bitch!" He thrust his arm forward to display his wound, flinging flecks of blood across his brother's velvet doublet. "Look what she's done to me!"

Quentin turned his lips in repugnance at the beaded droplets that bejeweled his doublet and lifted a hand to flick them away in disgust. "From what I've seen of her battered face, Forsworth, you deserved it," he observed. "And I cannot fault Elise for defending herself. Your manners are about as swinish as an ill-tempered old boar. I swear Mother never taught you anything."

"I'll take no more of your inane prattle, Quentin!" Forsworth cried. "Now let me have the wench!"

"Need I remind you, dear brother, that the wench, as you call her, is our cousin?" Quentin stressed the question as if he found it necessary to impress a lack-witted lad. "And I, for one, am appalled to see how you've abused her. In good conscience I could not give her over to you, knowing what you'd do. Now desist with this fool's play and be gone from here!"

Forsworth pulled back a fist, intending to let it fly into his brother's face, but with a swift flick of his wrist, Quentin slipped a dagger from its sheath and pressed its point threateningly into the leather jerkin that covered the lean waist of the other.

"Have a care for your life, Forsworth," he warned direly. "You could have more of your blood spilled right here and now, and I would consider it your just due. I'll not be cuffed about by you!"

"Are you going to give her to me?" Forsworth demanded.

Quentin's ridicule was blatant. "I do believe Elise struck the wits from your head when she hit you that time. Or was she right in saying you were addled before the event?" He dropped a hand on the younger brother's shoulder as if lecturing him soundly. "Go back to where you came from and see if you can staunch that flow of blood ere you bleed to death. I don't intend to give Elise to you. She's in my protection now, and 'twill be death to pay if you try to take her from me by force. I swear I will slice open your belly ere you take her."

Forsworth jerked away from the other's touch. "Get your hands off me, you Judas goat," he snarled and stepped awkwardly away, glaring at his brother. "Be warned, Quentin. I'm coming back for her."

The elder smiled tolerantly. "As you wish, Forsworth. I've no special love for you that I would mourn overlong at your loss. I always thought we were half-brothers anyway."

"Meaning?"

An amused grin slowly traced the handsome lips. "Meaning I believe you're a bastard child, Forsworth, of no kin to Bardolf Radborne."

"Damn you!" the younger shouted. "You're calling our mother a slut! An adulteress!"

Quentin shrugged casually. "I always thought you inherited your slow wits from some simple dolt, and we both know that my father was a man with a good mind."

"If he was so smart, why'd he let himself be poisoned?" Forsworth sneered.

"What do you mean?" Quentin questioned sharply.

Now it was Forsworth's turn to gloat as he indicated Elise. "Ask her all about it."

The older brother slowly turned his head until he could see his cousin over his shoulder. "What is he talking about?"

Elise wrung her hands in distress, knowing that Quentin had held his father in great esteem.

"Tell me!"

She jumped at his barked command and reluctantly revealed what she knew. " 'Twas rumored in my father's house long ago that Cassandra poisoned both my mother and your father."

"The bitch! I'll kill her!"

Forsworth chuckled in derision until the elder caught the front of the leather jerkin with such force that it nearly knocked the younger brother back upon his heels. Snarling his rage into his brother's face, Quentin shook him hard enough to rattle the teeth in his head.

"You bastard, I'll scrub your face from one end of this lane to the other if you don't stop that!"

Forsworth's humor was effectively squelched, and he gritted through grinding teeth, "I'm no bastard!"

"You're no brother of mine!" Quentin shoved him away in disgust. "Get out of here!"

"Not without Elise."

"Be gone from here!"

The younger started at the command, then his eyes went beyond his brother to fix the lady with a glare. "I'll make you sorry you were ever born, slut."

Elise did not try to hide her revulsion for the man. "My regret has always been that we were born blood kin. You can be assured I'll take hope that we're not kin."

"Watch for me," he warned. "I'm coming back to get you."

"Watch out, or she might get you first," Quentin scoffed.

Forsworth jeered at his brother's humor. "You needn't worry about me, brother. I'll not give this bitch another chance to sink her nails into me." Then with a final sneer, he turned and ran off down the lane.

A sigh of relief escaped Elise as Quentin faced her, but she realized by the pained look in her cousin's eyes that he was hurting inside. "I'm sorry about Cassandra and Uncle Bardolf."

"I should have expected as much." He heaved a sigh, calming himself. "There've been times when I've wished she wasn't my mother."

Elise laid a gentle hand upon his arm and murmured in gratitude, "Thank you for being here when I needed you."

Quentin swept her a solemn bow. "The pleasure has been all mine, madam."

"But why are you here?" she inquired, somewhat perplexed. "How did you manage to find me?"

"I went to the house and was told you were out in the garden. When I went to look for you, I saw where you'd been working, and then I heard the dog barking." He glanced back at the whining animal. " 'Twould appear that Forsworth has left you a present. Do you think he brought it to make amends?"

"Not likely," Elise answered dryly and, wiping her bruised and bloodied cheek on her apron, went to where the animal strained at the leash. The wagging of the short tail quickened as she loosened the tether and freed him, but he wove an eager, crisscrossing path in front of her skirts as she tried to walk.

A slow grin twisted Quentin's lips. "Forsworth was going to present that dog as a present to the Queen, but he's never been able to gain an audience with her. He was hoping she would be so fond of his gift, she would bestow a title on him."

"Clever woman, the Queen, to deny him access to her court," Elise commented, then looked up at her cousin with a querying brow raised. "Did you come for a visit?"

The smile faded from Quentin's face as he took on a serious demeanor. "I came to tell you that I've discovered where your father is being held prisoner."

"Where?" The question was expelled from her lips in a breathless rush.

"I'm afraid I'll have to show you. 'Tis too hard to explain."

Elise fretted anxiously. "Maxim isn't here, and I promised him I wouldn't leave the house unless well-escorted."

"Rumor is in the wind that the kidnappers are getting ready to move Ramsey, perhaps to send him out of the country again. 'Twould appear that every wasted moment is another stroke against us. Even now he may be en route to a waiting ship. If you take time to secure an escort, we may be too late. I've sent a message to Lord Seymour in London, making him aware of everything that is happening."

"But how will Maxim know where we are if I go with you?"

"He knows the countryside well enough to find the place where I told him to meet me. I can lead him the rest of the way."

A small frown betrayed Elise's bemusement. "But what benefit will my presence be to my father? How can I possibly help him?"

"You can tell the kidnappers that the treasure is on its way, that your husband will be bringing it to buy your father's freedom."

A strange prickling shivered down Elise's spine. From far off, she could hear Anne calling her, and with great care she asked, "Why would Maxim bring the treasure?"

"I've heard it said that he knows where it is. It only seems right that he would want to ransom Ramsey with it."

Though Elise would have denied the possibility of Quentin being the kidnapper, the question screamed at her. How could he otherwise know? How could he have received such information about Maxim and the treasure if not by way of the Queen's attendant telling him?

"I hear Anne calling me. I'd better go and tell her I'm all right." Cautiously Elise kept her steps slow as she turned away from him, explaining, "Besides, I must change my clothes and have my mount saddled. I'll meet you at the house."

Quentin followed on her heels. "I took the liberty of having your mare saddled for you, Elise. She's tied with my mount nearby. You must come with me now, or all will be lost."

"Really, Quentin, I must change my clothes," she insisted, trying to control the quiver in her voice. "Anne will be worrying about me."

He laid a gentle hand upon her shoulder, setting her heart to thumping wildly. "I must insist you come now, Elise."

She bolted into a run, startling Quentin by the sudden change in her manner. Realizing he had somehow blundered, he cursed and raced after her, easily overtaking her. He clasped both arms about her waist and, swinging her off her feet, clamped a hand over her mouth as he pressed his face near her ear. "Whether you struggle or not, Elise, you're coming with me. I need you to talk some sense into your father. He's been too stubborn for his own good."

Her reply was lost beneath his hand, and she fought against him with every measure of her being. It pained her terribly to believe that Quentin was the hated kidnapper, for she had truly liked him, and she could only marvel at how thoroughly she had been fooled.

Chapter 31

*I*F MAXIM HAD ONCE considered the fair Elise a thorn in his side, then Quentin must have compared her to a sharp stave. It took most of his strength and all of his resolve to bring her under control without setting up an alarm at the distant Bradbury Hall. He jerked his hand away from her mouth with a curse and stared almost in amazement at the neat curve of teeth marks left in the fleshy part. In the next instant she drew a breath to scream, and visions of a venging horde descending upon him from the house promptly filled his head. His need for haste in subduing the birthing squall was frustrated by her thrashing head and overactive teeth. Finally he jammed a kerchief into her resisting mouth and then sucked on a frayed knuckle. He caught up the long apron she wore and wound it around her arms and hands until those flailing and clawing members were both restrained. With a small knife he cut off a length of the apron tie and used it to secure the gag which she was wont to spit out.

Laboring against the resistance of this most uncooperative and tenacious sprite, Quentin lifted her in his arms and had to fight to keep her within his grasp as he made his way through the shrubs. She writhed like a slippery eel that refused to yield and gave his greater strength a severe testing as she kicked and twisted in a frenzied effort to escape.

"Dammit, Elise! Keep still!" he barked when he nearly dropped her.

A wild thrashing of her head accompanied her mumbled reply, and he knew he wasted his breath. His band of men stared in awe as he stumbled forth from the tangle of shrubs with a strangled oath, the best he could manage after receiving the full, backward thrust of her arm against his throat. He coughed and wheezed in air through his bruised pipes, seriously questioning his decision in going alone to get the maid. He soon found lifting her to the back of her steed was no less of a problem. The moment he turned away to fetch a cord to bind her with, she slithered down to the greensward. He stretched out an arm to catch her, but she ducked beneath the horse's neck and raced away as fast as her bonds would permit, much to the amusement of his men. Chasing her down, he scooped her up again and this time received the full thrust of her elbow to the jaw. He staggered in a daze for a moment, feeling as if his brain had just been jarred loose, and stumbled back toward the steed. He restored her once more to the saddle, then wrapped her skirts with the rope until she could scarcely move her legs. Taking no chances, he wound it around her waist and the pommel until she was lashed securely in place. Still, when he chanced to meet her glaring gaze, he read her unbridled hatred and her promise of dire recompense, should the opportunity present itself.

Quentin took the reins and, wrapping them about his hand, stepped into the stirrup of his own saddle, just as Elise kicked her mount hard with her heel. The confused mare did a skittering, sideways scamper, nearly dragging Quentin across the back of his mount. By dint of will, he regained his balance and settled into the saddle. Reining his mount close against hers, he raised his quirt and slashed the innocent mare viciously across the face. One glance at his sweating, snarling visage warned Elise that his fragile temper was close to the breaking point, and she would be better off biding her time under a meeker bent of spirit.

It was a long ride, and the afternoon light dulled as the sun lowered behind clouds in the western sky and slowly spread a reddish glow across the land. Elise knew only that they traveled in a general westerly direction. They made a short camp beneath the shelter of some trees and rose again well before dawn to continue their journey. It was close to evening of that day when they topped a long ridge that overlooked a shallow, boulder-strewn valley. Perhaps a furlong or so beyond the ridge the earth rose again to form a knoll, upon which squatted the tumbled remains of a deserted castle. Her first glimpse of the crumbling edifice reminded her of Faulder Castle, but in comparison, the other keep would have possessed a semblance of grandeur. This was hardly more than a shell of a place. Only a single tower at the far side raised its weather-beaten battlements above the crumbling walls as if in bold defiance of the elements.

Dusk had already begun to settle upon the land when they passed between two piles of rubble that evidenced the general location of a onetime gate. A pair of guards rose from the shelters to challenge them with crossbows at the ready. Quentin swept back the hood of his cloak to identify himself and dropped a hand to his thigh as he rode past, seeming pleased by the alertness of his men. As she watched him, Elise had the sudden suspicion that she had seen him in a similar pose somewhere else, but the impression was fleeting, and she turned her gaze to the handful of men gathered around a warm fire. Quentin snapped an order to them, and they hastened to douse the flames and stamp out the coals until all evidence of a fire was gone.

Quentin dismounted and, tossing the reins of his mount to one of his men, came to free Elise from the bonds that held her in the saddle. He lifted her down, but when her feet struck the ground, her knees buckled beneath her. He caught her and would have swept her into his arms, but she snarled her denial through the gag. With stubborn effort, she heaved herself away from him and leaned against the side of the mare.

Quentin smiled indulgently and reached out to free her gag. "Now behave," he cajoled as she glared at him. " 'Tis not in my mind to hurt you. I only want your company for a while, until your husband hands over the treasure."

"Where's my father?" Her words came out mangled by a dry, parched mouth.

"He's near," Quentin assured her. "No need for you to fret. He's in . . . ah . . . reasonably good health."

Elise disdained his bland smile. "I don't know what tempted you to ever do this horrible thing, Quentin. To think that you were once my favorite cousin. Now it comes to me that I'm not a very good judge of character."

"You know I've always been fond of you too, Elise." He lifted his wide shoulders in an indolent shrug as she gave him a dubious stare. "If not for me, Hilliard would have killed your father when they caught him spying on us in the Stilliards. When I argued that he was worth saving because of the treasure he had hidden, they dumped him on one of Hilliard's ships and took him off to Lubeck. If not for my threats to call a halt to the plot against the Queen, he'd probably still be there . . . or dead. Hilliard was not a very patient man. Ramsey would not have long withstood his torture."

"If you truly saved my father's life, then I must be grateful," Elise replied stiffly. "But you've brought havoc down upon yourself by keeping him prisoner and by taking me."

"I've heard of your husband's reputation," Quentin acknowledged. " 'Twould have taken a man of such daring to pluck Hilliard from his well-guarded nest, but I'm more wary. I've no intention of letting him know where or who I am."

"He'll find out. You can be sure of that," Elise warned.

"Then the game will become dangerous to both of us. He has what I want, and I"—he smiled ruefully—"have what he wants. An even exchange seems in order. Otherwise, the innocent shall suffer, and that I've no stomach for."

"No stomach for murder?" she queried with a delicate brow arched in doubt. "What of your mistress? What of Hilliard?"

Quentin heaved a laborious sigh. "When my life is threatened, I must take certain measures to guarantee my safety, though in truth they are against my nature. Still, what I've done to others, I'd be reluctant to do to you."

"But you'd still kill me if you had to," she jeered.

"Come along," he bade solicitously, tugging lightly on the rope. "I've answered enough of your questions."

"You won't get away with this, Quentin. If you harm my father, they'll be after you ..."

Quentin gave a sharp tug on the rope, causing her to stumble on the smooth stone as he pulled her along with him into the tower. "Really, Elise, all those dire warnings are not going to do a bit of good. They tend to weary me."

He paused just inside the tower and lifted a nearby torch from an iron sconce. Raising the flaming brand, he gestured to where stone stairs made a circular descent to the dungeons below.

"Now follow me and watch your step," he cautioned. "You could fall and hurt yourself."

Leading the way slowly downward, he held the torch high to light her way. Elise found the damp, mossy steps treacherous and her balance even more precarious with her arms securely bound by the skirt of her apron. They entered into the cavernous, torch-lit depths of the tower, stepped past a grating in the floor, and then passed a handful of guards gathered around a stout table piled high with dirty trenchers and the dried, crusted scraps of many a past meal.

One of the men shoved away the debris with his arm as he spied Quentin and sneered. "This rot eats at me belly," he muttered. "What I wouldn't give ta sink me teeth inta some tasty vittles. 'Ere needs be a cook here." He nudged an elbow against his neighbor's arm and leered after Elise as she passed. "Maybe her liedyship here can cook for us."

"I doubt it," Quentin retorted with little humor and squelched the man's laughter with a cold-eyed glare. "You'd better mind your manners with this one, or you'll answer to me."

"She yer new light-o'-love?" heckled a bold one with a chortle.

Quentin dropped the cord as he instructed his cousin, "Wait here."

Since there was nowhere she could go to effect an escape, Elise obeyed his directive and half-turned to watch as Quentin made a point of selecting a cudgel from a nearby pile of wood. Slapping it against the palm of his hand, he strode back to the man who had foolishly opened his mouth. That one was tall and broad of form and seemed confident of his prowess as he grinned up at the one who came to stand beside him. As the dark eyes fixed him with a stony stare, he shrugged and turned to swill his ale. He was just raising the tankard to his lips when the cudgel came down on top of it. The mug plummeted from his grasp, flinging ale in a whirling eddy as the stick continued downward across his arm, drawing a pained yowl from the man.

"Next time," Quentin cautioned almost gently as he bent closer to the grimacing man, "you'd better mind your manners, or you won't have an arm left to lift to your guzzling lips. Do I make myself clear?"

The bruised one eagerly nodded and as Quentin moved away, the man wiped in disdain at the wet droplets soaking into his breeches. Elise understood the message her cousin had just delivered to his troop. Even in his absence, she was not to be approached or harmed in any way. At least for this, she could be grateful.

In passing her, Quentin paused to slide the torch into an empty sconce and, glancing back, motioned her on. "This way."

Reluctantly Elise followed him down a pair of wide, stone steps and they progressed to where a wall of heavy iron bars separated a darkly shadowed cell from the rest of the room. Her cousin plied a large key to the massive lock and, lifting a ponderous bar, swung the gate open.

"Your chambers, my lady."

Elise moved cautiously through the door, having no ken what lurked in the blackened void beyond the bars. She turned in some indecision to Quentin and he reached to free her hands, then he swung the door

closed between them. He inclined his head toward
the corner of the cell where no light had reached,
and glancing askance, Elise saw only the end of a cot.

"Your father should be waking up soon. 'Twas only
a small draught of potion that was given to help him
sleep."

With a gasp Elise flew to the narrow bed and though
her blindly searching hands found a long, thin form,
she could not discern whether or nay the man was
kin.

"A candle, Quentin, please!" she begged with a sob.

"As my lady wishes." He fetched the torch and
thrust it into a nearby sconce.

Elise sank carefully to the edge of the cot, where
she stared down at the heavily bearded face of the
sleeping man. Even beneath the thick brush of whiskers there was no mistaking him. Her tears spilled
profusely down her cheeks as she took note of his
gaunt features and the thinly fleshed hands. His breathing barely lifted the wall of his chest, and almost in
fear she gently shook his arm, receiving little response.

Quentin called back over his shoulder for a man to
bring a pitcher of water and a rag. The one who answered his summons scurried in haste to do his bidding and was briefly allowed entry into the cell to
deliver the requested items.

"Here ye are, m'liedy," the small man said, setting
the pitcher on a small, rough-hewn table near the cot.
"Som'pin ta wash away the gentl'man's sleep."

Elise immediately dipped a cloth in the water, and,
wringing it free of droplets, she began to wash the
bearded face. Slowly her father roused to a vague
awareness, and for a long moment he rolled his head
and searched with his eyes as if his mind crawled
from a deep well of darkness. His gaze found her, and

his parched lips moved briefly. She bent closer as they moved again.

"Elise?"

"Oh, Papa!"

The cherished title was like a tender caress softly soothing him, and tears welled up in his eyes as he sighed the words. "My Elise."

Chapter 32

*T*HE WITHDRAWING ROOM of the Grand High Chancellor of the Order of the Garter and First Secretary to the Queen was not a small chamber, yet the space was filled with personages of such rank and prestige as to make the atmosphere almost stuffy. There were knights in breastplates of silver, dukes in fur-lined blanchets, earls in elaborately embroidered doublets, and such garments as to make Maxim's garb, though tastefully handsome, perhaps the plainest in the room, save for the somber black of the Secretary's own. That official had completed his noonday repast and ventured out into the antechamber to partake of the informal exchange ere the afternoon's business commenced. He had elected to join Maxim who possessed enough experience, position, and wisdom to be content with his way of life and could, for that reason, carry on a reasonable conversation without interjecting ambitious little remarks or clever insinuations or innuendos against a rival. Eager to know the outcome of his investigation, Sir Francis engaged him in a careful review of what he had discovered about the two murders.

"We've obtained a description of the barrister who visited Newgate," Maxim informed him. "And we've managed to find one of the Queen's ladies who actually saw the murdered woman with her lover a few weeks before the incident. Her description of the man is remarkably close to the one we received from the guards at the gaol. Tall. Dark-haired. Dark-eyed. Handsome. 'Tis my belief they're one and the same. I may also have a name we can lay to the man. The Queen's attendant led us to a page who had carried a couple of messages to the murdered woman from a man, and it seems that particular steward has always had a penchant for learning names of people at court and those associated with them. We need only to affirm that it was the same man."

"Why was Hilliard murdered?" Sir Francis inquired.

"Both Hilliard and the man's mistress could identify him, and with Hilliard in the gaol and destined to be drawn on hurdles at St. Giles-in-the-Field, he had reason to fear the agent would name him as a conspirator ere he retired from this world."

Sir Francis clasped his hands behind his back and jutted out his bearded chin thoughtfully as he scanned the room. Besides Maxim, he had more than fifty agents in his personal employ here in England and abroad in foreign courts. There were others in his hire whose work was obscure to all but him. Even now his man, Gilbert Gifford, was bringing evidence of the plot Babington and his accomplices had contrived in an effort to free Mary and assassinate Elizabeth. His spies worked with a high degree of efficiency, and the Marquess of Bradbury was one of his best.

The Secretary sighed heavily. "I wish the Queen was more appreciative of our efforts to keep her safe. My purse grows flatter by the day, and I'm ever pressed to ask Cecil to intervene in my behalf so I can fund these missions to safeguard her life."

"Lord Burghley knows her better than any of us,"

Maxim encouraged the man. "If anyone can get her to finance your endeavors, he should be able to."

"In the meantime I must be indebted to you. I'm aware that it cost you a goodly sum to find Hilliard out and bring him back here."

"Think no more of it. I'm grateful to have my honor restored."

"Aye, I thought I had lost a good man when Master Stamford brought accusations against you to the Queen, but it only opened a way for you to draw out Hilliard. I'm amazed at how well things worked toward that end."

"I nearly died because of it," Maxim observed in rueful retrospect.

"The reality of what happened to you could not be argued against. 'Twas not a ploy, and because it actually occurred, your flight to Hamburg was all the more convincing, enabling you to draw Hilliard in. Had you not come to me the night of your return to England and begged to be given a chance to prove your innocence, you'd have still been an affront to her majesty . . . a condemned man."

"I'm glad my loyalty to the Queen has been reaffirmed, so in years to come my children need not suffer her disfavor." A smile curved Maxim's lips. "Elise is expecting our first child later this year."

Sir Francis clapped him on the back in hearty congratulation. " 'Tis good news, indeed! May we drink a toast to your continued good fortune . . . ?"

"Your lordship . . . Lord Seymour?" A youthful lieutenant tentatively interrupted and cleared his throat nervously when Maxim turned to face him. A roughly garbed man with unshorn beard was pushing close behind the lieutenant, almost on his heels.

"What is it?" Maxim asked, amused at the hesitancy of the steward.

The officer seized the collar of the scruffy one's coat as that one tried to force his way past, but the peasant was determined to reach his goal and nearly dragged the lieutenant forward with him. With anger-reddened face, the younger seized the elder firmly and bade him to wait. Exasperated with this undisciplined man, he straightened his doublet with a jerk and forgot his awe of the Secretary and the Marquess.

"Your pardon, my lords, but this man claims to be a courier and has been sent with an important mis ... *ugh!*" He grunted in pain as the nondescript one elbowed him in the ribs and shoved his way to the fore.

"I be called William 'Anks, yer lordship," the impatient man declared. He reached inside his frayed tunic and drew forth a folded parchment sealed with a blob of featureless red wax. Squinting up at Maxim, he slapped the packet against the open palm of his hand. "I tooks a solemn oath ta deliver this missive inta yer 'ands an' was promised a gold sovereign from yer very own purse for bringin' h'it 'ere ta yez."

"The man's a thief!" the outraged lieutenant exclaimed.

Maxim plucked the required coin from his purse and flipped it in front of the straggly one's eyes. "Here's the coin to pay for your hire, but the letter had better be worth every bit of its value."

The unkempt messenger swept his hand above Maxim's, swooping the coin away in its descent, and leered triumphantly at the lieutenant as he passed the parchment on to the nobleman.

"Who gave you this?" Maxim asked in some confusion as he saw his full title scrawled across the front of the letter.

"I wouldn't be knowin' the man," the courier averred. " 'E wore a hooded cloak, an' 'twere pitch black when 'e come beatin' 'is fist on me door. I come a far piece ta fetch this ta yez, an', 'is lor'ship gave me no more coins 'an what 'ould pay for the barge ta come downriver. If not for 'im assurin' me I'd be rewarded well, I wouldna've even come." He tapped a finger against the front of the parchment. " 'E said h'it were important an' for yez ta read h'it at once."

Maxim split the seal with his thumbnail and lifted the letter up close to the light. As he read the contents, his face took on such a look of pained horror that the Secretary became alarmed. As he crumpled the letter, his features contorted into a snarl of pure rage, and a low growl rumbled in his throat, reminding Sir Francis of a wild beast on the hunt.

"Is aught amiss?"

The Secretary's words came to Maxim as if through a long tunnel. He fought the rage that threatened to send him howling in mindless pursuit across the hills and, with a dark, ominous frown, gritted out, "Elise has been taken hostage." He held out the parchment to Walsingham. "Her captor is demanding ransom for her release."

"Were h'it worth the gold sovereign?" the courier asked worriedly. From the expression on the nobleman's face, he had grave doubts that he would be able to keep his money.

"Take it and get out of here!" Sir Francis snapped over his shoulder and glared at the man's retreating form. He jerked his head to the lieutenant. "Tell Captain Reed to have that man followed."

When the Secretary turned back to Maxim, it was just in time to see him slip out the door. He continued to stare for a long moment, scrubbing the point of his neatly trimmed beard with the back of a thin knuckle.

Raising his hand, he flicked it, gaining the attention of a major of the Fourth Mounted Dragoons, and retired to his private chambers as that one made haste to follow.

Elizabeth was in counsel with a small group of northern lords when a message came to her from her First Secretary. A frown flitted across her brow as she read it, and when the meeting ended, she excused herself as gracefully as possible and reread the note. She penned a quick message to Lord Burghley, then summoned a colonel of the Third Royal Fusiliers and the commander of her agents.

Captain Von Reijn was working his way through a pile of manifests and lading bills in his Stilliard apartment when Justin came running up the stairs and, without so much as a tap of warning, burst through the door. The young man flipped the missive down on top of the desk where Nicholas sat and, without giving the captain a chance to read it, announced, " 'Tis from Maxim! Elise has been kidnapped from Bradbury."

Nicholas shot to his feet and slammed down a sheaf of papers he had been perusing. The oath that escaped his lips was such an unkind reflection on the parentage of the perpetrator of the deed that it gave Justin a very brief moment of pause. The two of them launched into a veritable frenzy of activity, igniting *Herr* Dietrich's curiosity, and though the afternoon was growing late, ere another hour's passing they were ready and gone with the cook following along at his own insistence.

Sir Kenneth was at his estate north of London, attending to a multitude of neglected affairs when the courier from Maxim arrived. He broke the seal of the letter and read the contents, then by way of the same courier, sent word off to Sherbourne. Taking the stairs three steps at a time, he crossed the landing and stormed into his chambers where he began to select the garb and weapons he would take.

Edward Stamford was the only one at the Radborne manor who managed to find the sweet relief in his dreams after Maxim returned to outfit himself for the journey and it was revealed that Elise had once again been kidnapped. The light tread of Arabella's footsteps on the stairs did not draw the attention of the household as she terminated her short visit there. She rode back to her husband's estate and, calling for a barge to be readied, prepared herself for a trip to Bradbury and beyond.

The twice-wed, once-widowed Cassandra indulged herself in what had become her favorite pastime of late, berating her sons who had not had the foresight to occupy themselves with duties beyond her sight and hearing. She was sure that either Elise or Arabella had gone to the officers of the court to seek a warrant for her arrest and was reluctant to venture forth from her current residence lest she be recognized and arrested. Her confinement chafed sorely on her need to range afield and secure support for the style of life to which she had become accustomed. Thus she vented her spite on her offspring and, try as they might, neither one of them could find an appropriate excuse to credit his absence.

'Twas much to their mutual relief that a shaggy messenger arrived and slowly, painstakingly repeated the words that the nearly illiterate Forsworth had bade him deliver. When he had finished, Cassandra rose from her threadbare couch and began to pace the floor. After a while the man lifted a fing·r to catch her attention.

"Ah . . . yer pardon me liedy, but 'is lor'ship was kind

'nough ta promise me a farthin' or two for me troubles."

Cassandra glared at the bold peasant for a space, then smiled and informed him sweetly, "Well, 'tis good that he did. The next time you see his *lordship* Forsworth, you must remind him of that fact."

Both of the sons in attendance snickered behind their hands and the disappointed messenger found his own way out. As the door closed behind him, Cassandra wagged a finger at the brothers and warned sternly:

"Listen to me! That measly Quentin has taken it into his mind to wheedle away our treasure for his own!" She smiled with such obvious evil intent that the hair crawled on the napes of both sons. She began to pace again and mumbled her musings aloud as she orbited the couch. "Forsworth said he followed Quentin and his small band of hirelings 'til it was plain they were taking Mistress Fine-and-Haughty to Kensington Keep..."

"That tumbledown castle?" one of her offspring scoffed. "They'll do good to find shelter from the rain there."

"Nevertheless," Cassandra continued, tossing a brief glare toward the one who intruded into her speech, "that's where they've gone."

"Why would Elise go with the likes of Quentin?" the other son inquired. "What does he have that we don't have?"

Cassandra's eyelids lowered until mere slivers remained for those pale gray orbs. Through that meager space she locked a disdaining stare upon the unwise son who had posed such a question. "You imbecile! She didn't go of her own free will! He took her! Carried her off by force, with his band of brigands giving him aid!"

"Oooeee! I bet that made her mad!" chortled the younger of the two. "Elise's got a temper hotter than a smithy's furnace."

Again the elder presented a serious question to his mother. "Why would Quentin want to take our cousin off to Kensington Keep when he berated us for taking her? He said himself she probably didn't know where the treasure was. If he believes that, what does he expect to gain?"

A moment of silence passed as Cassandra debated the question, and then a sudden light of understanding dawned. She snapped her fingers and faced her uncomprehending whelps. "He's had Ramsey all along! He was the one who took him! He must have! And now, thanks to my very good son, Forsworth, we can set him back upon his heels."

"What are we goin' to do?"

Cassandra barely made a full lap around the couch when she paused with a command. "Fetch some muskets and get ready to ride."

The pair collected their wits, a brief enough task to be sure, and the more serious one boldly dared another inquiry. "Where are we to get any horses?"

"Steal them if you have to, but get them!" railed the woman, and dismissed them with a flourish of her hand. "Now get out!"

The two brothers collided in their haste to obey, and the younger sprawled to the floor, tangled in the other's legs. Grinding her teeth in snarling vexation, Cassandra set her hands upon her narrow waist and strode forward to swing an expensively shod foot against the rising backside of the graceless one.

"Can't you do *anything* without falling over yourself?"

* * *

The first evidence of Elise's capture had come by way of the small dog who had scampered to the house in answer to Anne's call. He had barked and whined until she roused the household to perform a search of the distant labyrinth, and a short time later a pair of bloodied shears were brought back from the narrow lane. Recognizing them as the pair Elise had taken, Anne collapsed in a dead faint.

Fitch and Spence immediately took to horse to follow the trail left across the greensward where the horses' hooves had churned up the sod. Signs of their passage led them northward toward the lane, and once upon the road, the pair raced along, keeping a sharp eye toward the ground beside the lane to watch for a place where the band of riders might have left it. A double issue of stout, cloth-yard shafts filled the quivers slung upon their backs, and sturdy longbows were carried alongside. Spence bore a mace at his side with a pair of muskets tucked into his belt, while Fitch had chosen to outfit himself with a long-handled war axe and a brace of pistols. Their purpose was deadly, and their glowering eyes bespoke of their desire to serve vengeance on any who would do their mistress harm.

Maxim arrived at Bradbury sometime near midnight and paused only long enough to equip himself and saddle Eddy, then he rode out, not daring to stay overlong in the chambers he had shared with his wife. The weight on his chest was too great, the ache too deep.

The mists and vapors stirred by the cool night roiled in the low glades and hung motionless in the copses, but Maxim rode on like a venging nightshade. A pair of muskets was tucked in his belt, augmented by heavier dragoons lashed to his saddle. The long, ever-faithful, two-edged rapier hung at his side, and at the small of his back beneath his doublet, a slender dagger.

It was shortly after the rising sun had broken free of the horizon that he finally paused beside a well and gave rest to Eddy. He was there when a trio of riders came over the hill and, laying his hand to the hilt of his sword, Maxim stood and prepared to draw it forth. It was a moment before he recognized the pale hair of Nicholas Von Reijn and the two who accompanied him.

"Ho, Maxim!" the captain shouted, reining his mount to a halt. The animal chafed at the tight restriction enforced upon him by the bit and danced in a nervous circle as Nicholas posed the question, "Vhere are ve bound?"

"West!" Maxim answered, swinging into his saddle.

With a shout the captain touched his heels to the flanks of his steed. "Let's go!"

The villagers turned in alarm as the flying hooves thundered past on the road, and they gawked in awe as the four sped over the next hill with cloaks flying widespread behind them. Plumes of dust flew up in their wake to obscure their rapidly diminishing forms, and the rumble of their flight dwindled to an eerie silence ere the sounds of early morning returned.

It was shortly after midday when they paused on a hill to scan the countryside that stretched out before them. A pair of mounted riders raced ahead, and even from a distance the lean and stout forms of Fitch and Spence were easily discernible. With a shout Maxim brought the two men to a halt, and whirling their mounts about, the servants waited until they were joined by the four. Now they were six who rode together with a single purpose.

Near nightfall Maxim's small force reached the edge of the forest above a ridge. They made a camp and settled in to wait the coming of light. It was perhaps an hour later when Fitch, who had drawn the first watch, roused the sleepers with a low-voiced warning. "Someone's comin'. Two riders mayhap."

Maxim gave a quick glance at the night sky. A gusty nor'wester had blown in and ran its ethereal fingers through the tops of the tall oaks. A low scudding of clouds accompanied the wind and drifted over the face of the moon. He belted on his sword and gave quick orders that sent the members of his small band along both sides of the lane.

They did not have long to wait before a pair of dark shadows came riding along the lane. A grumbling comment from one of the riders intruded into the silence of the night and brought Maxim out of hiding. He stepped onto the road and waited their approach with arms akimbo.

"Ho! Sir Kenneth!"

The knight's horse was already skittish, and when he glimpsed the dark apparition that stood before him, he balked and did a sudden spin about, nearly unseating the travel-worn man. Kenneth barked a loud curse as he fought the frightened steed and finally managed to settle him down.

Sherbourne chortled and, pressing his mount near, clapped his friend on the back. "Only another reason for you to geld that stallion, my friend. One day he's going to spill your brains out."

Sir Kenneth cautiously dismounted with a mumbled, "Not ere I spill his."

Sherbourne came to earth with more grace and approached Maxim with long, swift strides. "We came as soon as we could," he assured him, clasping his lordship's arm in camaraderie. "Do you know where she's being held? Do you have a plan?"

"Nay to both," Maxim sighed, "but when I know

the answer to the first, then I'll know where to go with the second."

Chill raindrops began to slash down, and the men sought shelter in a protected niche beneath an outcropping of rock. Kenneth built a small fire, over which Dietrich prepared a fast, but palatable, meal, and the men gathered in the meager shelter to counsel and take nourishment.

Chapter 33

*T*HE PLACE OF MEETING had been carefully selected. It was a wide, clear valley with a small stream meandering through it. A narrow stone bridge provided access across the water, but beyond the cluster of trees that marched along the hillsides, there was not so much as a clump of brush to hide behind from there to the water's brink. The bridge could not be approached from any direction without a traveler being seen for a goodly distance. Even so, it would have taken either an utterly fearless or foolish soul to have crossed the planks of the bridge. Great gaping holes marred its footing where the underlying timbers had rotted away and the buttressing stones had tumbled away.

The sun rose high to mark the meeting hour, and still Maxim waited on the ridge beneath the shadows of the trees. His companions kept themselves well-hidden beyond a thicket, and from there they could observe the happenings of this first meeting. The green eyes flicked from one end of the valley to the next as Maxim searched for some sign of the kidnappers. Finally eleven mounted men came into view on a distant ridge. They rode along its edge for a time before one cloaked and hooded rider broke from their ranks and made the descent into the valley. In response Maxim urged Eddy down the hill and halted

him near the bridge. His adversary drew nigh the
opposite end and reined his prancing horse around
as his eyes skimmed the distant hills, then he pulled
the steed up with a jerk.

"So! We meet at last, Lord Seymour," Quentin called
almost pleasantly.

Maxim allowed a stiff nod to accompany his answer.
"I'm here at your bidding." His own gaze raised to
scan the ridge and the riders who waited there. "I
believe you have taken someone who belongs to me.
Where is she?"

"Safe . . . for the moment." Quentin adjusted the
hood to keep his face carefully concealed as he took
full note of the cold, steely glint in the green eyes.
He knew this was not a man to play games with. The
Marquess was deadly serious. "Have you the treasure?"

" 'Twill take a pair of days getting here. And of
course, you'll not be given the chests unless my wife
is returned . . . unharmed. Now how do you intend to
conduct the exchange so each of us will be content?"

Quentin lifted his gaze to scan the wooded ridge
behind Seymour and found no evidence that he had
been accompanied to the place. Still, he was not going
to underestimate one of such formidable reputation.
"I'll give you the father," he explained, considering
the nobleman again. "He will be tied to this bridge
and left bound and gagged. You may ask him if his
daughter yet lives and if he knows where she is. He'll
be able to answer both with a nod. You'll open the
chest of gold and display its contents, then close and
secure it with a rope. My men will have their muskets
aimed at you as you toss the rope across the bridge.
If you should make any attempt to come across or
release Sir Ramsey ere I've inspected the treasure myself and before my men and I have reached the safety

of the ridge, you both will be shot. Your wife is no more than a couple of hours' ride from here. I figure by the time you get there, I should be well upon my way."

Maxim scoffed at the proposal. "How will I know that you won't kill my wife and her father to hide your identity?"

"I'm leaving for Spain. I doubt any of you will follow me there." Quentin crossed his wrists and rested them upon the high pommel of the saddle. "The time of our next meeting will be at the same hour, the day after the morrow. Come with the treasure."

"I must see my wife ere you see a coin of the treasure. Bring her first, then I can go fetch Ramsey after I'm sure she's all right."

Jeering laughter accompanied Quentin's denial. "If I were to grant your plea, my lord, you might try to save your wife and the treasure, too. I need time to make good my escape. If I leave Ramsey with you, I can be assured that you'll make haste to reach Elise. You have no other choice."

Maxim's eyes flicked up to fix the shadowed face in the hood. "You use my wife's name with ease, as if you've been acquainted with it for some time."

"What does it matter how I say her name? She'll not be released until I have the treasure in hand."

"Quentin, is it?" Maxim queried.

Surprise shook Quentin's confidence, and almost breathlessly he asked, "How did you know?"

"You were not as careful as you thought you were," Maxim replied. "And there were some who were curious enough to find out who you were."

Quentin lifted a hand to sweep the hood back from his head, seeing no further reason in hiding his face. "If I were you, my lord, until this matter be done, I'd be most cautious about what is spilled . . . if you truly care for your lady."

"And if I were you, Quentin, until this matter be done, I'd be most cautious about how you care for my lady. I'll not belabor the reason why. Let's just say I'll not be adverse to following you to Spain to have my revenge."

With that stern warning Maxim reined Eddy about and sent him flying back up the ridge. He raced beyond the thicket and there halted the stallion as his men stepped from hiding. A vision of Elise lying upon a bed of stone drifted through his mind, but the blue eyes were sightless and the soft lips breathless in death. Maxim wiped a trembling hand across his brow to clear his mind of the nightmarish fantasy, but his heart still quavered with fear.

Sherbourne came forward to lay a hand on Maxim's knee and looked up with some worry on his face. "Is all well with Elise?"

A ponderous sigh slipped from Maxim. "Her captor has assured that she is well . . . for now. But he expects a treasure, and I fear he'll not be satisfied with what little I can offer on such short notice. As far as I know, no treasure exists. I've bought us time, perhaps a day or two, but that's all. We must seek out the place where they're holding her before the day after the morrow."

Quentin's men rode hard for perhaps half an hour or so, then they split into as many different paths as there were men. Most of them were to take circuitous routes and wait out the night ere they returned to the keep. Quentin, however, turned south and quickly found a thick copse of trees in which to hide. He dismounted, secured his mount, and selected a thick bed of moss where he dozed for a brace of hours.

Finally assured that no one followed him, he went to horse again.

Traveling swiftly, he was soon in the vicinity of Kensington Keep. After a wary circuit of the place that uncovered no trace of strangers, he made his approach to the ridge. He was weary from the long hours in the saddle and stretched to ease the ache in his back as he left the shelter of the forest and rode out along the ridge. As he neared the tumbledown edifice, his ears caught the sound of a woman's voice raised in angry argument. Slashing his quirt down hard upon his horse's flanks, he charged into the dubious confines of the courtyard and was surprised to find his mother and three brothers surrounded by most of his men.

"Here he is! Quentin, my good son! Where have you been? Tell these buffoons that I'm your mother and these"—she swept a hand to indicate her sons— "your own blood brothers."

"Half-blood, if that!" Quentin muttered the low grunt as he alit from the back of his mount.

"What did you say?" Cassandra's voice seemed overloud in the barren courtyard as it echoed back at her eldest son. "Speak up, Quentin! If I've told you once, I've told you a thous—"

"What in the bloody hell are you doing here?" he railed. He struggled to control his temper and continued in a slightly more subdued tone. "How did you find me?"

"Why, Forsworth told me that you had stolen Elise right out of his hands," Cassandra explained, launching a blustering excuse for their intrusion. "And of course I knew how you wanted to stand by your kin and help us as much as you could . . ." Her voice trailed off as she saw an angry glower darkening her eldest son's face.

"And of course," he mimed in whining tones, "you wanted to get yourself a share of the treasure!"

Cassandra assumed a crestfallen posture. "Why, Quentin, we just wanted to..."

"Get out!" he shouted. "Get out of my sight ere I commit mayhem on my own kin."

"Quentin!" Cassandra tried a sharper reproof. " 'Tis near dark and the nights are cold. There may be wolves out there... and we've no food..."

"Do you not ken, *Mother?* I told you to get out!" His bellow of rage echoed back from the surrounding hills as he pointed his arm rigidly toward the most obvious route of departure.

No longer able to deny his commands, his kin slowly mounted their weary nags and, filing in behind each other, made a doleful column of bedraggled riders as they left the keep.

Quentin watched them leave, then would have retired to the lower dungeon, but he found his way barred by the stout form of one of his guards. He stared at the thin, ratty beard of the man, noticing that it still bore the greasy signs of a recent meal before it finally penetrated that the man had something to say.

"Well?" The word was more of a challenge than a question.

" 'Ere be another one, sir," the man hesitantly apologized. "She said she knew ye."

"Another one?" Quentin could hardly believe his ears.

"Aye, sir." The man took heart. "This one's a foin liedy, I'd say. She come just afore 'ese other 'uns."

Quentin silently bemoaned the quality of henchmen available these days and gave voice to loud, plaintive wailings. "Oh, craven fates! I've come to my secret bastion without a word to anyone and am here beset by . . . relatives? Some unknown wench? My adversary need only tread the best-worn path to find me out! How can this be?"

The guard heaved an exaggerated shrug and stretched his eyeballs wide in mute, innocent denial. "I don' know."

Quentin slogged through the well-churned mud toward the tower door and, once within, found another guard leaning on a long quarterstaff as he leered down at a slight figure winsomely huddled on a stone bench. A shawl draped her head and was clutched tightly in a small fist beneath her chin. Quentin stepped closer and bent to peer into her face. "Arabella?"

Her relief was immediate. She came to her feet and threw her arms about his neck. "Oh, Quentin. I thought you'd never come!"

"What . . . ? How on earth . . . ? What are you doing here?" The question seemed inadequate.

"Oh, Quentin, darling." Her grip on him was desperate. "I just had to come and talk with you." She pulled away enough to look up into his puzzled frown. "You weren't at home . . . and then I recalled that once long ago you mentioned this place and said it would be a good place for us to hide from my father. I heard that Elise had been taken and knew how fond you were of her." She sniffed as she lowered her gaze. "I was wondering if you had decided to run off with her."

"My dear Arabella," Quentin cajoled and solicitously laid an arm about her shoulders as he began to guide her toward the stairs. "You simply must trust that I'd never leave you. Haven't we been together for some years now? Why, now that Reland is dead, I was going to ask you to marry me."

Arabella lifted starry eyes to his. "You were?"

"Of course." He gave her shoulder a reassuring

squeeze as they descended the dimly lit stairs. "You remember how quickly I came to your defense when Reland caught us together in the stable? I told you then that I'd always be there to protect you."

" 'Tis frightening to remember." Arabella wrung her hands in distress as the nightmare came back to haunt her. "I can still see him now, gaping at me as I huddled there in the straw. If only he hadn't come back so soon from his ride. He was so enraged, he might've killed me if you hadn't hit him over the head with your pistol. When he collapsed at my feet and I saw the blood coming from his head, I could hardly believe it when you told me he was dead." She heaved a trembling sigh. " 'Twas all so horrible! But you were right. 'Twas best to let everyone think he had been thrown from his horse. We didn't mean to kill him. The whole thing would never have happened had he not found us."

Her trust of Quentin was buoyed by her adoration as he led her to the gate of the cell where several torches and a pair of tallow lanterns now lit the area. Elise rose from the cot where she had been resting beside her father and approached the bars, only to be waved back by Quentin as he applied the key to the lock.

"Now see for yourself, my dear. Elise is here, as my prisoner, and I've made no plans to run away with her." He took Arabella's arm and urged her through the meagerly opened door. "Why don't you visit with her for a space and satisfy your curiosity. She can tell you that I only want her father's treasure so we can go away together."

Quentin closed the door gently behind the trusting woman and snapped the lock into place before he applied the key. As his eyes swept the cell, his gaze settled on a wooden bowl left on the table. It was still heaped with globs of greasy gruel, and apparently had gone untouched.

"The fare here insults the term 'food,'" Elise commented wryly. "It leaves much to be desired."

"I shall see that you get something decent to eat." He moved toward the stairs.

"Quentin?" Arabella's plaintive voice echoed in the cell. "Come back to me soon, my love. I don't like this place."

"Soon, love. When I finish my business."

"Quentin?"

He ignored her plea and mounted the stairs to disappear into the settling darkness.

Arabella turned to face Elise, but the accusing stare she thought would be there was not. Instead, there was pity in the deep blue eyes, an emotion she had played on for many years now. Only now, it served to prick her conscience, and wearily she sagged upon the empty cot to sort out reality from illusion. For too long she had wrapped herself in the protective armor of the latter. Perhaps it was time she faced the truth and realized just where she was.

Maxim despaired of success at finding a trail as night encroached. By the time darkness had descended hard upon the land, many furlongs had been consumed beneath Eddy's hooves, and though the gallant steed seemed to understand the urgency, even he tired of the relentless pace and labored to keep it up. Finally, after the animal had stumbled twice in the dark, Maxim had to admit failure. He drew the tired mount to a halt and waited for the others to catch up. A small rise situated deeper in the forest promised a safe and dry haven for a camp, and it was there Maxim led his road-weary companions.

The men shared cold rations that even Nicholas

and *Herr* Dietrich tolerated without complaint, then they spread their cloaks over beds of moss and settled for the night, all save Maxim. A troubled wakefulness haunted him and, after an hour of restless tossing, he rose to make a careful patrol of the area. He paused to lean against a tree and gaze out into a small glade where a doe and her fawn grazed in idyllic peace in the moonlit shadows. Slowly his gaze moved on, but everywhere his eyes ventured, a vision of Elise was already there. He was greatly troubled by the fact that he could not find her and that there was so little time to search. He cruelly castigated himself for having ever come up with the foolhardy notion that he knew of the treasure's whereabouts. If not for that tale, Elise might not have been taken, but then, he had to remember her cousins had tried a similar tactic long before.

Of a sudden, the doe raised her head and flicked her ears. The rasp of a twig on leather warned Maxim, and he stepped around slowly in the moon-cast shadow of the tree, his hand moving to the hilt of his sword.

"Rest easy, Maxim. 'Tis I." Sir Kenneth's soft whisper was hollow in the quiet of the night.

"Hmmm." Maxim acknowledged the knight's presence with a half-voiced sigh and returned to his musings, finding the glade now empty. There was a long silence as the two men savored the smells and sounds of the cool night. It was Maxim who finally broke the quiet.

"The fire will help banish the chill, and I guess 'twill do no harm."

"What do you mean?" Kenneth asked. "We made no fire."

Maxim tested the air again. "Someone has."

The knight sniffed. "You're right."

Maxim moved away from the tree. "It cannot be far. Rouse the others and let's search this out afoot."

Cassandra and her brood had retreated just far enough from Kensington Keep to be safe, a distance determined only by the weariness of their bones. The leader of the group sat huddled upon a rotting log, her cloak clutched close about her. Her grating, whining voice berated her sons as they labored to build the fire higher and secure enough comfort for her and thereby obtain peace for themselves.

"If only we'd brought some victuals." Her mewling filled the glade. "I'm withering with starvation."

"You didn't say to bring food," the youngest grumbled the reminder. "You only said to fetch muskets and horses."

"Must I think of *everything?* Aarrgh!" She coughed suddenly and waved an angry hand as a cloud of smoke from the dew-dampened logs engulfed her.

"Quentin's not living so high and mighty himself," drawled the more solemn son. "I saw some of that gruel they were stewing up. A body would almost be tempted to starve before eating that slime."

"I want to die! Right here and now!" Cassandra's distressed wail pierced the night. "If not from your foolery, then from some hungry beastie!"

The three sons froze with her comment, and their eyes searched warily for evidence of some creature in the shadows beyond their camp. They drew closer to the fire and faced outward, trying to penetrate the darkness. A nightbird chirped from somewhere close at hand, and a middle son whimpered. The undulating hoot of an owl drifted into the camp, and Forsworth fumbled for his sword.

Cassandra lifted her drooping head and glared at the three of them. "Get yourselves some rest!"

Her command made them all start, and finally they gathered their scattered wits. The camp grew quiet as the weary family settled down for the night and were finally drowsing when a distant howl drifted to their ears. Forsworth's eyes popped open, and he listened, his senses now fully alert. The howling came again, shivering down his spine. This time Cassandra leapt to her feet, then danced a frightful, shrieking jig as she trod in the edge of the fire where a small hot coal fell into her low slippers. A rustling through the trees brought the youngest one to his feet with a warbling wail.

"Wolves!"

A mad scramble ensued as the Radborne family fought each other to get to their mounts. Not caring how well the saddles and tack were affixed, in another moment the four were racing out of the forest astride wild-eyed nags who had caught the fever of their panic. Whether welcomed or not, they were bent on seeking shelter at Kensington Keep, for they doubted that even the bad-tempered Quentin had grown fangs long enough to match the wily wolf.

In the silence that followed their passing, Sir Kenneth slapped his thigh and chortled in high glee. "I never saw fur flying so hard to get someone out of a place before! Those nags will be spent ere a half hour's passing of the moon. Truly, if Sherbourne's wolf call had been any better, they'd have keeled over dead from fright."

With a grin Maxim raised his hand to signal his small band to move out. They had returned to their camp to fetch their mounts and now at a leisurely pace followed the sounds of the panic-stricken riders.

It was some time later, after watching the family's approach to Kensington Keep from the ridge, that Fitch and Spence went flying back along the road from whence they had come. Sir Kenneth had sighted a company of fusiliers before he had met up with Maxim's band, and now that their point of destination was determined, someone had to go back and lead them. 'Twas evident that a greater force would be needed to win the day.

Justin, Sherbourne, and *Herr* Dietrich tore off in the other direction to reach the nearest town before morning. There they could buy supplies and outfit themselves in rare form for the trip to Kensington Keep. As for the remaining three, they gathered their weapons and those things which would be needed to penetrate Quentin's defenses.

Chapter 34

A STRANGE CLANGING, clanking clamor drifted across the valley and, as the afternoon hour progressed, the persistent sound came ever nearer to the knoll whereupon Kensington Keep stood. In rising curiosity, the occupants of the tower crowded near the crumbling walls to scan the surrounding countryside and there glimpsed a trio of men approaching on horseback. Quentin could not stand the suspense. He was already in a temper, having had his sleep utterly destroyed by the return of his kin. This time they had proven even more tenacious about staying than he had been about their going, and he had finally given in, seeing no end to their arguments and protestations. He mangled a few curses as he swung into the saddle and rode out to meet the three whose mounts plodded lazily along. He soon discovered the source of the noise came from the last rider whose stout steed was loaded down with all manner of cooking utensils and paraphernalia. The rider in the van was old, wrinkled, and scraggly-haired, with shoulders rounded and stooped. As Quentin drew near, he saw that the fellow had a nervous twitch, which lent a perpetual squint to the right eye. The second rider was of stronger, more youthful form, but a wide bandage covered his eyes, and his mount was led by the elder.

"Good day ta yez, yer lor'ship," called the ancient.

"What are you doing here?" the frustrated Quentin demanded. He quickly rejected the idea that these sorry, ragged beings had anything to do with Maxim's men, but still there was need to be cautious. For all he knew they could be thieves out to steal what they could from him.

The stooped shoulders gathered in a brief shrug. "Jes' passin' through. Ain't no 'arm in 'at, is 'ere?"

"Passing through? With no intentions of stopping at Kensington Keep?" Quentin Radborne was suspicious.

"Don't see no purpose in it," the ragged man answered.

"Who are you? Where do you come from?"

"Why, 'at's me gran'son." The ancient gestured over his shoulder at the one who rode directly behind him. "The poor lad were blinded a few months back in a scuffle wit' a ruddy Irishman." Then the elder lifted his head and fixed a squinty gaze upon the last of the three. "An' 'at's me nephew." He thumped a finger against his temple. "But he's a mite slow though. Can't talk, ya know, but he can cook, 'at he can!"

"Cook?" Even Quentin had become convinced of their need for edible food. "Is he looking for work?"

"Well, yer lor'ship, he might be . . . that is, if'n ye're o' a mind ta let meself an' me gran'son here stay long 'nough ta show him what ye want. He only knows me hand signals."

"Anything!" Quentin agreed, then paused to caution, "But if you're lying about how well he can cook, you and the rest of your family will be booted out before nightfall. My men are not in a mood for any pranks and may well tear you apart if you cannot deliver what you promise. Do I make myself clear?"

"Ye got the makin's, yer lor'ship, ol' Deats can cook

'em up, 'at he can," the ancient answered with smug confidence.

"And by what name may you be called?" Quentin inquired of the ancient.

"Most just call me Justin." He tossed a thumb over his shoulder. "An' me gran'son here goes by Sherb."

Quentin gave a nod toward the tower. "Go on in. One of my men will show you where the kitchen is. 'Tis not much, but it's the best we have."

"Ol' Deat don't need much, yer lor'ship. Ye'll see."

Quentin watched them until they entered the gates, then he made a wide sweep around the cliffs that surrounded the keep, assuring himself that the three were not part of a larger group of miscreants tucked within the trees somewhere. Satisfied that the three had come alone, he rode back and was pleasantly surprised by the delicious aroma already wafting through the compound. His mouth watered as he entered the tower, and he found the two hard at work cooking and cleaning up the tables. The blind one sat before the fire, enjoying its warmth as he sipped from a mug.

"Care for some spiced tea, yer lor'ship?" Justin offered. "We brought it wit' us, we did."

Accepting a mug, Quentin savored the aroma a long pleasurable moment, then indulged in the warm liquid. He nodded his thanks to the cook as that one handed him a piece of flat bread cooked in a kettle of hot fat above the fire. His amazement knew no end as the sweetened bread created a luscious delight in his mouth, and he realized how hungry he was after avoiding the tasteless, greasy gruel that had become their main staple. Surely their plight was not because of a need of supplies, but for want of someone who could cook.

"I approve!" Quentin declared with enthusiasm. It

was the only thing that had met with his approval for days!

The old man chortled in glee, then winked at the tall man. "Just thought we'd give ye a samplin' afore we talk 'bout Deat's wages."

"Set a price and if it's fair, I'll consider it," Quentin replied magnanimously. A good cook was worth keeping satisfied . . . at least for the short time he intended to be around to enjoy the fare. Before a wage was due, he would be well on his way to Spain with the treasure. And now with a cook to see to the preparation of the food, he would not have to face a mutiny.

"The three of you can bed down here in the kitchen," Quentin directed. His eyes swept to a long box the newcomers had placed beside the hearth and he gave a jerk of his head toward it as he demanded, "What have you there?"

"Oh, ah . . . why, 'at's Deat's knives, yer lor'ship," Justin answered in a gravelly voice. He tottered over to the box and, lifting the lid, displayed the top layer. Long and stout-bladed cutlery was set in neat niches wedged into the wood of the shallow tray. "Deat uses 'em for butcherin', ye know."

Quentin licked his fingers, finding little reason for a close inspection of the lower trays of the box. After all, what was a cook without his knives? "I've some guests downstairs who'd be greatly heartened if they were given something worthy to eat. I'll escort you down when their food is ready." He made a casual excuse in an attempt to silence any inquiries before they were spoken. "They're prisoners of the crown and are being held 'til the Queen's men can come to fetch them, so I warn you make no attempt to free them lest you wish a much-shortened life. As to that"—he smiled as he slipped the key from his doublet and tossed it before their eyes—"I've got the only key, and no one enters or leaves the cell unless I'm there to open the door."

" 'Tain't a twitch off me nose oo' ye gots locked away." Justin shrugged indolently. "I'm just here ta settle me good nephew in as cook for ye."

"Good! Then we understand each other."

"Quentin!" The plaintive wail came from the small upstairs chamber which Quentin had once reserved for his own use. "Where are you, son? I'm hungry!"

The summoned one rolled his eyes heavenward as if in mute appeal, then almost angrily jabbed a finger at Justin. "You tell your nephew to prepare enough food to stuff down the gullets of that bunch of whiners upstairs. You'll find them in my quarters, and heaven help your hide if you delay!"

It was a short time later when Quentin's directive was carried out, and when Justin entered with a tray, Cassandra and the three Radbornes seized the food in a greedy frenzy. Snarling and snatching to prevent anyone else from having what they desired, they tore apart the fowl with their hands and teeth as Justin backed out of the doorway. He had once seen wolves feeding, and their display was somewhat reminiscent of a canaille of those beasts.

The mood was somewhat more tranquil among the prisoners in the dungeon. Elise had been slumbering beside her father on the cot before she was roused by approaching footsteps. She blinked sleepily as the key rasped in the lock and the door was swung open to admit a gray-haired old man who hobbled across the space. He placed his burden on the crude table beside the cot, then glanced aside at her as he rubbed a spilled droplet from the tray. His squinting eye opened and closed in a deliberate wink, prompting Elise to stare at him for a confused, uncertain moment, then a sudden dawning swept her and she recognized the man behind the disguise. He left her and climbed the stairs, but she knew what his presence meant. Maxim was aware of where they were, and he had already begun infiltrating the enemy's camp to secure their safety.

The only comments came from Arabella, who strode near the iron gate as it was slammed closed and once more secured. "So, Quentin! You lock the door again! 'Tis not that you've disturbed yourself to see to my comfort. Oh, nay! You've answered naught my tears and pleadings, but have steeled yourself against my cries. And now it seems you continue my imprisonment."

"I'm only protecting you from my men." Quentin excused his deed nonchalantly. "No telling what they'd do while my back is turned."

"Ha!" his mistress scoffed. "You've locked me away in here, and I finally begin to see that I mean nothing to you."

"Complaints! All I've heard since I've come to this place are complaints!" he grumbled. He motioned toward the tray. "See there! I've brought you food. Try it! Maybe 'twill sweeten your temper."

"I doubt it." Arabella's chilled tone denied the possibility. "To think that I've let you run my life all these years. Father was right! All you wanted was my fortune and . . ."

"*Your* fortune?" Quentin laughed aloud in jeering tones. "I worked harder for *your* fortune than you did yourself."

"What do you mean?" Arabella demanded angrily. "My father arranged the matches himself."

"That buffoon! He'd have settled for a mere portion of what you have in your possession now. I knew with your beauty you were worthy of an earl, or even a duke."

"You wanted me to marry someone else?" Arabella questioned in surprise. "But I thought you detested all my suitors."

"I did!" He shrugged and gave her a sneering grin. "At least the first ones. Their purses were of little value, and in his greed, Edward would have accepted them, for they had more than he. You ought to be thankful to me, Arabella. I arranged a better match."

Arabella shook her head, as if to free her mind from the confusing cobwebs. "I don't understand."

Quentin settled his arms akimbo in vexation and began to explain. "Dear girl, do you really think your life has been cursed? Nay, my lovely, your suitors fell beneath a stronger hand, except for perhaps one or two whose lives were snatched by fate ere I did a like service. I must say I found Seymour suitably wealthy, but the Queen's agent recognized me as a conspirator and it became necessary to lay the blame on him for that one's murder."

"You murdered the Queen's agent?" Elise interjected the question in amazement and turned to stare at her father as he laid a comforting hand upon hers.

"Quentin was the one who told the Hansa that I was spying on them," Ramsey stated in a raspy whisper. "I found that out from Hilliard himself. It amused him that an Englishman could hand over his own uncle to be tortured and starved."

Elise's head moved slowly until she glared at her cousin. "Don't ever give yourself airs above Forsworth, Quentin. You're wallowing in the same slime."

He seemed amused by her disdain. "I can hardly declare my innocence before so noble a lady. I vow my heart doth break at your slight, and truly, my dear Elise, I'm sorry I disappoint you, but my mother taught her sons well that we should look after ourselves."

"And so you do." Elise dipped her head, acknowledging his statement as one of fact.

Arabella railed at him. "You used me! All this time you used me!"

Quentin bestowed a lazy-eyed gaze upon his mistress again. "I'd have married you, Arabella. I told you I would. I had planned to right after you inherited Huxford's wealth and after a proper period of mourning had passed."

"How soon would you have killed me to gain that fortune?" Arabella asked caustically.

He pursed his lips thoughtfully and finally shrugged his brows. "Actually, you were quite suitable for a wife, and I rather enjoyed our interludes together. 'Twould not have been too soon, my dear."

"And to think I helped you murder my husband!"

Elise jerked her head up and stared at Arabella in amazement. "You helped him murder Reland?"

"Not exactly." Quentin's chiding chuckle raised gooseflesh along Elise's skin. "Reland was quite alive when I carted him away from the stable, but you believed me when I told you he was dead. True, he was unconscious, and because of that I was able to haul him off the cart and drown him without a struggle."

"You're detestable!" Arabella accused in roweling repugnance.

"Enough of this! I grow weary of your insults." Ending the discussion, Quentin strode quickly away, his boot heels clicking against the stone floor and echoing back to them.

"I've been a fool," Arabella moaned dismally. "All these years, I thought he loved me as I loved him."

Elise had no words of comfort to give her cousin, for her mind was already searching for ways to give her husband aid when he came to rescue them.

Chapter 35

*T*HE LIGHT OF LATE AFTERNOON had been obscured by a slow, misty rain that was more fog than drizzle. Maxim had searched out a shallow swale that would offer some shelter for an approach by foot to the south side of the keep. The three of them that remained were well-equipped, with rope, swords, pistols, and daggers. Maxim was the first to slide down the gully, and behind him came Nicholas and Sir Kenneth. They found good cover to the base of the knoll, and there they waited as they appraised the ramparts and crumbling stone wall. No guards could be seen, and it was quickly surmised that Quentin's men had gathered in the shelter of the tower, save for the two who stood guard at the approach.

The invaders squinted up into the rain and scoured the mound and tower wall for any sign of an opening, a niche, a crevice, or anything that would allow them to gain entrance to the place. Close beneath the stonework of the walls they discovered a smear of rust flowing downward, staining the cliff.

Nicholas pointed it out, being more familiar with scuppers and drains. "It probably leads away from the lowest level." He lifted a quizzical gaze to Maxim. "The dungeons perhaps?"

"Let's have a look." Maxim glanced aside to receive Kenneth's nod of approval.

"Let's go!"

Hardly half an hour later the three rested beneath a large opening covered by a rusty iron grill. A thin trickle of ocher water ran from the lower edge. Carefully they worked their way upward until they clung with the slightest of toeholds to the stone beneath the grill. Nicholas reached up a hand and tied one end of his rope to a rusty metal bar, then grasped the edge with his large hands, braced himself, and heaved. The grate moved, but only the barest measure. Sir Kenneth and Maxim applied similar efforts from their positions, and slowly they worked the barrier out of its nest. When it was freed, Maxim let the weight of it swing onto Nicholas's rope, and it was lowered to a safe resting place beneath them. Nicholas flipped the rope and the knot fell free, allowing him to gather it in and restore it to his shoulder.

Maxim had already entered the cramped drain and warned Kenneth to silence as the knight heaved his bulk into the opening. A dim light showed through two grate-covered openings in the ceiling beyond them. One was only a few yards away, while the other was perhaps ten yards beyond. Bars and a corner of an iron gate could be seen from the nearest, and when Maxim crept beyond it to the distant opening, he saw the boots of a guard seated on a stool and heard the sonorous rasp of his snores. Cautiously he returned to the first grate.

An examination proved that the grill only rested on a shoulder cut in the stone floor. It was a tight fit, but the three of them laid their shoulders against it and slowly heaved. The rust-encrusted grate moved reluctantly with a slight grating sound, and they froze to listen. The snoring continued without interruption, and with a trio of nods they forced it again. The grill loosened, and they worked it up and away, moving it aside onto the flooring. Maxim carefully raised his head to peer over the level of the flooring. No one moved. The guard, having propped himself against the wall, still slumbered amid blissful dreams. Maxim searched with his eyes through the deep gloom until he found three slumbering forms in the shadows of the cell.

The men silently lifted themselves out of the drain, and while Maxim examined the massive lock, Kenneth went to watch near the stairs and Nicholas moved swiftly and lightly to where the guard dozed. He straddled the man's sprawled legs before he clobbered him over the head with the butt of his pistol. He kept the man from falling with his left hand and returned him to a slumbering pose, then caught his feet in a quickly formed loop and slipped the rope under the bench and securely bound the hands, snipping off the excess cordage and returning it to his coil.

Maxim plucked a lead shot from his pouch and rolled it across the flooring of the cell toward the cot where a wealth of auburn tresses spilled over its edge. Elise sat bolt upright, immediately awake, and found that fond and familiar form standing just beyond the bars. It was his finger across his lips and the negative shake of his head that silenced the joyful gasp. She reached out and shook the man beside her. Slowly a bearded head raised, and she touched her father's lips with a hand to still his question, then pointed toward Maxim. His gaze came around to find the younger man, and a smile, the first for some months now, broke upon his countenance.

Maxim lightly tapped the lock, silently asking the whereabouts of the key, but Elise shook her head and mouthed the name "Quentin." She made a tucking motion as if slipping it into a doublet, then she came close to the door and reached through to grasp her husband's hand. They leaned together, and even the bars could not prevent their lips from touching briefly. When they drew apart again, Maxim smiled and, with his thumb, wiped a smudge of rust from her cheek.

He inclined his head toward the third form lying alone on the other cot, and Elise shaped the name "Arabella" with her lips.

Nicholas strode along the row of bars that surrounded the cell and gently tapped at each with a stout cudgel he had found. Toward the far end of the cell, he found several that did not ring, but gave forth a dull *thunk* instead. Flicking his hand toward Kenneth, he summoned the knight near. The pair of them grasped the lower ends of the bars and, flexing their knees and gritting their teeth, heaved upward and outward. One bar moved with a moan of yielding metal, then caught and held, while the other rusted base snapped and the bar lifted clear the measure of two handbreadths.

The sound of heavy boots and a protracted yawn echoed from the stairs, announcing the entrance of one of the guards who was coming to relieve the other. As his head came into view, he froze and his once-sleepy eyes widened as he saw three men staring back at him. He fumbled for his musket, but before he could raise it, Nicholas threw the cudgel, striking the piece from his grasp. The guard bellowed out a cry of alarm and, snatching a long rapier from his side, leapt to the dungeon floor where Kenneth met him with drawn sword. There was a rush of footsteps from above as the brigands scrambled toward the stairs.

Maxim stood away from the bars and lowered his musket. The first man to come into sight took a ball in the chest and slowly toppled to the floor. Another pistol spoke, and the next guard fell over his dead companion. Maxim replaced the empty pistols and his sword rang free as a half score guards clamored down the stairs. Elise smothered a scream as he was pressed back by the assaulting attack of a quartet of men, while Nicholas and Kenneth met a similar number with slashing, hacking sweeps of their long swords.

A sudden cacophony of screams rang from the level above them, and a moment later runnels of hot fat dribbled down the stairs. A handful of guards stumbled and slid down the slippery steps, holding their grease-soaked clothes away from the bodies while hardly daring to touch the bright red splotches on their faces.

On the upper level Justin threw open the long box and lifted the top compartment as Sherbourne tore off his bandage. The younger of the two seized his axe, while the knight claimed a mace and sword from the box. Dietrich chose a long butcher knife half the length of a sword, but twice as deadly. He butted away a stout guard with his ponderous belly and swung around with a vicious swipe. The other saw the blade coming and danced back on the tip of his toes and sucked in his breath just as the knife whizzed past, then he slithered senseless to the floor as a huge mallet followed the assault and caught him alongside the head.

Quentin had been in the loftier chambers with his family, demanding their departure at dawn, when the commotion alerted him. Savagely he snarled at his brothers, "Well, let's see how good you three are at defending my hide. Without me, there's no treasure at all."

Cassandra immediately jumped up and delivered swords to the hands of her offspring, then thrust out a finger toward the door in a command. "Go! Fight the filthy rabble who would dare attack your brother!"

Quentin smirked as he raced from the chamber.

Perhaps this one time it was to his benefit to have a family.

In the dungeons below Maxim had been pressed back toward the far wall by the advance of the guards. Still, he seemed the victor in the fray as he thrust out with his sword. One guard sank to his knees, and another struggled to hold at bay that whiplash blade that turned upon him and threatened at every quarter. He cried out as the rapier seared like fire through his ribs, then his own heavy sword clanged to the stone floor.

"Hold!"

Maxim glanced up, and his heart froze in his chest. Quentin had caught up a musket and now stood with its muzzle pointing through the bars a short distance from Elise's head. Behind him, his brothers had gathered and watched the proceedings warily. Maxim lowered his sword and Nicholas dropped the limp head of his opponent and let the fellow sink to the floor. From the level above, the sounds of scufflings and struggles continued, interjected with the clank of iron and the blunt thud of an axe.

"Stand back!" The flintlock was at full cock as Quentin's finger trembled on the trigger. "I warn you! Elise will only be the first, and my men will be upon you in a thrice."

In the frozen moment that followed, there came a sharp whine of a ricocheting ball from outside, and the dull thud of a distant musket shot. A volley of gunfire followed as a warning to the occupants of Kensington Keep.

"That should be the company of fusiliers," Maxim posed the conjecture, answering the unspoken question in the faces of the Radborne brothers.

No one moved, though it seemed now that the brigands sweated in fear and apprehension, then fate found her voice at this turn of events and took a hand. The first guard, whom Nicholas had bound so roughly, roused from his stupor and, with a shout of belated warning, lunged to his feet, or at least tried. The truss caught him as he heaved himself halfway up and arched him forward like a bow, just as the bench struck his knees from behind. He gave a whooping cry of dismay as he measured at least part of his length on the stones.

It was Ramsey who seized the moment of distraction. He and his daughter had worked a rusted end of his shackles free from its mount on the floor, then had carefully replaced it. Now he snatched it free and, flipping a loop in the chain, tossed it around the intruding muzzle of Quentin's weapon as he shoved Elise out of the way. He braced a foot against the bars and jerked hard. His strength was slight, but his surprise complete. The musket snaked through the bars until the lock struck a brace and snapped off with a sharp *ping* and rattled to rest somewhere in a dark crevasse.

Quentin drew back in dismay, rubbing his smarting hand, and reluctantly faced Maxim. That one raised his rapier in a quick salute and waited. Forsworth nudged his brother's arm and offered his own sword, and received a glare for his generosity. Neither of them noticed the guards making a careful retreat toward the stairs.

"I'm no swordsman!" Quentin mewled in fear. "You'd slay me as quickly as a helpless babe."

"You gave no quarter to the agent in my house," Maxim reminded him. "You bent no mercy on your mistress at court. I would say you've plied your skills quite well against women and helpless men."

"Mistress?" Arabella slowly shook her head and sank back to the cot, from whence she had risen at the onset of the fray. "Is there no end to his wickedness?"

Maxim passed his sword to Nicholas, took the pistols from his belt and handed them over to Ramsey along with the rearming pouch. He spread his hands as he taunted, "Does this meet your standard better? An unarmed man? Or must I be trussed and laid up like a fowl to await your thrust? What sort of coward are you, Quentin?"

The dark eyes narrowed as Quentin saw his chance, and in sudden glee he seized Forsworth's sword, but his haste made him clumsy. The blade spilled from his anxious grasp and rattled to the floor. He scrambled after it, and Maxim met him chest to chest over the fallen sword. Unrelentingly Maxim forced his adversary erect before his fingers could grasp the hilt. In frustrated rage Quentin lashed out, and the large signet ring he wore laid open a furrow across Maxim's cheek.

It was with immense satisfaction that Maxim levied a personal vengeance upon the man. A blow from his left drove Quentin back, and another fist to the full lips sent him stumbling further. Quentin shook the cobwebs from his head and, collecting himself, charged like a bull, closing and clutching at Maxim while his knee sought to thrust upward against his adversary's groin. Maxim flung him away, and Quentin stumbled over the bound guard and sprawled against the bars. He rubbed a bruised shoulder and glared up at his enemy, but made no move to rise.

"I thought I had gotten rid of you one time," Quentin growled.

Maxim smiled wryly. "I came back to take what had once been mine, and now I've come again to claim what is truly mine."

"You never had the treasure." It was a statement of slowly dawning realization. Quentin wiped a trickle of blood from his mouth with the back of his hand as he watched the Marquess with dark, brooding eyes. "You never intended to barter it as ransom."

"There *is* no treasure, Quentin," Ramsey declared from the cell. "At least none that *you* could spend. What I secured for my daughter was no more than documents assuring her the right of inheritance of my properties."

"But the chests you took from the Stilliards?" Quentin searched his mind for a reasonable explanation and could find none. "What did you trade at the Stilliards that you had to carry away in chests?"

Ramsey shook his shaggy head. "Those were only a few empty chests that I purchased for my daughter. That was all."

"*All!*" Quentin scrambled to his feet and demanded, "Why didn't you tell me sooner? Why did you let me go on believing there was a treasure?"

"If I had told you the truth, you'd have killed me," Ramsey answered simply. "Once you made the mistake of capturing me, you'd not have let me go free as long as I knew who you were."

"All this time! My attempts have been for naught."

"I'll take the key now," Maxim interrupted, and beckoned with his fingers. "Give it to me."

Quentin smirked as he slipped a hand within his doublet and removed the key. He waggled it tauntingly before Maxim's gaze, then he drew his arm back and swept it forward, sending the key sailing toward the drain. Elise gasped as Maxim dove forward to catch it. In the next moment her scream warned him and he rolled away just as Quentin's sword came plummeting down a bare inch from his head. Maxim tossed the key into the cell and whirled, catching his own rapier from Nicholas.

"Let us have this out with some trace of honor,"

Maxim cajoled, but Quentin only crouched and glared his hatred. "Come now. We shall see which of us is better. You may even best me."

Quentin lowered his face and stared at the sword in his hand. Of a sudden he leapt over the bound man and stumbled up the slippery steps, slashing wildly at Nicholas, who sprinted forward to intercept his escape. As Maxim raced after the man, he glanced aside, assuring himself that his friend had missed the murderous blow. Kenneth ran to give the prisoners aid in their bid for freedom and was soon hot on Nicholas's trail as that one followed Maxim.

Quentin dashed across the now-empty room littered with the bodies of his men. He bolted through the door and raced out into the courtyard, but immediately paused, seeing the ridge marked with a double column of mounted dragoons. Near them a line of fusiliers stood at the ready to block any attempt to escape. He glanced wildly about the courtyard, and the once-ancient Justin, the now-seeing Sherb, and the hefty cook slowly approached him. Maxim plunged from the doorway and was promptly followed by Nicholas, Kenneth, and the three prisoners.

Quentin backed along a tumbled wall near the edge of the cliff, his eyes wild as he searched for any avenue of escape. Maxim paced slowly forward, his sword ready, but not threatening.

"You've lost, Quentin. Your day has flown. Put an end to it. Fight me or surrender!"

"Then I choose to *have my day!*" Quentin shrieked, and flung the sword with meant intent. Maxim stepped aside, and when he looked again, he found Quentin reaching within his doublet. Drawing forth a pistol, the man waved it high and screamed a curse. *"Damn you, Seymour! You've hounded me for the last time!"*

The dark-haired man lowered the pistol's sights upon his tormentor, and Maxim flinched as a loud report sounded in his ear. He felt no searing pain, and Quentin gaped down at them as if confused. A small black hole had suddenly appeared in the middle of his forehead and, like a puppet dangling on strings, he began to turn. The rock upon which he stood loosened and pivoted with him. His sightless eyes ranged upward as he began to topple, then his arm jerked with a spasm, and the lead ball from his pistol whined high into the clouds overhead. The rock gave, and Quentin disappeared over the brink. The crash of falling rock faded, then ended somewhere far below.

The wind slashed a spattering of raindrops across the silent keep as if to wash away the memory of his passing. Maxim slid his sword into the sheath and turned to find Arabella standing in a frozen daze close behind him. Though her tears blended with the rain falling on her cheeks, she lifted her gaze to Maxim's and whimpered.

"I'm so sorry, Maxim. I'm so sorry for everything."

Elise stepped close to her side and removed the pistol from her hand, giving it over to Maxim. She led her cousin back into the tower as Kenneth stepped to the wall to motion the soldiers to advance speedily. What followed shortly were the arrests of Cassandra and her sons and all that remained of Quentin's men.

Maxim stared in amazement when the Countess Anne's conveyance came rolling toward the erstwhile gates. Behind it came a cart laden with perhaps a dozen of Bradbury's men armed with long knives, aging swords, quarterstaffs, and here and there a scythe. The Lady Anne Hall alighted from her coach and when Maxim silently pointed toward the tower, she rushed past him to assure herself of the welfare of her great-granddaughter. Within the chamber the elder rushed to Elise and her father, smothering both of them with thankful sobs and warm hugs.

"I hardly expected such an army to be raised to our support," Maxim commented aside to Sir Kenneth.

"I dare say the Lady Elise has that effect on people," the knight told him with a grin.

Maxim smiled and lifted his face to the cleansing rain, letting it wash away all the emotions of fear and anger that had so recently bound him up. Doffing his sword and belt, he handed them to Kenneth and then strode toward the tower. He clapped Nicholas's back in close camaraderie as he passed him. When he entered the tower, he stood for a long moment near the door as he watched Elise with her family, then she raised her gaze to him, and he saw all the love he had ever desired within those translucent orbs. She came to him and took his hand to lead him to her father.

"Papa, I would like you to meet my husband."

Ramsey rose and the two men clasped each other in an embrace of close kinship. Tears filled the eyes of the elder as he drew back to smile at his son-in-law. "God answered my prayers from the beginning and sent a protector for my daughter, a far more worthy one than I even dared ask for."

Elise stepped beside her husband and slipped her arm about him as she smiled into his warmly glowing eyes. "Never in the life of a maid has one found a more worthy protector. Once more you have fought gallantly in my defense and won the day, and again I stand in much awe of you. You are truly my champion, Maxim Seymour, and the love of my life."

KAREN ROBARDS

Shirlee Busbee
million-copy bestselling author

MIDNIGHT MASQUERADE 75210-7/$4.95 U.S./$5.95 Can
In the Louisiana horse country of 1812, Melissa and Dominic
find a love as turbulent and magnificent as the times.

THE SPANISH ROSE 89833-0/$4.50 U.S./$5.50Can
Although their families were bitter foes, nothing could distract
Maria and Gabriel from their passion—as they raged against
the one truth they feared to admit...and were unable to deny!

THE TIGER LILY 89499-8/$4.95 U.S./$5.95Can
The wonderful story of a beautiful young heiress, torn
between the conflicting emotions of defiance, suspicion and
wild passion aroused by the handsome, strong Texan who
controls her destiny.

DECEIVE NOT MY HEART 86033-3/$4.50 U.S./$5.50Can
A grand, sweeping novel set in the deep South that tells of
a beautiful young heiress who is tricked into marrying a
dashing Mississippi planter's look-alike cousin—a rakish
fortune hunter. But mistaken identities cannot separate the
two who are destined to spend their lives together.

LADY VIXEN 75382-0/$4.95 U.S./$5.95Can

WHILE PASSION SLEEPS 82297-0/$4.95 U.S./$5.95Can

GYPSY LADY 01824-1/$4.50 U.S./$5.95Can

AVON Original Paperbacks